# Stonedeer's Wrath

# Stonedeer's Wrath

---

*Book 1 Redemption, Book 2 Revenge,*
*Book 3 Resolve*

*by*

*James L. Stucci*

| | | |
|---|---|---|
| Library of Congress Control Number: | | 2015913181 |
| ISBN: | Hardcover | 978-1-5035-9545-3 |
| | Softcover | 978-1-5035-9544-6 |
| | eBook | 978-1-5035-9543-9 |

Print information available on the last page.

Rev. date: 09/26/2015

**To order additional copies of this book, contact:**
Xlibris
1-888-795-4274
www.Xlibris.com
Orders@Xlibris.com
719833

Dedications:

My parents Leo and Grace Stucci for giving me life and direction. Marius and Elinor Schlief my mother and father in law, for giving me Sandra Ann.

A special thank you to Steve and Linda Owens, for smoothing out my limited computer skills.

# BOOK ONE

## - *Part One* -

## Redemption

---

# CHAPTER 1

Dark, cruel eyes radiated hatred as they studied the large screen. The subdued light from the monitor cast an eerie glow on its feline features. His mind swam with the knowledge he would be the first of his kind to observe this alien scene, inflating his ego to even greater proportions. "Prepare triple life-support cubicles. Immediately!" He bellowed in his gravelly, sing-song voice.

A subordinate, working at a control module near by, turned icy eyes of objection toward his superior. Rising from his work, he joined him at the viewing screen. "Has "High One" forgotten the objective of this mission? He asked, in a nervous voice. "We are to procure only one specimen from every new world we discover. If any exists."

Rising, slowly to his feet, the leader struck a defensive pose. "I do not need the likes of such a low-born as yourself to dictate my duties to me! He said, in a voice dripping with malice. "Return to your station!"

Locking stares with his superior, the subordinate swallowed his fear and continued. "If I may be so bold, "high one" we may become over-crowded if......He said no more.

With a blur of motion, a furry, heavily-clawed hand shot out from the "high one", sinking, deeply into the chest of his subordinate; ripping out the organ he had used to pump his life fluids. Before the shocked creature collapsed to the deck, his eyes recorded the gruesome sight of his leader consuming his dripping, sill-pulsing organ.

A subordinate, working at another console, stood and stared at the macabre scene; a cruel act even for his kind. He froze, too afraid to move. Three had started out on this quest. If he didn't over-react two could, still, possibly return.

"Incinerate what's left of this upstart!" "Now!" The leader's voice blasted through the veil of his shock. "Unless, you would care to meet his presumptuous fate." Hurrying to do as he was bid, the sight of his leader's mouth, red with the blood of his comrade, lent speed to his big feet. Scooping up the ravaged body, he hurried down the passageway toward the incinerator room.

The steady hum from the ship's systems filled the confines of the control center. Like an irregular heartbeat, it pulsed out its power. Turning to the screen, once again, the brutal leader continued his scrutiny of the strange creatures he had detected just a short time before. The exorbitant fee he would receive at the conclusion of this successful mission would retire him, permanently, from this mind-wasting occupation. Space scavenging provided a lucrative lifestyle but not an end to his goals. A smile almost cracked his feline features as he licked a drop of blood from his furry paw; the first fresh meat he had eaten since the beginning of this venture.

The sound of his, now, second-in-command padding up the passageway tugged his thoughts back to the present. "Life-support in triplicate has been activated, "High One." "May I inquire as to the estimated time of occupancy?" He asked, nervously.

Turning, slowly, from the console, the leader cast a malicious grin toward his underling. Ignoring the inquiry, he said: "Very soon, now, we will have in our possession three specimens of a life form unknown to the "Nevoan" culture." "We will be magnanimously rewarded. Our deceased associate didn't realize the significance of the situation. He opted, instead, to cite protocol and his concerns about staying within the guidelines of regulations. He is no more, but we shall find the gratitude of the "Nevoans" most benevolent. Set a silent scanning course and prepare the neutralizing cloak." Assuming the position of his fallen comrade, he hurriedly complied. "Scanning pattern locked in, "High One", neutralizing cloak is at the ready. Awaiting your signal!" Nodding his shaggy head, the leader said: "Commence scanning maneuvers!"

A touch of a furry finger sent the alien ship hurtling through the heavens like a giant shadow: silent, deadly. The target: three unknown creatures from the planet they call Earth.

The star-filled sky hung over the night like an enormous chandelier, radiating its sparkling brilliance to Earth. Far below, three men surrounded a fire, capturing its warmth. Their attention was held by the vivid flames dancing off into the sky, fighting against the encroaching darkness. Like the logs being consumed by the thermal onslaught, so were their thoughts. The small site, they had chosen, would serve as home for the next three weeks. It provided them with a welcomed escape from the concrete and electric society, which held them in its bureaucratic grasp for most of the year. They looked forward to this rejuvenating adventure, together. Three weeks of hunting, fishing, and just plain relaxing. Using every precious moment of their time to untangle a year full of political suffocation. Each of them knew full well that soon enough it was back, again, to the fast-paced, plastic automations of their crowded lifestyles.

Brothers by birth: James, Gary and Gregory Stonedeer shared a closeness far-exceeding that of most sibling relationships. Orphaned at an early age, they became the charges of their Indian grandfather, Joseph. From that day on, they faced life as a unit.

James, age thirty, occupied his mind with the failures he had incurred over the last few years: a painful divorce, the loss of his Minnesota Peace Officer's boxing title and being passed over, once again, for the lieutenant's promotion.

"Maybe a clean start someplace else would be the answer." He thought to himself.

Gary, age twenty-nine, (nick named "Truck" because of his football exploits) replayed some of the gory scenes he had experienced while in Viet Nam. All the soap and water in the world, combined, would not be nearly enough to cleanse away the blood and gore he had waded through. Along with the many medals, he had received, was a serious head wound that left his speech partially out of normal. People, unaware of his injury, thought him slightly retarded.

Gregory, age twenty-eight, centered his thoughts on the decision he would have to make at the conclusion of this trip. A competitor company was experimenting with nuclear-powered computers and had offered him the position of "Director". The decision was hard for him to make. He had never considered himself leadership material.

As the fire burned low, they listened to the peaceful sounds of nature. Each night unveiled an orchestra playing a different song. An owl hooted out his refrain, in the shadowy forest, contributing to the nocturnal concert. A slight breeze ruffled the treetops, adding to the performance. The thoughts of the small audience varied, as they were being entertained.

Jim smiled across the fire at the sprawling figures of his brothers. So many things in their lives had changed, but the bonds that knitted them so closely together, over the years, remained as solid as ever. The strength and confidence they gave to one another helped them to surmount many obstacles in the past. Failures, as well as accomplishments, were equally shared

"I don't know about you two, but I'm going to have one more cup of coffee. Then, I'm calling it a night." He said, reaching for the blackened pot nestled in the coals. The smell of coffee blended perfectly with the pine smoke, wafting from the fire pit. The air was filled with a fragrant ambience. "We should get an early start if we expect to catch anything." He said as he finished pouring his coffee.

"Pour me a little more a dat mud as long as yer at it, jimbo!" Truck said, holding out his cup. "What time ya wanna get started?"

"Oh, I suppose around five or so." Jim answered. There'll be enough light by then without us running into anything."

"Hey, Greg! You want some more coffee?" When he didn't get a response he asked him again, "Greg?"

Roused from his trance, Greg refocused his mind on the present, mumbling to himself. "Sorry, Jim. I didn't hear you."

"More coffee?" He said, holding the pot out.

"No thanks, Jim. I've had quite enough for this evening."

As he set the pot back into the coals, a sudden breeze attacked their small fire, coaxing flames into licking the pine log, once again.

"How much we bettin on da biggest fish dis time you guys? Asked Truck. "I can use da extra cash."

"The same as usual, I suppose. Ten bucks each." Jim answered.

"Wonderful! Greg said with a big smile on his face. I will welcome another contribution from you rookies." He had won the friendly wager between them for the last three years in a row and claimed gloater's rights.

"You ain't got enough ass ta pull in da winner dis year, little brother. Truck interjected. Dat little minnow you hauled in last year is about da size of da bait I'm usin tomorrow."

"Truck! When will you start realizing that brain power will always triumph over brawn. Greg chided. I would be happy to give you a few lessons If you would like."

"An I could give you a few lessons, too, If ya want dem." Said Truck, jokingly, shaking his big fist across the fire at his younger brother.

Before his two brothers could continue their familiar bantering, Jim cut in. "I'll tell you what. Why don't you two stay up all night and argue about it. That'll make it easier for me."

"Unh uh, Jimbo. Truck said. You ain't gonna win like dat, again."

On one of their earlier trips, Jim had caught a large pike and it had spit the hook the instant he had brought it into the boat. It flopped out of the net and ended up between his two brothers, sound asleep on the deck. Before he retrieved it, it had attached itself to Truck's exposed hand. The loud bellow that emitted from the big guy's lips roared over the waves, close to bringing the dead to life.

"I swear, Truck, I didn't do that on purpose." Jim said, trying to keep from exploding with laughter. "I thought the damn thing was going to jump over the side, before I could get to it."

"You didn't have to bother cleaning that one. Did you, Jim?" Greg queried. He was, also, trying hard to contain the laughter that was waiting to erupt from the pit of his stomach.

When Truck finally realized what was happening, he had grabbed the fish with his other massive hand and squeezing it so hard, he separated the head, still clinging to his hand from its body Holding his hand out to the glow of the fire Truck said: "Yup! I still got da scars ta prove it, too. My ex old lady never bit me dat hard. An she could bite."

"From where I was sitting, Truck, they looked almost identical." Greg piped in.

Jim started laughing so hard, he fell over backwards from the log he was sitting on, holding his side.

"I don't think dats funny, Jim. He insulted my ex." Truck said, trying to keep a straight face.

Tears running down his cheeks, Jim sat up trying hard to fight back another laughing attack. "Keep me out of this, Truck. You and Greg work it out."

"Aw, dere's no use talkin ta dat short circuit. I get a headache when I try ta figure out what he's saying most a da time."

"I'm sorry, Truck. I didn't know you were that sensitive about the livestock you consider friends or wives."

Before Truck could fire his next round, Jim interrupted. "If you two are finished, maybe we should consider calling it a night. Unless, of course, you want to stay up all night, arguing."

"Aw, we wasn't really arguing, Jimbo. We was discussin."

"Ya! We wasn't arguing, Jimbo. We was discussin." Greg aped his big brother.

This set off another bout of laughter. This time, he was echoed by his two brothers. After the last ripples of laughter had subsided, Jim spoke. "This is just like the old days. We managed to find humor in everything we did. No matter what the situation was, we were there for each other. Let's hold on to it forever. Shall we?"

"I concur, one hundred percent, Jim. These last few years have been a tad rough for all of us. One can only hope, the future will be a little kinder."

"Amen ta dat! Truck said as he reached for the coffeepot. After filling their cups, he proposed a toast. To da best goddamn team in da world."

Clicking their cups together, in unison, each one captured the moment and added it to his collection of fond memories.

As they stood around the fire, enjoying the moment, a loud noise shattered the serene, stillness of the night. The effect it had on the three men was that of fingernails scraping along a blackboard. A few moments ago, they were enjoying the nocturnal whispers of darkness. Now, they were assaulted by the loud intrusion.

"What da hell is dat?" Truck asked, looking around, nervously.

"I don't know, but it sounds like it's headed this way. Jim said. Maybe it's a plane with engine trouble. A lot of bush pilots fly in this area."

"I don't think so. Greg said. It's moving much too fast for an ordinary bush plane. Aside from the fact, no pilot would venture into this area at his time of night."

As they searched the dark sky for the cause of the commotion, a curtain of tension enveloped them, riveting them to the spot. Closer and closer it came. The incongruous buzzing assassinated the familiar night choruses, thrusting deeply into the heart of nature itself.

"There! I see some lights!" Said Jim after a brief period of intense silence, pointing over the trees to their right.

"I used to be able to identify anything that flew by the color and location of its running lights. Said Greg. But those are totally unfamiliar to me."

"Dos are da strangest lights I ever saw." Added Truck.

"Whatever it is will be passing over us very shortly, gentlemen. Said Jim.

The eerie lights grew larger as they neared the campsite. Smaller fingers of light sprayed out from the mother beacon, tickling the ground in all directions. Its shape was very discernable, now. "V" shaped with a large, round dome at the very tip, it was approximately three hundred feet in length. The mini-spotlights that crisscrossed the area, beneath, seemed to cover every blade of grass in its well-executed pattern. The pale blue light, filtering down, silhouetted the ship against the dark background of the night sky. Like spidery legs, the rays of light walked over the ground, searching, reaching. About two hundred yards from where they stood, the strange craft changed direction. Like a giant eagle, it locked on to its prey, heading straight toward them.

"What in da hell is dat thing?" Truck asked, mostly to himself.

Dropping their coffee cups alongside the small fire, they backed up a few nervous paces.

"I think I'll be going home, now. Said Greg. I've seen quite enough. Thank you."

"I wish I had my camera with me. Said Jim. No one is going to believe me when I tell them about this."

Hovering almost directly above them, now, the lights captured each of the men, who stared up questioningly. The pulsating staccato of the engine quieted to a soft hum. Hanging like a giant chandelier, it stared back at the men from less than one hundred feet above.

The self-control exercises their grandfather Joseph had taught them while they were youngsters was the only thing keeping them rooted to the spot.

"When fear is controlled there is no panic." He would say. "Running from something you do not understand can lead to more danger. Acknowledge the fact you are afraid, then, find out why. By slowing your impulses to take flight, you make yourself less visible. The bolting jackrabbit is more exposed and likely to die. The jackrabbit that has patience lives to see another day"

All of grandfather's disciples had learned their lessons well. The thought of fleeing from the proximity of the strange craft coursed through their minds, but that's where it remained.

"Gentlemen! I have a strong inclination we are looking upon an "alien" vessel."

"Aw, come on Greg. Ya don't believe dat UFO crap, do ya?"

"He may be right, Truck. I have never seen a ship of this design before. Nor have I heard of one, this size, hovering as motionless. Look at it! It's frozen in the air."

"I think it's dos sneaky Russkies up ta dere old tricks, again."

"That is conceivable, Truck, but not very probable. Even with their highly-subversive methods, I don't believe their technology has evolved to this degree."

"Jim! Will ya listen ta da professor dere. He picks da damndest time ta give a lecture. Don't He?"

Once, again, Jim assumed the impartial role he had practiced a lifetime. He remained silent.

"I was purely making a speculation, not giving a lecture. To be perfectly honest, I am as ignorant of the situation as you are."

"Who ya calling ignorant?"

"Truck, if I may borrow one of your more intelligent phrases: Suck an egg!"

"Time out, you two. Let's concentrate on the situation above us. I don't know what it is or wants from us, but be prepared for anything."

"Any suggestions, Jim?"

"We have to find out what their intentions are. I haven't thought of anything, yet.

"How bout if we jus start walking. See if dey follow us or something."

"A good idea, Truck!" Lets do it!"

Moving in unison, they began slowly walking in the direction they were facing. Their legs wanted to rebel against the discipline that controlled their minds. Telling them to run for their lives. But it was set too firmly for them to have their way.

Looking over their shoulders, they noticed the strange craft was keeping pace with them from above. Not once did the distance, separating them, change. Like a giant shadow it pursued them, hauntingly.

As they walked, Truck bent over and picked up a large branch that had broken away from the forest.

"What, may I ask, do you intend doing with that?" Greg inquired

"Well, I sure as hell ain't gonna pick my teeth with it. He replied. If dos bastards wanna fight den maybe dis will even up da odds a little."

"Drop it, Truck! We don't want to show any outward signs of hostility. There isn't much we can do until they make the first move."

Flinging the branch away in frustration, he mumbled to himself.

"Jim! What do you suppose would happen if we made our way in different directions?"

"Your guess is as good as mine, Greg. Lets try it and find out. If anything happens, stop immediately. Barring any interruptions, we'll meet back at the truck. Okay? Let's go!

Without breaking stride, Greg and Truck veered off to the right and left. Jim continued straight ahead. They hadn't taken twenty paces before the confusion in the craft revealed itself.

Increasing in their brilliance, the strange lights showering down upon them, started radiating an intense heat. It began to get hotter and hotter with each step they took. Like an immense solar cloud, the relentless down pour of heat pelted them, mercilessly.

"Greg! Truck! Get back together, again!" Jim yelled through the suffocating onslaught.

Working their way back together, each man realized, now, just how serious their situation really was. Gasping for breath, they collapsed in a sweaty heap directly below the ominous vessel. Almost immediately, the stifling heat subsided and the probing strobe lights resumed their original glow.

"So much for that idea. Jim said. You guys all right?"

"Other than a touch of sun burn, I'm fine. Greg said. I think whoever, or whatever, they are want us to remain together."

"Aw, gee! I'm really sorry. Truck said, sarcastically. Maybe we should apologize ta dem. With that, he threw up his right hand with the middle finger extended. "Observe dis, ya bastards!"

"You may have something there, Truck." Jim said.

"What' dat?" The big guy asked, scratching his head.

"Maybe if we wave or do something they may interpret, as a peaceful sign, we may find out what their intentions are."

"Hell, Jimbo. Dey was da ones dat started dis shit." Truck said, Why should I be friendly ta dem. Look what dey done to us!"

"We feel the same way, too, Truck. But we have to do something. If you have a better suggestion, let's hear it. If not, for our safety, cool it! We have to remain clear headed about this."

"I'll clear a few a dos heads." He mumbled under his breath.

"Jim, I don't think our next move is necessary." Greg said, pointing up toward the ship. Look at that!"

Billowing out from the underside of the craft was, what appeared to be, a thick layer of green smoke. As they lay there, watching the swirling cloud descend upon them, the fears that each of them harbored began to surface. Like a heavy shadow, it settled over them, caressing their minds as well as their bodies.

"What, in da holy hell, are dey doin now!" Truck grumbled.

"It looks like a smoke screen of some sort. Maybe there leaving and don't want us following them." Jim said, trying to make light of their situation.

The density of the swirling cloak, not only cut off their view of the large craft, it also became difficult to see one another.

"I think this would be a fine time to leave, you guys." Jim said, trying to rise to his feet.

"Dis crap is starting ta get on my nerves, you guys. And, what da hell is dat smell?"

"You are absolutely correct, Truck. It is reacting on all of our nerves. At this very moment, I am experiencing a strange sensation. A lethargic feeling, I am almost positive, induced by gas."

"I feel it too, Greg. I thought I was just tired out from all of this, but I'm finding it difficult to concentrate."

Curling up into a big ball, Truck said: "I'm gonna take a little nap. Wake me up when yer ready ta go fishing."

As the last vestige of reality vanished, three huddled forms succumbed to the sedating fog. The green shroud gave them no warmth as it blanketed their minds.

# CHAPTER 2

The loud noise startled Jim, interrupting the serene stillness that engulfed him. As consciousness crept, slowly back into his mind, the scene that met his eyes convinced him he was in the middle of a nightmare. Bolting upright, into a sitting position, he stared in disbelief. Not more than five feet away, peering through, what appeared to be, metal bars, were three of the most hideous creatures that had ever polluted his visual senses. Yellow eyes, deep-set into bony sockets, stared back at him, unblinkingly. Radiating from the dark pupils were red veins that covered the entire eye in a spider web-like pattern. The large head resembled an inverted pear. The fat part, across the entire top, pulsed. A small valley was carved between the two short antennae on top. An oozing, horizontal gash, centered just below the eyes, took the place of a nose. But the most horrendous feature was the mouth, a large, vertical oval, surrounded by fleshy, sucker-like lips. Located within were two, large canines, one at the top and bottom, offset to meet in a pincer-like fashion. Judging their height at approximately six and a half feet, they stood on long, spindly legs that ended in splayed, toeless feet. Their long arms, extended from sloping shoulders, terminated in hands resembling double ice tongs. Four long, curved fingers, tipped with sharp talons, bespoke the fact they were well armed. The bluish-gray hue to the skin added to their ghoulish appearance. Except for hands and heads, their entire bodies were clothed in a silver colored fabric.

So overwhelmed by the strange images his eyes were projecting on his mind, he noticed, for the first time that he was entirely naked. As the three creatures continued their silent observation, he took an inventory of their surroundings. Across the cell from him lay his two brothers, breathing peacefully as in a deep sleep. Looking around, he judged the cell (or cage) to be about fifteen feet square. The bars were an inch thick and coated with a gray, velvet-like substance. They extended, vertically, about six inches apart, floor to ceiling, across the entire front of their cell. Polished to a high gloss, the floor looked as if it had been cut from a solid slab of white marble. Rubbing his hand over it, he noticed that unlike stone it gave off heat.

Looking over the heads of the three horrid spectators, he noticed many more cages, all connected and strung out in a large circle. The one they occupied being a part of this large circle. The ones within his view were filled with monstrosities of every shape, size and color imaginable. Every abomination that had ever auditioned for a nightmare was located here. If "Mr. Satan", himself, had been in the middle of the compound, cracking his whip, it wouldn't have surprised him. The most depraved minds in the world could not have even come close in conjuring up these rejects from hell.

Tearing his eyes away from this sideshow of horrors, he noticed the entire perimeter was filled with the strange creatures such as the ones that stood before him. Milling from one cage to the next in a slow procession, they all moved in the same direction. Running parallel to the cages about twenty feet away and inside the circle, were small metal structures, one adjacent to each cage. The walkway between the cages and small sheds was hard-packed and smooth, evidence of a considerable amount of traffic.

The ceiling of the cage, fifteen feet above the floor, was covered with a material resembling dark plastic. It was opaque enough to allow some of the sun's light to filter through. Slightly darker versions of the same substance served as walls across the entire back of the cage and on either side

The eerie sights, which bombarded his mind during these first, brief moments of consciousness, were absorbed in total disbelief. "God, tell me this isn't real! He shouted, as he rose from the cell floor to his feet. "It can't be!" He repeated to himself, in a lower voice. His sudden movements startled the three creatures observing him. As one, they moved back a few paces. Still staring at him, they resumed their silent vigil.

At the sound of their brother's voice, Greg and Truck were yanked back into reality, or unreality, given the situation. Looking around wide-eyed and speechless, they reflected the same shock on their faces Jim had experienced moments earlier.

"What in da holy hell is going on?" Truck asked, as they got to their feet and joined their brother.

"I don't know, brother, I just got here myself. Jim answered.

"Wherever we are, it is quite obvious we are not going to be treated as guests." Greg said. Looking around the cage.

As the three men stood together in the middle of the cage digesting the inexplicable collage of oddities surrounding them, a loud siren blasted the graveyard silence, the same noise that had roused Jim from his drugged status and delivered him into this nightmare.

Turning to their right, the three creatures moved on to the next cage. There were five observers, now, in front of their cage. Two of them, little more than three feet tall, appeared to be children. Like the previous group, they stood there staring in at them. Their large, yellow eyes drinking in the three strange creatures before them.

"Gentlemen, I have come to the conclusion that we have just become Earth's unwitting contribution to an "alien sideshow"

"Wha da ya mean by dat, Greg?" Truck asked.

"If I am correct in my assumptions, we are the latest attractions of a "Galactic zoo." The proprietors of which are obviously highly intelligent beings, capable of unlocking the mysteries of space travel."

"Are you saying we were abducted just to provide entertainment for these creatures? Jim asked. It seems like an awful lot of trouble just for that?"

"I'm not exactly positive, of course, but observe the manner in which they traverse from cage to cage. Stopping, staring, then moving along again. Not unlike the way we tour our local zoos. "Of course they conduct themselves in a more logical and civilized pattern. The controlled procedure of moving in the same direction, in unison, eliminates the random jostling one experiences in a disorganized crowd racing in all directions at the same time."

"I'll be goddamned if anybody's gonna through peanuts at me." Truck yelled, as he charged the front of the cage. The bellowing roar that froze many would be tacklers, on the football field, froze on his lips. The moment his hands came into contact with the bars, he was catapulted backwards into his brothers. Untangling himself from the heap, Jim bent over the still form of his large sibling

"Truck! You all right?" Concern reflected from both of their faces, when there was no response. They started shaking him and slapping him lightly, trying to bring him around.

"Come on, you big ape, Answer me!" Jim implored the big guy. After a short eternity;

"I believe he's beginning to respond, Jim. At least he's breathing normally, again."

As his eyes finally opened and color returned to his face, a bewildered expression stared up at them. Glossy eyed from the powerful blow he had been dealt, he sat up holding his head.

"Wha happened? He asked confusedly. I never been hit dat hard in my life."

Breathing a sigh of thankful relief. Jim said: "You were testing the bars to see how strong they were and almost electrocuted yourself. It's a good thing we were here to catch you. You've gained a little weight. Haven't you, brother?" He said, with a big smile on his face. "Now I know how it feels to be run over by a truck."

"I hardly believe this is the proper time for levity." Said Greg, in a more serious tone. He nearly killed himself and you make light of the situation."

"Aw, Greg, relax! Other den a little headache, I'm all right. Don' get so worked up about it!"

"He's right, Greg! They locked up our bodies but we can't allow them to lock up our minds. I'm just as concerned about the situation as you are. What's the matter with relieving a little of this tension? God knows we can use it.

Besides, there isn't a whole hell of a lot we can do at the present. Is there?"

"I'm all in favor of alleviating a little pressure from our dilemma. But, we also have to utilize our time constructively to enhance any chance of escaping."

The siren went off, again, signaling another shift in the rotating throng of spectators. With little more than a casual glance at the newest audience, they returned to their discussion.

"As weird as it seems, gentlemen, we are not dreaming! This is a dire situation! Until I am given a reasonable explanation for all of this I will, as you say, Truck, remain "worked up". Therefore, "my" sense of humor will be put on hold." Said Greg, in a serious tone.

"Let me work him over for a little while, Jim. He'll come around ta our way a thinking." Said Truck, with a big smile on his face. It couldn't help but spread to the faces of his two siblings.

"That's a great idea, Truck! Said Jim, as he looked at the bewildered expression on the big guy's face. Obviously, we're going to have plenty of time on our hands."

"I was just kidding, Jimbo! I'd never hit da little guy."

"That's not what I meant, Truck. I'm talking about a good physical workout every day. Not only will it provide a break in the monotony, but it will also keep us in shape. We may have to depend on our muscles as well as our minds, before too long."

"Kinda like getting ready for da big game. Eh Jimbo?

"Something like that, Truck. But this is a lot more serious than any game."

"Indeed it is! Added Greg. Not only are we ignorant of the rules. But, the slightest error, may sideline us for good. It is imperative that we maintain extreme caution in all of our actions until we familiarize ourselves with the authors of our dilemma. Having said that, I can't think of a better team I'd rather play for."

As they sat with their backs against the wall, at the rear of the cage, each man thought of his plight. The endless stream of observers parading before them was hardly noticed. Exhausted from their ordeal and the lack of a restful sleep, they soon succumbed to the embracing arms of "Morpheus", there only escape from this uncanny world, into which fate had cruelly tossed them.

The chill in the night air roused them from a restless sleep. Despite the warmth, radiating from the polished floor, their naked bodies shivered awake. How long they had slept, they had no way of knowing. But, sometime during the pursuit of dreams the sun had burnt itself out. It was replaced by a clear, starlit night. Moonless, though it was, the myriad of stars cast sufficient light enabling one to see for quit a distance. Devoid of the alien creatures, now, the only sounds came from a few of the strange malcontents caged within the circle.

After his eyes had adjusted to the subdued light, Jim noticed two round objects perched in the middle of the cell floor. Moving closer to inspect, he discovered two large bowls. Each one was about thirty inches in diameter and approximately twenty inches deep. One was filled with a clear liquid and the other contained a brown, gruel-like substance.

"Dinner is served, gentlemen! I think!" He said, raising the bowl containing the liquid to his nose and cautiously smelling it. Joining their brother, Greg and Truck bent over the bowl containing a brown, porridge-like substance.

"What da hell is dis stuff? Truck said, lifting the bowl to his nose and sniffing at it. It don't smell too bad, but it looks like crocodile shit."

"Surely they don't expect us to eat this swill. Do they?"

"I don't think we have much of a choice, Greg. Here, try some water! It tastes almost as good as the well water back home."

"I don' know about you two guys, but I'm so hungry I could eat da ass end out of a bag lady through a park bench. Here goes nothing!" Dipping two fingers into the mixture, he then placed them in his mouth.

"Do you find it necessary to be so primitively crude in everything you do?" Greg asked.

"Nah! It ain't necessary but I kinda got used to it over da years. Truck answered, still sucking on his fingers.

"Well, how does it taste, Truck?" Jim asked.

"Not too bad! He answered, as he stuck his fingers back into the bowl. I had a lot worse den dis in da service. Try it!"

Adding his fingers to the bowl, Jim tasted it, smacking his lips and trying to distinguish the flavor. "It really isn't so bad, Greg. We have to eat in order to stay fit. If this is all they intend giving us then we had better make the most of it." Jim said.

"Has it occurred to either of you, the possibility of drugs or even poison existing in the contents of these bowls?"

"Why would they do something like that, Greg? After going through so much trouble to get us here, I don" believe they want to harm us. Not their newest attractions!""

"Until I become aware of their underlying motives, I shall remain distrustful.

"Hell, brother, we don't trust dese freaks, either. But, we gotta eat. If we starve we ain't gonna be much good ta each other. So dig in, will ya and stop your goddamn yapping!"

The crude logic in his brother's words forced his fingers into the bowl. He tasted the mushy substance, fighting back a wave of nausea. "I must apologize to my taste buds for putting them through this traumatic ordeal." He said, in a lighter tone of voice.

A short while later, after they had consumed their first alien meal, Jim picked up one of the empty bowls and examined it. "I wonder what these are made of?" He said, turning it in his hands.

"It appears to be some kind of aluminum alloy, given its light weight. Said Greg. Similar to the material used in the fabrication of computer parts. Excellent craftsmanship!"

"Deh'd make good helmets, too! Truck said, placing the other one on his head. Nice and light!"

Giving his brother a reproachful look, Greg shook his head. "It is beyond me why you would even consider protecting your head, Truck! That would be comparable to putting armed guards around an empty warehouse. Wouldn't it?"

"What da hell da ya mean by dat, shorty?" Truck asked, removing the bowl from his head.

"Simply that our situation is not a laughing matter and you are not taking this very seriously! Greg replied. The three of us must make a concentrated effort to obtain any pertinent information that may be vital to us in our future plans. Anything we may see, touch, hear or even taste could, possibly, reveal something of importance."

"Ya gonna tell me dat looking at a couple a bowls is important? Not ta me it ain't!"

"I think you are missing the point of what Greg is trying to say, Truck." Jim interjected.

"I ain't missin nothing!" The big guy responded in a loud voice.

"No? Other than a few pounds of gray matter, I would say you were quite intact."

"Is dat so? Well, If you're so smart, "mister genius", maybe ya can tell me how da hell dey got dos things in here without us seeing em. Betcha didn't think about dat, did ya?"

Caught at his own game, Greg mumbled, almost too himself; "I most confess, I hadn't thought about that."

"Neither did I!" Added Jim.

"Well, you guys better start paying attention. Dis ain't no goddamn hayride were on, ya know. Turning the tables on his brothers, Truck continued to enjoy himself. Do I gotta do all da thinking around here?"

"Be that as it may, brother, I will concede to you this much. Greg said. You are, indeed, a master of sarcasm and pretty adept at rubbing salt in wounds."

Basking in the glow of his small victory, a big smile took over his handsome face. "Jus chalk dis one up for ol' Truck."

"Now that we've settled that, Jim said in a more serious voice, we have some work to do. Somewhere in this cell may be a hidden door. If we can find out its location, a close watch can be kept on it. But first things first." He rose to his feet and started searching the wall to their right. Greg duplicated the maneuver on the wall to their left. Truck probed the rear wall. Even with his long arms extended, the ceiling was still a good seven feet beyond his reach.

"Greg! Git on my shoulders and search da high spots." As Truck kneeled down, Greg hopped aboard his brother's massive shoulders. He finished his search of the high walls in no time at all.

"As long as you're up there, you might as well search the ceiling. Jim called up to them. I'll search the floor."

As Truck walked back and forth across the cell, Greg's probing fingers traced inquiring paths on the ceiling. As they neared the center of the cell, he called out, signaling his brother to stop walking. His fingers had detected a shallow groove. Following it around, he estimated its size to be about two feet square.

"What is it, Greg? Jim asked.

"I can't tell for certain what it is, but there's a two-foot square etching of some sort. Whether it's our proverbial "hidden door" or just a decoration, I'm not certain."

"See if you can open it!" Jim said, excitedly.

Plying his shoulder to the middle of the square, he pushed up with all his might. The unexpected force on Truck's shoulders caused him to lose his balance. Down they came, landing in a heap. Their momentum almost carried them into the lethal bars.

"You two okay? Asked Jim, helping them to their feet.

"For God's sake, Truck! If you couldn't handle my weight you should have said something. I could have put you on my shoulders, perhaps."

"Cool it, squirt! Ya caught me by surprise, dat's all. Truck said in mock anger. And don't make me laugh. If I got on your shoulders you'd only be three feet tall instead a four."

"I guess you two are okay." Said Jim, shaking his head.

"If it is a door, it is obviously well-secured from above, Jim. Said Greg, ignoring Truck's last barb. That leaves us with only one other recourse."

"And that is?" Jim asked.

"The three of us most alternate our sleeping periods and keep an eye on that door if, indeed, that's what it is. If there is the slightest indication that it is about to be opened, whoever is on guard must alert the others. While, at the same time, we must not reveal that we are aware of it and are capable of reaching it."

"I guess that's about all we can do, for the present. Jim said. I'll take the first watch!"

As his brothers lay down at the base of the back wall, he propped himself up in a corner. With his head slightly tilted, his eyes were on a direct line with the area in question.

After a few moments, Truck's voice invaded the silence. "When we git outta dis mess, I promise, I ain't never going fishing with you two, again. Whose big idea was dis in da first place?"

Two voices, almost in unison, shot back at him through the dark. "Yours!"

"Oh!" He mumbled.

Once, again, silence descended upon them.

* * * * * * * * *

The shrill blast, from the siren, brought Jim up with a start, introducing him to another day. Looking up, quickly, almost to make sure the door was still there, he cursed himself for having dozed off. He was startled, for the second time, by the sound of Greg's voice.

"Relax, Jim! Everything is in order. Sleep eluded me the second time around, so I doubled the watch. It's a wonder you were able to sleep with old diesel mouth, here." Nudging his big brother awake, he got to his feet.

"Whatsamatter?" Truck said, sleepily.

"If there was a way of developing that loud, snoring of yours into energy, we could fly home first class."

"Well, hell, little brother, all I gotta do is break your nose a coupla times. Den you'll breath jus like me." He said, shaking his big fist.

Backing away, in mock terror, Greg said; "That's quite alright. I rather like it just the way it is."

As he listened to his two brothers saying good morning to each other, in their usual manner, Jim noticed two creatures walking across the empty courtyard in their direction. "Better hurry up and change into something decent, you two. Our guests are arriving."

Looking through the bars, they watched in silence as the two creatures neared their cage. Their long, shuffling strides ate up the distance very rapidly.

"Are you gentlemen aware of anything different about these two individuals?" Greg asked.

"Dey look da same as da other creeps, ugly as hell."

"The only thing I see that's different is these two individuals are wearing black. All of the others were wearing silver." Jim ventured.

"Precisely!" Greg said.

"Maybe dere in charge a dis freak farm." Added Truck.

The two creatures stopped at the shed-like structure adjacent to their cage. Opening a door, they pulled out a cone-shaped apparatus situated atop a wheeled tripod. They pushed this machine to within a few feet in front of their cage and busied themselves with the dials and knobs at the side of the cone.

"I jus figured da whole thing out, you guys. We're on "Candid Camera" and dis is all a big joke."

But, the intensity reflecting from the eyes of the three Earthmen, said otherwise. A shroud of stillness smothered them as they awaited the unknown. The powerful grip of anxiety clutched at their emotions, allowing them, only, to stare and breath.

A loud, piercing staccato emitting from the cone, injected their minds so suddenly that it threw them onto their backs writhing and clutching their ears in agony. Every tissue of their minds and bodies was invaded by excruciating pain. The two creatures moved quickly, adjusting dials and pressing buttons. After what seemed like an eternity, the pain subsided and was replaced by a steady, but soft, buzzing in their minds.

A raspy voice echoed from the three walls of their cage. "Earth" creatures! Harm was not our intention." Looking up, in unison, the three men noticed one of the creatures talking into an apparatus connected to the strange, cone-shaped machine. His assistant continued to make adjustments. The language, although unlike any they had ever heard, was fully understood by the shocked trio.

The voice continued: "It was necessary to find the proper level of your brain's intellectual capacity. Starting at the level of the supreme "Nevoan" intelligence. I gradually reduced it to yours, a level not much higher than the primitive natives of "Elimar". This machine is a "cerebral implanter". It is capable of analyzing the brain tissue of any living creature. Once the comprehensive center is located, if one exists, impulses are transmitted to the area recording our language upon it. After we have concluded this process, you will be able to communicate in our language. It will seem to you as if you have always done so. None of your original languages or thought patterns will be damaged or erased during this enrichment period. In order for this process to develop correctly, you will be unable to move or talk until it is completed."

"Your purpose here is a glorious, honor. Selected from the barbarian planet, you call "Earth", you have become a part of "Zarnog's" universal collection of intelligence. All of your Earthly knowledge will be extracted from you and absorbed by him, as is the privilege of the "Leader Most High".

"We are the supreme race! All other life exists only to serve us! Conditions provided for the chosen subjects are far better than they could have obtained from the environments in which they were extracted. Servitude, is not only expected, it is demanded! Any converse actions directed against our great society will result in severe punishment. Loyalty and obedience will be rewarded. So, as not to confuse your low intelligence, you have only these two choices to make.

"Choose wisely!"

"After the machine has completed its analysis, sleep will come, immediately. Upon awakening, everything will seem as it was before. But, you will remember everything.

Welcome to civilization, Earth subjects!" Giving a curt gesture to his assistant, they quickly departed With the return of silence, the three men became aware, once again, of the tingling vibrations emitting from the machine holding them captive. Powerless, they lay in a vegetated state, while their minds were being excavated. All of their thoughts were exposed. Every particle of knowledge acquired in their lifetimes was, now, in the possession of the machine. On and on it went. The mental fingers clutching every thought, action and emotion their minds had ever experienced. After what seemed like a short forever, the tingling sensation subsided and was suddenly gone. Drained of all mental energies, the three men succumbed to a deep sleep. Mentally raped by the knowledge-hungry aliens, they were as infants in this strange world, naïve, vulnerable, expendable.

# CHAPTER 3

As the siren exploded, announcing another day, the collection of "universal" inmates stirred. The sounds, emanating from the alien zoo, protested the predicament of every individual and out of this entire orchestra of anomalies, no two sounds harmonized.

"Shut da hell up, ya ugly bastards!" Truck's voice boomed out, through the bars of the cage, blasting his two brothers annoyingly awake.

"I hope you derived some pleasure from that." Greg said, staring up at his big brother.

"Ya, as a matter of fact, I did! It's hard for me ta concentrate with all dat racket going on."

"I find that very hard to believe, Truck! When you and your "Neanderthal" friends get together, it sounds about the same."

Ignoring his younger brother, Truck turned completely around. Modeling the blue, close-fitting covertogs he wore, he said: "How da ya like my new duds?"

"I'm surprised they had one that would fit you, Truck." Said Jim, smiling.

"It says on da label "one size fits all." Dey kinda remind me of dos pajamas dey gave us at da orphanage. Da ones with da feet connected."

At the bottom of each leg of the covertogs were boots, with half-inch leather soles, sewn in.

"Very practical! Said Greg. It eliminates the possibility of losing ones shoes."

Hurriedly donning the covertogs, their nakedness was covered for the first time since their arrival.

"Well, at least a little comfort and courtesy has been accorded us. Greg said. Long over-due, though it was."

"A little less vulnerable, maybe, but after what happened to us, the situation has gone from serious to that of a life and death struggle. Jim said.

"Before I go down, I'll take a few a dos bastards with me. Said Truck. Dey ain't gonna make no slave outta me!"

"Truck! Didn't anything penetrate that cement block, you use for a head? This isn't a barroom brawl confrontation. Any show of hostility or rebellion, now, could very easily jeopardize our safety. I suggest a little passivity until we learn more. Greg continued. Roughhouse tactics will make matters even worse and probably get us killed. To put it in jock-strap language, too many penalties and we'll lose the game,"

"I agree with Greg, Truck. If we lead them to believe we're harmless, they may relax their vigil long enough for us to make our escape. We don't want to draw any attention to ourselves."

"Okay! Okay! I'll go along with it. If I gotta kiss dere ugly butts, I'll do it. But, when da time comes, I'm taking my shots."

"I'm sure we all will, soon enough, Truck." Jim said.

"Speaking of ugly butts, Truck, I'm sure there are plenty of farmers that would be grateful to have the use of your manure spreader." Greg said.

"Listen, pencil butt, you ain't got nothing to be so proud of, either. And what da hell ya laughing about, Jim?"

Putting on a sober face, hurriedly, Jim tried to contain the laughter exploding within. "It never ceases to amaze me, he said while taking a deep breath, the way you two remain so consistent. If these creatures over-heard your conversations, they'd put you into separate cages for fear of losing one of their exhibits. Isn't there anything the two of you agree upon?"

Greg and Truck, looking like two school-boys scolded by their teacher, gave their brother sheepish grins, causing him to give in to his laughter.

"I give up!" He said, as he walked to the other end of the cage.

Playing the game farther, Greg said; "You don't suppose it's possible we've hurt his feelings do you, Truck?"

"Nah! I think he's just a little homesick. Dat's all. Like da time he was at boot camp. Two days in da service and he was ready ta go AWOL. He jus needs a little cheering up."

Sitting with his back to them, a big grin on his face, Jim stared out through the bars. He knew what was going to happen next. But, before he could react, he was pinned on his back beneath his two brothers. Laughing and trying to squirm free, he, inadvertently, kicked one of his legs out brushing one of the bars.

"Time out, you guys! He said as he sat up. Check that out! I think they cut off the current to our bars."

As the three of them regained their feet, startling the latest group of observers, Greg said; "In the short amount of time they've had to diagnose us, I rather doubt it was sufficient, enough, to determine us as harmless."

"You forget, Greg. They know more about us as individuals than we do about each other. Something must have convinced them that we are not high-security risks."

"That's true, Jim. But, obviously, they haven't had a chance to scan Truck's tape yet. If they had, we'd all be in straight jackets by now."

"An da reason for dat, my puny brother, is because dey got so bored listening ta yours, dey didn't have time for da good stuff."

Their collective attention was drawn by a noise coming from across the compound. Marching in their direction was a cordon of ten black-clad creatures. Pushing and striking out at the spectators, they made their way through the crowd like a ship through a sea of ice. Each of them was armed with a short staff. Using them indiscriminately, the slow-footed residents fell in their wake, as they advanced toward their cage.

"What a lovely surprise! Said Greg, sarcastically, A visit by some of "His Majesty's" finest. Don't forget to salute!"

"I'll salute da coward bastards with a left hook ta dere melons!"

"Easy, Truck! Maybe we'll get some of our questions answered, now. Said Jim. Time for that later."

As the small patrol came to a halt, in front of their cage, one of them broke off and opened the door on the shed. Pushing a few buttons, he rejoined his comrades. Almost immediately, the bars across the entire front, of their cage, began to rise. Not until they were entirely swallowed by the ceiling did anyone speak or move. Staring at one another across the short space, alien vs. alien. They shared the same frozen tension produced by total unfamiliarity.

Turning his head, slightly, to face his brothers, Jim said, in a barely audible whisper; "Remember, no false moves until we find out what it is they want from us."

The foremost creature moved a step closer to the cage. "You will come with us, now, Earthmen!" He said in a language totally foreign, but, very familiar at the same time. Picture, if you will, that you are in the middle of a foreign country for the first time in your life, totally ignorant of customs, geography or language. A perfect stranger comes up to you and asks you for directions in his strange language and you are able to understand him completely. That was the stunning shock shared by the three brothers as they stepped down from the cage, onto the alien soil. That they could understand a language they never knew existed was thought shattering. The startled looks, conveyed in unison, the fact they were all conscious of this impossibility.

As they neared the patrol, they were immediately seized, two to a man. Their wrists held firm in the leathery, tong-like grip. Truck immediately shrugged off his would-be captors and brought his ham-like fist back, cocked for a crushing blow.

"No, Truck! Not now!" Jim yelled to his brother.

His fist, suspended in mid-air, was brought down quickly to his side. Resignedly, he offered his wrists up to be recaptured by his escorts before they could bring their staffs into play.

Sandwiched between the six creatures, with another two leading the way and another two bringing up the rear, the small procession drove through the crowd. Not until they were entirely out of the zoo compound, did the ten guards shoulder their weapons, without the slightest concern as to the destruction they had left behind.

They proceeded down a wide avenue surrounded on either side by connecting, dome-shaped buildings. None of them more than two stories in height. Their composition, as well as that of the pavement they walked on, was similar to the hard marble material that made up the floor of their cage. No two buildings differed in color. The brisk pace, of their captors, left little time for sight-seeing. If there was anything worthwhile seeing, it was well hidden. The monotony of the uniform string of buildings made one feel as if he were going in circles, confronting the same scene over and over again. The avenue, in which they traveled, was almost entirely void of other creatures. The few pedestrians they met along the way, scurried quickly out of the way of the advancing patrol.

"It's a wonder the owners of these cubicles are able to distinguish theirs from their neighbors." Jim thought to himself.

A short while later, they approached a large, open-spaced area sprawling directly in front of the largest building they had yet seen. Five stories tall with domes that seem to be covered in gold, it sparkled in the brilliant sunlight. Windows pigeonholed the five levels. On the second story, a large balcony, balanced on four massive, stone columns, hung directly above two wide doors. Five steps, ten feet wide, sat before them. Four sentries, with the strange metal staffs resting on their sloping shoulders, stood guard at the top of the landing.

Coming to a stop at the foot of the steps, one of the sentries addressed us in that alien, but comprehensive, language. "State your intentions, lowly Nevoans!"

The designated spokesman, of the escort, replied. "Lower than I, know then, that Tabor has been entrusted with the delivery of the three Earth, biological units. It is the desire of "Zarnog" our "Leader most high", to have audience with them. I will execute my duties, unless you are foolish enough to object. He said, with a snarl in his voice.

Realizing, for the first time, that he was confronting the infamous "Tabor", the sentry replied.

"Rather would I, Valdon, be burned out of existence by the "Sister" suns of Elimar than to interfere with the desires of our "Leader most high". You may proceed at once!" Nodding to his fellow guardsmen, they immediately swung the huge, double doors inward.

As they poured into the interior of the building, the one called "Tabor" almost knocked the insolent guard to the ground as he brushed by him. The hallway, they marched down, was composed of the same material as that of the exterior, allowing only for a slight variation of color. Both sides of the passageway were lined with columns, four feet in diameter, supporting the second floor. At the end of a long entryway, stood another set of massive doors. On either side stood two of the biggest creatures they had seen thus far. Seven feet tall, with arms and legs the size of half-grown oak trees, they stood as still as statues. Except for loin clothes, they were entirely naked. The staffs, they shouldered, were fully six feet long and they looked more than capable of handling them. The graveyard look in their eyes radiated hatred.

"Now dere's a couple a heavyweights!" Truck said to himself, in a low voice.

As the small party approached the doors, the two behemoths moved together, crossing their staffs.

Tabor came forward as the group halted. "I, Tabor, have arrived with the "Earth" subjects for the desired audience with our "Leader most high".

Shouldering his staff, one of the guards turned and went quickly through the door, closing it behind him. The remaining guard stood, menacingly, in the center of the doorway. He stared, maliciously, at the three Earthmen, murder dripping from his eyes.

"Cute bastard, ain't he?" Truck said in English, loud enough for his brothers to hear.

Glancing at his brother, Jim noticed him, staring back at the huge creature with a challenging grin on his face. Before he could warn him to "cool" it, the door opened, as the other guard returned. Nodding to his partner, they opened the other door and stood aside. As they were marched through the entrance, Greg noticed Truck winking at the monster, as they passed.

They were halted before three steps that led up to a raised platform. A huge, ornate chair took up most of the space. Seated upon it, was the most grotesque creature they had seen, up until this point. This monster was more hideous than any of the exhibits in its, own zoo. It seemed, as though, every new door that was opened to them, revealed a creature more hideous than the last.

An emaciated, wrinkled replica of horrors made them realize this was the first sign of aging they had noticed since awaking on this nightmare world. The robe, decorated with geometric figures, hanging from its thin, slanting shoulders, appeared many sizes too large. White, with a metallic sheen, it formed a backdrop for his purple body suit. The four digits, extruding from each tong-like hand, sported talons six inches long. Each one was painted a different, florescent color. The most shocking feature of all, though, was its head. Like the robe: It, also, appeared to be about three sizes too big. At first glance, it resembled a huge orange that had been left out under the sun to dry. Shriveled and wrinkled, it throbbed with a steady rhythm of its own. The blue veins covering it, moved like tiny snakes across its entirety to the, pulsing, drumbeat of its heart. If it had one, that is! The eyes, buried in deep sockets, glowed, fire red. The web-like veins, within, also moved with the steady pulse, going from dim to bright with every beat; not unlike the flashing of a neon sign. The two fangs, in the sucker-like mouth, were jagged and crusted with age. The macabre scene, before them, took only seconds to register on their minds.

The two, large doormen climbed the steps and assumed bodyguard-like positions on either side of the throne.

Tabor advanced a few paces to the foot of the platform. Bowing low from the waist with both arms extended tongs up.

"Zarnog! "Leader most high", I give onto you the Earth subjects for your pleasure!" Backing away, he positioned himself at the rear of his small patrol. Not for an instance did he look into the eyes of his "maniacal monarch".

What seemed like an eternity passed as the three men were subjected to the intent scrutiny of the "imperial Monster". "Let it be known, primitive beings, the privilege I have accorded you. Of all the orbiting bodies in all of the universes, capable of supporting life, you three have been selected representatives of your kind. To be added to my Intergalactic collection of intelligence and to help sate my overwhelming and unending desires for knowledge is the duty of all. I am "Zarnog", intellectual master of all universes. All species live only to serve me!"

The three Earthmen were emotionally frozen. The egomaniacal ramblings of this monster threatened their lives from every direction. Even the private secrets of their individual existences were in his possession.

Listening, patiently, but feeling the tension getting heavier and heavier, Truck, with a half smile on his face, shouted out loud enough for everyone present to hear: "Up yer ass, melon head!"

Glancing, nervously, at his brother, Greg said, in a low voice; "For God's sake, Truck, contain yourself!" He had no sooner spoken, before all hell broke loose.

Zarnog, with eyes glaring, foam trickling from his awful mouth, stiffened as in shock. One of the escorts, standing behind them, sent a painful blow to the middle of Truck's back with his staff. Before he went down, Jim and Greg were throwing punches at their brother's perpetrator, knocking him senseless. As the other guards advanced, to join in the fight, a loud, nerve-shattering voice echoed off the walls. "Cease this, immediately!" Zarnog, standing now, froze everyone's actions. Two guards picked up their fallen comrade, propping him up between them. Jim and Greg helped their brother to his feet.

"The next creature that moves or speaks, Nevoan or Earth dung, will be exterminated!" An ominous, silence, bombarded the small chamber, clinging to their souls. All eyes were locked onto Zarnog.

Scanning his small audience, sadistically disappointed no one was going to disobey, his rage-red eyes stared hauntingly into Jim's. "What is the meaning of the big one's words? Speak, now!"

Realizing the seriousness of the situation, Jim thought quickly, carefully choosing the right words. There was a strong possibility that they could be his last.

"Your Majesty, "up your ass, melon head", is a formal greeting used by all Earth people while acknowledging their superiors. He said, trying hard to maintain a straight face. Obviously, my brother wished, only, to pay homage to you, in his own way, from all of us. Our disadvantage is that we are ignorant of your "Royal" protocol. Therefore, his intentions were, greatly, misunderstood. Being strangers to your world, it is plain to see, we have a lot to learn. I, also, would like to apologize for striking your guards. I must confess, it is an act rarely used by us Earth people. We are protective of one another, yes, but we try to settle our differences in a more civilized manner most of the time. If we were given the opportunity to learn about your superior culture, I am positive, that in time, we could be a benefit to your greatness. I await your, merciful decision, "Great" one."

He stared at Jim with laser-like precision, trying to penetrate his mind and weigh the validity of his words. Finally, he spoke. "I trust that what you have said, Earth creature, is the truth. Upon it, your lives may depend. Out of my benevolent greatness, I will grant you the time you have mentioned. At the end of that duration I will judge your worthiness. If I learn that you have deceived me, you and your fellow species will be fed, piece by piece, to our hungriest exhibits."

Turning to the creature, in charge of the patrol, he said: "The Earth men are to be taken to the "Universal House of Knowledge". Their education will be placed in the guidance of "Mokar" the "High learner". When the "Sister" suns of Elimar have chased themselves one hundred times across our skies, they are to be returned to me. I will decide, at that time, in which capacity they will serve me. If any! Then, with a malicious grin on his horrible gap of a mouth, he said in a venomous voice: I hope you will not disappoint me! Dismissed!"

As Tabor bowed, Jim shot a quick glance at his brothers, urging them to do the same. As they straightened and turned to leave, Greg noticed a sardonic grin on the countenance of Zarnog.

The whole group was led out of the "High House" by the two, large sentries. This time, three Earthly smiles erupted.

"Way ta go, Jimbo!" Truck said, as they made their way outside. A sharp poke in his ribs, reminded him to be silent. Rubbing the painful area in the small of his back, Truck made a silent note to himself. "One a dese days I'm gonna squash dat bastard!"

They were led across the large, open area directly in front of the "High House" to a building of, almost, equal stature. Alien pedestrians scurried out of their way. The unfortunate ones, who lingered too long staring at the three Earthmen, paid the price of admission; a painful price.

Recognizing Tabor and his alien charges, the two sentries at the door, allowed them, immediate, entrance. In a small cubicle, off to their right, a creature sat at a table. He was writing in a massive log and hadn't noticed them, yet.

Tabor advanced toward the table and brought his staff down on the log with a resounding thud, startling the writer. "By order of Zarnog, these Earth subjects are to be entrusted into the care and guidance of Mokar. Notify him, immediately, that I may be granted an audience!"

Regaining his composure, the clerk rose to his feet. "You have a perverse way of gaining ones attention, Tabor. One day it will bring about your demise!"

"And when that day comes, it will not be at the hands of a useless scribbler. Tabor retorted. Now, do as I bid!"

As the two creatures stood there, glaring at each other, The three men were getting an education without even being aware of it. The higher a Nevoan's position was, in this cruel society, the more power he had. The ones with weaker positions were, constantly, made aware of this with cruelty and threats. No friends were every made in an individual's quest for status. It was the most important thing in their lives. And how they achieved it, didn't matter. Through this cold individualism, a society was born, spawning generation after generation of loveless, calculating beings.

Disengaging himself from the Icy stare of Tabor's lifeless eyes, the clerk exited through a door off to his right.

Strutting back and forth, as if he were, already, the king of his own castle, Tabor whiled away his impatience. He had killed many times to achieve his present position. His malicious, ambitions were too rampant to allow for complacency. His aggressive methods were well known. Those higher up on the power echelon always kept a guarded eye on him while in his presence. He would reach his goal or perish in the attempt. And only he knew what that goal was.

Taking advantage of this brief respite, the three men took a mental tour of their surroundings. Their eyes drinking in the anomalies they were confronted with. The familiar stone, indigenous to this society, glowed from the walls and ceiling with a light, blue radiation. The floors were of the basic white stone.

The table and chair were the only pieces of furniture in the large room. They were black in color and seemed to be made from some type of acrylic material. The huge log, sitting on the table, was covered with a beige, leather-like material.

A small, oval pool sat in the center of the room, spewing water from a sculptured likeness of Zarnog. Large banners hung on all walls, with the royal portrait emblazoned on them.

The round pillars supporting the ceiling, were, fully, ten feet in circumference. Two of them, facing one another from across the pool, appeared to have glass doors imbedded in them. The entire atmosphere of the large room was, methodically sterile. The purpose of its construction was, obviously, not for comfort or entertaining.

Their musings were interrupted by the return of the clerk. "Mokar will see you, now!" He announced.

With a malicious sneer on his face, Tabor brushed him, rudely, aside and went through the doorway. As his consort followed, quickly on his heels, the three Earthmen glanced at the clerk and noticed the hatred festering in his eyes, foam flecking around his yellowed fangs.

"Have a nice day!" Truck said in a low voice, as they filed past the livid creature. The prod in his back and the apprehensive looks from his brothers, wiped the smile from his face.

They were ushered down a long hallway, passed many closed doors. The glow, from the walls, was the only source of light. But, it was more than adequate. The passageway took a sharp turn to their right and emptied into a room resembling a library. All four walls were shelved, from floor to ceiling, and crammed to capacity with volume after volume of the leather-covered, logs. Sitting at a table, over-flowing with papers and an assortment of strange instruments, was a creature in bright, red covertogs. His tiny antennae peeked through a matching red cap that covered the entire top of his head. An insignia, emblazoned in gold, decorated the middle. Two tong-like hands cradled a cluster of stars. The men would find out, soon enough, this was the symbol of the supreme teacher of the Nevoan society. An aura of importance enveloped him. With a nod to his guards, the three Earth- men were ushered, directly, in front of the desk.

"I, Tabor, have been entrusted, the leader of the patrol started to say.

"You will acknowledge your superior by addressing me first by my position!" Interrupted the red-clad, creature that had not, as of yet, raised his eyes from the work in front of him.

The three men glanced at the shocked expression on Tabor's face. It was obvious that few talked to him, thus, and got away with it.

"Right on!" Said Truck loud enough for his brothers to hear.

Tabor was actually shaking from the ill-concealed rage exploding inside of him. The few seconds of deathly silence seemed like an eternity, when, at last, Tabor collected himself enough to, finally, speak.

"Mokar, High teacher of the universes and ultimate learner of the supreme "Nevoan" society, I, Tabor have been entrusted with the delivery of the Earth creatures. It is the wish of Zarnog "Leader most high" that you are to educate them in the ways of our society. In one hundred journeys of the "Sister" suns they are to be re-scheduled for audience with the "Leader most high". It was apparent, Tabor was struggling for enough self-control to finish delivering his message.

Looking up from his papers, for the first time, Mokar's gaze found the noticeably, shaken Tabor. Like a concert pianist, his timing was, methodically, perfect. Letting the audience hang on the, last, emotional note and deriving pleasure from the chords he had struck deep within the egomaniacal, Tabor.

"My" Recorder of progress", Solon, has already informed me. He, finally, spoke. Arrangements are already being tended to. Your conduct has, also, been brought to my attention, Tabor. It shall be duly noted in your "life appraisal". A scribbler, I may be, but one with the power to reduce a being to nothingness with a few, paramount, words. Your cruel and devious methods could become fleeting, meaningless memories if I so choose. I trust, in the future, you will enter my house with respect. Or, you will never leave it, again! Is this understood?"

Striving for composure, Tabor fought, with all his might, against the humiliation bombarding him. "One day he would rip out and eat the heart of this tormentor." He thought. But, for now, he had to endure.

"It is understood, Mokar." He answered, in a voice emotionally subdued.

"Very well!" Then, I believe we have nothing further to discuss. You and your subordinates are dismissed!"

"But, Mokar, will you not be in need of guards? The Earthlings may become hostile, if provoked."

"Then, they shall not be provoked."

When Tabor started to protest, Mokar interrupted. "May I remind you, Tabor, it is my duty in life to do the thinking, not yours. Dismissed!"

Turning, abruptly, to conceal his rage, he hurried out of the room, followed closely by his troops.

When the sounds of their footfalls had subsided, Mokar turned his attention and penetrating gaze back on the Earthmen

"If Zarnog deems it possible that you are capable of learning, then I most believe it, also. If I were in your position and given the same opportunity, I would want to learn as much about my enemies as I could. You are as strange to me, as I am to you. Maybe, with an objective understanding, it will be possible to educate each other. Do you have any questions, Earth men?"

The thoughts, going through the three heads were overwhelming. So much had happened and so fast. No amount of questions or answers could alleviate the bewilderment they felt. So, they just stood there, not knowing what to say.

It was Greg who, finally, spoke. "Mokar, may I have your permission to speak?"

"You have my permission, Earth man."

"In the short time we have been in your world, we have been subjected to abduction, humiliation, physical abuse and the entire slate of "Nevoan" hospitality. He said, sarcastically. How can anyone expect conformity from us, when we have not been shown one shred of decency?"

"I do not dictate rules and regulations, Earth man, but I, also, must abide by them. As long as I am allowed the freedom to pursue my studies, they are not my concern."

"Ya! Dat's good for you. Truck blurted out, excitedly. But, what da hell do we get if we play ball?"

Noticing the confused look on Mokar's face, Jim said, quickly; "Mokar, what my brother meant was, What kind of guarantee do we have that we will be treated any better for our efforts and why should we trust you?"

Looking, directly, at Truck, he said; "Obviously, you have many reasons for not trusting any "Nevoan". But, this one did you no harm. I can only assure you of one thing. As long as you are in my charge, you will be safe and treated fairly. I can promise you no more than that."

Looking at his two brothers, Jim spoke. "That's a lot more than we have received, so far. I think we should, at least, give it a try. What do you say?" It wasn't much of a choice, under the circumstances, but they all agreed

"Okay, Mokar! When do we start?"

"By the light of the first "Sister's" sun. He answered. But, for now, I will see to your living quarters."

As they walked out of the study and into the hall, Truck said: "By da way. Mokar, I like da way ya put dat bastard, Tabor, in his place."

"What is "bastard"? He asked, confused again. And what place did I put him in?"

Jim and Greg smiled at each other and shook their heads.

# CHAPTER 4

The first of the three "Sister" suns made her debut on the new day, shattering the darkness and bringing warmth to the alien world. Its light marched through the large, oval window, set high in one wall of the small compartment. Four "sleeping" shelves, covered with furs, jutted from one wall; three were occupied. A small bathing pool sat in one corner, foaming water in a whirlpool-like fashion. A long wooden table, with benches on either side, sat adjacent to the "sleeping" shelves. The abundant, marble-like, stone was of a grayish hue and reflected a depressing interior. The floor and ceiling were of the same material, slightly lighter in color. A large, wooden door stood between the table and the pool. Their new home was, approximately, twenty feet wide by forty feet long.

The three men, buried beneath the furs, were enjoying the only comfort that hadn't been stripped from them since their arrival on this world; sleep. Exhausted from the cruel orientation they had been subjected to and sleeping on the hard floor of the cage, they had attacked the inviting furs, greedily, immediately after being let into the apartment. Even Truck's loud snoring failed to interfere with this much-needed respite from their indignities. The prevalent thought on the minds of the three brothers, before retiring, was that upon awakening this impossible hellhole would be traded for the familiar realities of their friendly "Earth".

A key, turning in the lock of their door, brought the present, unwillingly, back into perspective. Startled by the sound, Jim sat up and stared, sleepily, at the door as it opened, admitting two, young aliens. Bearing platters, heaped with food and drink, they pushed their way in and set them on the table. Two guards, with the strange staffs resting on their shoulders, stood in the open doorway like statues, silently observing the two servants. As suddenly as they had come in, they were gone, locking the door securely behind them.

Laying back down on his furs, resignedly, reassured, once again that this was not a dream, he consoled himself with the only comforting thought that remained to him: "At least the three of them were together. Whatever the day had in store for them, they could always count on one another for support. He couldn't think of anyone else he would rather have on his team, in this strange situation."

Kicking himself free of the furs, which threatened to make him captive, once again, to their warmth, he arose and walked over to the table. Staring at the platters and pitchers, filled with food and drink, he was, suddenly, aware of how hungry he was. As he was about to give in to his stomach's demands, he stopped himself. "No! He thought to himself. I think I'll wait for the rest of the gang". With that, he walked over to the small pool and hurriedly got out of his clothing. Descending the three steps, he was soon immersed, up to his neck, in the warm embrace of the surging water. A faint, floral odor attacked his nostrils, pleasantly. As he floated on his back, he let his mind drift. The comforting tapes, from his past, played on his minds' screen. All of the loves, accomplishments and pleasures, he had experienced, surrounded him in his reverie. Serenity rocked him in her secure arms.

"How's da water, Jimbo? The bellowing voice of his large brother jolted him back to the present, so abruptly, that it forced his head beneath the water and he came up, gagging on the pint he had swallowed.

"Damn it, Truck. Don't do that! He said between coughs and gags. You scared the hell out of me".

"Well, excuse da hell outta me! He said. I didn't know ya was spacing out!" Sniffing the air, he continued. "Dat water smells awful purty, Jimbo". He said with his hands on his hips and a wink in his eye.

Suppressing a fit of laughter, at the, rather feminine, pose his brother struck. He said, "It is. Have some". With that, he pushed a cupped hand forward, sending a wave of water dripping down the front of Truck's cover togs.

"So! Ya wanna play rough, do Ya?" He said, quickly shedding his clothes. "I hope ya learned how ta breath under water." With a cannonball leap, he was soon in the middle of the pool with a headlock around his brother's neck. The two thrashing men threatened to evacuate all the water. Laughing and trying to get the best hold on each other, they forgot, for the moment, where they were.

"Did you two find it, absolutely, necessary to be so boisterous?"

The two men stopped, suddenly, looking up at the scolding, countenance of their younger brother.

"Some people do not rise as early as others. He continued. And I, personally, do not enjoy being awaken by the sounds of world war three."

Trying to look apologetic, without breaking out in laughter, Truck said: "Aw, wer sorry, Greg! We didn't mean ta wake ya. I know how much your rest means ta ya."

"As long as he is up, Truck, maybe he'd like to join us." Jim encouraged.

Before Greg could retreat two steps, he was pinned in the huge arms of his brother and thrown, in a perfect arc, into the middle of the pool. The stern look, instantly, left his face and he joined his brothers in a free-for-all.

A short while later, found them all clad in fresh clothing left on pegs at the side of the pool. Seated at the table, they were trying to analyze the contents of the platters. The strange fruits had a distinctively, exotic flavor. The reddish-brown meat had a taste similar to veal. The pale, pink liquid reminded them of peach brandy, only not as potent. It wasn't long before the three, Earthly appetites put a huge dent into the mass of food.

"Dat wasn't bad!" Truck said, belching and reaching for another piece of fruit.

"At least it is more palatable than the dog food they have been serving us. Greg commented. But, for Truck's sake, maybe they'll consider putting it back on the menu. You know, special order."

"How would you like a special order, shorty?" Truck said, shaking his big fist at his brother.

A key, turning in the lock, interrupted them.

As the door opened wide, Mokar strode into the room with all the self-assurance of royalty. The two watchdog guards stood their silent vigil at either side of the door

"I hope you find your arrangements satisfactory, Earth men! On this day, we begin your education."

As he talked, the two mini-servants began clearing the remains of the meal from the table. As they were bearing the large platters from the room, Truck reached out and grabbed another piece of fruit. Startled by this sudden movement, the tray slipped from his hands. Immediately, the two guards set upon the frightened servant with their rods. And, almost immediately, Truck let go with a perfect right and left felling the two guards.

Before Jim and Greg could rise and join in the fracas, Mokar cried out. "Cease, at once!"

To the guards, Mokar directed, "Assume your stations outside the door! To the servants, Clear this mess and dismiss yourselves!" And to Truck, I will overlook this overt act and charge it to your strained temperament. But, pay heed, Earth- man, if it occurs again, you will be severely punished! Am I understood?"

"Ya. But dey were hurting da kid and it was my fault." Truck implored.

"Regardless! No reason is a good reason for attacking my guards. The manner in which they choose to deal with the servants is not your concern. End of matter!"

As the two servants finished gathering up the scattered articles, the one who Truck had come to his defense stared at the big guy with awe. On the way out their eyes met. A big smile and an Earthly wink sent him confusedly on his way. The only thing he understood was that for the first time in his young life someone had been kind to him and had tried to help him. "The actions of the Earth giant would not be forgotten." He thought to himself.

Seated at the table, once again, the three men were listening to one of the many speeches they would hear from Mokar over the next few months.

"On this day, Earth men, we begin your educations. Zarnog has decreed a time period equivalent to six of your

"Earth" months. In that time, you will learn much about the flora and fauna of this world, our solar system and the history and mechanics of our great "Nevoan" society. Zarnog is curious to find out if the boasts of an Earthman are to be trusted. He said, looking at Jim. I say "will" learn because it is a matter of grave importance to you, under the circumstances. Your consumption of knowledge will measure the degree of your usefulness to our society. In other words, you choose your own destinies."

"It sounds to me as if a mild threat is imbedded in your words." Greg said.

"It simply means, you three have an opportunity to dictate the way you live your life on our world. Mokar answered. The only threat, to you, is not learning at all."

"Ya, I'd like ta know what's gonna happen ta us if we don't pass da course. Truck piped in.

"I cannot say, for certain, how Zarnog will react at the end of your educational tenure. But, there are at least three possibilities. If you are capable of absorbing most of the materials, there is a good chance a meaningful position will be assigned to you, such as one of my attendants. If mild interest is shown, your usefulness will be extracted through labor, maintenance, server or the mines. The position you achieve is entirely up to you.

"You mentioned three possible recourses at Zarnog's disposal. Two of them you have stated. What of the third?" Jim inquired.

"Termination!" Mokar said, hesitantly.

As the word grated out of the awful mouth, it echoed in the minds of the three men. Like a doctor telling his patient he had six months to live.

"What da hell did we ever do ta youse guys? And what gives ya da right ta pass judgement on us?" Truck bellowed.

"Take it easy, Truck! Mokar isn't responsible. He's just doing what he's been ordered to do. But, at least for right now we're still in the game. Right!"

"I ain't gonna be thrown outta dis game, either. By no one!"

His last words were directed at Mokar who shrugged and said, "That is entirely up to you, Earth man. Maybe it will provide the incentive you need, as you say, "to pass the course."

"Now that we know what we're up against, when may we get started?" Greg asked.

"Immediately! Said mokar as he led the way out of their quarters.

As they passed between the two guards, Truck rubbed the knuckles on his right hand and smiled. The two sentries backed off a few paces and followed them along the passageway that led to Mokar's study. Soon, they were seated at a small bench with logs and charts piled high in front of them.

"Let me begin by saying, you represent the first beings, other than my kind, that I have been ordered to educate. He said, as he sat down behind his own table. If I go too fast or you do not comprehend something, feel free to bring this to my attention. We are different beings from totally different worlds, so my methods will have to be modified, as to accomplish anything. I hope you take this as a form of encouragement when I tell you that in the past, I have always fulfilled my obligations to my students. Shall we begin?"

The planet "Elimar" is slightly larger in circumference than the planet Earth, approximately 28,000 miles. A rogue planet, belonging to no solar system, it is located thousands of light years from Earth. The elemental makeup of its atmosphere is almost identical.

Three satellite suns revolve around the planet, reflecting warmth and light, alternately, in the eighteen hours of daylight. As one would drop over the horizon, approximately nine minutes later, a trailing sun would rise. Thus, giving the affect of three sunrises and three sunsets. As the last of the trio of suns dipped over the horizon a period of nine dark hours would follow. From start to finish the whole process took nearly twenty-seven hours to complete.

The morning sun, "Brena", awakened the alien world. The midday sun, "Terba", which was closest to the planet, sprayed its hot rays, mercilessly, for the next six hours. Finally, the evening sun, "Persa", the farthest from the planet, cooled the planet down before it slipped into darkness. So, on any given day, the temperature went from a comfortable seventy degrees, "Brena", to the hot hours of "Terba", sometime exceeding one hundred and ten degrees, to the fifties and sixties of the evening sun, "Persa".

Having no moons, the dark hours are lighted, slightly, by a myriad of stars, adequate enough to make ones way by.

Four hundred "Sister" cycles equaled one Elimaran year. The three men had only half of that time to decide their destinies.

The Nevoans had come to Elimar from a distant solar system almost one hundred years before. Escaping their planet before its ever-encroaching sun finally consumed it. The mass exodus totaled one hundred and thirty thousand immigrants. The two large space ships that transported its mass of living cargo to Elemar, returned, immediately, in an attempt to rescue more of the Nevoans from their doomed planet. As fate would have it, they were added to the debris hurled, unendingly, through space. Along with it went the technology of Nevoan space travel. The settlers were soon to find out that the raw materials of their new home were too inadequate for building space ships. Only their contacts, with alien traders, kept them linked to the stars. It was one, such, alien "Scavenger" that had deposited the Earthly trio.

From the onset, the primitive tribes of Elimar were opposed to these invaders. Small bands obstructed any construction, destroying supplies and killing any pursuers bold enough to follow them into the hills or forests. The progress, of the invading aliens, was held to almost a standstill in the first few years, until a solar- electric barrier was built around the entire perimeter of their compound. It was just a matter of time before the high technology of the Nevoans developed enough to thwart any offensive actions of the natives. Soon, they were forced to abandon their villages and seek refuge in unknown areas. The roles were reversed. Now, the natives were hunted and enslaved. Any of the native villages, the invaders happened upon, were destroyed. The captured were put into breeding pens, eventually becoming labor, entertainment and sometimes, even food. Hunted continuously, the native villages became widely separated.

The "Yellow Heads", as they were called by the invaders, were a peaceful people, by nature. Until the invasion, they enjoyed a harmonious commerce among themselves. Tanned to a light, golden brown, with large, dark eyes, they are an attractive race. Artifacts, depicted in the logs, attested to the fact they were highly, cultured as well.

With sickened hearts, the three men continued their forced studies. They were trying hard to prevent the hatred they felt, for these cruel creatures, from over-shadowing their life and death, need to learn. So much to digest in the brief period of time allotted them. Fauna, flora, geography, politics; the list went on and on. The continuous bombardment of alien data started to take its toll on their Earthly minds.

"I don't think I'm gonna remember all dis crap." Said Truck, breaking in on the peaceful, silence.

There were about a dozen other creatures in the study, scattered about, in a library-like setting. A few of them turned in their direction, drawn by the sound of his voice.

"I resent da hell outta da whole situation!" He continued, out of frustration.

"We have no choice in the matter! Do we, Truck?" Jim said.

"But, it don't make much sense ta me. I never studied dis hard ta learn about my own planet!"

"Oh! Which planet might that be?" Greg piped in.

"Don't start on me, shrimp! I ain't in no mood.

"Listen! Both of you! Keep it down! Jim said, in a lower voice. We have to stick together on this and we don't have much time. So, let's not waste it!"

"Deres gotta be a better way den dis. Said Truck. I'm getting one hell of a headache!"

"What do you think our chances would be if we tried to fight our way out, Truck?" It was my big mouth that got us into this by telling Zarnog, with a little time, we could learn. And I think we can, too, at least enough to save our asses. So, hang in there! Greg and I will help you."

"Absolutely, Truck! Remember the final exams we helped you through before you graduated? Jim and I had to, practically, tie you down and sit on you in order to gain your attention."

"Ya, but dat was a different story. No jerk was threatening ta kill me if I didn't learn it."

"Just do your best, Truck. Jim Said. We'll get through this together. Okay?"

"Okay! I'll try, but I got dis feeling dat even my best ain't gonna be good enough for dat bastard Zarnog."

The apprehension, emitting from the three men, filled the room. The shroud of uncertainty weighed, heavily, on their minds. They forced their attention back to the massive logs, they knew, must be conquered.

So it went, day in and day out, absorbing as much knowledge of this alien planet as they could. Each man wondering, how high had Zarnog set the standards? Would their studious endeavors be enough to earn them a position on this alien world, or would they be marked for death. Time would tell. Would it be enough?"

# CHAPTER 5

Every day started out the same. After their baths, breakfast followed, served by the same slaves. The two guards keeping their vigil at the doorway, as the men ate, remained silently alert. Since that first morning, hatred for the Americans had taken root. The only break in the monotony was Toki, the slave Truck had saved from the beating. He would, always, make sure the big Earthman had the biggest and most tender portions of the food, hovering around him as if he were a God. Truck always smiled at him and patted the top of his head. Toki would respond with the closest thing to a smile that he could muster. His eyes would light up whenever the big guy would show him the slightest attention.

Slaves were forbidden to talk, while deploying their duties, a rule that irritated Truck. Every time he asked the pint-sized slave anything, he would look at the sentries with wide, frightened eyes, wanting to answer his Earth friend. But, the cruelties, he would suffer from the guards, outweighed his desire. One day, before their studies began, Truck brought the subject up.

"Ya know, Mokar, I'm tryin my best ta learn about dis place of yours, but, it's kinda hard when no one is allowed ta answer my questions. Sometimes ya ain't around an I wanna know something. Why can't da slaves and guards answer dem? It ain't gonna hurt nothing. Is it?"

"They are trained to delegate their tasks in silence, Earth man. They serve but one function at a time. To make them more proficient, in the discharging of their duties, all other distractions are removed." He answered.

"I understand dat, Mokar, but it would be a big help in learnin about you guys if we was able ta talk ta more a ya."

"I will take your suggestion into consideration, Earth man. There is some logic in what you ask for."

"You bet dere is, Mokar! Thanks for listening."

The very next morning, Mokar came into their quarters, while they were eating. "I have given much thought to your request, Earth man, and have decided to break with normal protocol. If it will enhance your knowledge of our great culture, casual intercourse, with my vassals, will be allowed, henceforth. But, I most give you fair warning, they will be on their guard against any subterfuge, on your part. Viewing your precarious situation, objectively, I hope this will benefit you in the training of your ignorant minds."

Looking at Greg, bewilderedly, Truck asked, in a low voice, "What da hell did he jus say?"

"He has given permission to the guards and slaves, of his house, to converse with us."

"Just, be careful about what you talk about." Jim added.

"Oh, dat's great! Dis is really gonna help. He said, excitedly. Thanks a lot, Mokar!"

"I will leave you now, Earth men. Your studies will begin shortly." With that, he left.

The long days turned into longer weeks as their forced education continued. Greg and Jim noticed Truck getting more and more irritable every day. No matter how much help they offered, the mood continued. Sweat poured from his stressed-out body, many pounds less than when they had started this life-saving challenge. They had just finished their super, after another trying day at the studies. The worried expressions on the three faces added to the depressing atmosphere.

"I gotta get outta here, you guys! I ain't gonna pass dis crap. I'm jus cutting in ta your study time and holding ya back."

"Can it, Truck! We're all in this thing, together, and we'll see it through as a team." Jim said.

"But, we don't have much time left and I ain't gonna remember it all, anyway. Da hell with it! I quit!" With that, he went and lay down on his bunk.

Greg chuckled, sarcastically, and shook his head.

"What's that all about?" Jim asked.

"I was just thinking if any of this was going to be beneficial to any one of us, not just Truck."

"You're not thinking about giving up, too, are you Greg?" Jim asked.

"No, Jim, I'm not. But, what worries me is how high the standards will be, set by Zarnog."

"You don't think Truck has absorbed enough of this to keep him alive. Do you?"

"Frankly, Jim, I don't know if any of us has. He answered. The very fact they are an extremely intelligent race, makes me wonder if any human can meet them.

"Well, we can't just give up!" Jim said, excitedly.

"I am not suggesting anything of the kind, Jim. We just have to find an alternative."

"An alternative, such as what?"

"Such as escape." Greg answered, in a low voice.

"But we'd all … Jim started to say.

"Be killed?" Greg finished for him.

After the chill, in the air, subsided, Greg continued. "Look, Jim, all we are accomplishing, at the present, could be for naught, if the powers that be find us inadequate in the end. Granted, it has provided us with some time, but the uncertainty of our futures has hung over us like a giant shadow. I, for one, would like to restore the privilege of dictating my own fate."

"I don't know, Greg. Jim said nervously. Maybe we have learned enough, or maybe Mokar could intervene for us."

"That's not much of an assurance, when you consider our lives are on the line. Think about it, Jim, even the few choices we've had, thus far, were forced upon us, which makes them nothing more than ultimatums."

They had been talking in low voices, just above whispers, as they did whenever discussing anything mildly, resembling insurrection. Their constant feelings, of being spied upon, kept them, always, on the alert.

"The only way we could ever hope to escape, this place, is with a little help. And I don't think we have too many friends here. Jim said, sarcastically. Without that, one, element, we'd be lost. Where would we go? How would we survive, even if we made it out of this prison?"

Unnoticed, Truck had made his way to the table, joining his brothers. "I gotta friend! He said, startling them.

"Surely, you can't mean that half-pint, Toki! Greg said. You're confusing gratitude with friendship? Besides, the fact, his dilemma isn't much better than ours."

"I don't care about dat. I know a friend when I see one."

"Maybe you're right, Truck. You have a history of acquiring strange friends."

"Listen, mini-butt, I ain't in no mood…

"Knock it off, you two! Jim interrupted. Save it for another time! We have more important things to discuss, at the moment."

With that, Greg and Truck gave him that, all to familiar, pouting puppy, expression, making him smile. Shaking his head, he continued. If you two were standing outside the gates of heaven or the pits of hell, waiting for admission, you'd find time to disagree about something. Will it never end?"

"Not very likely, Jim." Greg said, in a pseudo-serious tone."

"Uh-uh, Jimbo! As long as he's my brother, dat's da way it is."

Getting back to the discussion at hand, Jim asked. "Do you think Toki would help us, Truck?"

"I dunno. He's pretty scared a dese guys, himself, and I'd hate ta see da little fella get hurt cuz a me."

"We wouldn't want that, either, Truck. But, it's a chance we have to take if we want to get out of here. All we would need him for is to smuggle a few things in for us."

"Like what things?" Truck asked.

"Weapons, knowledge of the guards' watches, some extra food and something to cut through the grating on the window." Jim answered.

"Dat's a hell of a lot ta ask from da little guy." Truck said, with a sad expression on his face.

"Actually, Jim, we could lighten the load, considerably, by making copies of maps from Mokar's logs and putting some of our food aside. As far as weapons go, we should be capable of attaining our own, with all the training we've had."

"Dat's for sure!" Truck said, slamming one of his large fists into the palm of his other hand.

"This would, greatly, reduce the possibility of your little friend becoming in danger. Jim added. His knowledge of the guards' watch habits and a cutting tool, of some kind, would be all we would ask of him."

"Okay! I'll talk ta da little guy in da morning. But, I ain't so sure about dis."

Staring at the window, set high on the wall, across the room, a strange expression clouded Greg's face.

"What is it, Greg?" Asked Jim, semi-alarmed.

"I was wondering whether they've electrified that grating, as they did to the bars in the cage."

"I hadn't thought of that, Greg. But, I suppose we should find out. Shouldn't we?"

Walking over to the far wall, they stood below the square opening, perched ten feet above them. The last rays of the evening sun poured through, bathing the three men in its warmth. Staring up at it, they tried to discern, whether or not, it would reveal any dangerous secrets.

"Truck, give me a boost!" Said Jim.

"Just what do you plan on doing?" Asked Greg.

"Well, we're not going to find out anything from down here! Are we? I'm going up to have a look."

"For God's sake, Jim, use your head! You saw what happened to Truck, in the cage. There has to be a logical solution to this, without endangering your life."

"Such as what, Greg?"

Pausing to think, Greg looked at his brothers. "Such as, letting me go up! You wouldn't know a circuit from a cucumber. Besides, I'm lighter and you can catch me easier if I fly."

"I knew you'd think a something, squirt!"

"Squat, you big ape. Let's get this over with."

As Truck rose, easily, to his full height, the dubious window loomed, suddenly before Greg's eyes.

"Careful, Greg!" Jim's voice, whispered anxiously.

Beads of sweat broke out on his forehead, as he slowly reached out, with one arm, to discover the secrets of the cold unknown. Closing his eyes an instant before his shaking hand came into contact with the metal bars and opening them just as quickly when his brain received the message that it was safe. "Now I know how it feels to play "Russian roulette." He thought to himself.

His voice a bit shaky, he whispered down to his brothers. "It's safe! No current." Grabbing hold of the bars, he exerted a little pressure, checking to see if there were any weak spots. But, the alien metal stood strong and unyielding, even after he had hoisted himself, hand over hand, to the top, leaving his brother's shoulders.

"It's not very thick. He whispered, loudly, down to his brothers. But, it looks to be quite durable. May take some doing to cut through them".

"Is it mortared in, Greg?" Jim's voice came up to him in a loud whisper.

"Negative. The same material frames the outer perimeter, all the way around, and it also appears to be deeply recessed within the wall. If it's possible to do so, we'll have to cut through, at least, two bars to make the opening big enough".

"What does it look like, out dere, Greg?" Asked Truck.

So intense was his investigation of the window, he hadn't, yet, gazed beyond.

Fifty feet from the base of the building, they were in, stood a wall, approximately, twelve feet high. As he let his eyes travel beyond, he noticed an open field, flat and treeless, melting into a forest, about a mile, or so, in the distance. As far as his limited view allowed him to see, right or left, the view was the same.

Scrambling down from the bars, he remounted his brother's shoulders and soon had his feet planted on the floor, again. Walking over to the table, they sat down and Greg disclosed his observations to his brothers in a low voice. "We are in a very advantageous position. He started. This building, located on the outer perimeter of the city, is the first bit of luck since our arrival. It will definitely cut down on the odds of being detected."

"What kind of coverage will be at our disposal?" Jim asked.

"None, adequate enough, for concealment."

"Dat means we have ta escape in da night. Truck chimed in. Dere's our coverage."

"I agree, Truck. Hopefully it'll provide us with enough time to put some distance between us and this place."

"The next question is, gentlemen, where do we go? If we are successful enough to get that far, do we live out our lives as rogue scavengers, wondering aimlessly in this strange world?"

"I don't know about you guys, but I ain't gonna be nobody's slave. I don't care if I gotta live in a God damned cave, at least I'll be free."

"You'd probably feel right at home, too! Wouldn't you, Truck?" Greg poked.

Before Truck could fire back, Jim chimed in, in a slightly louder voice. What would our chances be of locating one of the native tribes and seeking safety with them?"

I would guess somewhere between a slight probability and none. Greg answered. Their nomadic life-style is the most important defense they have, against Nevoan attacks. Aside from the fact, they may be just as hostile as our present hosts."

"At least, dere easier ta look at. Truck chimed in. I'd take my chances with dem if we find em. I'm sick and tired a dis house a horrors!"

Shaking his head, he said to his brothers; "I'm just, now, realizing how impulsive and irrational my suggestion really is. Our success hinges on a score of contingencies; procuring the necessary tool, cutting through the bars, if possible, making it across the wall, eluding pursuit, surviving an environment in which we know little about and locating a tribe of people about whom we know even less. Aside from these few, minor details, I would say our chances are terrific."

"We don't need sarcasm added to the list, Greg! If you've changed your mind, just say so. We're all aware of the risks involved."

"I was merely putting our situation in its proper perspective, Jim. Weighing it out, objectively, we stand little chance of succeeding. On the other hand, we have only two choices. Don't we? Subservience or blind risk are options I find, discomforting."

Listening to his brothers making decisions was commonplace with Truck. The love and trust he had for them was all he needed. Whatever decisions were made, he accepted. His silent loyalty, more often than not, was the binding factor of their unity. This status, sometimes, carried more weight than the actual decision- making. The mundane realities of everyday life were his specialties. No one had absorbed more of nature's philosophies, from his beloved grandfather, than him.

"I, for one, am ready to take those risks. Said Jim. At least, it'll give us a common goal we can shoot for. Truck?"

"Da sooner da better". He answered, quickly.

"Greg?" Jim asked.

"You two have gone against my better judgement since day one. I guess it's foolish of me to think, because we're on a strange world and captives of even stranger beings that that would change. Let's do it!"

The very instant it was agreed upon, Truck's mind went into action: evasive measures, food, weapons, shelter. For the first time since their arrival, a genuine spark of interest was ignited within the big guy.

After further discussion, it was decided that Jim and Greg would distract the two guards, in the morning, by asking them questions about their weapons, homes, etc., while Truck took the young alien aside, availing him of his help. The first part of their plan, and the most important, would be set into motion.

Sleep became an elusive entity, as the three men lay down for the night. Their minds, filled with anticipation, anxiety and hope, fought against the 'Sand man'.

# CHAPTER 6

Another alien sunrise greeted the three, blurry-eyed Americans. The seeds of anticipation, planted deeply within their minds, bloomed into minor anxiety attacks. The sound of the key, turning in the lock, shattered the cloud of tension and startled the trio.

The guards assumed their positions, inside the doorway, while the two, small servants set out pitchers and platters on the table. Truck was seated on one of the benches, doing his best to remain calm. After making up their sleeping furs, Jim and Greg walked over to the guards.

"I've been curious, for the longest time, about your weapons. Jim said. Now that we have permission to ask questions, I wonder if you wouldn't mind, telling me a little about them."

"I will volunteer the information you request." Said one of the guards. However, I doubt whether creatures as ignorant as you may grasp its complexities."

Out of the corner of his eye, Jim saw Greg stiffen from the insult. Before his brother could react, he said: "If you go slowly, we may be able to understand."

"Very well. The guard said, in a condescending voice. This is a Draco, a lightweight staff made of metal alloys.

The power is produced by the "Draconium" crystals, stored inside. The controller unit, on the end, produces the degree of energy required."

"Could you give us a demonstration?" Greg inquired.

"We are ordered not to do so, unless it is in the nature of our duties." Said the other guard. However, if I were provoked, I would be forced to use it." He said, with a malicious look on his face.

"In that case, we shall forego the demonstration. Greg said, hurriedly. Would you be so kind and tell us more about the crystals?"

"They are harvested from mines, buried deep beneath this planet. They are the foundation of our economy. He continued. Their trade value is one thousand times greater than your "Earth" diamonds."

"What makes them, exclusively, a "Nevoan" resource, is the fact, only our superior technicians are capable of unlocking the secrets they hold. Enough questions! You there, slaves, remove yourselves!"

"Thanks for taking the time to answer our questions." Jim said, as they were passing through the doorway.

"It is my duty to obey the orders I am given. The guard replied. Left to my own devices, I would just as soon demonstrate on you inferior creatures and defecate upon you at the peak of your agony." He then left, locking the door behind him.

"Charming fellow!" Greg said, as he joined his brothers at the table.

"Well, How did you do, Truck?" Jim asked, in a low voice.

"It scared da hell outta da little fellow. But, after I got him ta stop shaking, he said he would try ta get us a cutting blade."

"Did he say when?" Jim asked.

"No! All he said was dat he'd put it in onc a dcm long fruit dey serve us. I feel bad about dis. He continued. If dey find out he's helping us, dey'll kill him for sure."

"If there was another way of doing this, Truck, without involving your friend, we'd do it." Said Jim.

"Ya. I know dat. I can't think a anything else, either."

As they finished their breakfast, silence crept in and joined them, once again.

The anticipation of breakfast, the next three days, ended in disappointment. Anxiety multiplies, while in captivity. The slightest shred of hope is clung to, tenaciously, with cracked and bleeding fingertips. Anything positive can mean the difference between total despair and tolerating a bad situation.

On the fourth day, as breakfast was being served, Toki looked at Truck, who was already seated at the table, and blinked twice. This was the pre-arranged signal.

Grabbing the long, gourd-like fruit in his big hands, Truck said; "Da old Indian never grew fruit as sweet as dese."

After hearing the words, that had been anticipated the last few days, Greg and Jim reacted.

"Since when have you been concerned about anything that went into that big mouth of yours?" Asked Greg.

"What da hell's da matter with you dis morning, shorty? Ya get up on da wrong side a da bed or something?"

"If you had an ounce of brains in that fat head of yours, you'd realize what this place is doing to us. But, you think this is some kind of picnic. I can't take it anymore."

"Come on, Greg, cool it! Don't take it out on Truck!"

"I would appreciate it if you stay out of this!" I don't need another big-brother, bullshit lecture right now." He answered, angrily.

"No more than we need tantrums from you, "Mister superior". So, just, shut up and calm down!"

Glaring at his brother, Greg lunged across the table and threw a right hand that caught Jim on the side of his head, knocking him backwards. Before he could recover, Greg pounced on top of him, pummeling him with lefts and rights. Rolling over and over, they ended up at the side of the pool. One more maneuver for position, and they entered the water with a splash.

The guards, watching the first few minutes with sadistic pleasure, decided it was time to break it up. It wasn't their concern for either of the Earth creature's welfare that prompted them into action. It was the fear they held for their superiors and what they would do to them for not performing their duties.

"Cease, At once!" One yelled, as the other used his "draco", none too gently, while encouraging the two men to separate.

"As much as your self-destructive attempts please us, we have our orders. No harm is to come to any of you until "Zarnog" tires of you. Out of the water, now!"

Dragging their soggy selves out of the pool, the two men looked at each other with mocked hatred.

"Seat yourselves and finish your meal! Quickly!" Roared one of the guards, as the other assumed his station at the door.

The three men ate silently, with lowered eyes. Each one knowing that to catch a glimpse of a pair of "Earthly" eyes, at this moment, would cause them to erupt into an outburst of laughter. Anticipation prompted them to eat their morning meal in record time.

Immediately after the departure of guards and servants, two sets of inquisitive eyes stared across the table at the big guy. Staring back at his brothers, like a guest panelist on "I've Got A Secret," he remained silent.

"This is no time for game playing, Truck. Jim said. Tell us, for Christ's sake!"

With a big smile on his handsome face, he reached into his left sleeve and pulled out a thin, metallic file, approximately, nine inches long. So stunned by the sudden appearance of the object, of so much anticipation, they just stared at it, speechless.

"The first chapter of our, much-anticipated, endeavor has just been completed, gentlemen." Greg said, smiling.

"And, the work and the risks, from here on out, become much more dangerous." Jim added.

"Well, let's get started, you guys!" Truck said, as he rose to his feet.

"Hold on, Truck! Jim interrupted. We'll be going to our studies, shortly, so we won't be able to accomplish much, now."

"A good place of concealment might be worth considering, at present, Jim." Greg chimed in.

"I'm way ahead a you guys. I was so sure dat my little buddy was gonna come through for us, I started thinking about a good hiding place. Da most logical place would be close ta da work, itself. Cuts down on da risk a being caught if we gotta hide it in a hurry."

"Well, what did you come up with, Truck?" Jim asked.

"We leave da thing up on da window sill. He answered. Ya can't see nothing from down here. Come on, squirt, I'll give ya a boost up dere!"

After he had climbed back down, from the massive shoulders, Greg looked at his brother. "I would never have figured you capable of logic. I'm astounded!"

"Aw, it's easy, little brother. It runs in da family."

"And I never realized you could punch so hard." Said Jim, as he rubbed the side of his head.

"Aw, It's easy. It runs in da family." Said Greg, aping his brother.

They laughed together, for the first time in a long while. As slight as their chance was, for escape, it was still a chance. An ounce of hope was worth more to their morale, at this time, than a pound of despair. Each of them felt, at that moment, somehow, some way, they would make it.

* * * * * * * * * * * *

"How's it going, Greg?" Jim asked.

Looking down from his perch on the window ledge, they had alternately occupied the last few days, Greg responded. "We're about halfway through this one, Jim. I hope this file holds up."

The bars were four inches apart. Two, twenty-four inch long sections had to be removed; leaving a twenty-four by twelve opening.

"At dis rate, it's gonna take forever." Truck said, from his station beneath the window.

"Another twenty-one days, to be precise." Greg said. Of course, this doesn't include any interruptions. Maybe we should double our efforts."

"I don't think that would be too wise, Greg. If we spend longer periods on that ledge, we'd be increasing the risk of being caught. Said Jim. This may be the only chance we'll ever get."

As the work was being done on the bars, they stationed themselves accordingly: While one worked away with the file, another would station himself by the door. The third would be directly under the window, ready to catch the one on the ledge if he had to drop down, suddenly. As usual, they talked in soft voices.

"Your logic outweighs our impatience, Jim. However, if we were able to procure another file, we could double our output."

"Uh-uh! Forget it! I ain't gonna ask da little guy ta take no more risks. It scared da hell outta him da last time."

"Jim and I know you want to adopt "da little fella". Greg mocked the big guy, with a smile on his face.

"How would ya like ta adopt a coupla black eyes, shorty?"

A slight sound, in the passageway, caught Jim's attention. "Get down! I think someone's coming!"

Greg stashed the file and dropped, quickly, into Truck's arms. They had no sooner seated themselves at the table, when the door burst open. The two guards stepped inside the doorway, as Mokar walked over to the table.

"Greetings, Earth men! I have just received word there is a feast, on the morrow, honoring "Zarnog" and the Nevoan conquest of this planet. He has ordered you to attend and exhibit the progress you have made."

"Pardon me, Mokar. Greg interrupted. Our allotted time has not been exhausted. We still have much to learn. A confrontation, such as this, may be a bit premature, when you consider the fact our lives are at stake."

"Do not concern yourself about the time limitations he has imposed upon you, Earth man. This is merely a feast to pay homage to him. It is not the final confrontation. In fact, I feel as though, it is more of a test for me."

"Why would he wanna test you, Mokar?" Truck asked.

"Why, to find some discrepancy in my ability to teach, of course. Answered Mokar. It is the way of our society. If one is found to be incapable of fulfilling his obligations, he is demoted. Failure is considered a weakness."

"How can any incentive survive while working within a system founded on negativism? Asked Greg. Without motivation there would be no attempts made at all."

"Fear is the highest motivator of all, Earth man. The status, of being "High Learner, is coveted by many. I am, almost, as well protected as Zarnog, himself. Any lesser position is vulnerable to assassination and constant changeover. I am motivated enough by that fact, alone, to retain my present status. Is it so different on your world?"

"Yes and no, Mokar. Jim added. We, also, have the fear factor as a motivator, in some instances. But, at the same time, we are provided with many choices."

Mokar took a seat at the table next to Truck. His interest piqued.

"Some pursue careers that may improve their prestige. He continued. Wealth, travel, entertainment, the feeling of accomplishment, self-satisfaction and many other factors may provide incentive. Our history is dotted with infamous leaders whose primary tool was fear. They were, quickly, overthrown when people stopped being afraid."

"Be that as it may, Earth man, the fulfillment I receive, in my present capacity, provides me with enough desire to retain it. I trust, you and your siblings will do nothing to jeopardize my interests. I will collect you, shortly after "Brena" has cast her first light. Rest well, Earth men!"

With that, he rose and walked out of the compartment, followed by his guards.

As the lock clicked and the sound of footfalls evaporated down the hallway, they sat frozen to the table, breathing three sighs of relief.

"Dat was cutting it close, you guys!"

"You're right about that, Truck! Jim said. From now on, while we're working, we'll have to maintain absolute silence. I allowed myself to get caught up in your little argument and I let my guard down for a moment."

"An excellent idea, Jim, but where are we going to locate a muzzle to fit him?" Pointing at Truck.

"I gotta muzzle for you, dwarf. Truck said, shaking his fist across the table at his brother. And it'll fit perfectly!"

"I'm glad you two appreciate the seriousness of the situation. We'd have a hell of a time if we didn't agree on anything. Wouldn't we?"

The sarcastic humor caught his brothers off guard, for a moment. As long as he had their quiet attention, he added; we've had enough surprises for one night. I don't think we should resume our work on the bars for right now. We have other things to think about."

"What do you think Zarnog expects to see tomorrow, Jim? This brief assimilation into his society hasn't produced any major changes."

"I think it's our conduct he's concerned with. Our first impression wasn't very positive. I think if we show no signs of aggression, he may consider that progress."

"Perhaps, if we leave Truck at home we may survive the day."

"Keep it up, squirt, and you may not go ta da party, either."

"One thing is certain. Jim, quickly, interrupted. Mokar has treated us decently. If we jeopardize his position, we forfeit our chances of escaping."

"I guess, one might say, we are forced to be on our best behavior even if it kills us." Greg added.

"Dis is kinda like going onna blind date. Truck put in. If she don't like da way ya act, it's all over."

"Something like that, Truck. But, if we all maintain level heads, we should have no problems."

"Well, gentlemen, shall we begin our work-out and retire a little earlier than usual? Greg asked. I have this feeling, tomorrow is going to be an eventful day."

Ever since they received accommodations at "Mokar's Motel", their nightly regimen included a vigorous workout. Staying on top of their physical condition was as important as the mental aspect. Each one knew, sooner or later, muscle would be needed to accomplish their escape. The food they were given was plain, although, nutritious. With little else to do but study, there was adequate time left over for the improvement of their bodies. Adhering, religiously, to this routine, it wasn't long before they were in the best condition of their young, lives. The only things missing were the Earthly tans they had worn before the abduction and a few pounds of lazy flesh.

Their Indian grandfather had shown them many exercises for improving their physical and mental reflexes.

"The mind should be exercised much more than the body, when preparing to confront a foe." He used to say. "Search out his weakness before attacking. This will conserve strength for the time it is crucially needed. Rushing into a bear's den, to do battle, can only get one dead. Knowing when the bear sleeps will get the bear dead."

The old Indian's three protégés, had practiced these principals, faithfully. Their lives, on this ominous world, could very well depend upon how well they learned their lessons. Could three Earthmen fit into an alien scenario? Could they, dare hope, to carve a comfortable niche in this unfriendly world? Time would tell! And, time was running out.

# CHAPTER 7

The small entourage, that made its way across the large open plaza, consisted of Mokar, the three Earthmen, and the two watch-dog guards. Tabor and his boys confronted Mokar earlier, trying to convince him more guards were needed for the escort. Mokar waved him off, telling him to stay out of his affairs

The warmth, of the morning sun, brightened the faces of the three men. Trapped indoors, for so long, this unexpected break in routine also brightened their spirits. Walking side by side, with heads held high, they stepped out with a brisk pace. They showed no fear, on the outside. But, each of them harbored a multitude of concerns within.

A huge crowd, milling about in front of the "High House," parted as soon as Mokar and his three alien charges were recognized. The stares from the three Americans was returned a thousand-fold. Fear, frustration and hopelessness flowed from their eyes. Being a member of the Nevoan society was a form of incarceration, in itself. The only thing that separated their plight from that of the three men was, they were holding the keys. As they climbed the wide steps, the great doors swung inward admitting them into the semi-darkness of the waiting hall. They were immediately surrounded by, no less than a dozen, of "His majesty's" finest.

"What means this, Tabor?" Asked Mokar.

Remembering their last confrontation, Tabor remembered to address him with his respective title. "Mokar, Learner Most High", I have been instructed to escort your party directly to the quarters of "Zarnog, our "Leader Most High". He said, nervously.

"This is, rather, out of the ordinary, but, lead on, Tabor."

Moving down the passageway, past the throne, banquet room, they came to a spiral ramp-way. Following the corkscrew route, they came to a halt before a large gilded door at the top level of "High House".

Banging his staff, three times, against the wide door, Tabor awaited summons. It was opened immediately by one of Truck's heavyweight friends. The other giant stood directly across from him. As usual, they were both in their silent, venomous moods.

"I Tabor, High Protector of Zarnog, have arrived with the lowly Earthlings. Notify Zarnog, at once!"

"I got your lowlys!" Truck said in a subdued voice. It was the first time any of them had spoken, since leaving their quarters. A mixture of Nevoan and Earthly eyes stared at him reinstating silence. The defiant smile, however, remained on the big guy's face.

Turning on his heel, the one who had opened the door, departed. His counter-part moved directly in front of the entrance, glaring at Tabor.

Soon, the other guard returned and escorted them inside. Tabor's men waited outside the doors.

Zarnog was reclining on a pallet over-flowing with furs. His volcano-red eyes followed them into the room, reflecting no welcome.

Coming to a stop, just below the island of furs, Tabor stepped forward and, as he saluted, the rest of the party followed suit.

"Zarnog, Leader Most High, I give unto you the Earth creatures. Stepping quickly aside, he escaped the malicious gaze of his leader. It fell, instead, on a trio of unflinching, Earthly eyes. Not one trace of fear was revealed. They would not allow themselves to be intimidated.

"So, Earth insects, we meet again! I trust your stay, thus far, has been interesting. He said, with slime running out of his cesspool mouth. By now, you must be aware of the superiority of our supreme culture and the honor you have been bestowed. Mokar, what have you to say about your charges?"

The alien educator had been standing directly behind the trio of Earth subjects. His great mind was trying to decipher his leader's evil motives. What did he have in store for these three creatures? He wondered.

"Zarnog, Leader Most High, the task, you have set before me, constitutes a great challenge. Although they exhibit signs of mild learning ability, they will never evolve to the Nevoan intellectual level. Aside from that, I have discovered a similarity with our own culture. They have evolved to the point of having varying degrees of intelligence. Therefore, they can not be classified as beasts."

The three men felt like a herd of cattle on the auction block, everyone talking about them while they remained, stupidly, silent. The nervous looks they gave to each other, communicated, the fact, they were all on the same page.

"Individualism exists, denoting intellectual evolution." Mokar finished.

"We shall see at the end of their allotted time, which function they will serve best. If any! The royal monster said, grinning maliciously. One bit of progress, I am witnessing, is their improvement in conduct. As a small reward for your labors, Earthlings, you will be allowed to partake in our great ceremony this day. I requested this audience to remind you that our methods and ideals have served us well since the beginning. They will not be changed to accommodate inferiors. Doubtless, you will deem some of the events, taking place today, as cruel and without purpose. Any overt expressions of your disagreement or disgust will be taken as a sign of disapproval of our great society. It will not be tolerated! Your behavior will be under constant scrutiny."

"Zarnog. May I speak, most "High?""

"Be quick, learned one! I have many things to attend to before the festivities begin."

"It is my opinion, oh High one, the Earth creatures are not ready for intercourse, at the present. I have taught them nothing about Nevoan etiquette."

"Then they will begin their lessons, immediately! Today, they have my permission to do as Nevoan's do. They must learn or they will perish. It is, entirely, up to them. Dismissed!"

The tension, in the room, attacked their minds. Standing erect and silently, absorbing this exchange between Zarnog and Mokar, the three men knew, as one, they were to be part of the days entertainment, the proverbial, letting loose of the lambs in the lion's den.

Greg looked as if he were about to say something and caught an elbow in the ribs from Jim. Truck was mentally busy with the scoreboard. The Nevoans had a big lead. But, there was still plenty of time left in the game.

They were, quickly, escorted back to Tabor's men, waiting outside of Zarnog's chambers and led to the banquet room. Except for slaves scurrying around, placing food and pitchers on the tables, the large room was almost vacant. From every wall, hung banners depicting Zarnog's likeness. That was the extent of decoration. Upon the raised platform, a long table sat in front of Zarnog's throne. Two, small tables sat on the main floor; a dozen feet in front of the royal table. Three wide steps led up to it.

At least, two hundred long tables were set up in orderly rows, each capable of seating fifty people. Mokar and his small party were seated at one of the two small tables, directly in front and five paces from the steps leading up to the thrown. Tabor and his henchmen occupied the other small table, across from them.

"Ain't dis great, you guys! We got ringside seats and big brother can really watch us, now."

"Precisely, Truck! And, at the same time, he can exhibit his latest acquisitions for the entire congregation."

"Yes, Earth men. You will be under a considerable amount of scrutiny this day. I have a heavy investment in you, also. So, I will add to the weight of observation; only because I do not wish to see all of our hard work go for naught."

As they talked, a steady stream, of the creatures, made their way to the tables. The crescendo, from so many conversations, grew louder as the banquet hall grew more crowded.

"Mokar! What did Zarnog mean, when he said; "Today, we have permission to do as Nevoans do?" Jim asked.

"Simply, that you are free to wonder about and partake in the activities and entertainment if you wish to do so. You may mingle with the populace and, in essence, become accustomed to Nevoan etiquette. However, I must warn you. There are restrictions! You are not to leave this chamber, at any time. Nor will you be allowed to approach Zarnog's table uninvited. Looking over at Tabor's table, Mokar added, in a lower voice; you will be followed by one of Tabor's subordinates, at all times."

"It would seem that Zarnog is exceedingly, anxious to see us fail. Greg interjected. This unexpected liberty could be fatal, especially when one is totally ignorant of Nevoan social skills. This could be paramount to our safety, before the day is over."

"Could you give us a few do's and don't's that may help us get through this?" Jim asked.

"It may not be enough, under such short notice. But, I can give you a few suggestions. Mokar answered. Never lose eye contact, with a Nevoan, if confronted. This will be taken as a sign of weakness or fear. Never interfere in another's dispute. This would suggest that one or the other, involved, is incapable of settling his affairs. Looking at Truck, he continued. If, at any time, a slave is being abused, walk away. They have resigned themselves to lives filled with such treatment. Always, if known, address another Nevoan by his full title. This shows respect."

"Boy, you guys got a lotta rules. Truck interrupted. I hope I can remember dem all."

"It is difficult to recount that which is a natural part of ones life, especially, under such short notice. But, I hope that this will be of some help. So intent, have I been, teaching Geography and History, I totally, ignored social etiquette."

"Your information is appreciated, nevertheless, Mokar. Greg said. Speaking for all of us, we shall try to adhere to these principles of conduct."

"Then, it is I who shall be the appreciative one, Earth man."

A loud gong resonated through the vast hall, gaining the attention of the gathered audience and silence fell upon them, almost, immediately. Led by his two, behemoth ghouls, Zarnog, in all his purple splendor, strutted through the doors. He was followed, closely, by four smaller figures, clad in white.

A quiet aside, from Mokar, informed them these were Zarnog's mates; smaller versions of "His Ugliness".

As the party mounted the steps to the royal table, they were offered a collective salute from the alien multitude.

After the females were seated and the two giants assumed their posts, one on either side of the throne, Zarnog spoke. "Today, we celebrate our "Landing Day." He began, in his loud, gargling voice. A long time ago, our great culture was almost eliminated by a totally, insurmountable cataclysm. But for the superior intelligence of our supreme race, we would now be extinct. We have carved the second Nevoan society so deeply, into this world, we are, once again, the dominating factor. In time, we will aspire to our former greatness.

All during this royal discourse, the three brothers were impressed with the silent respect that was accorded him. The huge crowd was, absolutely, frozen. The great leaders of their world were not given, any way near, this much silent courtesy.

"We most multiply and become stronger, yet. Zarnog continued. Every living being must be made aware of their ultimate purpose in life; to serve me, your "Leader Most High." Therefore, I command every female unit, within the reproductive stage, impregnated, before the third sun lightens our skies on the morrow. Our greatness shall never be decimated again. I have spoken! Let the festivities begin!" He finished, as he sat at the table.

The three men sat there, dazed by what they had just heard. The concept of assembly-line sex, added to their growing list of reasons to rebel against these ego-inflated aliens.

"Mokar! Jim spoke, breaking the nervous silence. You mean to tell me, this is the way Nevoans propagate. Even that choice is taken away from them? It seems so impersonal, calculated."

"That is precisely what is intended, Earth man. Our forebears practiced random selection. Interpersonal contact not only caused over-population, it, also, interfered with their ability to serve. Regulating reproduction, every five of your Earth years, balances workloads and stabilizes our population. Is it so different on your world? He asked.

"Quite different! Greg joined in. Spontaneity, the choice in your selection and pleasure are three important factors in motivating sexual activity. Love is another. But, it isn't always necessary."

"There are a few countries, on our world, that would benefit from your method of birth control. Jim added. They have, literally, over-produced themselves into starvation, disease and death."

"I'd like ta know how you guys do it." Truck joined in.

A bewildered look came over Mokar's face. "I do not understand your question."

"What Truck is asking is, what type of physical activity takes place between the male and female during impregnation?"" Greg interjected.

"Why, absolutely, none. Mokar answered. Male reproductive fluids are injected into the females, Mechanically. In ten circuits, of the "sister" suns, the fertilized egg is withdrawn and cultivated in the "House of Life.""

"Comparable to the test-tube babies on our world." Greg added.

"You guys take da fun outta everything. Don't ya?"

"We derive pleasure from more important things then reproductive habits, Earth man. My work, for example."

As they talked, servants ran in and out, leaving huge platters and pitchers, heavy with food and drink, on every table. The vastness, of the great hall, was becoming, somewhat, diminished by the over-flowing crowd. Like a giant beehive, it buzzed, loudly, with conversation. Arguments had, already, erupted in different areas. As they observed this alien scene, they, also, felt the weight of many eyes boring into them. The heaviest scrutiny came from Tabor's group. Added to this drone, was the horrible sucking sound the Nevoans make while eating. Their repulsive, sucker-like lips would hold a large piece of food, while the pincer teeth moved up and down. This shredded the food into small chunks that were inhaled down their throats. Like mulching machines, they consumed great quantities

The manners of the royal monster and his four mates, was little better. Conversing, with food and slime dripping from ones repulsive mouth, was the norm.

As not to offend Mokar, the three men made no comment and finished their meal in silence. Heads bent low, over their plates, they shut off some of the grotesque sights surrounding them.

A short while later, festivities were interrupted, once again by a loud gong. This time it came from directly behind Zarnog's table. Like turning off a radio, silence struck immediately. Zarnog rose from behind his table.

"We have in our midst three visitors. He began. Creatures from a far away planet they call Earth. Even though they are far below our intellectual level, I have accorded them the honor of attending this glorious occasion. They will be allowed to mingle and socialize, if they choose, for the duration of this glorious occasion. At all times, will they be treated as we would treat one another. Do your best to make them feel welcomed." This last, said with a malicious sneer on his ugly countenance.

"In the keeping of our great tradition, the fruits of the world, just conquered, are sampled by the victorious. He continued. It is time for drinking the "Nectar of Conquest"! All shall partake!

As he spoke, slaves scurried through the crowd, filling cups. A liquid, resembling pink milk, was poured into the three men's cups, also, as the slaves hurried about, serving everyone.

"A taste of this new world, to increase our hunger for more of the same, a sip of a new life, discovered, to serve the imperial Nevoan society. We consume this small token, as our forbears consumed many worlds. Strength and wisdom be ours!" He shouted.

With that, every creature in the room drank. The brothers followed suit. But, they did not drain their cups. After the first sip hit their taste buds, waves of nausea were fought down. The taste was that of salty, sour milk.

"What da hell is dis stuff?" Truck asked, between gags.

"I could not tell you before the toast was offered. He said, in a subdued voice. Had I, you may not have participated. That would have been a grievous affront to Zarnog. Sometimes deceit is necessary to prevent more serious consequences."

"Okay, Mokar. Jim said. Your concern is appreciated. But, please, tell us what it is we just drank."

In a low, hesitant voice Mokar said: "It is the milk of the impregnated native women, we have captured, mixed with the blood of their newborns."

Three Earthly faces ran the chameleon gamut of colors, going from pale white to sickly green. Before either of his brothers could register their disgust and possibly complicate the situation, Jim spoke in a low, controlled tone. "So this is what a super intelligent race considers civilized behavior. To us, it is the most disgusting, barbaric act one could subject another to. We will never fit into your inhumane world, Mokar."

"I do not make the rules, Earth man. But, I must abide by them. You must adhere to these same rules, if you wish to survive our world."

"Your rules do not apply to us, Mokar. Jim continued. Can't anyone, on this hellhole, get that through their

Goddamn heads? We are human beings, not stray dogs to be forced into obedience. We were born free and all that we wish is to die free."

"And, if your bonds were severed, what then? Mokar argued. Would you live an empty life on this planet, to starve? Without intellectual stimulation, what would life be worth?"

"What is life without choices? Greg joined in. The scant selection we would have out there, would be welcomed after being subjected to all this great "Nevoan" hospitality. There is, also, the possibility these barbarians, as you call them, are capable of caring and kindness. Elements you Nevoans are devoid of and necessary factors for human happiness."

"Choose your words carefully, Earthman! Should they fall among the wrong persons, they could be your last." Mokar said, nodding toward the adjoining table.

"I gotta walk, you guys. Dis bullshit is pissing me off!"

As he started away from the table, Jim said: "Hold on, Truck! I'll go with you."

As they were leaving, Greg noticed two of Tabor's men rise and follow his brothers, through the milling crowd. Turning toward Mokar, he asked: "What happens to the captives after this disgusting assault is made upon them?"

"The females are put into breeding compounds with selected male natives. The rest of the men are sent to the mine or used where uncomplicated labor is required. Their strength and endurance make them perfectly suited to these tasks."

"We have groups of people on my world that specialize in the same way. Greg said, with a sad smile on his face. They're called horse breeders."

"What is horse?" Asked Mokar.

"A large, four-legged animal with limited mental capacities, sometimes used for hard work."

"Ah, then we do have similar practices!" Said Mokar.

"Letting out an exasperating sigh, Greg shook his head.

\* \* \* \* \* \* \* \* \*

Across the large room, his brothers came to an open area. Double circles, side by side, were engraved on the floor. It was completely surrounded by raucous spectators. Combatants, holding long staffs, with padding on the ends, stood inside of the rings. A third person, holding a remnant of green material, over his head, stood in the center of the abutting circles. When he brought this arm down, the two opponents began flailing at each other with their staffs.

Jim turned and asked a spectator what was going on. He, quickly, learned these were the rings of justice. A small dispute was being settled here. The just opponent was the one remaining in his circle at the end of the skirmish. The one, knocked out, was considered guilty. He forfeited all, or part, of his property to the victor. More serious disputes, usually, ended up with the loss of a limb or even one's life. This method, of discovering justice, had "Medieval" undertones. Jim thought.

Four or five of these small physical debates were in full swing, simultaneously. As they observed one particular pair of fighters, Truck glanced across the circles and looked directly into the eyes of an old acquaintance; one of the guards that stood watch over their quarters. This, particular, one had tasted his knuckles while attempting to abuse his servant friend, Toki. Unable to resist, he brought up his big right hand and started to rub his knuckles. An ear-to-ear smile accompanied the gesture. The color, in the guard's eyes, went from raging red to hellfire orange.

Catching his brother's motions, out of the corner of his eye, Jim, quickly, assessed the situation. "Knock it off, Truck! We don't want any trouble."

"Don't worry, Jimbo. I'm jus having some fun with da creep."

But, peace was not to reign on that day.

No sooner was the match over, when the infuriated guard was talking to the starter. A small conference took place and one alien was sent trotting toward the throne. A split second later, the loud gong rang out, again. All activity ceased, immediately. All eyes focused, collectively, on the throne. Zarnog rose from his royal seat.

"As you are aware, I have given our Earthly guests, restrictive, freedom on this momentous occasion, a privilege, never before, given to an outsider. The circles of justice are at the disposal of all here, tonight. He continued. Having been given a temporary Nevoan status, the big Earthling has been challenged by Kalvar, guard of "High House.""

A shroud of tension hung over the three Earthmen. It was dispelled, slightly, by Mokar.

"Zarnog, Most High, may I speak?" He asked, nervously.

"I will hear you, learned one!"

"Most High one, these men are strangers to our world. Our customs cannot apply. He argued. They still have much to learn about our ways."

"That is, ordinarily, true. But, because of my benevolent nature, were they not given the honor of doing as Nevoans do?"

"Of course what you say is always true, "Leader Most High." But, what property does the Earth man have to forfeit in this contest?"

"That, in which he had when he arrived. His life! Enough of this discussion! Let the contest begin!" He bellowed.

The three men were surprised, but just as suddenly, realized what this whole scenario was really about. This false façade of Zarnogs was nothing but a smokescreen to camouflage his sadistic nature.

Greg had worked his way through the swarming ocean of hatred and joined his brothers at the first sign of conflict. The worried look on their faces greeted him.

As the alien audience surrounded them, Kalvar stepped into one of the circles directly in front of them. Zarnog had a bench moved in close and now was seated at ringside. Drooling in anticipation, he glared maniacally at them. To go to these lengths to derive such cruel, bloodthirsty pleasure, was, indeed, the demented workings of a diabolical mind.

"Any suggestions, Jim?" Greg asked, as he nervously scanned the rabid crowd.

"Only one. He answered, holding back the panic he was feeling. But, it would be suicidal. The odds are slightly against us."

"Approximately five thousand to one." Greg added, off-handedly.

"Hey! Whatta you guys worried about? I'll kick his butt. Besides, I been waiting for a chance ta get back at dese bastards for da way they been treating us."

"I guess there is no other alternative, at this time. Is there? He said, his voice cracking. Watch out for yourself, brother."

Looking into their eyes, Truck saw the genuine concern and love he had seen so many times. Clapping them both, soundly, on their shoulders, he turned and stepped into the circle. Staring across the short space, that separated them, Truck smiled at his opponent. He had been in this sort of situation many times in his life. One's composure, at this time, carried as much wallop as a hard punch. The psychological aspect could be the difference between winning and losing. He would not let his team down.

The two gladiators were handed staffs six feet in length. The last ten inches, on either end, were honed to razor-sharp blades. Zarnog's lust for blood would not permit the tame use of padded staffs. This was the championship fight. Winner takes all.

The starter stepped between the two circles, as he raised his green flag. Before his hand had begun its downward motion, signaling the start, Kalvar lunged out past the outstretched arm and almost impaled Truck's throat. Only a reflexive move to the side prevented him from digesting steel. Now, the only things between them were their staffs. The missed attempt seemed to shake Kalvar, somewhat. It even failed to wipe the smile off the Earthman's face.

"Dat's da last chance yer gonna get, ya ugly bastard. Now, it's my turn. Truck said, confidently.

Moving back and forth, in their limited spaces, like two caged cats, they searched for lethal openings. Each man refused to give ground.

Greg and Jim refused to give up their positions, nearest the circles, as the jostling crowd pushed forward for a better view. They would stay close to their brother, at all costs.

A fake step to his right and a fast lunge to his left sent Truck's staff into Kalvar's side. The wound, although superficial, bled profusely. It wasn't long before he was slipping and sliding and finding it hard to keep his balance. His large, red eyes reflected the color of defeat. With his life, slowly oozing out of him, he made a desperate lunge at Truck's midsection. Leaving himself wide open, in his wild attempt, Truck easily turned the staff aside, dipped low and brought the other end up, and almost through, the alien's midsection. The death stare, in Kalvar's eyes, signaled to the audience he was dead on his feet. Before he could crumple to the floor, Truck, with his great strength, lifted Kalvar like a limp rag doll. Hanging from the end of his staff, he flung him twenty feet away. The lifeless body fell into the crowd, staff and all, knocking down several onlookers. Because the contest was finished so suddenly, Zarnog hardly got his money's worth. More than one alien mouth hung open in awe.

Jim and Greg rushed to Truck's side, anticipating more trouble.

"Do you think you might have over done it, just a little, Truck?" Greg asked.

"Ta hell with dem all! Bring dem on, one atta time, and I'll kick dere insect assholes so hard dey'll be walking on dere lips!"

"Calm down, Truck! We don't need any more attention! Got it?"

"Ya, I got it. He answered, breathing a little easier.

Thousands of alien eyes were locked on the trio. Silence hung, like a crushing cloud, above their heads. One false move, at this time, might prove to be their last.

"Earth men, come before me!" Zarnog's voice thundered across the short space.

Moving to within five feet of where the monster was sitting, their senses were set at full alert. This might be D-day.

"I must commend you, Earth man! That was quite a display, especially by a creature ignorant of our weapons. Obviously, you have done something similar to this, before. With a little practice, you would almost be as lethal as my two personal attendants, Krol and Nebon."

Truck couldn't resist beaming a wide smile at the two, huge freaks, standing behind Zarnog.

"This strange look you have on your face, what does it mean? Zarnog asked. I've observed you using it many times."

"It's called a smile, Zarnog. Jim interjected, hurriedly. He knew that his brother was still on an adrenaline high and might say the wrong thing. Earth people use it when they are feeling good or when they see something funny."

"Ya, like dem two wimpy creeps ya got working for ya."

"Shut up, Truck!" Jim said, in a nervous voice.

"Your words carry the tone of animosity, Earth man. Zarnog said, looking directly at the big guy. Do you believe you could defeat them as easily as you did that weakling Kalvar?"

"Any two of us could knock da shit outta dem, barehanded. He wouldn't give up. Dere big, but dere dumb."

"For God's sake, Truck, shut your mouth! You trying to get us killed?" Greg piped in, with panic in his voice.

"Naw, I'm jus tired a dese bastards telling me dat dere better den we are. It's time we show em. Whatta we got ta lose?"

Greg and Jim looked at each other and acknowledged, silently, the truth in their brother's words.

Zarnog, himself, deescalated the potential disaster. "That request will be granted to you, Earth man. But, your death will have to wait. I have more important matters to attend to on this glorious day. It is too bad you were not hatched into life as a Nevoan. He said, as he rose from the bench. Your hatred would have won you high status." He, then, turned and made his way back to his table. His two dogs stared daggers at Truck, then followed their master.

When things returned to normal, or abnormal, as it was, the three men made their way back to the small table. They had won a small victory. The enemy was not invulnerable and they were aware, now, Earth men were not passive pushovers. Mokar was already seated, but he had overheard their conversation with Zarnog.

"Your sibling's loose tongue will bring about your demise, if it is not curtailed." He said.

"Given our situation, it makes little difference. Wouldn't you agree?" Said Jim. If we breathe at the wrong time, because of our ignorance of your rules, we're apt to meet our ends, anyway. At least, if we assert ourselves, we'll have some idea from which direction the "grim reaper" will come."

"Do all Earth beings harbor this reckless, mental energy?"

"Only the people forced into giving up their freedom. Greg answered. Fortunately, this represents only a small percentage of Earth's population."

Another lull interrupted the noisy audience, as the two main doors were flung apart. Four of His Majesty's finest escorted a man and a woman to the foot of the thrown. The first Elimaran natives the three men had seen, in the flesh. The female hugged a small baby to her bare breasts. Gray hides hung from the hips of both. This represented their only article of clothing. Golden blonde hair crowned bodies deeply tanned. The woman's was braided tightly to her head. The man's hung shoulder length and was tied back, Indian-fashion, with a hide strip going around his head. Their dark, oval eyes, slightly larger than humans, stared straight ahead, proudly. His well-muscled body stood an inch or two over six feet. Several scars gave evidence of a healthy but hazardous life-style. The female was five or six inches shorter, but, stood no less proud as the male. The baby, at her breast, suckled away without a care.

"Dey look almost human." Said Truck, in a low voice.

One of the escorts addressed the royal head. "Zarnog, Leader Most High, I, Selbo, a protector of boundaries, bring to you a gift on this momentous occasion. They were captured in a raid on a small, yellow-head encampment. This man, alone, is responsible for sending six of my troop to meet their ancestors. If he had not come back, to aid this female, he would have escaped, also. I give him on to you for your supreme pleasure." He finished.

"What must it take, for you pitiful animals, to concede to our superior dominance? We offer you a better life, one without hunger or danger. Yet, you slap the Nevoan society in the face with thievery and murder. It is your duty to serve and honor the most, supreme beings in existence. Your futile attempts to disrupt Nevoan progress will only come to the same conclusion many beings, in the past, have discovered. Total extinction! He bellowed. Assimilate into our great society or be consumed. Bring the new-born to me!"

Before either of the two natives could react, one of the escorts ripped the baby from her arms and held the squealing infant out to one of Zarnog's huge bodyguards. While the rest of the escort was trying to restrain the two natives; alien, earthly and native eyes watched in horror, as the two henchmen stretched the infant out before Zarnog's repulsive face. Leaning slightly forward, the royal beast attached his drooling, sucker-like mouth on the tender throat.

The screams from the woman and the curses of the three men lasted longer than the gurgling noises of the infant.

"You dirty son of a bitch!" Truck yelled, as he charged the throne.

Greg and Jim were just starting to rise from the table when Mokar grabbed the staff from a guard, standing near by. He, quickly, stunned the two men into unconsciousness. "Take them back to their quarters, quickly!" He ordered the same guard.

As they were being dragged out of the fracas, he turned his attention back to the throne area. The native male had, finally, managed to shrug his restrainers and was flailing away, right and left. Greatly out-numbered, he was pummeled from every, possible angle. Only his hatred kept him on his feet.

The big Earthman faired a little better. But, he too, was covered with blood. He had snapped the neck of one of the giants and was trying to reach Zarnog, who, in all the turmoil, still held the dripping, lifeless body of the infant, in his tong-like hands.

Finally, it was over as suddenly as it had begun. In the struggling, mass of bodies, it had been impossible to bring to bear the stunning power of the staffs. A slight opening had revealed itself and Truck joined his native partner in oblivion.

Livid with rage, Zarnog spoke. "Chain these two animals together and send them to the mines, on the morrow! They will pay the rest of their lives for this sacrilegious assault. He roared. Death is too quick! They must sweat and bleed and remember this day, always. Let the metal serpents, around their necks, burn into their minds and serve as constant reminders of their assault on the most Supreme Being in existence. Take them away!"

On this alien eve, three Earthmen and one native shared the same dark unconscious, oblivious to the agonies they would awaken to.

# CHAPTER 8

Before the first sun greeted the new day, a private meeting was taking place in Zarnog's quarters. Seated on a pallet, over-flowing with cushions, the regal monster glared at his guest. Summoned at this early hour, Mokar stared back, anxious to hear the reason for this unexpected call. The cold reception and Zarnog's sadistic silence he was used to. It did not intimidate him, as it was meant. Many times had he been beckoned to his leader's quarters to advise the maniacal tyrant on various issues. The treatment was always the same.

"I have a task for you, "Learned" one. He finally spoke. A minor one, but never the less, one that has to be handled with tact for it to achieve its full impact."

"I will do my…. Mokar started to say, but was interrupted.

"Wait until you have digested what I am about to say, before answering! Zarnog ordered. You have grown quite fond of our Earth pets, so the task may not be an easy one from your perspective. The sacrilegious act, perpetrated by the big Earthling, would ordinarily constitute an immediate death penalty. For a brief moment, he managed to inflict fear upon the most superior being in existence. Unfortunately, my humiliation was, also, engraved on the minds of many of my loyal servers. Never, before, in my entire reign, have they seen this look on my supreme countenance. They will not forget! I will not forget!"

He paused, for an instant, breathing hard and blowing mucous through his repulsive air hole, froth bubbling from his horrible mouth.

"In my haste, he continued. I ordered him and his fellow combatant chained and sent to the mines. There, to spend the rest of their worthless lives in hard labor and degradation until they perish. I deprived myself the pleasure of seeing them torn apart and fed to our hungrier specimens. I have been cheated!" He bellowed with rage.

By now, the veins in his bulbous head were doing a serpentine, mating dance. The angry fires, in his eyes, flared blood red.

"To rescind this order, now, would be to admit that I have made a mistake. Omnipotent rulers are above this."

Mokar patiently awaited the royal dissertation to conclude and the facts to surface. So far, Zarnog had revealed nothing concerning him. To interrupt him at this point of his insanity would be hazardous to his health. So, he sat there, silently.

"Because of my highly-evolved, mental network, Zarnog pushed on, I have conceived the perfect solution. First, an edict will be imposed on all my servers. To wit; Any person who mentions, aloud or otherwise, the incident that occurred shall forfeit their life. I have no doubt, whatsoever, my loyal charges will forget, entirely, the fear their leader expressed on that night. Sadistic elation over-flowed these last words.

"As to the second part, my learned Teacher, I entrust to you. Mokar's antennae were on the alert for the first time since this royal babbling commenced. He had experienced many of Zarnog's tirades. As long as they didn't hinder him, in his pursuit of knowledge, they usually went in one antenna and out the other

"You will convince the Earthlings their sibling was torn apart and the pieces were fed to our most vicious exhibits. The seed most be planted in their minds that this is an example of what happens to those audacious, unfortunates who feel they are mighty enough to do harm to your leader."

After the shock level registered normal, once again, Mokar spoke; choosing his words carefully as to survive another confrontation with this demented Monarch.

"Leader Most High, your reasons for doing this are well-guarded. I do not understand. How will this benefit your magnificence?"

"Yours is the occupation for solving riddles, Learned One, not mine. But, I will disclose my reason for you. Actually it is two-fold. After the knowledge that their sibling no longer exists is conveyed to them, they will devote more time to their studies and become more productive to the Nevoan society. If they were aware their sibling was still alive their every effort would be concentrated on joining him."

"But, Mokar took a risk interrupting the benevolent beast. Might they not rebel, upon learning of his demise? Earthlings are more close-knit than most of the Universal species I have studied."

"Initially, I would imagine, their anger will curtail their studies. But eventually they will get over it and get on with their adaptation into our society. One thing is certain, learned Nevoan, never again will they be threats to my supreme being. Broken and tamed just like my other exhibits.

"And the other reason, most High One?

"Ah! Yes! The major reason, also. Not having the pleasure of observing the rending of the Earthly parts, I will extract my satisfaction from the grief this ploy will bring from the other two, watching the hate pore forth from those Earthly eyes whenever we are in the same room. Not quite as exhilarating as physical torture, but, a small rebate from a hasty decision will provide me with a little satisfaction."

"You may, also, notify them because of the loss of their sibling and the grief they will contend with, I, in my sympathy to their situation, have removed all time limitations on their progress. From here on out, they may

proceed at their own pace and grieve as long as they wish."
He said, drooling ecstatically.

"Pouring honey on the wounds you have inflicted will
still leave the wound." Mokar thought. Zarnog was a master
Nevoan, to be sure. Only his diabolical mind could have
conceived this cesspool masterpiece.

"That will be all, Learned One. Keep me informed as
to their reactions. I want to know all the delicious details."
He said, with a sardonic grin.

"I shall do as you bid, Leader Most High."

Quitting the Royal apartments and "High House" in
record time, he slowed his pace when he reached the open
square leading to the "House of Knowledge".

"They were just alien creatures to be studied. He thought
to himself. Why should it matter to him what happened to
them? But, the strange thing was, it did. Empathy was
something every Nevoan was devoid of, and, yet, he was
concerned. "Why?" He asked himself.

"That bastard!" He said aloud, borrowing one of the big
Earthman's expressions. This was not going to be an easy
thing to do.

# CHAPTER 9

As the morning sun spilled its warmth into the small compartment, a door opened. Mokar and two guards, carrying chains, made their way, stealthily, toward the two unconscious Earthmen. The ends of the chains were fastened, securely, to the small columns at the foot of their beds. The shackle ends were snapped shut around Earthly ankles.

Mokar assumed, upon hearing the news he was ordered to convey, they would react violently. For the safety of all involved, restraints would be necessary. Until their anger was completely vented, their movements would be severely limited.

Paralyzed by the alien shock emitted from the deadly rods they called "Draco's", the semi-comatose embrace held them firm. The long swim back to consciousness would be rewarded with a much more devastating blow.

Mokar was about to defer his twisted mission until a later time, when one of the Earthmen stirred.

Looking up at Mokar through blurry, bloodshot eyes and taking a moment to put his surroundings into focus, Jim asked. "What Happened?"

An antiquated emotion stirred inside of the Nevoan. Hidden away for so long, it confused him. "What was it?

He thought. Why was it so hard for him to do this? Just as suddenly the thought of losing his position surfaced. He would do as he was bidden.

"I was forced into using physical means to prevent you and your sibling from jeopardizing your lives. As it is, I have some bad news to impart."

Shaking his head, as he sat up, Jim looked, first, at his brother Greg, still out like a light, then at Truck's empty sleeping platform. Like a cold bucket of water over his head, it hit him. Everything that transpired the night before flew back into his conscious mind.

"Where's Truck?" He shouted, in a panicked voice. As he was about to maneuver into a sitting position, he noticed for the first time, the chain around his ankle. Looking up, slowly, into Mokar's eyes, fear and anger erupted. You son of a bitch, what have you done with my brother?"

The sound of his brother's voice brought Greg back to the present. He quickly assessed their situation. Despair exploded in his head. He lunged out of his sleeping furs and fell upside down in front of Mokar.

He ordered the guards to lift the struggling Earthman back onto his platform. Waiting for the Earthmen to quiet down, he steeled himself against the pair of murderous eyes. Finally, he spoke.

"Your brother was exterminated, last night, while attempting to assault Zarnog."

Jim and Greg looked at each other, shocked. Silence pervaded the small room as the mournful meaning of those words took root in their minds. Then, the pain, anger and frustration merged into an emotional volcano.

"You God damned bastards! Greg screamed. We did you no harm. Unchain me! Let me spend the last of my life killing you murderers. Why couldn't you just leave us alone? Truck! Truck!". He sobbed.

"Why didn't you kill us, too, Mokar? Jim shouted. What insane entertainment are we to provide? Tears streaming down his face, he continued. We loved our brother. You have taken him from us. Kill us now, monster, because if we get the chance a lot of you freaks are going to hell. To emphasize his anger he yanked, with all his might, on the chain. Are the Nevoans such shit-faced, cowards they have to chain unarmed men?

"The chains are only for your safety Earth man." Mokar answered.

"That's bullshit, Mokar! One on one there is not a Nevoan in existence that we could not tear apart with our bare hands. Tears blurring his eyes, he continued. "Work hard you said and we would be protected. Learn about your society and we would be allowed to survive. This is our reward?" Wracked with grief, he lay back down, exhausted.

"Earth man, I would share your grief, if I was allowed to do so, but, it would be my death. I did all I could do to prevent this from happening."

"You expect us to believe that? After what has happened. You must be insane! Greg screamed. We trusted you. We tried to learn about your kind. Unfortunately, no one took the time to learn about us. You killed a big part of us when you killed Truck. You would be better off putting us back into that cage. I will kill the first one of you bastards I get my hands on."

After a moment of tense silence, Mokar spoke. "Earth men, whether you hear me or not, I will speak. Make of it what you will. I was the one who immobilized you, last night. Had I not, you would, also, be dead. Your sibling moved too quickly for me to intervene. There was, absolutely, nothing in my power I could have done for him. I am trying to understand your anguish. If my work was, suddenly, taken away from me, I would be angry; a loss I would feel greatly. I was not responsible for your sibling's death. Your arrival has presented me with a great challenge. I have learned much about you and your planet. All of these things I have mentioned, only to make you understand there are characteristics in Nevoans, also, which distinguish one from another."

The two men stared at the ceiling, uncaring. The burden of their loss was crushing. No words could ever explain this loss to anyone.

"The chains were put on because I foresaw your reactions to the loss of your sibling. If I had not been learning anything about you, how would I know this? Mokar continued. When or whether they are removed is entirely up to you. There is nothing you can do for him, now. But, there is much you can do for yourselves. Zarnog has revoked the time limitation he had put upon you. With no restrictions, there are many things you can accomplish. Do not throw your lives away!"

"Mokar! Jim cut in. Do you realize the pain your people have caused us? Ripping us from our world and everything we knew, abusing us mentally and physically, treating us like lowly beasts. The list of Nevoan hospitality goes on and on. I want no more to do with you monsters. Release me, now, and I will avenge my brother."

"How many of us would you have to kill to fulfill your revenge, Earth man? Eventually you would be killed. I offer you a chance to stay alive. Your death or the deaths of many of us will not bring him back. Besides, Zarnog has given me specific orders to….

"To hell with your orders! Greg cut in, loudly. Just give us the chance to die like men. I guarantee that ugly son of a bitch, Zarnog, will get his money's worth and then some."

"The end result is quite evident, is it not? Why would you forfeit your lives while there is an alternative?"

"Do you call living under a microscope and being threatened every time you turn around an alternative? Jim asked. It's nothing but imprisonment. Nothing you could ever say would alleviate the crimes perpetrated against us.""

"Be that as it may, Earth men, I will continue to assist you if you change your minds."

As they started out of the compartment, Greg asked: "Where is our brother buried?"

Mokar turned around, slowly, and said; "I do not understand what you mean, Earth man."

"What have you done with our brother's remains?" Greg clarified.

Mokar hesitated before answering. This piece of information, Zarnog had added to exercise his sadistic muscles. Grief and pain were tools of his trade.

"What was left of him was divided and fed to the most voracious exhibits."

"Mother of God! How could you? Jim cried. You claim to be the most civilized beings in existence. Why? Why?"

On hearing this desecrating news, Greg had swung his head over the side of his sleeping platform and vomited the alien feast from the night before.

Mokar hurried out of the compartment, followed, closely, by his guards. His morbid task completed, he sought the sanctuary of his library. "Why was this bothering him?, confusing him? What were these strange feelings stirring inside him? Mokar thought. Of all the tasks he had done for Zarnog none had ever bothered him before. "The price I pay to retain my position gets steeper all the time."

Back in the small compartment the two Brothers, laying on their platforms, stared into space. Each trying to absorb the blow, so cruelly dealt them. Their aching hearts and anguished minds released a flood of tears. The "Big" guy was gone, forever. Now, there was just the two of them. All the things they had shared, together, were, suddenly, memories.

"Jim, what should we do?" Greg asked, breaking in on the solemn silence.

"I don't know! At this very moment, I want to commit mass murder, squeeze every drop of alien blood out of existence. But, of course, that's impossible. A second choice would be suicide. But, then, I'd be throwing away any possible chances of avenging Truck. It won't be the same around here without him. I miss him, already!" He sobbed.

"My sentiments, exactly, brother. Our hatred of these beasts multiplied last night. We could end it all with one, impetuous assault. Or we could become model citizens."

"What are you getting at, Greg?" Jim asked, confused.

"We had a plan, Jim! The three of us! Even with the pressure of the time limitation weighing us down, we were working on our escape. The only spark of interest, igniting

Truck, was working on our plan. I, for one, would feel bad if we threw it all away. Especially now, since the time factor is no longer a problem. We owe it to the big guy to accomplish what we started. He wouldn't have thrown in the towel because of one player being sidelined and you know it!"

"What you say makes sense, Greg. But, I don't know, whether or not, I could keep my anger in check long enough to accomplish anything. What they did to our brother makes my blood boil."

"Then, what we have to do is channel that negative energy and use it for a positive purpose. We can do it, Jim!" We have more of an incentive, now, than we ever did. Maybe it's fate!"

"Aw, bullshit, Greg! Truck didn't have to die to provide incentive for us. We already had that."

"Maybe so. But, to throw it away now wouldn't prove anything, either. I want to live long enough to accomplish what we started. If I have to use Truck's death as impetus, so be it!"

"It'll be a lot harder, now. Jim replied. They took out our heavyweight."

"True, again, Jim. But, we also gained all the time we'll need. Besides, do we have anything better to do?"

Nodding his head in agreement, Jim replied. I suppose, the first thing we should do is talk our way out of these chains. We made a lot of threats and they may keep us in them for quite a while."

"Maybe not, Jim. Their whole society is based on threats and violence. They have no concept of love and caring as we do. To them, a loss is something to take advantage of. Not to mourn. I think, if we talk to Mokar in the morning, he'll free us."

"That's another thing, Greg. Mokar did save our hides, whether we want to admit it or not. We said some pretty harsh things to him. As mad as I am at these bastards, I wouldn't do him any harm. He's been pretty fair with us."

"I don't think we'll have to worry, in that regard. Mokar almost seemed human there for a moment. Like he wanted to apologize, but didn't know how. By tomorrow, our threats will be forgotten."

"Okay, Greg. I'll give it a try. But, there is one condition."

"And what's that, Jim?"

"I know you've never been the aggressive type, like Truck and myself. But, I want your word that, if we should manage to escape, we spend the rest of our lives, on this cruel planet, waging war against our brother's murderers. His tears and aching heart poured out as he said; I will never feel at peace knowing they are carrying on with their lives while our brother was deprived of his."

Reflecting on his brother's words Greg replied; "That is true, Jim. I have dealt differently with conflict, all my life. There was never a need for aggression, on my part. But truck's death changed all that. Till the last breath of life leaves my body, I vow to fight these monsters. As Truck always said; I'm ready to start kicking ass."

As the alien silence fell, once again, Earthly tears poured forth in farewell.

# CHAPTER 10

A sharp pain brought him awake with a start. Running a hand down the side of his right leg, he came in contact with damp fur. Instinctively, his powerful grip crushed bone and flesh while ripping it away. A loud squeal emitted, echoing off the walls of the dark, damp cell. It was followed by a sickening splat as it was hurled against one of the same. Adjusting his eyes to the semi-darkness, Truck took a slow survey of his situation. The floor, upon which he lay, was strewn with dirty straw, half-gnawed bones and animal waste. The mildewed walls surrounded an area approximately ten feet square and rose another ten feet to a cracked, wooden ceiling.

The metal collar, around his neck, trailed ten feet of chain. It ended on the collar attached to the neck of the still-unconscious native, lying at his side. Both men were covered with a multitude of cuts and abrasions. The long talons of the Nevoans had shredded his body suit into rags. The hide loincloth of the native had managed to survive intact.

After assuring himself, that no serious damage was done, he continued his survey. Dim light trickled through a small grating set in a door. The high ceiling was filled with gaping cracks and looked as though it would give way, soon, from the rotting moisture.

A scuttling sound from one of the corners opposite him brought his attention to another creature emerging from a hole in the floor. Only a foot long, it scurried across the floor on six insect-like legs, bristling with stiff hairs. Two yellow eyes perched on stalks six inches above the head. A round, gaping hole surrounded with inward-curving teeth gave testimony this was an eating machine. Two more followed, immediately. They converged on the still-quivering body, Truck had provided for them, at the base of the wall. Using sharp pincers and their horrible mouths, they quickly reduced their former comrade to nothingness. The small appetizer finished, six horrible eyes locked onto Truck and his companion.

Groping for something to toss at "Satan's pets ", Truck's fingers closed around some small bones. His movements brought the gruesome trio a few steps closer. Rising to his feet, he flung a piece of bone as hard as he could. It clattered on the wall behind them, missing them by inches. But, this sudden act of aggression was enough to send them scurrying back down the hole.

"Coward bastards!" He said aloud.

Stretching and stomping about for a few moments, he managed to restore circulation into his cramped and aching muscles. Upon glancing down, he noticed the native staring at him.

After sizing each other up, Truck took a step forward and offered his right hand in friendship. "The name's Gary Stonedeer". He started to say.

Quick as a cat, he was on his feet in a fighting crouch, staring across the short space at the Earthman.

Stopping in his tracks, Truck continued to say; "My friends jus call me Truck."

With his hand, still extended, he smiled across at the confused native. "I ain't gonna hurt ya!"

Eyes, never leaving the Earth mans, he cautiously reached for the proffered hand. As they met, Truck closed his big hand and shook it a couple of times. "Glad ta meet ya."

Sitting down with his back against the damp wall, Truck asked; "What's yer name?"

Knitting his eyebrows and shaking his head, the blonde giant sat chain length in front of him.

"Ah! So dat's what it is. Ya can't unnerstand me. Don't worry about dat, pal. It looks like we're gonna get plenty a time ta learn."

Picking up the chain, Truck examined the links. Running his fingers in and out of the thin loops, he searched for a flaw. Taking three feet of slack in his massive hands, he pulled with all his might. "So much for dat." He said resignedly, leaning back against the wall.

His companion stood up and stretched the chain taught. Truck got to his feet, anticipating the native's intentions. The combined alien and Earthly strength proved futile against the metal umbilical cord.

"Strong shit! Truck exclaimed. See if ya can find a rock or something ta smash it with." Remembering the native couldn't understand what he was saying, he knelt down and pantomimed someone smashing something with another object. The native nodded his head and started searching. As he walked toward the corner where the little horrors had retreated, he was pulled backwards, nearly falling over. Turning, quickly, he launched himself on the Earthman, throwing both of them onto the grimy floor. Using his greater strength, Truck threw him off. Like two cats, they were on their feet, quickly.

"What da hells a matter with you?" Trucked asked, keeping his eyes on the circling native. A slight grating sound brought his attention back to the corner. Pointing toward it, he said; "Dat's what I was trying ta warn ya about!"

The native looked in time to see the ugly trio vomiting from the hole. A quick leap put him at Truck's side. Looking at the big guy it dawned upon him what had happened. He had misunderstood the stranger's actions. Smiling, he held his right hand out. It was quickly covered by Truck's massive paw.

"Dat's more like it, pal!" Motioning to the native to sit as far from the creatures as they could.

"We gotta start communicating so we can get along. Pointing a finger toward his own chest, he said; "Truck!"

Getting the idea, the native pointed to himself. "Bantor!" He said.

"Bantor! Truck repeated.

Shaking his blonde head up and down he smiled.

He then tried to pronounce the Earthman's name. Pointing a finger, he said; "Ta- rok!"

After many repetitions it still came out "Ta-rok" so Truck left it at that.

As they talked, their hellish audience had advanced to within a few feet and had multiplied. No less than eight pair of hungry yellow eyes devoured the twin mounds of meat in front of them.

"Christ! It looks like a family picnic and wer da main course. What da hell are dose things, Bantor?" Truck asked. Pointing toward the creatures, he made Bantor understand what he was trying to say.

"Sleva!" His native friend said.

"Sleva!" Truck repeated. "Ugly bastards ain't dey?" Scooting over as close to Bantor as he could get he knelt down on one knee. He grabbed up the slack chain. A little more than three feet of doubled chain hung from his hand. He had the right leverage, now, as he waited for the creatures to get a little closer. Raising his arm, slowly over his head, he let the end of the chain rest against the small of his back.

Bantor sensed what his companion had in mind and moved even closer, giving him even more slack in the chain to work with. With his left hand he groped around in the dirt floor, searching for a weapon, coming up empty.

A louder scraping echoed from the mouth of the hole. Another "Sleva" pulled itself up through the hole and spilled itself out on the dirt floor. This one was at least three times larger than the others. As it made its way to the front of the pack, its subordinates parted, making room for it.

"Here comes da Grandfather!" Said Truck, as it came to a stop a few feet in front of them.

The two, yellow eyes focused on them, while slimy drool dripped from the putrid, garbage-disposal mouth.

Sweat, dripping down his arm, made the chain feel slimy. Tightening his grip, he waited. The next slightest, alien move would be his signal. The stillness in the small confines was suffocating. One more element had been added, for the first time; human sweat. The putrid stench attacked their senses as they waited.

As fast as it takes to tell, the larger creature struck. Faster than it takes to tell the chain was a blur, catching the nightmare in mid-leap; smashing it into the filthy floor. Like the propeller of a plane, the chain continued to lash out death. Besides "Big Daddy", five others were dead or dying. The remaining four ran up the white flag and disappeared into the black exit. Before the last one was totally out of sight, Truck was up kicking the mess he had made down the hole after them.

"Dat oughta hold dem for a while!"

Sitting down, once again, they stared at the hole, listening to the crunching slurps of the feasting survivors. Thankful their flesh wasn't on the menu.

"I wonder how long derc gonna keep us here. Truck said aloud. I'm getting kinda hungry."

Almost on cue, the small door to their cell burst open admitting six, well-armed Nevoans.

"On your feet, beasts! You are leaving!"

The captives didn't have to be asked twice for an invitation to leave the cesspool suites. Sandwiched between the six escorts, they were quickly ushered out of the palace dungeon, up and out into the courtyard. Six more guards, with bags over their shoulders, joined them.

As the first sun cast its rays onto the alien world, the small patrol herded its prisoners out of Nevoa. Three uneventful days and nights later the small escort literally deposited their, half-starved, charges into a large, open-air pit. The ten-foot drop knocked the wind out of the chained men for an instant.

The large depression was two hundred feet across and perfectly round. Carved into the perpendicular walls, along the entire perimeter, were small cave-like openings. Peering into a few of these holes as they walked around familiarizing themselves with their new home, they noticed they were of different depths and widths.

"Dis mus be da motel!" Truck guessed. But, where da hell is everyone?"

A few entrances up the line revealed a pair of dirty, callused feet sticking out of its mouth.

Bantor bent down and gently shook the owner. A startled groan emitted from the lair followed by an emaciated head, as the old man sat up. His dark eyes, stared back at the two men, in confusion and fear. His chest heaving as though he had run a long distance, he rose to his feet.

Laying a hand on the bony shoulder, Bantor spoke softly, repeating the word "Kaba" once or twice. The old man yelled out "Bantor" and embraced the blonde giant. Happy tears of recognition flowed from the corners of his old eyes. Pulling away, he pointed at Truck. Bantor announced, "Ta rok" and then pointing at the old one, he said; "Kaba!"

Truck held out his hand and said; "Glad ta meet ya, Kaba!"

He looked questioningly at the proffered hand and then to Bantor, who took the hand in his and shook it as he smiled. Then he placed the bony paw in Trucks and it, too, was shaken.

Sitting cross-legged in front of the opening, they talked. Truck assumed they were fellow tribesmen. He listened to the singsong rhythm of their language. Bantor pointed at him once or twice. Probably relating to the old timer all that had transpired since the two had met, Truck thought.

The sound of voices and shuffling feet, coming from above, interrupted the powwow. A large ramp, three feet wide, twenty feet long was slid over the edge, into the pit. Sweaty, dirt-encrusted men of all shapes and sizes flowed into the crater. Trance-like, each one made his way to one of the small caves. With hardly more than a curious glance at the two, chained men, they filed past. The parade of fatigued, stumbling men didn't cease until it numbered more than seventy. As the last foot met the dirt of the pit, the ramp was immediately hauled up and over the edge. Guards were dispersed around the top at twenty-foot intervals. The dust had hardly settled before all was still, once again. An occasional snore or a mournful groan, were the only telltale signs the pit was occupied.

The cave next to Kaba's was unoccupied. Motioning to Bantor to follow, Truck went in, on hands and knees, to investigate. The smell of human waste slapped him in the nostrils.

"Have ta do a little housecleaning." He said to himself.

The small cave measured approximately, ten feet deep and six feet wide. But, it was only four feet high.

Room, enough, to accommodate the two of them. Backing out, he gestured to Bantor to check it out for himself. A few moments later, he came out, shaking his head and wrinkling his nose. Truck grabbed his own nose with two fingers and shook his head up and down in agreement. This caused the blonde native to throw his mane back and shake with laughter, slapping the also-laughing Earthman on the back. Neither man realized it, at the time, but their friendship would evolve into the greatest relationship between aliens any planet had ever known.

Shortly before the last sun had burned itself out, a gong sounded. Like a tidal wave of zombies arising from their graves, the men withdrew from their sleeping caves and converged on one end of the pit. Two large kettles were lowered, at the ends of ropes, and hung suspended three feet above the ground. Kaba, whose only job was meting out the portions, stood behind them with two ladles in his hands. As the men passed before him, one scoop of water and one scoop of mealy gruel were poured into their bowls

Truck and his chained counterpart fell in at the end of the line. Before they pulled even with the chow buckets Truck yelled out to the guard above; "We are new prisoners an we ain't been given no bowls!"

"You will be given bowls on the morrow. Tonight you may use your hands or go with out!" He said, with a sneer on his ugly face.

"Well thanks a lot, pal. Next time I see your mother, I'll tell her what a good job yer doing. Shit breath!"

Stepping in front of Kaba, he put his hands together and drank the water from them as it was poured from the ladle. Keeping them together, he watched as Kaba deposited the thick slop from the other ladle in his hands. Or I should say, over his hands. Shaking his head, he moved forward, a little, so Bantor could receive his share of hospitality. The sadness, in Kaba's eyes, told them that he was forced to do what he did. They understood.

Sitting with their backs against the wall, in front of their small cave, they slurped their meal as fast as they could, before it ran through their fingers. As they dined, the two buckets were raised and Kaba joined them. Licking his fingers clean, Truck burped and patted his stomach in mock satisfaction. Bantor looked at the mess in his hands and offered them to the Earthman. Truck couldn't shake his head fast enough, in polite refusal. This caused Bantor to roar with laughter. Truck wasn't the only one with a sense of humor.

As Bantor and Kaba conversed, Truck listened. He, also, observed Kaba setting both of his bowls aside, half finished. He figured the old man was saving it for later on and thought nothing more of it until a large, fat barrel of a man strode up to them. This was, by far, the largest person Truck had ever met on two planets. Like an eclipse, he stood over the three of them. He said something to Kaba, who was shaking like a leaf. Bantor asked Kaba something. The old man lifted the bowls from the ground and started to give them to the large man. Bantor intercepted them and placed them back in front of the old one. Before he could turn around, again, the big man aimed a punch at the side of his head. It never landed. Truck perceived a conflict and was ready. Kicking out, with his muscular leg, he caught the Sunday-puncher in the knee, knocking him off balance. Before he could rise, Truck was on his feet and waiting. The fallen giant also regained his feet, surprisingly fast for one with so much bulk. As the battle of the dust bowl approached, the on-lookers moved in closer for a ringside seat. Glaring across at the Earthman, fat man shook with rage. No one had ever opposed him since his first day here. His bullying methods had kept him well fed, while the weak perished around him.

This stranger, with blue eyes and black hair, would die. Bellowing like a bull with his balls in a vise, he charged with head lowered and arms outstretched. A split second before he was on him, Truck grabbed one of the reaching arms, pivoted and flipped the mountain of flesh over his head in a perfect arc. He landed on his back a dozen feet from the smiling Earthman.

Rolling over and shaking his head, the maniacal glaze in his eyes and saliva foaming from the corners of his mouth, spoke for his anger.

"I think ya better go home, now, buddy!" Truck said, in a serious voice. "I don't want ta have ta hurt ya."

Staggering to his feet, with homicide on his mind, he charged the Earth man with all his fury. Ducking under the tree-trunk arms, Truck turned and planted a rock hard fist behind the exposed ear. Down he went, as if a roof had collapsed upon him. He did not get up, this time.

The entire audience was shaking their heads and mumbling among themselves. No one was more surprised than Bantor who was six feet of chain from all the action, on Truck's left. Many of the spectators came up to him, said a few words and slapped him on the back.

Bending over his fallen adversary, Truck noticed he was breathing heavily, as if in a deep sleep. Kneeling between his legs and grabbing an arm, he pulled the giant onto his shoulders and rose. His Earthly muscles rippled through the tatters of his body suit. Pointing here and there he made them understand he was taking sleeping beauty home. Kaba touched his arm and pointed to a large cave up ahead. If you have ever carried four hundred pounds of lard while walking in soft soil, then you will recognize the powerful act displayed by the Earthman.

Depositing his burden on the doorstep of his cave, Truck smiled and said; "You'll feel much better after a good nights sleep."

As they walked back to their caves, the sun made its farewell plunge over the horizon. Sitting with their backs against the wall, they reveled in the first night breezes, cooling their weary bodies.

"A helluva a way ta start my first day on da job." Truck thought, aloud.

## CHAPTER 11

At the sound of a gong, the filthy occupants pulled themselves from their sleeping holes into the new day. Scratching and dusting what little dirt would not adhere to their bodies, they made their way toward the chow buckets. The collective silence, from so many gathered men, was eerie; a reflection of spirits broken, long ago.

Truck and Bantor had already taken their places in line, holding their newly acquired bowls. Observing the zombie-like migration, in their direction, a wave of depression passed over them.

"I ain't gonna let dese bastards get ta me!" Truck thought, as he looked into the lifeless eyes of the men shuffling before him. When a person has thoroughly convinced himself there is no hope, there is nothing left but to die. And these men seemed pretty resigned to their fate.

Eating their meager breakfast, which was a repeat of the night before, both men contemplated their situation in silence. Chained together, as they were, made even the slightest possibility of escaping that much more difficult. But, they would not give up hope.

Bantor had decided, long ago, he must learn to trust his chained companion. "Had he not come to his aid at the palace, kept them both from becoming dinner, while in the dungeon and probably the thing that carried the most weight, defending his uncle from the bully, Corba. Yes, he thought, He liked the big man. It would be an honor to teach him the "Kletta" language, a privilege, never before, accorded to an outsider.

Kaba joined them, interrupting their thoughts. "Morning, little buddy!" Truck said, beaming a huge smile in the old man's direction.

Kaba did not understand the words. But, his smile said it all. He returned it in kind.

As the two natives conversed, Truck looked around the compound for his fat "friend." Spotting him, sitting in front of his cave, Truck waved. The glare, returned, emitted from a face that was purple from his right eye to his right ear lobe. "I think he wants ta be friends, now." He said to himself, smiling and winking back.

Kaba and Bantor had caught his actions and stared, questioningly at the big Earthman.

Shrugging his shoulders and smiling, Truck said; "Da hell with him if he can't take a little joke." Pointing across the compound at the steaming behemoth.

Bantor, recognizing the humorous taunt, burst out laughing. He told Kaba. Soon, they were both laughing. The infectious sound, of the native laughter, induced Truck to join in. "A man could do a hell of a lot worse, as far as friends go." He thought.

A gong sounded, signaling the start of the workday. The long ramp was lowered to the floor of the crater. Up they went, single file, until every man, except for Kaba, stood at the top. A long, low, stone structure stood fifty yards off to the right. "Most be da guards barracks." Truck thought.

Herded across a mile of dusty desert, they came to the entrance of a vast cavern. Located at the foot of a lofty cliff, it stood like an open wound. Guards, on either side, handed out a pick or shovel to every other man. They were led down a steep incline a half a mile into the bowels of the planet. Metal bowls, set into depressions, on either side, held burning oil.

A short while later, the passageway leveled out. Guards were assigning working areas. When it was the chained duo's turn, a guard explained the procedure.

"One will dig, the other will shovel." He said. Holding up a piece of dark blue crystal, he continued. "This is "Dracon". It is the most precious commodity in all of the Universes. One transport cart is to be filled, each working day. Food and water will be withheld, until completed.

The pace, you set, is entirely up to you." He said, with a malicious sneer on his face.

"Now! To work! End of orientation! With that, he strode back up the passageway, toward the surface.

Their designated working area was a twelve-foot long, seven-foot high tunnel, barely seven feet wide. Four oil bowls burned, dimly, giving it the atmosphere of a crypt. A four by four wheeled, metal cart, approximately three feet deep, stood empty at the back of their small depression. They, quickly, moved it up toward the entrance.

With Bantor on his left, Truck started swinging the pick, digging deeply into the hard, compact earth. A few more swings and he was rewarded with a fist-sized chunk of blue crystal. Gathering it up, he showed it to Bantor and deposited it in the cart.

Nodding his head in acknowledgement of what needed to be done, he attacked the mine wall with his shovel. Working this close together, one or the other was in constant danger of being hit with pick or shovel. Only their impeccable timing prevented this.

On and on, they labored, extending their tunnel a few feet. But, barely covering the bottom of the cart with the crystal. Sweat drenched them, covering their bodies completely. Dirt clung to their bodies, turning into mud from their exertion.

A half an hour later, they stopped. Their muscles pleaded with them for a rest. Guards patrolled the main passageway, checking on their progress from time to time. Giving their charges a cursory glance, they returned, quickly, to the surface.

Truck wiped a sweaty, dirt-encrusted hand across his face, as he caught his breath. He looked at his partner with a newfound admiration. Bantor had matched him, stroke for stroke, without relenting. Each of the men was reassured there was no dead weight at either end of the chain that united them. It was only mutual exhaustion that caused them to stop and regain a second wind. The cart, three quarters full, by now, stood testimony to their arduous attack on the mine wall.

They had talked very little during their excavation. It wasn't because they couldn't understand one another. They were conserving their energy for the dirty task before them. Truck avowed, to himself, as soon as he could communicate well enough to make himself understood to Bantor, escape plans would be discussed. He could never help his brothers, by remaining here. This place would kill him, before too long. They were on his mind, constantly. Somehow, some way, he would be with them, again.

The sound of approaching footsteps invaded their tunnel and their thoughts. Getting to their feet, they waited, alertly.

"So, beasts, I catch you shirking your duties, and so soon!" Raising his staff, he advanced. Backing the two men against the wall, he came even with the three-quarters full cart and stopped. "What is this? In the short time you have been working, you could not have collected so much dracon. It is not possible!" He said, glaring at the two men.

"Well, we didn't pull it outta our ass, pal!" Truck said, noticing the surprised look on the ugly face.

Turning abruptly, he hastened up the tunnel, disappearing.

"I don't know what da hell we did, pal. But, I think we better get back ta work." Picking up their tools, they continued the assault on the dirt wall.

A few moments later, the guard returned, trailing one of his superiors. Peering into the cart, he said; "You are to be commended, beasts! No one has ever shown this much progress, in such a short amount of time. It appears, your workday will be completed well in advance of everyone else. Once again, the "Leader most High" has made the right decision."

"Well, if ya feel dat way about it, why don't ya give us some water?" Truck replied. We'd probably work even faster if we could have a drink once in a while."

"It is not our job to make your life easier, beast. Our major objective is to squeeze as much labor out of everyone sent to us as possible. Because I complemented your progress, does not entitle you to any reward, because, there are none. When you perish, there will be an immediate replacement. No one lasts long in the mines. With a sneer on his face, he said; "Keep up the good work!" Turning, he walked up the passageway, followed by the other guard.

"I got news for ya, shit face, Truck yelled up the passageway. I ain't gonna be here much longer!"

Some of his anger was taken out on the dirt wall, in front of him. The rest would remain in reserve, keeping him alive until he joined his brothers again. At least, he hoped so.

The hated blue crystal grew steadily higher, in the cart. Until, at last, it was above the rim. The two, exhausted men sat down, admiring their accomplishment. A big smile cracked through the dirt caking the Earthman's face.

"Well, we did it, pal! Thumping the native on his back. It was returned with a smile and a reciprocating thump on the Earthman's back.

Throwing their tools on top of the cart, they started pushing it up the passageway. All of a sudden, Bantor let out a cry of pain. He had stubbed his toe on something sharp, protruding from the dirt floor. Looking down at the native, groaning and holding his foot, Truck knelt down to investigate. The skin on Bantor's right, big toe wasn't broken. But, the swelling was already starting. Probably a bad sprain, he thought. As he was about to raise himself up, his hand came into contact with the hidden obstacle. Pushing aside a little dirt, he uncovered a seven inch long piece of metal that tapered to a point. It was part of a pick broken off by a past employee.

Holding it up for Bantor to see, he smiled. "I think we jus found a way outta dis place."

As the big guy fumbled for a place to conceal it on his person, the sound of approaching footsteps froze them, for an instant. Bantor grabbed the piece of metal and hid it under the hide flap of his loincloth. As the guard made his way up the tunnel, he was nearly run over by their cart

"Where da ya want dis crap? Asked Truck. And where's da water?"

Turning, the guard made his way up the main tunnel. "Follow me!" He said.

After a short distance, they turned down another tunnel that branched off to their right. The grade was steeper than the one they had come down, initially. The two exhausted men had all they could do to keep up with the guard. A short distance later, daylight poured through an opening, directly ahead. Staggering, at last, into the daylight, they squinted against the brightness.

"Dump it there!" Said the guard, pointing down.

Looking around, they noticed they were in a low, natural crater. The deep depression was filled half way up with the fruits of many laborers. It sparkled back at them like a giant blue eye.

After tipping the cart, adding their contribution, they followed the guard back to the original entrance.

As they entered the dazzling brilliance of mid-day, they discerned a water bucket sitting on a flat rock in the shade of a sprawling tree. A guard dipped a ladle into the bucket and held the dripping offering out to the men.

Truck took it from him and handed it to Bantor. Surprised by this act of unselfishness he smiled and accepted it. Taking a small drink, he handed it back to the Earthman. Truck did the same. Back and forth it went, until it was emptied.

Grabbing the ladle, impatiently, the guard told them to sit down and left to take up his post.

They sat with their backs against a large rock, breathing the fresh air deep into their dusty lungs and stretching their legs and arms out to relieve the cramps in their aching muscles.

A small group of guards watched them from a short distance away. The chained captives paid them no heed as they luxuriated in the sunshine and fresh air, which was worth more to them, at this moment, than anything else.

"I wonder if Jim and Greg are all right. Truck thought. Dese bastards are gonna pay for what dey done to us. I swear it!"

Bantor's mind was on Cinda, his woman. "Was she still alive?" If she was, he would find her and make them pay. The Nevoan leader "Zarnog" had killed their child. The horrid scene had triggered nightmares that would not end until that cruel monster died a slow, horrible death at his hands.

A short while later, two men staggered out of the entrance, received water and collapsed by their side. By the time the third sun was half spent, nearly all of the men were finished for the day. The last eight were, literally, dragged out of the mine.

Half filled carts meant half rations. Three quarters full meant three quarters rations, and so on.

It was plain to see why so many died. Even at full rations the body burned up much more fuel than it was receiving. Death was inevitable, under these conditions.

When the last of their large "family" had joined them, they were herded back to their dust-bowl prison. They headed toward their small caves, for some much needed, rest. Bantor and Truck did likewise, but for other reasons. After burying the pick end, they sat with their backs against the walls, facing each other. Light filtered in through the opening, a few feet away.

"We gotta start learning how ta talk ta each other. Truck opened. We got da tool we need ta break dese chains, but we gotta understand each other if wer gonna escape."

Bantor stared at him, understanding the big man's need to talk. He, also, felt it was important to communicate, especially under their circumstances. The chain, connecting them, kept them close to each other. But, a shared language would bring them closer even yet.

Through signs, English, Elimaran and sand drawings, they started. Day after day, week after week, they continued. While their communications grew stronger, every day, their bodies grew weaker. Too much work and too little fuel were taking their toll on them. If they didn't make their attempt, soon, they would never make it.

# CHAPTER 12

As the third sun dipped below the horizon, three men sat huddled in a small cave, talking in whispers. "What we need is some sorta diversion. Truck said. Its gotta be long enough for us ta get over da top."

"I have given this much thought, my sons. Said Kaba. I am too old and would only hold you back."

"Uncle! I will not hear of such talk! You are elder man of our tribe, now that Sorbo has passed to his ancestors. We need your knowledge." Bantor said anxiously.

"Knowledge is useless unless it has a chance to spread. I will not deprive your knowledge from growing. I have lived long. Each day a part of my life travels to be with my ancestors. Soon, I will be whole, once again, in their presence. You are young and strong enough to make change in this world of ours. My time is nearly spent."

"This saddens me, greatly, Uncle. You have been father and tutor to me since my sire disappeared. But, if this is your wish, I will respect your decision."

By listening very closely, Truck understood what was happening. "Hey! Don't worry about it! After we get outta here, we'll come back and set everyone free."

"Ta rok of another world. Kaba said. You have taught this old one much. Your way of making the best of this hopeless situation has lifted my spirits and brought joy to my heart. The Elimaran fires will always welcome you. Now, continue with your plans or neither one of you will ever warm your backsides on friendly fire."

The few moments of silence, necessary to digest and accept Kaba's decision, dampened the atmosphere in the small cave. The last few months of degradation were lessened, only, by the encouragement they gave to one another. The setting of the third sun, on the following day, would mark their attempt.

They talked long into the night. Two hours before the first sun erupted, they were, finally, asleep. It had been decided Kaba and one of his cronies would create a diversion at the south end of the crater. Shouting and arguing, they hoped to draw the guard's attention. Truck and Bantor would make their way toward the north end, away from the diversion. The sentries at this end were thinly dispersed, about fifty yards apart. It was their hope Truck would have enough time to lift Bantor over the top and climb their connecting chain before the guards closed in. After that, it would be a foot race.

Bantor knew the direction, in which his village was located, but was unfamiliar with the immediate landscape. Whether there were mountains, forests or rivers to cross, he had no idea. Whether food would be available, in this area, was also unknown. To the determined duo, these were sacrifices they would gladly make, in their pursuit of freedom.

If they were successful in reaching his village, step two of their plan would be implemented, an all-out assault on Nevoa to liberate his woman, Cinda, and his friend's brothers. Considering, the only weapons they had were desire and the element of surprise, this would be a monumental accomplishment.

They had managed to cut through one link on their chain, but for appearances, left it connected. One hardy pull, and they would come apart. They would do so, shortly, before their assent of the wall. When they were safe, they would attempt to remove the collars.

All the next day, they planned to work at half speed. It was a trade-off they would have to make. Their penalty would be half the amount of water, but, the strength they would need later, will not have been depleted.

They talked, quietly, of their plans, going over them again and again. There was no room for error.

They would work in streaks. When they weren't resting, they tore into the compacted earth, furiously. Not until the cart was half full, did they slacken their pace.

When they heard the guard's approaching footsteps, they picked up their tools and went through the motions of men hard at work. After they receded down the passageway, they rested. All the long day, they played this game. Each man suffering his share of anxiety attacks.

"Soon, Bantor, we'll be outta here. Da first thing I wanna do is find a river or lake and scrub dis crap off a me. Den, we gotta find enough food ta feed an army. I never been dis starved, for so long, in my life."

"If we do escape, Ta rok, I will lead you to a land so beautiful and abundant with game, it will satisfy our needs many times over."

"When we escape, pal! Ya gotta start thinking positive."

"I am trying very hard, my friend, but there are so many negatives to consider."

"Dat's where people make their mistake! Dey take too much time thinking about all da things dey can't do. Try thinking bout all da reasons ya have for wanting ta get outta dis place and don't let nothing stop ya."

"The confidence and optimism you express, so often, is starting to become contagious. I will not burden myself with negative thoughts any longer, my friend."

"Dat's good! Without you, I don't think I could find my way around dis place. We need each other!"

"Do all of the men from your world think as you do, Ta rok? Are they all so confident?"

"No. Not all a dem. We got our wimps, too. Course, its hard ta tell how a man is gonna react in a hard situation.

Some a da sissies could become heroes. Some a da tough ones might faint. It's hard ta say."

"It is like that on my world, also, Ta rok. Unexpected courage sometimes comes from the least expected sources. I wonder how I would react if my world and everything familiar to me was ripped away."

"I think you'd do just find, pal. Ya got da right spirit."

"So, it is as I expected! You have not done enough work to merit a rest. On your feet, lazy beasts!"

Unbeknownst to them, the guard had crept up on them while they talked. They were on their feet, immediately, ready to resume work. But, the guard was not ready to let the slight discretion pass. He advanced upon them swinging his staff.

"I will teach you to shirk your duties!" He said, aiming a blow to Bantor's midsection. It never landed.

Intercepted by Truck's shovel, it was deflected sideways.

"Just go about your business and no one gets hurt!" The Earthman said.

Glaring back at the big man, his eyes red with rage. "You dare oppose your superiors?" Raising his staff, he aimed a blow at Truck's head. It was deflected, once again, by Truck's shovel, just as a vicious arc from Bantor's pick ended six inches deep in the creature's ugly skull. Dead on his feet, he froze for an instant, before crumpling into the dirt. Fire red eyes stared at his executioners.

"I fear I have just jeopardized our plans, Ta rok. Because of my hatred for these monsters, I could not stop myself, nor did I want to!"

"Don't worry about it, pal. Da bastard had it coming. It was him or us and I kinda like it better dis way."

"Do you think we should make our attempt, now, Ta rok, before they discover the body?"

"Dat seems like da thing ta do, but, we'd never get through all da guards at da entrance."

"We can't just sit here and wait for them to discover the body! Bantor said, nervously.

"Well, let's make sure dey don't find it den!" Said Truck.

"I do not understand!" Said Bantor, confusedly.

"We bury it, dump our cart, as if it was full and get outta here like we was done working."

"Will they not become suspicious when there is no guard with us?"

"I don't think so. Wer usually da first ones done and dere used ta seeing us all over dis place. If dey ask about da guard, I'll think a something."

Without wasting any more time, they dug a shallow grave and, hurriedly, covered the body, laying his staff along side him. Throwing their tools in the cart, they pushed it, speedily, toward the dump area, hoping they would not cross paths with another guard while in route. Luck was with them. They dumped the cart and made it almost to the entrance before encountering another guard.

"Hold there, beasts! Where is the guard assigned to you?"

Having prepared himself for the inevitable, Truck answered. "Dere was a disturbance down one a da tunnels. He told us ta go on ahead to da entrance. He even threatened us with our lives if we didn't do as he said."

"May we go, now? Bantor asked. We had another full cart, as usual, and are very tired and thirsty."

"You may go, beasts! I will check on this matter, later."

After drinking their water, they lay down in the shade. Each man struggled to keep his nervousness from showing. If they were found out before being herded back to the crater, their lives would be forfeit.

As the day wore on, the majority of men had completed their work. Conversation was at a minimum. This type of slave labor left only enough energy for resting and breathing.

At least two pair of eyes cast furtive glances at the opening, every once in a while. The next few hours or so would tell them if all their plans were for naught.

The last two men were ushered out of the mine with stinging blows and curses. One of them broke from the guard and charged toward the water bucket.

"Stop that beast! Shouted one of the guards. He has not done enough work to merit even a sip of water."

One of the guards, protecting the water bucket, launched a blow, catching the desperate man in the throat. He crashed to the ground. His neck bent at an impossible angle. He would never need water, again.

After designating two volunteers to drag the body away, they were ushered to their feet and started on the short march back to the crater. It was the longest march for Truck and Bantor since their arrival. Any moment, they expected all hell to break loose. Their nervousness made the short trek seem like a cross-country safari.

Relief showed in all the faces as they poured down the ramp, into the crater. Double relief showed on two. As they made their way to the cave, Kaba and his friend, Valon, joined them. Bantor, quickly, explained what had transpired. After digesting this information, they agreed, unanimously, if the attempt was not made this night, they would get no other chance. Once the guard's disappearance was noted, questions would be asked. Truck and Bantor, having seen him last, would be the first on the chopping block.

"When Valon and I start the commotion, you should be in position to make your attempt. The strange ritual, you two have been practicing, should make your presence less conspicuous."

Every night, just before the final sundown, Truck and Bantor would jog four times around the entire perimeter of the crater. This served two purposes. One: Their frequent presence, outside their cave, was a nightly occurrence, tolerated by the guards keeping their vigil around the circle. Two: They knew their legs would be put to the test if they succeeded in getting over the top. The brutal work they did, offered very little exercise to their legs. The nightly regimen was exactly what the doctor ordered.

"Valon and I have decided that you will have our rations tonight. There is no telling how long it will be before you are able to find sustenance."

"Uncle, I would not have you go hungry on my account." Said Bantor.

"Me neither!" Added Truck.

"We have all hungered for something in our lives. It won't be the last time. Said Kaba. The added fuel may make the difference in your attempt, hence, the difference in our escape.

"Listen to the wisdom in your uncle's words! Valon interrupted. We shall eat tomorrow. You may not. This small sacrifice is for our salvation as well. I know you will be back for us, one day."

"You can bet your last buck on dat, pal! Truck joined in. Wer gonna get everyone outta here, even Kaba's fat friend, Corba. Dat is, if we can lift his big butt up far enough."

The warm laughter dispelled some of the tension in the small cave. Each man hung on to this brief respite from the dubious undertaking they were plotting. Any distraction was welcomed, at this point.

Kaba reached behind and withdrew a large, patchwork hide. Holding it out to Truck, he said; "This will offer a little more protection than your present attire."

"And more acceptable on this world than those enemy rags you now wear." Valon added.

"Where in da hell did ya get dis?" Truck asked, examining the strange pelt.

"Every man, that was able to, cut a scrap from his meager loincloth. I had ample time to fit it all together using a sharp stone and thin strips of hide for binding."

"Only one person refused to contribute." Said Valon. I think you can guess who that was."

"Fatso!" Answered Truck, affirmatively.

"Uncle! Will he not make trouble for you after we're gone?"

"I think not, my son. He has no love for our Earthly friend, here. But, he has even less for these monsters that invaded our world. He wishes to leave as much as the rest of us. Besides, Valon added a little more insurance by telling him if anything happens to me or anyone else, because of his bullying, he would be left behind."

"I pray it shall be as you say, uncle. If I discover he has done you harm, in my absence, I shall send him to his ancestors with my bare hands."

"Empty your mind of these thoughts, my son. There are more important matters to think about."

While they were talking, Truck pulled the tattered remnants of his covertogs off and was trying to figure out how to put the native garment on. With Bantor's help, he was, finally, able to cover his nakedness.

The simple garment is cut in a "T" shape. The horizontal strap is tied around the waist, behind the back. The long flap in front is passed up between the legs and pulled through the strap in back. The excess material hangs down the back of the thighs.

"Well, how do I look, you guys?" He asked.

"If not for your black hair and blue eyes, I would say you have Elimaran ancestors." Valon offered.

"Less likely to be mistaken for an invader by a native spearman." Kaba added.

"Give my thanks ta everyone, Kaba. I swear on my grandfather's grave, I'll be back ta repay em all."

"You have already done that, my son, by planting the seed of hope in all of us, giving us something to live for. Kaba said, as he stood up to leave. Try to get some rest before the eating time. We will talk more, later."

After Kaba and Valon had left, the two men were able to sprawl out full-length in the small cave.

"I hope dis is da last time I look at dese ugly walls. Back home, only animals live like dis."

"Some of my people live in caves, Ta rok. Much cleaner and larger, of course."

"Hey! I didn't mean ta offend ya, pal."

"No offense taken, my friend. Hopefully, after tonight, I'll never have to sleep in one again. To sleep in the long, sweet grass, under the open sky is the only luxury this man desires."

"Amen ta dat, pal."

As stillness invaded their cramped quarters, each man focused on the part he would soon play. Nervous anxiety coursed through every thought. In a few hours it was do or die. No awards would be given for coming in second. Sleep rejected them, as they lay, staring into the dark, contemplating the fate this night would bring them. One way or another, they would soon be rid of this harsh existence.

The eating gong sounded, startling them from their mental meandering. As they took their place in the line, Corba fell in behind them.

"Man from another world, I would let you know that no one has ever bested me in a physical contest. He said in a subdued voice. I would not speak of this before now, because it is something I have never experienced. I did not know, before, how it felt to lose. I was angry at first, but since have salvaged a little solace in knowing it took someone from another world to do it. I would offer my hand in friendship."

Truck covered the proffered hand with his and thumped the behemoth on the shoulder.

"No hard feelings, pal. Glad ta have ya on da team."

Bantor, looking skeptically at the big man, asked' "Why have you waited until now to show your friendship? The dispute, you had with Ta rok was many suns ago."

"The venture, you will attempt, shortly, is known to everyone." Corba replied.

"If you are asking to come with us, the answer is no. Bantor interjected. The misery you have caused my uncle and others through your bullying will not be forgotten by this one."

Before the situation could get out of hand, Truck refereed. "Hey, buddy! Give him a chance ta talk. Let's hear what he's got ta say."

Corba, feathers ruffled, glared at Bantor. "I have two reasons for approaching you at this time. Neither one is to ask for employment in your quest. One; I have pride. To acknowledge ones better is the right thing one must do. I have already acknowledged Ta rok as my better before it was too late. My second reason for this confrontation is to make my contribution to your quest.

Reaching into a pouch, hidden beneath his hides, he withdrew two stones. "These will help make you more comfortable on your journey. Placing them in Truck's hand, he said; "May your ancestors guide your trails." Turning on his heel, he went to the very end of the feeding line.

"What da hell da ya make a dat, Bantor?" Truck asked, while staring at the stones in his hand.

"Hide them away, safely, my friend. They will be extremely useful in our travels."

"What are dey, anyway?" Truck asked, tucking them beneath his patchwork skins.

"They are a hunter's most prized possession. Firestones! Corba must have secreted them away since his incarceration. Bantor shook his head at the surprise. This one may have been a little hasty in his appraisal of the "fat one". To offer them up to another is no small act of generosity."

After receiving their share of food and water, they sat in front of Kaba's cave, chatting with Valon.

"Kindness comes from the most unexpected sources. He said, after he was apprised of Corba's gift. I would not have conceived that one parting with as much as his sweat."

"Be that as it may, they will aid us, greatly, in our endeavor. If we get that far." Bantor said.

"When we get dat far, buddy. When!" Truck repeated.

Kaba joined them and was quickly filled in on the latest happening. He didn't seem as surprised at Corba's kindness as the others.

"Sometimes we forget who the real enemy is because of petty differences. Corba is an Elimaran and would die, as fast in the protection of his world, as would any man. Our grievances with each other weigh considerably less than the atrocities perpetrated against us by these invaders. Corba, also, caught me by surprise. Kaba continued. First, by being at the very end of the eating line. Second, by pledging to aid Valon and myself in the diversion."

"By my ancestors!" Quipped Valon.

"By mine, too!" Added Truck.

After finishing their double portions of food, Kaba suggested they try to rest a while. He would rouse them shortly before the last "Sister" sun retired from the sky.

At the entrance, of their small cave, was, yet, another surprise: Two pairs of sandals, made out of layers of soft leather.

"Dese will sure save our feet a hell of a lot of wear and tear." Truck said, as he slipped on the larger pair, lacing the thongs half way up his calf.

After donning his sandals, Bantor spoke. "I have been giving it much thought, my friend. We both have loved ones held in captivity by the invaders and we are both anxious to free them. This one would propose a slight change to our plans."

"Whatta ya trying ta say, Bantor?" Truck asked.

"The men, here, have made sacrifices to aid our escape. I would suggest, upon reaching my tribe, we return, in force, and free these poor men. Many of them may not last much longer."

The only thing Truck wanted, on this strange world, was to be with his brothers. The anticipation of that day was overwhelming. But, these gentle natives had all but adopted him. Bantor had become like another brother. Besides, the chances of freeing his brothers were pretty slim without their aid.

"I suppose our personal plans can wait a little longer, Bantor. Dey sacrificed a little for us, we can sacrifice a little for dem."

"Ta rok! You are, truly, an Elimaran at heart! Bantor exclaimed, thumping the big guy on his shoulder."

"You gotta have a little American in yours, too, pal." Truck said, returning the thump.

We better try ta get a little shut-eye, now. It won't be long before da shit hits da fan."

Crawling into their cave, hopefully for the last time, they tried to relax their tensed muscles and over-burdened minds.

After a brief silence, Bantor asked; "What is shit and fan?"

"Go ta sleep, pal. I'll tell ya some other time."

# CHAPTER 13

The sound of gravel crunching, under feet, roused the occupants of the small cave. The tension in the tight confines hung like a blanket of fog, blocking any attempts at sleep.

Kaba stuck his grizzled head into the opening. "The time is here." He said, in a low voice.

With their new sandals, donned in a hurry, metal spike concealed, the two men emerged from the cave.

The third "Sister" sun was close to finishing the last leg of daylight. Then, darkness would fall upon them. It was the only ally the two men had in their bold attempt at escape.

Their plan was to climb out of the pit, on the north end, and out-distance any pursuit, before darkness hid them. To make a mad rush, in total darkness, would be foolhardy. All it would take, to seal their fate, would be to run into an obstacle, hidden by the night, turn an ankle or become separated. Bantor would have no trouble navigating his way back to his village. But, the big Earthman would become, hopelessly, lost.

A slight wind stirred the dust, in the compound, as the two men started walking around the perimeter at a steady pace, beginning their nightly routine. Without showing any outward signs of awareness, they observed more men than usual sitting or loitering in front of their caves.

The sentries, walking the rim of their prison, were at their normal distance from one another. Periodically, the four of them would stop, assuming positions around the crater similar to the four points of the compass; north, east, west, south. Approximately one hundred yards was kept between them at all times. Every ten minutes, they would move again, in unison, a quarter of the way around the crater. Their third quarter rotation would be the moment Truck and Bantor were anticipating. By that time, the sun would be close to sinking over the horizon.

Their point of departure, at the north end, would be situated half way between two of the sentries. They hoped the fifty yards, or so, would allow them sufficient time to climb over the rim and establish enough distance between their pursuers.

As they continued their way around the dusty perimeter, each man was locked into his own thoughts. "We only have one shot at dis. Truck thought, while wiping gritty sweat from his eyes. If dey stop us, dey'll kill us for sure. I wish I coulda seen one a dese freaks run. I got no idea how fast dey are. Ah, da hell with it, he continued with his musings, It's better den wasting away in dis shit hole. Besides, I owe it ta Jim and Greg ta try."

Bantor wasn't even sure they would get over the top. But, they had to try. The daily drudgery, of the mines, was killing them. His heart longed for his captured mate, Cinda, and the dark forest and lush fields around his village. His Earth brother had enough confidence for both of them. "He would not let his big friend down; no matter what the outcome."

The sentries, maintaining their silent vigil, ten feet above, saw nothing unusual among the meandering men. Their laxity and blasé' approach to their duties were attributed to long stretches of service in this desolate waste and their egotistical concept of themselves. "No one would ever think of escaping from the most superior beings in all of the universes." Their concerns, as far as security went, were perfunctory, at the most.

One quarter rotation had been completed so the two warriors slowed the pace a notch. They would slow up, even more, the closer it came to making their attempt. They had to conserve as much energy as they could for their race with the sentries and the diminishing light from the third sun of the day.

Truck glanced at the blonde native, matching his own Earthly stride. In a low voice, he said; "Don't worry, pal! We'll make it!" A grin and a wink added to it eased the tension, somewhat, but not entirely.

"Ta rok acts like we are going to a celebration. Does it not weigh heavily upon you what we dare to attempt?" He asked.

"Course it does, pal. But, I ain't gonna show no fear. Animals can smell fear and I ain't sure if dese ugly bastards are animals or not. Besides, you're doing enough worrying for da both of us."

Another rotation had just been completed by the sentries. The next time they came to their rest stop, the plan would be put into motion.

Kaba and a small group of men were congregating in the south end of the pit, the area opposite their exit point.

They had decided the best route to follow, after climbing out of the pit, would be to head directly toward the setting sun: north, by our Earthly compass. This would lead them in the direction of a thick forest about two miles away.

Adjusting their pace, as to arrive at the given exit point when the sentries stopped for their ten minute hiatus, the two men slowed their pace even more. The distraction Kaba and the others were about to stage, would be the final signal. Timing would be crucial. Taking the focus off of them, for even a brief moment, could mean the difference between success and failure.

An instant before they arrived at the exit point, a loud commotion erupted at the far end of the pit. Kaba and a group of men were arguing loudly. A few were grappling, raising clouds of dust, while a ring of spectators shouted and cursed at the combatants.

The two closest guards, fifty yards to their right and left, above the rim, were engrossed in the melee, enjoying the scene. Their hatred of the natives and the tedious duties that surrounded them, left little room in their alien hearts for compassion. Let them destroy one another. It would save them the trouble in the end.

Walking the last few feet, to the base of the wall, Truck grasped the chain in his powerful hands and quickly severed it as the weakened link popped apart. Bending slightly, at the waist, he laced his hands together and shouted to Bantor. "Time ta go, pal!" Placing one foot in the Earthly hands, he was catapulted over the rim of the pit by Truck's enormous strength. Scrambling to his feet, he hurriedly lowered the end of his severed chain back into the pit. He had barely enough time to plant his feet before the weight of his friend pulled against him, nearly toppling them both back into the dusty crater. Within a heartbeat, Truck was at his side, making a desperate dash to freedom. From the time the chain was severed to the start of their frantic exodus, took, only, a few moments.

A quick glance, over his shoulder, revealed to Truck, the guards were, just now, aware of their escape. As they turned in their direction, he saw them raise their staffs and pointing them in their direction. The distance between them and their nearest pursuers was approximately seventy-five yards.

Suddenly, small explosions started kicking up the dust around their fleeing feet. Replays, from Viet Nam, flashed across his mind as he, automatically, deployed a zigzag course. Bolt after bolt of deadly energy spewed from the alien staffs, throwing dirt and moss in all directions.

Hearts beating against their chests and tortured lungs sucking in great gulps of air, they fled. Their sweat-drenched bodies already covered with a thick layer of flying grit, added even more weight to their dilemma.

Risking a quick look over his shoulder, Truck realized they had widened the gap from their nearest pursuer. The relentless barrage, however, grew steadily closer, pelting the ground inches from their tired bodies.

The large copse of trees was about a mile off in the distance. But, to the nearly- exhausted men, it seemed as if it were on the other side of the planet. The sun was nearly spent, which didn't help their situation any. One misstep, at this moment, would put an end to their dream.

Looking at his blonde friend, matching him stride for stride, Truck's respect for the courageous native grew even greater. He'd have him on his team any day. He also knew that he had taxed his physical output to its limits. Another hundred yards and they could lose themselves in the shadows of the forest. It looked like a hundred miles to the desperate men. They knew, as one, they would die on their feet before quitting. They almost did!

About twenty yards from the sanctuary of the nearest trees, Bantor let out a cry of pain. Tumbling head over heel, from the impetus of the ball of energy that struck him, he lay still.

Coming to an immediate stop, Truck turned and looked backward at his friend, laying face down, a few feet behind him. He noticed their pursuers were a good two hundred yards away, but, coming on steadily.

Racing to his side, he bent down and lifted the unconscious native to his shoulders. Taking a long, rasping breath, he turned, once more, and entered the forest. Fifty feet of meandering around the boles of the leather-like trees he turned left, paralleling the edge of the forest. His mind had warned him, long ago, that his body was completely tapped out. But, on he went, as if in a sleepwalker's trance. "I can't give up! He thought to himself. Jim and Greg need me! I can't let them down any more than I can let down Kaba and the rest of the dying men in the pit."

His mental vacation prevented him from noticing the sudden drop in the forest floor. Legs, still churning in desperate flight, he fell through the air like a skydiver who suddenly noticed he had forgotten his parachute. Clutching his unconscious friend more tightly, his last vision was that of a tree coming at him from below and slapping him in the face.

Before the last light of the day spilled over the horizon, the two men were already in darkness. No sounds of pursuit or anything else, for that matter, reached their resting minds.

## CHAPTER 14

"Jim! Give me a hand with this, will you?" Greg shouted, struggling with a large barrel of grain.

Walking over to help his brother, he grabbed the handles on the barrel and they dumped some of its contents into a trough situated just within the bars of a large cage. Its shaggy occupant, the size of a horse, cowered in the farthest corner. Two black eyes peered out beneath the thick black hair on its head. Its six legs were folded beneath its Quivering body. The "Quavo" was plucked from its home on one of Saturn's moons.

"Poor bastard! Jim said, lowering his end of the barrel to the ground. I know, exactly, how he feels."

"If it wasn't for the fact we scored a tad higher in the "Nevoan" intelligence test, we may still be in one of these cages ourselves. I'd go back in there in a heartbeat if I could only have known what would happen to us. Greg added. At least Truck would still be here." He finished, tears threatening to erupt from his eyes.

"I'll second that! Said Jim. In a heartbeat!"

Five days after the devastating loss of their brother, they had approached mokar with a proposal. They would continue their "Nevoan" education in the latter part of the day, but they wanted some type of work to do in order to break up the tedium of being locked in. Greg, also, blew a little smoke up his alien butt about their willingness to repay The "Nevoan" society for all they had done for them.

Mokar, the intelligent creature he is, thought to deny the request because of the double meaning in the Earthman's words. But, after further thought, he decided that sooner or later societal interaction would be inevitable. So, he granted the request.

They were appointed to the care and feeding of the exhibits in the "Universal" zoo. Mokar figured it this way: The entire Nevoan settlement was surrounded by a force field. Where could the creatures of Earth, possibly, go? They depended on him for their existence in this cruel society. Let them mingle and work. It was, after all, their lives that would be forfeited if they made the wrong decisions.

Their daily routine went something like this: Shortly after the first of the "Sister" suns peeked over the horizon and their morning meal completed, they were escorted by Mokar's watchdogs to the zoo. There, they were turned over to "Porda", the head honcho. After feeding and watering the strange exhibits, they would begin where they had left off, the day before, cleaning the next cage in line. Since assuming their new positions, they had completed cleaning nearly every cage in the large ring of attractions. Then, they would start the whole process again.

Halfway through the heat of the second "Sister" sun, approximately midday, they would be escorted back to their compartment. After a refreshing dip in the scented pool and a change of clothing, they would eat a meal. A brief rest period and they were back in the presence of Mokar, absorbing the Nevoan culture and geographical data of the planet. Shortly after their evening meal, they would continue their assault on the stubborn bars of their window. Days ran into weeks and their routine never varied. For all, outward, appearances, they were model, hard-working citizens of the Nevoan society.

Their busy schedule had its dividends. The physical labor hardened their tanned bodies, preparing them for the arduous task ahead. The hectic pace, also, served to alleviate some of the mental anguish caused by the death of their brother.

"How's it going up there, Greg?" Jim asked, in a subdued voice.

Greg, perched on the window ledge, ten feet above the floor, answered without turning from his task. "Another quarter inch, or so, should do it. That is, of course, this blade holds up."

"You want me to take over for a while? Jim asked. You must be getting tired."

"I'm okay, Jim! He answered, sawing away at the bar. I must be on an adrenaline high, now that we're this close."

Jim looked up at his brother and smiled, his own anxieties surfacing. "I know what you mean, Greg."

"If they managed to finish the job this evening, by this time tomorrow night, they could be on their way."

Of course, the most important factor in their escape plans was, yet, to be realized. The force field, around the settlement, had to be neutralized. A vital piece of information was revealed to them by Toki, the little servant; the location of the control unit. The second bit of fortune was finding out that it sat in the middle of the zoo compound. Their chores kept them in close proximity with the tall, metal box on a daily basis. The central location of the zoo, within the Nevoan settlement, made it the logical site for the control box. The Draconium crystals, in the central unit, radiated invisible rays outward like the rays from the sun, to other crystals buried around the entire perimeter of the settlement. There, they were refracted upward. Thus, creating an impenetrable barrier. Any solid object coming in contact with this wall of energy was immediately repelled with lethal results. To activate or deactivate the energy field was a simple matter of adding or removing the crystals from the control unit, which sat in a small metal shed. The door on it was always closed, but never locked. However, there was always one of Porda's flunkies in the vicinity at all times. A diversion would have to be created, lasting long enough to immobilize the unit.

"We did it, Jim! Finally!" The sound of his brother's excited voice trickling down upon him, startled Jim back into the present. Looking up at his brother perched on the ledge and holding up a two-foot section of the bar in his hand, Jim smiled. Greg's sweat-drenched face smiled back in return.

"Wedge it back in place and get down from there." He said, as he walked across the room and stood beneath the window.

Greg, hurriedly, stuffed small pieces of fur ripped from their bedding, between the severed ends of the bar and wedged it back into its original position. Grasping the window ledge he lowered himself down to Jim's shoulders and then to the floor. Walking over to the table and sitting down, they stared at each other. A moment of silence passed between them as they mentally celebrated the culmination that weeks of hard work had, finally, produced.

"If everything goes smoothly tomorrow, we should be out of here just after dark." Jim said, in a low voice.

"Have you come up with any good ideas for neutralizing the force field?" Greg asked.

"Just one, but I don't know how good it is." When Greg didn't respond, he continued. "When we get to the "zoo", first thing in the morning, Porda and four of his five men are usually congregated around the supply shed. The fifth man is loitering near the shed controlling the force field. Between these two areas are cages that obscure the view from one to the other. I propose you keep Porda and the others distracted long enough for me to take out the lone guard and disable the energy system. I know it's easier said then done, but it's all I could come up with. What do you think?"

"Sounds good, Jim! Except for a couple of vital elements you've overlooked."

"Such as?" Jim asked.

"I should be the one to work on the force field and the elimination of the guard. I'm not saying I know more about it than you do, but I might recognize something similar to a computer part or some other component I'd be familiar with, while you might not."

"Secondly, he continued. We have to decide what to do with the body after I take him out."

"You sound pretty sure of yourself, little brother. You realize, of course, our chances of escaping will be shot if you fail. Don't you?"

"I know you are much more qualified in that sort of thing, Jim, but after what they did to Truck I won't let us down. Besides, I need the on-the-job training."

Of the three brothers Greg and Truck had the closest relationship. Although anyone within ear shot of the two would have guessed they disliked each other. Quite the opposite, they would kill for one another. The horrible end of their brother's life by these cruel beings was enough to turn a reverend into a "Rambo."

Looking at his brother in a new light, Jim replied: "I have faith in you Greg, but killing isn't easy, especially the first time. If you think with your heart, instead of your brain, you're apt to make a mistake that may cost you your life. Once you've made your mind up there can be no hesitation."

"My heart and my mind are in agreement, Jim. This is not just for Truck. We have to do this for our own welfare. Our brother's memory will be with us all the way."

"Okay, Greg! You got the job! I only wish I could devise a way for all our brother's perpetrators to come to the same, cruel end."

"That's it, Jim!"

"What?" He replied to his brother, questioningly.

"The perfect solution for getting rid of the body. Those big carts we use to remove the refuse from the cages are sitting near the supply sheds. I'll just grab one, do the deed and dump it in. I'll cover it over with the straw-like bedding and at the opportune time, feed it to "Mr. Xarta.""

Jim's eyes went wide and a big grin curled the corners of his mouth as the morbidity in his brother's suggestion struck home.

The "Xarta", a twelve -foot long, five-foot round eating machine, from a distant galaxy, was the perfect garbage disposal. Nearly eight hundred pounds, with a head three quarters the length of its body it resembled a crocodilian nightmare. Two large, black eyes with fire-red pupils perched on short stalks on either side of its head. Its entire body, from the tip of its stubby tail to its snout, was covered with leathery scales. The cavernous mouth was filled with triple rows of razor-sharp teeth in, both, upper and lower jaws. Six short legs, ending in sharp hooves, supported its murderous bulk. The "Xarta" was definitely not a vegetarian.

"Giving them a taste of their own medicine, eh Greg? No pun intended. I just hope it doesn't spit the bastard out."

"I doubt it, Jim. I understand they are capable of digesting even the most repulsive garbage."

"What do you think will happen after they discover him missing?" Jim asked.

"What can they do? We'll be working just as hard as ever. The only period of time that could be in question would be the time it takes for the diversion. Hopefully, it will be so brief as not to draw much attention."

"That's true! After all this time, they're use to seeing us working in different areas of the compound, apart from one another. I just hope they stay in their normal routine, tomorrow."

After discussing a few more minor details, they crawled into their furs. Each one hoping it would be the last time under these conditions. A new beginning or a merciful end awaited them.

# CHAPTER 15

The short march to the "Zoo", through the deserted streets, did little to alleviate the anticipation within the thoughts of the Earthmen. Sleep had played tag with their unconscious minds, as their anxieties danced to the beat of a loud drum.

As they were led toward Porda and his men, they counted five, which meant one other would be near the energy shed. While Porda barked out orders, two of his men were busy hauling out buckets and other equipment from the back of the supply house to the short porch at its entrance. The other two stood, one on either side of the door.

"So, Earth vermin, you arrive at last! Be forewarned you will work harder than yesterday or be subjected to the wrath of Porda!"

It was the same greeting every morning. Boasts and threats were the life-blood of this society.

"And a good day to you, Sir! Jim said. We would have been here a lot sooner but we got a flat tire along the way." He continued, sarcastically.

"Your words are strange, Earth dung. I hope the meaning carries no undertones of insolence."

During this intercourse, Greg had made his way to the front of the supply shed. Finding one of the large, two-wheeled carts empty, he began throwing rakes, scrapers and other supplies into it. One of the sentries eyed him, for a moment, but saw nothing unusual and turned his attention back to the sound of Porda's voice.

Staring back at the large alien, Jim risked a quick glance and noticed Greg rolling the large cart toward the middle of the compound.

"It would be foolish, indeed, to incite the wrath of Porda. Jim said, smiling at the ugly creature. I am aware of the enormous power your status entitles you."

Actually, by Nevoan standards, his position was slightly above the over-seeing of slaves in their draconium mines. In other words, on the lower end of the Nevoan power chain.

The look on Porda's face was almost human. Glaring back at the American, he analyzed the sincerity of these words. Like one caught between boast and embarrassment, his fired-red eyes reflected indecisiveness.

"Explain yourself, low-life, before I......

"Before you what? Jim interrupted. Beat the hell out of me? Fire me? Who else would work for these shit wages? You don't even have a dental plan, for christ's sake."

At the first sign of their leader's agitation the four subordinates moved in a little closer. It wasn't concern for Porda's well being that piqued their interest. No, they hated their superiors as any true Nevoan would. Their curiosity and inbred distain for anyone or anything other than themselves was the drawing factor. There was, also, the possibility of doing some harm to another creature.

As the alien quartet drew closer, anticipating the sadistic opportunity of bringing their weapons into play on living flesh, Jim was thinking fast for a way to deescalate the situation.

An injury, now, would jeopardize their plans.

"Porda! Before your men get too exited, I think you should hear what I have to say. It could be to your benefit."

Raising a clawed hand, Porda halted their approach.

"What could you say that would possibly benefit me?" He asked, glaring at the human as if he were an insect.

"This entire collection of species is very important to your society, especially to Zarnog. I know your boss puts a lot of pressure on you and your men for its proper maintenance."

"That is of no concern of yours. You are no more than a working specimen of this same space garbage."

"True, Porda! However, we are at least capable of communicating in your language and have aspired to this fine position. We clean, feed and water to preserve Zarnog's pets."

Porda looked at him with raging red eyes and seemed ready to set his hounds on him, but he continued, hurriedly.

"I don't think he would find you very reliable if your charges started dying off."

Flecks of drool seeped from Porda's horrid mouth as he said: "You forget how easily Zarnog extinguished your sibling, as if he were a speck of dust. You would not be missed."

"You misunderstand me, Porda! I was not referring to myself. There is an exhibit that is very sick. It won't eat or drink. When I cleaned its cage, I noticed blood on the floor. I think I know what the problem is."

"What makes you think you can help the beast? Your intelligence level isn't too much higher."

"According to Nevoan standards, I agree, Porda. We're not much higher. But, on my world, my brother and I cared for many types of animals. I think I can help!" Jim said, hoping to extend his stay on this hellhole world for a while longer. These volcanoes facing him were close to erupting.

Porda's alien mind digested the Earth creature's information. Was this a ploy to diminish his anger? Zarnog was obsessed with these alien creatures that filled the cages. He'd better not risk losing any.

"Show me this sickly beast, at once!" He bellowed.

Escorted by Porda and two of his men, Jim breathed a small sigh of relief. They walked to the far end of the compound in the opposite direction to which his brother had taken.

* * * * * * * * * *

As Greg walked away, pushing the cart in front of him, he was aware of the loud voices receding in his wake. Trusting his brother could deal with the situation, he continued on until he arrived at the center of the compound. He stopped in front of a huge pile of straw bedding mounded ten feet high. Emptying the tools from the cart, he grabbed the long-handled pitchfork and proceeded to fill the cart. Looking to his left, he spotted the lone guard loitering next to a large, metal shed.

"Beautiful day isn't it?" Greg yelled across the dozen paces separating them. When the sentry didn't respond, Greg continued filling the cart. "I have to draw him in closer." He thought. After a few more pitchforks of straw fell into the cart, he had decided. Backing into the cart, as if by accident, it toppled over, spilling its contents.

"Would you be so kind and help me set this cart upright?" He yelled over to the guard. Shouldering his staff, he walked over to the human. "It would seem, even a minor task such as this, is too complex for Earth dung such as you." He said, as he stopped a few feet in front of Greg.

"My humble apology for disturbing you, kind sir." Greg said, at the same time he jabbed the pitchfork into the throat of the creature. The force of the thrust was so powerful, the tines buried in his throat, lifted the creature off the ground. The deadly staff went flying from his grasp. By the time he landed, he was already dead. The creature just didn't realize it at the time. Trying to force a scream out of his horrible mouth only produced a spurt of thick green fluid that choked off all sound.

Pulling the fork out of the oozing throat, the Earthman quickly replaced it, with all his strength, into the bulbous head. He would have struck for the heart if he knew where it was located, or if it even had one.

"This one's for you, Truck, and it's just the start." Leaning on the fork until the last alien spasms expired, he suddenly realized, other than the small game on his own world, this was the first creature he had killed that he wouldn't eat. "I would do it again and again for you my brother." He thought. And I may have to before this is all over with. Pulling the fork out of the alien head, he hurriedly scooped up the dead Nevoan and tossed it into the cart. After throwing straw on top, to conceal it, he made his way over to the shed, furtively looking around to see if anyone had observed his murderous act. Throwing the door open, he discovered one large crystal, situated on top of a tripod. Rays emanated around it, giving it a halo effect. Sitting on a ledge, just below the activated crystal were a dozen more in reserve. Racing back to the scene of the crime, if you will, he grabbed the pitchfork and returned to the shed. Using the wooden handle, as one would a pool cue, he knocked the glowing crystal of the tripod. Gathering it up, along with the reserve crystals, he hurried back to the body, lying lifeless in the cart. One by one, he crammed them down the throat of the creature.

"Eat hearty, you son of a bitch." He said to himself. Grabbing the handles, on the cart, he started away from the area. After covering just ten feet, he suddenly realized he had left the alien's staff behind. Dropping the cart handles, he rushed back and hid the staff in the mound of straw. Returning to the cart, he continued toward one of the larger cages off to his left. Sweating profusely from the adrenaline rush he was experiencing, he, at last, stopped his momentum in front of Mr. Xarta.

The cold black eyes, sitting on their short stalks, stared back at Greg. Moving to the control box, across from the monster's cage, he pressed a button and raised the front bars of the cage approximately twelve inches. Then, scooping the body from the cart, he pressed it into the opening. Mr. Xarta did the rest. Rushing to the front of his cage, which was his usual feeding pattern, his compactor mouth attached to the lifeless alien and sucked him out of sight in less time than it took to tell. Returning to the control panel, Greg lowered the front bars flush with the floor, thinking to himself that Mr. Xarta could have inhaled the body right through the bars without him having to open it. Moving a few cages down, he went through the motions of cleaning a cage occupied by a less voracious exhibit. "All had gone well, he thought. With a little luck, they would be out of this alien prison very soon."

From the time he had left Jim's confrontation with Porda until providing lunch for the Xarta had consumed approximately fifteen Earth minutes. When he pushed his cart toward the supply shed it was abandoned except for the two sentries lounging in front of the entrance. Pushing the cart up the ramp, he unloaded the tools and began filling the cart with food for the varying diets of the exhibits. As he was about to leave, he saw his brother approaching. Porda and his two guard dogs escorted him. As they neared where Greg was standing, he noticed Jim's covertogs were almost completely covered with blood. Resisting his first impulse to rush to his brother's aid proved to be a wise decision. For soon he learned it wasn't his brother's blood that covered his clothing. Removing a splinter the size of a ruler from a two-ton herbivore, from a distant galaxy, was the cause.

The rest of their short workday was, pretty much, routine. On their short march back to Mokar's palace, both men anticipated the privacy of their quarters more than any of the other days spent on this heartless planet. What they would learn, from one another, could decide their fate.

* * * * * * * * *

"By the time I bound up that huge foot with the remains of a discarded covertog, I was covered with her blood. The creature was so scared it whimpered the entire time. The only anxious moment, I had, came at the end when it rose from the floor and started toward me. Porda and the rest of his sadist bastards were really getting their kicks, and it looked, for a moment, like they were going to get their money's worth. All of a sudden, the creature just stopped in front of me and started licking me with her two-foot tongue. I was never so relieved in my life. I put my arms around that shaggy head and hugged her. Disappointed, that I wasn't going to be disassembled, Porda opened the cage and let me out. He didn't say a word all the way back to the supply shed."

"There, little brother! I told you my story. Now, you'd better tell me a better one. A story with a happy ending, I hope!"

They were seated at the table in their apartment, awaiting their mid-day meal. Both men fought the anticipation, churning in their guts, until they had bathed and changed into clean clothing.

Greg stared across the table at his older brother. The impassive mask, he wore on his face, gave no hint of success or failure. Jim was crazy with anxiety and ready to explode.

In a low voice, Greg said: "The force-field has been deactivated. We leave tonight!"

Jim hadn't realized he'd been holding his breath as his excitement whooshed out.

"Way to go, little brother! Reaching out, he gave Greg a playful slap on the cheek. "Was it hard to dismantle it? Any trouble with the guard?"

"Keep it down, Jim! We don't want to advertise before we've made travel arrangements." He smiled at his brother's elation, which threatened to make him join in before he could answer the question.

After relating the incident to his brother, a glassy stare came to his eyes.

"You all right, Greg?" Jim asked, concernedly.

"Yes. He answered, in a far away voice. I killed a creature, today. Although not human, he might just as well have been. At first I was scared. Then, when it was over, I felt elated. Pay back for what they did to our brother."

"You did what was necessary, Greg. Sometimes it's the only way."

"I know you're right, Jim. But, having ridden that emotional elevator and taking the creatures life, I felt good about it."

"Change is scary, little brother! But, if we don't we'll die, for sure, without a chance in hell for survival."

"Well, be as it may, I earned my wings today. You don't have to worry about me doing the right thing, from here on out." He said, in a saddened voice. Now that we are one player short we'll both have to work a little harder. We can do this!"

The afternoon sun plummeted beneath the horizon. It was followed, moments later by the rising of the evening sun. The two Earthmen, waded through their evening meal, methodically and attended their last session in Mokar' study. Whether they were successful, or not, their Nevoan education would cease. Each one contemplated the fate only the alien night would reveal.

# CHAPTER 16

A large branch crashed through the foliage above and landed with a thud, on the human body, forcing the air from his lungs. Trying to catch his breath, Truck sat up and hurled the branch from his chest. Within a few moments, his breathing returned to normal. Lying back down, exhausted, he let his eyes answer the quarries of his fuzzy brain. Groping with his hands, on either side, his first question was answered. A thick matting of furry, gray moss cushioned his body. Staring up through leafy branches of a huge tree, his mind kicked into second gear. He started to remember how he had arrived into this strange situation; Escaping, Bantor falling, plunging into nothingness and sudden blackness.

Turning his aching head to the right and then left, he spotted his alien chain-mate lying ten feet from him. Sitting up, slowly, he took an inventory of his body parts. There were very few areas that didn't cry out in pain, but nothing seemed seriously injured. The deep gash, on his forehead, above his right eye, was crusted over with dried blood. This was probably the most serious of his injuries. He thought.

Slowly, rising to his feet, he tested his legs for breaks or sprains. Finding nothing to concern him, he walked over and knelt down by his unconscious friend. He was breathing as if in the middle of a deep sleep. Dried blood matted the blonde hair on the left side of his head, above the ear.

Grabbing a handful of loss moss, he wiped away enough of the mess to reveal a five inch long furrow about an inch wide and down to the skull. It started at the back of the head and ended just above the right ear.

Pressing a finger into the gaping wound revealed to Truck the skull was undamaged. It was a grazing shot, nothing too serious. Tearing a strip of leather from his piece-meal garb and packing the wound with moss, he patched it up.

"Dat's da best I can do for ya now, Buddy!" He said to the unconscious native. We gotta find us some water, so I can clean it up."

The dim light, filtering through the tree, at first made the big Earthman think it was close to nightfall. So concerned for his friend, he had not, as of yet, had time to explore his immediate surroundings.

"I'll be right back, little buddy! He said, aloud. Don't go anywhere!"

Ten paces from the bole of the tree, they had landed in, he parted the hanging branches and felt the full heat of the morning sun, as he stepped out into the open.

The huge tree they had, literally, fallen into, resembled a weeping willow of his world. Truck thought. Not in its color, bark, or shape of leaves. But, it had the same sprawling, droopy branches that formed an umbrella-like closure beneath the tree.

Looking up, he noticed a cliff towering seventy-five feet above the tree. The tree, itself, was at the least, a fifty-footer.

"Dat was a hell of a jump!" He said to no one.

Continuing his circuit of the tree, he noticed about a mile off to his left, an object glimmering in the morning sunlight.

"Dat could be water!" He said, squinting into the glaring brightness.

Ducking under the canopy of branches, he was, once again, beside his silent friend.

"I can't leave ya here, pal, and I ain't got a bucket so yer gonna have ta go with me. He said aloud.

Hoisting the native over one broad shoulder, he forced his way through the branches.

What he hoped was water was closer to two miles away, not one. But, to the almost totally exhausted Earthling, it seemed like a hundred.

Step after weary step, he trudged on. He stumbled, at times, but caught himself at the last moment. He knew, if he gave in to the pleading of his mind to rest his body, he would, in all likelihood, slip into unconsciousness for days.

He couldn't allow that to happen. His native friend needed help worse than he did.

Sweat found its way through the heavy layers of dirt and caked blood. It flowed into his eyes, stinging them. Blinking only blurred his vision and added to his discomfort. On and on, he walked, until, suddenly, he was knee-deep in a small, cool stream. At first he just stood there. Then, his mind caught up with the reality of the situation and he laughed out loud.

"We made it, my friend!" He said, as he waded back to the bank and gently deposited his native burden in the shade of a large bush.

Crawling the few paces back to the stream, he buried his head in the cool, reviving water, drinking deeply. Pausing, a while, to keep from getting sick, he looked around for something, in which, to carry water. A few yards, downstream, he spotted some large leaves floating alongside the bank. On closer observation, he noticed that they were, actually, attached to the bank with long, narrow roots. They resembled the lily pads that covered some of the lakes on his world. Yanking one free, from its grip on the bank, he curled it into a cone and dipped it into the stream.

He, quickly, returned to his fallen comrade and cradled his head in one massive arm, while slowly pouring the liquid life between his cracked, dry lips. The water ran back out, at first, but then, with a sputtering, choking cough, the native responded. His eyes flew open to look into the smiling, grime-caked countenance of his Earth partner.

"Welcome ta paradise, little buddy!"

"What happened?" He asked, reaching a hand to his bandaged head and groaning.

"Take it slow, pal! You'll be as good as new in a few days!"

Staring up at Truck, he touched the side of his head and asked, "How did it happen?"

"One of dose bastards ricocheted a bullet off da side of your skull. It's a little bigger den a scratch, but it'll be okay in a little while."

Noticing, for the first time, the big Earthman, also, had blood on his face. "Ta rok ! You, too, are injured!"

"It's just a little scratch I got when I fell. I'll tell ya all about it, later."

Closing his eyes, Bantor looked as if he were slipping back into unconsciousness, once again.

Shaking him, gently, Truck said; "No time for sleep, now, little buddy. I want ya ta get your butt inta dat stream. I wanna clean dat hole in yer head."

As the native nodded, Truck grabbed him under the arms and slowly helped him to his feet. He half carried, half dragged him to the shallow stream and laid him belly down on the bank with his head hanging over the water. After Bantor had drunk his fill, Truck removed the makeshift bandage and started to clean the ugly wound. Bantor noticed it and asked Truck how he knew to use moss on his wound.

"Da tribe, I come from, use it all da time. Grandfather Joseph taught me dat when I was a kid."

"Our tribes have similar ways, Ta rok. It is used for many different purposes by my people."

Washing the strip of leather in the stream, Truck said; "I don't see any of dat stuff around here. I might have ta go back ta dat tree we fell in."

"We fell into a tree?" Bantor asked, confusedly.

"I'll tell ya all about it after I fix dat head of yours." Truck said, walking out of the stream.

"You will find the moss, you need, under that tree, over there." Bantor answered, pointing upstream and to his right.

In a matter of minutes, Truck had gathered what he needed and was busy making a compress for his friend. After the leather strap was secure on Bantor's head, Truck got up, removed his loincloth, and plunged into the small stream. It barely came up to his knees. But, lying on his back, he let the gentle current ply its invigorating fingers to his many aches.

Bantor, soon, joined him, enjoying their first luxury in how long? Weeks? Months? Who knew?

After a long while, Truck rose up from the soothing embrace of the rejuvenating water and looked around. "I'm getting kinda hungry! He said. "I wonder if dere's any food around here."

"Leave that to me, my Earth brother! I will find us something to eat, in a while. But, at this moment, I wish to enjoy the soothing caress, of these waters a little longer."

"Sounds good ta me, pal! Truck said, settling back down in the water. Being hungry ain't nothing new to us, is it?"

"Not for much longer, my friend." Bantor answered.

Eventually, they did vacate the lulling waters of the small stream, because their hunger outweighed the soothing comfort of the water.

The sharp piece of metal, broken off of one of the picks they had found in the mine, was used, along with a large rock, to remove the collars from their necks. Throwing them and the chains into the stream, both men vowed they would never, again, be anyone's slaves.

After washing their tattered loin clothes and hanging them on a bush to dry, they dozed for a short time in the shade of a small tree.

Truck awoke to a fire with two strange looking carcasses spitted over it. Bantor was seated across the fire peeling the skin off tuber-like objects with a sharp flake of rock. It was pitch dark, except for a sprinkling of stars in the alien sky.

"So, my Earth brother decides to wake. Bantor smiled from across the fire. I thought I was about to enjoy this feast by myself."

"How long did I sleep?" Truck asked.

"The last of the" Sister" suns extinguished her light a short time ago."

"Ya shoulda woke me so I coulda helped get da food.

"Ta-rok, each man knows best how much rest he needs. Bantor said. The ordeal you have gone through to get us here merited much sleep."

"But your head! You need lots a rest, too. Truck answered.

"I will rest when I see my people, again. In the mean time, we both will have much time in which to heal."

Truck got up and retrieved his loin clothe from the bush. Slipping it on, he squatted by the fire. "Dat sure smells good! What is it?" He asked.

"It is called a "Paca". They live in the trees their entire life. Bantor said, as he placed the tubers in the fire. I was fortunate enough to bring them down with a couple of well-placed stones."

"Smells like da roasted squirrel we ate back home. Dere tree hoppers too. Truck said, closing his eyes and inhaling the aroma. Are dey almost done?"

"Do you think that would matter, at the present?" Bantor asked.

"Uh uh!" Said Truck, as they simultaneously grabbed the meat from the fire.

Scorched in places, raw in others, it tasted like home cooking to the half-starved men. Even the potato-like tubers, slightly bitter, disappeared in short order.

"Dat was da best chow I've had in a long time. Truck said, licking the grease from his fingers. My compliments to da chef!"

"Hunger always produces compliments, my friend. When we reach my village we shall really feast. If we ever reach it, I should say. It is a long way off." Bantor said, mournfully.

"When we reach it, pal! Truck said, confidently. We got dis far and no one is gonna stop us!"

"Are all of you Earth people so positive? Bantor asked. You and your siblings have suffered even more than my people. Strangers to everything we see and yet you remain so sure of things."

"It's all you got in dis situation ta keep ya going. My brothers, probably, think I'm dead, but, I know dey ain't gonna give up. Dat's da way we are."

"I am glad you are that way, my friend, for, it too, gives me hope. Now, tell me all that has transpired since our escape attempt was burdened by my weakened state."

Throwing another branch into the fire, Truck told his native friend the whole story.

"And den I gave you some water and you started ta come to. I thought I lost ya dere for a while, pal."

"It is, truly, amazing, that one, from another world, would show that much concern for a stranger. I have known close friends that would not do that for one another."

"Den dey weren't friends ta begin with!" Truck said.

"That may be, but, from here on out, my possessions are your possessions, your pain is my pain. I will never forget what you have done for me, as long as I live."

"Dat's okay, pal. Just live a long life and show me da way home. Truck said, smiling form across the fire. I'm jus glad you were da one dat got hit and not me. I don't think you coulda carried my big butt."

"I would have tried. I'm sure you know that. But, I think I would have found a softer tree to land in."

Native and Earthly laughter erupted in the alien darkness, disturbing the serene stillness.

A soft breeze blew through their small campsite, stirring the coals in the fire pit. The sudden glow reflected off of two determined faces. Worlds apart, as far as cultures go, but, solidly united never the less.

"What's da plan for tomorrow, pal?" Truck asked, adding another branch to the fire.

"I think it is best to remain here for a while and restore our strength. The journey, that lays ahead, will require it."

"How far are we from your village?" Truck asked, rubbing the side of his injured forehead.

"If we travel, steadily, through most of the three "Sisters' suns, each day, we may be there in twelve cycles."

"Dat seems like an awful long time. We got a lot a people ta rescue, Bantor! Maybe we should leave in da morning."

"If we do, as you suggest, my friend, who will be there to rescue us when we collapse from exhaustion? I have as many reasons as you to hasten my decision. But, the condition we are in, we could help no one."

"Yer talking like my grandfather, now. Truck said, staring into the fire. He had a saying for everything. I never knew anyone in my life so close ta nature. He talked to da animals, the land, everything."

"It would have been an honor to meet your grandfather. Bantor said. He sounds like a man of my tribe."

"He woulda liked you and yer people, too, Bantor!"

A cold breeze wafted through the small campsite. Borne in the wake, was a nerve-rattling roar.

"What da hell was dat?" Truck asked, nervously looking around.

Unfazed by the eerie sound, he had heard many times before, Bantor replied from his seat near the fire. "That is "Kazor", the king of death. We must pass through his domain to reach my peoples' village."

"Ya mind telling me what a "Kazor" is, little buddy? Truck asked. Remember, I'm a stranger ta dis place."

"Forgive me, Ta-Rok! I forget your knowledge of my land is limited. A "Kazor" is a murderous beast. It stands twice the height of the tallest man and may weigh as much as five of you. It walks, upright, on two heavily clawed hind feet. It, also, has two short arms, in which it uses to hold its prey. Its head is long and flat, split almost the entire length by its cavernous, fang-filled mouth. Its eyesight is poor. But, the stare from these living coals is enough to inflict terror in the bravest heart. Its wrinkled, leathery skin, a dark gray in color, is almost impervious to our spears. However, there is one vulnerable area, on the beast. Situated on the under belly is an area about a foot wide which is extremely soft. Getting past those terrible jaws and clawed feet, there is still the massive tail to contend with. It is covered with bony spikes, as long as a man's arm. It kills not only for food. It kills for the pleasure of killing. He continued. It is told, through the legends, that one such monster devastated an entire village; men, women and children."

"So, my Earth brother, you will have no difficulty recognizing "Kazor" If you are unfortunate to come upon him."

"Sounds like one, tough bastard!" Truck said, throwing even more wood onto the fire.

"Tomorrow we will make weapons and gather what food we can for our journey. But, tonight, we most rest and strengthen our tired bodies."

"I don't know if I can sleep with dat big son of a bitch out dere. It sounded pretty close by."

"He is quite far away. Go to sleep, my friend." Bantor said as he stretched out beside the fire.

Tossing another handful of branches into the small blaze, Truck, reluctantly, gave in to his fatigue. Curled on his side, sleep did not come immediately. His thoughts turned to his brothers. He had to make it, for their sake. Suddenly, sleep fell upon him like a living thing, feeding on his exhaustion. Kazor was just a dream.

# CHAPTER 17

The evening sun had exhausted itself only moments before. The stars that speckled the night sky filtered their dim light into the small compartment. The two men, each carrying a fur bundle headed toward the window. Looped over the shoulder of one of the men was a braided rope, made from the extra furs of their bedding.

Bending low and bracing himself against the wall, beneath the window, Jim waited for Greg to mount his shoulders. Adjusting his balance, when he felt his brother's weight, he straightened up.

Greg, reaching up, locked his fingers around the bars, above the windowsill, and pulled himself up. He, quickly, removed the severed bars that had been held in place by wedging bits of fur between them. Tossing the two, foot-long, sections, on the soft turf, outside the window, he called down to Jim, in a soft whisper.

"Toss the bundles up!"

Catching them, he quickly lowered them to the ground, outside. Taking the braided rope, from his shoulder, he tied a slipknot to one of the bars. He lowered an end down to Jim, who, quickly, scrambled up to join his brother on the ledge.

"Aren't you going to miss all this?" Jim asked, smiling in the dim light.

"Not in the least! Greg answered. After you, big brother."

Quickly, scrambling down the ten feet to the ground, he was, immediately, joined by Greg. With a quick flick of Jim's arm the rope detached itself from the bar above. As Greg recoiled the rope over his shoulder, Jim found the two severed bars and fixed them inside the fur bundles. Each grabbing one, they raced across the short distance to the wall. Tossing them over the ten-foot barrier, Greg leaped to his brother's shoulders and gained the top. Lowering the end of the rope to him, Jim pulled it taut. Greg, feeling the tension, lowered himself down the other side. Two quick tugs alerted Jim that he was over safely. Greg looped a couple of turns around his waist and braced himself to take his brother's weight. When Jim felt the slack taken out of the rope, he scrambled to the top of the wall. Hanging by his hands, he dropped to the ground, joining his brother. Gathering their meager supplies, they hurriedly raced off into the night.

Everything had gone as planned, so far. But, they still had better than a mile to cover before reaching the forest, trying to put as much distance between themselves and their prison before the night sky reached its starry, chandelier potential. Their bundles slowed them down, a little, but, their adrenalin made up for it. Like two marathon runners, they flew across the uneven course. The spongy, moss-like grass absorbed the shock of their footfalls. Noiselessly, they streaked toward the forest that, naturally, seemed farther away than it actually was. But, since the beginning of time, freedom has lent wings to fleeing feet. Both men kept a steady pace. Sweat glistened from their bodies, even though the cool night breeze slapped them in the face. Both men were well conditioned. With a lot of spare time during their captivity, they had not been idle. To prepare themselves for this moment, both men had done their homework.

Risking the chance of stumbling over some unseen obstacle, Jim took a quick look over his shoulder. Neither man had spoken, since their frenzied rush to freedom began, to conserve their energy and, also, to eliminate one more element of detection.

Smiling to himself, he broke the silence. "We can slow our pace, a little, Greg! There's no one in pursuit."

The vast amount of time it took planning, foraging, cutting through the bars and preparing for their escape had culminated into a matter of a few hectic moments. The elation that flowed through the hearts of the two Earthmen, as they pounded toward the security of the, not so distant, forest, was overwhelming. But, on and on they raced. Until they were, finally, surrounded by the towering trees. Collapsing against the bole of one, they recaptured their breath and slowly allowed the realization, of what they had done, saturate their minds, hearts and the very depths of their souls.

"We did it, Greg!" Jim said, as tears of relief leaked from the corners of his eyes.

Reflecting his brother's elated feelings, Greg choked back a sob as he said; "It would be ecstatically complete if there were three of us sitting here."

Tears of grief, elation and relief were absorbed by the alien soil. The two brothers sat quietly for a long time, letting their Earthly emotions run its full gamut.

The alien night had just started to bloom into its full garden of stars. Some of its brilliance trickled through the tightly laced branches of the alien treetops.

"You okay?' Jim asked, after a while.

"I'm fine, Jim." He replied, while reaching into one of their fur bundles for one of the hollowed out gourds filled with water. Quenching his thirst, he passed it to his brother. Reaching back into the bundle, he came up with a map. They had copied it from one of Mokar's massive logs. Unfolding it, he studied the alien symbols.

"If this map is correct, the heaviest concentration of native activity lays north of our present position. We'll have to detour around one of their draconium mines in about three days, then, continue on our present course. In a couple of weeks we should be able to make contact with one of the tribes. That is, of course, they haven't reverted to their nomadic ways, again. Then, we may never locate them!"

"We'll find them, Greg! No matter how long it takes." Jim said, stuffing the gourd back into one of the bundles.

Refolding the map, Greg stared up through the lacy canopy, at the twinkling stars beyond. "I just hope God has decided to join us on this adventure. We're, definitely, going to need his support before this is over."

"Don't worry about that, Greg! Truck has already recruited him for our team."

"Of course! You're right, Jim. Greg said, getting to his feet and placing the map back into his bundle. I must not let this emotional blanket weigh us down."

"Between the two of us, Greg, we can carry the weight of our loss as we carried each other in life. Jim said, as he, also, regained his feet. He picked up the other bundle and said; Let's put as much distance from this place as we can. We can rest when the morning sun comes up."

Shouldering their meager belongings, they plowed through the strange forest. The starlight, filtering down on them, through the interlocking branches, cast an eerie glow, giving the leafy verdure, surrounding them, a surrealistic appearance. Other than an occasional sound of something rustling through the laced branches, overhead, their trek through the forest was accomplished in, almost, complete silence. The mossy carpet cushioned their footsteps, muffling any traces of sound. Even the soft, night breeze failed to penetrate this leafy haven. Hour, after hour, they plunged ahead, trying to travel as straight a course as possible. The dark, eerie shadows keeping pace with them, step for step and wearing on their, already overloaded, minds. Toward morning, they were rewarded by the discovery of thinning foliage just ahead of them.

As the first sun of the day crested the horizon, they could distinguish an opening in the thick growth of the leafy shroud that had blanketed them throughout their nocturnal passage. They had spoken very little during the entire march, walking single file and leaving, barely, one set of prints in the spongy moss-like carpet. They left, hardly, a whisper of their passage.

Twenty yards, before the forest receded into open, rolling hills, they came upon a small brook. Barely three feet across and only a few inches deep, the spring-fed water skirted the forest and extended its liquid finger into the hills beyond.

"This looks like a good place to rest." Jim said, kneeling beside the small stream and taking a drink of the clear water.

"I didn't think we'd ever be rid of this depressing forest!" Greg said, joining his brother. After drinking their fill, they sat with their backs against on of the huge trees. Their water gourds refilled, they ate some of the fruit from their meager stores.

"I think the first thing we should do, after resting, is to construct some weapons. There's an ample supply of wood, that's for sure. If we could only find a suitable material for bow strings, we'd be in business."

"I've given that a lot of thought and I believe I have come up with a solution. Greg said. These covertogs, we wear, are made with a tough fiber. If we could, somehow, unravel it I believe it would serve our purpose, until we are able to bring down an animal more suited to our needs."

"What would I do without you, Greg?" Jim said, smiling at his younger brother.

"I'm sure, you would have figured out something. He said, reflecting his brother's smile. Sometimes the obvious solution is right under one's nose."

"Well, right now, I think we should rest up. Jim said, throwing a fur to his brother and wrapping one around his own body. They've probably, just now, discovered us missing. It would be, at least, six or seven hours before they could catch up with us."

"Do you think that maybe it would be a wise move if we slept aloft in one of these grand trees?" Greg asked, sounding a little nervous.

"I haven't seen any signs of predators or anything big enough to harm us. Answered Jim. I think we'll be safe, enough, right where we are,"

Curled up in their furs, a few paces from one another, each man hoped this was true. After a few moments neither one cared. The emotional gauntlet they had run, coupled with their physical ordeal, soon lulled them into a sound sleep.

# CHAPTER 18

The morning sun cast its warming rays on the two slumbering men curled next to the dying embers of their fire. Opening his eyes and greeting the new day, Truck glanced across the fire pit at the sleeping native. Rising to his feet, he brushed some of the grass and twigs, that had slept with him, from his huge body. Walking the few yards to the stream, he removed his loincloth. After a quick drink, he waded into the knee-deep current and lay down flat in the cool water. The invigorating liquid revived not only his tired, aching body, but his hope as well. Thoughts of weapons and survival were interrupted, as Bantor, splashed into the stream a few feet from him.

"Welcome to the new day my friend."

"And a good morning ta you, pal. Truck answered. I hope ya slept well. We got a lot ta do today."

"Thank you, Ta-Rok, I feel much revived."

Finishing their bath and breakfasting on roots and nuts, that grew close by, they started searching for the materials needed in making weapons.

Bantor cut down four eight-foot lengths of saplings with a sharp-edged stone. He, also, found two, thick tree limbs to be made into clubs.

The Earthman collected lengths of flexible vines and chunks of sharp-edged stone.

"If da skins a dos critters we had for supper were just a little bigger, I could make bow strings for us."

"What are bow strings, Ta-Rok?" He asked, as they sat around their new fire.

"Ya mean ta tell me ya don't know what a bow and arrow are? What da yos guys use ta hunt with?"

"We use spears, mostly, but throwing clubs and stones work also." He answered.

"Pal, if I can find da material tough enough ta use, I'd build us a weapon dats been used by da tribes back home for a thousand years. A powerful weapon dat can kill from a long way off."

"What such material would you need, Ta-Rok?' Bantor asked, excitedly, intrigued by the prospect of a new weapon.

"A hide large enough and tough enough to be able ta stretch, without breaking, when it's cut into long, narrow strips. Or, maybe, some tough grasses or flexible vines can be used. I don't see none a dos around here."

Staring across, at the big man, a sudden thought popped into Bantor's mind. "Would the bark of the Crometta tree serve the purpose?" He asked.

"What's a Crometta tree? Truck asked.

Smiling at his friend, Bantor replied. "The very same tree whose arms we fell into, recently, and cushioned our fall. Its bark is very strong and flexible when soaked in water for a short time. And, unlike other bark, it does not dry out with age. Our women make rope, cords, baskets and many other things from it because it is easy to work with and lasts a long time."

"Dat sounds like it might work. Truck said. Where can we find one a dese trees?"

Rising from his seat, by the fire, Bantor said; "Follow me, my friend."

Walking to just such a tree, standing fifty yards away, Bantor began making long, shallow slits in the bark with a sharp flake of stone. He peeled away a section three feet long and barely a quarter of an inch wide. Handing it to Truck, he waited.

The big man wrapped the ends around each of his massive hands and pulled with all his strength. The surprise, on his face, when the bark didn't break, elicited a smile from Bantor.

"Dis will do da trick, little buddy! He said, smiling back. I could feel it stretching a little, but I couldn't break it."

"So, you think it will meet our needs?" Bantor asked.

"You bet yer ass it will. Truck answered. If you can cut me strips like dis about seven feet long, I can do da rest."

Turning his attention toward the tree, Bantor began cutting in earnest. The excitement coursing through his body had to be toned down a few notches so his mind could guide his hand into making long, accurate cuts. "How many will you need, Ta-Rok?" He asked.

'I'll make us two bows. Truck answered, looking over the natives shoulder. But it's nice ta have extra strings just in case. Cut em as straight as you can so dere aren't any weak spots. I think five or six oughta be plenty."

Nodding his head, the native renewed his attack on the tree. "While yer doing dat, I'll cut da wood for da bows and make us a couple a throwing hatchets and maybe a good axe."

"I won't even ask what an axe or throwing hatchets are." Bantor said, over his shoulder.

"Yer gonna love em, pal!"

"I am sure I will, Ta-Rok. New weapons are always welcomed."

"We can worry about making da arrows later."

In the next few hours both men busied themselves with their given tasks. Truck found two supple saplings that had the right flexibility, six feet long and nearly two inches in diameter. Stripping the bark, with a sharp flake of rock, Truck set them aside. Stoking the embers in the fire pit, he added more wood. Soon, he had a small blaze going. Next, he went down to the small stream and found four rocks that were approximately the same weight. He, then, cut four forked branches of fairly equal size. Trimming them of their leaves, using a sharp flake of rock, he cut lengths of bark from the same, giant tree Bantor was working on.

For the next three days, stopping only for food and rest, they had completely armed themselves. Each man now owned a sturdy bow, arrows in a bark quiver fletched with the same material and tipped with sharp points of stone, sharp stone knives and two long spears bearing fire-hardened needle-sharp tips. Truck had, also, made a large, stone axe.

"In the new dawn, Ta-Rok, we will continue our journey. These new weapons have given me more hope than I have had in a long time. I feel certain that I will see my people soon."

"Now yer talking my kind a language, pal. I'm getting kinda anxious myself."

They were sitting on the bank near the stream resting from the exertions of the last three days, discussing their next moves. The new weapons had increased their spirits one hundred fold. The warm sun and slight breeze whispering through the boughs of the small forest provided the perfect background for their feelings. They had decided to hunt along the way rather than take up more time in replenishing their supplies. The nuts and berries they had found, with an occasional critter they were fortunate to knock out of the trees had sufficed them for now. They were confidant, that with the addition of the new weapons, they would be eating meat every day.

Movement in the branches of a tree, twenty yards from the stream they had been traveling along, brought Bantor to his feet. Truck joined him, immediately.

"What da ya see, pal?" Truck asked, grabbing his bow.

"Our dinner, I hope. Bantor answered. A nice fat Pava." Wading across the stream, he approached the tree quietly. Stooping, he picked up a couple of stones from the bank and was about to launch them when Truck interrupted him.

"Hold it, little buddy!"

At the sound of the voice, he turned and watched the big Earthman notch an arrow on his bow, aim and let loose. Looking up into the tree, he saw the arrow fly true and bury itself in the neck of the furry tree dweller. It toppled from its perch, dead before it hit the ground at Bantor's feet.

He stared in awe at the furry creature, so easily dispatched and then at Truck as he waded across the stream, joining him.

"If I had not seen, with my own eyes, how easily you killed the pava from that distance I might never have believed it could be done. Even after you had explained the power and capability of this weapon to me I had doubts. It is almost magical!"

"Dere's no magic about it, pal. All it takes is a little practice. Truck replied. Old Grandfather put a bow in our hands as soon as we could walk." He finished, as he knelt down and pulled his arrow from the furry neck. Checking it for any damage, he replaced it in his quiver. He had made twenty arrows, apiece, for himself and Bantor, each one two feet long. He had tipped them with sharp, stone points. With the absence of any bird life, on this world, he had fletched each arrow with small strips of the resilient bark.

"I hope, some day soon, to honor this weapon by becoming as accurate as you." Bantor said, still in awe of the feat he had just witnessed

"All it takes is a little practice, pal, and we'll have plenty a dat along da way. Lifting the little animal, that weighed, approximately, ten pounds, by its hind feet, he gave it to Bantor. I killed it. You cook it! He said, walking across the stream toward their small encampment. Try ta save da hide, if ya can." He added over his shoulder.

The rest of the day was consumed by the gathering of roots, nuts and berries. Their survival relied, heavily, on this alien "produce". Fresh meat may not be available, on a daily basis. They were stored in a bark pouch, with a strap attached, made to sling over one's shoulder. Truck, also, brought down two more of the furry tree dwellers. Their flesh was cut into strips and slowly dried over a separate, smoky fire. Also, drying over this fire was one of the Pava hides. Bantor had removed the flesh and bones through the opening at the neck, after severing the head.

After, virtually, turning the little creature inside out, he scrapped away all the flesh, muscles and ligaments, still attached, leaving it in the shape of a bag with feet and tail still attached. When the native was satisfied that it had dried, sufficiently, he took it down to the stream. Using wet sand, he scrubbed it thoroughly. After rinsing the sand and bits of flesh from it, he hung it from a tree and let it dry. After a while, he turned it right side out so the fur was, once again, on the outside. Tying a strip of fur, from one of the other hides, each end to a forepaw, he filled it with water and hung it back on the tree limb.

"I was wondering what we were gonna carry da water in." Truck said,

The sound of the Earthman's voice startled Bantor. Looking up, he saw him walking toward him from the forest. He was carrying a pole on his shoulder fully eight feet long and approximately three inches in diameter.

"If we were in my village the women would weave water-tight containers. I am limited in that area of creativity so I decided to make a water bag from one of the hides. I believe it will serve the purpose."

"It'll do just fine, little buddy. Truck said, smiling at the native. Between da two of us, I think we can handle any problem dat comes up." He added as they walked back to their campfire.

"May I ask what Ta-Rok intends doing with that pole?" He inquired as he checked the meat drying over the fire.

Truck sat on the ground next to the fire and began stripping the bark from the small tree. "Da other night when you was telling me about dat kazar creature I started ta do a lot a thinking. I made dat big axe not jus for cutting trees but in case we ran inta one. Den I thought we would have ta be real close to it in order ta use it. He continued, still scrapping bark. So I thought, a long heavy spear might be jus da ting we need. I'll splice dat sharp piece a metal, we found in da mine, to it. If we get attacked, bows and arrows may not stop da bastard. So, I guess you can say, dis is da last resort."

"I don't think there is another person, other than Ta-Rok, capable of wielding such weapons. But, my concern is the extra weight slowing us down." Bantor replied, with a glum look on his face.

"Don't worry about dat, pal. I can handle it. I'm jus trying ta even up da odds a little against dat big sonnuva bitch out dere."

"Forgive me, my Earth friend! My eagerness to see my people, again, causes me to be too hasty and clouds my thinking. He said, apologetically. I have forgotten, many lives depend on our success."

"No need ta apologize, pal. We're both anxious ta see our families, again."

Working through the rest of the daylight and well into darkness, the two men completed preparations for their long journey. Everything was packed away for a quick departure with the rising of the first "Sister" sun. Curled close to the fire, to ward off the night chill, both men fought their way through the dubious meandering of their minds. Exhaustion, finally, won out, alleviating their plight for a few, brief hours.

# CHAPTER 19

The two brothers followed the meandering stream north, staying as close to their water supply as the terrain allowed. In and out of low-lying cuts, through small copses of leather-barked trees, it flowed north to south, its depth and width changing at every turn. To throw off pursuit, they would use the shallow flowage to cover passage. A bow, slung over their shoulders, a woven grass quiver filled with arrows depending from a vine rope, hung down their backs. Each carried a lance, six-feet long with fire-hardened points. Their cover-togs were now sleeveless and came up to mid thigh, the cut material used in making bowstrings. The fur bundles, tied around their wastes contained maps, two gourds of water each, a small amount of alien fruit and the two pieces of metal bars they had laboriously removed from the window of the prison abode. This made up the sum of their worldly possessions, or unworldly possessions, as it was. They had risked a two-day lay over in their camp at the edge of the woods for the preparation of weapons. Alternating their sleep periods, they kept a constant vigilance. It would seem the egos of the Nevoans could not justify the pursuit of, just, two low lives such as they. That was just fine with the Earthmen. They had left at first sun. Both men hoped that somewhere along this waterway native life existed.

Halfway through the heat of the second sun found them in the middle of one of the many forests they had traversed, while following the winding stream. A movement in the branches, fifty feet ahead and slightly off to his right, caught Jim's attention. "Hold it, Greg!" He said in a low voice, as he reached for his bow and notched an arrow.

"What is it, Jim?" Greg asked, as he, also, as he brought his own bow to the ready.

"Another one of those furry critters we've been seeing. I don't know about you, but I'm getting tired of roots and berries. Aiming his bow toward the thick branch, occupied by the animal. I sure hope its edible!"

The audible twang of his bow sent the arrow on its lethal course. It ended with a thud in a branch about two feet above the creature. Almost simultaneously, a second arrow followed that buried itself in the furry chest. The momentum of the arrow toppled the animal backwards off its perch. A moment later it was on the ground, lifeless.

Walking over to secure his prize, Greg bent over and plucked the arrow from the bleeding flesh.

"Nice shooting, Greg! Yelled Jim. I could have sworn I had it dead center."

"You, probably, would have if your arrow hadn't been deflected. Greg replied. I noticed a branch quiver, just before impact."

"Are you trying to make me feel better about missing, Greg?" Jim asked, starring at his young brother.

"Yes I am! Greg answered. But, if you feel that badly about it I'll let you clean and cook it." Smiling as he started to make a fire a few paces from the stream.

Smiling, himself, Jim picked up the alien carcass and moved to the fast-moving brook to clean it.

A short while later, both men were wiping grease from hands and mouth. "I don't know what it is called, but it sure was delicious. Jim said. It tasted a little like rabbit."

"Almost! Greg said, belching. At least we know of one edible creature on this strange world."

Drenching the fire, they broke camp and continued following their liquid guide. Mile after mile, they traveled, with very little change in the scenery. Toward the end of the third sun, they set up camp in the remaining shade of a stand of trees. As they sat on the bank, eating the remains of their roasted pava, a large animal emerged from the forest, across the stream, twenty yards from where they sat.

"What, in two worlds, is that? Greg asked, pointing and rising slowly from the ground.

"I don't know, Greg, but I think we should find a nice, high tree to sit in."

The huge, gray creature stood about eight feet tall and was all of a thousand pounds. Its enormous hind feet sunk into the muddy bank as it bent to the stream to drink. Its long, horn-tipped tail strung out behind for balance. Its huge, hippopotamus-shaped head held double rows of sharp, encrusted teeth. Its two, small forelegs dug into the muddy bank and acted as a tripod for the huge head, while it drank. The two, beady eyes were almost closed as it sucked gallons of water into its huge stomach. A slight breeze, blowing in their direction, brought the fetid stench of the creature to their Earthly nostrils.

"Back up, slowly, Greg and put some trees between us." Jim whispered nervously.

He didn't have to be told twice. Retreating, as cautiously as they could, their eyes never lost sight of monster. As luck or fate would have its way, Jim's first step backwards found a dried branch that had broken away from the forest. A loud crack, sounding like a gun shot, in the quiet setting, raised the creature's head from the stream. The beady, cold eyes fixed on them like radar. In an instant, it came bounding across the stream toward them.

"Time to go, Greg!" Jim yelled, racing toward the patch of heavy trees to their rear. Greg was one step behind him. They reached the trees about twenty yards in front of the animal. Despite its size, it was, surprisingly swift. The monster's great bulk allowed it to crash through the small trees the Earth brothers had to dodge. It was gaining on them, rapidly.

"Split up, Greg!" Jim yelled, as he veered to his left. Greg, simultaneously, took of at a right angle. "Meet you back at camp, later!" He yelled, over his shoulder.

The confusion this caused, in the creature, is probably what saved them; for the time at least. Watching as his; or her, prey scurried to the left and right slowed its momentum. Before the puny mind could decipher which one to pursue, it was too late. By this time, both Earthmen were aloft in the branches of large trees. When the creature finally moved, it plunged full-speed straight into the forest and was soon, miles away.

After waiting for almost an hour, straining his eyes and ears, Jim decided to make a move. "Greg!" He yelled, at the top of his lungs. He waited. No sound filtered back to him from the gloomy shroud. "Greg!" He repeated, straining his vocal chords to capacity. Once, again, the eternal wait. Silence. Just as his mind was about to switch into is panic mode, he thought he heard the sound of a faint voice, off in the distance.

"Greg!" He yelled, echoing through the forest. Climbing down, from his perch, he waited for a reply. There it was, again! Faint, but no doubt, a voice. His first instinct was to rush, headlong, into the gloomy woods, in pursuit of his brother. Logic took over and he retraced his steps, as best he could, back to the stream. Stopping, every so often, to listen for friend as well as foe. A short while later he came upon the small brook. Heading down stream, for approximately one hundred yards, he almost stumbled over their fur bundles lying alongside their small campsite. Grabbing the bows and arrows, spears and furs, he found a tree easy to navigate. He was, soon, safely perched on a high limb, over-looking their campsite. He didn't have long to wait, before he heard a slight, rustling sound a short distance away. The sound was, steadily, closing on his area. A moment later, Greg walked out of the woods and into their campsite.

Relief erupted from his heart and into his lungs as he said, in a loud voice; "What took you so long?"

Startled by the sound of his brother's voice, Greg came to a sudden halt as he waited for his heart to catch up with him. "Dammit Jim, I wish you wouldn't do that!"

Throwing their equipment down from his perch, he was quickly at his brother's side. "Are you all right?" He asked, giving Greg a resounding thump on his back.

"I was until I arrived here." He answered, smiling back at his brother.

As they retrieved their gear, constant glances were hurled into the darkening gloom behind them.

"I thought our adventure on this world was all but over, for a while there, Jim. That creature snuck up on us so suddenly."

"You're right about that. Jim replied. Up until this happened, we had no idea such a creature, even, existed. I think we should get as far away from here as possible, before total darkness sets in, and find a nice, comfortable tree to spend the night."

"The sooner the better, big brother!" Greg replied, as he started walking upstream.

Miles later, just as darkness fell, two men slept an exhausted sleep. Curled up in a constructed nest, high above the forest floor, their dreams and nightmares battled in shapes and colors unimaginable before this day began.

# CHAPTER 20

Bantor stopped and shaded his squinting eyes against the midday sun with a well-tanned hand. Pointing with his other hand, he said; "In two cycles of the "Sisters", Ta-Rok, will be in my village. Over that far ridge and through the "Forest of voices", I will be home."

"What's da forest of voices? Truck asked, wiping the sweat from his eyes.

"The forest that protects one side of my village." Bantor answered.

"Was dis gonna be a surprise or ya want ta tell me about it?"

"Forgive me, my friend. Once, again, I assume you are knowledgeable about my world. The native said, with a smile. Legend has it that long ago "Kazor" destroyed an entire village, existing in the middle of that forest. The creature ate until he could eat no more and, then, he tried to bury those he had not eaten. The screams and moans, of the unfortunate people, echoed throughout the woods and would not stop until the last one was buried. It was a large village and this, particular, "Kazor" was very old and died before the last of his victims were either eaten or buried. To this day, the voices of the unburied can be heard in this area, making their plaintive cries into the night. Of course, the elders, of our tribe, know it is only the wind flowing through the thick branches causing the sounds. Their morbid sense of humor kept this from the rest of the people and they use it to frighten unruly children. When these children became older and found out the truth, they, in turn, continued the façade to keep their own children in line." He finished.

"It's kinda like da boogey man story we hear at home. Truck replied. You better be good or da boogey man will get ya. He chuckled. I guess people are da same wherever ya go."

"I guess they are, at that." Bantor replied.

They were standing at the summit of a very large hill, resting from their long march. The closer they got, to his village, the more the pace quickened. Earlier, this same day, they had come across an opening in one of the forests, they had traveled through and almost walked upon a large kazor. Luckily, for them, the huge beast was at rest and they skirted around it. According to Bantor, the beasts only sleep one day out of ten. Their insatiable appetites and pure lust for killing, keep them constantly on the move. When they, Finally, gave in to these rest periods, they are in a depleted state, close to death. One could walk right over them and they wouldn't stir. Of course, no sane person has, knowingly, tried to prove this theory. For obvious reasons!

The two, weary travelers would take their word for it, also. After that close call, they slowed the pace a notch and kept a more vigilant watch.

Their routine, toward the end of the day, was pretty consistent. An hour or so, before the last "Sister" burned herself out, they would eat and practice with their weapons. Bantor was becoming quite proficient with his bow. He could hit a target, the size of a large gourd, eight out of ten times, from a distance of fifty feet or more. The emotional celebration, he elicited, after his first kill; a small "Pava", caused the big Earthman to explode in laughter. He respected and loved the blonde native as he did his own brothers. The chains that had held them together, in the beginning, were long gone. But, now they were even closer! The red scars encircling their necks, from the collars, were still noticeable. Wounds from the past acted as reminders of future revenge.

They decided to set up camp in a copse of trees, situated in a small valley. Truck had found the little spring by, literally, walking into it up to his knees. They both decided their tired minds and bodies needed rest before something serious happened.

As the last of the day's suns slipped below the horizon, they sat near their small fire eating some of the dried meat. The night sky had not yet blossomed into its full garden of stars. A cool breeze massaged the glowing coals of their fire sending sparks into the sky.

"How soon da ya think we can organize your people inta a rescue mission?" Truck asked. Bantor, sitting across the fire, looked up from the piece of stone he was working on. "Upon hearing our story, I don't think we will have long to wait, my friend. The atrocities these beasts have committed, against our ancestors, has multiplied our hatred even more than the cruelties we suffer at present."

"I don't understand!" Truck replied, confusedly.

"Less than five generations ago, our people were numerous. They had comfortable lives, trading with the many villages that shared this land. The only worry was old "Kazor", who would, sometimes, attack a village. They would band together and kill it, or at least drive it away. When the "Nevoan" creatures landed on our world, they decimated thousands of people, scattering them into many isolated villages. With their powerful weapons they killed any man unfortunate enough to get too close. The women, of entire tribes, were enslaved. He continued, with tears starting to glisten the corners of his eyes. Our people will die off the face of this world, without a trace, if we stop fighting.

"Ya know, we had a situation like dat, back home. Da Indians got tired a being pushed offa dere land. So dey got together and pushed back. Da tribes banded together and won a big battle. Why don't you guys join together and kick dese sonnuva bitches outta your world?"

"That would be possible, Ta-Rok, if we knew where each other was located. He answered, while adding a few sticks to the fire. These alien creatures, through their blood lust, have isolated all of our tribes almost to the point of extinction. No one travels far from his village for fear of never returning. We have not seen any strangers for many years. But, we have hope! If wc havc managed an existence, other villages may have survived, as well."

"How many warriors do you have in da village?"

"Ta-Rok, they are all warriors! Bantor said, staring hard across the fire at the American. Every man, women and child! From birth to death, it is every person's duty to avenge our ancestors and reunite our peoples."

"Dat's my kinda tribe, pal! I'm looking forward ta meeting every one a dem."

"I know that every one of my people will, also, welcome you into their hearts, as I have."

As the brisk night settled over the two men, hope kept them warm.

# CHAPTER 21

The third sun had just risen, beginning the cooling cycle, leading into nightfall. Greg and Jim were rounding the base of a large hill when the sound of voices sent them scurrying for cover. Huddled low, beside a large boulder, they watched in wonder as the scene enfolded before them.

A group of forty or fifty men were stumbling through a large passage between two hills, not more than fifty yards from where they hid, Some were being helped by their comrades. The remnants of hides, they wore, were as filthy as their bodies. Six Nevoans prodded the collection of miserable men with their long staffs, cruelly motivating them to quicken their pace. Two were at the head of the column, with the other four equally distributed along the line of straggling men, driving them like cattle.

"Jim, we have to help them! Greg said, in a low voice. Those miserable bastards won't last long if we don't."

"I'm way ahead of you, little brother! Jim replied, as he rid himself of everything except his bow and arrows. Come on! We're going on a goose hunt."

"What, on Earth, are you talking about, Jim?" He asked, starring, confusedly, at his brother, while notching an arrow.

"Just like the goose hunts Grandfather took us on when we were younger. You remember what he told us?"

"Of course! Pick off the geese furthest back, on the "V", as not to warn the next one in line and move your shots forward. But, do you think we can get close enough to accomplish this? There's a lot of open space separating us."

"Right now there is, Greg. But, they're heading toward that defile, in the hills, a short distance off. At the slow pace they're moving, we should be able to use the little coverage we have and get there ahead of them. Then, as they pass us by, we can pick them off, one by one, moving up to the pair in front. I don't think those poor unfortunates will give us away."

"That seems to be the only logical chance we have of aiding them, Jim. Let's do it!"

At the last instant, they decided to take all of their belongings with. They worked hard to get them and they had no way of knowing how long it would be before they could retrieve them, if they were fortunate to survive this impulsive mission, that is.

Keeping what cover the terrain had to offer between them and their goal, they took off at a right angle from the marching men. After about one hundred yards, they cut to their right, paralleling the direction the group was heading. Reaching the small, well-worn cleft between the two, small hills, they raced up the mounds, one on either side and concealed themselves the best they could. They didn't have long to wait, either. The two creatures, leading the stumbling, bedraggled men, entered the small valley. The curses of the Nevoan guards, in addition to their lethal staffs, prodded the men along. In a matter of moments, the end of the column passed beneath them.

Rising, slowly, from his hiding place, Jim raised his hand. Greg duplicated his actions from across the narrow divide. Moving like two cats, they crept down to the bottom of the small hills and pursued their prey.

When they had closed to within twenty feet, they let go their arrows. Two, barely audible, thuds resounded as they sunk to the hilts in the bulbous heads of the aliens. Without a sound, they dropped in their tracks. A few of the exhausted men turned to see what had happened. Starring at the two men holding strange weapons, they were given the universal sign for silence; a finger to the lips. Turning back to their march, they proceeded on.

"So far, so good!" The two men thought as they followed the human train. Pausing, briefly, they recovered their arrows from the lifeless bodies. It was decided, before starting, to target the heads of their enemies because they had no knowledge of other vital spots on the creature's anatomies.

Re-notching their bows with the same, bloody, arrows, they moved on toward their next targets. In order to do this, they had to work their way up the column of struggling men, one on either side, to get close enough to the next two Nevoans. The stares of the captives were the only, outward signs experienced. They remained silent, as they trudged along.

Within moments, two more arrows had found their marks. Silently, they were removed from the lifeless flesh. But, this time, an excited murmur was elicited from the marchers. Watching these two strangers slay their tormentors, was like water to a thirsty man. It revived their spirits, to a degree, and, as human nature goes, it was hard not to emote under these circumstances. The strange stirrings were enough to catch the ears, or in this case, the antenna of the two leading aliens. Turning, as one, to detect the source of this mild commotion, they detected the two Earthmen moving toward them. The brief pause that intervened, while they tried to assess the situation and, at the same time, search for their companions, was their undoing.

Thunk! Thunk! Two wooden missiles of death buried themselves into the ugly heads. They were dead on their feet before gravity hurled their bodies to the ground.

Native and Earthly eyes studied one another. They had done it! The two brothers looked at each other with satisfied smiles, on their faces, and took in deep breaths as if they had been holding them for quite a while.

"Good shooting, Greg!" Jim said, walking toward his brother.

"And you, also, big brother!" Greg replied, as they walked over to the dead Nevoans and retrieved their arrows.

Looking back at the collection of half-dead humanity, the stares from the eyes that held them in silence, sent pictures in the minds of the Earthmen of Auschwitz and other camps of death, they had seen on film.

"Any suggestions as to what we do now?" Greg asked.

"I think we should introduce ourselves, first. He answered, as he walked up to the nearest men in the column. My name is Jim and this is my brother Greg. He said. We are happy to be at your service!" He held out his hand to the man in front of him. A bear of a man, I may add.

This elicited a murmuring of voices, as a glint of recognition of the gesture reflected from the giant's eyes. He took the Earthman's proffered hand and shook it. A big smile blossomed through the filthy countenance. He mumbled something in a language unknown to the Earthman. Jim shook his head, letting the man know he did not understand him. The giant nodded and pointed to himself. "Corba!" He said, thumping his chest with a huge hand. He repeated it twice more.

"Corba!" Jim said, pointing at the huge man and watched as he shook his head, acknowledging that the American was correct.

"Thumping his own chest, Jim said, in a loud voice "Jim!"

The big man looked back at him and tried to pronounce the name. It came out sounding like "Gem".

Jim shook his head and repeated it. "Jim"! He said, once again, thumping his chest. And, once again, "Gem" came out of the native's mouth.

"I think that is as close as he is going to come to pronouncing your name, Jim!" Greg said, smiling.

So "Jim" became "Gem" and "Greg" became "Gug", no matter how many times they repeated it

As "Gem" and "Gug" circulated through the throng of half-starved natives, they dispersed what little food and water, they had. The big man accompanied them, keeping up a constant stream of his language. Over and over, one word was becoming more prominent than the others. "Ta-rok"! Many others, in the group, were using the word, also. The Earthmen, naturally, couldn't figure out what it meant.

A while later, the entire group, was splashing into the same stream the brothers had been following. The big man, Corba, had led them here. It was obvious, immediately, to the brothers, this was a luxury they had not enjoyed for a long time. Drinking and splashing in the shallow, cool brook, they reminded Jim and Greg of children frolicking at a beach, on a hot summer day back home. The invigorating liquid restored their spirits and made them feel human again. Each one acted as if he had been given a second chance at life. In essence, they had. The Earthmen had no idea of the atrocities they had been subjected to. But, just the same, they were happy to have been responsible for providing it.

"I wish there was a good restaurant, nearby. Greg said. These poor men look to be in need of a good meal."

"Maybe we could shoot some of those little creatures, if they're around here. Jim replied, looking around at the half-wasted humanity.

"It would take quite a few of those tiny creatures to satisfy these appetites. What we need is something the size of an elephant." Greg replied.

They counted forty-nine men, with themselves included. "Maybe two elephants would be better. Jim said, as he, also, stared at the skeletal images cavorting in the stream.

Almost on cue, a native approached and motioned them to follow him. Walking through the thin forest, away from the stream, he cautioned them to silence as they approached the end of the tree line. Gazing out, on the open plain, they discerned a herd of large animals. Long, dark brown hair covered their bodies, giving them the appearance of the musk ox on their world. That's where the resemblance ended. The long heads were the only areas devoid of the thick, shaggy hair. A long horn protruded three feet high above the large, single eye. The wide mouth, at the end of the long snout, held solid rows of large molars. The only evidence of a nose was two gill-like openings located at the end of its snout, one on either side. It appeared to be about six feet high at the shoulders. Four, thick legs supported the massive body. In comparison to its length, they appeared to be stubby. It had to weigh two thousand pounds, if it weighed an ounce. They counted a total of twenty-three. Each was absorbed in consuming the moss-like grass, which grew, profusely, around everyone of these alien forests.

Their native guide pointed to the beasts. "Lurda"! He said, in a low voice. He, next, pointed to the bow, hanging over Jim's shoulder, and made the motion of shooting it.

"I think he's asking us to kill one of those beasts, Jim! They must be edible!"

"I think you're right, Greg! But, I don't think a puny arrow is going to do the trick. They must weigh a ton."

"If we get close enough, Jim, we just might hit a vital spot. All we can do is give it a try."

"Oh, what the hell! Jim replied. If our ancestors could bring down a buffalo, with it, we might be able to do the same."

Each of the Earthmen notched an arrow and motioned to the native to remain where he was. They exited the forest and flattened out on the soft, green carpet. Using elbows and feet, they slithered, on their bellies, toward the herd. A small stand of brush, approximately twenty yards ahead, was the only landmark between them and the herd. Even if they reached it, undetected, it would, still, leave them a shot of, at least, thirty yards.

Silently, like a couple of serpents, they slid over the soft greenery and soon were concealed by the stunted bush. In quiet voices, they singled out a large animal that had its behind pointed in their direction. The single eye, intent on its grazing, was shielded by the creature's large body.

Standing, slowly, each man left the concealment of the small bush. In a low crouch, one on either side, they crept at right angles and gradually paralleled the animal. As they were about to cross its line of vision, Greg leapt forward and shouted at the top of his lungs. The beast's head came up and eyed its antagonist. Undecided, as to which way to turn, it stood there, bellowing its fear to the world. Before it could make up its mind, two arrows protruded from its rib cage, followed, shortly, by two more, which buried themselves in the muscular neck. Its bellowing roar, increasing in volume, sent the rest of the herd scampering, hurriedly, toward the distant hills.

The huge animal was quivering with rage and pain. White foam, mixed with flecks of blood, began running out of its mouth. One of their arrows had found its way into one of the beast's lungs. But, it was far from quitting its life, as it charged the sources of its pain. Greg took off running in the direction that would take the beast directly across Jim's path. He, being the faster of the two men, was the decoy. Jim, who flattened himself to the ground after loosing his arrows, rose up when the animal was directly in front of him and let go of two more arrows, in quick succession. One penetrated the large, single eye and the other buried itself in the animal's throat. As soon as the second arrow had left his bow, he didn't stick around to admire his marksmanship. So it was he didn't observe the huge beast stumble to the ground, letting out its last Earth-shaking bellow and die. He didn't stop running until he heard his brother's voice shouting. "He's down, Jim! We got the bastard!" Stopping, suddenly, he hurried back and joined his brother. Both were sucking in huge gulps of air. Cautiously, approaching the large animal, they nudged it with sandaled feet.

"All this excitement has sure piqued my appetite." Greg said, smiling.

"I could do with a bite myself." Jim replied, smiling back at his brother.

A few moments later, they were joined by the entire throng of ravenous men. Smiles of appreciation and sound thumps on their backs were all the rewards the brothers needed.

The mob made quick work of the carcass. Armed with sharp flakes of stone, the hide was removed and the huge body was quartered and carried back to the camp, just inside the small forest. All that remained at the sight of the kill was a large red stain and a head minus the tongue. Either the natives had a lot of faith in the two strangers, having seen how easily they had dispatched their captors or the hunger pangs, in shrunken stomachs gave them enough reason to anticipate a successful hunt. Whatever reason it was, upon reaching the camp, a large fire was already blazing and a whole quarter, of the kill, was spitted over it.

Desperation, which exudes the final ounce of hope in a person, versus the confidence of the hunting skills of two, perfect strangers; the bottom line was, they would not go to sleep, this night, with empty stomachs.

The Earthmen found out, soon enough, Corba, the giant native, was not their chosen leader. His enormous size and bullying techniques, instilling fear among the natives, were his only qualifications for leadership. This became evident when a pair of hungry hands reached for a piece of meat, from the roasting quarter hanging over the fire. Jim and Greg joined the others as they watched, in horror, the scene that enfolded before them.

Corba grabbed the hungry soul, by his throat, and threw him against a nearby tree. The force was so great you could hear the audible crunch when the man's head came into contact with the tree and gray matter oozed out of the crushed skull, before the body hit the ground.

The men, closest to the fire, scurried back a few paces for fear of receiving the same treatment of their fallen comrade.

Greg rushed over to the fallen native, hoping to assist him. The body only twitched in its death throes and then lay still.

"What the hell is wrong with you?" He shouted across the short space, separating him from the big man.

Corba just stood there, with a cruel grin on his ugly face. He said something to the rest of the men, making them back up even further from the fire.

As Greg rose to his feet and prepared to launch himself at the cruel ogre, Jim beat him to it. Covering the short space, in two steps, he sent a roundhouse right toward the grinning face. It landed, solidly, on the jutting jaw. The impetus, of the powerful blow, toppled him backwards. Somersaulting once, he lay still, out like a light.

The horrible scene, that followed, took only moments to accomplish, but will last forever in the minds of the two Earthmen.

The body had not even finished its backward plunge, before the natives were on it. With large rocks and branches, fists and claws they pulverized the bully into a huge, blood pudding. Shocked into immobility, the two Americans watched. Moments later, two natives dragged the remains of Corba into the woods. He would hurt them no more!

After the participants, of the murder, which were all who had the strength to walk, returned from cleansing themselves of the gore, in the stream, one of them approached the brothers. Taking them by their arms, he led them to the fire. Handing Jim a large flake, of sharpened rock, he pointed toward the meat.

Recovering from his shock, Greg said, "I believe he wants you to dole out the meat to everyone."

When he had hacked off a fair sized chunk of meat, he offered it to the native who had brought them to the fire. He shook his blonde head and pointed to first Greg and then to him.

"I believe we are being honored, Jim. They want us to eat first."

"Okay with me!" Jim said, handing the chunk of meat to his brother. After he cut a chunk for himself, he handed the primitive knife to the native and smiled at him.

Smiling back at the Earthman, he expertly carved the roast. Before long, every man had his share.

Long into the rest of the second sun and well into the evening sun, they tried their best to communicate. With sign language, drawings in the dirt around the campfire and a few words, English and native, they gleaned enough, from one another, to learn of each other's plight. They had been held captive for a long time, they didn't know exactly how long, in an open, cave-strewn pit. They dug in a mine for some type of rock, day in and day out, until they died. From the appearance of their emaciated bodies, it was obvious they were ill fed. Many times, during this period, that word kept cropping up. "Ta-rok". The brothers assumed he was a chief or some important leader. The man, who earlier, had led them to the fire, was named "Lando". It was through him most of the communication took place. It was, also, learned there were a dozen more of their elders still in the pit.

This was causing a little tension among the men. Some wanted, only, to rest long enough to regain some of their strength and head directly back to their individual villages. The majority wanted to help those unfortunates back in the pit.

"If Jim and I help to rescue your people, would we be accepted in your village?" Once, again, with hand motions and drawings, this too, was communicated. Lando said some words, in his language, loud enough for everyone to hear and placed his right hand first on Greg's and then on Jim's right shoulders. The loud sounds, exhibited by the natives, could not be denied. They were cheers of acceptance. Greg and Jim returned the gesture, which brought on even more cheering.

Only six of the Nevoans remained to guard the pit. Even though they had them outnumbered, the lethal staffs, they wielded, very easily evened the odds. It was decided, after a good night's rest, to construct weapons and work on regaining their health. In a few days, they would be much better prepared for the arduous task ahead.

After bidding Lando and the rest of the men a good night, they curled as close to the fire as they could. Their furs, they had given to the more sickly. The adrenalin, from all the excitement and finding a home on this strange world, was all they needed to keep them warm. Although, still strangers, they were no longer alone.

# CHAPTER 22

Greg sat naked on the mossy carpet, trying to unravel the remains of his covertogs so he could make bowstrings. The two Earthmen had been given a large piece of the Lurda's hide. At this very moment, expert hands were working on it, making it pliable enough to provide loincloths for them.

Jim was off with a large party scouring the forest for the proper materials to be made into bows, arrows and spears.

Lando approached and squatted down, across from him. He pointed at the long threads, in Greg's hands, and made a gesture with a confused look on his face.

Greg grabbed his bow and pointed to the taut cord, pulling on it to emphasize his intentions. "I don't have any idea how many I can make, before I am completely naked in your world. He said, smiling at the native. There may be enough material to string five or six bows."

Shaking his head, Lando got to his feet and bade Greg to follow him. He had not understood the Earth stranger's words but he understood the predicament. They walked toward a huge tree, resembling a willow with its sprawling, drooping branches. The dark, gray bark, encasing its trunk, resembled burnished leather.

Taking a flake of rock, from a fold in his ragged loincloth, he made two, long shallow cuts in the bark, about a quarter of an inch wide. He peeled it off and handed it to Greg. Then he made the motions of wrapping something around his hands and pulling it apart.

"I understand! Greg said. You want me to test its strength. With that, he wrapped the ends around either hand and pulled. To his surprise, the cord didn't break! He exerted his full strength and, although, he could feel it stretch a little, it remained intact.

The big smile, on Lando's face, was immediately mirrored by the Earth mans. "What is this called?" Greg asked, giving Lando a quizzical look.

"Crometta!" The native answered, giving the tree a sound slap.

"Crometta!" Greg repeated.

Lando shook his head and smiled, again.

"This is going to help our cause, immensely, and save us a lot of time." Greg replied, taking the stone flake from Lando's hand and cutting a strip about six and a half feet long and less than a quarter of an inch wide. Holding it up in one hand, he used his other in a counting gesture. He, then, pointed to all of the men in the camp.

Lando understood. He would cut enough bark strips so everyone of them would have a bow.

When Jim came back with his heavily laded men, Greg showed him the bark cord. He was just as impressed as his brother. "Thank God, you found an alternate solution to the problem. I don't know how much longer I could have tolerated looking at your bare butt." He said, laughing at the hurt expression on his brother's face.

Three days later, after much collective effort, found the entire band of men fully armed. The training, in the use of these strange weapons, however, consumed a few extra days. When they were satisfied a fair modicum of accuracy was attained, plans were made to attack the pit. It was decided, in two days, at the dawning of the first sun, they would make their attempt. The few, who had opted to set off for their own villages, had a change of heart. To a man, they would attack their enemy together. They believed the new weapons to be magical, despite the Earth brothers insisting otherwise. They did, however, get them to believe the more they practiced the stronger this small army would become. Now, they had a weapon capable of killing from a distance, as did their enemies. Hope loomed a little larger in their deprived souls.

Greg had taken a small hunting party out and they had downed two more of the shaggy Lurdas. Drying racks were set up over small fires. Even after eating to capacity, they would carry the majority of it with them in hide packs.

The native garb, the two brothers now wore, consisted of a long piece of hide wrapped around their waste, passed between the legs, from front to back and over itself, once again, to hang down behind them in a flap. What remained of the alien garb was thrown into the fire. But for the color of hair and eyes, the two brothers could have fit comfortably into any native tribe on this planet. It was, also, noticeable their native cohorts accepted them more, now that the enemy attire was gone.

Lando was talking to a group, nearby. Many times he would point toward them using that word. "Ta-rok". Jim walked over and got his attention. "Ta-rok. He said, looking quizzically at the group. As one, they began pointing, first at him and then at Greg. Shaking his head, he walked back to where his brother was sitting, by a small fire. He was fletching another arrow with the amazing bark, tucking it into narrow grooves, he had cut, in the end.

"I'm beginning to believe the word "Ta-rok" means stranger. Jim said. Then, again, it could mean leader or chief. Aw, the hell with it. I give up!"

"Don't let it worry you, Jim. There is a lot we don't understand, at present. Greg replied. Now, we will have plenty of time to learn. Here! This might cheer you up a little! Reaching behind him, he withdrew two Lurda horns. They had been honed to sharp edges and needle points. Six inches from the thick end, it was wrapped with layers of bark, forming a hilt. Sand and water had been used to scrape it to a smooth finish. The slight, over-all curve and the dark ivory sheen made the sword into a thing of beauty that was, nearly, eighteen inches long.

"These are beautiful, Greg! Jim said, as he accepted one from Greg. Who did the work?"

"Lando. Greg answered. He used to be a carver in his village before he was captured. They, usually, break up a piece this big and make all sorts of things; jewelry, tools, knives, ornaments and so on. When he gave me the two horns, in honor of the kills we had made, I wasn't sure what to use them for. Then, the slow, natural curve gave me an idea. I communicated to Lando what I wanted and he did the rest."

"Except for the material, it resembles an old cavalry sword." Jim said, admiring the workmanship.

"These go with them!" Greg said, reaching behind him for a second time and coming up with two hide scabbards, with long cords attached.

"Well, I'll be damned, Greg! Any more surprises hiding back there?" He asked, holding the scabbard and slipping the ivory sword into it.

"That's it! Greg answered. I salvaged some discarded remnants, punched a few holes and there you have it."

"Thank you, brother. I owe you one."

"As usual." Greg said, smiling.

After a short pause, Greg continued. "I've been thinking. If everything goes as planned, tomorrow, where do we go from here?"

"We go with Lando to his village, I suppose. Why do you ask?"

"I meant beyond that, Jim. All their tribes are so isolated, from one another, because of the Nevoans."

"What are you getting at, Greg?" Jim asked.

"I was thinking if we could organize all these isolated tribes, if we can locate them, bring them together and train them, we may be able to rid this world of Nevoan supremacy."

"That sounds logical, Greg. But, these people have become so set in their ways, because of the atrocities perpetrated against them. They've become autonomous. Their fears prevent them from venturing too far from their own borders. For almost one hundred years they've remained isolated from one another. Where would you, even, start?"

"Why, right here of course! We have representatives from many villages with us now. If, or I should say, when we celebrate our over-whelming victory, tomorrow, these same people will take word of it to their villages. If you remember, Jim, a few short days ago many of them were ready to go their separate ways. We've already planted the seeds. All we have to do is nourish their confidence. He paused, starring at his brother for a brief moment, then, continued. They've, already, become infatuated with the new weapons. When they become more proficient with them and discover the lethal power they have, at their disposal, it might make the difference between a secluded life and safe commerce with the other villages. Like I said, Jim, it has already begun."

"When do you think the proper time to brooch this to them would be, Greg? If we put this on them, now, some may turn tail and head for their villages tonight. It might make the others even more nervous about tomorrow. Jim said. You have to realize that for their entire lives they have been on the defensive side. Asking them to take the offensive against these powerful aliens is almost unheard of. I'll leave it up to you, little brother. It's your idea."

"Okay, Jim. I think the appropriate time to disclose this to them would be, soon, after our victory tomorrow. There will be a few more people, at this time, and, perhaps, another tribe to be heard from.

"You sound pretty confident, little brother." Jim said, smiling.

"It runs in the family, Jim. Besides, I have, at least, one more score to even up."

"His name wouldn't be "Zarnog" by any chance. Would it?"

"That wasn't just a lucky guess, Jim. You want him dead just as much as I do."

"You bet I do! Interjected Jim. Our personal grievances have nothing to do with these people, however."

"On the contrary, Jim! Our best chance of accomplishing this would be to go in force. We need them as much as they need us."

"Okay, Greg. Jim said, after a while. We'll give it a shot. After all, we really have nothing to lose."

The damp, chill of the night, eventually, drove everyone closer to the large fire. Hopes, dreams, nightmares, pain, tension, death and life were, also, drawn toward the fire, and burned more vividly, in the minds of the small group, then the yellow flames attacking the wood.

# CHAPTER 23

A child's voice, screaming in the distance, brought the two travelers to an abrupt halt. For only a heartbeat, they hesitated. Then, as one, they rushed toward the source of the sound. Breaking into a small clearing in the forest they were traveling through, they espied a Kazor working arduously at a cleft between two large boulders. The screaming came from within.

"Ta-Rok, the beast has a child trapped. We must lure it away."

Before he had finished speaking, Truck had rid himself of his gear and was charging toward the creature with his enormous spear.

"Get away from da kid, you son of a bitch!" He yelled, as he covered the space separating them.

The sound of his voice caused the creature to swing around, directly in the path of the charging American.

Standing over seven feet tall, it roared at the puny human. Slime dripped from its cavernous, fang-filled mouth. Its small, red eyes glowed with flames from hell. The audacious nature, ingrained in its puny brain, made it invincible. It stood its ground. It did not react until four feet of the heavy lance was imbedded, firmly, into its scaly breast. The impetus was so powerful it toppled the creature over backwards. Truck was flung over its head. The lance, still gripped in his huge hands, snapped. A blood-thinning roar emitted from the beast, as Truck struggled to right himself. The creature, mortally wounded, but didn't realize it, also regained its feet. Screaming its rage at the human, blood pumping around the broken shaft that extended from its chest. Its small forelegs reached the author of its pain and pulled it out, causing a torrent of green life fluid to erupt from the gory hole. Before it could decide its next move, an arrow imbedded itself into one of its eyes. Taking his attention away from the creature, for the first time since the start of this perilous encounter, Truck noticed Bantor standing about twenty paces to his left. Before the native notched another arrow, he threw Truck's huge axe toward him. Catching it deftly, by the haft, the American awaited the charge. Only a dozen paces separated him from the roaring beast. Its puny mind, making it hesitate long enough to remove the arrow from its flowing eye socket, gave the two men time to react. Bantor's second arrow glanced off the side of the horrendous head. It charged the native, voicing a murderous chorus.

Bantor dropped his bow and set out for the nearest tree. The very instant it was distracted, Truck, also, charged. Leaping upon the back of the huge beast, he clenched his powerful legs around its thick, slippery neck. The strange feeling, of a weight pressing on its back, caused it to come to a complete stop. Its lethal, horn-tipped tail lashed at the burden.

Bantor, perched safely in a stout tree, fifty paces away, could only stare in horror at the gory scene enfolding before him.

Truck held on to the beast with one hand embedded into the useless eye socket. In his other hand he wielded the massive axe. Blow after blow, he dealt to the monster's head, virtually turning one side to pulp. Still, the beast, not knowing it was already dead, because the message hadn't reached its puny brain, fought on. It lashed its tail, again and again, at the small creature on its back, sometimes narrowly missing, sometimes slashing American flesh.

Bantor scampered down from the tree and rushed to aid his friend. He was too late! The creature had crumpled to the ground and lay still. So, too, was his friend. Green fluid from the beast, mixed with the red blood of the Earthman, as they lay married together in a macabre heap.

Dragging his comrade from beneath the scaled creature, he laid him on his stomach. Grabbing handfuls of moss, he began staunching the numerous flows. Most were superficial, but a few were deep. Blood oozed from everywhere, but no spurts were detected. Luck was with his Earth friend, Bantor thought. No main life vessels had been severed. The massive loss of blood had carried his friend into unconsciousness. His breathing was very shallow. "I must get him to my village, immediately!" He said to himself.

Calling to the young boy, who still cowered between the boulders, in shock, Bantor had him carry their equipment. Hauling his unconscious friend onto his shoulders, they made their way to his village.

"If you were ten times as heavy, my brother, I would still bear your weight. You must survive! We have many things to learn from one another."

A short while later, they entered his village. Friends and family, alike, acknowledged the emergency and eased the American from Bantor's shoulders. Relieved and exhausted, Bantor, too, was taken to a hut and mercifully gave in to his weariness. The last thing he remembered, before surrendering to the comforting arms of "Morpheus", were vivid flashes of putrid green and Earthly red.

# CHAPTER 24

The six alien sentries cast eerie shadows into the large pit. The failure of their comrade's return from the mine put them in a nervous state. The only thing that kept them from abandoning their obligations was the wrath of Zarnog. Casting wary glances in the direction of the mine and barely going through the motions of their given duties caused them to be much less attentive of the small group of men huddled, together, in the pit. Their major concern lay outside the miserable hole. What unknown force had delayed their return? Not concern for their friends, because they had none. It was the strength they gained in numbers. Now, they felt weak, vulnerable. These miserable inferiors, below, were not worthy of protection. They should leave! But what logical reasons could they give to Zarnog that would merit their existence? None!

They continued their quasi-vigilance like robots. Their unfocused demeanor prevented them from noticing the large group of men that completely encompassed the huge crater. The group was split into two parties. Greg led the force coming from the west, Jim from the east. Both halves would meet in a pincher formation, completely surrounding the pit. A flaming arrow, launched into the sky, would be the signal to attack. Both men hoped the element of surprise would minimize their loses.

When word was passed through the line that both halves of the encircling force were in position, they waited in silence. Whether there was one miserable soul or one hundred in the dreaded pit, it would, still, be worthy of the attempt.

Jim noticed the alien sentries constantly looking toward the south. He passed word to the men positioned in that direction to hold their ground, to wait until the rest of the small army attacked. This way he would have drawn their attention by engaging them from the north, east and west. The southern contingency would delay and then come in from behind.

Greg gave the signal and the wad of moss was lit and the arrow sent toward the heavens.

Three sides of the circle closed in on the aliens, and as Jim had hoped they would, they fell back toward the only avenue open to them; south. The first salvo of arrows downed three of the aliens. The remaining three closed together and sent a volley from their lethal staffs that downed six of the natives. Word was sent to the southernmost group to attack. They sent a lethal arc of arrows toward the remaining defenders. Two of the three were hit instantly and went down. The third and last, of the aliens, dropped his staff and started running away from the pit. He covered, barely, twenty-five paces before he, also, lay dead on the ground, his body bristling with arrows,

The cheering, that arose, from the impromptu army, was harmonized by the poor individuals in the pit.

Of the six natives, struck down by the alien staffs, four survived. Their victory was sullied by, only, two fatalities.

Men were sent out to collect arrows and staffs. Others tended to the four wounded men. The bodies of the six aliens were left where they had fallen. The ramp was slid into the pit and the dozen half-starved men were helped out of their prison. They were fed and tended to.

The bodies of the two fallen natives were placed on a huge platform of branches in the middle of the pit and set afire as a testimonial that no other native would suffer and die in this pit. They would be the last!

"What I wouldn't give for just one Stealth bomber. Greg said. I'd level this wretched place so, never again, would it house suffering unfortunates."

"I wonder how many poor souls died here at the hands of those dirty bastards. Jim added. As long as we live, Greg, there will be no more."

"As Truck would say, Jim, amen ta dat."

It was decided they would make camp in the forest north of the pit. When all were fully recovered, they would head toward Lando's village. They had found out, earlier, his was the closest.

Later that evening, as Jim and Greg sat around the fire discussing future plans, the last survivors from the pit approached them. They were accompanied by Lando. It was communicated to the two Earthmen these poor individuals would follow them to the end of their days. Before they left, a strange thing happened. The oldest of the survivors, Kaba, held out his hand to Greg who naturally accepted it and they shook hands.

It wasn't until much later, when they were preparing for sleep, that the significance of the gesture struck home. As they curled close to the fire, Greg sat up, suddenly. "Jim! That old man from the pit, Kaba."

Startled by the tone in his brother's voice, Jim also sat up. "Yea, what about him?" He asked.

"Did you notice anything strange about his behavior?"

"Same as the others. I couldn't understand him either. He was polite, though, offering to support us anyway he could. We even shook hands on it." Jim answered.

"That is the part I am confused about. He'd only been with us a few hours and already he's displaying a good old American custom. Shaking hands like he'd been doing it for a while."

"He probably picked it up from the others. They're use to seeing us doing it."

"In the short time he's been here I doubt he's had much time for anything but convalescing. Greg said. I'll have to ask him about that in the morning. If I can make him understand me, that is."

"You do that, Greg! Now go to sleep!" Jim said, lying back down. But strange thoughts occupied Greg's mind far into the night. Soon, exhaustion won over and he, too, slept.

# CHAPTER 25

The buzzing sound of many voices forced Truck's eyes open with a start. He stared at the soft light filtering down on him through the thatched ceiling of the hut. Confused, as to his surroundings, he sat up quickly. Too quickly! The pain, shooting through his entire body, made him wince. Unconsciousness threatened to recapture him. As he lay back down, the throbbing pain subsided slightly. His battle with the "king of killers", was it yesterday? Came back into focus. Did I win? He wondered aloud. The outcome was fuzzy. All he could remember, in the end, was falling and a heavy weight crushing him.

Turning his head to the side, he spotted a wooden bowl filled with water. Reaching slowly for it, he drained the contents with loud, long gulps. How long have I been here? He thought. And, where da hell am I?

Alongside the water bowl was a small pile of fruit. It vanished in short time. His thirst and hunger slightly sated, he was about to attempt crawling out of the sleeping platform, when he heard footsteps approaching the hut. A young native girl, perhaps ten or eleven years old, came through the frond curtain, hanging over the hut's entrance. She was carrying a wooden platter, laded with food and a pitcher of water. A short hide skirt was her only apparel. Her long, golden hair was held off her face with a leather thong wound around her head.

"Good morning, sweetheart! Is dat my breakfast?"

The sound of Truck's voice startled the girl. The platter clattered to the dirt floor, scattering its contents. Her large, dark eyes got even larger as she turned and raced out of the hut.

"I still have a way wit da women". He said to himself, smiling, as he watched the young girl scamper away.

A few minutes later, Bantor burst through the entrance. He was followed, closely, by a man and woman. Sandwiched between them was the young boy who was trapped in the cleft of rock by the Kazor.

"So, Ta-rok, I see you have decided to join the living, once again! Bantor said. We were quite worried about you, my friend."

"How long have I been out cold?" Truck asked.

"Five journeys of the "Sister" suns have passed since you decided to ride the "Kazor. Bantor answered. The killer of killers, though, is not as fortunate."

"What happened, Pal? I can't remember much toward da end."

"I will tell you, my brother. Never before have I seen a man do what you did. Clinging to the neck of that monster and swinging your huge axe. It was a sight you see but once in a hundred lifetimes. Old Kazor was doing about the same amount of damage to you with his huge, spiked tail. As blood poured from both of your bodies, it was just a matter of time before one or both would be dead. I managed to put an arrow into one of its eyes before it turned on me and the rest of my arrows flew from their holder. By the time I reached safety in the branches of a large tree, both of you were on the ground in a huge puddle of green and red blood."

"Five days! Truck said, exasperatedly. I must a got my ass kicked big time. Tanks for getting me here."

"No thanks is necessary, Ta-rok. Consider it a favor returned."

After a short silence, Bantor continued.

"This woman and her daughter made you comfortable during that time. Ta-rok, this is shara. Her daughter Lea is still running down by the stream. What did you do to her?"

"Must be my personality. Truck said, with a smile. Thanks for taking care a me, Shara. I didn't mean ta scare your little girl."

"It is we who thank you." Said the man standing behind the boy. Stevo would be dancing with his ancestors if not for you. We owe you much."

"I'm jus glad we was in da neighborhood." Truck said, reaching out and tousling the hair of the small boy.

"My name is Tonio. Said the boy's father. You may use my hut and my fire for as long as you may live. We can never repay you." He finished, with tears of joy glistening his kind eyes.

"I don't wanna put ya outta your home." Truck replied, starting to rise from the sleeping platform.

Placing his hands gently, but firmly, on Truck's shoulders, he pushed him back down. "We are comfortable. Rest and regain your strength." With that, the small family left.

"Ta-rok, of another world, this is our way of expressing gratitude. To share one's fire with a stranger is to extend friendship. To allow one's abode to be used by a stranger is to suggest total acceptance. A man's family and home are his most treasured possessions. It is the greatest honor he could have paid you for saving his son's life."

"I have a lot ta learn about your ways Bantor."

"We both have much to learn about one another, my friend. When this conflict with our enemies is ended, hopefully, we will have all the time of two worlds to do so."

"Amen ta dat, Bantor."

"Now, my Earth brother, get some rest. I will send someone to bring you food and clean up this mess. Try not to frighten whoever it is."

"I'll try my best, pal." Truck said, smiling, as Bantor left.

There's only one more thing that could make this occasion even happier, Truck thought to himself. If only Jim and Greg were here. They'd love these people. Tears escaped from the corners of his gentle eyes. Soon, we'll be together again.

A short while later, a young girl carrying a large platter of food, nervously entered the hut. Her dark eyes stared at the bed. The Earth stranger was fast asleep. His loud snoring startled her for an instant. But, this time she set the tray down alongside the bed and smiled. "This man saved my little brother from a horrible death. I will never fear him again." She thought to herself. Very quietly, she retrieved the fallen platter and its contents, scattered on the floor, turned and left the hut.

# CHAPTER 26

Four days after the "Victory of the pit" Greg was sitting against one of the giant crometta trees. Across his lap lay one of the alien staffs. After their conquest, the alien barracks was searched. No fewer than fifty of the lethal rods were recovered. Sleeping furs and food was also salvaged.

Then, it was burned to the ground along with the bodies of the dead alien watchdogs.

They set up camp, the next day, approximately two miles north. A small copse of trees with a stream running through it, bordered a moss-covered plain abundant with Lurdas. Many of the large omnivorous were killed. The once, raggedy, half-starved band of men were soon adorned in clean loincloths. Besides their new attire, each wore a spark of hope in his heart, as well as a few pounds of needed fat around their waists.

Two more had died during the night. Not from the brief conflict, but from the war they had waged against hunger, filth and hopelessness. It was decided a few days of rest would benefit not only the suffering individuals, it also provided time to practice with their new weapons.

Greg was fascinated by the power the alien staffs produced. He was determined to unlock its secrets. It would be a big boost to their arsenal. Storming the alien city with primitive bows and arrows might not be enough.

A small catch, barely noticeable, at the butt end of the five -foot long staff, unlocked a panel. Out fell a piece of the blue crystal. "So, I have found the battery compartment." He said aloud. After replacing the crystal, he accidentally found another panel six inches from the butt end. This panel slid aside, revealing two buttons. Pointing the rod toward the treetops, he pressed a button. Instantly, he could feel a feint vibration through the rod.

This must be the stun mode, he thought. Quickly repressing the same button, the vibration stopped immediately. Pressing the second button sent a ball of bright energy ripping through the leafy ceiling. As branches and leaves cascaded down upon him, he leapt to his feet.

"Bingo!" He yelled, shaking with excitement.

A few of the natives, standing nearby, raced for cover, stringing their bows for action.

"Take it easy! I have unlocked the alien secrets of this weapon."

Bidding them to follow him, he headed toward the open plains. Soon, he spotted what he was looking for. Standing over her calf, a cow Lurda browsed on a small bush, approximately eighty yards away. Pointing the alien rod in her direction and sighting down its length, he pushed a button. A ball of energy flew from the rod, accompanied by a slight whistling sound.

The natives stared in awe, as the large beast crumpled to the ground. The small calf sped off toward the rest of the herd in the distance. They raced toward the fallen beast, slacking off their rush the last few yards only as a precaution. The shaggy beast was more than adequately armed for killing if one wasn't wary. But, this one lay still. After a few sandaled feet had prodded it, they rolled it over on its side. Greg's shot was not a direct hit, but the ball of energy had ripped open one side of its massive head, spilling part of its brain on the mossy floor.

Praises of gratitude and good-natured thumps on his back were being given when Jim and several other natives rushed on the scene. "I saw you from that rise over there, he said, pointing to his left. So, little brother, you have unlocked the mystery of that weapon!"

"Actually, Jim, it was by pure accident. Greg said. It's so relatively simple, I'm surprised it took me so long. Naturally, I couldn't wait to try it out. I don't think I need to tell you, we've added some very powerful weapons to our antiquated arsenal."

"That's why I suggested collecting them before we burned that building, Greg. I knew, sooner or later, my little brother would figure it out." Jim smiled, as he added his thump to Greg's back.

"Do you realize how much this bit of luck is going to increase our chances of success? I'm ready to kick ass right now."

"Me too, Greg! But I think it best we train our native army in its use. Unless, of course, you want to go storming into Nevoa like Butch Cassidy and the Sundance kid."

"Perhaps you are right, big brother. To suffer their ending wouldn't accomplish anything. Would it?"

"Not if we want to avenge Truck. No it wouldn't"

As they talked, the natives had busied themselves with the butchering of the big animal. In the days that followed their victory, they had amassed quite a larder. Food had been preserved for the days ahead. Weapons and clothing were made. The Earthmen had shown them how to make traveling tents out of the tough Lurda hides. The lives of the group had improved many times over. With hope, once again, instilled in their souls, they were truly reborn to the world.

Later that evening, as the two Earthmen sat around their small fire, Lando joined them. The stocky native, although only forty years of age, was considered one of the elders in his village. They had observed him delegating orders and leading different working parties and seemed to be respected by the other men. He was also the designated liaison between the two cultures. His pleasant way of dealing with situations, also, gained the respect of the two brothers.

As he waited for the two Earthmen to finish fletching the arrows, he added another branch to the fire. Patience was, also, a big part of his make up. He felt more than just respect for these two strangers. He loved power and saw in these strangers a way to achieve it. Although they had given him and his fellow sufferers a new lease on life, their value toward his future plans would be inestimable.

"Good evening friend Lando. Jim said, setting another completed arrow aside. What can we do for you?"

Through words, gestures and drawings in the dirt, he communicated to them, in five risings of the "Sister suns" they would be sitting around a friendly fire in his village. He assured the Earthlings that his brethren would accept them and adopt them into their hearts, as he had. He, also, communicated his entire village would assist them in their venture. A short while later, he shook hands with them and went back to join his men.

"Doesn't it make you feel good to know you won't be spending your entire life, on this planet, all alone? Jim asked, as he watched the retreating native. Our plight could have been a whole hell of a lot worse."

"I just hope we get the opportunity to realize that situation. Greg said, staring into the fire. If only one of a thousand things goes wrong, we won't have to worry about it."

Jim stared at his brother for an instant and then added his gaze to the fire.

"Amen ta dat, brother."

# CHAPTER 27

Bantor's village consisted of almost one thousand inhabitants. This site had been established only twenty years earlier. Five times, in its history, the village had been relocated. The ever-encroaching arms of the alien invaders prevented them from staying in one place for any length of time. In the one hundred years of their settlement, the invaders, ruthlessly, conquered village after village. Sending out patrols of a thousand men each, they scoured their new world, killing and capturing thousands of natives. Slowly, the native population decreased. Resettling in areas further and further from their enemies, they, soon, became isolated from one another. As their numbers dwindled, commerce and communication between them became almost extinct.

A ten-foot high fence, constructed from poles consisting of young crommeta trees surrounded the entire village. Two wide gates, one located on the north side of the village and one on the south side provided the only means of passage to the outside. Huts were located on the outer fringes of the perimeter, just inside the fence. In the center was a huge hut. It was a place for socializing, problem solving, community projects and celebrations.

Two streams ran through the village, making the grounds within the palisade very fertile. Small gardens surrounded almost every hut. Melons, squashes, gourds and berries grew abundantly. Each household tended their own plot. Any excess was stored in a root cellar, located in the Tribal hut. In the advent of hard times, this emergency cache could be used by anyone who asked for assistance. Hunting parties were sent out daily. All kills were butchered and doled out, equally, to every hut.

As Bantor led the limping Earthman around his village, a small group of men, women and children followed them. Each one of them wished to get closer to this stranger who had slain the "King of killers". Looking back over his shoulder, Truck noticed a young girl, using a hard wood branch as a crutch, struggling to keep up with the following crowd. He turned and threaded his way toward her. She was about seven or eight years old with the largest and darkest eyes he had yet seen, among these natives. He, also, noticed her right leg was missing from the knee down. A large scar ran from the corner of her right ear and ended at the side of her mouth. When the wound had healed, it left that side of her mouth drooping down. His heart went out to her, immediately.

He knelt down and waited for her to continue forward. But, she stopped. Two frightened eyes stared back at the huge Earthman.

"What's yer name, sweetheart? He asked, with a big smile on his face.

"Are we going too fast for ya?"

The girl just stood and stared.

"Holding his arms out to her, he said "come on, I'll give ya a ride."

To the surprise of everyone, the little girl hobbled slowly up to the big guy.

Lifting her up, crutch and all, he placed her on his massive shoulders.

"Now ya got a ringside seat." He said, as he made his way back to Bantor at the head of the crowd.

As they continued the tour, Bantor smiled. Many others did so, also.

When they reached the shade of the Tribal hut, they all sat on logs, surrounding a large fire pit. At night a fire was lit and kept burning until dawn. It was a comfort to these people and also kept them from running into anything in the dark.

After all were seated, Bantor asked Truck to tell everyone about his ride on the "Kazor".

So, with the little girl perched on his shoulders, he did so.

Later, as everyone walked back to their respective huts, shaking their heads in awe of his heroic feat, Truck asked Bantor where the little girl's house was.

"She lives four huts up from the one you abide in. Over there! To the east."

"She's a quiet little girl, ain't she?" Truck said, reaching up and patting her head.

"Three years ago, Tarok, Gia was like any of the young girls of the village, talkative, inquisitive. She accompanied her mother and father on a hunting trip one day. Our women hunt, skin and carry their weight, just like the men. On the way back, they were spotted by a patrol consisting of about fifty invaders. Sabo, her father placed her high in a tree. He, then, proceeded to decoy the aliens away from the area. Everything worked fine with very few of his party lost. After a while, he and his mate, Mara, circled back to retrieve their daughter. Mara stayed hidden in bushes near by, while Sabo climbed to his daughter. Before he could reach her, he was blown out of the tree. He was dead before his body hit the ground. A few of the invaders had circled back to the same area. Seeing her father falling, little Gia screamed. Their next shot blew off Gia's leg. As she tumbled downward, a branch lodged itself into her cheek stopping her fall. The invader's watched the motionless, mutilated body swaying at the end of a branch for a few moments, then hurried to join their comrades. Moments later, Mara came out of concealment and retrieved her daughter. Her husband's headless body was later recovered. Since that day, Gia has not uttered a single word."

Tears threatening to leak out of the corners of his eyes, Truck reached up and lifted the girl from his shoulders. He hugged her broken little body to his chest. "I shall avenge your father, little one. I promise you!"

"Her hut is over there! Bantor pointed directly ahead. I will meet you back at the "Tribal" hut, later." With that, he was gone.

Working in a garden, along side the hut, was a tall native woman. Dirt clung to her body from head to toe. Sweat made small streams in the grime that clung to her bare breasts. Her golden hair glistened from the moistness of her labors.

When she noticed the big stranger, carrying her daughter, her eyes went wide with alarm. Dropping her digging stick, she rushed toward them. As she neared them, she noticed her daughter's little arms wrapped around the big man's neck. This canceled her impulse to snatch her away.

"I got a special delivery for a woman named Mara. Is dat you?" Truck asked, with a big smile on his face.

"Yes! I am Mara." She replied, questioningly.

"Den here ya are. He said, placing the girl, gently, in the waiting arms. And, by da way, it says on da package ta handle with care." Truck winked at the bewildered woman and headed back to his hut, thinking to himself. "Dat was da most beautiful woman I ever saw. I gotta get ta know her better."

Mara stared after the retreating stranger. "I wonder what all that was about?" She thought. She would soon find out.

# CHAPTER 28

The third "Sister" sun had just taken her place, in the sky, when a group of weary men crested the top of a high hill. It overlooked a long valley, studded with trees and small ribbons of crystal-clear streams. At the far end of the valley, approximately two days away, a small lake reflected the sun's rays like a huge diamond sunk in the Earth. Their elevated perch eased itself, gradually, into the fertile valley below.

Lando, standing beside the two Earthmen, pointed toward the lake and with a big smile on his face uttered some words. "Landos village!" They were made to understand.

The lake was the first body of water they had seen since their arrival on this world. They knew the many small streams they had crossed had to have originated from some place. With the absence of mountains, in this area, the streams either started from underground springs or a larger body of water higher up.

"I believe that is the most beautiful handiwork of "mother nature" I have ever seen on two planets." Jim said, losing himself in the view.

"A pristine picture, indeed!" Greg echoed.

At the base of the long slope was a cluster of trees, scattered on either side of a small stream. They had decided to make camp there for the night. Small fires were built and water bags were replenished. Sentries were posted. As night settled over them, they crowded closer to the small fires, chatting happily about loved ones or favorite places they would, soon, be seeing. Long ago, many had given up on this dream. Until these strangers came into their lives, many of them had stopped living. Their bodies still functioned and they carried out the arduous tasks demanded of them. But, they had stopped hoping and dreaming. Every day was their last. They ate. They slept. They worked. Mechanically! Now, they were whole, once again. Because of two strangers! What ever was left of their lives would be lived in their honor.

As the glittering stars began spraying their brilliance into the darkness, Greg and Jim were listening to Lando and some of the men from his village as they talked. The oldest man in the group, Kaba, who was from a different village, seemed to be disagreeing with Lando about something. Both were pointing toward the brothers every now and then. After a few more moments, voices rising, the old man got up and walked toward the small stream.

Wondering what all that was about, the two brothers looked at each other and shrugged. No arguments, or any other form of discord among the natives, had occurred since the death of the bully, Corba. The situation seemed to be unsettling for some of the others, also. When either of the two brothers looked at anyone, the natives looked away, avoiding eye contact. Some of the men, in the small group, retired to their furs much earlier than usual. Lando sat there, staring at the retreating back of the old man, as he walked into the darkness. The haunting roar of a Kazor, miles in the distance, came right on cue, adding to the, already, "chilly" disposition of the group.

"I don't know what it is, Greg, but I think something is going on. Lando and that old man were definitely arguing about something. I didn't need an interpreter to figure that out. And, I think it has something to do with us."

"I noticed that, also, Jim. The others are acting a little suspicious, too, averting their eyes whenever I look in their direction."

"I think it would be wise to sleep in shifts tonight, little brother. We still don't know who to trust on this world."

"I agree, Jim. Go ahead and get some sleep. I'll wake you in a few hours."

Crawling into his furs, he said to his brother; "If something should come up before then, feel free to wake me."

"You can count on it, Jim." Greg replied as he laid his ivory saber beneath a fold in his furs, at his side.

An hour later the small fires had subsided to glowing coals. The cool breath of the night breeze blew life into them, now and again. The last of the men had finally surrendered to the warmth of his furs. The nocturnal sounds of the natives blended with the night's harmony.

Adding a few pieces of wood to the fire, Greg strained his ears for sounds that didn't coincide with the darkness. The night sounds his Grandfather had trained them to listen for on his own world were imprinted deeply in his mind. But, this wasn't his world. What should I be hearing? He thought to himself. To pick up any discrepancies in the night's orchestra one had to have been born here. I wasn't! It's going to be a long night.

His revelries were interrupted by a different noise, startling him to full alert.

Crack! The sound of dried wood being crushed by a skulking foot was the same on any world. We have a visitor. Be on guard!

Drawing his ivory saber slowly from beneath his furs, Greg squinted into the darkness. The seconds that last a lifetime, in these situations, were slowly counting down. A shadow, to his left, silhouetted itself against the starry night. It moved toward him, keeping away from the glow of the fading coals in the fire pit. A fortuitous breeze invaded the night, stirring them into brief life and revealing the old man, Kaba, hovering close to the ground. His sleeping fur covering him from the neck down. As he approached within two feet of him, Greg brought the ivory tip of his sword up to the throat of his night guest.

"Stop right there! He said, in a voice loud enough to get the old mans attention, without raising the whole camp. Move and you swallow about a foot of ivory!"

Rising from his furs, Greg convinced the old man to rise, also, with a little pressure on the ivory blade. Walking sideways and stretching out his leg, he nudged Jim awake.

"What is it, Greg? He asked, sleepily. My turn, already?"

"We have a guest, Jim. It's that old man, Kaba."

Rising to his feet, fully awake, now, Jim said; "Well, little brother, put the coffee on. It looks like it's going to be a long night."

And, a long night it was. For the next two hours the three men struggled to communicate. The shocking impact, of what they learned, took the two brothers on a roller coaster ride through the gamut of emotions again and again.

Kaba, through sign language, drawings in the dirt and the few words they understood of each others language, described a big man, strange to this world, who escaped the pit with one of his kin. Ta-rok and Bantor were shackled together. A heavy chain around their necks connected them. Because of this closeness, they, fast became friends. Ta-rok learned the people's language and told him of his two siblings, held captives by the invaders."

Two sets of Earthly eyes, wide with hope, glistened from the light of the small fire.

"Describe this Ta-rok!" Greg demanded, barely able to contain the emotional volcano threatening to erupt.

After Kaba communicated the approximate height and weight of their brother and the fact that he talked funny even after he had mastered the language, tears erupted like an emotional river beyond flood stage.

Kaba, also, told them that their escape was successful. Bantor's village was, also, his. The two men were to lead his people in an attempt to rescue the unfortunates in the pit.

"I don't think there is any doubt about it, Greg. Truck is one of a kind. It couldn't be anyone else."

"I'm trying hard to believe, Jim. But, Mokar informed us that Truck was dead. Why would he lie to us?"

"I think that bastard, Zarnog, had something to do with it. He, probably, threatened Mokar or promised him something. I, honestly, don't know."

"Well, what should we do, big brother? Believe this old man or go with Lando to his village?"

At mention of Lando's name, Kaba shook his head and, after a while, made the two Earthmen understand that Lando was not to be trusted. "I will take you to my village while enough strength remains in this old body. Then, you will know, for certain, if indeed, it is your sibling."

"A little hope is better than none at all. What do you say, Greg?"

"Up until a few hours ago, we were still in mourning for our departed brother. If there is the slightest chance this old man is telling the truth we have to go for it. Let's do it!"

Before dawn was in its infant stage, introducing another day to this alien world, they left.

# CHAPTER 29

The new sun peaked over the horizon, revealing three, heavily burdened men traveling at a brisk pace. Surprisingly, the old man didn't slow them down that much. But, they knew, he would not be able to sustain this pace much longer. They made frequent rest stops. Kaba was their guide. If anything happened to him, they were lost.

After hearing their brother was still alive, from the old man, they would have run the entire way. But, run where? They set a pace that rebelled against their anticipation. More than anything, they wanted to be reunited with their brother, as fast as possible. Unfortunately, Kaba had lost most of the spring in his step through years of humiliation and degradation by his captors. Actually, they were all slowed down, considerably, more than usual by the heavy loads they carried.

Besides communicating the news of their brother, Kaba also informed them that Lando, upon returning to his village, had no intentions, what so ever, of helping them in their quest. They would have, virtually, been made slaves to his ministering, making weapons and training men in the usage of bow and arrow and the alien weapons. Lando was, basically, a coward. His village consisted of only three or for hundred people. His father was lead-elder and would never consider stepping outside his small realm. Like father, like son, Lando had no intentions of changing this.

Upon hearing this, they decided to collect all the alien rods and as many bows and arrows as they could carry. Kaba gathered as much food as would fit into a small hide bundle. Two hours before the first sun, they departed.

When they, finally, communicated to him that they wanted to know how long it would take to get to his village, he shrugged his shoulders and told them he didn't know. Yes, he knew the way! But, he was old. In his youth, maybe, ten or twelve cycles of the suns. Now, he had no way of giving them even a vague estimation. His agonizing ordeal, in the pit, had drained most of his life.

Through out the day, they plodded on. Their rest periods were getting longer every time they stopped. So, by halfway through the last sun of the day, they decided to make camp. Poor old Kaba! He barely had strength enough to eat a little dried meat and crawl into his sleeping furs. Within minutes, he was snoring away.

They decided not to make any fires for a few days. Although, it didn't seem likely Lando would send anyone in pursuit, the brothers decided not to chance it. Being this close to a reunion with their "departed' brother was foremost on their minds. A few cold nights wouldn't bother them in the least.

As they lay, in their furs, Greg asked; "Why do you suppose it took Kaba all this time to impart this information to us? He's had ample opportunities along the way."

"I've thought about that, Greg. Maybe he wasn't sure if we were the same brand as Truck. Or, maybe Lando threatened him if he told. I don't know for sure. But, I'm just happy we found out before it was too late to do anything about. According to the old native, had we reached Lando's village our chances would have been very slim to have left it."

"All the times we heard the word, "Ta-rok" I should have guessed it was their way of pronouncing "Truck"."

"How could we have known, Greg? Their language is so different from ours. That word could have meant anything, for all we knew."

"Another thing I can't understand is why Mokar lied to us. Toward the end there, I thought I detected some human-like characteristics. "I guess I was wrong about that."

"No! I don't think you were wrong, Greg. I noticed some changes in Mokar myself. Especially, after he told us Truck was dead. I think that ugly, son of a bitch, Zarnog, forced him to do it, threatening to remove him from his position if he didn't. One more reason for me to pop his head like a pimple."

"Then, he would be extremely fortunate if you get to him first, Jim. I wouldn't be as humane as you."

A brief lull, in their conversation, allowed each of the men to pursue their own thoughts. Their anxieties would multiply each and every waking day, until they were united with their brother.

"You know, Greg, I don't think Lando's men totally agreed with what he had planned. I saw guilt on every one of their faces, before they had a chance to turn away."

"After all we did for them, I should say so! We, essentially, gave them back their lives. I don't think I could look anyone directly in the eyes, either, if I were in their position."

"It's harder than hell, trying to find a place to stay in this world. Isn't it "Gug?"

"Amen ta dat, "Gem!"

They laughed like they hadn't laughed for a long time. Actually, not since the three of them were together.

"I just hope Kaba's village has a few more honest people than the one we were about to call home. Jim said, after a while. From the "Nevoans" you'd expect it. But, these people are almost human, in every aspect."

"I guess it's prevalent, in any world. Greg said. At home, we didn't have to go far to find the very same thing. One might say, it's more than, just, human nature."

A short time later, heavy eyelids gave way to gravity, shutting out the rest of the alien night.

# CHAPTER 30

The Earthmen kept a steady, but regulated, pace to allow for Kaba's aged step. During their trek, they were not idle. Absorbing enough of the native language, they pieced together a rough outline of their brother's mysterious ventures. As they traveled over the uneven countryside, the mid-day sun beat down on them. Anxiety motivated their weary bodies. The old native shuffled along trying his best not to add to their burden. He would die free and on his own two feet, before he would voice a complaint. To expire in his own village, surrounded by familiar faces, was his only desire.

The brother's anticipation was lessened, slightly, by the need to keep the old native healthy. Without him, they would wonder aimlessly in the alien wilderness.

As they crested a small hill, they worked their way down the other side into a valley thick with crometta trees. Off to their right was a sheer wall of rock that dropped down from a small mesa. Licking at the foot of the stone escarpment was a small brook.

"I'm getting kind a tired. Jim said, giving his brother a quick wink. I think we should stop here for the night."

"I agree, Jim! It's the most compatible spot we've come upon in quite some time; water, shade and plenty of wood for our fire."

Kaba smiled. The two Earthmen never stopped this early in the day. He appreciated their kindliness, however. "Are all the people, from their world, so thoughtful?" He wondered, as he walked along the stream looking for edible plants. A few yards further, the small stream turned to the right, almost lapping at the base of the cliff. Approximately twenty feet above the stream, up a gentle slope, he espied a dark hole, sunken into the stone. Hurrying back to the others, he informed them of his discovery. Soon, the three of them were studying the small opening. As Kaba and Greg stood by with drawn bows, Jim picked up a handful of gravel and threw it into the opening, which was about four feet in diameter. Approaching from both sides of the dark entry, they peered inside. The sun's light penetrated about five feet into the small cave. It revealed no living thing. Bending low, Jim entered. When his eyes had adjusted to the dimness of the interior, they beheld a cave approximately eight feet deep by twelve feet wide. The sandy floor was littered with small pieces of scorched wood, bones and animal droppings; evidence of previous renters, men and animals. Beginning at the small opening, the roof slanted upward to a height of ten feet. He called to the others and they joined him. Kaba smiled and conveyed to them that they should spend the night here. Greg asked him why and Kaba pulled him by the arm until they were outside, once again. When Jim came alongside, the old man pointed to a grove of trees about one hundred yards away. Beneath one of the trees sat their answer. A Kazor was snuffling its ugly head into the branches above, probably searching for dinner.

"I think you are absolutely right, my old friend. Greg said. It would be much safer in the cave."

Jim couldn't agree fast enough. "Absolutely!"

It didn't take them long to transfer their belongings into the small cave. A good supply of firewood followed, moments later.

"I think it would be the safest thing for us to eat some of our back-up rations, because, I for one, am in no mood for hunting." Jim said.

"I agree, big brother. I think it would, also, be wise if we made our doorway a little smaller."

Kaba smiled at the nervous antics of his two foreign friends.

A short time later, a small pile of good-sized boulders was piled up alongside their doorway. A few of the bigger ones were rolled inside the cave. Later, when they were ready for sleep, these would be wedged into place. Armfuls of grass were also gathered to cushion their sleeping furs.

Kaba beckoned to them to join him around a small fire he had built just outside the cave entrance. Sitting with their backs against the cool stone facing of the cliff, they stared across the flames at the old native.

"I am old, my friends. He said, as he threw another branch into the fire. I have walked many trails in this world. As the "Sister" suns continue to chase each other through the heavens, my trails get longer as life gets shorter. This old man would not have burdened your travels, while in my youth. We would, probably, have reached our destination by this time. But now, our marches are shortened. My legs easily weary."

"Kaba! Jim interrupted. Even if Greg and I knew our way around your world, we, still, wouldn't abandon you. You are so much like our own Grandfather. He taught us how to survive, in our own world. You are doing the same for us, in this world."

"I agree, whole-heartedly! If Jim and I have to take turns carrying you, then so be it! We are all going to enter your village together!"

"The news you gave us, about our brother, pumped new life into us, just as we instilled new hope and life into you and your companions with our fortunate arrival. Jim continued. So! We will hear no more talk about separation. We started together and we will finish together. One way of another!'

Tears welled up in the old eyes. After years of degradation, in the pit, kindness had been a stranger to him. "I will enjoy your company, my Earth friends. I will try to cheat my ancestors out of a visit for a while longer. But, I must give you this." He reached behind him and handed a piece of leather to Jim.

Looking at the strange markings that covered its surface, Jim asked; "What is it?" He handed it to Greg, who also looked bewildered.

"If my time should happen to expire, before we reach my village, this will show you the direction. I will explain it more to you, in the morning. Now, I must rest!"

As the last of the "Sisters" plummeted beneath the horizon, the three companions were settled into their snug cave. Boulders were wedged into place, except for a one-foot opening to allow the smoke from their small fire to escape. Feeling more secure since they had left "Mokar's" Hotel, weariness quickly closed their eyes. The news of their brother's sudden resurrection added emotional weight to their travel-worn bodies. But, it was a comfortable weight they were happy to bear.

# CHAPTER 31

The first sun of the day had just begun spraying its rays over the quiet village. Early risers were, already, tending gardens, bearing water skins to one of the two streams flowing through the village or lulling in front of their huts.

Truck walked, stiffly, through the peaceful setting, carrying a bundle under one, powerful arm. The wounds, from his battle with the "King of Killers," were healing nicely. However, the soreness in his muscles kept him from moving at his normal pace. The nods and smiles he received, from passing villagers, made him feel glad he was part of this friendly group.

Stopping, in front of one of the huts, he hesitated, slightly, before knocking on the doorframe. After a few moments had passed, he realized no one was home. Taking the bundle, from under his arm, he placed it in the doorway. As he turned to leave, he ran right into the woman, Mara, knocking her off her feet.

"I'm sorry, pretty lady! He said, as he reached down and lifted her to her feet. I shoulda been watching where I was going."

Little Gia, stood a few feet back, leaning on her crutch. Her big eyes grew even larger, in adoration for the American.

"What do you want?" She asked, rather defensively, as she brushed herself off.

"I brought a present for da little lady." Truck answered, as he retrieved the bundle he had placed in her doorway.

He held it out to Mara. As she took it and unwrapped it from the fur, the quizzical look on her pretty face made Truck smile.

"What is it?" She asked.

"It's a wooden leg! He answered. I had a lotta time on my hands, da passed few days, so, I started ta carve a piece a wood. Before ya know it, I started thinking about little Gia. She might like it. Ya mind if I try it on her ta see if it fits?"

Never, before, had Mara been confronted with such a strange idea. She hesitated a brief moment, until she felt Gia tugging on her short skirt. Looking down, into her daughter's pleading, dark eyes, she relented. "If Gia does not mind, I will allow it." She said, with the curious look, still, on her pretty face.

Holding his arms out to the little girl, who came willingly, he sat her on a low bench. Retrieving the bundle from Mara, he knelt in front of her.

The hollowed, cup-shape, at the top of the wooden limb, was filled in with layers of soft fur. He, gently, placed the stump of her leg into this recess and pulled the leather, attached to the top of the wooden leg, halfway up her thigh.

Long, leather, thongs were wrapped securely around it, fixing it firmly in place.

"Is dat too tight, Gia? He asked, concernedly.

The little girl shook her head.

"Its gotta fit snug. But, ya gotta tell me if it's uncomfortable. Okay?"

Once, again, the little head nodded, affirmative.

"If you're ready ta try a few steps, I'll help ya." Truck said, making last adjustments on his handiwork.

She held her arms out to the big guy and slowly slid off the bench. Truck took the crutch from her and tossed it aside. "You ain't gonna need dat thing anymore, Sweetheart!"

Taking her hand, he led her slowly around the compound in front of her hut. She looked up at the big guy and they traded smiles. She was reluctant to put any weight on the wooden limb, at first. But, she soon relaxed enough to trust the new leg. As they turned back toward Mara, he let go of her hand. "Go to your mother, darling!" He said, staying close to her, just in case.

She stopped and stared up at Truck, indecision in her eyes.

"Go ahead! You can do it!" He encouraged.

Her first few steps were tentative. But, as she approached her mother she became more confident and increased her speed. She was doing fine until one miss-step threw her balance off and she fell, with a thud.

Mara rushed toward her daughter, but stopped in her tracks when she heard Truck's voice.

"No! He shouted. She has ta learn how ta pick herself up, just like da other kids."

By that time, Gia had already regained her feet and continued toward her mother. Mara knelt down and enfolded the girl into her arms. Their tears mingled together along with loud, happy sobs. A third set of tears was added as Truck made his way back to his hut. So overwhelmed by Gia's success, he had to be by himself. "I can't let her see me crying like dis. He said to himself. Dey need someone ta be strong, especially now."

He stopped at one of the streams, took a drink and threw some water in his face. "Dat was a beautiful sight! I'll visit dem later." With that, he continued on toward his hut.

"Ta-rok!" Bantor's voice invaded his thoughts. He and several men were in the large, open space behind the Communal lodge. Targets of hides, filled with grasses, stood at the far end. Each of the dozen men held a bow and a quiver of arrows.

"We have a small problem! He continued, when Truck had joined them. The new arrows, we have made, do not fly true."

"Let me see one a dos arrows!" Truck said, borrowing a bow from one of the men. Notching the arrow, he let it fly toward the target, twenty-five yards away. It went high, a foot off to the right. "I see what ya mean! Dat should a been dead center."

"All of the arrows, from this new bunch, are doing the same thing, Ta-rok."

Taking another arrow from a quiver, he studied it for a few moments. "Here's da problem, right here. Truck exclaimed. Two a da reed fletches are higher den da other one. Dey gotta be even."

With the absence of feathered wildlife on this planet, they were forced to substitute a light, but stiff, reed to fletch their arrows. It grew, profusely, around most streams.

Borrowing a flint knife from the man closest to him, he trimmed the end of the arrow until it was even. Grabbing up a bow, he notched the arrow and let it fly. It hit the target almost dead center. Handing the bow back to his owner, he said; "My old Grandfather taught me how ta adjust an arrow. "Even a crooked branch can be taught to fly straight with a little patience." He quoted the old Indian.

"Your Grandfather would have been welcomed among my people. Bantor said. His wisdom, in you, will benefit us, greatly."

"He would a loved it here, too, Bantor."

"My uncle, Kaba, was much like your Grandfather, Bantor. He, too, raised me and taught me how to use the wilderness for survival. I pray his spirit has not yet joined our ancestors."

"I'm ready ta go and rescue dos poor bastards anytime ya say, Bantor!"

"Soon, my friend. But, first you must regain your strength. The training must continue with the magic weapons to improve our chances. If we are too late to save my uncle and the others, they will be avenged with the extermination of every invader who has infested our world."

"Everything is gonna be all right, pal. Truck consoled his native friend. There a tough old bunch. We'll see dem real soon."

"I hope you are right, Ta-rok. Whether they are alive or not, our fate will be decided.

"Amen ta dat, pal!"

# CHAPTER 32

A horrible roar shattered the nocturnal stillness of the alien night. The three men, in the small cave, came awake, instantly. The loud intrusion filtered through the small, stone-filled entrance, vaporizing all traces of sleep.

Peering through the small openings of their haven, the author of the disturbance was revealed. By the glow of the existing embers of the small fire pit, outside the cave, Kazor swung his large, ugly head from side to side, bellowing his dominance into the night. Snorting and snuffling between eardrum-shattering roars, the large beast ambled, slowly, toward their retreat.

Throwing an armful of branches onto the sleeping coals of the small fire pit, inside the cave entrance, Jim yelled to the others to grab their weapons.

The trapped men didn't have long to wait before the rock barrier, to the entrance, exploded inward, narrowly missing them. It was immediately replaced with the ugly, tooth-filled maw of the Kazor. Eyes, glowing red, he tried forcing his way into the cave. Fortunately, for the three men, its body got wedged into the entrance, halfway inside the cave.

Arrows, bouncing off the tough, leathery head only managed to infuriate it more. Its fetid breath and nerve-rattling screams inundated the narrow confines of the cave, nearly deafening the three warriors.

Its large, rear quarters, wedged tightly in the small opening, it swung its massive head back and forth, desperately, trying to reach its breakfast.

Kaba darted off to the side, grabbed a burning branch from the fire and flung it down the monster's throat. Screams of agony intensified the roars and doubled its efforts to squirm closer to its tormentor.

"I think you pissed him off a little, old man." Jim said, loosing another arrow.

Finally, a well-placed arrow imbedded itself into one of the eyes, followed closely by another that flew into the large mouth and secured itself in the hungry throat. The gurgling screams emitting from that eating machine would have won first place in a talent show held in Hades.

With all their arrows, either dangling from the tough hide of the beast or laying too close to it to retrieve, the three men resorted to throwing rocks.

After a short eternity, life started to ebb from the relentless lizard. Its great head sagged lower and its tiny forelegs started making scrabbling motions. The roars subsided into gurgling spasms. By all accounts, the great monster was dead long ago. But, its diminutive brain hadn't received the message yet. Finally, the death-dealing head crashed to the floor of the cave, sending up a cloud of dust.

The low, gurgling sounds, emitting from its putrid throat, were its last.

The three, dirt-encrusted men stood in disbelief, exhausted. Muscles and minds ached from the strenuous ordeal. Smiles on their faces cracked some of the grime and the sudden silence brought reality back into focus.

"We did it! We killed the bastard!" Jim exalted.

"As Truck would say; "Dat was one, tough, sonnuva bitch!" Greg added, as he wiped some of the dirt from his face.

Kaba just stood there, smiling. His old heart was beating a tattoo on the inside of his chest cavity.

"It's starting to stink like hell in here, guys. Jim said. I think we should get some fresh air. Don't you?"

After enlarging a small gap, next to one of the Kazor's powerful hind legs, they retrieved their arrows and the rest of their possessions and piled them outside the cave. The first of the "Sister" suns tickled the new day awake by spilling her rays over the horizon.

Sprawled around a fresh fire, the three combatants, slowly, dispelled their exhaustion.

"What a way to wake up! Greg said, smiling. Exhilarating! But, I'd never want to do it again. Thank God, we came out of it unscathed."

"Along with thanking Kaba for finding the cave.
Jim added. I think the outcome would have been quite
devastating had we been caught out in the open."

After a quick dip in the stream to remove their battle
grime, they packed their belongings and doused the fire.
Munching on dried meat, they continued on with their
journey. Each man happy to be alive and more than ready
to embrace whatever the new day might bring.

# CHAPTER 33

Three days later, Bantor and Truck sat outside his "rented" hut.

"I have decided, Ta-rok,! This day will be spent in final preparations for our quest. The morning sun will see us on our way."

"I'm ready anytime you are, pal! My wounds are almost healed and I know I ain't gonna slow ya down. Truck replied. How many a dem da ya think will go with us?"

"All of them, if I asked, Ta-rok! Some will have to stay behind to protect the children and elderly. Their job will be the hardest."

"Why is dat, Pal? Truck asked. Dey ain't gonna be doing any fighting.

"No! But, they will be the ones to mourn those who do not return. And, I fear, most will not."

"I gotta agree, pal! A lot a dese good people will be lost. But, if ya don't do nothing, now, all could be lost in da future. We don't know if my brothers or your mate are even alive. But, it don't make no difference. We either rescue dem or avenge dem."

"I know what you say is true, my Earth friend, but logically, the numbers are overwhelmingly against us. Their force, alone, poses a big problem. If we can not figure a way through it, we will accomplish nothing."

"Dat isn't da biggest problem, pal. Da biggest problem is you worrying so much. The Earthman said, smiling. Relax! We'll think a something. Just like when we got outta dat shit hole."

"I wish I were as positive as you, Ta-rok. Then, it was our own two lives in the balance. My whole village faces a fate unknown, in this venture. I know it is a risk that must be taken, but, I wonder who will be left to benefit from it."

"We can't worry about dat, now, Bantor. All we can do is put our best team in dere and hope for da best. Here! Have some more a dis fruit. He said, tossing one of the long, green succulents to the native. It's full a vitamins ta build strong bodies. Wer gonna need dem!"

Catching it, Bantor started laughing. After a while, he said; "How is it you can make light of every situation that falls upon us? Are your siblings the same way?"

"No! Dere kinda like you. Truck answered. Dey do all da worrying for me, too. All I do is think about what's gotta be done and don't think about what's gonna happen. It leaves more room in my mind for da battle plans.

Their conversation was interrupted when Mara and Gia approached them. In the little girls arms was a small, fur bundle. It did not affect her balance in the slightest, as she strode into their presence. Mara was adorned in a hide shirt that was diagonally cut, in front, from the right thigh to, slightly, below the left knee. Her long, golden hair fell, naturally, over her shoulders, almost to the small of her back. Small, purple flowers peeked from her locks. Gia's outfit was a carbon copy of her mother's, even to the flowers in her hair.

"We are sorry to disturb you, but, Gia insisted on bringing a gift to Ta-rok."

"Uh, ya weren't disturbing nothing. Truck stammered. Bantor and I was just chewin da fat."

Looking toward the cold fire pit, Mara said; "I see no fat!"

"Ta-rok and I were just discussing some future plans. Bantor said, coming to the big guy's rescue. Now, I have a spear that needs mending. Smiling at Truck, he got up and left.

Pointing to a log, Truck asked; "Would you two ladies like ta sit down?"

Nodding her head, Mara sat.

Gia walked up to him and offered him the small bundle.

"Ya didn't have ta get me nothing, sweetheart." He said, as he accepted the package. Folded inside the fur was a long knife, made from Lurda horn. Leather thongs were wound around the end, forming a comfortable grip. The blade, itself, was polished to an ivory sheen and honed to razor sharpness.

"Dis is beautiful! He exclaimed, smiling. Thank you very much, little darling. He reached down and gave her a bear of a hug and placed her alongside him on the log.

"Did ya make dis yourself, Mara?"

"It was made by my mate, Sabo. It was one of his favorites." She answered, solemnly.

"Uh, I don't know what to say. Truck thought. Maybe you should keep it as a memento."

"I do not need knives or other material objects to remember." She replied, placing her hand over her heart. He will always be here."

"I'm sorry! Truck sputtered quickly. I didn't mean ta make ya sad."

"Do not worry, Ta-rok! You have put happiness back into my daughter's life. For that, I am happy. And, I thank you." She said, as she stood.

"Come, Gia. We must prepare our supper."

Picking up the little girl, he gave her a big hug, as he stood, then he put her down. "Thank you, sweet heart. You come back and visit me. Okay?" She nodded her head and walked toward her mother. Before she reached her she turned around and said, in a sweet voice; "Thank you, Ta-rok!"

Mara stared at her daughter and unleashed a flow of emotion from her eyes. Kneeling down, she enfolded her into her arms.

Truck stood there, stunned. Then, a big smile crossed his face and he said; "You are very welcome, my dear."

Mara stared up at Truck. "She has not uttered a single word since her accident. For this, also, I have you to thank."

"No ya don't, sweet lady! Gia did it all by herself. It was just a matter a time. Ain't dat right, Gia?"

"Yes, Ta-rok." She replied, a big smile on her face.

As he watched them walking away, he said to himself; "Dos two would make some man a beautiful family. If everything works out all right, who knows?"

# CHAPTER 34

The second "Sister" sun beat down on the large hunting party. Four of the shaggy Lurdas had, already, been slain and butchered. As men scraped hides and cut the meat into transportable pieces, others were scouting for more herds in the area. Bantor and Truck had brought down two of the large beasts themselves.

As they and twelve others stood on a small rise, they spotted a small herd about a half a mile north of them. Carrying bows, arrows and spears they started off toward their prey. Normally, a hunting party would not even consider taking more than two or three of the beasts at one time. In this case, a tremendous amount of meat had to be cured to sustain the native army, on their mission and also provide enough for those left behind.

This herd consisted of one large bull, six cows and two calves. The shaggy heads were down, busily mowing the moss-like grass, as the sun beat down on their carpeted bodies. A small stream bordered them on the right. To the left, of the herd, approximately a half a mile away, stood a small copse of trees.

Bantor would lead six men up the side of the stream, to the right of the herd. Truck would lead the other six, to the left, in a wide arc toward the trees. There, they would remain in hiding. On a signal, Bantor and his men would drive the herd toward the trees.

As Bantor's group neared the herd, they crossed the narrow defile, caused by the steady flow of the water. Peering over the edge, of the small ravine, he spotted one of Truck's men waving a hide. The signal! Charging onto the moss-covered plain, they had spread out along the stream, effectively blanketing the herd from that side.

At the first sound of the approaching men, yelling and waving scraps of hide, the herd bolted toward the trees. The short legs, of the bovines, tore up the turf in their wild stampede. If the chase had lasted for any length of time, they would have been far out distanced. As it was, the herd came within twenty paces of the trees and turned north.

Men, strategically, placed along the front fringe of the trees, began loosing their arrows into the large beasts. Truck, at the very end of the stand of trees, bolted out. Yelling and firing his bow, the bawling herd turned back toward Bantor's charging group.

Five of the cows and one of the calves were down, twitching and screaming out the last of their lives. One of Bantor's men managed to get a spear into the hindquarters of the remaining calf. As it fell to the moss-like turf, it added its frightened voice to the horrible choir. The large bull stopped in its tracks. Arrows dangled from its furry pelt. Mucus blew from the leathery snout, its large, dark eye sadly registering the decimation of its family. His sides heaved as he tried to recapture some oxygen back into its starving lungs.

The calf, with the spear protruding from its rump, screamed its rage and tried to regain its feet. A man raced up to it with drawn bow and put it out of its misery. The old bull had had enough. It lowered its head and charged toward the native.

Truck continued his frantic dash until his foot discovered a hidden root. Rolling over and over on the soft sod, his quiver of arrows was scattered over the plain. Throwing his bow aside, he, quickly, regained his feet. Drawing his newly, acquired knife, he raced after the charging bull.

The man, with drawn bow, stood over the calf and let his arrow fly. The bawling stopped, only to be replaced with shouts of warning. Only then, did he notice the charging animal. Flinging his bow aside, he took off running. Only twenty yards separated him from destruction.

Truck pumped his muscular legs on an intercept course, from the left and slightly ahead of the bull. Covering the last few yards with a new burst of super effort, he leapt upon the shaggy back of the beast. Just before his momentum threatened to topple him from his perch, he reached out and grabbed the great horn. Shifting his weight, he braced himself for the ride of his life. To his surprise, the beast slowed his pursuit of the fleeing man and concentrated his every effort to dislodge the strange creature on its back. Throwing the great head from side to side, it started twisting and bucking in great leaps.

The natives looked on in shock. Never before, was this imaginable. Their bows were useless, at this range. They feared hitting their Earth brother. All they could do was try to keep pace with the strange spectacle Truck held on for his life. One hand was clutching the ivory horn, the other stabbing, repeatedly, into the great neck with his long knife. He didn't realize the irony of the situation. Trying to dispatch the beast with a horn knife from one of its own relatives. The huge animal refused to forfeit its life. Doubling its efforts, to rid itself of the terrible pain, it raced, frenziedly, across the plain. The big man knew if he lost his grip, he would be mashed, horribly, into the alien sod. He had to hang on! He thought to himself. Who would rescue Jim and Greg if he didn't?

He stabbed with all his strength, causing huge, gaping gashes in the muscular neck. Blood was everywhere! The Lurda's great horn was slick with it. But, yet, the Earthman refused to loosen his grip. After a short forever, the powerful creature started to falter. It slowed its pace, slightly, and started spewing blood from its nostrils. A few more, staggering, steps and it fell over on its right side. Releasing his grip, Truck flung himself, safely, to the side, rolling free. From his prone position, he watched the Lurda steal its last few breaths from life and lay still. Pulling himself up into a sitting position, the big American sent a silent prayer to his creator.

Moments later, he was being helped to his feet by Bantor and surrounded by the rest of the hunting party. Taking the bloodied knife from his hand, Bantor asked him if he was all right.

"Dat was a tougher sonnuva bitch den dat old lizard!" He said, with a big grin on his blood-smeared face.

Grinning back at his big friend, Bantor said; "Well, Tarok, you have just completed wrestling the last of the three largest creatures on my world."

Looking quizzically at the native, Truck said; "Ya mean two, don't cha?"

"No, my brother! I mean three! You have defeated the kazar, the Lurda and Corba."

The loud laughter that echoed over the, silent plain would have scattered herds from miles away.

"Let us butcher these animals and get you back to the village. Bantor said. All this exertion is not doing your healing any good."

"Ah, all I need is a little nap. Truck answered. Den I'll be as good as new."

# CHAPTER 35

The evening sun was half spent, when a large crowd congregated around the Tribal hut. The hunt was a big success. Most of the meat would remain to provide for the village when the native army left for battle. The store of dried meat would be used on their march.

As men and women sat around making repairs to weapons, packing supplies or just chatting, the atmosphere was a mix of anticipation, excitement and dread. Many knew, they would not return. But, none would refuse to go. They knew, in their hearts, if some sacrifices were not made now, eventually, their people would face certain extinction.

Earthen pitchers of "Tova" were passed among the crowd. The intoxicating liquid, made from the long, green succulents (by the same name) was used only on special occasions or, as some would say, for medicinal purposes.

As Bantor and Truck sat among a large group of men, discussing plans, the young girl, Lea, who had attended to his needs while convalescing, approached them with a platter filled with cups and a large pitcher.

"Ah, Ta-rok! Let me introduce you to "nature's nectar." Grabbing the pitcher, from the platter, he poured a cup and handed it to the Earthman. Pouring a second cup, he set the pitcher down on the platter.

Raising the cup of greenish liquid to his nose, the big man sniffed at it. "What is dis stuff? He asked. It kinda smells like plums."

"Tova! Bantor answered. We use it only for celebrations. Taste it, my friend."

Bringing the cup to his lips, Truck took a large swallow. The big smile, on his handsome face, conveyed, to the gathered crowd, that he liked it. And, just as quickly, the smile evaporated and his eyes widened. "Wow! He snorted. Dis shit is strong!" He said, trying to catch his breath.

The cluster of men and women, surrounding him, erupted into laughter. Bantor, after the laughter had subsided, said; "I am sorry, Ta-rok! I should have warned you, Tova is for sipping, not swigging." The look on his friend's face caused him to erupt into even more laughter.

"Now ya tell me! Truck replied. It goes down nice and smooth and den it explodes in yer head. I like dis stuff!"

"Sip it, my friend, but not too much. We have a very busy day on the morrow."

"Ya don't have ta worry about dat, little buddy. I'll have a clear head in da morning. He said, taking a small sip. Ya gotta give me da recipe, for dis stuff when we get back."

"I promise, Ta-rok! As you say, "when" we get back I will show you how it is made."

Later, as darkness started to blanket the day and most of the people returned to their huts, to make final preparations, Bantor, Truck and a handful of others sat around the large fire. Spirits ran the entire gamut among the village people. From total despair to the confident feeling that, soon, they would be free, from their oppressors, circulated through their minds. Whatever their feelings, everyone volunteered. Seven hundred men, women and older boys were selected. The rest would remain to protect the village.

They would leave as soon as the first "Sister" brightened the day. Traveling light, each would carry a hide pack, Truck had taught them how to make. Dried meat, water gourds, extra arrows and spears, and sleeping furs were the only creature comforts they would know for some time.

"Well, my friends, I think we have addressed all of the important requirements. If the morning brings new questions or suggestions we shall discuss them then. Get what rest you can, now."

Everyone rose and filtered toward the individual huts, each one wondering how much sleep their emotional battles would allow them to get and if this would be the last time they would know the familiarity of their own abodes.

As Truck and Bantor walked through the village, each was absorbed by their own thoughts. A tall, young boy stepped out of the night shadows, startling them.

"May I have words with you, Ta-rok?" He asked, hanging his head.

"Sure, Kid! Come on over ta my house."

Bidding Bantor a good evening, they walked in silence towards Truck's hut. When they reached it, Truck pointed to one of the logs situated around the fire pit. "Have a seat, pal. He said. What's on your mind?"

The young native took a seat and stared at the dirt between his sandaled feet, for a moment. "I am Roca! He said, hesitantly. It is I who was saved from the charging Lurda, earlier today. I am grateful to you."

"Aw, no need ta thank… Truck started.

"Please! I must say what is in my heart, before I lose courage, once again.

Truck just stared across the few paces at the young native, trying to figure what was on his mind.

"When I felt the breath of the beast, on my backside, I was frightened! He said, in a quavering voice. I did not stop running until I was back in the village. I feel shame. He said, with tears in his eyes. Others have told me of your efforts to save me. Things I should have witnessed with my own eyes, had I not been so afraid. I feel like such a coward! I am sorry."

Truck observed the young native, feeling remorse. He knew how to handle the situation. As the tall, young man rose, as if to leave, Truck stopped him.

"Sit down, young feller! He said, in a commanding voice. I wanna tell ya a little bit more about today.

The young man quickly regained his seat, on the log, and stared at the huge American.

"Ya weren't da only one dat was scared, today. Ya shoulda seen da pile a crap on dat bastard's back. I didn't think I was gonna make it, either. When I saw ya running, I had ta do something ta slow dat big bastard down. He smiled at the youngster, as he continued. After I was on his back, I asked myself; "What da hell did I do this for?" But, by dat time, it was too late ta change my mind. So, I just hung on ta dat sonnuva bitch until he stopped running. Ya see what I'm trying ta say? A man does what he thinks is best, at times. You had ta run ta save yer ass and I had ta hang on ta save mine."

"But, I should have stopped and helped you. Roca interrupted, fresh tears streaming down his cheeks. Instead, I ran away like a frightened child."

"If ya woulda did dat, you'd be walking with your ancestors right now, my boy."

"Maybe that would have been better than becoming a coward." He retorted.

"You're not a coward. As a matter a fact, I saw ya run. With dat speed you can be on my team any day. It'll come in handy one a dese days and I hope I'm dere ta see it. Truck said, smiling. Besides, a coward wouldn't feel bad about what he did. Look at you! You're miserable because a what happened. But, ya ain't no coward."

Staring at the big man, he started to feel a little better. If this stranger, to their village, was willing to accept him after what had transpired, then maybe he should accept it himself.

"Thank you, Ta-rok. He said, much relieved. I will never let anyone down again. I promise you!"

"I know ya won't, pal. Truck said, walking over and putting an arm over the youth's shoulders. Now, go home and get some sleep. We got a big day ahead of us."

As he watched the youngster fade into the night, he smiled. "He'll be just fine. He said to himself. Now I'd better get some sleep, myself."

# CHAPTER 36

A few days after their battle in the cave, the three men rested on a high knoll. A small cluster of trees shaded them from the hot, mid-day sun. Poor old Kaba, sat against the boll of one of the trees, looking like death warmed over. It appeared, this journey would outlast the old man. The two Earthmen, grime saturated and travel weary, stared across the few paces at the native.

"If his village is too much further, I'm afraid the old chap isn't going to make it." Greg said, concernedly.

"We offered to build a litter and carry him. He refused. What else can we do?"

"Perhaps, an extended rest might help. Greg added. Since it was revealed to us our brother still lives, we may have, unconsciously, increased our pace."

"But, Kaba hasn't complained once. Jim replied. He is just as anxious as we are, to reach his village."

"True! His stubbornness would kill him, long before he'd complain. Greg said. After all he has endured, his desire to reach his people might exceed his capabilities."

"Then, we have to slow down, for all our sakes, Greg. We depend too much on him. We'll start looking for a likely

spot, to spend the night, as soon as we get moving again."
Jim decided.

Before the second sun was completely spent, they had
set up camp in a narrow, tree-lined valley, alongside a cool,
bubbly brook.

"I think a little fresh meat is in order. Greg said. There
should be a few edible ruminants in these trees."

"A good idea! Jim said, shouldering one of the Nevoan
"Death Rods". It's too bad these weapons were bundled
together and out of our reach, in the cave. They would have
made short work of that monster. Let's hunt with these,
tonight, little brother."

"Fresh meat would be a nice change. Kaba interjected.
Gnawing on dried meat always puts me to sleep." He
finished, with a big smile on his wrinkled face.

"Now that we know, what has been slowing you down,
maybe we should hunt every day. Jim said. Greg and I
couldn't figure out what was making you lag behind so
often." The two brothers smiled at the confused look on
the old man's face.

As the two Earthmen disappeared, into the woods, Kaba
started preparing a fire. "Their hearts are purely native, by
nature. He thought. Their desire to be reunited with their
sibling is no greater than my desire to be with my people.
Sleeping ancestors awaken and give this old man strength

enough to return to his people! That is all I will ask of you, ever."

Plodding through the quiet forest, they scanned the treetops. A slight breeze stirred the very tops of the trees and coaxed them into a gentle swaying. Very little reached the forest floor. Sweat formed a sheen on the two, robust Americans.

After a few miles further, into the dense forest, their luck hadn't improved. Other than a few wind-motivated branches, the alien forest remained still.

"Slim pickings, Greg. You think we should go much further? It would be a damned shame if we got lost, at this stage of the game."

"It doesn't look too promising, does it? Greg replied. We might as well start making our way back."

They hadn't taken five paces when, suddenly, a loud noise caught their attention. It froze them in their tracks.

"Sounds like men shouting. Jim said. But, I'm not sure from where."

"I think it's coming from that direction." Greg said, pointing to the left of them.

Picking their way, as fast as the terrain would allow, they headed toward the mysterious disturbance. Breaking into a small glade, awash with sunlight, they came upon a scene as prehistoric as it gets. There, not forty paces from where they stood, four natives were in the midst of a losing battle with the "King of death". One man was limping, badly, from a large, bloody gash in his right thigh. The four men surrounded the beast, doing their best to keep it at bay with their spears. As it charged at one of the natives, another would rush in from behind and deal it a wound. The wounds in the tough hide were superficial, however, and the men were tiring. The eventual outcome was easy to foretell.

All of this, the Earthmen observed in a few, brief moments. Shouldering the alien weapons, they sighted down the ends of the rods. Two, whistling bursts of energy flew simultaneously toward the beast.

To the stunned surprise, of the natives, the ghastly head exploded in a gory cloud of leathery flesh and green blood. As the giant lizard toppled onto its side and completed its death throes, they became immobile. As the shock subsided, slightly, they looked around, searching for the author of this magic. As one, they spotted the two strangers moving slowly toward them.

"Top of the day, gentlemen!" Greg said, as they came to a stop a few paces from the numbed natives. They stood there, frozen, starring at the two strangers. Not until the man with the gushing wound fainted, did anyone move.

Jim grabbed a handful of loose moss and applied pressure to the gaping wound. Greg poured water between his lips, from a small gourd hanging at his side. A few moments later, he sputtered back into consciousness. He looked up at Greg and uttered something in his native tongue.

"I'm sorry sir. I am unfamiliar with your language."

"I think we had better get him back to our camp. Jim said. Maybe Kaba can do something for him."

All of a sudden, one of the natives reached out and grabbed Jim by the shoulder. Before he could react, the native spoke. "Kaba"?

Jim looked at the man and nodded his head, affirmatively. "Yes! "Kaba".

The one who had spoken conferred with his comrades. He walked back to where Jim was standing and started talking, excitedly, in his native tongue. After a while, he realized he wasn't being understood so he repeated, "Kaba"? Looking around.

"I think he is inquiring as to where Kaba might be located. Greg said.

Jim pointed behind them and off to their right. "Kaba"! He reaffirmed.

The native nodded and said something to the two standing behind him. They, immediately, picked up their wounded comrade and started walking in the direction Jim had pointed.

"Looks like we have four guests for supper." Greg said, as they hurried after the four natives.

They, soon, picked up their previous trail and the two brothers led the small group back toward their camp. A half an hour later, they arrived. Kaba had his back to them as he bent over the fire, roasting tubers. Hearing their approach, he turned to look. He was on his feet in an instant, a physical act that belied his age. Rushing toward the natives, he put his hands on the shoulders of one and then another, while jabbering away in his language. The natives responded in kind. The smiles and jubilant chatter told the brothers all they needed to know. They had found a few of Kaba's Tribal kin.

A while later, they sat around the fire, chatting. The wounded man, by the name of Santos, was resting, comfortably, in borrowed furs, near by. His wounds, cleansed and dressed, he slept peacefully. Introductions were made. Tonio, the spokes-person was in the lead of this small scouting party. Roca, the youngest of the group, towered over the others. Varga was the quiet one.

After Kaba had conveyed to them that these two strangers were Ta-rok's siblings, the last of their reserved posture vanished.

Tonio related to Kaba, just this morning, seven hundred of his people had left the village and were on their way to do battle with the invaders. Many scouting parties, such as his, were sent out in advance in the hope of detecting any Nevoan forces in the area. Word had come to their village, through hunting parties, that many were in the vicinity. Tarok and Bantor believe it is they the Nevoans seek because of their escape.

After kaba had related this information to the brothers, through the use of their unorthodox communications system, Greg spoke.

"Kaba, if you please, ask them how long it will take us to reach them." The anticipation, almost, flowing out of his throat.

After exchanging words with Tonio, Kaba conveyed to them that, shortly, after the first of the "Sister" suns has risen, the entire army would be in this area.

"Santos cannot be moved. We will wait for them here! I am sure, he said with a smile, your anxieties and mine will leave little room for sleep this night."

Kaba was more accurate, in his assessment, than he could ever know. The long, alien night was an eternity for the two brothers.

# BOOK ONE
## - Part Two -

## "A New Beginning"

# CHAPTER 1

"Sister" dawn had just poked her early head above the horizon, brightening the new day. The six men, bundled in their warm, fur cocoons, had not yet greeted her. A seventh man rushed upon the peaceful scene and quickly roused its sleeping occupants.

Scrambling, quickly, out of their warm furs, the two Earthmen listened to the native jabbering away with Kaba and his kinsmen. The old man, quickly, communicated to them, enough to answer their questions.

Varga, the quiet one, had arisen a few hours earlier and decided to scout the area. A short distance, to the east of their position, he spotted a party of invaders traveling toward them. He said they were, approximately, five miles away and moving steadily.

"Perhaps, we should head for the forest. Greg said. It seems to be the only coverage we have in this area."

Kaba shook his head, pointing to the west. "We must warn my people of this approaching danger." He communicated to the brothers.

No one had to be told twice. Quickly, gathering up their belongings, they vacated the area. Roca and Varga supported the injured, Santos, between them. They had gone about a mile or so, when Jim looked back at the two natives bearing their wounded comrade. They were laboring to keep up. He, also, noticed the leather compress, around Santos' thigh was soaked through with blood. Calling out, to the others, he brought them to a halt.

"Greg! We have to do something for that poor guy. He's going to bleed to death, before too much longer. Besides, they're having a hell of a time keeping up."

Taking a piece of leather, out of his pack, Greg bent over the bleeding native and tied it, snugly, over the wound. "This will stem the flow, temporarily. He said. But, once we're on the move, again, I'm afraid he'll lose more blood. I don't suppose there is an ambulance, near by. Is there, Kaba?" He said, in futility.

"Great idea, brother! Jim said, dropping his fur pack on the ground. All we need are a couple of stout poles." Taking a flint knife, from his pack, he scanned the thinning trees around them.

Suddenly, the lights got a little brighter in Greg's mind. Grabbing his knife, he joined his brother. The five natives stared after them, questioningly.

Soon, they had cut down two saplings, of approximate size and stripped them of their smaller branches. The natives sat and stared, as the two strangers secured the poles to a large fur, by means of leather thongs.

Noticing, for the first time, the quizzical looks on the faces of the natives, they looked at each other and laughed. "They haven't a clue have they Jim?"

"Let's show them and get this show on the road, Greg?"

Placing the litter, alongside the injured man, they, carefully, lifted him on to it. As they picked up the ends and started walking away, they looked back at the natives. The quizzical looks were, now, replaced with big smiles. After Tonio and Varga replaced the Earthmen, at the ends of the litter, they retrieved their belongings and continued on their way. Santos even had a smile on his ashen face.

While the two brothers had been preparing the litter, Roca had made a short surrey. Retracing their steps, he had scouted out the Nevoan pursuers. He informed them, they were only a few miles behind and it appeared, they were onto their trail.

Redoubling their efforts, they tried to gain back the distance they had lost. All of them were weary, from the ordeals suffered during the course of their adventures. Kaba looked in need of a litter, himself. Adrenaline was the only thing that motivated their feet.

No less than fifty of the ugly aliens were in pursuit. Their deadly staffs were balanced on sloping shoulders. The long, spindly legs ate up the terrain at a greater rate than the native prey. It was inevitable. Before too long, they would be over-taken. To complicate matters, even more, the terrain had changed. They were, now, traveling up a gradual slope, leading to the crest, of a wooded hill. The sweat-drenched humans and natives, alike, were almost at the point of exhaustion. Kaba stumbled and fell. Jim helped him up and half carried, half dragged him toward the top of the hill.

"I think we should set up shop, when we reach the top of this hill, Greg. Kaba's out on his feet and the rest of us can't go much further." Jim gasped.

Twenty more yards and they were at the summit, where they collapsed behind a large, fallen tree.

"So close, yet, so far!" Greg muttered, half to himself.

"What?" Jim asked, trying to catch his breath.

"Our fate, on this world, has dealt us another twist. Greg replied, exasperatedly. When we retired to our furs last night, we both envisioned the reunion with Truck, on this day. Now, this!"

"Don't give up the ghost, yet, little brother. We might be able to hold them off, until the reinforcements get here. Jim said, smiling and trying to bolster his brother. If those bastards continue to follow our trail, this is a pretty good vantage point."

Pointing down the slope, they had just climbed, Greg replied; "They had better get here asap, Jim. Look!"

About a half mile down the gradual rise, the first of the aliens came into view. Following closely, at their heels, came the rest of the ugly pack. They had not, yet, become aware of their small party, hidden behind the fallen tree.

Kaba broke in on their observations. His excited antics turned their heads in his direction. He was pointing down the slope, at their backs. Staring in the general direction, indicated by his animated gestures, they disclosed a large throng of people, approximately, three miles off.

"My God, Greg, they're here! Jim said, excitedly. Maybe it isn't too late, after all."

"I have an idea, Jim! It's impossible for us to outrun them, so, we send Kaba and his kin ahead, while we slow them up. Greg said, quickly. They haven't noticed us, as of yet."

"It's about all we can do, Greg. I convey to Kaba what we intend to do."

Kaba's eyes grew large and he, adamantly, refused to abandon them, after Jim had communicated, to him, their intentions.

"You must go, Greg interjected, or all will be lost!"

"I agree with my brother, Kaba. Jim added. It is the only way to insure the survival of, at least, a few of us and your people must be warned of the encroaching danger."

Kaba stared at the two Americans, digesting the wisdom in their mad plan. All he could do was nod his head, solemnly and accept it.

"Send the fastest one of these men, ahead, to warn your people and then the rest of you follow, as quickly as you can." Said Jim.

Kaba placed his hands on the shoulders of the two Earthmen. "May all of our ancestors carry you, safely, through this day."

Words were then tossed back and forth, between him and his tribesmen. Roca relinquished position, at one end of the litter to Tonio and tore off down the slope, at break-neck speed. The others followed, closely, behind him.

The two Americans, sadly, watched them go for a moment, then, turned their collective attention back to the ever-encroaching aliens.

"I wish I had a few grenades, brother."

"To hell with the grenades, Jim! A stealth bomber would be nice."

Keeping low, behind the fallen tree, they unpacked the bundle consisting of the deadly "alien" weapons. Leaning them against the tree, alongside each other, they waited.

Less than three hundred yards separated them, now, and still they gave no indication they were aware of the two men.

"How close do you think we should let them get, Greg? You know these strange weapons better than I do."

"I could say; wait until you see the whites of their eyes, Jim. But, we are, both, aware of the fact, they don't have any white around their eyes. So, we go to plan B. I think we should lay down a barrage at about one hundred yards. We don't want them too close."

"Remember what I said about "Butch Cassidy and the Sundance kid?" Jim said, smiling.

"Yes I do. Greg answered. What about it?"

"They made their mistake by thinking they could charge through the whole Mexican army. I think we'll pass on that option."

"I'm, so, relieved to hear that." Greg said, smiling.

Slowly, the unsuspecting aliens, climbed up the gradual slope to, within, one hundred yards of the Americans. They marched two abreast, keeping a six-foot space between them. Their easy gait was perfect for traveling long distances, without becoming fatigued.

Gazing at each other, the two brothers, silently, acknowledged how much they had meant to one another in their lives. They would not, easily, forfeit this feeling.

"Good hunting, little brother!"

"Likewise, Jim. Let's take a few trophies, shall we?"

The alien rods jumped to life in their hands, vomiting sphere after sphere of screaming energy into the alien horde. The first ten creatures vanished. Gory limbs and other clumps of twitching flesh spread out on the ground. The fortunate ones, at the rear, dove behind trees, rocks and clusters of bushes. Confusion was something they had never experienced. Never before, in their long history, had their own weapon been used against them.

The two men poured volley after volley into the partially hidden creatures. Trees exploded into toothpicks and many bodies remained hidden long after their heads exploded into a brainy gel that covered a good many of their comrades. The survivors, quickly, fanned out to the right and left, trying to squeeze the source of their destruction with a pincer-like maneuver.

"We can't let them get behind us Greg. Move to your right, as far down this tree as you can get. I'll do the same to the left."

Grabbing a few of the deadly staffs, each, they moved out. The aliens were swift, however, the two Americans were comfortable with this situation. Many years of stalking prey and becoming one with their surroundings benefited them now.

"Use your senses, in situations such as this. As a last resort, use your legs to remove your ass from danger." Grandfather had taught them.

Using the limited coverage, offered by the strange terrain, The Earthmen blended in with the landscape. Eyes and ears on alert, they waited.

It wasn't long before the large, splayed feet, of the creatures, began making slight slapping sounds on the soft moss. These incongruous sounds ran contrary to the quiet nature of the strange forest. Closer and closer, they came. Their awful, blood-shot eyes scanned the forest. They were visible to the two brothers, now, spread out at least fifty feet apart. It was evident, the Nevoans had never done much of this particular type of fighting. They were loud, careless and visible.

The creature, closest to Jim, was only twenty feet away. To use his weapon, now, would only reveal his position, inviting a quick death. As he lay in a tangle of roots, at the base of a tree, he slowly laid the weapon aside and drew his ivory knife from the thong around his waist. Concealed beneath the roots, he waited. He slowed his breathing and focused on his target.

Ten feet, five feet, the creature came stealthily on. As it passed within a foot of him, the American, silently, sprang from concealment and buried the ivory knife, deeply, into the bulbous head. Without a whisper of noise, it folded to the ground. Quickly withdrawing his knife, he pulled the body and its weapon beneath the roots and waited for signs of detection. None came. But, the next alien in line did. He, too, met the same fate as his comrade.

Grabbing his alien firearm, Jim slunk, quietly, into the shadows. Before he could completely conceal himself behind a large boulder, an explosion shattered it a foot from his head. Shards of the alien rock imbedded themselves into his neck and right cheek. The loud, echoing in his brain, momentarily, stunned him. Crouching low, he made a dash for a fallen tree a few yards ahead. He threw himself flat, behind the wooden barrier, an instant before the area around him erupted into a storm of flying turf and wood.

Crawling down the length of the large tree, he pulled himself out of danger for the moment. As he lay there catching his breath and feeling the blood trickling from the multiple wounds, in his face, he heard explosions erupting fifty yards to his left.

"I hope Greg is hanging in there." He said to himself, as he plotted his next move.

Peering through an opening in the rotting tree, he watched the alien army approach, thirty feet away. They were still concentrating their fire on the opposite end of the tree, where he had just vacated. As they began to pinch in, toward this area, he made a quick count. At least twenty of the bastards were still in the hunt. Not counting the ones still on Greg's ass.

"I guess it's do or die time." He said to himself, as he rose suddenly from his position. Firing as fast as he could push the button, he showered the creatures with a cloudburst of death. The surprised creatures, still standing, fired back, missing wildly in their haste. In the confusion, he tried to pick up the sounds of explosions coming from the area his brother occupied. He couldn't detect anything from that direction.

"Good bye, my brother!" He said aloud.

All of a sudden, an explosion struck the tree, directly in front of him. The concussion hurtled him ten feet backwards, through the air. Just before he slipped into oblivion, he thought he heard human voices shouting all around him. Then, he heard nothing more.

## CHAPTER 2

The first bit of consciousness, seeping back into Jim's mind, came in the form of a ringing sound, vibrating in both ears. Opening his eyes, he stared at the soft light filtering down on him through the thatched roof. Turning his head slowly, he took in his surroundings.

A young woman sat a few paces from him on a low stool. Her golden hair formed a perfect backdrop for her kind and lovely face. When she noticed him observing her, the large, dark, beautiful eyes sparkled.

She rose from the stool and gracefully walked to a small table, situated alongside his sleeping platform. She poured water into a cup, from a large pitcher, and offered it to him.

She was dressed in a short hide skirt and leather sandals. Her long hair was held off her face with a leather thong. Sprigs of purple flowers were tucked, neatly throughout the golden tresses. Her large, firm breasts rose and fell in perfect harmony. Her smooth skin, tanned to a coppery brown, glistened with health.

Smiling at her, he accepted the cup. "This must be heaven! He said, as he drained it, quickly, with long, thirsty gulps. How long have I been out?" He asked, handing her the empty cup.

She shook her head and said something, in Kaba's language. Smiling at the Earthman, she turned and left the hut.

The ringing in his ears had lessened to a quiet hum. Running his hand over his face, he detected numerous wounds, already scabbing over. The bandage on his neck felt wet.

"The battle! Greg!" He said out loud. Sitting up, quickly, he swung his legs from beneath the furs and sat on the edge of the platform. "Did he make it?" He asked himself, his mind in a panic.

Suddenly, the frond curtain, hanging over the entryway, parted. Standing there, with a big smile on his face, was his lost brother, Truck.

"Welcome home, Jimbo!" He said, as he covered the few paces and picked his dazed brother from the platform and gave him a big bear hug.

"Truck! He said, returning the hug. Am I ever glad to see you, again!"

Spilling tears over each other's shoulders, they held on for several moments.

"Greg?" Jim said, questioningly, while trying to restore oxygen to his lungs.

A sad look clouded Truck's moist eyes. Releasing his grip on his brother, he said; "He's in another hut, still out like a light. He was shot in da head. Tears rained and the sorrow he felt stuck in his throat. He's breathing okay, but dey don't know if he's gonna make it or not."

"Take me to him, Truck!" Jim said, as he started toward the entryway.

"Jim! Take it easy! You need your rest too. Maybe a little later."

"The hell with rest, Truck! I want to see him now!"

"Well, now dat ya put it dat way, follow me."

A few moments later, they entered another of the small huts. A woman was bent over Greg, bathing a deep gash on his left temple. The ashen color and shallow breathing told a very bleak story.

"Dis woman is Lona! Truck said. She has been watching over our brother since you guys got here."

The attractive woman paused long enough, from her ministering, to smile and nod her head at the two men in acknowledgement.

Kneeling down on the opposite side of the sleeping platform, Jim stared at his little brother. His arms were outside the furs. From forearm to shoulder, they were pockmarked with a multitude of small wounds.

Looking up at Truck, Jim asked; "How long have we been here?"

"Dis is da third day, Jim."

"And he's been like this from day one? No changes?"

Truck shook his head "We thought da both a you were already dead. When da fighting was finally over and we found ya, it didn't seem possible ya were still alive. Dos ugly bastards were laying everywhere. How in da hell did you guys keep dem off of ya?"

"I'll tell you all about it later, Truck. When Greg is better."

As he looked down on the still body of his brother, tears overflowed his eyes.

"It's not fair, Truck! We went through hell to get here. All we thought about was staying alive, so we could be united, once again. The dams broke in his tear ducts and flooded freely down his cheeks. He can't die! Not now!'

Truck knelt down, beside his sobbing brother and put a massive arm around his shoulders. Adding his tears to the emotional pot, he said; "Da big boss up dere will pull him through. You'll see! We gotta lot a catching up ta do."

"Hang in there, Greg. Jim said between sobs. Don't you dare leave this team!"

"Amen ta dat, big brother. Now, I better put your ass ta bed. Ya gotta get your strength back."

"I'm staying right here, Truck! Jim said, vehemently.

"Hey dere doing everything possible for da little guy. You'll just be in dere way. Trust me Jimbo. Dey'll make him well. Truck wasn't going to give his brother any room for objection. He continued. Dey brought me back from da dead. I'll show ya my scars one a dese days."

Rising to his feet, he took one more look at his brother. "You win, Truck. He said. I'll get some rest. But, promise me you'll wake me if anything changes."

"Dat's a promise, Jimbo. And I know it will be good news, too.

Truck escorted him back to his hut and within a few moments he, too, was sleeping.

"Do's two had one hell of a battle. He said to himself. It's a miracle dere both still alive. All mighty father, please, help him. I wanna sit down with da two a dem an tell dem how much I missed dem."

Looking up at the starry sky, as he walked the short distance to his hut, he stopped and said; "Big coach, up dere, ya gotta take care a your players. He continued, as a fresh flood of tears flushed his eyes. We got a big game ta play and we need dem ta help us win. It's up ta you, coach. Thanks for listening."

"Tomorrow is another day. He thought to himself, as he continued toward his hut. I pray all three of us will be here to enjoy it."

# CHAPTER 3

Truck, Jim, Bantor and a handful of others, were sitting around the Tribal hut. Truck was doing his best interpreting for his brother, as he told them of his battle. When he had finished, Truck filled him in on the rest of the story.

"When we finally got dere, on dat hill, dere was only a handful a dos ugly bastards still standing. Our arrows finished dem off in a hurry. Dat's when we found you two guys. We found you right off da bat. Greg was about forty yards away, almost completely buried under a ton a tree branches and dirt. Both a you guys was in pretty bad shape. We carried ya back ta da village and here ya are."

"Truck! How do you say "thank you" in their language?"

He told the proper words to his brother and Jim turned to Bantor and repeated them.

"Bantor smiled. "I am doing my best to learn your tongue. Your sibling and I have become brothers, also. It is we who thank you for killing our enemies. The last we met was when the creature "Zarnog" was killing my newborn son. I have been told, by Ta-rok, you two had come to my aid. "Thank you"! He said, in almost flawless English.

Truck pointed to a tall, young man. Roca, here, is da real hero of da rescue. Without his speed, bringing us word of da battle, you two guys would, still, be up on dat hill."

Jim smiled and nodded at the young native, who smiled back.

"How many of them were there, Truck?" Jim asked.

"When we finished off da last seven or eight, da body count was over fifty."

"Truck! Jim asked excitedly. Tell me you collected all of the native weapons."

"We took everything, Jim. All of da strange weapons, backpacks and bows and arrows and we even found a fur bundle lying behind a fallen tree. Dere was twenty more a dem alien rifles inside.

"Those are the ones Greg and I collected when we liberated the men from the pit."

"Ya! Kaba told me about dat fight. Dat was da worst place I ever been in, I'll tell ya dat."

"Greg might argue with you on that. Jim said smiling. When he's better we'll show you how to operate those weapons. I'm sure you'd agree they will come in handy."

"After ya show dese guys how ta use dem, we'll have our artillery. He said with a big smile on his face. After a brief pause, he continued. Ya know, about da time we got word about yer battle in da hills, we was on our way ta dere city. About seven hundred warriors was ready ta kick ass.

Bantor decided dat dis was a good sign an decided ta return ta da village. When da little guy gets strong enough den we're really gonna kick some ass."

"I hope you're right about that, Truck. He didn't look too good. His healing may take a little time."

"Dese guys, indicating the villagers gathered around them, have been treated like hell by dos bastards all a dere lives. A little more time ain't gonna make no difference. Besides, He said, beaming a fresh smile, da reinforcements are here."

"I just hope, for all of our sakes, it happens sooner, rather than later." Jim said, a cloud of worry shadowing his eyes.

"Stop yer worrying, big brother! No one looks pretty when dere shot in da head. But, I just know da little guy is gonna pull through. It's only been about six days and we ain't going no place until he gets better."

Bantor said something to Truck, in his native tongue. Truck nodded his head and turned to Jim. "Bantor was wondering if ya could show him how da strange weapons work. I didn't tell him dat you wanted ta wait til Greg gets better, before ya showed him. But, I'm kinda curious myself about dem. If ya don't want to, I'll tell him ya don't feel up to it."

"That won't be necessary, Truck. After all they've done for us, it won't hurt to show them now. Actually, my brother,

other than a slight twinge in my neck, I'm one hundred percent."

After relaying his brother's answer, to Bantor, a man was sent to retrieve one of the weapons from a storage room near by. Moments later, he handed it to Jim.

"We got a practice field, over there, Jim." Truck said pointing, as the whole group made their way toward it.

"This won't do, brother! Jim said. For the safety of all, I think we should go outside the village. Once you see what happens, you'll understand why."

Exchanging a few words with Bantor, they immediately exited the village. A short distance away, they stopped. Jim pointed to a small tree sitting on a hill, approximately fifty yards from where they stood.

Sighting down the length of the blue rod, he pressed a button. As one, the entire body of people gasped and took a few steps backward. A yellow ball of energy whistled out of the end of the staff and hurtled toward its designated target. An instant later, the tree exploded into hand-sized pieces. Turning toward the group of stunned witnesses, the Earthman smiled.

"Dat was amazing! Truck said, as he took a place alongside his brother. Dis, sure as hell, is gonna help our cause and we got a hundred a dese things. He said, excitedly. Dey don't look too hard to use, either."

"Actually, it's quite simple. The hardest part was discovering the firing mechanism. Want to give it a try?"

"I thought you'd never ask." The big man said, taking the weapon from Jim and sighting down its length. He pushed a button and the rod started to vibrate.

Reaching over, carefully avoiding the end of the rod, Jim pressed a button on butt end of the weapon.

"What da hell was dat?"

"Sorry, Truck! That was the button for the stun mode. You remember how that felt, don't you? He said with a smile. This is the button for the firing mode. Don't touch it until you've sighted in the target."

"Ya sure dere ain't nothing else ya wanna tell be big brother?"

"That's it, Truck. He said, reassuringly. Go ahead and shoot!"

So, once again, Truck sighted down the length of the rod. The target, this time, was a boulder lying on the same hill as the destroyed and still-smoldering tree. A ball of energy vomited from the shaft, once again. It struck the rock, squarely, reducing it to dust.

"Wow! I gotta get me one a dese things. He yelled. Bantor! Here! Give it a try." Handing it to the native, he explained its secrets in his tongue.

Nodding his head, in understanding, he aimed at a small tree, forty yards away. The shot was a little off its mark, but, a large hole was blasted close by.

A big smile covered his face, as he handed the weapon to Jim. So it went for the next hour. Each native, in turn, had a chance to use it.

Afterward, as they walked back to the village, Jim turned to Truck and said; "Now we have about twenty-five people that can help us train others in its use."

Truck translated this to Bantor who was still smiling.

As they entered through the village gates, a small boy rushed up to them. He said some words, excitedly, to Bantor and Truck.

"Come on, Jim! It's Greg!"

They took off running.

# CHAPTER 4

A dubious shroud cloaked their minds, as they raced through the village. As they approached the hut, Kaba was on his way out. He held up his hands, gesturing them to stop. He turned to Truck and spoke. "Many days has your sibling battled with his ancestors, pleading with them for another chance to live. I think he has, finally, convinced them to leave him for a while. He is awake. But, he is still confused. Rest is all that is needed to make him whole again. Smiling at the brothers, he understood their anguish. Do not stay too long."

Smiling back at the old man, Truck enfolded him in a crushing embrace, as he said, along with tears of happiness; "I love you, my old friend."

Jim, standing rigidly nearby asked; "What did he say, Truck?"

"He said dat our little brother is gonna make it. But, he needs lotsa rest."

The vigorous hug was repeated, on the old man, who was still trying to catch his breath from Truck's mauling.

"Thank you, Kaba!" He said, as they rushed passed him and entered the hut.

Propped up, in a sitting position, he stared at his brothers as if from far away. A slow smile cracked his chafed lips, as he said in a low, raspy voice; "It is about time you two hooligans come to visit your ailing brother."

Rushing over to him, one on either side of the fur-covered pallet, they embraced their brother. They stayed that way for quite some time. Not a word was spoken, but their hearts melted together. No one relinquished their hold, for fear of losing each other, once, again.

It was Greg who first spoke. "I need some air, gentlemen!"

Untangling themselves and wiping the tears that had saturated their faces, they stared at each other.

"Dis is great, you guys! Truck sputtered, through his sobs. Da team is back together again. Look out, ya sonnuva bitches, we're coming!"

They laughed together for the first time, in how long? Weeks? Months? They had a lot to catch up on. Thank God! They would have another chance to do so.

Seeing how weak and weary he looked, they didn't stay too long. Telling him, they would check in on him, periodically, they started to leave. Lona, the woman who had attended their brother's needs and who had been a silent witness to the warm reunion, told Truck she would take good care of his sibling. "I have plans for this one!" She said with a quick wink and a big smile on her attractive face.

When they were outside, Jim couldn't help but notice the big smile on his brother's face. "What did she say to you that was so funny?" He asked.

"I think she has da hots for our little brother." He answered, as they walked across the compound.

"I must admit, Truck. They are an attractive people. Aside from their large, dark eyes, they are as human as we are. I know, when I first came to in that little hut, one of the first things my eyes revealed to me was this golden-haired angel sitting on a stool, smiling at me. God, she was a beauty!"

"What was her name, Jimbo?"

"I'm afraid I wasn't able to communicate with her. I'd love to find out, though."

"Den, I think ya start learning da language and go after her. It looks like we're gonna be here for a long time."

"That is an excellent idea, Truck! While Greg is convalescing, we should get together, every day, and you can teach us."

"I ain't no teacher, Jim. You should know dat, by now. I'm still trying ta learn it, myself."

"At least, you can get us started, my large brother. Besides, you owe it to us."

"Whadaya mean I owe it ta ya?" Truck asked, confusedly.

"Do the words, "final exams", ring a bell? Jim said with, a smile.

"Ya, still, holding dat over my head, after all dese years? Truck smiled back. Okay! I'll do it! But, don't blame me if ya end up talking funny."

"I don't think its contagious, my brother." Jim said, laughing at the same time.

"Keep sassing da teacher and ya won't learn squat."

Jim continued laughing and was soon joined by the big guy.

After a while, he said; "It feels good to laugh again. Especially, now that we're all together, once more."

"I missed dat too, Jim. We can't let nuthin do dat to us, again."

"As you always say; "Amen ta dat", Truck."

Putting his arm over his older brother's shoulder, he said; "Come on, Jim! I wanna introduce ya to two more beautiful ladies."

A few huts, further up the line, almost adjacent to the "Tribal" hut, they stopped. Before they even walked up to the door, a little girl, with a peg leg, rushed into Truck's waiting arms.

"How ya doing, Sweetheart? Is dat leg giving ya any trouble?"

"I am fine, Ta-rok. She replied in a sweet, little voice. My new leg feels a little snug, today."

"Let's have a look at dat, little darling." He said, placing her gently on a low bench and removing the wooden leg.

Looking over the big man's shoulder, as he was busy with the leg, she pointed to Jim and said; "Who is that, Ta-rok?"

"Dat's my oldest brother, Jim, Gia. He's gonna live with us in our village. Why don't ya give him one a your big smiles and say hello ta him."

Jim, standing a few paces back, listened to them jabbering away. A big smile, from the little girl, prompted him to respond in kind. "Hello!" He said, giving her a little wave.

Truck looked back at his brother and said; "Jimbo, I want ya ta meet Gia. I made her dis leg so she could play wit da other kids. Dat crutch she had, was always getting in da way." Removing some of the fur stuffing, from the top of the hollow leg, he retied it around her stump.

"Dere ya go, little lady. He said, as he lifted her to her feet. Try dat out!"

"You fixed it, Ta-rok! She cried out, after taking a few steps. It feels real good, now."

He scooped her up in his arms and said to Jim; "She's growing real fast. Every week, or so, I gotta make some adjustments. Looking into her dark eyes, he asked her where her mother was.

"She went to the stream to get water. Said the little girl. Are you going to eat with us, Ta-rok?"

"Not tonight, darling. Jim and me has ta go see my other brother, Greg."

"What's the matter with him, Ta-rok? She asked. Is he sick?"

"Yes he is, sweetheart. But, he's gonna be alright in a few days."

Jim just stood there with a big smile on his face. Watching the big man interact with the child, brought a lump to his throat. Here was one of the toughest men he had ever known, in his entire life. Fortunately, for most of those, he had touched, in his life, his heart was as big as his biceps.

"I think I'm gonna have ta make ya another leg pretty soon, little lady. You're grown up so fast!"

"Will I get as big as the other girls, Ta-rok?"

"Sure ya will, Gia! He said, as he sat on a log with the little girl propped in his lap. If ya take after your mother, your gonna be taller den a lot a dem other girls."

It was hard to believe those big eyes, of hers, could get any bigger, but, they did as she said; "Really, Ta-rok?"

"I can promise ya dat, sweetheart!"

Jim, sitting on a log, a quiet observer, finally spoke. "She really adores you, Truck. But, that comes as no surprise. He continued, smiling across at the happy pair. Even when you were a youngster, kids and animals would follow you around all the time."

"It's da "Stonedeer" charm, Jimbo. We all got it! It just comes naturally!"

"If you say so, brother. But, I think you received the biggest helping."

As they sat there, enjoying each other's company, a woman entered their midst. She was balancing two large skins, filled with water, hanging from a yoke that rested across her shoulders.

Placing Gia on the log alongside him, Truck rose and covered the short space between them and stood in front of her. "Let me give ya a hand with dat, Mara." He said, lifting the yoke, easily, from her shoulders, water skins and all, he hung it on pegs set into the side of the hut.

"Thank you, Ta-rok. Those bags seem to get heavier with each trip I make to that stream."

"Ya should a sent Gia ta find me. I would a got it for ya."

"What you were doing was more important than hauling a little water, Ta-rok. Your ailing sibling needed you by his side."

"I got some good news, Mara. I talked ta Kaba a little while ago and he told us dat Greg is gonna be okay. He said, with a big smile on his face. We even got ta talk ta the little guy."

"I am happy to hear that, Ta-rok! She said, smiling back. You have told me how much your siblings mean to you." She finished, staring in Jim's direction.

Looking, quickly, at his brother, Truck said; "I didn't mean ta ignore ya, Jim. Every time I get near dis woman, I kinda forget about anything else. Let me introduce ya.!"

"Mara, dis is my oldest brother, Jim." He said in her native tongue.

Mara smiled and said something to Jim. Truck, quickly, interpreted.

"Mara says dat it is a pleasure to finally greet you. She's heard a lot about you two guys."

"Tell her, the pleasure is all mine and that I wish us all to become good friends." Truck did so and the three of them stood there smiling at one another.

"Truck! Jim said, after a while. I'm going to go back and check on Greg. It was more of an excuse than anything else, to put an end to the embarrassing feeling he had, because he was unable to communicate. I'll see you later."

"Okay, Jimbo! Tell Greg I'll see him in a little while."

Nodding at Mara, he turned and left.

Gia came over to him and asked; "Is your brother going to learn how to talk right like you did, Ta-rok?"

"Yes he is, little lady. I am gonna teach dem."

# CHAPTER 5

Ten "Alien" days later, they were congregated in the shade of the "Tribal" hut. The three Earthmen, Bantor, Kaba and about twenty others sat off to one side. Their battle scars healing nicely, along with an abundance of nutritious food and rest, their strength and spirits were almost fully rejuvenated. Their daily endeavors to learn the native language advanced them, quickly, to the head of the class. They had enough working knowledge of it to, at least, make themselves understood. Truck was proving to be a pretty good instructor. This opened a whole new world to the brothers. Unfortunately, it also added new problems.

One day earlier, Jim had sought out the beautiful woman who had cared for him, while he convalesced. He had learned, through Kaba, her name was Sanda. To express his appreciation and thank her were his only intentions, at this point in time. However, it was to escalate into something much bigger.

He saw her by one of the streams, early one morning. She was in the process of washing leather garments and placing them on flat rocks to dry. Her long, golden tresses, still damp from her morning bath, captured the early rays of the sun, reflecting its glow in an aura of warmth. Her statuesque body moved gracefully as she worked. Clad only in a brief, hide skirt, the Earthman let this beautiful scene imprint itself upon his mind, for a brief moment, before he acted.

"Well! Here goes nothing!" He said to himself, finally mustering up enough courage to approach the lovely woman. "Good day!" He said, stopping a few paces from where she knelt over the stream. If he had gotten any closer, she may have detected the sound of his heart, beating against the inside of his chest.

Looking up, at the smiling man, she smiled in return. "Good day to you, also. She said. You are looking much better."

Struggling for the right words, he finally said; "Your care and kindness has made me so. I thank you!"

"There is no need for "Thank You", Earthman. We are all born to care for one another. Is it not so on your world?"

"In most instances, but not all. He replied awkwardly. I think the majority of people are compassionate, by nature, but not all of them are willing to make the attempt."

She rose from the edge of the stream, with another wet bundle in her arms. She had taken a few steps toward the drying rock, when she tripped and lost her balance. Jim caught her around the waist before she hit the ground, breaking her fall. The wet leather bundle ended up draped, dripping, over his head.

They stood there staring at each other, for a few moments. Then, she started laughing.

Removing the wet leather from his head, he offered it back to her, echoing her laughter. Shaking the water from his head, he lost himself in the musical sounds of her amusement.

After a while, she retrieved the dripping garment from him. "I am sorry, Earthman. I am so clumsy, at times."

"Sorry is not necessary, Sanda. He said, staring into her sparkling eyes. We are born to protect one another. Is this not so on your world?" He asked, with a big smile radiating from his face. Besides, it was my pleasure."

She looked at him, quizzically, for an instant and started to laugh again. "You make me laugh much, Earthman, even with your words. She smiled. I like to laugh."

"And, you do have a beautiful smile and laughter. He said. Please! Call me Jim!"

"Gem?" She repeated, looking at him questioningly.

"Nodding his head and smiling, he knew that was about as close as anyone around here would come to pronouncing his name correctly.

"Sanda!" A harsh voice interrupted the sublime moment. A burly, bearded man entered their midst. The two Pranas, hanging over his shoulder, were thrown on the ground at her feet. Prepare these for my evening meal!" He said in a loud and intimidating bellow.

Jim could see Sanda cringe. The beautiful smile vanished from her face. It was, immediately, replaced with a look of abject fear.

"Borsa! I was just...

She didn't have a chance to finish. The gruff native lashed out with the back of his hand. The blow caught her on the right side of the jaw. She was knocked to the ground, instantly, a trickle of blood flowing from the corner of her mouth.

This happened, so suddenly, Jim didn't have a chance to intervene. But, when the brute aimed a kick at the cowering woman, he hit him with a shoulder, knocking him off balance. Down he went, almost rolling into the stream. Regaining his feet, surprisingly fast for a big man, he glared at the American. Confusion showed on his hairy face. His bullying tactics had never been challenged before. The audacity of this stranger immobilized him for an instant. Pointing a finger at Jim, he said; "This is none of your concern. Go your way and tend to you own affairs!"

"This is my concern! Jim said, helping Sanda to her feet. Where I come from, men do not harm women."

"Then, I, Borsa will send you limping back to that place if you touch my woman again." He bellowed.

"I don't think so, fatso! I'm thinking about opening a restaurant in this neighborhood and staying for quite some time." The Earthman said, sizing up the big man. If there were to be a confrontation, he would be at a considerable height and weight disadvantage.

Sanda stood in shock. She liked the Earthman. She didn't want any harm to come to him. The constant state of fear, surrounding her since Borsa had entered her life, prevented her from getting too close to anyone. Borsa had hurt too many people since he joined their village.

"When I get through with you, your own ancestors will not recognize you!" He roared, as he charged toward Jim with outstretched arms.

Just before contact, Jim lowered his body and caught the bulky native with his shoulder into the soft mid-section, lifting him off his feet. Describing a perfect arc, the momentum of the charge deposited him in a heap ten feet away.

Jim looked down at the infuriated native and said; "Now take your big ass home and don't ever lay a hand on this woman again. If you do, I'll happily kill you!"

Eyes flaring hatred, he rose from the ground, drawing a knife from his belt. "Now you will die!"

Jim reached to his side and realized he was unarmed.

A small crowd had gathered, attracted by the loud voices. The two combatants hadn't noticed, until now, so intent were they on one another. Jim searched the faces in the crowd and noticed Greg and Truck making their way toward the front.

As Borsa was just about to resume his attack, his arms were pinned to his side by Truck and he was, quickly, stripped of his knife. Releasing the infuriated native, he said; "No fair cheating. If you're gonna fight my brother, ya gotta do it man ta man."

Turning back toward Jim and staring at the crowd, the fight went out of him. No one had opposed him, since coming to this village a year ago. He was used to getting what he wanted by intimidation and using his great strength.

Before the situation had a chance to escalate into something more serious, Kaba intervened. "Borsa!" He shouted. You have been warned before about this behavior. Soon enough, everyone will have their fill of fighting. Cease at once! He paused for an instant, staring at the big man. Although these three men are strangers to our village, they will be accorded the respect given to all our people."

"I do not need an old man telling me what to do. I am not a stranger here. He is!" Borsa bellowed, pointing at Jim.

"Not all of us are old, Borsa. Bantor interjected. Do as he says!"

Glaring at everyone around him, he stomped off.

Jim turned to Sanda. "Are you all right?" He asked.

"I will be fine, Earth… Gem. She said smiling. I must finish my chores, now." She turned and hurried toward the stream.

Moments later, they were sitting under the "Tribal" hut and Bantor was filling them in on Borsa.

"He came to our village more than a year ago. Traveling a great distance from his village to hunt the Lurda. At this time, he became lost. One of our scouting parties found him wondering around half starved. He has been here ever since. He is a cousin of your old nemesis, Ta-rok, Corba "the terrible".

"I wonder what happened ta dat bozo. Truck mused. He sure caused a lotta trouble in dat pit."

"He is dead! Greg answered. When Jim and I liberated a party of men returning from the mine, he was among them. A short while later, he crushed a man's skull. Jim laid him out flat and the other pathetic souls literally tore him apart."

"That explains Borsa's behavior. Said Jim. It must run in the family."

"If he continues to abuse people is this village, he may suffer the same fate." Kaba chimed in.

"Is he her mate, Kaba? Sanda's?" Jim asked.

"Not in the true sense. Kaba answered. Before Borsa arrived, Sanda had many suitors. She was interested in only one. His name was Talos. He went out with a hunting party and was never heard from again. Borsa was, also, a member of that party. Many feel he had something to do with Talos's disappearance."

Not long afterward, he moved into her hut. No suitor has dared approach her because they fear Borsa."

"I got a feeling dats gonna change in a hurry." Truck said, smiling at everyone and winking at Jim.

# CHAPTER 6

A few days later, Truck spotted Bantor sitting alone in front of his hut. The native was deep into his thoughts.

"Morning, Bantor!" The big man said, taking a seat on the log beside him.

Coming, suddenly, out of his revelry, the native smiled at Truck. "Good day to you, also, my brother."

"What's da matter, pal? Ya look like ya lost your best friend."

"I may have, Ta-rok. He replied, solemnly. I do not know if my mate lives or not. Maybe I am being selfish, my Earth brother. But, since our escape, I have thought of nothing else other than to be united with her, once again."

"Den I think its time ta do something about dat. Truck said. Greg and Jim told me da other night dey was feeling good and raring ta kick ass. I think we should have a meeting and get da show on da road."

"I do not wish to rush things, Ta-rok. You, too, are still healing. But, the day that monster deprived me from holding my new-born, in my arms, forever and separated me from my mate, I have had an emptiness in my heart. At the same time, my mind is overflowing with revenge."

"Ya don't have ta convince me, Bantor. Me and my brothers have a bone ta pick with dat bastard, too. And, I think, da sooner da better."

A short time later, the majority of the village was assembled in and around the "Tribal" hut. Excited murmurings were sprayed throughout the large crowd.

"We all know what we must do! Kaba began. A short while ago we were prepared to do battle. Now, with the renewed strength of our Earth allies and the mastering of the "alien" weapons, we are even more prepared. Our storehouses are filled to capacity, because of this. Unless there are any objections, I say, in two journeys of the suns, let our quest begin. Kaba paused and looked out at the large crowd. As frightening as this prospect was, no one objected.

The total unity, of his people, made the old man smile with pride. He nodded to Jim, who was seated to the left of him.

"Forgive me if I distort your beautiful language. I will do my best to explain to you. He started, drawing small pockets of laughter and understanding from the crowd. The strange weapons will be in the hands of those we have trained. They have practiced many hours and have grown quite proficient in their use. Anyone curious, as to how they work, feel free ta ask me or my brothers."

"De're getting pretty good with da bow and arrows, too. Truck interjected, with little Gia seated on his lap. I think we're ready da send dos bastards home in a hand basket."

"What is hand basket?" Asked Gia.

"Dat's a place where dey can't hurt no one, ever again, Sweetheart." He said, smiling down on the little urchin.

She smiled back at the big guy.

Mara, seated at his side, said; "Your language is difficult to understand, at times, Ta-rok."

"I could not agree with you more, Mara! Greg chimed in. After spending a good part of our lives acting as his interpreter on our own world, now, I suppose we'll have to do it here, in your language."

"Greg and I feel we were put on this world to help people understand our brother." Jim added, smiling.

"Dere dey go! Truck said, returning his brother's smile. Ganging up on me again."

The laughter, sprinkling through the large gathering, helped to alleviate some of the tension.

After a while, Bantor spoke. "Soon, we will all be aware of our status on this world. Many will not return. If I learn my mate has already joined her ancestors, I will be counted among them."

Staring at the young man, who had become a son to him, Kaba spoke. "There is not a person, dwelling in this village, who does not seek revenge. The cruelties dealt by them, among our people, in the last one hundred years will take many suns to eradicate. Each of us must strive to exist and rebuild our lives." His last words were meant, specifically, for Bantor.

"We all have someone or something to live for. Jim said, staring across part of the crowd at Sanda, much to the chagrin of Borsa. If we work together, on this, most will succeed and realize their future goals."

"Obviously, we will be out-numbered! Greg joined in. But, this can work to our advantage. Small groups, applying pressure at strategic positions will do us more good than an all-out, frontal attack."

"Four of us, among you, have been inside their walls. Jim jumped back in. We know how to shut down the lethal force field, surrounding their city. Diversions will have to be made, while a small party puts it out of commission."

"A decoy could be used. Added Truck. Kinda like dat "Trojan Horse" ta get dem ta open da gates."

"That is a possibility, Truck. Greg chimed in. But, you must remember, there was scant coverage in front of the gates."

And so the discussion went on. Well after the fires were lit, to stave off the encroaching darkness, they talked. More were optimistic this time then the previous trial run. Specific objectives made them feel this mission was more than just a shot in the dark. Each group would carry out differing functions. One depended upon the other for success; decoys, artillery, scouts and assassins.

Greg and Jim would lead a small party inside the walls, via a tunnel, in hopes of diffusing the lethal power curtain.

Bantor, who had become adept with the "alien" weapon, would over-see the artillery.

Truck would be in charge of the snipers, bowmen who had become deadly accurate with the Earthly weapon.

Roca would lead the main diversion, and probably the most important one, at the main gate.

Over seven hundred men, women and older boys constituted the total force against an alien enemy of one million or better. Everyone volunteered, even the elderly and women with infant children. They were given the responsibility of protecting the village.

The only allies the prevailing army would have would be surprise and luck. They would find out, all too soon, if these were enough.

As the fires burned lower, in the pits, the majority of the vast gathering had ventured off to their own huts. A few scattered groups lingered, enjoying each other's company.

Lona had invited Greg to her hut, once again. He left, sheepishly, under the knowing grins of his two brothers.

Jim, Truck, Mara and Gia were the sole occupants of the "Tribal" hut. The little girl was sound asleep in Truck's huge arms.

"I had better put her to bed. Said Mara, rising from her seat on the log. She has had a long day. Do you wish to join us, Ta-rok, or have you more planning to do?"

"I'm kinda tired, myself." He said, rising from the log and casting a huge grin in his brother's direction.

"I'll walk you home." Said Jim, smiling as he realized the significance of his words.

As they made their way, through the slumbering village, Jim wondered how Sanda was doing. Since his brief encounter with Borsa, it took every bit of his restraint to keep from beating the hell out of the bully and sending him packing. "Women, like air, land and water should always be cared for and protected." He remembered his old Grandfather saying. "His day is coming! He thought. I promise you that!"

As they neared the woman's hut, Mara bid him a good night. Taking the still-sleeping Gia from Truck's arms, she carried her inside.

"Well, Jimbo! It looks like were gonna be busier den hell, in dese next days."

"I just hope we're not biting off more than we can chew, Truck. But, I guess it has to be done. He said, draping an arm over his brother's shoulder. Eventually, they would be exterminated from their own world."

"You're right about dat, big brother. If dey don't do this now, dere ain't gonna be many more chances."

The serenity of a nocturnal setting has a tendency to lull those, still awake to enjoy it, into a calm state. Hardship doesn't appear to be as serious as you thought it was, during the day. Stress loosens its hold on our minds. The dark quiet baths our souls in hope.

As the two men, silently, thanked their God for bringing them together and thought about the perilous adventure ahead of them, loud shouting, from a hut further up the line, invaded the night quiet.

"That sounds like Borsa! Jim said, as he raced in the direction of the commotion. Truck was close on his heels.

"But, Borsa, it is my duty to my village. Sanda's voice echoed into the still night. I must go with them!"

"You are my woman! Borsa's gruff voice rasped. You go only where I say!" The sound of something breaking followed his words.

Rushing into the small hut, Jim discovered Borsa standing over the woman. She was lying in the remains of a small table that had been shattered, alongside the sleeping platform. Blood was running from her nose.

Without hesitation, Jim grabbed the big man by the back of his neck and pulled him out of the hut. A powerful shove deposited the bully into the cold fire pit.

"I warned you once before, you son of a bitch, to keep your filthy hands off of her. Jim roared, lividly. Tonight, one of us is going to sleep in hell!"

Regaining his feet and wiping ashes out his eyes, he glared at Jim. "You dare enter my hut uninvited! He bellowed. I will kill you for this!"

"Bring it on, fat ass! This dance is long over do."

Looking over Jim's shoulder, he pointed. "I see you have brought your sibling to help you."

Truck, standing a dozen paces away, said; "Dis fight is between you and my brother. I ain't gonna butt in. Then, a big smile transformed his face, as he said; "You'd already be dead if dat's what I wanted ta do.

With his attention momentarily distracted, Jim was taken by surprise. Borsa charged into him like a mad bull, pinning his arms to his side and driving him to the ground. Gasping for breath, he lay there, pinned to the ground, under three hundred pounds of unyielding flesh. Before the last of the life-giving oxygen was driven from his lungs, he brought his knee up with a vicious thrust to Borsa's groin. It was enough to loosen the death grip, slightly, allowing him to pull one arm free from the crushing pressure at his sides.

Punch after punch, he launched on the bearded face. Nose and lips bleeding and one eye already starting to close, he released his grip on the American and staggered to his feet.

Restoring oxygen to his starved lungs, Jim groggily regained his feet. The cruel eyes of the bully went wide as Jim waded in.

This wasn't supposed to be happening! He thought to himself. Everything he had ever caught in his powerful embrace died there.

A left hand came as a blur out of the night and broke his nose. The next, a right hand, crushed his jaw.

Borsa staggered backward, instinctively staying on his feet. His eyes were wide in panic. His entire face, dripping with blood, in atonement for all the weaker individuals he had harmed.

On, the American came. Reeling blow after blow on the face, into the ample stomach, it didn't really matter. In his rage, as long as it contacted flesh he was happy. This bastard would never be allowed another chance to abuse anyone.

Finally, the big man toppled over on his back, his face swimming with blood and American knuckles. He was out cold, barely breathing. Still, the relentless attack continued. The face turned to pulp right before his eyes. Even after he was jerked to his feet, from behind, Jim's fists kept searching for that ugly face.

"Whoa, Jimbo! Truck yelled. Take it easy! I think he's had enough."

Relaxing every muscle in his body, he collapsed into his brother's arms, exhausted. Staring at what used to be borsa, he sank to his knees.

Truck kept a comforting arm over his shoulders. "It's over, Jim. Relax! Da bastard had it coming."

After a while, enough air was restored to his lungs, enabling him to speak. "I couldn't stop, Truck! After what he did to Sanda, I didn't want to."

Kneeling over the bleeding bear of a man, Truck said; "He ain't gonna hurt no one, again, Jim. He's dead!"

"Another set of arms encircled his neck. "Are you hurt, Gem?"

Looking at the beautiful tear-streaked face, he noticed her puffy nose still leaking blood out of one nostril. "I am fine, Sanda. He said in a quiet voice. He won't hurt you ever again."

Looking over his brother, who was still kneeling by the body, he noticed Bantor and several others, staring at him in awe. What would be his punishment for having killed one of their people? He wondered. He would gladly do it again if anyone tried to hurt Sanda.

"We observed the entire incident, Earthman. His visit to his ancestors was long over do. Said Bantor. We will take care of the body." It took three men to accomplish this. Then, they all departed.

"Ya gonna be alright, Jim?" Truck asked.

"I think I'll be better than I ever was. Jim answered, rising to his feet and putting an arm around Sanda's waist.

"Well, I think I'll go home den. He said, with a big smile on his face. "Sleep well big brother."

"As well as you will, Truck." He replied, returning the smile.

Quiet, once again, returned to the night. At least two more people were happier than before it had begun.

# CHAPTER 7

The "Army of Destiny" passed through the village gates, shortly after the first sun brightened the new day. Over seven hundred men, women and older boys set out with hopes of ridding themselves of their alien oppressors.

Each "soldier" was outfitted with bow and arrows, sharp flint knives, spear, water gourd, sleeping furs, firestones and an adequate supply of dried meat. Over one hundred trained men carried the alien weapons across their shoulders. Confidence and determination was in the hearts of the majority. Doubts and fear were in the souls of the rest. Some, possibly all, would not return.

The Earth brothers, along with Bantor, were at the head of the mass of novice warriors, stretching a half a mile behind them. Six scouting parties, consisting of ten men each, were fanned out two miles ahead of the main body.

The estimated travel time, to the enemy city, would be, approximately, fourteen days if the large envoy could maintain a twenty-mile-a-day pace and avoid any major incidents. They had waited a lifetime for this moment. A few days here or there wouldn't make much of a difference, at this point.

The spirited group in the lead conversed among themselves as they trudged along. "I still don't agree with some of the selections made for this venture. Jim said. On my world, women were rarely put on the front lines."

"That is not the way of this world, Earth brother. Bantor replied. Every person born is instilled with a sense of duty and loyalty to their village. The choices, they make, are their own. If they wish to stay behind and protect the weak or go into battle, they would be fulfilling their obligation."

"We are well aware of these natural-born decisions that have to be made. Chimed in Greg. But, at the same time, it makes it extremely hard to concentrate fully, on the battlefield, when your mind is preoccupied with your own preservation and protecting someone alongside of you whom you care deeply."

"I wish, with all my heart, I could experience that situation. Bantor responded. To have my mate fighting alongside of me, at that moment, would give me great pleasure."

"I am truly sorry, my friend! Greg replied, feeling selfish. I completely overlooked your dilemma."

"I am, too! Added Jim, sheepishly. Forgive me!"

There is no need for apologies, Earthmen. I understand your concern."

Truck, marching along to their rear, overheard the conversation. "You guys worry too much! Da women can take care a demselves all right. Some of dem are even better with da bow and arrow den some a da men. He said. Dere's even a few carrying dos rods dat are better den a lot a da men."

The three men in front of him remained silent, so he continued. "At least, while dere here, we can protect dem. Just think about how much worrying you'd be doin if dey was left back in da village."

Bantor and his two brothers smiled at each other.

"I hadn't thought about that, Truck. Said Greg. But, you are absolutely right! From now on, I shall leave the worrying up to you."

"Fat chance a dat happening!" Truck responded, returning their smiles.

The mid-day sun had just replaced her sister, sending its relentless heat down upon the advancing natives. The moss covered plain, was devoid of trees. In the distance, a thick forest beckoned to them with its promising shade.

Not one word of complaint was uttered throughout the entire ranks. As they made their way toward this refuge, from the tortuous rays beating down on them, their pace seemed to quicken.

Periodically, a man from one of the many scouting groups would return and inform them of the situation ahead. In the first five hours of the trek, their luck was holding strong. No enemy movement had been spotted. Surprise was paramount to this mission.

After the last scout had been sent back to rejoin his party, Bantor looked back at the following horde. He noticed the ones at the far end picking up the pace. A cool respite from the punishing sun provided incentive to their tired legs and it rested, invitingly, just a short distance away.

"When we draw near the forest, I think it wise for the four of us to filter back through our people and check for any problems. Bantor said. We must be strong, when we reach our destination. We will rest ahead!"

The brothers agreed as one. They hadn't had a chance to check on the women since leaving the village. Their time was implemented, in these last five hours, by discussing strategy and keeping a vigilant watch for approaching danger. If only one set of alien eyes discovered them, it could jeopardize their mission. They must stay alert!

As the head of the column neared to within one hundred yards of the forest, the four men dropped back and made their way through the ranks of tired troops, reassuring all they met as they passed.

Gazes of uncertainty reflected from the eyes of many, already resigned to the likelihood, this might be the last journey they would ever take. The nervous banter vibrated through the crowd in small waves. Sprinkled throughout the advancing army were smiles and occasional laughter. But, the overall consensus was; morale was ebbing.

"If the confidence of these poor natives doesn't show improvement, what kind of mental condition will they be in once we reach our objective? Jim asked himself. Because of the overwhelming odds they were about to face, everyone had to be sharp. Time will tell, I guess."

Just then, he spotted Sanda making her way toward him. Her lithe movements and dust- covered beauty made him smile. "How you holding up, Sanda?" He asked, helping her off with her backpack.

"A little tired, Gem. She answered. Other than that I am fine."

He gave her a big hug and a quick kiss on the forehead. "You are, definitely, the prettiest sight I have seen all day." He said, with a big smile.

"Considering there hasn't been too much to gaze upon this day, other than hills and moss, I will still take that as a compliment." She responded, smiling up at the Earthman.

"You know, where ever we go, you will always be the most beautiful sight around."

"Thank you, Gem! She said, a little uncomfortably. It will take me a while to accept compliments, again."

"You may take forever, my dear." He said, looking into her beautiful eyes.

Since the night he had killed Borsa, they had become constant companions. At first, he wanted to be with her, to comfort her. Soon, he realized he needed no excuse at all. He was in love with her.

The emotional and physical degradation, she had experienced, left deep scars. They would take time to heal and he had all the time of two worlds to help her.

Greg and Truck had found Lona and Mara in the crowd and joined their brother.

When the entire body of travelers was safely concealed in the luxurious cool arms of the forest, they split into small groups.

A spring was located, belching its sweet, ice-cold liquid into a large pool. They drank their fill and replenished their water gourds, while others frolicked in the pool located just yards away. Refreshed, after removing the dust and grime accumulated during their arduous march, they appeared to be in better spirits.

"This is just what the doctor ordered! Jim said, resting against the bole of a large tree. Their confidence needed a little dusting off."

"Dat sure felt good! Truck said, removing water from one of his ears with a finger. He had been one of the first to plunge into the cool pond. How long we gonna be here?" He asked bantor, seated on a log a few paces from him.

"I am anxious to leave, shortly, Ta-rok. He answered. But, this place is good for them. When all feel rested, will be soon enough."

"Dat answers my question! Truck replied, with a confused expression on his face. At least, I think it did. Rising to his feet, he held his hand out to Mara. Come on, sweet lady! Let's go for a walk." A knowing smile passed between them as she accepted his hand and they disappeared into the woods.

"Don't get lost, Truck!" Greg yelled after them, smiling.

Lona, sitting at his side, whispered into his ear. The flush of red covering his face, told the others she wanted to go "exploring", also.

Rising to their feet, Greg quickly stammered; "Lona wishes to see how her cousin is faring." With that said, they left.

"I thought her cousins were all too old to make this trip. Jim said, smiling. Aren't they back at the village?"

Sanda gave him an elbow in the ribs and smiled back at him. "Yes they are, Gem! But, I don't think they intended to find her."

He exploded into laughter at his own naivety and was soon joined by Sanda and Bantor.

"There must be something magical in this spring water. The native leader chimed in. Everyone wishes to go exploring."

This precipitated more laughter.

Jim thought to himself. He, too, would like to kidnap Sanda, take her to a quiet place in the woods and make love to that beautiful body, cover her gorgeous lips with kisses. But, she was not ready. All in due time, he sighed inwardly.

Bantor felt uncomfortable. "These two are not leaving on my account. He thought to himself. Maybe I should make up an excuse and leave them alone."

"Bantor, something has been bothering me since the decision was made to attack the invaders." Jim said.

Abandoning his previous plan to leave, curiosity kept him rooted to the log. "What is it that troubles you, my brother?" He asked, staring questioningly at the Earthman.

"You are well aware that my brothers and I were held captives in their city for, God only knows, how long."

"Yes! It is common knowledge to everyone." Bantor replied, looking at the American questioningly.

"While we were there, Jim continued, we were treated half-way decent by a couple of the residents. Mokar, their "High Teacher" and the little slave "Moki" were vicariously instrumental in our escape. Mokar gave us the knowledge of this world and the various native tribes and the little slave brought us the tool we needed to cut our way to freedom. Jim paused, staring across at Bantor, who still had the confused look on his face. Unknowingly to Mokar, at the time, the use of his information helped us locate some of your people."

Bantor, sat in silence, wondering where all of this was leading to.

"If, or I should say when, we gain entrance to their city and the killing begins, will none of their lives be spared? Or, will the killing not stop until the last of them are wiped out of your world?"

Bantor hesitated for a moment before he spoke. "In all of my existence, I have never had to consider the possibility of this situation becoming a reality. You have seen with your own eyes, the horrible deeds they are capable of. I hated them before they murdered my newborn and subjected my mate to humiliation and other degrading horrors."

"But, Bantor! Jim interrupted. You know, yourself, there are Zarnogs, Borsas and Corbas wherever one goes in this world. Would you condemn the majority for the vicious acts of a few? Jim continued. I love all the people in this village. But, I hated Borsa for the pain and abuse he dealt to Sanda."

"You ask me to pick and choose the ones I will allow my people to kill? He asked, perplexed. How can I do this?"

"No, Bantor, of course not! Jim cut in. I do know, some of them will not bear arms against us. The ones I have mentioned will be among them. We both understand this is a war, kill or be killed. If someone is trying to harm you, by all means, defend yourself."

"Then I see no possible solution, Earth brother. In the midst of a conflict, all are vulnerable."

A veil of quiet fell over them for a few moments. Each man pondering what he had just heard and what he felt inside.

Sanda, silently listening to the debate, spoke. "Both of you are good men who think not only with your minds, but also with your hearts. I have suffered at the hands of both invader and my own kind. My father and mother were killed by the invaders. I hated them all. What could I do? No one had ever shown me any kindness. Borsa abused me every chance he could. I hated him! But, other men have been kind to me. Patting Jim on the arm, she continued. This man protects me and professes his love for me. Should I overlook this and continue to hate all men because of what Borsa did to me?"

Both men stared at Sanda. The meaning of her words was quite evident. "A kindness given is given in return".

After a few more moments of silence, Bantor rose from the log. "I believe it is my turn to cool off." Running toward the pool he leapt in, causing a big splash.

# CHAPTER 8

A few hours later, the weary group of travelers felt, somewhat, refreshed and began making preparations to leave. The cool refuge was alive with a positive atmosphere, much better than they had arrived with. As they exited the serene woods, at the same point they had entered, Bantor spotted a lone figure racing in their direction. He recognized Roca's long strides, quickly, eating up the distance between them. Soon, he stood before the leader, gasping for breath. "Bantor, you must hurry! He said, excitedly. A large party of invaders has Parva's group surrounded."

"How far away are they?" Bantor asked, in alarm.

"They are holding up in a small gully, about, a mile from where we stand. His young lungs, finally, back to normal. I will lead you to them!"

Turning to the brothers, who had overheard the exchange, he said; "Drop back and inform the rest. The faster ones must hurry to the front. The others must follow at their best pace!"

It wasn't long before a third of the army's numbers followed, followed closely on Roca's heels. The sandal-shod feet of the party flew over the mossy plain in urgency. They could not allow their numbers to be diminished. Every man was a vital instrument in this venture and would be protected at all costs.

As they neared a slow rise to a ridge, Roca slowed his pace, slightly. When Bantor pulled alongside, he informed him of the situation just ahead of them. "Parva and his men are trapped in a small rock-strewn gulch fifty yards from here. The invaders must have surprised them from this same rise we are approaching. He continued. I was returning from my party, beyond those hills to the left, when I came upon them. I had to give them a wide berth so I wouldn't be detected."

Unnoticed by the two lead men, the three Earthmen had pulled even with them. "How many of them are there?" Jim asked.

"I counted about one hundred, while I hastened to bring word. He answered. There may be more or less."

As they approached the summit of the small ridge, they slowed their pace and slowly peered over the edge. The scene below didn't look too promising. Closer to two hundred aliens were pouring a relentless barrage into a cluster of large rocks, twenty-five yards before them.

The invaders were spread out in a horseshoe formation, slowly enclosing the circle. Their backs were to the native army spying down on them.

Every now and then a figure would rise from the rock barricade and loose an arrow, in futility, toward the encroaching danger. They didn't have much time.

As the last men joined them on the ridge, orders were given to spread out. Using whatever cover availed them, they advanced as quickly as they could on the rear of the alien army. If they didn't attack soon, the trapped men would be lost.

"Now!" Shouted Bantor, as he loosed a bolt of energy into the back of an unsuspecting alien.

As one, the native army rained bolt after bolt of energy and arrow alike. In moments, the invaders were reduced to small groups of individuals, fleeing east and west for their lives. They were hunted down to the man. The native invasion was still a secret!

Two of the beleaguered men from the scouting party were dead. The rest suffered various wounds, only one seriously. Not one man or woman, among the charging rescuers, suffered as much as a scratch.

As they waited for the rest of the main body to catch up, they patched up the wounded men and buried their dead comrades. The alien carcasses were piled together in shallow graves and covered with rocks. Almost two hundred more of the alien rods were added to their arsenal.

"If luck continues to favor us at this rate, it would be possible to decimate the entire Nevoan population within a year." Greg said.

"It's kinda like da bear baiting some people use at home. Truck added. Dis will help us, big time!"

"I do not understand why, of late, they are sending out so many patrols. Said Bantor. Small groups of ten or twenty would scatter around the land, killing a few unwary natives. The large party that attacked your siblings in the hills and now, this."

"I think, when we destroyed their mining camp and killed their caretakers, we hit them where it really hurts. Said Jim. Their whole economy revolves around that blue stone."

"Undoubtedly, Jim! That is a big part of the reason. But, I feel Zarnog's over-inflated ego is the primary factor. Greg piped in. It's a good bet, nothing like this has ever occurred to the great "Nevoan" race since they polluted this world."

"Dat's okay with me. Said Truck. Let dat bastard keep sending em to us. Before ya know it, dey won't have any more ta send."

The main body of the native convoy had finally caught up. It was decided they would head for the little tree-lined valley, Roca discovered on his return. It was a little better than three miles to the east.

As the third sun of the day had nearly given up its place in the sky, the entire hoard was comfortably entrenched within the narrow confines of the fertile valley. A small, shallow stream flowed through its entire length. Sentries were posted. No fires were lit. Ten new men were sent out to replace the wounded scouting party, three miles ahead.

Small groups huddled together. The quiet emanating, from so many people, was uncanny. Left to their own devices and under different circumstances, they would be celebrating. Tonight, no unnecessary noises would give them away. After the victorious battle, earlier, confidence soared. Many of the vague, frightened looks that fogged eyes in the beginning now held a sparkle. Laughter was more prevalent than before.

As most of the native horde succumbed to the beckoning warmth of their furs, a small group huddled around Bantor. Furs were draped over shoulders, to ward off the brisk night chill. In the distance kazors screamed their warnings into the darkness. The starlit sky sparkled down on them, adding to the peaceful ambience.

"For almost three days, old kazar kept Graci clinging to the high branches of that tree." He told the small audience. The story of how his mother and father had met was a favorite among his people. Leota and Graci were the former head man and head woman of their village. Bantor had been urged by Lona to tell the story for the benefit of the Earth brothers.

"Leota, as he was known to do, was off alone, hunting. Bantor continued. On this given day, he was tracking a Lurda he had wounded. When he had noticed the Kazor lounging under the tree, he started to give it a wide berth. Just then, he detected movement in the foliage, above the large beast. It was Graci! She, too, liked to go off by herself foraging or hunting." Bantor smiled at the rapt audience. He never tired of telling his story and they never got tired of listening. This night was special. He had three sets of Earthly ears piqued. "Leota was in a quandary. He continued. He had but one spear left and his knife. Maybe he should race back to the village and get help. But another look at the unfortunate girl, in the tree, told him that that would not be wise.

"Her skin was reddened from the thermal rain and it looked to him that one good shake of the tree, by the beast, would dislodge her from her precarious perch."

"Hidden behind a tree, he made up his mind. Dashing across the twenty yards separating them, he lowered his spear. As fate would have it, the "killer of killers" turned while he was still a few yards away. His momentum carried him into the beast and his spear became imbedded into its left eye.

"Screaming its rage and wrenching the spear from Leota's hands, it charged the impetuous native. Doing a quick about face, he raced back to the tree he had previously hidden behind. Scurrying up into the safety of its branches, an instant before the tooth-filled jaws manicured a little foliage inches from his feet."

Jim stared around at the small group trying to pick up some sort of hint as to whether this story was fact or fiction. The three women who had, obviously, heard this story many times before sat entranced. Truck winked back at him when he noticed Jim looking in his direction. Greg just shrugged, letting him know he was thinking along the same line of thought.

As Bantor paused to take a drink of water, he looked at the faces in the small group. Expectant eyes told him to continue with his story. "It is getting late, my friends. Maybe I should finish my story another time."

"Not if ya want me ta come over dere and squeeze da rest of it outta ya pal. Truck said, smiling. Now, get on with it!"

"Yes! Please continue." Greg said, intrigued.

Nodding his head, bantor continued. "All that day, Leota and Graci conversed from their leafy havens. Our village was much bigger then. They had never met until now.

"She had been trapped in that tree since yesterday morning. The hot sun was taking its toll. Her lips were cracked and her body was baked red.

"Leota! She yelled. If I don't get some water, soon, I fear I shall faint right out of this tree."

"I have a full gourd! He said, holding it out so she could see. Come on over and I'll share it with you."

This caused Graci to start laughing and she almost lost her grip on the large branch she was clinging to.

Concern for her safety wiped the smile off of his face in a hurry. "I didn't mean for that to happen. He shouted across the distance. "I am sorry!"

"No need to apologize. She said in her sweet voice. You would not be in this predicament if it weren't for me. It is I who is sorry."

"Before we say or do another thing, I want you to take your wrap off and tie yourself to the tree. He shouted. I'll figure a way out of this." Looking around him, he observed the tree he was in was not close enough to another. Escaping from one tree to another was out of the question. Next, he searched through the branches in his abode until he located a relatively straight branch, approximately, six feet long and two inches in diameter. Taking out his knife, he quickly cut it from the mother tree. He pared away the smaller branches protruding from it and started carving the end into a long, sharp point.

"I have an idea! He yelled across at Graci. I'll only have one chance at it to make it work, so listen, closely. If I can lure that beast close enough, I might be able to put out its other eye. If I am successful, get out of the tree as quickly and quietly as you can and head back to the village."

"I will not leave you in danger, Leota!" She replied.

"Don't worry about me, Graci. I'll be right behind you. But, just remember, the Kazor has excellent hearing. Be as quiet as you can. Okay?"

"Very well! She replied. As long as you are leaving with me."

"Here goes nothing!" He said as he descended lower in the tree. When he attained a point he thought would be just above the creature's reach, he started yelling and shaking branches. He got the beast's attention, as it sauntered closer to the limb he was balanced on. Green ooze bubbled from its punctured eye, as it raged its frustration. Tapping it on its head with his rustic spear, he yelled over to Graci. Get ready!"

Taking careful aim on the one good eye, he let go of the branch he was clutching to. Swaying, slightly, on his perilous perch, he gripped the end of the spear tightly with both hands and plunged it down with all the force he could muster.

The sharpened point sunk into the eye with a squish. The roars intensified, as the beast staggered around in circles, now, completely blind.

Descending, quickly, Leota yelled. "Run Graci!"

The need for a quiet escape was unnecessary. The bellowing roars drowned out every natural sound indigenous within a five-mile area. The two captives eventually made their way back to the village. From that episode on, they were inseparable. They mated and I am the result of their immense love for each other." He finished.

After a brief lull, the night calm returned.

"What happened ta dem?" Truck asked, when he realized the story had come to an end.

"One day, about twenty summers ago, they went out with a hunting party. They were never heard from again. My mother's sibling, Kaba, has raised me as his own son."

"Now, my friends, it is time to rest. We have many miles to make up tomorrow."

As the last of the weary horde crawled into their sleeping furs, a distant roar disrupted the nocturnal quiet, an ironic tribute to Leota and Graci.

# CHAPTER 9

For the next six days and over one hundred miles later, the large group trudged, steadily, on. No enemy patrols had been sighted during this time. The closer they came to their objective, however, the more ambivalent they became. It was something they knew must be done. But, the outcome was in question. Small arguments had to be quelled, on a daily basis. There was even talk, by some, of abandoning this "fool hardy" endeavor and returning to their village.

The mid-day sun had just taken its place, in the heavens, when Bantor called a halt. "I think it would benefit everyone if we were to take an extended rest period. He said to Jim, walking alongside him. The grumbling gets louder with every mile. A small herd of lurdas has been sighted a few miles from here. I think a short break to rejuvenate their travel-weary muscles and a little fresh meat might restore spirits."

"That sounds good to me! Jim replied. I'm getting a little tire of dried meat, myself."

As the column came to a stop, bunching up behind the lead man, he informed them of his intentions. Word was spread throughout the following throng. Camp was quickly set up at the foot of a small escarpment. Many trees dotted the immediate area, providing sufficient shade for the weary mass. Springs bubbled their life-giving liquid from five different locations, scattered at the base of the cliff.

Greg and Truck had started the day in the company of Lona and Mara. Sanda walked with a group of women further back in the moving mass.

It wasn't long before Bantor had a group of fifty men sitting around him. Drawing a map in the dirt at his feet, he informed them where the herd had been last seen. "If we are fortunate enough to locate them in this area, we can descend upon them from the surrounding hills. Parlon, returning from one of the scouting parties, believes they will remain there for a while. He counted one old bull, twelve cows and six calves. The old bull was spotted first, standing on a rise and guarding his family. That is the one that must die first or his alarm will scatter the rest."

The Earthmen volunteered to take out the guardian.

After a few more preparations, they left camp. Besides bows and arrows, each man shouldered one of the alien weapons.

Bantor, walking abreast with the three brothers, scanned the horizon. "Over that next ridge, about a mile away and we shall find out if they wait for us."

As they walked in silence, Truck began thinking about Bantor's story from the night before. "Bantor! He said. Do ya think dere's a chance of your parents being alive?"

"I cannot say, Ta-rok. Hope lingers in ones heart for a long time. Especially, when it is for the ones you love so dearly. But, after many summers, it dwindles. A part of me still wishes to believe they were taken captive and I might, yet, find them. But that part of me gets smaller and smaller as the summers go by."

"Don't give up hope, pal! Dey could be hidden in dat city someplace. If dey are, ya can bet your ass we'll find em."

"Your optimism has helped me many times before, my brother. Thank you! I shall not give up hope."

As they walked a little further, in silence, Bantor came to a sudden stop. "Ta-rok! He yelled. Does this area not seem familiar to you?"

Turning in a slow circle and scanning about him, the big guy answered. "I don't think so. Why?"

"We passed this way after escaping the pit. One days march in that direction, pointing to the left of them, would bring us in the area."

"As long as we are this close don't you think we should take this opportunity and investigate? Greg chimed in. They may have started up operations again."

"Ya gotta agree ta dat, Bantor. We don't want dem bastards hurting anymore people. Do we?"

"After we return to our camp, we will discuss it. Bantor answered. But, now, let us continue our hunt."

A short time later, the herd was located, surrounded and slaughtered in its entirety. They were skinned and butchered, quickly. The meat was wrapped in the tough hides and hung from poles, balanced on sturdy shoulders. Amazingly, the hunt had taken only a few hours. After surrounding the herd, the alien artillery made quick work of it. The most strenuous part was hauling all that meat back to camp.

As no alien patrols had been detected in the surrounding area, for quite some time, Bantor felt safe enough to light fires. Soon, the smell of meat roasting permeated throughout the camp. Because of the promise of fresh meat and a prolonged rest, tempers mellowed and friendly banter, once again, found a home.

"If we send out a scouting party, in a couple of days we would know for sure whether or not the pit is active again. Said Bantor. If it is not, the extra exertion will have been placed on only a few. All are weary from traveling."

"And if it is?" Jim asked.

Then, the majority will be well rested and we will liberate those poor souls. Bantor answered. Ta-rok and I, along with six others, will form the scouting party. We know the fastest and safest route to the pit and mine."

The huge assembly of natives fanned out from the small escarpment, dotting the mossy plain with activity. Many fires burned in their midst, giving a soft glow to the encroaching dusk. Laughter and song peppered the peaceful atmosphere from one group or another. The succulent smells of roasting meat and vegetables contributed to the serene ambience.

"May I interject something I've given considerable thought to?" Greg piped in.

The discussion continued. Many observers had moved closer to the small group of men, listening silently.

"What is on your mind, Earth brother?" Bantor asked.

"It concerns the mine and the abundant store of crystals Truck told me about. We can destroy their pit and buildings continuously, but they will just rebuild."

"What are you getting at, Greg?" Jim asked.

"The only sensible thing to do is close down their economy. Obliterate the source. With these weapons, we have captured from them, we are more than capable of doing some damage."

"Dat's a damn good idea, little brother! Truck joined in. We could seal dat mine entrance and bring da mountain down on dat pile a glass. I think it's worth a shot, Bantor."

"Once the situation at the pit is learned, we will take that walk to the mine, Ta-rok. I promise you! Get some rest, now! We leave at first light."

As most of the people retreated to their furs, Jim walked with Sanda toward one of the springs. Taking a long drink of the cool liquid, they splashed themselves and removed some of the dust clinging to their bodies.

Sitting alongside the small pool with his arm draped, protectively, over her shoulders, they listened to the nocturnal orchestra. A teasing breeze crept upon them, now and then, raising goose bumps on their flesh. The many fires, scattered up and down the small valley, flickered in the night breeze, revealing the skeletal remains of their carnivorous repast. The night sky twinkled down on them from a multitude of stars.

"Your world is very peaceful at night, Sanda. Jim said, interrupting their solitude. It makes one wish it would last forever."

"Is it so different from the nights on your world, Gem?" She asked in, in a soft voice.

"Oh, we have places which are serene constantly. But, most of my world has accustomed itself to bright lights, fast paces and loud noises. He answered. Sometimes a person has to travel for quite a distance to find a little peace."

"I would not feel comfortable knowing I would have to escape to enjoy a little serenity. But, I can understand what it would feel like. She replied. Every time Borsa started to abuse me I wanted to run away to that safe place."

Jim sighed and looked away from her. She noticed the pained look on his face before he had turned and asked him what was wrong.

"Borsa is dead!" He said, looking back into her eyes.

"Uh, I know that." She said, confusedly.

"Sometimes, I'm not so sure you do, Sanda." Before she had a chance to respond, he continued. "Ever since that day I opened my eyes and saw you sitting there, I wanted you; heart soul and body. I know I am a stranger to your world and I don't pretend to know all of your customs, but, in my way, I have tried to let you know how I felt about you. At first, I thought maybe I was doing something wrong. But, there are no laws, on any world, against caring for someone. Borsa is still the problem. While he was alive he was hurting you. Even after his death, he is still causing you pain."

"I am sorry you feel that way, Gem. After all you have done for me I never meant to hurt you." She responded, her eyes glistening with tears.

"I know you didn't, Sanda. But, when I see Truck and Mara and Greg and Lona together, sharing their lives, I wish for the same."

"But, Gem, We spend much time together. Are we not sharing life?"

"Yes! The part of you that is not afraid pays me a visit every day. But, most of who you are is hidden away in the past."

"What do you want me to do, Gem? Am I to pretend it never happened?"

"Of course not! He said. We never forget our past, especially the bad things that happen."

She remained silent, tears leaking from the corners of her beautiful, dark eyes.

"My parents were killed in an accident, when my brothers and I were very young. Our Grandfather adopted us. Being the eldest, my hurt was more severe than my two brothers. It was hard for me to start trusting, again."

"What did you do, Gem?" She asked.

"For a while, I drew from the strength of the people around me. Soon, I was relying on my own strength and my confidence began to build. Grandfather used to tell us; "It is easy to let someone get close to you when feelings are high. But, during the sad times, closeness is needed the most. Trust others during these low times and, soon, you will learn to trust yourself, once again."

"Many, here, are concerned about you, Sanda. If you don't start trusting, you may never untangle your emotions and remain trapped in the past. He continued. I have fallen in love with you and just want you to be happy. If you want me to stay away from you until you've had time to sort things out, I will. If it will help."

"Oh, Gem! I didn't realize I was hurting so many people! She sobbed into his chest, as he wrapped his arms around her. I am so sorry."

"My darling! He said, holding her tightly. You are hurting yourself more than you are hurting anyone else."

The night was turning cooler, as they clung to each other. Their hearts and minds also bonded as they contemplated the situation.

"Gem! Will you spend the night with me, in my furs? She broke the silence. I am tired of being alone."

"It would be my pleasure, Sanda, if that is really what you want."

"Yes! That is really what I want!"

As the night continued its quiet journey toward day, they made their way, together, toward her furs.

# CHAPTER 10

As the first sun trickled her light and warmth over the horizon, the large throng of people rose from their furs and embraced the new day. Fires were started and many sat around drinking tea and picking at the left over roasts, still skewered over the large, cold fire pits. Some waited their turn at the small springs, with gourds and water skins in hand. The overall attitude had improved considerably during this short respite.

It was even more evident in at least two. Jim and Sanda had risen before the slumbering camp stirred. They had bathed in one of the small pools and made love, again, as the warm rays from the first sun joined them. The noticeable spring in their step and smiles on their faces advertised their undeniable love for one another. Although they had slept little, they welcomed the new day and all it would bring. As they approached a small group clustered around a fire, their happiness was so obvious it spread to the others.

"Good morning, big brother! Truck greeted. Ya look like ya just won da big lottery."

Smiling back at the big guy and looking down on Sanda at his side, he replied. "I think I did, Truck!"

Lona, seated next to Greg, held out two gourds of steaming tea. "Would you like some tea? She asked. It's a blend I've been experimenting with."

"Thank you! Said Sanda, accepting it from her. It smells delicious!"

"Umm. This is good! Said Jim, after taking a sip. What's in it?"

"I took some leaves from the Crometta tree, dried and crushed them. Then, I did the same with the thin roots connected to the floating leaves in streams. Add a pinch of crushed Hermus vine and a little honey and there you have it. She smiled. It's quite simple, actually!"

"You never give yourself enough credit. Said Bantor. Your cooking skills are well known. Everyone looks forward to sampling one of your new creations."

"Thank you, Bantor! But, compliments are not necessary. I just enjoy cooking."

"Maybe dat's what puts da starch in my root. Truck said, with a big smile on his face as he looked at Mara. Why do ya think I'm always asking for seconds?"

The true intent of his words caused the small group to erupt into laughter. So contagious was it, everyone within earshot joined in.

A short time later, the levity of the small gathering shifted, as talk defected toward battle plans. Preparations were made and an hour later Bantor, Truck and six others left camp. Burdened with only their weapons, they traveled at a fast pace. The mossy terrain, silently, cushioned their strides, as they moved toward their objective. Making their way down a gradual incline, they entered a small, boulder-filled depression. It, slowly, opened up into a broad plain, ringed on two sides by low, tree-studded hills. Off in the distance, approximately a mile away was a high ridge.

"When we reach that large hill, we will rest." Bantor said, pointing directly in front of them.

"Dis is starting ta look familiar. Truck enjoined. If I'm right, wer about halfway dere."

"Right, my brother! We should see it from the top of this approaching rise."

As they neared the high promontory, Bantor and Truck hoped upon hope they would find the pit vacant. For almost one hundred years, it was synonymous with pain and degradation to his people. Today it would end, if they were fortunate. Scrambling up the long, slanting side of the ridge, they slowed their momentum as they neared the top. Peering, cautiously over the rim, they espied their objective, nearly three miles away.

To those who have spent even one hour in that dehumanizing hole, the sight of the ugly depression was unforgettable. They were still too far away to detect any movement, so they rested.

"I think our safest route would be to circle wide to our right and approach it from the low hills to the south of it. Said Bantor. It will provide us with a little coverage, at least."

"Dat should be close enough for us ta see if dos bastards are starting dere shit again." Added Truck.

Picking their way down the steep slope, the eight men were soon jogging across the mossy carpet. A short time later, they came to the foot of a small cluster of hills. Crawling to the top of one, they peered down at the pit, only two hundred yards away. All their questions were answered, as they detected movement around the edge of the pit.

Two alien sentries lounged around the near end, with their backs to the observers. Their lackluster approach toward duty was a familiar sight to the two former tenants. Once before, this had contributed to their plans. For all of their purposed intelligence, the Nevoans lacked in the area of security, especially in this forsaken outpost.

"Only two sentries, Ta-rok. You realize what this means?"

"Most a dem poor bastards are in da mine working dere asses off. Truck replied. Dese guys don't give up. Do dey?"

"If they keep the same schedule we were on, they won't be back for many hours. What do you think, Ta-rok?"

"I say we kill da two sonuva bitches down dere, free who's ever in da hole and head for da mine."

"I do not feel like waiting an entire day either, my brother. Let's do it!"

Using what coverage the terrain allowed, they made their way toward the unsuspecting aliens. They got to within fifty feet of them, before one happened to turn in their direction. Before he could utter a sound, his body pieces were flying into the pit below. His comrade's gory debris followed immediately. Looking cautiously around for other sentries that may have been hidden from their sight, they approached the lip of the "hell hole" and peered into it.

Two dirt-encrusted, emaciated faces stared up at them. The gaunt look in their eyes told the rescuers that these poor men were far beyond being shocked by a little bloody carnage raining down on them. The eight men, quickly, wrestled the huge ramp into the pit and helped the two elders to the top. "Darbo and Pella had Kaba's old job. They served the hungry mine workers their two skimpy meals.

They soon learned from the elders, the other sixteen men had left earlier for the mine. They were escorted by six of the aliens. This new group of laborers had been here about two months. Seven of the original number had already perished.

The two old natives were led to the shade, near by, provided by a cluster of large rocks. They were given water and pieces of dried meat, which was a feast to their starving bodies. After assuring them they would be back soon, the eight natives set out toward the mine, less than a mile away.

As they passed through a small depression in the hilly terrain, they could make out the ominous mine loaming over the mossy plain five hundred yards ahead. Truck and three of the natives veered to the right. Bantor and the rest made their way toward the left.

They knew the alien "watch dogs" would be loitering around the mines entrance. One or two of them might be inside checking on the human gophers, toiling within its depths. Alien egos wouldn't allow for sentries, which made their approach from both sides easily attained. Hidden behind large boulders, they worked their way to within thirty yards of the yawning mine entrance.

Four aliens, clustered together, sat on large rocks, chatting. Their deadly staffs lay on the ground at their side. If the old men from the pit were correct, two more were in the mine or nearby.

At a signal from Bantor, the four aliens were reduced to a quivering heap of body parts. Immediately after firing they rushed the entrance, four on either side of the dark opening. They didn't have long to wait. Two of the creatures rushed from the cave, drawn by the low whistling sound made by the alien weapons. They were, literally, blown apart, after having taken only three paces into the daylight.

"Collect all the weapons and hide what is left of the bodies. Bantor ordered. Ta-rok! You and I will bring those poor men up into the sunlight. Grabbing burning torches from just inside the entry, they made their way into the foreboding depths. Exploring the shallow cuts to right and left of the main tunnel, they soon had a parade of bedraggled men following them. As they walked into the last cut, off the main tunnel, their torchlight reflected off of two filthy, emaciated faces. Bantor dropped his torch and rushed the two men, enfolding one of them in his strong arms. The surprised native stood there, frozen.

As soon as Truck saw Bantor drop his torch and dart into the narrow cut, he raced after him, anticipating trouble. The scene he bolted into was anything but. As one exhausted native sat with his back against a dirt wall, Bantor and the other native sobbed onto each other's shoulder.

"Leota, my father! Long have I thought you dead! How is this possible, after all these summers?" Bantor asked, with tears streaming down his cheeks.

"Take me out to the sunlight, my son. There, I will tell you everything."

By the time they finished marching the last man out of the mine, the first few had already drunk their fill and were resting in the shade. The dried meat, the men carried, disappeared into the half-starved stomachs in record time. It would tide them over until they returned to their camp.

Bantor sat with an arm draped over his father's shoulder, deep in conversation. Truck noticed, even through the layer of dirt, caking Leota's face, except for a few age lines and a sprinkle of silvery hair, they could have passed for twins. Both courage and determination shun through. While the other "miners" rested, Truck joined Bantor and his father and listened to Leota's story.

"Your mother and I were hunting pava in a thick forest about ten miles from the village. We had been successful, as four of the furry beasts hung from our shoulders. As we were making our way back to the village, we were detected by a large patrol of invaders. They, quickly, surrounded us. It was obvious they wanted to take us alive, as they hadn't fired their deadly weapons. I managed to kill two of them with my knife, before I was knocked unconscious. We were roped together with ten other captives, from different villages, and herded toward their city.

Graci and two other women were separated from us and we were led toward a large building. It is here they manufacture the deadly rods. For almost twenty summers I toiled, making those accursed weapons, all that time not knowing if Graci was alive or not. About two months ago, a small group of us were delivering some of these weapons to another part of the city. We passed a small party of women, laboring over large cooking pots. I spotted Graci, dropped the load I was carrying and raced toward her. I never made it. Graci saw me and started in my direction. One of the creatures hit her with his staff and she fell. I managed to wrest his staff away and started swinging. I busted a few heads, before I was knocked unconscious. The next day, they sent me to the mines. That was the first time I had seen my mate, since entering their city nearly twenty years before. Then, having her ripped away from me again, is more than I can endure."

"Father! We will free mother and all the rest. Bantor interrupted. Do not give up hope! Soon, we will not have these invaders to fear."

Looking at his son and the small handful of comrades who had liberated him, he smiled. Your army may have big hearts, my son, but you are far, outnumbered."

Bantor smiled back at his sire. Three short miles, from where we sit, are seven hundred friends and relatives. We are on our way to attack the invader's city."

Upon hearing this, the spark in Leota's eyes got even brighter. "Now, there are seven hundred and one." He said smiling.

"But, father, you need to regain your strength! I will appoint a small company to escort you, safely, back to the village.

"I will regain my strength, when your mother is by my side, once again. The elder replied. As everyone of her oppressors falls under my knife, I will feel rejuvenated."

Truck, listening and observing in silence until now, spoke. "He's your father, alright! He said, with a big smile on his face. Stubbornness must run in da family."

Staring at the big Earthman, Leota asked. "Who is this man and why is his talk so strange?"

"Forgive me father, and you also, Ta-rok! This reunion has made me forget my manners. Father! I would introduce you to my "Earth" brother, Ta-rok. He has saved my life countless times and inspired hope in me. Ta-rok! I would introduce you to Leota, my sire and leader of the Kletta village."

"I am happy ta meet ya, Leota!" Truck said, sticking out his right hand.

Staring questioningly at the proffered hand, He said; "I do not understand."

Taking Truck's hand in his, Bantor shook it. "It is a sign of friendship on Ta-rok's world."

Even more confused, Leota started to say something.

"I will explain everything in time." Bantor interrupted.

Turning to Truck, Leota said; "It is enough to know, for now, that you have aided my son. Extending his hand toward the big man he added; I am sure that, we too, shall become good friends."

Shaking the hand, Truck said, with a big smile on his face; "You can bet your ass on dat!"

The confused look returned to his face, as he looked at his son.

"Dere's one more thing I gotta do, before I leave. Said Truck. Get dese men moving and I'll meet ya back at da pit." Grabbing one of the alien weapons, he got up and raced into the alien mine.

Bantor gathered up the resting natives and began the slow march back to the pit. Although half starved and exhausted, the dirty troop of men had a slight spring in their step, put there by hope.

Approximately half way back to the pit, they heard a loud rumbling sound and felt a slight vibration beneath their feet. Staring back toward the mine, they observed a dark cloud spewing from it. It wasn't long before the slight breeze blowing from that direction, caught up with them. Soon, everyone was covered with dust from head to foot. It was hard to distinguish the rescuers from the rescued.

"What is happening?" Leota asked.

"I do not know, father. But, Ta-rok could be in danger!" Bantor answered, as he made his way through the thickening dust cloud. He was, approximately, one hundred yards from the mine, when he noticed someone heading in his direction. As the cloak of flying particles abated slightly, he recognized Truck stumbling toward him. Racing across the short gap separating them, he was soon at his side.

"What have you done now, Ta-rok?" He asked, putting an arm of support around the massive shoulders.

Startled for an instant by the sudden voice of his friend, trickling into his half-plugged ears, he stopped. A big smile cracked some of the dirt on his face, as he said; "I closed dat god damned mine down for good!"

By the time they had rejoined the others, most of the dirt was removed from their faces. The dust cloud had finally settled and they had spotted a small spring along the way. They helped each other excavate the clogging grit.

Truck explained what had happened shortly Bantor and the others had left the mine area. He had made his way through the mine to the vast pit they used to collect the crystal rock. Firing the native weapon into the pile of blue crystal had set off a chain reaction.

"Da moment I fired inta dat pile a glass, I started hearing dese popping sounds all around me, like little explosions. I raced like hell ta da entrance. Big chunks a rock was falling all over da place and just as soon as I got outside da cave, da whole mountain came down. I took off running as fast as I could, but dat dust cloud caught up wit me. I must a swallowed five pounds a dat shit."

Listening, incredulously, to his story, Bantor said; "Because of what you have endured, my brother, many people have been spared the degrading hopelessness we were forced to undertake."

"Ah, dere was nothing to it, Pal. Thanks for coming back an looking after me."

"That is what brothers are for, Ta-rok, to look after one another."

A little more than an hour later, the six men and their charges were comfortably settled in the large encampment. As the last sun of the day faded, dreams of victories, reunions and new beginnings grew. Tomorrow already seemed a better place.

# CHAPTER 11

A few days later found the small army marching soundlessly over the mossy plain. The closer they got, to their objective, the more scouting parties were sent out. A little more than twenty-five miles separated them from their fate. Except for Leota, all of the rescued men had returned to their respective villages. Vows of solidarity and aid were promised. But, they all knew, because of the distances between the scattered villages, reinforcements would be a long time in coming. In spite of this fact, spirits remained high. Leota, the headman of their village, had returned. He was loved and respected by all who knew him. The younger people had heard enough about his leadership to be inspired.

As he walked at the head of the large human wave, he chatted with Bantor. The nutritious food and quality rest, he had enjoyed over the last few days, strengthened his abused body and mind. The kindliness he received from friends and relatives took his spirits to a higher plateau.

Bantor looked at his father and noticed a bemused expression on his face. It wrinkled the brow, of the old leader, with deep creases.

"Are you all right, my father?" He asked.

"I am much better than I was a few days ago, thanks to you. Very soon, now, I will be reunited with my heart. Then, I will be a very happy man my son."

They walked in silence, for a while, when Bantor asked; "And, what if mother already walks with our ancestors? I have, long ago, given up hope of ever seeing either one of you again."

"Ah, hope is a precious thing. Is it not? He answered. Sometimes we hang on to it far too long. But, it will not make any difference in the end. Your mother and I will be together one way or another."

Looking at his father, with a touch of alarm in his voice, Bantor replied; "You talk as though you do not plan on returning to our village. You are headman of our people. We need you!"

"If a man is not happy, does it really matter where he settles? Leota answered. I would not make a good leader, with part of my heart missing."

"Father! I have missed my mother, as I have missed you. Bantor responded, excitedly. My mate, Cinda, is also a captive of the invaders. Many others care about me and depend on me. My Earth brothers have cleared my way of thinking. I was not going to return to the village without Cinda. Now, it would be selfish of me to throw my life away. He continued, more passionately. I will fight for more than just the love of my mate. I will fight for the survival of my people!" Bantor was so angry about his discovery, of what his father proposed, he quickened his pace and soon was far ahead of the trailing crusaders.

Leota smiled to himself. Bantor was a true product of his loins. The same heated determination flowed in his veins. Then, he thought to himself; "Could a man still be happy after the loss of a soul mate? Was there anything left worth living for? I will discover the answer to that, soon enough."

A little ways back in the flowing throng, Jim, Truck and Greg walked alongside Sanda, Mara and Lona. Truck notice Bantor bolting from his father's side. "I'll be right back!" He said, as he raced after the native. Quickly, catching up with him, he asked; "What's da matter, pal?"

"Nothing that would concern you, Ta-rok!" Bantor snapped.

"Hey, buddy! Put dos barking dogs on a leash for a while and let's talk."

Bantor looked at the big guy, questioningly, for an instant and then smiled. "I am sorry, Ta-rok! After what my father has been through, he now has a death wish. He says he will not return to the village, without my mother."

Truck stared at the native, shaking his head. "Dis shit kinda runs in da family. Don't it?"

Bantor threw his head back and laughed. After a few moments he said; "No matter what the situation, Ta-rok, after talking with you it never seems so serious. How do you manage to do that?"

"Everything has a way a working itself out, pal. Wasting time worrying ain't gonna change things. Truck answered. Ya just gotta trust dat when da situation dos come up, ya do da right thing."

"My father feels the same way I did, when I began this venture. I hope he, also, has a change of heart."

"Well, den, get your ass back dere and talk with him. Ordered Truck, with a big smile on his face. Keep letting him know dat your dere for him. Pretty soon da light'll go on in dat dark place, just like it did for you."

"Thank you, once again, my brother. Bantor replied, placing his hand on Truck's shoulder. Your words have lightened my concerns."

"Hey! Dat's what pals are for." The big man said, as he turned and headed back to join his brothers. Bantor slowed his pace and let the large following catch up with him.

"I see I am not the only one anxious to get to that cursed city. Leota said, as he caught up to Bantor. But, for the comfort of some of the slower people, maybe you should slow your pace slightly."

Bantor looked at his father. The big smile, on the older man's face spread to his. "Yes, father! You are right. We must conserve their strength as much as we can."

They walked in silence, for a while, absorbing the hilly landscape and losing themselves in their own thoughts. The third sun of the day had just assumed her duties. Its rays, less intense then her previous "sisters", poured down on them just as relentlessly. The large, dusty horde trudged on. No complaints were voiced. This far into their quest, it was much too late for them. But, the monotony of the uneventful trek was starting to show on some of the faces.

"So, my son! Tell me about this woman of yours." Leota said, breaking the silence.

"Father! In the short five years we were together, Cinda had become my soul mate. We were inseparable! Our time together was one adventure after another." Bantor replied.

"Did you have any children?" The elder asked.

A sad look came over Bantor's handsome features, as he answered. "We had a daughter named Kelijo. She was only two months old before the evil leader of the invaders, Zarnog, murdered her. Moisture threatened to leak out of the corners of his eyes. My Earth brother, Ta-rok, helped to make the mourning less painful."

"These Earth men always seemed to be helping someone. He thought to himself. Maybe they have special powers."

"I have one more reason to hate these creatures. Bantor continued, anger flaring from his eyes. My daughter shall be avenged!"

Looking compassionately at his son, Leota asked; "Do you think Cinda still lives?"

"Yes, father! She will live forever in my heart, if not at my side. One way or another, I have given my word, to those who are concerned about me, to rid our world of these monsters."

"You really believe you will be alive to see that day?" Leota asked.

"Maybe not, father! But, our people will."

They went silent for a few, long moments, each man pondering their future.

The terrain, ahead, dipped slightly into a large, forested valley. A ribbon of silvery water sparkled in the afternoon sun, as it snaked its way through the lush vegetation.

After a while, the elder spoke. Bantor! My intentions may have been induced by the separation of your mother or the pain and degradation I suffered while enslaved. You, yourself, have endured the same dilemma. My emotions have distorted my reasoning, as they did yours, once. Will you help me to lead our people?"

"You needn't have asked, father! But, yes, of course!" Bantor replied, emotionally.

"And, will you promise, also, to give me many grandchildren?"

"Only if you promise to be there to play with them, father!"

"Like you, my son, I will try my best to survive."

They both stopped and looked deeply into one another's eyes. Tears of relief ran from the corners as they embraced each other. They stayed that way for a few emotional moments. The hot, dusty caravan caught up with them and crowded around. When they finally broke apart, Leota spoke. "Now, I think we should get these tired people into the shade of those trees. We will enjoy a long rest, before our final march."

"Amen ta dat!" Truck said, as the Earth trio and their women joined them.

The confused look on Leota's face caused Bantor to start laughing. It spread to the Earthmen, who soon added theirs.

As they made their way toward the trees, Leota stood rooted to the spot, wondering what all that was about. "I have a lot to catch up on. He said to himself, as he headed toward the trees. But, now, it will be more worthwhile."

# CHAPTER 12

As the light of the early "sister" brightened the new day, an aura of nervousness arose with it. In, approximately, seven or eight hours, they would be in sight of their goal; Nevoa. They would attempt to end a culmination of over one hundred years of pain, degradation and oppression. Many of those, in the human throng, had lost friends or relatives. Revenge motivated some, but not all. The majority was there out of loyalty to their people.

The three Earth brothers had one more reason to fight. These people had opened their hearts and homes to them and adopted them into their lives. They were "alien orphans" a short while ago, with nothing to look forward to. The proliferation of these people was paramount to their survival. In short, their futures must be earned.

Feelings were as varied as the number of people, gathered around the main fired pit. Leota stood on a large boulder, looking out over his faithful followers. Standing near by was Bantor, the three brothers and their women.

"Before this day is finished, my people, many changes in our lives will have occurred. Some of us may not be returning to our village. Leota shouted. A short time ago, I had convinced myself I would be numbered among those unfortunate souls. He paused. My son has taught me that life is made up of many reasons for living. Not just one. Looking down into Bantor's eyes, he said. I vow to you and to all my people here today, as your leader, I will fight for the continuance of every man, woman and child as long as I have breath."

The large crowd roared its approval, as Bantor brushed the tears from his eyes and smiled up at his father. When the noise dwindled to a steady hum, he continued. "Among you, today, are five of us who have been inside the treacherous city. Once before, our Earth brethren have disarmed the lethal energy barrier. For us to be successful, we must shut down its operation, once again. One of our Earth friends has approached me with a plausible solution to this problem. I will, now, let him explain this plan to you." He finished, dismounting from his perch upon the rock. Greg, immediately, replaced him.

"First, I must apologize for the fact I am not too well-versed in your language, as of yet. But, in time, Jim and I will be speaking as well as our mentor, Ta-rok."

The smile that had started on Truck's face faded, suddenly, as the large crowd broke out in laughter. Being the brunt of his brother's little joke, he soon joined in the laughter. When the noise had settled down, Greg continued. "The plan I propose is simple. However, It will be risky. The crystals, which are the source to the energy field, around the entire Nevoan settlement, are buried a few feet down and approximately eight feet apart. We obtained this information, while incarcerated in the "House of Knowledge". It is the duty of every inhabitant, of that city, to know this. What I propose is to dig a small tunnel under the force field. The location of this tunnel will be on the fringe of the least-populated area, but, closest to the master source. Greg noticed a lot of murmuring and doubtful head shaking throughout the crowd. He continued, quickly. "Aside from myself and my brother Jim, two other volunteers will be requested. If we are fortunate enough to penetrate the city, we will endeavor to make our way to the source and deactivate it."

A voice carried to him, over the stirrings of the crowd. "I have been close to the invader's city. The terrain, surrounding it, is barren of tree and bush. You will, surely, be detected!"

"You are absolutely correct, my good man. Greg answered. We would have to use the only coverage availing itself, to make this successful; Darkness! He said, pausing to take in the reaction of the crowd. Approximately one mile from the city is a dense forest. He continued. We will remain hidden there until dark. Then, cover the short distance toward the city."

"What about sentries? Another voice erupted from the crowd. This party, you suggest, would be vulnerable to night eyes. Wouldn't they?"

"A very good question, sir! Greg replied. In the duration of our captivity, we noticed no night watch. The invaders rely on their force field to the point of invulnerability. After a brief pause, he began again. "The stone barrier inside of the force field can be, easily, surmounted by two men. After the tunnel is dug, the two volunteers will make their way back to the main force, secreted in the forest and direct them to join us as quickly as possible."

Another voice droned from the crowd. "What makes you so sure you can destroy it, if we even make it into the city?"

"Sir, I am sure of nothing, in this quest. But, if you have a better idea, please share it with us." Greg replied.

Silence fell, once again, through the crowd.

"Small groups will be deployed around the city in strategic positions. They will be appointed ahead of time." Greg finished. Nodding to Leota, he stepped down from the rock.

Remounting the stone perch, the old leader studied the faces in the bemused crowd. Anxiety, indecision and fear reflected back to him. "If what we are feeling now is the last time our kind must experience this, then we are fortunate. He opened. Remember the loved ones we have lost. Our ancestors had to endure over one hundred years of the same. Day after day, their lives were in turmoil, because of these invaders. We have but few allies on our side, to aid us in our cause; surprise, revenge and hope. I can only pray, they are adequate enough to help us. In these next few days, we shall find out! He continued. Twenty years ago, my decision was made for me. I do not want to spend another twenty years hating something. I wish to spend the rest of my days, on this world, loving and caring for my people and in peace. I am determined to make that happen. Raising his voice even louder, he asked. Is this what you want?"

The crowd erupted. "Yes! Yes!" Repeated over and over again. The concentration of so many voices raised in unison, echoed into the twilight. If enemy patrols were out and about, the fighting would have begun sooner than expected. The small scouting parties, scattered ahead of them, were the only buffers between the two factions.

Tonio and Roca volunteered to accompany Jim and Greg, on their tunneling venture. Each would carry one of the alien weapons and a knife. The lethal rods would be slung over their backs, by leather thongs, in such a way as not to impede their flight across the open terrain.

Gathered around a small fire, Jim drew in the dirt an outline of the alien settlement. Making marks in certain areas where the strategic strike zones would be located. The native army would be divided into five groups.

Truck would lead one hundred of the finest marksmen with the bow, picking off as many of the enemy as silently as possible. The more they eliminated before the alarm was sounded the better their odds for victory.

Bantor had almost two hundred rod-bearing sharp shooters. When the bowmen were detected and stealth was no longer their ally, the heavy artillery was to pour a relentless barrage into the aliens.

Leota led another two hundred men, armed with bows, arrows and light spears. Their prime objective was to contain the military barracks, which housed over five hundred alien warriors.

A man named Gorza would lead another two hundred on a direct assault of Zarnog's palace. If they could get the "master monster" to surrender, it would prevent a lot of casualties.

Tonio would lead the rest in a raid of the prisoner's compound, once his tunneling duties were finished, employing the aid of all he released. Sanda, Mara and Lona were in this group.

By the time most of the details were worked out, the third sun had finally surrendered to darkness. The night was cool, but not uncomfortable. No fires were to be lit during the night or any other preceding the battle. There was enough adrenalin flowing to keep them warm enough. Emotional conflicts accompanied each person there, as they sought their furs for the night.

# CHAPTER 13

The next day found them safely encamped among trees, below a steep cliff. Seventy-five feet, at the top of the escarpment, was a dense forest. Approximately one mile from the Nevoan settlement, it hid twenty alert, native scouts. The small stream, flowing at the base of the cliff, was alive with activity. Dusty garments were washed, while others further upstream, splashed in the cool, shallow water. Small groups gathered, discussing final preparations for battle. Work parties busied themselves, cutting poles and planks out of the forest for the tunnel project. Knives, arrowheads and spear points were honed to razor sharpness.

"The most logical point for the tunnel would be close to the "House of Knowledge", in the same area where we made our escape from. Jim explained. We make our way to the front of the building and cross the open square to the "zoo".

"Are there no sentries in this area?" Tonio asked.

About twenty spectators were clustered around, listening intently.

"The only sentries we have ever noticed were those in front of the monster's palace. Greg chimed in, pointing to the area in the dirt map at his feet. They are located at the top of the wide steps, directly in front of the large double doors."

"By coming up from behind the building, here. He pointed to the drawing. Moving to the front, from both sides, we should be able to quietly, take out the sentries. Jim added. The entrance to the "zoo" is approximately one hundred yards across the compound. Hopefully, darkness will conceal our movements at this time."

"Our next problem is the guard or guards inside the "zoo" itself. Greg jumped back in. The power station, unless it was moved since we disabled it, sits directly in the middle. Approximately seventy yards away, on all sides, sit the cages containing Zarnog's "pets". A few shrubs exist in the area. Otherwise, it is open ground. The small detail, led by Jim and myself, must be able to distract and dispatch the guards as quickly and quietly as possible."

"Will the creatures in the cages not alarm the guards?" Bantor asked.

"There is little possibility of that happening. Jim answered. "From sunrise to sundown they are consistently filling the air with their complaints."

"If all goes as planned, or I should say "when" all goes as planned, Bantor said, smiling. How long before we can begin our assault?"

"Within seconds after disabling the force field, one of the men in our party will ignite an arrow and send it skyward." Greg replied.

"Hopefully, enough bodies will have traversed our tunnel and made their way toward the front gate. Jim added. When Roca's gang starts its assault on the front gate, from the outside, the backs of the Nevoans on the wall should be exposed to our arrows."

"If they are not in place before Roca and his men start harassing the main gate, these men will be easy targets for the invaders." Leota cut in.

"Yes! They would be. Greg responded. That is why timing is of the utmost importance. One group most back up the other."

Truck and most of the others had been sitting quietly, listening to the plan unfold, going over and over, in their minds, the roles they would play. All their hopes hinged on the force field being eliminated. From the outside, no weapon would be effective and they would be slaughtered. Once their element of surprise had run its course, they would, still, be terribly outnumbered. Some of your better coaches would say, "The best defense is a good offense". They had no choice but to go full speed ahead. If they relented, even for a moment, they would be crushed by the superior weight of numbers. The contingencies for success were vastly against them. They had to tunnel under the force field, without being crushed by its power, scale a ten-foot wall, amass the bulk of their soldiers behind a building, dispatch sentries, deploy patrols to designated areas of the city, disable the force field and protect each others backs. All of these elements had to be implemented without being detected.

"I wanna know what wer gonna do with dos poor bastards locked up in da zoo. Truck, finally, chimed in. We can't just set em free. Some a dos things are pretty mean."

"Truck! You spoiled our little surprise! Greg said, trying to keep a straight face. We were going to give them to you so you could start your own circus."

The small group erupted with laughter, when they saw the confused expression on his face.

Realizing it was at his expense, once again, he played along. "I hear you and Jimbo got lotsa experience cleaning cages and feeding dem. You two will be da first ones I hire." He replied, with a big smile on his face, coaxing more laughter from the group.

In a more serious tone, Jim responded. "We can't worry about them until the dust has settled, Truck. When we're finished with our endeavor, we'll deal with it."

During the remainder of the day men were busy cutting down trees for battering rams, tunnel supports and making the necessary tools for digging. Weapons were being fine tuned, once again. More scouting parties were sent out, blanketing a five-mile perimeter around their camp. To be detected, at this point, would undo everything.

Small arguments flared up throughout the camp, some of them physical. They were short lived, however, as the disputants realized why they were here. On any given battlefield, in any given army, there were always a fair number of deserters. One hundred years of oppression and degradation far outweighed their slim chances of victory. Although, many had considered leaving, the infinitesimal possibility of an alien free life kept them united.

As the day's last sun was halfway spent, the large group collaborating on strategy had dwindled down to Leota, Bantor and the three brothers. This close to their objective, fires were out of the question. As they lounged on the bank of the small stream, chewing hard, blackened chunks of dried meat, Leota asked a question.

"A settlement as large as this, I find it hard to believe they have so few sentries. How is this possible?"

"I think there are two reasons that would explain this. Greg answered. "One". Their inflated egos find it hard to accept that anyone would dare enter their city uninvited. "Two". They feel their force field is infallible."

"That's true! Added Jim. Only Zarnog's insecurities dictated guards being dispersed in and around the palace."

"Dat's because dat ugly bastard, on da throne is a coward. Truck interjected. He needs lots a dogs around him ta do da biting."

"I just pray the dark cloak of this night will be our ally. Leota said in a sullen voice. Other than the spirits of our ancestors, imploring us to avenge their devastated mortality, it is the only one we have."

On the other side of camp, Sanda, Mara, Lona and a handful of other women sat in a close group. They were braiding long strands of Lurda hide, to be used in climbing the wall. Everything depended on getting enough people inside the alien city to execute their plan. The light chatter they shared, masked the heavy doubts filling their minds.

"I want four children! Lona said. I think the first is growing inside me as we speak."

Mara and Sanda looked at one another, for an instant, then, started to laugh.

"I don't think I said anything funny." Lona said, looking at the two women.

Mara and Sanda put their arms around the confused woman and continued to laugh.

"What is wrong with you two?" She asked, looking left and right at the women, as they squeezed her tightly between them in an affectionate embrace.

It was Sanda, who stopped long enough to catch her breath. "Only a few days ago, Mara and I told each other the same, good news. We wanted to tell you when not too many were around to hear."

"You mean to tell me, we are all pregnant?" Lona responded, as she joined in with tears of joy running down her cheeks.

Sanda and Mara just shook their heads up and down, as not to interrupt their blissful laughter.

After a while, Lona asked. "Have you told your men?"

Both Sanda and Mara shook their heads.

"No! Said Sanda. They have enough to think about. When this is over it will be announced and added to our victory celebration."

"The very reason I decided not to tell Gug!" Lona replied.

"Hopefully, this will be over before we get too fat to crawl through tunnels." Said Mara, with a wide smile.

"When we are finished here we should find them and get a little...Uh, ...sleep." Said Sanda, eliciting laughter again.

As the whole camp turned to their furs, some, possibly for the last time, an eerie pall fell upon them. By this time tomorrow their fate would be decided, one way or another. Would it be freedom? Or, would it be eternal rest?

# CHAPTER 14

All of the following day was spent climbing the steep cliff. About halfway up, a shallow crevice was discovered. It provided a perfect path as it rose, at a gradual angle to the top. Thus, saving a lot of their energy.

As the last of the "sister" suns closed her eyes, darkness fell upon them. The last of the seven hundred native, warriors finished their climb to the top of the cliff. They had started navigating the steep path, two hours earlier. It was just barely wide enough to accommodate single-file movement.

As the last native crested the summit and was embraced by the leafy arms of the small forest, the night was only minutes old. Separating into their appointed attack groups, they made their way, silently through the dense woods.

Jim, Greg, Roca and Tonio would make their way over the mile of open terrain, three hours in advance of the following army. Hopefully, it would provide them with enough time to finish the tunnel. Strapped to their backs, along with their alien weapons, were digging tools and lengths of wood.

Nodding at Truck and Bantor, who were directly behind them, they dashed out of the forest and raced toward the Nevoan city.

"I'll meet you guys at da pass." Truck said to himself, as he watched them speed away.

Organizing themselves into their given groups, they would utilize this time to go over any last minute details.

Within a handful of minutes, the four men neared the target area. About fifty yards from the deadly barrier, they slowed their pace. Restoring oxygen to their lungs, they replaced speed with caution and walked, slowly, up to the invisible menace. Four sets of eyes scanned the night for any unwanted visitors. All remained still.

As they closed to, within, twenty feet of the estimated location of the force field, Roca removed a long pole from the bundle on his back. The other three men stopped and silently observed. Holding the ten-foot pole before him, Roca moved toward the force field. Because it was invisible, they had decided this method would be the only way of locating it. Dangerous? Yes! But, they had to know, precisely, where to start their tunnel. The margin for error was zero.

One tentative step after another produced a river of nervous sweat, on the young native's body. This was, without a doubt, the most dangerous prey he would ever face. A few more steps, then, suddenly, the pole was ripped from his hands and flung into the night behind him. He was shocked to a standstill.

Jim and Greg were, quickly, at his side. "Roca! Are you all right?" Jim asked.

"Yes! I am not hurt. He answered, breathing heavily. I was overwhelmed with its power."

Greg advanced another two paces in front of them, estimating the distance to the killer force to be about four feet.

"I wouldn't get any closer, Greg! Jim said, over his brother's shoulder. We'll have to start digging right from here!"

Tonio and Roca brought up the digging tools and started hacking at the mossy turf. After penetrating the spongy carpet to a depth of about one foot, they broke into the loose soil. There appeared to be enough clay in the mixture. It would keep the tunnel from crumbling on top of them. In a matter of minutes, the two natives had a three-foot round, two-foot deep hole.

As they worked, Jim and Greg removed the small bundles of wooden braces from their backs. Hopefully, these would be adequate enough to keep the tunnel from collapsing upon them.

Working in tandem, the Earthmen relieved the two sweating natives. As the depth of the hole reached five feet, they decided it would be safe, enough, to start tunneling their way toward the city.

Only one could work at a time, now. Slowly, they inched their way through the resisting soil. Fortunately, it was moist enough to keep it from falling back on them. The short, wide pieces of wood were wedged into place, holding back enough of the dirt so as not to undo their dirty efforts.

As they worked, quickly, at least one set of eyes watched the building tops for movement. The few windows, facing their precarious position, remained dark. The spot, they had chosen for the tunnel, was advantageous for two reasons. It was situated directly behind Zarnog's palace, where the only visible sentries were located. Only the ten-foot stone barrier would have to be surmounted to reach it. The second reason was that it was in a straight line with the forest, which concealed their army, barely one mile away. Once it was navigated, the large buildings would, effectively, shield them from prying eyes. From the front of these buildings, the zoo's entrance was only seventy-five yards away. Of course, the aliens lackadaisical regard for security was a boon to their endeavors.

"Greg! Hand me that long pole!" Jim ordered. Upon receiving it, he slid it down the tunnel. Only four feet protruded from the entrance. When the entire ten feet spanned their tunnel, they estimated they would be in the safe zone. This would put them on the other side of the lethal force.

"Another four feet and we can start working our way toward the surface, Jim. Greg informed his half-buried brother. I pray our calculations are accurate."

All four men were thoroughly encrusted with dirt. In the dim light of the first of the evening stars, they blended in, naturally, with their project. As one man burrowed into the slowly yielding soil, a second man, directly behind, scooped the dirt out toward the entrance. A third man flung the accumulated dirt out of the five-foot entranceway. The fourth man rested and scoured their surroundings for any signs of movement. Working at breakneck speed, they relieved each other every ten minutes.

Twenty minutes later, the long pole was inserted into the tunnel. It spanned the entire ten-foot length. Tonio was at the end and started digging his way to the surface. Roca was sent racing toward the forest to collect the native army.

Moments later, Tonio announced he had broken through to the surface. Working even faster, they shored up the narrow tunnel with the remaining boards and scooped out as much of the loose soil as they could. Their surface hole was, approximately, six feet from the base of the stone barrier. Once they had assured themselves that all was still quiet. They dove back down the tunnel and rejoined Greg. They didn't have much time to congratulate themselves, as the first of the small army joined them.

Jim looked at Greg and asked. "How long before daylight?"

"I would say, no more than two hours at most. Why? What's on your mind?"

"I was just wondering how many bodies we could get inside the city, in that period of time." He answered.

"Depending how fast we can get them through the tunnel and over the wall, I would say the majority might make it. That is, of course, our handiwork doesn't come tumbling down."

"Then, I think we better get busy, little brother!"

Like cattle, prodded through the stockyards, the natives disappeared into the fragile tunnel, assailed the wall and joined their silent comrades, crouching in the shadows of Zarnog's foreboding palace.

Bantor and Leota were among the last group to arrive. Truck, Sanda, Mara and Lona stood alongside, staring at the crusty Earthmen. "These are the last of us. Said Leota. I have sent Roca and his men off toward the main gates. We can only pray they cause enough of a distraction to keep alien eyes locked in their direction."

"If there were another way, my father, we would attempt it. Those men will expose many to our arrows. We will reduce their numbers."

"I hope you are right, my son. Their sacrifice is necessary." He said, sadly.

"Before this day is over, my father, there will be many sacrifices."

As the last group lined up for its turn on the "subway", Greg looked back at Truck. "Truck! He said. I think you should bring up the rear, just in case you happen to get stuck.

You wouldn't want to hold up the parade. Would you?" A big smile cracked some of the dried mud on his face.

"Yea, and I could save ya da trouble of crawling through dat hole, by drop-kicking your little butt over da wall, too!"

Smiles were still evident on the dirt-encrusted faces as they emerged, safely, on the other side.

# CHAPTER 15

## THE SIEGE

The guards, lulling at the top of the wide steps, were silently eliminated with a few well-placed arrows in their bulbous heads. Jim, Greg and six natives set off immediately through the ominous shadows toward the "zoo". The battle had begun!

As they stole into the waning blackness, designated groups deployed to other areas. Truck would lead a group into the "monster" monarch's palace. Bantor and Leota would make their way toward the female prisoner's compound. Tonio led his large patrol toward the guard's barracks. As silent as the night, they melted into the alien shadows.

The siege would commence when a flaming arrow was sent into the dark sky, signaling the successful endeavor of Jim and Greg.

The slain sentries, outside the palace, were quietly removed to the deep shadows behind the massive building. Their lethal staffs were, quickly, employed by five capable natives.

Speaking in whispers, Truck, gave a quick sketch of the interiors layout. "Every time we visited dat bastard, Zarnog, he had two big pets standing guard at da inner doors. Once we get inside, all we got between us and dos doors is a row of big columns. If all of us goes in at da same time, dere gonna see us. Dat's why I'm taking only three a you guys with me. Da rest a you just wait here until we need ya. Picking three men, he said; "Now, all we gotta do is wait for da signal."

As Leota, Bantor and one hundred men, cautiously, approached the female compound, the only movement they detected came from the front of the large double doors. Two sentries milled about. Their weapons leaned against the building, a few paces from them.

Dividing into three groups, they quickly separated. Using the cover of darkness, the building was soon surrounded. Bantor and Leota's group was situated directly across from the entrance, occupied by the two sentries. A large shed hid them from view.

The old leader's heart raced with hope and dread at the same time. "Was his beloved Graci on the other side of those walls?" He wondered.

* * * * * * * * * *

Roca's group consisted of one hundred of the fleetest natives in the village. Their mission would be the most dangerous, after the fighting began. Racing through the last of the night's dark cloak, they drew within fifty yards of the ominous gates. Once the night decided to surrender to the day, they would find themselves in an extremely vulnerable position. With almost no protection against enemy eyes or firepower, they would have to rely on a running battle. By using their speed and marksmanship to harass the guards at the top of the wall, they hoped to distract them long enough to take the focus off of their fellow comrades within. This was a necessary diversion to cut down on the numbers against them. To accomplish this ploy, timing was imperative.

Each man carried a crude shovel. While half of them dug shallow trenches, the other half kept a silent vigil, focusing on the walls. They would lay in the shallow retreats, covered with dirt and moss, to await the signal. Roca looked, sadly, about him. Most of them would never see their village again!

Jim and Greg weaved their way through the alien community, as silent as wraiths. Their native companions followed their lead to the letter. Stopping frequently behind an alien hovel, every now and then, they listened and watched for the slightest nocturnal incongruity. Eventually, their stealthy progress placed them at the entrance to the "zoo". The gate to the large entertainment park stood wide open and unattended, as they knew it would be.

After easing their way, cautiously, through the gates, they headed toward the storage shed lying twenty yards to their right. Halfway across, a signal from Jim froze the others in their tracks, while he silently covered the remaining distance. A slight noise had caught his attention, an instant before. Peering, ever so tentatively, around the entryway, he noticed one of "his majesty's" finest curled up on a pile of grain bags in a shaded corner of the shed. The horrible gash of a mouth bubbled and wheezed, denoting a state of heavy, alien sleep. The eyes, because of the absence of lids, stared up at the roof. The creature's weapon leaned against one wall, at his side.

Drawing his ivory dagger, Jim moved, slowly through the entryway, toward the creature. But, the best laid plans of mice and Earthmen go awry. He hadn't taken his second step when his foot bumped against a rake, sending it skidding against the side of the metal shed, shattering the night calm.

The creature was on his feet in an instant, reaching for his weapon. Before the tong-like hand could close upon the lethal rod, seven inches of ivory penetrated its brain. In the instant it took, to realize his blunder, Jim acted, throwing the razor sharp weapon across the ten feet separating them. Rushing toward the crumbling alien, he eased the body quietly to the dirt floor. Pulling the blade out of the oozing eye socket, he wiped it off on the alien's covertogs and replaced it in his belt.

"Nice job, James! His brother's voice called softly from the entryway, startling Jim. A little noisy, perhaps, but, efficient just the same."

"I hope I didn't set off any alarms, Greg! I was a little careless."

"Don't worry! All is quiet! Greg replied. When you didn't exit the shed, immediately, I figured something was wrong."

"There is something wrong here, Greg! In all the time we spent slaving in this stinking place, I can't remember them having more than one guard at night and he was stationed near the crystal control shed."

"Maybe this one is the lone sentry, Jim. He just decided to take a little nap."

"I guess we'll soon find out, little brother. Jim replied. I want four of our men to stay near this shed, covering our backs. The other two will go with us to the control shed."

With that said, the four men darted through the ever-lightening shadows toward the crystal nemesis. Cruising to a cautious stop, approximately twenty yards from the target, they espied not one, but five, alien sentries lulling around. Three were standing off to the left, conversing. Two were milling around to their right. Only one played the professional role of the sentry. He circled the small shed, looking about him every so often. His lethal staff balanced on a sloping shoulder, at the ready.

As they clustered quietly in the shadows of the waning night, Jim motioned for them to retreat further back from the watchdogs. He ordered one of the natives to go and retrieve the others at the shed.

"I see that old bastard isn't taking any chances, since our last visit here. Greg said, in a hushed voice. What's the plan, Jim?"

"When the others join us, we spread out and open fire. The complaints, coming from some of those cages, tell me it will be light soon. Jim whispered. Their anguished cries should muffle the sound of our approach.

Shaking his head in agreement and remembering the raucous awakening they were subjected to on that first dawn in this strange world, Greg replied. "We should have known then, from that auspicious beginning, our endeavors on this world would not come easily."

"When the firing begins, I want you to make your way to the shed and disable that god damned thing once and for all. Jim continued. Take one of the natives with you and have him fire the signal arrow the instant you have accomplished your task. I am afraid the time for stealth is long past, my brother. It's time to get this show on the road!"

As the natives joined them, they slowly surrounded the unsuspecting creatures. Jim turned to Greg and in a soft voice said; "Take care of yourself, little brother!"

Greg looked into his brother's eyes, for a brief second. "Likewise, big brother." He replied. Then, he was gone. He was fifty feet away from the target shed, before he heard the lethal hiss of the first barrage. The lone sentry, near the crystal shed, turned toward the disturbance. Before he could take his first step to investigate, his head exploded and his body crumpled to the ground.

"Nice shot! Greg said to the native kneeling at his side. Now, get that signal arrow into the sky as soon as possible." He said over his shoulder, as he dashed toward the shed.

The dark night sky was on the verge of capitulating to the light of the new dawn. Its last attempt at keeping the world locked in its ebon embrace was failing. The new day was starting to emerge, victoriously.

Greg made short order of the crystals and tripod, scattering the blue stones in every direction. It would buy them the time they needed. If this mission proved to be successful, they could come back later and totally dismantle the deadly shield stone by stone.

Gathering the native, who had accomplished his mission, they rushed back to join in the battle. He slowed his momentum, as his eyes took in the scene directly before him.

Jim and three of the natives were on their knees, scanning the perimeter. All four of the alien sentries lay scattered about in meaty, oozing heaps. Two of the natives were also down. Both of their bodies looked like jigsaw puzzles, with many pieces missing. The odor, permeating the air, was that of an electrical storm, that had belched lightning, mixed with cooked flesh. From his position on the ground, next to one of the mutilated natives, Jim looked up. Blood trickled from a series of minor wounds on his face and body. Tears of loss dripped from the corners of his eyes and mingled with his wounds. He stared at Greg, questions in his eyes. "The force field? The signal arrow?" He asked.

Two nods and a thumbs-up sign erased a few pounds of anguish from Jim's mind.

"Okay! He said, rising to his feet and staring briefly at the two dead natives. Let's get back and help finish this damn thing once and for all.

\* \* \* \* \* \* \* \* \*

Before the flaming arrow was halfway through it arc, Truck and his three men were through the massive doors and concealed behind one of the large columns. Fifty feet in front of them were the double doors, leading into Zarnog's chambers. One of the giant sentries sat cross-legged on the floor. His lethal staff lay across his lap.

Before the small group had a chance to move up to the next column in line, it happened. One of the native's staffs, inadvertently, clanged off the huge column. The sound resonated through the vast room, like a rifle shot.

The alien sentry was on his feet in an instant, firing blasts in the general direction of the sound he had heard.

One of the natives, who had the misfortune of peering around the column at that instant, crumpled to the floor with half of his head missing.

When the sentry discovered the fallen native, he let loose with a relentless barrage that kept Truck and the remaining two natives hugging the columns even closer.

Realizing, eventually, a stray shot could decimate their numbers even further, Truck acted. Diving to his left and rolling to a kneeling position, he fired his weapon. The shots took the sentry in the throat and slammed him against the double doors. Before its body had even bounced back, the two natives at Truck's side added their contribution to the melee. The giant's body was, Literally, dissolved into a slimy pool of green ooze.

As they rushed toward the door, they noticed it was starting to open; the other guard. Truck arrived, just as the other giant came through to join his comrade. As the creature started to raise its weapon toward one of the natives, Truck brought his staff down hard, on the tong-like hands and drove his elbow into the creature's throat. The deadly staff clattered to the floor and the alien flew backwards into Zarnog's front chambers. Before it could regain its feet, Truck and his two native allies had the situation under control. One of his men grabbed up the fallen weapon, while the other aimed his own at the giant, now on his feet and gasping for breath.

"Don't shoot! Truck yelled. Let's hear what dis bastard has ta say."

Staring at Truck, the memory light went on in the ugly mind. "So, Earth dung, you have returned! The large creature responded, unafraid. The malevolent look in his eyes focused on the Earthman. If not for these puny hill-dwellers you would be dead already!"

Not understanding the alien words, bubbling out of that horrible gash of a mouth, the two natives looked at Truck. "Shall we kill him now, Ta-rok?" One of them asked.

A mischievous smile spread over Truck's face. "Not yet! He said. I want you two ta go through dat doorway, he said pointing, and haul dat royal bastard out here. You'll, probably, find da coward hiding under his bed. I'll watch him!" He said, glaring at the big alien.

As the two natives backed away from Zarnog's behemoth bodyguard, Truck moved, sideways, to the door they had come through. Pulling it closed, he threw the latch on it, locking them inside.

The large alien stared, questioningly, at the American, unable to glean the slightest trace of fear on his countenance. The strange look on the face of this inferior was causing consternation within his evil mind. The familiar look of dread, reflected back at him in the eyes of his countless victims, was absent.

Truck continued to smile at the giant, sizing him up. The creature outweighed him by a good fifty pounds and towered over him by at least six inches. "Maybe I shouldn't risk it! He thought to himself. It would be so easy, just, to blast his ass outta existence, like we did to his partner. But, I can't get Bantor's little baby outta my mind."

His revelries were interrupted, a moment later, as the two natives entered the room. Between them they, literally, dragged "his highness" across the room. The mumbling monarch trembled with fear. The huge bodyguard made like he was going to intervene.

"Don't get any ideas, pal! Truck said, in a loud voice, glaring at the creature. He, then, set his weapon in the stun mode and jabbed it into Zarnog's side. As the body hit the floor, Truck turned to his native allies. Get dis garbage to da back a da building and see dat he's well-guarded." Walking over to the double doors and throwing the latch, he opened them. He, then, handed his weapon to one of the natives, as they dragged Zarnog from the room.

They stopped and stared questioningly at the big Earthman. Before either could speak, Truck said; "See dat wer not disturbed, for a while." With that, he closed and locked the doors behind them.

Turning back to the large alien he said; "How bout you and I dance a little bit. What da ya say?" This time, the big grin on his face didn't mask his intentions.

The meaning of the words was lost upon the alien. But, the aggressive posture struck by the American as he advanced across the room, made it perfectly clear. "You have made a big mistake, Earth scum! The creature said, as he prepared himself for the attack. No one has ever defeated me! You are about to die a horrible death!"

"Well, don't just talk about it, ya ugly bastard! Come and get some!"

Glaring at the American, through eyes as red as the pits of hell, he lowered his head and charged across the remaining space, with arms outstretched.

An instant before the ice-tong hands could bury themselves into his flesh, Truck ducked to his left and buried his right fist into the giant's midsection. It was a powerful blow. In the past it would have stopped anything he hit dead in its tracks. However, the creature's momentum carried it passed Truck. He stopped a few paces away and turned back to face the Earthman. The blood red coloring of its features and the viscous foam, bubbling from the horrible gash of a mouth were the only indications Truck's punch had done any damage. Before it could charge again, the Earthman moved in, throwing lefts and rights at the bulbous head, careful not to land any punches on the horrible mouth. The two pincher-like fangs would have ripped his hands apart.

The giant moved back a few paces. Then, it started flailing its long arms in defense. One long talon slashed a fleshy furrow across Truck's left shoulder. Without missing a beat, the Earthman waded in and planted a hard thrust to the creature's throat. Both of its tong-like hands went, immediately, to the injured area. It was in distress! Before it could recover, Truck placed a devastating kick into the same area; a kick that had once launched a football seventy yards.

The creature started to topple. Before it hit the floor, The Earthman came up from behind and placed his powerful arms around the thick neck, twisting. As they staggered around the floor, Earth sweat mixed with alien mucous. The creature flailed its arms in panic. It was weakening.

With a last mighty effort, from his tired arms, an audible cracking sounded and the creature fell to the floor, its head facing in the opposite direction. The alien's weight pulled Truck down with it.

Disentangling himself from the dead alien, Truck struggled to replace the oxygen in his lungs. After a while, he regained his feet. "Now, dat's what I call a party!" He said to himself, as he turned toward the door. It was only then, he realized, it was already open and a crowd of native faces smiled at him. As they made their way to the outside, one of the natives asked him if it wouldn't have been easier if he had just shot the creature.

"Yea! You're right about dat. But, he woulda died too fast and I wanted ta give da sonnuva bitch a slow funeral."

\* \* \* \* \* \* \* \* \*

The alien dawn erupted with the staccato-like blasts of the alien firearms. The haunting screams of the dying, both native and alien, blended in, creating a horrific harmony. The Nevoans manning the wall, poured from the two large shelters, located at the top. They were armed and ready. Before they could direct their fire on the invading natives, within their walls, Roca's party sprang from the dirt and poured a deadly barrage into their backs. Half of the aliens fell. The other half retaliated by returning a merciless rain of fire on the racing natives below their walls. It was deadly! These alien soldiers were chosen for the wall duty because of their marksmanship. One third of Roca's party was blown into oblivion and many were wounded. Roca, himself, suffered a serious wound to his left arm. Then, it happened! A flock of arrows darkened the early dawn sky. Many missed their targets. Many did not. When the wave of deadly missiles diminished, not one alien was left standing on the wall. The aerial scythe had, quickly, hewn the weeds from the garden.

Gathering his men together, Roca veered toward the heavy gates, leading into the city. Before they could get close enough to blast their way through them, they suddenly swung open. A handful of their native comrades, bows slung over their backs, struggled with the heavy obstructions. As the Roca party neared them, the opening was already ten feet wide. Adding their collective weight to the task, the city was, soon, wide open and vulnerable to them. One of the bowmen shouted to him, as he passed through the gates. "We must hasten to the alien barracks. Our men are under heavy fire!"

As Bantor and Leota stepped over the bodies of the dead watchdogs, they entered the structure holding the female prisoner's. Hope was foremost in their hearts. Their minds were alert for hidden enemies. The dim light filtering through the small windows set high in the walls, cast gloomy shadows about them. The graveyard silence fell upon them like a heavy cloak.

"Light some torches! Leota ordered, in a quiet voice, nervously dreading and anticipating this moment at the same time. Be prepared for anything!"

The brief moments, it took to light the torches, weighed heavily on the two men. What would they reveal?

When the torches were, finally, passed forward, one of them made its way into Leota's trembling hand. As it quickly ate its way through the gloomy shadows of darkness, it revealed a group of women huddled in a corner. There were at least twenty of them. Disheveled, dirty and barely clad, the fear saturated faces stared back at them. The gaunt looks, in their eyes, reflected the tremendous amount of abuse they had endured. The odors, permeating the small prison, were appalling.

"Move these poor souls out into the fresh air! Leota ordered. Quickly!"

Once the women realized what was happening and who their rescuers were, voices were raised in joy. Hope, which had vanished through the years of degradation, resurfaced. Tears, that had forsaken those hapless eyes for so long, gushed in a river of happiness.

One woman rushed out of the huddled mass and into the arms of Leota. The impetus, of her impassioned fervor, caught the old leader by surprise, knocking him over backwards.

"Leota! Is it really you? Graci cried out as she clung to him desperately. I am not dreaming?"

Stunned to the very roots of his soul, Leota wept and clung to the half-starved woman just as fiercely. "I am here, Graci! I'll always be here for you!"

Bantor, who had just reentered the enclosure, stood in happy shock, observing. For many summers he had no parents. Now, he was reunited with both. He, quickly, joined them, adding his tears of happiness. "Mother! I welcome you back!" He said between sobs.

"Bantor! My son! She uttered, before a fresh torrent of happiness drenched the small huddle. These cruel invaders separated me from my little boy, but, I am thankful to be alive to see this young man in his place."

Long moment passed before they rose from the dirt floor and made their way out into the early morning light, still clinging to one another. "We have many years to make up. Leota said. Much has happened in that time. But, now, we must concentrate on our mission and put an end to our suffering once and forever." He appointed ten men to stand watch. For their protection and because of their weakened condition, he decided it was best to leave them here. Rations of food and water were doled out and care was given to the weaker members.

"Mother! Bantor asked. Have you heard mention of a woman called Cinda? She was captured with me more than a summer ago."

"I am sorry, my son! I have been with most of these women, since I arrived. She answered, seeing the look of anguish in his eyes. I do not know of her. But, there are other women scattered throughout the invader's village."

"Thank you, mother. He said in a subdued voice, as he hugged her. If she still lives, I will find her! Then, he walked away.

Graci looked after her son and then brought her focus back to Leota in askance.

"Cinda is his mate. He answered the silent question voiced with her eyes. His pain is of the same nature, I have carried, until moments ago." I hope it ends well for him, also." He finished, hugging Graci to his chest. He was almost inclined to stay at her side.

"Oh, Leota! You must help him find her!" She sobbed into his shoulder.

"I will do everything I can to aid him, my love. He said, as he finally broke away. I will be back, shortly. We will end this, now, to prevent any further suffering to our people. I promise you a better future." With that said, they left to join the battle raging near the alien barracks.

* * * * * * * * *

Most of the alien citizens opted to stay inside their dwellings. The military faction, of the Nevoan nation, was the aggressive side shown to countless victims throughout its history. The non-military side was looked upon as inferior, oppressed and treated almost as badly as the native slaves. Production of every invention, vital to Nevoan prosperity, was their responsibility. From the raising and preparation of food to the manufacture of weapons, these individuals dedicated their lives. Yet, they remained unrecognized. The irony of it was, their productivity and ingenuity was the nurturing factor keeping them from extinction. The military regarded them as one-dimensional insignificants, performing menial functions.

The only requirements needed to become one of his majesty's finest, was an evil mind and a voracious appetite capable of consuming all who stood in one's way of advancement; mother, father, children, superior officers.

This divided society would be the cause of its downfall. While the brains of the outfit, so to speak, proved to be non-threatening, the natives had only the alien army to contend with. Of course, there were a few of these, otherwise peaceful, residents who offered resistance. They were, quickly, cut down by native bows and arrows and deadly bolts from the lethal rods. Unfortunately, in times of war, discrimination is marginal.

A small contingency was deployed to contain the alien citizens in one area. Another patrol, consisting of fifty native marauders, concentrated on hunting down and destroying alien soldiers, scattered about the city.

High upon the walls of the army barracks building was a protected catwalk, encircling the entire structure. Small slits, in this refuge, were spaced ten feet apart. In every one of these, protected, positions, an invader took deadly aim at the approaching natives. Bodies, of both alien and native flavor, lay scattered at and around the base of the building. There was, virtually, no protection within fifty yards of the imposing structure; advantage aliens.

Leota, Bantor and the three Americans huddled behind a small shed, in conference. Raising his voice above the explosive sounds of battle, Leota spoke. "Too many of our brethren have perished in this attempt. If we continue this frontal assault, many more will follow. He paused, looking around at all of the dead and dying natives, lying in bloody heaps. The smell of burning flesh permeated the air. The screams of the dying hurled their complaints at the living. Maybe it would be wise, at this time, to gather our survivors and retreat from this evil city. To continue this futile assault may doom us all." He finished, with a heavy heart.

"But, father, the sacrifices we have already made will be undone. Bantor interrupted. Our suffering, at the hands of these invaders, will only begin again if we do not defeat them. We must continue!" He implored.

Looking at Bantor with glazed eyes, he answered. "My son, a leader must consider what is best for his people. At this moment, there seems little hope of accomplishing this mission. We must acknowledge our inability to continue and thank our ancestors we have come this far. At least, we will have a chance to prepare for the future."

"This is the future! Bantor shouted, angrily. If we fail now, our suffering will only continue. Soon, there will be no one left to decide any future."

The three Americans looked at each other. Mixed feelings ran through their minds. This was one of those "damned if we do, damned if we don't" situations. Finish it now, one way or another. Or, spend the rest of their lives, on this planet, battling for survival every waking moment.

Before Leota could respond to his son, Jim interrupted. "Leota, there might be another solution to this situation."

Staring at the Earthman, Leota waited for him to continue.

"If we can persuade Zarnog to command his men to surrender, we will save countless lives on both sides."

"Dat's a great idea, Jimbo! Truck chimed in. I know I can make dat bastard see da light." He said, smiling and rubbing his big fist.

"In all this confusion, I wasn't aware of his capture. Leota responded. Where is he being held?"

"Behind his royal palace. Greg answered. Right where we entered this God-forsaken nightmare. That is, of course, our comrades haven't repaid him for all the kindness he has shown them in the past."

A new look of hope came into Leota's eyes. "Bring him here with all haste! He ordered. Turning to Bantor and smiling, he said. Tell our men to cease firing and retreat to safety. Immediately!"

While Bantor rushed, to do his bidding, a small attachment was sent to retrieve the royal monster. During the time it took to bring him to the forefront, the native barrage had diminished. The alien defenders, on the walls, aborted their firing moments later.

The most prominent sounds, now, were the heart-wrenching screams of the mortally wounded, making their final pleas for life.

The small squadron of natives approached the leader. Sandwiched tightly among them was Zarnog, stumbling along and trying to keep up with the fast pace. His hands tied behind his back, he quivered with fear and stared out at the world through guilty, fire-red eyes. By the numerous scrapes and bruises, on his body, it was obvious small debts had, already, been repaid to the suffering account of the natives. It was amazing he was still alive, after all the atrocities he had perpetrated against them.

As they halted in front of Leota, the mighty, alien leader sagged to the ground, mumbling in a low voice.

Staring at the creature, the native leader tried to suppress all the hatred he had for the cruel monarch. This thing was the architect of all his suffering and deprivation over many years, the same monster that had almost succeeded in extinguishing his people from the face of this world. He fought the ardent urge to tear him apart where he lay groveling.

"Raise him to his feet!" Leota commanded.

Two men, one on either side, grabbed Zarnog by the arms and set him on his feet.

"I am Leota, leader of the "yellow heads". He began. The strange Nevoan words flowed from his mouth. Every one captured by the invaders was forcibly made to speak and understand their language. Bantor and the Earth brothers were the only others who could do so.

"I wish to put an end to our differences once and for all. It has lasted far too long and caused many thousands to visit their ancestors prematurely. Leota continued. Those of us, who still exist, have been subjected to suffering, degradation and sorrow, at your hands. I command you to order your charges to throw down their weapons and cease hostilities, at once!" Pausing for affect, he added in a malicious voice. You cannot imagine the pain you will suffer if you do not heed my words."

Quivering like a young sapling being tossed about in a slight breeze, he stared back at Leota. "What guarantee do I have that you will not kill us all, once we are disarmed?" He asked, as drool and slime spewed from the awful openings in the hideous face.

"Unlike your kind, we dwell on peace. Killing someone, even though they deserve it, serves no purpose if it is not a benefit to my people's welfare. Leota answered. If my orders are realized the killing will stop. If they are not carried out, I have only one guarantee."

"What is this one guarantee?" Zarnog asked.

"I will take you with me, back to my village and keep you alive as long as I can. Every day I will have you tortured, so slowly that you will not want to see another sunrise. We will vent upon you all the agony and humiliation, from a lifetime filled with degradation and fear." Leota finished, with a sneer on his face fit for a Zarnog.

Quivering even more noticeably, Zarnog spoke. If I agree to your wishes you will set me free and leave here in peace?"

"I do not believe you are capable of understanding the concepts of freedom and peace. Leota responded. However, I will confiscate all your weapons, and destroy the machines that produce them. Then, I will depart your city and hope I will never have to return."

When the beast remained silent, Leota continued. "The atrocities you and your kind have instilled, upon us, make it understandable I had wished to exterminate every invader on my world. But, that would make me just as cruel and uncaring as you. I do not believe our coexistence will be realized for many generations to come. I can only promise that you will be allowed to exist in your little part of the world. However, I swear upon my beloved ancestors, if another native is ever hurt by your kind, because of your orders, every invader will be exterminated! Do you understand these conditions or should I give you a personal tour of my village?"

The words couldn't have come out of that awful mouth fast enough, as Zarnog replied. "I will agree to your wishes, "yellow head".

"Cut him loose!" Leota ordered.

As a native produced a knife and severed the bonds from Zarnog's wrists, Bantor turned to Leota.

"But, father, who will pay for the murder of my child and the suffering my mother was forced to endure? They cannot be forgotten! Let me kill him and avenge these wrongs. I beg you!"

"Bantor, my son. I know the wounds, from these grave incidents, will take a lifetime of healing. He said, placing an arm over Bantor's shoulder. At least, this way, we will be together, alive, to comfort one another. It is a hard decision to make. Believe me! But, it must be so." Releasing his son, he turned toward Zarnog. "Now, do as you were told!" He said, in a loud voice.

The royal beast obeyed. He shuffled forward to within twenty feet of the barracks and stopped. "This is your master, Zarnog, leader most high. He said, fear rippling his voice. Throw down your weapons and desist all hostilities. At once!"

Overwhelming silence smothered the air. Even the plaintiff voices of the dying natives dropped off in volume. The majority of eyes were focused on the reaction of the alien soldiers manning the wall. The rest sighted down their lethal rods, targeting Zarnog's back. The slightest bit of subterfuge, on his part, the war was back on, minus one monarch.

Within moments, alien rods started raining down from the walls above. All of the alien defenders stood up from behind the ramparts and stared down at the scene below.

On orders from Leota, two natives moved alongside of Zarnog and escorted him back to their group. After the natives had collected the fallen firearms, Leota made Zarnog call his men from the walls and assemble in the area directly in front of the building. Men were, then, sent in to collect any weapons left behind and to make sure all of the invaders had vacated.

\* \* \* \* \* \* \* \* \*

When word was spread throughout the city, that Zarnog had surrendered, fighting came to a virtual standstill. Every living soul, man, woman, child, alien and native alike, amassed in the great square adjacent to the "Royal" house.

On the high steps in front of the palace, was a group of people. It consisted of Leota and Graci, surrounded by Bantor, the three Americans and their women; Sanda, Mara and Lona.

Bantor stood apart from the others, shoulders drooped and sadness in his eyes.

Jim walked over to him to see if he was all right. Before he could say a word, Bantor spoke. "Everyone here has good reason to celebrate, my Earth brother. My reason does not exist. I must resign myself that Cinda is gone forever and now walks with her ancestors. It grieves me so. But, at the same time it gives me closure. I will never wonder, if she still lives. My question has been answered."

"Do not despair, yet, my friend! Jim said, in a concerned voice. We haven't completed our search of the city. There is still hope!"

"Thank you, my brother. But hope only goes so far and lasts so long."

Jim remained silent, feeling his friend's loss. They stood, shoulder to shoulder, observing the alien mass. At this time a native group of six men were making their way through the thickly packed crowd. In the middle was a tall woman. As they made their way toward Leota's group, at the top of the wide steps, Bantor lifted his sullen eyes in their direction, let out an ear-piercing yell and raced off in their direction. When Jim finally joined him, he was in the arms of the tall woman. He knew, then and there, his friend had found his mate, Cinda.

One of the six natives that had escorted her had made his way up to Leota and was explaining to him how they had found her and three other native women hiding in the officer's quarters. One of the officers, they found out later it was the three American's friend, Tabor, and nine of his men had refused to surrender and were killed after a lengthy battle.

Clinging to each other as if life depended on it, which it probably did to Bantor, they mingled their love and tears together. After a while, Bantor separated himself from Cinda and hand in hand walked her up to Leota.

"Leota, my father, this is my mate, Cinda."

Reaching out both arms and enfolding her into a loving embrace, he said; "I am very pleased to, finally, meet you my daughter. I welcome you into my family."

"It is my pleasure, also, Leota, my father." She replied.

After tears had dried and introductions were made, life returned to a normal semblance once again. Leota took charge. Facing the huge crowd of aliens, assembled before him, he spoke. "People from another world, we wish you to know that to exist in life, certain rules need to be followed." The sudden silence of the enormous crowd was stunning. Everyone was looking around as if to assure each other this was actually real.

"Rule number one is to allow each and every man, woman or child the right to live a happy life. Rule number two is to follow ones beliefs. But, at the same time, never to force another being into following these beliefs against his or her will." He paused, picking out a few nods of affirmative in the crowd.

"Once we leave this city, in light of the past atrocities imposed by your cruel leader, it is very unlikely we shall ever return, unless invited. I cannot see this happening in a long future. Many wounds have been opened. Only time will heal them. Your cruel leader, Zarnog, has been found far from wanting. His evil tactics have jeopardized any possibility of commerce between our cultures. However, it is fortunate, a likeness exists in both of our societies. Not everyone is motivated by cruelty and blood. A few of my people have lived among you. They have made me realize that some good exists in even the cruelest of societies. If we were to leave today and the existing hierarchy remains, nothing would change. All of this would be for naught. The suffering and degradation would begin once again. One among you, I have been told, has exhibited a humane and fair outlook on all life. This person, of whom I speak, is Mokar, the high learner."

At that moment, the large door behind them opened and the grand teacher stood among them. The three Earthmen and Leota had spoken to him earlier and he had agreed to lead his people.

Mokar turned toward the massive crowd and spoke. "There are many among you who feel an educator is a weak candidate for this high status. Cruelty bound us together in a state of constant fear for too long. Fairness and hard work will bind us together to build an even greater society. We wake every day in constant fear that it may be our last. I say to you, now, in time we will all awaken with a feeling of accomplishment and an anticipation of better things to come. I ask you to put your trust in me."

The alien crowd erupted in a loud cry of desperate acceptance.

Jim, Truck and Greg approached Mokar.

"Ah, my three favorite Earth students." He said.

"We just wished to thank you for showing us the way out of here." Jim said, with a smile on his face.

"Precisely! Greg chimed in. Without the education, you so graciously provided, we would have failed our survival course."

"I am so glad I could be of assistance. Mokar replied, sarcastically. Even the big one, here, I see, absorbed enough of my teaching to survive this world."

"You bet I did, Mokar! Truck joined in. By da way, how's dat little fella doing, Toki? He was a slave in your house when we was here."

A strange look came into Mokar's eyes, before he answered. "A short while after your siblings had made their escape, Zarnog interrogated everyone in the "House of Learning" and found out the little slave had assisted them. He had him exterminated."

"Shock and tears dripped from the Earthman's eyes, at the same time. "Dat dirty sonuva bitch." He said, as he walked away, trying to conceal his sorrow. He didn't want to be around anyone, at the moment. As a matter of fact, no one saw him, again, for most of that day.

# CHAPTER 16

Warm tears of sadness mingled with the bitterness of revenge, as the big Earthman made his way through the surging mass of alien bodies. His strong legs knew exactly where they were taking him, the very instant his mind had conceived the plan. Through the close-packed crowd, he wended his way like an ice cutting ship through a sea of soft ice. He worked his way, quickly, toward the dome-shaped domiciles of the civilian population. Eventually, he found the one he was looking for. A group of six native sentries stood guard, spaced out in a circle around the small abode. They smiled and nodded their heads in welcome as he approached.

"How's dat royal pain in da ass doing? He asked, as he joined them. Not giving ya any trouble is he?"

"No trouble at all, Ta-rok. One of the natives answered. What is it that takes you away from our great victory celebration?"

"Aw, I ain't much for crowds. He answered, trying to keep the rage and sadness, roiling within, from giving him away. Seeing dat I was in da neighborhood, I thought I'd drop in an ask his highness what he plans ta do with dos poor creatures he's got locked up in da zoo." He lied.

"One moment, Ta-rok. We'll bring him out for you." Another native joined in, as he turned toward the entrance of the small structure.

"Dat won't be necessary, pal. The big man said, stopping the native. I thought I'd take him for a little walk through da zoo. Give da royal bastard a little exercise, while we talk."

"But, Ta-rok, Leota has given us specific instructions to keep him confined, under close watch. If we parade him around, he is apt to stir up trouble. Isn't he?"

"We ain't going to parade him around. The Earthman smiled at them. I am! Da zoo is deserted. Everyone one is in da square celebrating. Why don't you guys go and join dem."

Looks of relief showed in their eyes. Here was a chance to break the boredom and join in on the festivities.

Quickly, Truck extended his lie a little further. "You guys have been guarding him all day. Take a little break and in a couple hours I'll bring him back."

"Do you wish a couple of us to accompany you, Ta-rok?" One of them asked.

"Nah! I think I can handle him by myself. He said, shaking his big fist, while eliciting big smiles from their faces. You guys get outta here, now, and have some fun. I'll see ya later!"

As one, they turned and made their way back to the palace.

Without hesitation, Truck went through the small entryway, leading into the well-lit apartment. Zarnog reclined on a low divan, in the middle of the room. More, well-deserved, bruises were in evidence, on his ugly features, small tributes for the "kindness" he had shown others in the past. When his bloodless eyes focused on the large Earthman, he rose, quickly, to his feet. "What do you here, Earth creature?" He asked, alarm registering throughout his alien system.

Staring at the repulsive murderer, Truck fought against the overwhelming urge to rip him apart with his bare hands. Instead, he composed himself, somewhat, and replied. "I got some questions dat need answering and I thought ya might need a little exercise. So, you and I are going for a little walk."

Quivering with fear, Zarnog replied. "I do not wish to go anywhere with you, Earthman!"

Covering the few paces separating them, in a flash, Truck grabbed the royal pain by the back of his neck and held him so their faces were only inches apart. "I don't give a God damn what you wish, your hind end. Ya don't have a choice! With a powerful shove, Zarnog went flying through the entryway and tumbled to the ground outside.

Truck followed him, immediately. "Get up ya sonnuva bitch! You and I are gonna take a little walk through da zoo."

Quaking with fear, Zarnog managed to regain his feet. Truck grabbed him, none too gently, by one of his arms and off they went.

"What are you going to do to me? The manic monarch whimpered, in a frenzied voice.

When Truck didn't answer, the deposed leader continued. I am still the "High" leader! You cannot treat me in this manner!"

Truck remained silent, steering his alien cargo through the maze of domiciles that fronted the "zoo". By the time they reached the middle of the zoo compound, Zarnog's devious mind was almost in a state of shock.

They made their way to the front of one of the exhibits, Truck half-dragging the babbling alien. There, they stopped.

"Ya know, in da two worlds I been on, I never met an asshole as sick as you, man or beast. The American said, breaking his silence. Look around at all a dese poor creatures. Not one a dem ever did anything ta you or asked ta be here. But, feeling dat you was better den everyone else gave ya da right ta hurt dem. Me and my brothers were made ta feel da same way. It didn't matter ta you if we was hungry, scared or hurting. But, we survived it all. He continued, staring into zarnog's eyes that reflected indifference. Look at dem, ya sonnuva bitch! Truck bellowed, as he rushed to within six inches of the alien's face. Dese creatures are suffering, all because of you. My little friend, Toki the slave, suffered because he was a good little kid and wanted ta help us. Ya murdered da little guy because of his kindness."

Zarnog was trembling so violently, he leaned against one of the small control sheds to keep from falling. "I beg of you, he babbled, don't kill me! I was just doing what was my right to do. All of these beasts are meaningless and provide nothing more than entertainment. Gaining courage by listening to himself talk, he continued. We are far superior to these beasts. Even the slaves deployed around my kingdom are mine to do with as I please. Is it so different on the world you come from, Earthman?"

In answer, Truck took a step toward the sputtering creature and launched a right hand to the side of the bulbous head. Zarnog dropped to the ground, writhing in pain.

"Dat little slave happened ta be my friend. You will never hurt another living thing, again!"

With that said, he walked over to the control shed and pressed a button. The bars, in the front of the cage, directly behind where Zarnog lay, raised two feet. Walking over to the stunned alien, he picked him up and wedged him into the opening feet first.

Zarnog's eyes glowed red with panic and, as he felt needle-sharp teeth sink into his legs, he screamed at the top of his alien lungs. He was dragged into the middle of the cage. Truck moved back to the shed and pushed a button that dropped the bars back down.

Zarnog continued to scream in well-deserved agony as he watched mister Xarta eat him alive, consuming his legs, slowly working that mulching machine mouth up his torso. The horrible screams subsided, only, when the dagger-like teeth were halfway up the alien chest.

Truck stared in silence. No remorse or regret took up space in his heart or mind. At that instant, his only wish was that Mr. Xarta wasn't such a fast eater. He turned around, slowly, looking at all of the caged unfortunates. "Dat was for all you guys, too. He roared. I wish I coulda done more for your entertainment." He smiled.

Glancing up at the bright sky, he said. "Toki, thanks for being my friend." The tears dried on his face, as he made his way out of the zoo.

# CHAPTER 17

The third sun of the alien day was halfway through its cycle, when the big Earthman trudged, slowly, up the wide steps leading into the "House of learning". Mara stood at the top, watching him approach. "Ta-rok! You gave us all a big worry. She said. Where have you been?"

"I had a lot ta think about, darling. So, I went for a long walk around da city." This way he only swept half the truth under the rug.

"Are you all right?" She asked.

"I am now! He answered, giving her a big hug. Thanks for asking."

"Leota is inside. He wishes to speak with you." She said, as they made their way through the huge double doors.

Mokar had opened his house to the native army, offering the large, first floor atrium to accommodate their numbers. Out of the seven hundred native warriors who started this venture, less than five hundred remained. Deployments were scattered throughout the city, gathering their dead and collecting any over-looked firearms. Their physical presence also discouraged further uprisings.

As Truck approached, Leota and a small group were in deep discussion. Mara went off in search of Sanda and Lona.

"We have, but, two recourses at hand. Leota said. We can bury our dead here or carry them all the way back to our village and do it properly."

"With our numbers decreased, father, it will impede our progress by many days." Bantor said.

"Not to mention what affect the decomposition of the bodies will have on us." Tonio added.

"Leota! At the risk of sounding disrespectful of your methods for dealing with the deceased, I have a proposal that may be worth considering." Jim interjected.

"All ideas would be worth considering at this time, my Earth friend. Please, continue!" Leota urged.

"On my world many cultures practiced, what is known as "Viking" funerals. Jim continued. The Vikings were a war-driven race that traveled far and wide, conquering many countries. Because of their constant, warring nature, they didn't have the luxury of carrying their dead back home. So, they made funeral byres and burned their fallen heroes. They believed, the souls of these individuals traveled to their ancestors much faster in the rising smoke, fueled by their own bones."

"That is an excellent suggestion, Earthman. Leota said, noticing the nods of approval throughout the small group. They shall be honored in the tradition of our Earth brothers, bringing us even closer together."

"And what of our wounded? Rocca chimed in. Do we burn them, also, because they may impede our homeward progress?"

Leota stared into the eyes of the grief-filled warrior. "Roca! He said. We have all lost friends and kin, this day. That much we will leave behind us. But, rest assured, every wounded soul will be cared for and, if need be, carried on our backs until we reach our village."

Staring back at Leota, through tear moistened eyes, he responded. "I am sorry for having spoken so, my leader. My heart has taken control of my mind."

"Given the present circumstances, Rocca, I believe you have spoken the true feelings of this entire tribe. No apologies are necessary! Leota replied.

"Leota! Greg joined in. I, also, have an idea that will aid us greatly on our return trip."

Truck sat toward the back of the small group, leaning against one of the massive pillars. Mara had brought him a handful of dried meat and he gnawed away, ravenously. He wasn't ready, yet, to be confronted by Leota. He had a pretty good idea what he would hear. In the mean time he was keeping a low profile and listened.

"I will hear your idea, Earthman?"

"While my brothers and I were Zarnog's captives, Jim and I were given the job of feeding the zoo exhibits, as well as cleaning their cages. During this period, he continued, we came into contact with some of the most vicious creatures on, at least, two worlds. At the same time, we also had contact with some extremely tractable specimens."

"What is it you are trying to tell us, Earthman?" Leota interrupted.

Truck was on his feet in a flash, making his way toward the front of the group. He was caught up in the excitement of his brother's idea. "We build da biggest goddamn wagons ya ever saw and dey'll take us home." Truck interrupted, answering for his little brother.

Leota stared at him. His eyes gave away little. "So, our lost Earth brother has returned. We must have a talk, later. He said. But, at this moment, I want you to tell me what a "wagon" is."

Truck looked toward Greg, hoping he'd pick up the ball, again. He was much better at explaining things. Even though, Truck couldn't always understand some of the words he used to describe whatever it was.

"A wagon, Leota, is nothing more than a long box placed upon axles and rolled along on four wheels. If we employ some of the most tractable creatures, in Zarnog's collection, they will be hitched to these wagons and take us home in comfort." He finished.

The three brothers looked around at the people in the small group. Blank faces reflected the total ignorance of what he had just said. "They haven't the slightest clue as to what we're saying. Do they?" Jim offered.

"They'll grasp the concept, soon enough, Jim. Once they see what it is we are trying to accomplish." Greg added.

"Ya mean ta tell me dat dere are some tame beasts in dos cages? Dey all look pretty dangerous ta me." Said Truck.

"Well, my large sibling, if you hadn't decided to seek employment as a miner and traipse around the country, you would be aware of this. Greg joked. Jim and I could have used the help."

"That's true Truck! Jim joined in. A few of the bigger ones even called for you by name, after you left." He finished, with a big smile on his face.

"Yeah! Like I really had a choice! Truck responded. Dat was da worst time I ever had in my life. I wish I coulda been dere, instead, shoveling shit alongside my brothers." He finished, with a big smile in return.

Before anything further could be discussed, Leota broke in on the group "We have had a long day. I think it would be best if we all retired and commence with these ideas at the first sun."

The battle-weary natives didn't offer any resistance as they made their way to their furs. Watches had been deployed around the city. No more fighting was anticipated. But, it was better to be safe than sorry.

Before the brothers separated for the night, Truck turned to them and asked. "By da way, you guys, which a dos beasts asked about me when I was gone? I didn't even know dey could talk." The three of them shared a good laugh, then, said goodnight.

The big Earthman was halfway across the large open space when Leota intercepted him.

"Ta-rok let us go and take in some of the night air. Shall we?"

Without saying a word, the big American fell in beside him and they made their way through the double doors and into the alien night. One native was on duty, at the top of the landing. He nodded to them, as they moved down the wide steps. Twenty yards from the base of the steps and out of the earshot of the sentry, Leota stopped and turned toward Truck. "The men I ordered to stand watch over the alien leader came to me in a state of high panic. They, reluctantly, told me what happened. None of them wanted to bear bad news against you, however, they had no choice. "Can you blame them, Ta-rok?"

"Nah! Dey was just doing dere job." Truck answered.

"Good! Leota responded, looking into Truck's eyes. Now, you can tell me what you have done with Zarnog."

Standing straight and holding his head high, he responded. "I killed da bastard! He murdered da first friend I made on dis world, a friend dat helped my brothers escape. Besides dat, da sonnuva bitch murdered Bantor's baby, your little grandchild.

"He has murdered a lot of my people, my friend and, undoubtedly, deserved to die. But, we can't go around killing for revenge. That would take a lifetime to accomplish."

"I know dat, Leota. But, if anyone tries ta hurt my family or my friends, I gotta do what I gotta do."

The set look in Truck's eyes dissuaded Leota from trying to make him see it differently. "Where is the body? He asked, instead. I will send men to retrieve it and hide it somewhere far from the city. There may be some who have not yet broken their bonds with the cruel leader. It could cause us more problems if this was discovered."

"Dere's no need for dat, Leota. Truck answered. Dere ain't no body!"

"But, no body? Leota replied, confusedly. I do not understand."

For the next few moments, Truck told him all about his ghoulish deed, omitting no details. And, he still didn't feel any remorse or regret because of it.

"I hope you will always count me among your friends." Leota responded, after listening, incredulously, to this gentle giant's gory deed.

"You can bet da house on dat!" Truck said.

Leota just shook his head and smiled, as they made their way up the steps. "We are so fortunate this one is loyal to us." He said to himself.

# CHAPTER 18

The first sun of the new day was just starting to warm and lighten the alien world. Spirits were up a hundred-fold, as the natives scurried around in anticipation of their Earth brother's ideas. Few, if any, had the faintest notion of what was to come. Never the less, they volunteered to a man.

After raiding the alien workshops, Truck had discovered heavy-duty axes and saws. Well-equipped, he selected twenty-five warriors to accompany him into the small forest that had, only a short while ago, provided refuge for their invading army.

The shops also revealed, stacks of components for the deadly weapons, assembly required. Long steel rods were stacked on pallets, according to thickness, in one corner. Various pins and drilling equipment were also discovered. Obviously, the Nevoans were way ahead of the natives as far as technology went. The equipment and material, located in the alien "K mart", would serve their purpose well.

Jim and Greg selected twenty natives to accompany them to the "zoo". Armed with long, braided, Lurda hide ropes, they made their way around the compound. The brothers knew, from experience, the precise cages, holding the most tractable creatures. From their previous employment, they knew the ones they could trust. Spending hours manhandling the beasts from one side of their cages to the other, so they could remove the soiled bedding and scatter the fresh without being eaten or trampled, gave them a pretty good idea of what they were looking for.

The "Quavo" was the creature Jim had removed the large splinter from. How long ago was it? The furry beast followed him out of the cage like a puppy, once its long tongue lashed out at the Earthman, establishing familiarity and recognition of a kindness once done to him. The noose slipped around the thick, shaggy neck was, almost, unnecessary. The beast followed, closely, behind the Earthman on its six stubby legs. It stood five feet at the shoulder and weighed, approximately, twelve hundred pounds. Anatomically, It resembled the Lurda, with the absence of the lethal horn and disposition. And, like the Lurda, it subsisted entirely on the moss that covered most of this world. Its long, bushy tail swished side to side continuously.

The next beast of burden, they selected, was the "Galbor". It was the size of an ox, about fourteen hundred pounds. Long stiff, yellow hair covered its body, entirely, except for the head, which Flattened and narrowed, slightly, toward the end of its muzzle and its slit-like nose. The two dark eyes were set, one on either side of its hairless head. Directly below, the long snout, sat its wide mouth filled with molar type teeth for grinding the grains and grasses of its diet. Its four legs were the size of small oak trees, supporting its barrel-shaped, tailless body. It was a little skittish, at first, retreating to the back wall of its cage. After a few words, in a soothing tone and gentle strokes on the long muzzle, Greg was able to lead it out of the cage.

Another animal, that had made their employment much easier at the time, was the "Cragon". A three-legged tripod of power, it stood nearly seven feet tall. Its one powerful front leg was longer than the two thick rear legs, so its wide body had a sloped appearance. The small tail, held constantly erect, twitched constantly from side to side. Its short, soft fur could change colors from a dark brown to a fire red, reflecting its mood. The eleven hundred pounds was evenly displaced over the tripod frame. Near the top of the giraffe-like head were two dark eyes, set in two-inch bony stalks. A fleshy hole at the end of its short muzzle served as its mouth. Two gill-like openings sat below the small cup-shaped ears on either side of its head. It was not the prettiest creature. But, it was safe to work with. When it moved, it resembled a lineman charging out of a three-point stance. As a matter of fact, when Jim was in the cage cleaning business he had nicknamed it "Bronco".

The fourth creature, seeking employment in their working menagerie, was the "Harban". Weighing nearly sixteen hundred pounds, it was the largest of the group.

Standing six feet high at the shoulders, it resembled a cross between a Tibetan yak and an old English sheep dog. Long, black hair draped over its entire body. Its large round head grew, like an extension, from its thick neck. Two large, dark eyes were barely visible beneath the black shaggy mane covering its head. Wide nostrils perched, above a large oval mouth. Ears flopped from the sides of its massive head like mud flaps. Six long legs fitted, comfortably, beneath the tubular-shaped body. If it had a tail, it wasn't noticeable through the thick carpet.

Nervousness was the name of the game. Not only for the beasts, but, the men as well. As they herded their alien "cattle" together, Jim shouted out orders to his men. "Give them a lot of slack, until they settle down. These creatures have been penned up and mistreated for a long time. Exercise a little patience and they'll come around."

"Jim! What about these other unfortunates? Greg asked, as he led the "Galbor" around the compound, with the rest of the horrific herd. What will become of them?"

"You know as well as I, Greg. Most of those beasts are vicious and unpredictable. We can't take any chances!" Noticing the bemused look on his brother's face, he continued. "I'm sure Mokar will assign responsible individuals to look after them."

"Maybe you're right, Jim. He answered, resignedly. We don't want to jeopardize the safety of these people, now.

Especially, after all we have gone through. Fortunately, for us, we sent Truck off into the forest. He would have insisted we take all of them home with us." He finished, with a big smile on his face.

"You're right about that, Greg!" Jim said, smiling back at his younger brother.

In the next few hours, they worked the animals all over the zoo compound. After it seemed the beasts were capable of comprehending orders of "stop" and "go" they made their way out of the zoo and headed toward the large square in front of their quarters. The stares of bewilderment, they received from the Nevoan citizens, followed them with every turn. Six men held on to the leather halters, trailing behind each animal. This would accustom the animals to pull against a resisting force. The weight of the men, pulling on the straps, simulated the weight of the wagons. The Earthmen each walked between a pair of the large creatures, leading and coaxing them forward against the resistance. They wanted to observe which two would work best as a team. As only two large wagons were being constructed, the right tandems were imperative, over the long haul to their village. They faced a large task! Not only were the animals of different breeds, they were of different galaxies.

A short while after they had made it to the open square, Truck and his men arrived. Staggering under the weight of split logs and rounds six inches thick, cut from trees three feet in diameter, they halted at the foot of the wide steps. Truck walked over to where Jim and Greg had tethered the four beasts. They were in the process of feeding and watering them.

"Dose are da strangest horses I ever saw! He said, as he stroked the long hair of the "Harban". I hope dis idea of yours works, Jim. Some a dese natives are gonna need a ride home."

"I think it'll work out fine, Truck, once we get all the wrinkles ironed out." Jim replied, as he stared at the sweaty, sawdust-covered body of his huge brother. "It looks like you accomplished your job, also."

"Yeah! Truck replied. It was kinda slow going at first. But, once dey got used ta da axes and saws, it was a piece a cake. I think we got enough a da stuff. We left a pile of it, already cut, in case we need more."

"Well, it's about time you showed up! Greg said, as he joined them. For a moment, there, I thought we were going to have to send out a search party to rescue your big butt."

Grabbing his brother in a big bear hug, he squeezed him against his sweaty chest. "I was so afraid I'd never see ya again, little brother. I really missed ya!" He said over Greg's shoulder, smiling at Jim.

"Let me go, you big ape! Greg sputtered into Truck's massive chest, trying to break away from the powerful grip of the crushing hug. You smell worse than these animals!"

Releasing his struggling sibling, he winked at Jim. "Ya know I never get lost, little brother. But, thanks for worrying about me."

Brushing off the sweat and sawdust and catching his breath, once again, he looked into his brother's laughing faces and joined them.

"Maybe we should get washed up. Leota has a big victory feast preparing. Jim said. He sent out a hunting party earlier and I hear they've had good success."

"I can get in ta dat! Truck said. I could eat da ass outta two orangutans!"

"Now, dat's what I call hungry!" Greg mimicked his brother.

"Amen ta dat!" Jim joined the party, as they walked up the wide steps, laughing as they went.

# CHAPTER 19

The large banquet hall buzzed with activity. This time, It was filled with the sound of native voices. "King" Mokar had offered its use to accommodate the native feast. He had, also, contributed a substantial amount of the gourd-like fruit, grown by his agricultural experts. Mokar was the only alien in attendance. Native-Nevoan relations were not to the point of social interaction and probably never would be. That was just fine with both factions. As long as one another was allowed to live peaceful lives, with no intervention, intercourse was unnecessary.

Seated at a large table, just below the royal throne platform, the Americans and their companions dined heartily. "Hey, Mokar! Truck yelled across the table. Ain't cha gonna sit on da throne?"

He stared across the table, at the Earthman, watching him tear into one of the large fruit, with juices running off his chin. "Never, again, will a Nevoan leader stand over his people. He replied, looking at all the native faces. I most take my place beside them, while guiding them into this new life."

"Spoken like a true leader! Jim said. More are apt to change if they see their king working alongside them."

Most of the natives, sitting around the table, had no idea what was being said. Only those who had been incarcerated and subjected to the "photo cerebral implants" understood. Other than the three Earthmen, Leota and Graci, Bantor and cinda, no one else comprehended.

"Both of our peoples' future generations will benefit from this. Leota joined in. A day may come when friendly commerce may exist between us. One hundred years of sorrow will take a long time to heal. Now, at least, the wounds will not grow any deeper."

"Indeed! Greg chimed in. Nevoan technology combined with native woodsmanship would be a boon to both societies."

"I agree, my Earth student! Knowledge of all things belongs to everyone. Mokar replied. If it is not shared, little growth would be made by any society. I am, first and foremost, an educator and I would be content to instruct anyone, native or Nevoan in improving their lives."

"Maybe, in the future, there will be some from our village ready to take that challenge. Said Leota. The important thing is we have made progress stemming the suffering, which has gone on much too long."

After a brief pause, Truck broke back in. "Dis is a lot more relaxing den da last time we was here. He said, looking around at all the happy natives, celebrating in the large room. Not as exciting, though! A little music and dancing would, really, liven dis party up."

"You'll have to pardon my large brother. Greg said. He's easily bored, if there is too much discussion and not enough small wars taking place." He finished, with a big smile on his face.

A look, as if he were scolded, came over Truck's face. With a big smile, he said; "We could always dance a few rounds and entertain dese people, little brother."

"I would, Truck! But, you always insist on leading all the time and keep stepping on my feet." Greg returned, smiling.

Before Truck could throw the next verbal punch, Jim intervened. "I had meant to thank you earlier, Mokar, for allowing us the use of a few of your zoo exhibits. They will aid us, tremendously, in our journey home."

"My Earth student, I have always felt the incarceration of creatures, solely, for the purpose of entertainment, was a great waste of intellectual progress. The observance, of beasts from galaxies far removed from us, is like watching our suns rise and fall every day. We take for granted they are there. But, we know little about them. The time we squander, in this ritual forced upon us, could be put to better use."

"Never the less, your generosity is appreciated! Greg said. Those animals and the use of your shops will help us, immensely."

"As far as I am concerned, Earthman, you can take the entire collection home with you. Mokar answered. Personally, I think it nothing more than a useless distraction."

"There is one of us, here, who would gladly take you up on that offer, Mokar. Jim said, looking across the table at his large brother. Truck has a history of collecting strange pets."

Ignoring his brother's remark, Truck asked. "What'll happen to da animals we leave behind? Ya ain't gonna kill dem or anything like dat, are ya?"

"Enough killing has already been done, my Earth friend. Mokar answered. They will be attended to as usual. There are those among us that find them fascinating. Why? I don't understand. But, rest assured, they will be cared for."

"Thanks a lot, Mokar! I was kinda worried about dem. Da ones we take home will be taken care of. You got my word on dat!"

"I am relieved to hear that. Mokar replied, a bit sarcastically, as he rose from the table. I must leave you now. I have matters to attend to. If any assistance is required, feel free to ask for it." With that said, he left.

As the third sun of the day spent the last of its brilliance, the celebration was coming to a close. The last of the celebrants made their way out of the large room, seeking the warmth of their furs. The hard labor, they had willingly volunteered for, was a needed distraction, a reprieve from the destruction and blood they had experienced. The anticipation and excitement, revolving around the "Earth" inventions was just what the doctor ordered.

A small party remained at one of the tables, talking. "How long before these inventions, of yours, will be ready? Leota asked. I'm sure you are just as anxious to return to our village as the rest of us."

"The wagons should be completed within five cycles of the "Sister" suns. Greg answered. We have located everything we need in their workshops. It's just a matter of putting it all together."

"The beasts, we have selected, will be trained and ready by that time. Jim added. If there were more to choose from, we could all ride home in style."

"Unless, of course, we allow our brother here to do the selecting. Greg chimed in. Then, we may be here for quite some time."

Smiles blossomed around the table, as they all stared at Truck.

"I think he's just jealous dat I always had a good relationship with da animals, all my life." Truck replied.

"Oh! We're well aware of that, Truck. Greg shot back. Jim and I have seen a number of your dates."

The hurt look on Truck's face was so comical it, caused joint laughter among the small group. It wasn't long before he joined them.

After the humor, of the situation, had dispersed, Leota spoke. "It is decided, then. In five cycles of the suns, we shall start our journey home. If our Earth brothers' inventions are completed and live up to their expectations, we, as a village, shall be indebted to them."

"There is no need for gratitude, Leota. Jim said. We are just as anxious to return to the village as the rest of you. The kindness you and your people have shown, adopting us and giving us a home on your world makes us indebted to you."

"Our Earth brethren will, also, have another surprise waiting for them when we reach our village." Lona said, winking and smiling at Mara and Sanda. The three beautiful blondes laughed conspiratorially, as the whole group stared at them questioningly.

"What surprise?" Truck asked.

"When we are home, Ta-rok, you will find out." Mara said, smiling into the big man's confused gaze.

Jim looked at Sanda and received a beautiful smile in return. "I think you will, also, be pleased, Gem."

As the Earthlings stared at each other, in a quandary, Leota spoke.

"I think we should retire for the night. Much work is to be done, so we must get an early start."

As they made their way out of the great hall, Leota asked Truck a question. "Ta-rok! What is "music" and "dancing"?

"When we get home, pal, I'll tell ya all about it. He answered. I think you'll like dem."

So, Leota sought out his furs and like the three Earthmen had many unanswered questions to accompany him. "I cannot reach my village soon enough." He said to himself.

# CHAPTER 20

The first sun of the day fell on the busy natives, as they toiled with the construction of the "Earth" wagons. Everyone wanted to be involved with this project. The excitement pushed their adrenalin level to new heights. As the day grew so, too, did the contours of the wagons. The beds were almost twenty feet long and eight feet wide. The rough-hewn planks were made smooth, by many eager hands, rubbing fine sand over them with flat rocks. The wheel rounds were three feet tall and six inches thick. Metal rims were pounded onto the edges to give it strength and durability. The hole in the middle, where the axle passed through, was also lined with metal. Some of the long metal rods, they had found, were nearly four inches in diameter.

It took a while to learn how to operate a certain machine that bored holes of many diameters. But, with the requested assistance of Nevoan manpower, they were quickly mastered. The strange machine was powered by the same quartz rock that gave the lethalness to the Nevoan weapons. Acting much like a laser, it easily bored holes of various sizes through the metal rods. Hubs and pins were fitted around the wheels, holding them firmly on the axles. A huge metal pinion was fitted through the center of the front axle, allowing it to swivel and turn in the wagons given direction. The large box, on each of the wagons, had three-foot high fences along all four sides.

Other groups worked on braiding the tough Lurda hide into reins and harnesses. Others worked on carving large wooden yokes to hold the beasts in place. No comfort features were built into the wagons; such as leaf springs or shock absorbers. It would be a bumpy ride but it would serve the purpose. Greg kept a practiced eye on all proceedings. Drawing from memory, rather than professional experience, he did his best with what availed him.

Jim, Truck, Bantor and a small group continued to work with the four beasts of burden. Their progress, in training the creatures, was steady, but, not without mishap. Stomped feet were suffered by those slow afoot. Small nips, from an irritated animal and collisions with the beasts added to their bruises. The tractable animals were becoming more docile as the days passed. Maybe it was the freedom, from the oppressive cages, combined with the first kindness they had been exposed to, since their abductions. Whatever it was, their adaptability was becoming more noticeable as the days wore on. These reasons, besides, all the food and water they could hold, was shaping them into compliant beasts of burden.

The group of trainers, also, decided, through trial and error, which pair would work best together. They matched the ox-like Galbor and the three-legged Cragon not only because of their size, but, because of the length of their stride. Neither beast would hinder the other's progress. Jim's six-legged pet Quavo would be matched with the massive Harban, because their docile personalities fitted well together.

While they were getting the alien giants accustomed to the harness and yoke, only the Cragon showed any aggressiveness. A little patience and a short while later it settled down and adapted to the change. Jim continued to use the exercise of having some of his native charges pull on the reins, while prodding the beasts ahead. They had considerable loads to pull. He wanted them prepared when they started their journey, a few days from now. Getting them accustomed to the pull on their harnesses, soon, became commonplace. They accepted the resistance and continued to pull ahead until given the command to stop. Looking at the creatures, Jim concluded, they had resigned themselves to this strange activity because it was a much better life than they had ever known on this world. It was ironic. But, it coincided with the plight of him and his brothers. They had resigned themselves to better lives. They, also, were free of their cages.

The next few days flew by, in a flourish of labor. The wagons were almost completed and their beasts of burden were fully trained. They hoped! All that remained were the final tasks. Hunting parties had been sent out and improved their supplies, for the long march home. The weapons, they had captured, would be piled in the wagons, along with the injured. Many of the blue crystal rocks had, also, been collected. It would have been, nearly, impossible to gather them all. The ones they left behind would power Mokar's machines and used in a positive manner. The new leader had assured them "a peaceful society had no use for weapons of destruction". So, the natives had no qualms about taking all of the lethal rods they could find. There were so many, Leota ordered groups of men to take the majority into the hills and bury them, along with most of the blue crystals. There was no possible way for them to haul all of it with them. Their beasts of burden had even lightened their load, considerably. By having adapted to a diet of domestic grasses and moss, the need to haul food for them was eliminated.

Everything seemed in readiness. Tomorrow, they would begin their journey.

# CHAPTER 21

The strange procession, flowing through the massive Nevoan gates, would, probably, never be repeated again. The time it would take to heal the gaping wounds, caused by the aliens, would make intercourse unlikely for many generations to come.

Seven hundred uncertain natives had begun this revolution to gain their freedom, a short eternity ago, with little hope of returning. One hundred years of constant turmoil was just too overwhelming. Very few, at the onset, believed there was little chance of defeating these powerful invaders. Loyal to the last native, they knew they had to make the attempt before their numbers dwindled to the point where resistance would no longer be possible. More than two hundred lives were the physical prices paid, to the "Grim Reaper", for their freedom. The emotional price tag was even higher.

Mokar and a few of his trusted scholars watched the native contingency pass through his gates, probably for the last time as an eyewitness. He, also, believed there was little chance of commerce between the two cultures. The last one hundred years of atrocities would take twice as long to heal. He was, sad to say, a witness to most of them.

"If our wanderings, on this world, should ever place us together, again, I vow to you and your people, it will be a peaceful encounter. Mokar said to Leota. Our short coexistence has evoked enough hatred and cruelty to fill all eternity. There will be no more!"

"We, too, shall pass in peace if ever we should meet. The native leader replied. The end of hostilities will give us both the time we need to heal our wounded world and make it a better place to live. Rule well, Mokar!" He said, as he passed through the gates.

The Earth brothers had met earlier with the new Nevoan leader. Gratitude was expressed to him for helping them to survive a cruel society, ruled by an even crueler monarch. He had shielded them from Zarnog's evil tactics on many occasions and virtually kept them from getting killed. In spite of himself and the dictates of his society, he had become their first friend in this friendless metropolis. Before they parted, he bestowed upon them several leather-bound folders. The flora and fauna of this world were illustrated in detail. One of the huge tomes contained a vast collection of maps. The Nevoans had not been idle in their one hundred years. They had mapped out a vast area, radiating from their city for hundreds of miles in all directions. This information would be invaluable to anyone wishing to do a little exploring on this world.

Greg and Truck commandeered the two wagons. Jim walked alongside the animals, coaxing them on and easing their nervousness, every now and then, when they became a bit skittish around the large group of native travelers.

The wagons were loaded with a large supply of the lethal weapons and precious quartz rock. Alongside these piles, forty wounded natives tried to find comfortable positions on the bumpy ride. Extra furs, food and other supplies surrounded them.

This was a, totally, different group of travelers, who covered the moss-carpeted terrain with a spring in their step and hearts freed from one hundred years of heavy suffering.

Jim looked about him and smiled. "How long ago was it? He thought to himself. Weeks? Months?" The pleasant aura would accompany them all the way back to their village. An emotional transition had, definitely, taken place, during this period of time. The trek to the alien city was more like a funeral march. For many of the sacrificed souls, it was. The returning caravan was a continuous, celebratory parade with no complaints to weigh them down.

He walked ahead, to the lead wagon. Greg sat on the driver's seat, patiently urging the three-legged Cragon and the Galbor into a steady pace. The four long reins clutched comfortably, two in each hand.

"How's it going, Greg?" He asked, as he jumped up and straddled the sideboard.

"Rather good, actually. Greg answered. Considering the fact they were in cages a few days ago. If someone only had a camera, what a picture this would make."

Jim smiled at his brother's enthusiasm. "If you notice them lagging in their harness or stumbling, stop immediately. We have a long way to go, so don't put too much stress on them."

He sat in silence, for a few moments, observing the smooth, working rhythm of the two beasts.

"They seem to be in sync. He said, after a while. We'll coax more out of them, as they gradually get used to it."

"How long do you estimate before we reach the village, Jim?"

"I have no idea, little brother. But, I'll tell you one thing, at this pace and the restored spirits of these people, it won't take as long as the trip going out. They have nothing left to complain about." He finished, as he jumped off the wagon.

"That, in itself, will increase our speed considerably." Greg agreed.

"I'll talk with you later. Jim waved. I want to see how Truck's doing."

"By the way, Jim. You wouldn't happen to have any extra air freshener you could spare, would you? That three-legged beast smells worst than Truck after pizza."

Jim chuckled, as he made his way back to the other wagon. They had decided to stagger them through the marching horde to provide more accessibility to their supplies. It would relieve some of the burden from the weary travelers over the many miles.

As they continued to put miles between them and the alien city, the terrain started to change. Low, rolling hills rippled the landscape. It was dotted, every so often, by small patches of forest. The springy, moss-covered plain was more than firm enough, as not to impede the steady progress of the large wooden wheels. To save a little wear and tear on the working beasts, they weaved their way around most of the hills and obstacles. Even though, they were on a snake-like course, no one seemed to mind. They had accomplished what most of them had deemed to be impossible. This journey home would be a relaxing and healing experience.

The morning sun was halfway through its cycle. Leota informed everyone they would stop and rest when it had run its course. The overall demeanor of the natives was so improved and adrenalin was so high, time went quickly by. The rest periods were mostly for the benefit of the animals. The happy energy, exuding from the natives, made it difficult to relax. The well-earned exhaustion from their victory and travels would follow them all the way home. Then, they could rest.

As Jim walked back, toward the second wagon, the contentment radiating from everyone created an emotional epidemic. Tears were as vividly displayed as laughter. Many friends and relatives would be mourned, during this journey and for a long time to come.

"How's it going, Truck? He asked, as he jumped aboard. Are they working together pretty well?"

"Dere doing fine, Jimbo. Truck answered. Dat big one dere has been farting so much I think it's acting like ether on da wounded men. Most a dem have been sleeping since we left."

Jim laughed, as he looked into the back of the wagon. Sanda, Mara and Lona were ministering to the wounded men. "Everything okay back there, girls?" He asked.

"They are doing just fine, Gem. Sanda answered. With a lot of rest, in time, they will be back to their normal selves."

"And don't let your sibling deceive you, Gem. Mara chimed in. Not all of that foul wind is coming from the animals."

Truck heard this and looked at Jim with a big sheepish grin on his face.

Looking at the guilty expression, on his brother's face, made Jim laugh so hard, he almost lost his purchase on the wagon. "Just take it nice and easy, Truck. Jim said, after catching his breath. Don't push them too hard." He finished, referring to the animals.

"I'll try, Jimbo! But, I think I ate too much at our celebration. Bouncing around on dis wagon ain't helping either."

"That's not what I …. Jim started to say.

Truck cut him off with his roaring laughter and they both erupted into a duet of humor.

"I'll see all of you later. Jim said, as he dropped down from the wagon. You wouldn't happen to know where Leota is, would you?" He asked.

"The last I saw he was at the rear of our column. Lona Joined in. He was with Graci, Bantor and Cinda."

"Thanks! I'll catch up with all of you at our first rest stop." With that, he hurried to the tail end of the marching throng.

A short while later, he spotted Leota strolling hand-in-hand with Graci. Not a care in the world or eyes for anyone else but each other, they followed the anxious horde.

Bantor, his arm draped over Cinda's shoulders, moved at the same pace. "Like father, like son." Jim thought, as he joined them.

"I just wanted to let you know, our little experiment is working out well. The wagons are holding up and the animals are doing just fine."

"There is not a person in this village who is not indebted to you and your siblings. Leota said. You have made comfortable travel possible for our wounded and hastened our return home. Many may not have made it, but for your Earth inventions."

"Thank you, Leota! But, we are the ones who benefit from your kindness. Jim replied. Our new lives, on this world, would have been quite different had we not met. We share our Earth knowledge willingly, not only as a slight payment for your generosity but to improve all of our every day lives. So, we both gain from this arrangement. We are loyal citizens of your village, now, and these new things we bring from our world belong to all of us."

"I have this feeling inside, the Earth wagon and training wild creatures to do your bidding, is just the beginning. Bantor joined in. Ta-rok has told me about many strange things."

"You're right about that, Bantor. Jim answered. We have a lot of new ideas to discuss. But, I'm sure you will find them interesting."

"And, the nice thing about it, my Earth brother, we have a lifetime to realize them."

"Amen ta dat!" Leota said, eliciting laughter from the small group.

A short while later, a halt was called to their march. A small forest accommodated them with its soothing shade and the small brook running through it. The first leg of their journey, toward the rest of their lives, had been completed.

# CHAPTER 22

Progress was steady and uneventful, in the next five days. Miles melted behind them, with each setting sun. The spirit of the small army reached a new plateau, as they got closer to their village.

Squeals, from their four beasts of burden, had the same affect as an air-raid siren. They were picketed down wind, a short distance from the slumbering camp, for obvious reasons. There were many, among them, who thought Truck should have been picketed down wind also.

Disengaging himself from Sanda's side, Jim leaped out of the warm furs. Lighting a torch, at a fire pit, he rushed toward the frightened animals. Before he had covered half the distance, he heard the blood-curdling roar of the "king of lizards".

They were camped in a large hollow bordered on two sides by large hills. Shade trees were scattered throughout the area, but not thickly. Movement, at the top of one of the hills' was silhouetted against the star-lit sky. The "killer" was still a good five hundred yards off, but moving steadily in their direction.

Jim put his arms around the shaggy head of the Quavo and felt the shuddering fear. Others had joined him, by this time. Greg, Truck and Bantor were soothing the other animals.

"Hey, Jimbo! Truck yelled across to him. I think we should go up dere and blow dat sonnuva bitch ta hell."

"I agree, Jim! Greg chimed in, over the panicked symphony emanating from their beasts. We can't let it get near these animals!"

Most of the camp was gathered around them, curiously searching for the author of the disturbance.

"Let's do it!" Jim replied.

Armed with the powerful rods and bows and arrows they advanced toward the malicious menace. Some of them carried lit torches, dissolving a part of the night's dark cloak. This was unheard of, to most of them. You ran from the Kazor. You didn't rush to embrace him.

When they had reached a point approximately fifty yards from the approaching monster, they fanned out in a semi-circle. The faith they had in the new weapons and the invincible feeling of power, radiating from the group, kept them rooted to the spot. Even then, the murdering creature stood their nerves a good test.

"Everyone, draw a bead on the bastard. Jim yelled. Wait for my order to start firing."

When the Kazor got to within twenty yards of them, it stopped. Its puny mind was confused. "Why were these delicious weaklings not running away from me in panic?

This has never happened before." It seemed to be thinking. If it was capable of logic, that is. Contaminated slime dripped from its cavernous mouth. Teeth, brown and rotting from age, were still intimidating, never the less.

Before it could decide its next course of action, it was too late.

"Fire!" Jim shouted.

Arrows and bolts of energy rained, in a killing storm, toward the beast. In a brief instant the Kazor exploded into a thousand slimy chunks that flew into the night and buried themselves, Forever, into the soft moss. Only one round had been fired from each weapon. More was not necessary. The rapid destruction of the large creature left the group of men in awe. The nervousness and doubt, prevalent only moments before, was replaced with smiles and shouts of victorious joy.

As they made their way back to the encampment, they stopped to check on the animals. They were calm now and munched on the springy moss.

"You know, Truck, that Kazor was probably a mile away when our animals picked up its scent. Do you know what this means?"

"You betcha, Jimbo. The big guy answered. We got four a da best watch dogs in da world."

Walking toward the center of their camp, they noticed the main fire had been relit. Nearly everyone had been roused from their warm furs by the sudden racket, shattering the nocturnal calm. Leota and a large group were standing around the fire. These men had not taken part in the glorious slaughter.

As they approached, Leota looked at them questioningly. Because of the swift manner, in which they had dispatched the beast, they were only gone a handful of minutes.

"So! The vicious beast ran off into the night when it saw you. Yes?" He asked.

"No, father! Bantor answered. There are pieces of the Kazor, so small, scattered over the moss, a child could carry them."

Leota stared in amazement at the group of victorious men. "It is a fortunate thing we decided to take some of these strange weapons back to our village. We are safe, because of them."

"They destroyed the beast, quickly. Greg joined in. But, at the same time, our safety this night is a direct result of the vigilance of our animals. Their alarm roused us in time to defeat it."

Leota stared at them, still amazed at how quickly the most dangerous animal to walk in his world was eliminated. "Once, again, the gratitude of the entire village goes out to you and your siblings, for making this possible."

The tranquility of the night was disturbed, for the second time. The loud cheers of almost five hundred voices, raised in unison, doing the damage this time around.

The three Earthmen looked at each other, embarrassedly, as the loud demonstration of appreciation subsided.

"Leota, are we not members of this village and counted among your people?" Greg asked.

"Why, of course!" The leader answered, confused by the question.

"Then, from this moment on, any brain child conceived by myself or either of my siblings will be accredited to the entire village. Future celebrations, then, can be shared by everyone, because we all worked hard to implement them."

"I agree with my brother! Jim added. We had the idea. But, it took the entire cooperation of the village to make it work. We're just happy they alleviated one of our problems and you had the confidence to let us make the attempt.

"And, dere's a lot more where dose came from. Truck added. I promise ya dat!"

Many of the natives, by now, were starting to reclaim their warm furs and retire for the second time that night. The fire burned a little lower, in the large pit. Sanda, Mara and Lona sat off to its side drinking their "special" tea, another mysterious ritual they shared. Another unanswered question the three brothers added to their stockpile of wondering.

"Let us retire to our furs. Leota said. An early start to our journey puts us that much closer to home." Nodding to the three brothers, he put his arm around Graci and strode off into the night.

Bantor and Cinda had put the heat back into their furs, shortly after they had returned from dispatching the Kazor.

Greg and Lona bid them goodnight and departed. Smiling at each other.

Jim and Sanda joined Truck and Mara around the diminishing glow of the fire.

"What makes that tea so special, you girls are drinking all the time?" Jim asked.

Shaded smiles appeared on the faces of the two beautiful blondes. A sparkle in their eyes added to the bewilderment of the two men.

"We will tell you all about it, when we reach the village, Gem. Sanda replied. But, it is late and I am tired."

"I am too!" Mara joined in. They both planted kisses, on their men's cheeks and left.

"What da hell's going on with dos three dames? Truck asked, watching them make their way across the dark encampment. Dey been acting strange, lately."

"I, honestly, don't know, Truck. Jim answered. I guess we'll just have to wait and find out. Come on! He said, rising from his seat by the dwindling fire. Let's go check the animals one more time and hit the sack."

Long stakes had been driven into the ground and lengths of braided Lurda hide, attached to them, prevented the beasts from wandering off. But, they were long enough to allow them to move around and graze on the moss and low bushes scattered nearby.

As they approached, the Quavo lumbered toward Jim and put his big shaggy head into position for a good scratching.

"Dat animal sure loves ya, Jimbo." Truck said, as he made his way over to where the three-legged Cragon stood. At sight of Truck, the ugly tripod moved toward him and started licking his face.

"It looks to me like you, also, have made a friend my brother." Jim said, laughing at the comical sight.

"Yah! Stinker and me get along pretty good, too. He replied, rubbing the alien head.

"I don't think you have to tell me what you two have in common." Jim said, smiling.

The massive Harban and the greyhound-looking Galbor kept chomping away at the turf, undisturbed by the attention their teammates were getting.

A short while later, the two brothers joined the rest of the weary travelers in slumber. Every day, from here on out, would be an adventure for them. A whole new world was at their disposal, awaiting an Earthly touch of excitement and change. The possibilities were limitless and they were ready for the challenge.

# CHAPTER 23

An audible cracking sound and the sudden tilting of the wagon, to his right, caused Truck to react. Pulling on the reins, he brought the animals to an immediate stop. Jumping to the ground, he saw the cause of the problem. The large wooden wheel, on the right forefront, was broken completely in half. Problems, such as this, had been anticipated. Four of the "spare tires" were mounted around the sideboards of each wagon.

Truck went to the rear and unlashed one of them. He, also, took a large wooden mallet out of an equipment bag, inside the wagon. Walking back to the broken wheel, he used it to remove the metal pin that secured the wheel to the axle. He, then, employed a dozen men to raise that side of the wagon, removed the broken wheel and replaced it with the spare. As he was pounding the securing pin back into place, Jim came up to him to see what the problem was.

"We got our first flat tire, Jimbo! But, we're almost ready ta get rolling again." He said, replacing the large mallet and broken wheel in the back of the wagon. The metal rim would be salvaged, once they got back to the village.

"It's fortunate Greg had the foresight to have extra wheels made. Jim said. When we get home, we can carve spoke wheels. They'll last a little bit longer."

"By da time we're done building we're gonna have a pretty comfortable village. Eh Jimbo?"

"You got that right, Truck! He answered. You must be getting a little tired. You want me to take over for a while?"

"Yah! Thanks Jim. My butt's getting kinda squishy."

"Thanks for sharing that with me, Truck. Jim replied, as he climbed into the driver's seat.

"Wait a minute, Jim! Let me check dos other wheels, before ya start." After he had completed his inspection, he waved to his brother. Good ta go, Jimbo."

As Jim moved ahead, he yelled over his shoulder. "Check the wheels on the other wagon, while you're at it, Truck!"

"Will do, Jimbo!" The big guy yelled back, as he moved on.

The terrain, they were traveling through at present, was becoming more uneven. Small hills dotted the landscape. It was almost impossible, to skirt around every one of them. More often, now, they had no choice but to go up and over the top of some of them. Although they were small hills and the grades were not that steep, it was taking its toll on the animals. Rest periods became more frequent and lasted longer. Yet, no one complained. They were still making much better time then they would have had they been carrying their wounded and supplies on their backs. Besides, the animals assured them all peaceful nights of secure slumber.

As the days wore on, anticipation was at its highest point. Familiar landmarks were starting to reveal themselves. They set up camp, for the evening, in a small copse of woods, surrounded on three sides by large hills. A large spring-fed pond nestled at the base of one of the slopes. The happy banter, filtering throughout the encampment, gave testimony to the many anxious men and women who were more than ready to bring this journey to a climax.

The glow of the large communal fire reflected upon the travel-weary faces. Each one contemplated, in their own way, the joyous reunions with family and friends soon to be. A hunting party had dispatched a dozen Lurdas, shortly before making camp. They were, now, quartered and spitted over many fires, throughout the encampment.

The three Earthmen had just returned from settling the animals down for the night and checking them for any injuries. Other than being weary from their struggles against the wagons, they were just fine.

Leota walked in front of the fire, from where he had been standing with Graci, Bantor and Cinda. "I don't believe I have to tell most of you, in just three journeys of our "Sister" suns, we will have reached our village." He began, his voice resonating through the night and quieting the crowd.

"What we have accomplished was only a dream, a short time ago. The resourcefulness of our three Earth citizens, coupled with the loyal efforts of the entire village, made this possible. A Man or woman, who wishes to hunt or travel throughout our world, can now do so in safety. I salute your efforts." Looking out, among the crowd of nodding, smiling people, the overwhelming pride of being their leader moved tears into the corners of his eyes.

"Upon the return to our village, my son has agreed to lead search parties into the wilderness to locate other villages. He continued. The maps and charts, donated to us by the new, alien leader, will be their guide. Detailed, in some of these maps, are the locations of other settlements. In the near future, commerce will be established and the growth and prosperity of our people will increase."

A thunderous cheer, of agreement, erupted from the weary audience. Some of them had relatives or friends hidden away in these lost tribes. The natives, who didn't have friendly contacts with these other tribes, looked at it as an adventure to travel and explore.

After the verbal celebration had subsided, somewhat, Leota spoke again. "Many new and exciting things are now at our disposal. Some of them will seem strange, at first. But, in time, we will adjust to them. In the end, we will all benefit by them."

As the fires burned low and many pounds of Lurda flesh had been consumed, the conquering natives eventually succumbed to sleep. The dark, star-flecked sky cast an aura of peace and hope, as it watched over their dreams.

# CHAPTER 24

From a distant rise in the terrain, about two hundred yards away, a small figure was seen racing down the slope toward them. The travelers, at the head of the caravan, passed word back that someone was approaching. Soon, a young boy, of about ten or eleven years old, came panting into their midst. Leota was summoned forward and soon stood in front of the boy, who was struggling to catch his breath.

"What brings you here, my son?" Leota asked, kneeling down and placing his hands on the boy's shoulders.

Puffing himself up to his full height, he said, proudly; "I am Toran, a sentry for my village!"

It was, soon, discerned that Kaba used some of the older boys as lookouts. For the last few weeks, he had them situated at high points around the village awaiting the arrival of the returning army.

"You have done your job well, Toran! Leota said. I am happy that you are counted among us."

"Thank you, my leader." He responded. After having accepted a drink of water, he turned and raced back toward the village to spread the word of their return. The excitement, flowing through his young body, fueled his legs into high gear. He practically flew over the rough terrain and soon was out of sight.

"That is one happy camper! Said Jim, who had silently witnessed the event. He'll have bragging rights for a long time and the envy of every youngster in the village."

"My happiness is magnified a thousand times that of the boys. Leota said, his eyes starting to well with tears of relief. I have been away for much too long. It is time to go home, my Earth friend."

The short distance, separating them from the village, was covered in record time. If they had had four legs and horns sticking out of their heads, it would have resembled a herd of thirsty cattle stampeding toward a water hole. Even the four, tired beasts of burden were caught up in the excitement. Greg and Truck had all they could do to keep them from speeding off with the rest of the horde.

Eventually, every grimy, travel-worn body passed through the wooden gates, into the village. The happy bedlam, that transpired, sounded like a "New Year's Eve" celebration, after everyone was deep into the cups. It was an emotional drunk. Screams of joy, as well as ululations of mourning filled the late afternoon air.

Greg and Truck decided it was best to draw the animals up just short of the gate. There was no way of telling, how they would react in this situation. They staked them out where they stood and strode through the gates, for the first time in how long?

Small groups were straggled all about the entryway to the village, laughing, hugging one another and crying. Some, in the throes of disbelief when they heard about the loss of a loved one or friend, cursed their ancestors for allowing this to happen.

As they made their way through the mob of celebrants, a little old man came up to them and enfolded both of the Earthmen into his bony arms. "It is good to see you two are still in this world." Kaba said, staring at them through moist eyes.

"Kaba! Ya old sonnuva gun! Truck shouted, hugging the old man back, fiercely. I'm glad ta see dat your still kicking, also."

As he was being squeezed between the two Earthmen, he happened to look back through the open gates. "What, in the name of my ancestors, are those?" He asked, pointing behind them.

"We will be glad to tell you all about it in time, my old friend. Greg answered. But, not at this moment."

Kaba just shook his head and kept staring at the animals. "I will anticipate that story, my son."

"Ta-rok!" A small voice screamed, loud enough to be heard over the homecoming hullabaloo.

Searching the crowd, for the author of the familiar voice, Truck spotted her. Leaning on her crutch and standing apart from the merry mob was little Gia. Mara was alongside her, with one arm draped, protectively, over the young shoulders.

Plowing his way through the sea of celebrating natives, he was at her side in a few heartbeats. Picking her up, he hugged her to him. "I missed you, little one!" He said, as tears of happiness flowed into her blonde curls.

"I missed you, too, Ta-rok!" She said, placing her arms around his neck and squeezing tightly.

Mara stood, silently, adding her wet smile to the family reunion.

After a few moments, Truck set her down. Noticing, for the first time, the crutch she was leaning on, he asked. "What happened ta da leg I made ya, darling? Did ya lose it?"

"No, Ta-rok. She answered. It is too small for me. I can't wear it anymore!" She finished, with tears bursting from her blue eyes.

Kneeling down in front of her, Truck hugged her to him. "Don't worry, little one. I'll make ya a bigger and better one. I promise!"

After waiting for the tears to finish running their course, he wiped her face with his big hand. "Ya know why dat leg of yours doesn't fit anymore, don't ya?" Truck asked.

"Why, Ta-rok?"

"Cause yer growing up ta be da prettiest lady in da world. Just like your mother dere. He said, smiling at Mara. Da bigger ya get, da bigger I gotta make da leg. Just keep growing, sweetheart. I'll always be dere for ya. Okay?"

"Okay, Ta-rok." She said, smiling up at the big man and hugging him around the waist.

Handing the crutch to Mara, he picked her up and sat her on his shoulders. "Let's show dis little one, here, what we brought her." With that, they headed toward the gates.

# CHAPTER 25

The community fire burned brightly, spreading its warm glow into the darkness and illuminating the many faces gathered around it. As the happy crowd reveled in the familiar security of this occasion, young boys and girls filtered through the crowd serving the potent melon drink, "Tova". Many were already deep into their cups. The volume of the celebration echoed, loudly, into the nocturnal darkness. Intimate groups were scattered all about the communal fire. Leota, Bantor and the three Earthmen were situated nearest the fire. Their women sat alongside them. Gia was in her usual place, seated on Truck's knee.

Rising from his seat, by the fire, Leota faced the large crowd. As he scanned the happy faces, relief, joy and sadness reflected from his kind eyes. It would take time to smooth out the lines that creased his face. Stress, hopelessness and deprivation were the cause. The wounds to his soul ran even deeper.

"My people! He began, silencing the boisterous crowd a few decibels. I have been away for many suns. Much has occurred since then. The joy in my heart can never be expressed and the debt to those responsible can never be repaid." He paused, for a moment, letting his gaze encircle the entire collection of faces and then continued.

"The many brave souls, who are not with us to share in this momentous occasion, have not perished in vain. To their last breath of life, they battled so that we could live out our lives free of oppression. We will do them honor by living these lives in harmony." He finished, taking up his seat by the fire.

A thunderous roar exploded from the attentive crowd, with such enthusiastic force, it shattered the night's calm for miles around.

"Dat was beautiful! Said Truck. I don't think I coulda said it better."

"I know, damn well, you couldn't!" Greg chimed in, smiling at his large brother.

Leota shook his head and smiled. "Thank you, Ta-rok! It would take a lifetime to express, in words, what their sacrifices mean to us. Unfortunately, I am not allowed that luxury. As leader of this village, I must dwell on the living."

"If you would allow it, Leota, my brothers and I could erect a shrine in their honor. Jim said. It is a common practice where we come from."

"An excellent idea, Jim! Greg joined in. There are many, in this village, who are experts in working stone."

"Memorials have already been etched in everyone's hearts. Said Leota. But, I suppose we should start getting used to more of these Earthly concepts."

"Speaking of ideas, Leota, my brothers and I have many we wish to propose to the village." Jim jumped in, enthusiastically.

"If they are as beneficial to my people as your "Earth Wagon", propose away. Replied Leota. But, this can wait until the morning. Tonight we celebrate!"

"Amen ta dat!" Said Truck, lifting his cup in salute.

"I, also, have ideas to discuss with you, my father." Bantor chimed in.

Leota looked at all of them and smiled. "I have to be the most fortunate leader of any people, to be surrounded with so many willing contributors. I am truly blessed!"

As some of the glow dissipated from the communal fire, so did the large crowd. People started wandering off to find the security of their huts, they had not experienced for a long time. To sleep a restful sleep, uninterrupted by war, beasts or nightmares was a luxury, they now could afford. They had paid dearly to attain it.

Before too long, the three Earthmen, their women and Gia were the sole occupants enjoying the last warming embraces of the communal fire.

Sanda, smiling, looked at the other two women. "I think this is the right moment to share our secrets.

Mara and Lona nodded their heads and returned the smile.

The three Americans stared back at them, questioningly, anxiously awaiting long overdue answers to questions that had plagued them for miles. But, before any of them could utter a word, Mara spoke.

"We are all with child!"

The stunning announcement entered the three Earth minds so abruptly, it shut down their capacity to breathe or speak for a few moments. Everything stood still! The familiar sounds of the night even took a brief intermission. Then, in a wave of ecstatic appreciation, the Earth trio erupted. Hugging their women and kissing them, they all started talking at once.

"I knew dere was something going on. Truck said, smiling. But I was too stupid ta figure it out."

"When did you find out for sure?" Jim asked Sanda.

"Why wouldn't you let us share this with you?" Greg asked Lona.

"If we had told you, you would have sent us back to the village." Mara answered.

"We only learned of this shortly before we reached the alien settlement. Sanda added.

"The "special" tea, you were wondering about, is to enhance the flow of "Mother's" milk." Lona chimed in.

Silence prevailed, for a few moments, while all of this was being digested among the Earthmen. Then, Truck broke the tranquility.

"Are you sure dat wer da fathers?"

The shocked looks on the women's faces and the huge grin on Truck's ignited convulsive laughter.

Gia looked from one to another, trying to understand what was going on. Everyone was laughing and hugging. The three men were shaking hands and slapping each other on the back.

"Ta-rok! Why is everyone to happy? She, finally, asked. What is going on?"

"Yer gonna be a big sister, darling! He answered, hugging her to him. Your momma is gonna have a baby."

A big smile cracked her pretty face. "I hope it is a little girl! She said. Boys are, too, rough!"

"I agree with you, Gia. Greg said, looking at Truck. Some of them are."

"Dat's true, little brother. But da ones dat play with computers all dere life are harmless. Ain't dey?" Truck shot back.

"Before Greg could shoot back another round, Jim intervened. "You guys keep this up and I absolutely refuse to be Godfather to your kids."

The looks on the women's faces, thinking the men were seriously arguing, caused another moment of laughter.

A short while later, they said their goodnights and made their way back to their huts. Each one of them was overly exhausted, especially on the emotional side. Sleep would be slow in coming. But, none of them minded in the least. Now, there were three more reasons to make life on this new world that much more pleasant. The two cultures would soon blend in a peaceful harmony. It had already begun in the wombs of the native women.

# CHAPTER 26

A little more than one "Earth" year later, the first sun of the day cast its light down on the waking village. Its warming embrace dispelled the night chill, rousing many of the residents from slumber. The early morning "Sister" reflected her brilliance off of the many strange inventions, throughout the settlement.

Two stone wells stood beside each of the streams, running through the village, one at the north end and the other to the south. Wooden buckets, hanging above each one, swung on grass ropes, as they waited to scoop the clear, cold water to the surface. It had taken many days of cooperative teamwork, by the whole village, to accomplish this. A few, minor casualties incurred. But, it was worth the injuries. The overall health of the community had improved drastically.

A stone monolith, eight feet high, stood in the center of the village. A memorial to the natives who had perished in the "Alien" war, it would always remain the focal point of the settlement. Inscribed on its surface was a tribute. "THEY DIED SO WE MAY LIVE". Any given time of any given day, a group of natives would be gathered there. Many had lost friends or family and felt a connection with their loved ones, through the stone memorial. Many just stopped to say thank you to all the men and women who had sacrificed themselves for them.

A playground was built near it so the children, of the village, would always be aware of the ones who made their peaceful lives possible. It was complete, with swings, slides and teeterboards. A tall, wooden flagpole stood off to one side of the playground. Perched at the top was a grass-woven, dyed replica of old glory. The natives had no banner of recognition, depicting their village. Leota had agreed to adopt the "Stars and Stripes", as part of their heritage.

It was not uncommon to see wooden bicycles, tricycles or wagons, lying in wait for their young riders, around many huts. Wheelbarrows and four-wheeled carts were, also, scattered about.

A large shed stood at one end of the settlement. Inside, it was filled with tables, chairs, shelves and other wooden furnishings in various stages of construction.

A tall flagpole stood off to one side of the playground. Perched upon the top was a grass-woven, dyed replica of "Old Glory". The natives had no banner of any sort depicting a symbol of their village. Leota had agreed to adopt the stars and stripes as part of their heritage.

A large corral, for their beasts of burden, had been built near the front gates. The animals flourished in their new environment. They had become so tractable and adapted to their new lives, it was not unusual to see them led through the village with children perched high on their backs.

Leota had given the Americans free reign to pursue their Earthly ideas. His enthusiasm, to every proposal, allowed for the increasing comfort and security of his people.

The three brothers experienced the best lives two worlds could offer. Every waking day, they discussed new ideas. Once agreed, they conferred with Leota, who usually gave them permission to implement them.

They all had families to take care of, now, so many ideas stemmed from this. Strollers, cribs, toys and other inventions, for comfort and amusement, spread through the entire village.

Sanda had given birth to identical twins; a boy named Arius and a girl named Elino. They were happy, healthy and naturally spoiled.

Mara had given birth to a little girl. They named her Pali. It was not an unusual sight to see Truck walking through the village with Gia, with her brand new, state-of-the-art leg, walking at his side, pushing a carriage with her little sister in it.

Lona had, also, given birth to a little girl. They named her Johi. Greg was so fascinated by her, Lona didn't have much more to do other than feed her or clean her after a mess occurred. Greg absolutely refused to do the diaper patrol.

One, significant, factor would distinguish their offspring, throughout their lives on this world. Each one was born with thick, black hair adorning their little heads. The three Earth fathers enjoyed the idea that, after they had outgrown this life and passed on to the world of ancestors, their children would be living representatives of their home world, Earth.

Bantor and Cinda had a baby boy. They named him Julo, in honor of Leota's deceased brother. When all of their babies were together, Julo, with his peroxide blonde hair, stood out like a piece of butterscotch candy in a box of licorice.

Bantor's forays, into the wilderness, had proven successful. Two of their disassociated, cousin tribes had been located. Through information, gleaned from these tribes, other villages would soon be located. Commerce had already begun and a handful of friends and family were reunited. In time, the people would be undivided. Their world would enjoy the freedom and privileges, once experienced by their ancestors.

Jim stood in the entryway of his hut, looking out at the village, proud to be a contributing factor in its growth and comfort. Sanda lay buried in the furs, still, sound asleep. The twins had kept her up, most of the night. They, too, slept soundly, nestled safely in their cribs.

"A man couldn't ask for anything more than this." He said to himself, smiling at his beautiful family.

He noticed Greg and Bantor walking his way and ventured out to join them.

"Good morning! He said. What brings you two out so early in the morning?"

"Good morning, Jim! Greg replied. Truck sent word to us to meet with him outside the front gates."

"He said he had a little surprise for us. Bantor joined in. After experiencing all of these Earthly ideas, so far, I doubt that I shall ever be surprised again, in this lifetime."

As they walked through the village, Leota shouted to them. He was talking to a group of men, in front of the memorial stone.

"Greetings to this new day!" He said, as he joined them.

"And to you, my father." Bantor replied.

"Good morning, Leota!" Said Jim.

"Where are you three bound?" The leader asked.

"Ta-rok wishes us to join him outside the gates." Bantor answered.

"My large brother wants to share another one of his, so-called, surprises. Greg said, smiling. I can hardly wait!" He added, sarcastically.

As the four men passed through the gates, they spotted another group of men fifty yards away. Making their way closer, they noticed each man was wearing some kind of leather hat on his head. Truck was in the middle. In one of his large hands, Jim noticed, was a leather, oval-shaped object. "Oh my God! Jim said, in a low voice, smiling. I knew this was coming, sooner or later."

"Good morning to ya, guys! Truck said, with a big smile on his face. Ya wanna play some football?"

# BOOK TWO

## Revenge

# CHAPTER 1

Large, splayed, feet pounded over the moss-covered terrain, leaving barely a whisper in their passing. Crimson fluid seeped from a wound in its right shoulder. Life, slowly ebbing from its exhausted body, the creature struggled forward. The long ground - eating, strides, were now reduced to an agonizing shuffle.

Murderous creatures, from the far north, had over-run its settlement, decimating over half its population. The Nevoan leader, "Mokar", had sent out many runners to locate one of the "Yellow head" tribes to secure aid. "Froban" was one of these designated emissaries.

Standing a few inches above six feet tall, his inverted, pear-shaped head sat upon sloping shoulders. Short antennae, taking the place of ears, sat on the top of his head, one on either side. A shallow indentation, at the top, separated them. A horizontal gash sat, directly, below two, large yellow eyes. Red veins radiated within, in a spider-web-like pattern. The horrible mouth was an oozing, vertical opening, oval shaped and surrounded by fleshy nodules. Two teeth were visible. They were, actually, fangs. One at the top and the other on the bottom, they met in a pincher-like fashion. Long arms ended in tong-like hands.

Sharp talons extended from the four fingers. His long, splayed feet each sported four toes. He was clothed in a gray, stretch material, leaving only his head and hands exposed. Needless to say, "Froban" and his entire race would win very few beauty contests.

He was captured two days later by the invader's scouting party and along with nine others was marched back to the Nevoan city. He managed to escape shortly before they reached it. The throbbing wound in his shoulder was evidence he did not get away unscathed.

Since losing the war with the "Yellow heads, (their word for the native tribes indigenous to this world) nearly eight years earlier, all of their weapons had been confiscated by the victorious natives. The invasion, by this latest faction, found Froban's settlement defenseless. In short order, the Nevoan population was reduced by almost half. The remainder was, quickly, enslaved or driven off.

Weakened by the steady oozing of his life fluids, Froban was having difficulty willing his feet forward. If he succumbed to the pain and allowed his body to stop moving, if only for a brief instant, he knew his life and the hopes of his kind would be forfeited. After six, agonizing days his torn body finally convinced his weary mind it needed a rest. He took a few more, staggering, steps and collapsed on the mossy plain. His mind implored him to regain his feet, but, his body ignored it. He sank into the dark void of unconsciousness.

\* \* \* \* \* \* \* \* \*

The planet "Cirema" is warmed by three, alternating, suns. The morning sun woke the world with her moderate rays and during her six and one half hour tenure, sometimes reached temperatures in the eighties. As this sun fell over the horizon, moments later, it was replaced by the mid-day sun. Temperatures, exceeding one hundred degrees, were possible. As the horizon swallowed the second sun, another six and one half hours later, It was replaced by the evening sun. Temperatures as low as sixty degrees, cooled the world before tucking it in for, yet, another six and one half hours of darkness. In reality, each day played witness to three sun rises and three sun sets, in its, approximate, twenty-seven hours. The natives, simply, referred to them as the "Sister" suns.

As the first "sister" sun sprayed her warm rays onto the sleepy world beneath her, a small group of men crested a high ridge, over-looking the mossy terrain. Mounted on domesticated "Lurdas", they scanned the vast wilderness, in search of prey. The small hunting party had left their village an hour in advance of the first sunrise. The sturdy beasts, they rode, picked their way, sure-footedly, over the rolling landscape. Only two short years earlier, these same animals roamed wildly over the mossy tundra. Their ferocious nature and hardiness made them well-adapted to their surroundings. Of all the creatures on this planet, they were second only to the dreaded "Kazor" in unpredictability and tenacity. This lizard-like monster roved their world, killing and eating at will. Standing nearly eight feet tall, it walked on two thick hind legs. Besides its large crocodilian mouth, filled with row after row of dagger-like teeth, it had a long, heavy tail with five-inch-long barbs on the end. It was the personified killing machine.

The three transplants from Earth, James, Gary and Gregory Stonedeer, had introduced the natives to their methods for domesticating feral beasts. By capturing them, shortly after their weening stage had transpired, they were slowly acclimated to a subservient life among the natives. Once their lethal horns, which could grow to a length of eighteen inches, were removed, they, eventually, became almost as docile as the herds of cattle back on Earth. Those born into captivity, assumed the status quo. In the short time this experiment had been in progress, their domesticated herd had grown to over one thousand. Hunting parties were more often for the capturing of the beast rather than killing them for the meat. This experiment served two important purposes. "Lurda" meat was the main staple of the native diet and, now, would be readily available. They were kept in large holding pens outside the village. A group of men and women specialized in the butchering, preserving and storage. No one would ever suffer from hunger.

The second issue and the paramount reason was safety. The danger involved, while hunting these animals, was extreme. Countless numbers of men and women had lost their lives, in the endeavor, under the trampling feet or through fatal encounters with the lethal horns.

Breaking the wildness out of these alien bovines, to the point they were tractable enough to carry a rider, was another work in progress. The three Earth men took over this responsibility, along with the aid of some of the braver natives. They began by strapping hides, filled with stones, onto the backs of the calves. By, gradually increasing the amount of weight, as it grew, they accustomed the animal to tolerate pressure, to this area, eventually, the weight of a man.

As the beast grew older and more tolerant of the unnatural weights, halters and reins were slipped onto their heads. When it was deemed they were comfortable, with the new paraphernalia, it was time for a rider. Because it was their idea, to begin with, the three Americans got the job.

After sustaining their share of bumps and bruises and landing time and again on the mossy sod, they were almost at the point of discontinuing the experiment. It was Jim who remembered how the Indians of Earth broke their wild ponies. Leading the animals into one of the shallow streams, surrounding their village, they found the water limited their powerful muscles and they, eventually became more tractable. It, also, made the ungraceful landings a tad less painful. Before too long, a stable of almost two hundred, compliant mounts was gathered. Hunting and traveling could, now, be done in relative safety.

Sitting, comfortably, on his shaggy mount, one of the men spoke.

"Do you gentlemen realize, approximately, nine short years ago we were sitting in front of a fire at our favorite fishing camp on earth? Pointing at the wide expanse that lay before him, he continued.

"None of this was even, remotely, conceivable! We have been fortunate to share in the beauty of two worlds. It's overwhelming!"

His older brother, Jim, mounted alongside him, looked at his sibling and considered those words, before he spoke.

"I never thought of it in that light before, Greg. But, I have to agree. We have been pretty fortunate. Our seeds were sown on Earth, scattered into space and took root here. We didn't have much of a say in the transition. But, I wouldn't change a thing even If I could."

The second youngest of the Earth trio, Truck, piped up behind them.

"Dere ain't too much I miss about dat old planet, except our Grandfather and a few friends. I got everything a man could ever want right here!"

"You, sure as hell, can't find friends of that nature on this world. Can you, Truck? Greg chided, smiling across at Jim. These people are a lot more civilized. Aren't they?"

The look, on the big man's face, ran from serious to confused to comprehension when he noticed the smiles on his brothers faces.

The other two men in the group, Tonio and Roca added theirs as well. They were more than used to the antics of their adopted Earth brethren.

"Perhaps, Ta rok will find a new tribe of people who know how to celebrate properly." Tonio chimed in.

"Or, maybe, he could teach us how to be more primitive in our celebrations." Roca added.

"Okay, you guys! Truck said, smiling. I think I got da message!"

"Thank God! Greg continued. Now, we can enjoy another eight years of peace."

"How would ya like a piece a dis, shorty?" Truck asked, shaking his fist.

Jim was taking it all in, as he had many times in his life. Greg and Truck were consistent. The smile disappeared from his face, as his eyes detected something lying on the mossy turf, about seventy-five yards in the distance.

Pointing in the direction, he brought the other's attention to it.

"What do you guys make of that?" He asked.

"By da color of da clothes, it looks like one a dos Nevoan fellas!" Truck guessed.

"Let's get a better look!" Jim said, spurring his mount into a gallop.

Followed closely by his comrades, they soon approached the object in question. In a moment, they were there.

"You were right, Truck!" Jim said, dismounting and kneeling at the side of the inert body. In moments, he surmised, the creature was still alive. Barely! Grabbing a water skin, hanging from the side of his mount, he poured water into the horrible gash of a mouth. Truck tore up a handful of moss and began working it into the wound in the creature's shoulder. Moments passed, before the creature started to recover. Water sputtered from its mouth and as its eyes focused on the natives, it made an attempt to regain its feet.

"Take it easy, my friend! You're in no condition to move!" Jim said, gently pushing him down to the mossy turf.

Relaxing, somewhat, his eyes darted from one man to the other, as he spoke.

"Are you of the "Yellowhead" tribe?" He asked.

Memories rekindled in the Earth man. A language imprinted on his mind, almost nine years earlier, by these very same beings when they had held him and his siblings in captivity, came back to him.

"Yes! I am of the Yellowhead tribe! Jim replied, flawlessly, in the Nevoan language. Tell us what has happened to you!"

Surprised, for an instant, to hear his own language flowing from a native tongue, he answered.

"I an Froban! I have been ordered by my leader, Mokar, to secure aid for my people."

"Mokar is our friend! Jim replied. How may we help you?"

Tonio and Roca listened in amazement, as their Earth brothers conversed in this strange language. They were never held captive by these beings and, thus, were ignorant of the language.

"Many suns have passed since strange creatures entered our settlement, slaughtered hundreds and took many as slaves. Some of us were able to make our way to the outskirts of settlement, into hiding. I was captured, but I managed to escape, after killing two of the invaders. Unfortunately, a third wounded me with his long spear. I thought my life would run its course, before I could find assistance for my people."

"Don't worry about nothing, buddy! Truck chimed in. Were gonna fix you up and see what we can do about helping our old friend, Mokar

"These invaders, Froban. What did they look like?" Greg asked.

The exhausted Nevoan stared, vaguely, at the Earth man, remembering.

They were as tall as our tallest citizen. They had long hair the color of night skies, covering most of their bodies. Dark eyes were wide-set and penetrating. Their narrow heads ended with long wide jaws filled with many pointed teeth. They carried weapons, such as the ones wielded by your people for cutting down trees. Long spears and knives completed their armament. However, their most devastating weapon was the way they used their teeth. With my own eyes, I have seen throats ripped out and people being consumed while still alive."

"Let's get this man back to the village! Jim said. When he's properly rested and strong enough, we'll learn more."

They lifted the injured Nevoan and laid him, gently across the back of Roca's mount and made their way back to the village.

"Where in da hell did these bastards come from?" Truck asked no one in particular, as they spurred their animals into a steady gallop.

"I haven't the slightest idea, Truck! But, I think we'll soon find out!" Jim answered for everyone.

Time would tell how, horrifyingly, true those words prove to be.

# CHAPTER 2

Five days later, the area around the "Tribal" hut was filled to capacity. The wide- open space, in the center of the village, was used for celebrations, discussion forums or just a general gathering for socializing. Small storage huts were located in this area. A large, stone-lined fire pit sat close by, ready to shed its warmth and light on any nighttime activities.

On this night, the focus of curiosity was on their Nevoan guest. He represented the first of his kind to have ever set foot inside a native village by invitation. His serious wound had been treated and his strength had been almost completely restored. He was seated next to the native leader, Leota. The Earth men and their mates, Sanda, Mara and Lona completed the small group, at the center of attention.

Leota, like his Earth brethren, was also a captive of the Nevoans in the past and could converse in their language. In a voice, slightly louder than the anxious murmurings of the large gathering, he spoke.

"If our Nevoan guest would be so kind as to relate his reasons for being among us, I will translate for my people." He addressed Froban, in his own language.

Staring, nervously, out at the inquisitive audience, he began. "I am known as Froban. With my first words, I am compelled to convey my gratitude to all responsible for extending my life. My forefathers had almost convinced me to join them."

Leota translated for his people. Nods of approval bobbed through the crowd, acknowledging the Nevoan's etiquette.

"My purpose for being among you is to employ aid for my people. Froban continued. We have been invaded by strange beings from the north. The population of my settlement has been reduced by half, since the murderous attack began. We had no weapons at our disposal, in which to offer any resistance. Many were taken prisoner. The fortunate few of us, who were not slaughtered or enslaved, fled and are now scattered in the forests, many miles from the settlement."

After translating this to his people, Leota asked their nervous guest a question. "What did these invaders look like, Froban?"

"Never, before, have I seen such as these! He replied. Tall and covered with long, dark hair, they appeared more animal in the way they moved. Their dark, slanted eyes sat far apart. Each one contained a slash of yellow through the center. They had long snouts, ending in wide jaws and filled with sharp, pointed teeth. Openings on the ends of their long snouts, one on either side, appeared to be used for breathing purposes. Small openings, toward the tops of their heads, to the side of each eye, appeared to be used for hearing. Two arms and two legs, muscular and hairy, ended in sharp claws on hands as well as feet."

Anxious looks reflected back at him, when Leota translated for them. The noise level had, also, increased.

"What kind a weapons did dey have?" Truck inquired, in a voice that carried above the boisterous crowd.

"Long spears, with sharpened points, were their primary weapons. Froban answered. They, also, wielded stone axes and knives. However, their teeth and claws did most of the damage."

"Does Mokar still live?" Jim asked.

"He was among the group of survivors I was sent from. As far as I know, he still lives." Froban replied.

When Leota relayed this information to the vast crowd, it resulted in mix feed back.

Comments, such as, "Let them suffer the way we did at their hands". "Why should we get involved? It won't bring our loved ones back," Echoed from the crowd.

Leota looked upon the faces of his people. It was easier to agree with them then not. All of the anguish experienced by them, at the hands of the Nevoans, would take a long time to dissipate. Maybe, never! He thought. "Should he risk the lives of his people to help those who had oppressed them for over one hundred years, accounting for the loss of many loved ones? A decision had to be made and it wasn't going to be an easy one.

Jim glanced over at the Nevoan, who was staring, dejectedly, at the ground between his feet. Although he could not understand their language, the negative vibrations, exuding from all these Yellowheads, he understood perfectly.

"Leota! May I speak?" Greg shouted.

"Please do!" Leota replied, relieved.

Raising his voice a few octaves above the tumultuous crowd, he managed to gain their attention.

"Peace is just another word. He began. If it is not totally accepted by the heart, mind and soul of an individual, it can never be, truly realized. The generations of suffering, people have endured, cannot be ignored or forgotten. Although my siblings and I suffered for only a short period of time, at the hands of the Nevoans, it was long enough to fester hatred for them. We, too, lost dear friends when we were uprooted from our world and every thing we knew."

He hesitated, long enough, to look over the entire crowd before continuing.

"Ask yourself this! If the situation was reversed and we were the ones seeking aid from the Nevoans, would they agree to help us?"

"I'd like to believe they would. Assisting the victims of war is just as important to the victors. "Peace" is not a conditional word. Both sides must learn how to rebuild trust."

"I agree with my brother!" Jim joined in. Needless to say, everyone has suffered from our war. Both sides! To insure future peace, we must lay our past differences aside and do what is right. Ignoring the present situation could cause dire consequences in the future."

"On da world dat we came from, dere were powerful countries dat bullied da weaker ones. Truck added. When dey conquered and took over, dey kept da people from making any progress. Kinda like dos animals, in dat Nevoan zoo. Dey were forced to live behind bars. But, you all saw what dos beasts could do when dey got dere freedom. Dey helped us all get home. Didn't dey? Da same thing can happen again if we give dese people a hand."

The animals Truck was referring to were four alien herbivores abducted from their worlds by the same space traders that had abducted him and his brothers. They shared much the same fate as they did. After the victory over the Nevoans, The Earth men trained the four animals to pull large wagons, loaded with native casualties, back to their village. For the rest of their lives the villagers allowed them to rove freely among them, as a reward for their services. The last of the gentle beasts expired a few years earlier.

The crowd had quieted, considerably, digesting the Earth men's words. The thought of more strife was unsettling. For many, emotional wounds from the last conflict were still unhealed. However, the refusal of assistance to their former enemies, would weigh heavily on some native consciences. Was there a righteous solution to this dilemma?

Sensing the animosity, radiating from the crowd, Froban put his fears in check.

"Would the Yellowhead leader permit me to speak?" He asked.

"By all means, Froban! Speak!" Leota answered.

Stepping before the crowd, he returned their stares. The fate of his people was in his hands. He must not fail them!

"In the past, I have warred against you. It was my duty, as a soldier of Nevoa, to do so. I did not think of life or death in the same light as you people do. Since hostilities ended eight years ago, my people have gone through a transition. We do not feel superior to the world we live in. The life we enjoy, now, is without circumstances. It is a life we wish to continue."

He paused, briefly, to allow his heart rate to lessen. It was his responsibility to convey, to these people, the "Nevoan" side.

"We are different beings! However, suffering is indiscriminate. He continued. We do not mourn our losses in your manner. But, our wounds need healing also. With your assistance, both cultures may continue to do so."

Nodding, slowly, to Leota, he regained his seat.

Leota translated and looked out at the boisterous crowd. He had to agree with the Nevoan. No one survived a war unscathed. The victorious, as well as the vanquished, were left with physical and emotional reminders.

"If no one has anything more to add, I suggest we break up and meet back here after the first Sister sun has lighted our paths. At that time, a vote will be taken. Think hard on this, before you make your decisions. Let your hearts dictate which stone you cast."

As the mob of perplexed natives made their way to their abodes, the Earth men, Leota and their mates sat around the dwindling fire. Their Nevoan guest had been escorted to his quarters.

The women had remained quiet, during the entire proceedings. Talk of another bloody conflict had them, dreadfully, concerned.

"The wounds from our last battles have not yet been heeled, Ta-rok! Mara said, worriedly. Is it upon us again?"

"Nothing has been decided, my daughter! Leota interjected. We shall find out in the morning in which direction our hearts will take us."

"Don't you go worrying your pretty little head, in da mean time, darling! Truck did his best to sound convincing. Every thing is gonna work out okay!"

"I'm not so sure about that, Truck! Jim said. Judging from the reaction of that crowd, It's hard to say which way they'll decide."

"Which way will be the right way? Sanda asked. Do we help these people or ignore their pleas, because of past grievances?"

"I can't bear the thought of another bloody conflict! Lona chimed in. However, at the same time, to do nothing would be an even bigger travesty."

"I believe, if our people decide with their hearts and do not allow the wounds of the past to cloud their judgment, the right decision will be made." Leota added, hopefully.

As the starlit night showered her nocturnal rays down upon the quiet village, sleep eluded most of its occupants. An ambiguous aura accompanied each native, as they pondered the dilemma confronting them. For more than a century, the authors of their frustration, pain and emotional anguish had perpetrated a relentless assault against them. Eight years of peace was, hardly, enough time to quell the sorrow in their souls. Now, the Nevoan people were being subjected to this same devastating circumstance. Was there enough room, in native hearts, to rise above their prejudices and provide assistance?

The new day would not come soon enough. Minds and hearts would be at war, throughout the long night.

# CHAPTER 3

The first sun of the new day had just peeked into the slumbering village. Children were already in the play area, enjoying all the Earthly creations, slides, seesaws, swings. When James, Gary and Gregory Stonedeer were adopted into this village, eight, short years earlier, Leota had given them free rein to their Earthly imaginations. The comforts and life styles, of the natives, had improved drastically. Wells were dug to ensure healthy drinking water, solid abodes were built, utile furnishings, such as chairs, tables and cabinets were produced in small workshops. Toys, bicycles, carts and other forms of amusement delighted the youngsters. The wooden barricade, surrounding the entire perimeter of the large village, had been reinforced. Catwalks, with four guard houses, one on each corner, added to their security. The old "Stars and Stripes", from the Earth men's country, had been adopted by the villagers as their identifying symbol. It flew from a twenty- foot pole in the middle of the play area.

"Remember, always, to aim at the center of your target. This will allow for the varying path of the arrow." Jim explained to his young audience. The bow and arrow were two more useful implements the brothers had introduced to this world. Almost from the day they started walking, native children were instructed in their use. By the time they reached their early teens, they were proficient, enough, to become welcomed additions in the defense of their village.

"Father! My weapons are so small, I don't think I could bring down an infant "pava".

(A pava is a small, tree-dwelling rodent, hunted for its tasty meat)

"When will I be able to hold a man's bow?" Jim's oldest son, Marus, complained.

Before Jim could answer, Lenora, Marus's twin sister, chimed in.

"You have to learn how to shoot the infant's bow and hit something with it first. She said with a giggle. You need a lot of practice!"

Although Marus was the older of the two, by a few minutes, he was shorter than his sister and they were, forever, in competition with one another.

Before marus had a chance to respond, to his sister's teasing, Jim intervened.

"You both are growing so fast. It won't be long before you earn that right. When that day comes, I will help you both to make a much more powerful bow."

Bomar, two years younger than his twin siblings, sat, quietly, with his mini bow and arrows in his lap. In some ways, he was ahead of the others. Each one had to construct their own weapons. This was a part of their early training. His workmanship was almost perfect. The old saying was "never trust in another person's weapons". Bomar, also, asked more questions than the other two put together.

"Father! Bomar said, right on cue. Does tendon make the best bow strings?"

Smiling at his youngest, Jim answered.

"It is the most consistent I have found, so far, Bomar. It doesn't dry out as fast, like some other materials I've used. So, it lasts longer. However, if you should find yourself in an emergency situation, the bark of the Crometta tree, woven grasses or even thin flexible vines would, also, work until the time you are able to acquire it. At the least, they would help keep you alive until then."

"Good morning, my Earth friend! Leota greeted, as he approached the small group. Pardon my interruption, but, may I have a word with you?"

"And a good morning it is! Jim responded. Of course! Have a seat!

You kids, go inside! Your mother has prepared breakfast." He ordered.

Leota sat down and stared across the fire at the Earth man, approvingly.

"Your young ones adapt to this lifestyle as easily as you and your siblings did, when first you came among us."

"Yes, they have, Leota!" But, they probably won't bother our leader, as much as we did, with Earthly ideas. Jim replied, smiling at the old leader. Every thing they see and do is just another normal aspect of their every-day lives."

"If all new generations were as willing to contribute as much to our people, as you and your siblings have, I would, happily, look forward to being bothered until I meet my ancestors." He replied, smiling.

"That, too, may come to pass, Leota. Many of the youngsters, in this village, are pretty creative."

"One can only hope." Leota said, with a sorrowful lilt in his voice.

Observing the sullen expression on the old warrior's face, Jim asked: "What is it that bothers you, my friend?"

Slowly, refocusing his eyes on the Earth man, he answered. "Bantor's party is long overdue. They set off, more than six weeks ago, to explore new territory in the northern region. This, coupled with the Nevoan invasion, has me concerned. Froban told us their attackers came from the north."

"You worry too much, as always, my friend! Jim replied. Bantor may have found something interesting that would take up a little more time. As for the area he is exploring and the direction, from which the invading army came from, my be nothing more than a coincidence."

After a short while, Leota responded. "It is most likely, as you say, my Earth friend. But, unfortunately, the concerns I have, for my only son, battle with the concerns I have for my people. They may be, even, stronger!"

"I know, exactly, how you feel, Leota! Jim said, as he looked through the doorway of his hut, at his family. It goes with the territory of being a father!"

After a short while, Leota rose from his seat.

"Thank you, my friend, for allowing me to spread my sorrow a little thinner, in its telling. Now, we have a vote to take!" With that, he strolled up the path toward the Tribal hut.

A short while later, ever adult in the village was gathered there. Leota and the Nevoan, Froban, were seated alongside the large fire pit, in the middle of the meeting area. They conversed in low voices.

The three Earth men and their mates were milling through the boisterous crowd, from one group to another. Heated discussions erupted from all directions. The significance of an individual's vote, on this day, could prove to be historic. Many of them had grown complacent, during the eight years of peace. Their feelings were: "If the Nevoans stayed in their own back yard, we would stay in ours." Most of them were willing to settle for a divided world. A coexistence, with all its amenities, was not important to them.

Some allowed the loss of family or friends to rekindle their hatred for the Nevoans. They believed, they should be left alone to fight their own war.

"It didn't make any sense, at all, to risk further lives in defense of the killers of their fathers, mothers, sisters, brothers and other loved ones."

A few discussions led to the morality of the situation. "The downtrodden deserved assistance, regardless of who they were, despite past transgressions!"

As they joined Leota and the Nevoan, at the center of this beehive of uncertainty, they noticed a large, clay jar sitting on a table. The opening, at the top, was covered with a hide lid. A narrow slit, approximately six inches long, had been cut into it. Leota explained its purpose to them, earlier. Each one of the voters concealed a small stone, either black or white, in their hand. Next, they placed their hand through the slit in the hide and dropped their vote, privately, into the jar. A white stone signified a "yes" vote. A black stone signified a "no" vote. It was a, relatively, democratic inception on a, relatively, uncivilized world.

Leota rose from his seat. Holding his arms above his head, he captured the crowd's attention. Soon, the noise level ebbed, enough, for him to begin.

"My people! We gather here on this day, on the dawning of a very serious situation. The decision, I ask you to make, will be a difficult one. It comes in the aftermath of a victorious war against a people who, for more than one hundred years, squeezed the life out of our tribes. Many of our loved ones, now, walk with their ancestors because of this. The pain, we suffered, lessens over the years. However, it still lingers among us."

He hesitated, momentarily, as he scanned the apprehensive faces of his people. Not a sound was uttered, as they waited, anxiously, for him to continue.

"I battled with sleep, the whole night through. I kept asking myself, over and over again, am I capable of balancing my emotions long enough to make a decision I will be comfortable with? Almost twenty years, before our final battle with the Nevoans, a major portion of my life was stolen from me. During this period of time, I developed a festering hatred that occupied every waking moment. I wanted nothing but revenge, until my ancestors called me to join them."

Wiping the tears from his face, he paused. The crowd realized their leader was exposing his pain to them and appreciated his openness. They became, respectfully, silent. Everyone knew he was referring to the abduction of his mate, Graci.

"Each of you, among us, can tell his own painful story. He began, again. This hatred was eating away what life was left to me. My son Bantor, our three Earth warriors and many others made me realize "life" consists of many components. To throw it away, because one part has been removed, leaves all the other parts abandoned. It, then, becomes a selfish affront toward the rest of our loved ones and to the village.

"The Nevoan people, whom we have been at peace with for the last eight summers, now, are in the need of our assistance. They are another piece of our existence, whether we realize it or not. I, for one, will go on record by extending my hand to them. What we could accomplish, together, toward our futures, would take precedence over the heartaches of our past."

Leota returned to his seat. Graci smiled at him, proudly, as she offered him a cup of water.

"Leota! May I say a few words?" Jim asked.

The leader, emotionally drained, nodded his assent.

Making his way to the front of the crowd, he began.

"My friends! I agree with our leader! But, for reasons he has not stated. My brothers and I would not be among you, today, if it were not for the aid of a few Nevoan individuals who went against authority. Everything we held dear had been stripped from us. Yet, our heart-felt memories remain. Our war, with the Nevoan people, is long over. However, there are many who choose to remain emotionally mired in the past."

He paused, briefly, scanning the multitude of faces filled with indecisiveness.

"After doing a lot of soul-searching, I have made my decision. My conscience will not allow the annihilation of an entire race of people, because of past transgressions. I would offer my assistance to these people. My heart and mind are in agreement!"

As Jim took his seat, Leota observed the reactions of his people. The negative feedback, filtering through their ranks, didn't sound like it boded too well for Nevoan futures. He rose from his seat and addressed the gathering.

"If no one has anything more to add, at this time, I suggest we cast our votes!"

After a few moments passed and nobody offered, a long line formed, snaking its way toward the large jar. An eerie silence fell over them, broken only by the sounds of shuffling feet and the clink of stone votes as they collected in the bottom of the jar.

The nevoan sat alone, downcast. He had done all he could to help his people. But, he feared for the worse.

As the crowd, slowly, ebbed away, seeking their individual abodes, each person hoped their decision was the right one. Tomorrow would unveil the results of their collective consciences. The survival of an entire race of people, could, lay in the balance.

# CHAPTER 4

The three Earth men and a small group of natives gathered at one of the wide streams, bordering the village. Six young Lurdas were held in check, by mounted riders, with the use of braided hide ropes. The young bovines, eight months old, were the last of the selected animals to be broken.

"I do believe it is your turn, Truck! Greg called out, to his large brother. Try not to hurt him!" He added, with a big smile on his face.

"Thanks for da concern, squirt! I'll try ta be careful with him." He replied, sarcastically.

Led to the middle of the shallow stream, by two young natives, The bull was sandwiched between them with their own mounts. The reins were passed to Truck, who quickly leapt upon its back. About the time he was getting settled, onto the furry saddle, The big creature started thrashing around, in a whirlwind of panic. Twisting and turning, bucking and dipping, it tried to rid itself of the unnatural weight on its back. Truck held on for all he was worth. Even with the removal of the lethal horn, the Lurda was still capable of doling out a lot of pain or even death.

After fifteen minutes had lapsed, the young bull showed no signs of tiring. The big Earth man absorbed the gut-wrenching punishment, from the animal, but, refused to relinquish his perch. Holding, tightly, to the reins and squeezing his powerful legs into the animal's sides, he anticipated every move the animal made. Except one! The beast stumbled and fell forward onto its front knees, catapulting its Earthly cargo, over its head, in a perfect arc.

As Truck lay flat on his back, in the cool water, the animal regained its feet. Staring across the ten paces separating them, man and beast used this respite to replenish their starving lungs with oxygen. Truck regained his feet.

Greg, Jim and the rest of the natives were quick to react. But, before they could start forward, to drive the animal away from their brother, He yelled out.

"Don't anyone move!" He, then, started walking slowly toward the panting beast. I wanna try something! When he was within an arms length, of the Lurda, he reached out very tentatively and started rubbing the furry snout.

The mounted men stared in awe, ten paces away from the big Earth man's daring display. Barely a breath was heard.

The large, single eye of the beast, wide with fright, stared fixedly at the two-legged creature before him. When Truck began talking softly, to the shaggy creature, the nervous tremors that rippled through its body started to subside. When he placed an arm, over the animal's thick neck, talking in soothing tones, he was not rejected. After a very long moment he retrieved the reins, hanging from the beast's muzzle and started walking it in a wide circle, through the shallow stream. After a short while he stopped and eased himself, carefully, onto the creature's back. A few moments later, he coaxed the animal out of the water and dismounted.

"I knew ya could do it, big fella! He said, giving the young bovine another hug around its powerful neck. Ya just needed a little more time! Dat's all!"

As the rest of the group joined him, Jim spoke.

"What in the hell is the matter with you, Truck? You know how dangerous these animals are!"

"I agree, Jim! These, definitely, are not creatures you can use psychology on!" Greg intoned. Relief, as well as anger, reflected from his voice.

Staring at the scolding countenances, of his two brothers, Truck shook his head. "Whatta you guys getting so worked up about? I could tell he was tuckered out. So was I! All I was trying ta do was let him know dat I wasn't going ta hurt him. After dat, it was easy!" He finished, with a big grin on his face.

"I suppose he's right, Jim. Greg cut in. With all the practice he's had, with his primitive friends back on Earth, I guess, it just comes naturally to him.

"After watching how far dese animals can fling dat skinny little ass of yours through da air, maybe you should use some a my expertise." Truck replied, smiling.

"I may just do that, you big ape! Greg shot back. But, in the future and for all of our sakes, try to limit your risk taking. Hospitals are a long way off!"

"You're up, Greg! Jim interrupted. This will be the last one for today!"

When they had first started this experiment, The Earth men had tried breaking three animals at the same time. The ensuing chaos ended in near-fatal results. Needless to say, that idea was, quickly, abandoned.

As their young assistants were herding the next beast, into the stream, a rider approached from the direction of the village. As he neared, they discerned Tonio, riding at full gallop. When he was among them, he reined his mount to a stop.

"Leota has requested everyone to join him in the meeting place!" He informed them.

A short while later, Jim and his "rodeo" gang were turning their furry beasts loose in the small corral, outside the main gate. As they made their way through the village, they detected a nervous energy emitting from the moving populace. Soon, they spotted their mates and a few other women clustered around the Tribal huts. When they were among them, Sanda took Jim aside.

"Sarva has returned from Bantor's group! She began. He has informed Leota they had been overwhelmed by strange creatures. They might be the same creatures that had attacked the Nevoan settlement!"

Many alarming thoughts raced through the Earthman's mind. "Where and when did this happen? Were Bantor and his men killed or captured?" He looked around and discovered Leota and Graci in the middle of the meeting area. They were surrounded by a small group of women. Graci was in tears.

Truck and Greg were at Jim's side. "Sanda! Stay with Cinda! He ordered. Come, my brothers! Let's find out what all of this is about.!"

They made their way, through the milling crowd, toward Leota. As they approached, Graci was being led away by a few of her female friends. The three Earthmen stopped, in front of the leader. Their collective silence was a sign of respect and acknowledgement when they noticed the emotional pain reflecting from his saddened, liquid eyes.

"This day has begun poorly, Earth friends! He said, sullenly, his voice heavy with heartache. Earlier, I was informed, the decision to aid the Nevoan people was voted against. Just, Minutes ago, I found out a vicious assault was perpetrated against my son and his party, adding to my emotional burden. He continued, his voice cracking, straining against the agony he felt. "As leader of these people, I know a decision must be made. As a father, I have already made my decision!" A silent moment fell over them, as they acknowledged the meaning of his words.

"We are ready to assist you, in any way we can." Greg responded.

"Amen ta dat! Truck added. Let's kick some butt!"

"The sooner the better!" Jim joined in, making it unanimous.

Fresh tears found their way down the sides of Leota's cheeks as he stared, in appreciation, at the three Americans.

"It would seem, I have relied upon you three Earth men, more in the recent past, than I have upon my own people. My spoken gratitude, for your loyalty, is far from being a sufficient reward. I will be indebted to the three of you, long after I am feasting with my ancestors."

"There is no need for gratitude, Leota! Jim replied. Bantor is our brother, also! If we have to go by ourselves, we'll find a way to rescue them."

"I agree! Greg chimed in. But, in light of what has occurred, I don't believe there will be one person in our village, who would not be willing to volunteer his services."

"I can only hope, what you have said comes to pass. Leota replied. Soon, we will find out, how large our rescue party will be. With that said, he turned toward the vocal crowd and raised his arms. When the noise level dwindled to an excited murmuring, he spoke.

"There are two major issues, concerning us all, I must impart to you at this time."

A multitude of quizzical expressions reflected back to the leader. The crowd chorus diminished even further, as they waited in anticipation.

"The foremost issue concerns the results of our voting. He continued. The majority has elected not to offer aid to the Nevoans. As your leader, I have always strived to remain impartial to your decisions. However, as a conscientious member, of this world, I am disappointed! The Nevoan people are now experiencing the same dilemma that plagued our people for more than one hundred summers. Some of you may be thinking, "It was long overdo", or "they deserve it!" But, I ask you, here today, when will it end? Who will be next?"

Staring out at the mass of questioning looks, Leota fought to keep his emotional struggles in check.

"I believe it will end when cultures put their differences aside and unite in a common cause. As to who is next, I can answer for all of us, here today. We are next!"

This bit of information stunned the crowd into silence. Their collective attention grew more vivid, as they focused, questioningly, on Leota.

"A short while ago, a messenger from Bantor's party returned home. He bore unsettling news, concerning everyone in this village, even more so unsettling to a father.

I was told they were attacked by strange creatures while making their way through the northern region. After he described these creatures to me, I realized these were the same beings that had attacked the Nevoan settlement. He told me many lives were lost. The rest were captured and herded toward the north. Our messenger,

was scouting an area south of the party, at the time. He caught up with them, shortly after the battle was over. He watched, from a distance as his comrades were tied together and driven north. He felt there wasn't much one man could do, against such overwhelming odds. So, he decided to make his way back to us with this information. If he had not succeeded, many of us, here tonight, would have gone to our ancestors, not ever knowing what became of our loved ones."

The attitude of the gathering went through a metamorphosis. The complacency of the majority had, suddenly, switched to a unanimous attack mode. Something had to be done! Earlier reluctance, to get involved, was now changed by this personal affront.

"The lives of our surviving brothers and sisters lie in the balance. Leota continued. I, myself, along with our Earth brethren, have made our decisions. Who will join us?"

The entire assemblage erupted in shouts of allegiance. An aura of fervid energy circulated among them. Pacifistic ideals about war were abandoned. They had been violated!

As the shouting continued, and the volume of the rabid revelers increased, Jim looked over at their mates and a few other women, clustered around the main hearth. He did not want them to become involved with another war. They were celebrating just as avidly as the men. He frowned. Worry had already begun to set in.

Greg noticed the look on his brother's face and understood immediately.

"Leota! He shouted in a loud voice. May I speak?" He asked.

"If you can gain their attention, long enough, speak away, my Earth friend." He answered.

Raising his arms above his head, he walked up to the edge of the boisterous crowd.

"May I have your attention for a moment?" He implored in a loud voice.

After a short while, the volume ebbed enough so he could be heard.

"I have an idea I wish you to consider. He began.

You are all aware of the fact my brothers and I have trained a small number of Lurdas to allow riders on their backs. We have, also, trained almost two hundred men who are capable of handling the beasts."

The noise level dropped even lower as he continued.

"What I propose is to outfit two hundred mounted warriors and set out, directly, for the Nevoan settlement.

Upon reaching it, we liberate them and recruit them for our mission to rescue our brethren."

Many voices began rising in objection. The loudest belonged to Sanda, Mara and Lona. Soon, the entire female contingency was voicing their disagreement.

Up until present, only men were used while handling the powerful beasts. Because of their unpredictability and tenacious natures, the risks were great. No woman would be endangered in this experiment.

It was Mara who spoke up first.

"What of the women of this village? She asked. Do we not have friends or relatives counted among Bantor's group, also?"

"I agree! Sanda joined in. Since the beginning of time men and women have fought, side by side, in the defense of their village and loved ones."

"We are all aware of how valiantly our women are capable of fighting. Jim interjected, while looking over at his mate. What my brother is suggesting would give us a smaller, more mobile unit capable of striking quickly. Under the present circumstances, if we are to save any of our brethren, speed is of the essence."

The female component, of the vast audience, raised voices in objection. Small arguments erupted, raising the volume to an ear-splitting crescendo.

"Silence, my people! Leota commanded, in a bellowing voice.

He did not have long to wait before the crowd, once again, became civilized.

"I would have to agree with our Earth brothers. Nothing would be accomplished in a prolonged, massive assault. Native, as well as Nevoan, lives lie in the balance. We must act with haste! At this time, I will leave the selection of men and other details of the plan in the capable hands of our Earth brothers. I have spoken!"

# CHAPTER 5

Two days later, the first "Sister" cast her brilliance upon a scene never thought possible, throughout the history of this planet. Two hundred natives, mounted on shaggy Lurdas, made their way, steadily, across the moss-covered plain. They had departed their sleepy village, two hours before the first light had trickled over the horizon. Each man was outfitted for war. Hide bags, fastened to the broad backs of the beasts, contained only the bare necessities needed for the survival of this quest. Sleeping furs, water bags, fire starters and an ample supply of dried meat. Their armament consisted of a "Draco" (A lethal rifle-like weapon capable of discharging bolts of energy over long distances. They had been confiscated from the Nevoans, during their war eight years earlier). Bows, with an ample supply of arrows, long lances with fire-hardened points, flint and

Ivory knives completed their weaponry. Special holders had been designed, to hold these implements of destruction, securely, to the backs of their mounts.

Riding three abreast, the small cavalry snaked its way over the rolling landscape. A comfortable pace was maintained to adapt their novice mounts to a regular routine and to build up their endurance. It was a six or seven day trek. They had to do it, gradually.

The last few days had been hectic. Choosing men, gathering supplies, consulting their maps and outfitting each of the mounts had made it necessary to work in shifts. Time was of the utmost importance! Many lives were at stake, both native and Nevoan. For

all they knew, their endeavor might, already, be too late. But, try they must!

The plan was to converge on the Nevoan settlement with all haste, provide whatever aid they could, after liberating the people and, hopefully, employ some of the survivors to join them when they continued north in pursuit of the invaders.

Prior to the devastating assault on the Nevoans, excluding the trio of Earth men, a third race of beings, on this world, was unheard of. Where did they come from? And why did they project themselves into bloody focus with their murderous attacks? What good reasons could they have had for promoting this reign of death? These questions and many others occupied the minds of the crusaders, as they put miles of familiar real estate behind them. Their bovine mounts followed natural, herding instincts by keeping pace with one another in uniform procession.

The three Earthmen led the columns of cavalry men, as they pushed their way through the treeless plain. At their present pace, the time it would take to reach the Nevoan settlement would be less than half of what it took them, eight years earlier, when the trek was made on foot.

Four scouting parties, consisting of three men each, spread out around the encroaching army, a few miles off, to alert them of enemy eyes. Stealth and mobility were the main assets of the small force. Because of the overwhelming odds facing them, clandestine tactics would be consistently employed.

While selecting recruits, for this perilous mission, nearly every man in the village had volunteered their services. An army of nearly two thousand warriors would have been, readily available. This would have lessened, considerably, the odds against them. However, the valuable time, lost in preparation, would have been the down side. To march this massive body of soldiers all the way to the gates of the Nevoan settlement, would take twice as long and, drastically reduce the chances of rescuing their brethren. As it was, each man was selected for his ability to control the unpredictable lurda and his mastery of all weapons of war. Needless to say, if the three Earthmen had broken a thousand more of the shaggy beasts and trained more men to ride them, confidence levels would have been much higher. A lot of good men were left behind. Some of them were proven veterans of the war with the Nevoans. They pled their cases, for employment, louder than the rest.

Among those left behind, was Leota. In the last moment, much to the surprise of the Earthmen, he withdrew.

"The love I have, for my son, might force me into making a hasty decision. He had told them.

"My heart compels me to join in this endeavor. But, my mind tells me to be objective, for the sake of all of our brethren. I entrust our Earth brothers with this mission. Their judgments will not be clouded by a father's love. I will stay behind and help protect our village."

They all realized the leader's heart ached to be with them. However, a modicum of relief was attained as a result of his withdrawal. Riding into battle with one's mind swimming in emotional turmoil could, possibly, cause other problems. The success of this mission was going to be difficult enough, to begin with. Added emotional weight would only decrease their chances.

There were many willing people, in the village, who would have, gladly, taken his place. Among the foremost were the mates of the three Earthmen. Earfuls of objection were heaped upon them. Only when the importance of the village's defense was stressed to them, did they appear slightly mollified. If the small cavalry failed in its attempt, to eliminate all perpetrators, the village was vulnerable to an, eventual, attack. The three brothers were relieved the women would not be involved in this dangerous undertaking. They realized the women were just as capable of doing battle as most men, probably even more than some. But, for the same reasons that prompted Leota's withdrawal, they felt relieved not to be carrying the extra emotional burden.

It had been decided, earlier, the two hundred mounted warriors would be divided into four squads. Three would be commanded by each of the Earthmen. Tonio and Roca headed the fourth. They felt the men would be better utilized if split into more maneuverable units.

The two hundred and first member of the mounted crusaders was Froban, the Nevoan messenger. He rode double with Roca. When first informed he would be riding on the back, of one of these shaggy beasts, all the way to his settlement, he was on the verge of bolting from the native village and making his way back, as fast as his fleeing feet could take him. It took a lot of convincing, before he finally accepted the fact, this would be the most expedient recourse for rescuing his people. His, already, pallid skin took on a grayish hue as he clung, resignedly, to Roca.

Thoughts varied among the troops, as the sure-footed bovines carried them steadily across the rolling terrain. Self-doubt and confidences waged an emotional battle every step of the way. This was evident even among the veterans, who constituted the majority of the small vanguard. Their bravery, in the previous conflict with the Nevoans, was the deciding factor on their resumes, qualifying them for selection ahead of others. The balance consisted of youths as young as sixteen years of age. Their misgivings ran a little deeper, having no experience in the art of killing. The veteran warriors did their best to alleviate some of their anxiety and assured them, if they did what they were told to do, this mission would be a successful one. They hoped, once their young wings were tested, they would do just fine.

As the second "Sister" sun crested the horizon, spraying her hot rays, relentlessly, over the weary warriors, a rider could be seen, in the near distance, galloping toward them.

"Heads up, you guys! We got company!" Truck announced, breaking a long silence.

As the young scout came to a halt, at the head of the column, he informed them all was secure for at least the next five miles ahead.

"Darma and the rest of the scouts will wait for us at the first resting stop!" He finished, reining his mount alongside the three Earthmen.

On maps, magnanimously, contributed by Mokar, the new Nevoan leader, at the end of their war, their current route was segmented with designated resting areas. The one up ahead, would be their first. Many saddle-sore warriors anticipated the opportunity to stretch their legs and regain some circulation to their butts.

"Thank you, Novar! Jim responded. I think everyone is ready for a rest. Especially, the youngsters!"

As the scout retreated, to inform the trailing cavalry, Jim turned to his brothers.

"When we reach our first stop, check on the status of the men in your squads and the condition of their mounts. We can ill-afford any injuries to either."

"Especially, since we've down-sized our forces. Greg added. I still contend, we could have, easily, put two warriors on each mount."

"We had no way of measuring the capabilities of these animals, Greg. Jim replied. We're still in the learning process!"

"I don't know about you two, my butt is barking da way it is! Truck joined in. Two fellas, riding together, would really be miserable!"

"You don't have to worry about that, Truck!" Greg chided.

"Why's dat?" Truck asked, looking, questioningly, at his younger brother.

"We would not have done that to your poor animal." Greg answered, with a wide grin on his face.

Jim and others, within earshot, broke out laughing.

"Keep it up, squirt and I'll lighten da load on your animal, in a hurry!" Truck shot back, shaking a big fist at Greg.

"Seriously, Truck! His sibling continued. Maybe the two of you should consider trading places, once in a while."

"If I kick dat scrawny butt of yours you'll be too sore ta ride. It's a long walk ta dat Nevoan city!"

"There they go again! Jim thought, shaking his head and smiling at his two siblings. No mater what the situation was, the harmless threats and slights, they threw at each other, always had a way of removing the seriousness from it."

"At least I would arrive in one piece! Greg shot back. That poor beast, of yours, may end up crippled for life!"

"It's a good thing the two of you are not riding double. Jim intervened. That animal would have deposited the both of you into the moss, miles back!"

Truck looked over at Greg and winked.

"We better be quiet for a while so General Custer, here, can plot out our next strategy!" He said, throwing Jim a mock salute with his middle finger extended.

Three Earthly smiles were at the forefront of the small cavalry, as the mid-day sun continued to pelt them with her thermal onslaught. One mile ahead, a small forest beckoned them to share in its cool embrace. The first chapter, to this quest, had already been written. Hopefully, many more would follow.

# CHAPTER 6

As the last of the native cavalry nestled into the welcoming shade of the small forest, men were already busy filling water bags, hobbling mounts, or submersing themselves in the invigorating water of a small stream. Morale was still positive, despite the apprehension suffered by some of the younger warriors.

Most of the army sat in a circle around the three Earthmen, as they fielded questions and conveyed their knowledge of the Nevoan settlement. They were the only ones among them who had experienced it, first hand, while held captives by the Nevoans years earlier.

"When we get close to the settlement, small scouting parties will be deployed in advance. They will go in on foot, because of the minimal coverage in this area."

Jim announced.

"We have no way of knowing, at this point, whether or not, the invaders are still within the confines. Once the area has been deemed clear of unfriendlies, we'll send in half of our troops to search for survivors and secure the area. The rest will be staggered around the outside of the settlement to guard against a possible trap."

Looking around, at the weary faces, he observed nods of acknowledgement. Everyone had to be on the same page in order for this mission to be successful.

"Our numbers are few, gentlemen! Greg joined in. Each of you will be playing a vital role. Do not, under any circumstances, take any unnecessary risks. Cover each others backs at all times!"

"If these creatures have existed in our world, all along, why have they decided to attack us at this time?" A voice queried from the crowd.

"What do they want from us?" Another asked.

"Hey! Truck yelled, as the volume emitting from the excited men intensified.

"We can't worry ourselves about why dey attacked when dey did. We just gotta find a way ta stop dem from doing it again and hurting more people. If we could read dos murdering bastards minds we'd have all da answers. But, we can't!"

Staring at his large brother, a smile spread over Greg's face.

"I hate to admit it! But, I think Truck has hit upon a possible solution to all of our unanswered questions." He began, excitedly, looking at Jim.

His two siblings stared back at him, questioningly.

"If just one of those cerebral analyzing machines still exists, among the Nevoans, it could help us immensely! At the least, we would be able to understand their language."

Lights of understanding flicked on, in the minds of Jim and Truck. Memories of the cruel machine, which had excavated all of their Earthly knowledge, and placed it at the disposal of the former Nevoan leader, Zarnog, came flooding back to them. This "Mind Rape" had been an initial part of their orientation into this strange world.

"An excellent idea! Jim agreed. It would, definitely, give us an advantage over our enemies."

"I would not have thought of it, had Truck not mentioned "Mind Reading". Greg replied. I hope all of that thinking hasn't given him a headache."

"I don't get headaches, midget. But I know how ta give dem!" Truck said, shaking his fist and smiling.

Jim conveyed their, tentative, plan to the rest of the small army. As improbable as it was, this small positive, in the overwhelming task ahead of them, managed to induce a slight measure of hope. If all went accordingly, the tides of war could turn in their favor.

Knowledge of one's enemy was probably the most important factor, in any given war, and possibly the difference between victory and defeat.

"If this machine still exists, we would be more than half-way to realizing our goal. Jim continued. Our next objective would be the capture of at least one of the creatures."

"No problemo! Truck replied, slamming one big fist into the palm of his other hand, with a vicious smack. We'll get dem for ya. Won't we guys?"

A unanimous cheer of agreement echoed from the gathered warriors, shattering the peaceful ambiance of the cool forest.

When the noise level of the excited troops subsided, somewhat, Greg spoke.

"If we are fortunate enough, to recover one of these machines, I think it would be an excellent idea if everyone took the opportunity to listen to Truck's old tapes. Jim and I wouldn't have to interpret for him anymore."

The gathering erupted into laughter, when they observed the look on Truck's face.

"Dat's da gratitude I get for coming up with a good idea." He responded, with a big smile on his face.

After a short while, Jim spoke.

"I think it best, at this time, everyone check on their mount and get some rest. Our journey will continue in a few hours."

\* \* \* \* \* \* \* \* \*

Much later, that same day, before the mid-day sun had expired, one of the perimeter scouts reported in. They had discovered a large herd of lurdas, three miles ahead, but, still no sign of the enemy. They could not afford to waste valuable time in the pursuit of fresh meat. Many lives depended on their expediency.

"It's tempting!" Jim said to his brothers, alongside him, as they led the native cavalry over the rolling landscape.

"The thought of a nice juicy roast is alluring." He turned and winked at Greg, riding to his left. They were, both, well aware of Truck's voracious appetite and constantly teased him about it.

"I know what you mean, Jim! I can almost feel the succulent greases dripping down my chin." Greg replied, continuing the game.

"Keep it up, you two jokers and yer gonna find it hard ta ride when I kick your scrawny asses. Ya know, damn well, all dis riding makes me hungry!"

"If our comrades are still alive, I know they'd appreciate the small sacrifices we're making." Jim said, in a more serious tone.

Once, again, silence prevailed. Each man consoled themselves with his own thoughts. Jim's musings reverted to events, years ago, when the three of them were united once again. While in captivity, Jim and Greg had been informed by Mokar, the "High learner" of the Nevoan people, their brother Truck had been killed. They had discussed an escape attempt, earlier. After a short mourning period for their sibling, who they thought dead, it was decided, they would continue with their quest for freedom.

After accomplishing this goal and putting themselves far from Nevoan clutches, they happened upon a group of filthy, half-dead natives trudging across the mossy landscape. Six Nevoan soldiers drove them on. Cruel curses and painful blows, from their lethal staffs, hailed down on the weary group. The six tormentors were quickly dispatched, by the deadly bowmanship of the two Earthmen. They, eventually, learned these half-starved individuals were part of a Nevoan labor camp.

After a short period of time was spent building the strength, spirit and confidence, of this raggedy group, an assault was made on the open pit, which had been the living quarters of the downtrodden men. Others were liberated and the Nevoan contingency was eliminated. Among the rescued group was an old man named Kaba. After a while, the two Earthmen learned their brother had been a recent resident of this same pit. He had managed to escape, along with Kaba's nephew, Bantor.

Immediately, upon hearing this, the two Earthmen and the old native abandoned the group they had been traveling with and stole off into the night. Kaba and Bantor were from the same village and the Earthmen believed that's where they would find their brother. During the trek, Jim and Greg managed to rescue four of Kaba's villagers.

A few sunrises later, they were embroiled in a deadly battle with fifty Nevoan soldiers. Severely wounded, they were found by an army of natives from Kaba's village and nursed back to health. Their "dead" brother was there to greet them, when consciousness returned. A large-scale attack was launched on the Nevoan settlement. After their victory, peace had reigned on their world for the last eight years. Now, they were confronted with this latest crisis. If their comrades still lived Jim knew in his heart, as well as his mind, some way, somehow, they would rescue them.

As the evening sun was well on her way to surrendering, to the encroaching darkness, the exhausted travelers took refuge in a small, tree-lined glen, surrounded on three sides by low-lying hills. No fires were lit. None were needed. "Hope" provided enough warmth, as they succumbed to the embraces of their sleeping furs.

# CHAPTER 7

Five, uneventful, days later found the native cavalry on the outskirts of the Nevoan settlement. A contingency of a dozen men, led by Roca and Tonio, was sent out in advance of the main force. Jim called a halt behind a rise of low hills, approximately, two miles from the settlement's main gate. Now, all they could do was await word from their scouts. The time was spent checking and rechecking their mounts and making certain all weapons were up to their deadliest standards.

Each man knew his assignment. When the word was given, they would assume their designated positions. Apprehension cloaked them, with a cloud of uncertainty. Even the veterans exhibited signs of nervousness. War did not allow for any concrete certainties. Their fate would be determined by their actions.

Observers were posted at the tops of the hills, hiding the native cavalry. The three Earthmen were, also, at the summit of one of these rises, silently scanning the barren two-mile strip, leading into the Nevoan compound.

"We'll have, absolutely, no coverage from this point on! Greg said, breaking the silence. Whether we advance on foot or mounted will make little difference. We're going to be highly visible targets."

"We'll know more, when our scouts report in. Jim responded. For all we know, the invaders may have, already, vacated the premises."

"I don't think we gotta worry too much about da coverage, Truck interjected. If all dey got is spears and axes, we should be able ta get close enough without risking any of da men. We got da big guns. Don't we?"

"My only concern for stealth is the safety of the hostages, if there are any. Jim replied. A full-out attack may incite the invaders into mass murder. If we can deploy a surprise assault, we stand a better chance of rescuing them."

"We're about to find out, gentlemen! Greg said, pointing in the direction of the settlement. One of our scouts approaches!"

Moments later, Roca crested the hill and stood before them. Catching his breath, he made his report.

"Shortly after penetrating the Nevoan city, we discovered a party, consisting of ten of the beasts, congregated outside one of the buildings. He began. We approached to within throwing distance, before we were discovered. Roaring like crazed animals, they charged into us. Using our power weapons, we quickly dispatched eight of them. The two, remaining, dropped their weapons and fled. They were captured within moments and bound securely. After placing them under heavy guard, I hurried back here to make my report."

Truck handed him a water skin. While he was quenching his thirst, Jim asked him if the had seen any hostages.

"Tonio informed me he had noticed movement inside the building, guarded by the invaders. I don't know for sure if they were Nevoans or more of the beasts because I rushed off to bring you my report."

The majority of the cavalry was clustered around them, by this time, and had heard Roca's information.

"Everyone, get mounted up! Jim shouted. We leave, immediately!"

In moments, their loyal animals were being spurred across the mossy route to the city. The mounts, belonging to the advance party, followed behind. Each one tethered, by lengths of hide cord, to one of their mounted brethren. In a handful of moments, they covered the short distance and came to a halt in front of the massive gate, leading into the city. Tonio and two other natives were there to meet them. As the entire cavalry dismounted, Tonio approached the Earthmen.

"Tonio, my friend! Jim greeted, as he shook the native's hand. What news do you have for me?"

"The battle has begun, my brother. We have eliminated eight of the creatures. Two were captured and are, now, under heavy guard. Tonio replied. We have, also, rescued four of the Nevoan citizens."

"Good work! Jim replied. Lead me to them, if you please!"

"Before I do as you ask, Earth friend. He hesitated. I feel I must prepare you for this most horrible sight, of which you are about to witness."

"Whatta ya trying ta say, Tonio?" Truck asked.

Looking at the big Earthman, with a sad expression on his face, he continued.

"The four Nevoans, we have rescued, have parts missing from their bodies and are barely alive! We were unable to learn anything further, because of our ignorance of their language."

"Take us to them, immediately!" Greg ordered.

In a matter of moments, they were standing in front of the most macabre scene they had ever laid eyes upon.

Two of the Nevoans lay on the ground, staring up at them. Both, arms and legs, had been severed from their bodies. The other two, (the lucky ones? if you will), were missing their arms. They stood alongside their dismembered comrades, staring through lifeless eyes at the Earthmen. Bloodied, dirt-encrusted rags hung from the ends of their festering stumps. Cords had been wrapped, tightly, above the wounds, to prevent them from bleeding to death. The putrid smell, of impending death, permeated the air. The gaunt stares, from the four maimed beings, reflected the excruciating hell they had experienced.

"My friend! Jim began, in the Nevoan language, as he knelt beside one of the legless victims. Why was this done to you?"

Staring up at the Earthman, surprise reflected from his large eyes that this non- Nevoan was capable of conversing in his language.

"How came it to be you are familiar with my language?" The Nevoan asked.

"I will tell you at another time! Jim replied. Suffice it to say, all of us here have come to aid the Nevoan people. Now, please, tell me why this has happened!"

Grimacing in pain, the dying creature struggled to continue. "For many days, the beasts have been using us to provide sustenance. Each cycle of the "sister" suns, they remove a part from us with their sharp weapons. We were forced to observe, as they consumed our flesh."

The horrified looks on Earthly faces, were stared upon, questioningly, by their comrades. None, of which, understood the language. Jim translated the repulsive act, perpetrated against these poor souls, by the heartless beasts. A cloud of apprehension settled over the gathered natives, shocking them into silence. It was inconceivable any race of beings could commit this atrocity against another. Would they be next on the menu?

A few, tense, moments passed before the Nevoan started talking again.

"We numbered twenty-five in our group, to begin with. After these ruthless beasts plundered our city, killing anyone who wandered across their paths, they herded us into this building. He pointed to his left. For five cycles of the suns, they kept up a relentless assault. I believe some of my people were fortunate enough to have escaped."

"Do you have any idea as to why this group was left behind?" Jim inquired.

"Before your companions carried what is left of us, from the building, we had not been permitted to see the light of day. The beasts came upon us, only once each cycle, to sate their hunger. Knowledge of anything else, pertaining to this invasion, was shielded from us." He finished, weakly.

Jim squeezed his saddened eyes shut and shook his head. Their latest adversary would not be content with just the destruction of all in its path. If left unchecked, the existence of all they held dear, on this world, would, literally, be consumed.

Turning toward his men, with moist eyes, he gave orders.

"Deploy your men around the outside perimeter of this settlement. He said to Tonio and Roca.

"Truck! Greg! We'll take our men and do a sweep, of this entire village, dwelling by dwelling! If there are any of those murdering bastards lurking around, kill them! We already have the captives we need for our experiment."

"Whatta we gonna do with dese poor guys? Truck asked. We can't just leave em lying on da ground like dat!"

"Have a few of your men carry them to one of the dwellings. Jim answered. Make sure they are provided with plenty of food and water. Then find Froban so he can stay with them and provide assistance."

"I think we should dispatch riders to search for Mokar and other survivors. Greg suggested. My best assumption would be, he is held up in the very same forest that hid our invading army years ago."

"That would be my guess, also, Greg. Jim agreed. It's the closest refuge outside the village and a logical area to start our search."

* * * * * * * * *

Many hours later, the entire Nevoan establishment was pronounced secure. No other hostiles had been discovered. Watches were dispersed on the high walls, surrounding the settlement, observing the barren waste in all directions. Many mounted patrols had been sent out, in search of the missing Nevoans. The majority of the army were involved with cleaning up the carnage left behind by the marauding beasts. Body parts of all descriptions, sizes and colors were collected and added to the massive funeral pyres, blazing in the center of a large, open square. More than a few of the hardiest warriors lost their lunches when confronted by the globs of unidentifiable flesh and nauseating odors. In one area, of the settlement, they had discovered a massive mound of bones, picked clean by the ravenous appetites of the invaders. It stood as a morbid monument of devastation they had caused. When the three Earthmen first observed the two creatures that had been captured, it took all of their Earthly objectivity not to add their wicked bones to the fire while they were still alive. This, however, didn't stop Truck from wading into the two of them, trying his best to break them in two. It took a lot of physical persuasion, by many people, to pull him away from them. The ghoulish beasts had to be kept alive in order for them to implement their experiment. That, in itself, was the only saving factor that availed itself to the heartless creatures.

# CHAPTER 8

As the first sun of the new day strived to remove some of the chilling atmosphere, cloaking the Nevoan city, men were already resuming their gruesome tasks from the day before. It was impossible to estimate the number of bodies being consumed by the funeral fires. Body parts were still being recovered. Men pushed hastily-built carts, heaped with Nevoan refuse, from all reaches of the city.

The three Earthmen were taking their turn at the fire. Using make-shift shovels and pitchforks, they fed the grizzly remains into the blaze.

"This is the last of it! Tonio said as he approached the Americans with a cart less than half full. That, which remains, could not be gathered up." He finished, his eyes glistening with sadness.

"Thank God for that! Jim replied. We can't afford to spend much more time on this anyhow. If Mokar and the other Nevoans are not located by the setting of the last "Sister" sun, tomorrow, we begin our journey north."

"I agree! Greg responded. We've done about as much as we can. If they ever return, their transition will be a little easier. It would have been advantageous, for us, had we located one of their machines and someone capable of operating it. But, our time is crucial."

"How do you feel about it, Truck?" Jim asked.

The big man had been working furiously, at his chore, all morning, almost in complete silence. When he didn't respond, Jim tried again.

"Anything you want to talk about, brother?"

Truck stopped shoveling and stared across at his older brother. The moisture, dripping from his kind eyes, wasn't caused, entirely, by the smoking fire.

"I took a walk through da zoo early dis morning, before you guys were up. He paused, choking back his words. Dos animal bastards slaughtered everyone a dos poor creatures, in dere cages. Dey had less chance den da Nevoan people. Dey couldn't escape!"

Pausing, momentarily, before he spoke, Jim stared back at his brother. Here was one of the toughest men he had ever known in his life. Physical attributes aside, Truck also possessed a large space in his heart, filled with concern and compassion, for all the misfortunates in life. Equal amounts of fury and caring emotions made him what he was, a grizzly or a teddy bear.

"If everything falls into place, we'll soon have our revenge, my brother. You don't have to worry about that!"

Greg, working a few paces apart from his brothers, had been listening to their conversation. He knew when his big brother fell into these emotional doldrums, they could last for a long time. He had to do something!

"My condolences, for the loss of your friends, Truck! He began. Now, if you don't mind, pick up the pace a little. We'd like to finish this gruesome task, some time today!"

Jim looked at Greg in askance. They were well aware of the fact, Truck always out-worked them. Catching a glimpse of a slight grin, on his younger brother's face, he understood.

A slight smile cracked the saddened countenance, on Truck's face, when he registered Greg's attempt to alleviate some of his pain.

"If I didn't love ya, shorty, your scrawny ass would be barbecued, by now." He returned, with a full smile on his face.

"Amen ta dat!" Jim chimed in.

Soon, all-American laughter prevailed over the macabre scene.

A short while later, their ghoulish task completed, the entire native force, other than the sentries on the walls and the guards keeping watch on the prisoners, congregated in the open square, adjacent to Mokar's residence.

"Have all the search parties checked in?" Jim asked, addressing the crowd.

"All but one! Tonio replied. Roca's party is still unaccounted for!"

The second sun was almost half way through her cycle, bathing the native warriors in its splendor.

"If Nevoan survivors are not discovered, before this day has ended, we will leave this settlement with the rising of the first sun." Jim announced.

Cheers of acceptance echoed from the small gathering. Everyone was more than ready to leave this "city of death" far behind.

"We have accomplished all we could do here. Jim continued. If any survivors do return, I am sure they will be appreciative of everyone's efforts. I commend all of you, for bearing up under this gruesome ordeal!"

"If none of the inhabitants resurface, by tomorrow's first sun, we will proceed with our original plan. Greg interjected. We will travel north and, hopefully, discover the trail of these merciless defilers. No avenue will be overlooked, in the pursuit of our brethren."

"And when we find da bastards, we kill dem all! Truck added. I ain't gonna take no prisoners!"

A roar erupted from the audience, boisterously voicing their agreement.

"I see you haven't lost you knack for inciting riots." Jim commented, shaking his head.

"Dis is just da beginning! Truck returned, with a wink. Wait till da main course gets here!"

The next few hours were spent discussing tactics, resting up and looking after the welfare of their mounts. The beasts had been cordoned off in an area near the main square of the settlement. This mossy tract provided for their sustenance. Large vats, found in one of the Nevoan workshops, were filled with water from a near by stream.

A large structure had, also, been discovered, containing Nevoan produce. The men were more than happy to supplement their dried meat with these strange fruits and vegetables. The three Earthmen had sampled these delicacies years before, while in captivity.

The Nevoan, Froban, had joined them, shortly before the third sun of the day was spent. When not involved with cleaning up the ghastly remains, scattered about the city, his time was devoted to the aid of his four dying comrades. They had seen very little of him, since entering the settlement.

"How are your four buddies doing?" Truck asked.

"All have left this world, but one. He replied. Soon, he will follow them!"

"I wish there was more we could have done for them, Froban." Jim joined in.

"Their spirits had left them long before you rescued them, Earthman. However, your concern is acknowledged and I find it necessary to compel gratitude to you and your men, for your kind gestures. When my people return, they will be made aware of this."

Jim interpreted for the small group, still in attendance, which nodded its approval.

Turning back to Froban, he said, "The majority of my people believe the Nevoans would have responded in kind, if the situation was reversed. Past grievances have clouded some minds, because emotional wounds have not yet heeled."

"The same sentiment runs rampant in my settlement, also. Froban replied. Mokar has introduced us to a different way of life. However, existing among us are individuals who will not let go of the past. I related to this group, until a short while ago. Whether my people return or not, I, Froban, vow to assist you in your endeavor."

"We need all da help we can get, pal! Truck chimed in. Dos bastards started dis crap, but, we sure as hell are gonna finish it!"

"This is the name for the creatures who attacked my people?" Froban asked.

"Dat's just one a dem! Truck piped up, before either of his two brothers could interject. And dere's a lot more where dat one came from!" He finished, with a big grin on his face.

"Suffice it to say, Froban. Greg jumped in. It is a word, used by my people, when their enemy is unknown." He finished, casting a hard stare at his smiling brothers.

"Bastards! Froban repeated. It is an appropriate title for their kind."

Now, three Earthly smiles, one grin away from all out laughter, were reflected.

Moments later, in a more serious tone, Jim asked Froban if he thought any of his comrades, if still alive, would join forces with them.

"When I relate to the others how we had become benefactors, because of your selfless labors, they will be eager to participate. Revenge is, also, a strong motivator." The Nevoan replied.

At this time, one of the wall sentries rushed into their midst. "A large group of people is headed toward this city." He announced, catching his breath.

Before the last words had left the sentries mouth, The Earthmen were racing across the square. The rest of the gathering was in close pursuit. Weapons were retrieved, along the way. As they gained the catwalk, adrenaline was running high. Soon, they were adding their gazes to the sea of apprehension, as they waited.

It wasn't long, before they discerned men riding lurdas. They were followed, closely, by hundreds of Nevoan citizens.

"They've located them! Jim exalted. Tonio, if you would be so kind, mount up your squad and offer assistance."

"I'll go down and make sure dos bastards get lots a food and water." Truck volunteered, as he raced off.

Unnoticed, Froban had followed the group of men when they had raced to the top of the wall.

"The eyesight of your sibling must be failing him. He said to Jim. Those who march toward us are not the "bastards". They are your people and mine."

Greg and Jim looked at the naïve Nevoan and broke out laughing.

# CHAPTER 9

"For three long cycles of our suns, the invaders killed at random. Some paused, long enough, to feed upon the slain."

Mokar held court in the large, open square fronting the "House of Learning". He commanded the attention of hundreds of his people, as well as the native contingency.

"Our only recourse was to go into hiding. Their veracious appetite for flesh and blood was our only ally. While they fed upon our slaughtered comrades, it allowed us the time we needed to make our escape. So intent were they, with their bloody banquet, we were not detected.

He paused, staring out at his large audience.

"Mokar! Could you give us a rough estimate as to the size of the invader's army?" Jim asked, breaking in on the Nevoan leader's thoughts.

"It was impossible to decipher numbers, Earth friend. He answered. When the swarm overwhelmed us, our time was spent in evading them long enough to flee the settlement. Because of our defenseless status, it was the only recourse availing itself to us."

"Do you have any ideas as to why you were not pursued?" Greg asked.

"I have given that much thought, Earthman! Mokar replied. My conclusions suggest the invaders were not interested in occupying our city or expanding their boundaries. They were on a hunt and their main objective was food."

Jim interpreted for his men. The faces of the natives ran the gamut from shock to fear and, finally anger.

Apprehension multiplied in the minds of the younger warriors, as well as some of the veterans. The inconceivable thought of engaging, in battle, a race of beings intent on making you a smorgasbord was unsettling.

"For two cycles of our suns, we fled south across the mossy plain. We stopped only when we were hidden in the depths of a large forest. Because of our lack of weapons, I was reluctant to send observers back to gather information concerning our settlement. I did not wish to lose anymore of my people. It was at this time, I sent messengers out seeking aid."

"I'm glad we was able ta find you guys! Truck chimed in. For a while dere it looked like dos bastards killed everyone of ya."

"Gladness belongs to the Nevoan people you have rescued, Earth friend. Mokar replied. Gratitude, also, belongs to you and your people for purging our city of the carnage cast upon it. This magnanimous gesture will, forever, be foremost in my mind!"

"Mokar! Jim broke in. I know this is sudden, considering what you and your people have just suffered. But, I was wondering if you would be willing to join forces, in a campaign against these beasts. Some of our people have died at their hands, also. Others have been taken prisoner."

"Thoughts of retaliation, for the loses we suffered, entered my mind long before we had entered the sanctuary of that distant forest. He answered. Were it not for our lack of weapons, we would, already, be engaging our enemy."

An Earthly light bulb flickered, vividly, in Greg's mind. "What if I were to say to you, we had the means to arm every Nevoan who thirsts for revenge. Would that influence you decision?"

Jim and Truck looked at each other, questioningly, for only a brief instant. Then, the lights flickered on in their think tanks, as well.

"There is not one Nevoan citizen, in this entire settlement, who would reject the opportunity to avenge the atrocities imposed upon us. He answered, staring at the Earthman. The weapons, carried by your small army, are few. They could not possibly come close to arming all my Nevoan warriors. What do you propose?"

"Many weapons, confiscated during the war between our peoples, lie buried a short distance from where we sit. Jim jumped in. Once we have ascertained their condition, it would be possible to arm many men."

"Dat's a great idea, you guys! Truck agreed. I'll take my squad and go check it out, right now!"

After they had gone, armed with any digging tools they could find, Jim explained to the rest of the men what they planned on doing.

The addition of hundreds of Nevoan soldiers, to their small cavalry, bolstered confidences ten fold. After having observed, close up, the havoc and carnage the enemy was capable of causing, reinforcements were more than welcomed.

Shouts of appreciation erupted from the crowd. A little encouragement, at this time, was just what the doctor's ordered.

Froban, sitting on Mokar's left, had been silent until now.

"Mokar! I have already pledged my assistance to the native army. He began. Their nurturing methods prevented my life from leaving my body and making a painful journey to meet my forefathers. I sit before you, on this day, only because of their timely intervention."

"Your perseverance has given us all another chance at life. Mokar interrupted. I have been apprised, by our Earth allies, of the debilitated condition you were in, when first they found you. The undying praise of every citizen, yet alive, belongs to you. As a token of our collective esteem, I appoint you to lead our warriors."

"I accept the status, willingly, my leader. Froban responded. You will not be disappointed."

Jim and Greg nodded their heads in approval and smiled, at the promoted messenger. What he had endured, while seeking assistance for his people, more than qualified him for the position. He had heart!"

After a brief lull, Greg spoke. "Mokar! There is another matter we wish to discuss with you. I believe it would help us, immensely!"

"What is the nature of this issue, Earth friend?" Mokar asked.

"If we were allowed access to, just, one of the photo cerebral implanters, once used by Zarnog, we might be able to get some answers, as to why your settlement was attacked." Greg replied.

"With the demise of our former leader, all instruments of deceit and destruction have been eliminated. Mokar said. However, one of the devices, of which you refer, has been preserved as a curiosity."

"Would you or anyone else be capable of operating this machine, if it still functions?" Jim asked, hopefully.

Mokar stared at the two men, for a moment, before he spoke. "In what manner can one of Zarnog's toys avail us an understanding of our attackers? The Nevoan leader shot back. I am unable to comprehend what this is pertaining to."

"We have captured two of the beasts involved with the desecration of your settlement. Greg answered. Jim and I believe, if we can explore the minds of these creatures, we might gain an understanding of their motives, precipitating this atrocious assault."

"If the only thing we manage to accomplish, through this experiment, is an understanding of their language, it would still be a huge advantage for us." Jim added.

Nodding his bulbous head, Mokar replied. "Your conjectures have convinced me this is worthy of an attempt. I will do all I can to assist you. Now, I would look upon these defilers of my settlement."

A short while later, the group stood in front of a small dwelling. Four natives, with "Dracos" balanced on their shoulders, stood guard.

"Bring the prisoners forward!" Jim ordered.

The four sentries hastened into the dwelling. Seconds later, they reemerged, dragging the two, furry creatures out and depositing them, none too gently, on the ground, in front of the curious audience.

Dark eyes, with vertical streaks of yellow at their centers, stared back at them, maliciously. Hide straps, wrapped tightly around their long, furry muzzles, prevented them from using their sharp teeth on anyone. Arms, tied securely behind their backs and leather hobbles attached to their legs, completely immobilized them.

Mokar stared openly at the two creatures, as if he were trying to read their minds. They glared back at him, defiantly.

"If any intelligence exists, in these two beasts, it is deeply hidden. Mokar remarked. Your attempt to expose it may prove to be a futile one."

"It would be worth the effort, Mokar. Jim replied. The possibility of vital information could be lying just beneath the surface."

"Let us hope it is not buried too deeply, my friend. Mokar added. Let us go, now, to Zarnog's old palace and recover this machine."

# CHAPTER 10

Mokar, Froban, Jim and Greg, Tonio and Roca congregated in Zarnog's old "Royal" room. They waited, patiently, for one of Zarnog's former assistants to arrive.

"Do you remember our first visit to this room?" Jim asked his brother, staring around at the vast chamber.

"Indeed, I do! Greg answered. Our large brother nearly succeeded in making our stay, on this world, a short one. Your timely, but bogus, intervention bought us a stay of execution."

"Older brothers come in handy, sometimes. Jim replied, smiling as he reminisced. We were all in a state of confusion, at that time, just trying to survive the ordeal."

"So, tell me! What excuse did Truck have before this incident took place?" Greg responded, with a big smile on his face.

Jim laughed at, yet, another verbal jab, thrown by Greg, at their large sibling.

Their musings were interrupted by the approach of an elderly Nevoan.

"Delcor, my old comrade! Mokar greeted. I see you still walk in this world."

"Just barely, old learner. Delcor responded. What is all this about?"

"Do you still possess knowledge of the cerebral implanter? And, are you capable of operating it?" Mokar inquired.

"The cerebral implanter? That device has not been used since the demise of Zarnog." Delcor replied.

"We are all well aware of this! Mokar shot back. If you would be so kind and answer my questions."

"The many years I spent, operating that machine, have ingrained a permanent memory. Yes! I am still capable of running the device, if it is still in working order." He answered.

"Can you tell me, now, why this is so important?"

"Suffice it to say, my old friend, the knowledge you possess may save many lifes."

Once again, a questioning look reflected from Delcor's face. But, before he could inquire further, Mokar interjected.

"Send word to me, immediately, when the device is prepared for use."

Having said that, he turned and led the small group out of Zarnog's chambers.

Delcor stared, quizzically, after them as they filed passed. "What is all this about?" He wondered.

As they made their way toward the center of the open square, they noticed Truck and his squad of men resting in the area adjacent to Mokar's palace. Their arduous labors left them covered with dirt from head to foot. Even more noticeable was the mound of Nevoan weapons, stacked six feet high and spread fifty feet across the square. Although they were covered with a film of grime, it was still an impressive sight.

"It looks as if you've had a successful day, my brother." Jim said, as they joined the tired group.

"You're right about dat, Jimbo! Truck replied. Dere were more still buried, but, dis is all we could carry. We, also, got a hide filled with dos crystal rocks."

"There appears to be, approximately, one thousand weapons here, Jim. Greg exclaimed. To clean and restore them for use will take us an enormous amount of time. Time we can ill-afford to squander."

"You're right, Greg! Jim agreed. But, with a little help from our Nevoan allies, it shouldn't take too long."

Turning to Froban, who was observing the scene alongside him, He spoke to him.

"Chosen leader of the Nevoan army, I need your assistance!"

"To ask is to command, Earth friend. How may I help?" He answered.

"If you would be so kind and have each of your volunteers secure a weapon, from this pile, and prepare it for use, would save us a lot of time. Jim replied. If any remain, I will have my men finish."

Froban shouted orders to the vast group of Nevoans, who had congregated around the stock-piled weapons. In no time at all, the immense stack of Nevoan weapons vanished. The first ones taken were, already, in the final stages of restoration and proclaimed fit for use.

The three Earthmen had been standing off to the side. They watched, in amazement, how efficiently Froban's soldiers carried out this task.

"I believe if you had brought back another thousand weapons, my brother, they would have gone to good use. Jim commented. There still remains a large number of Nevoans, awaiting the opportunity to adopt them."

"If ya want me ta go back and get more, just say da word!" Truck replied.

"That won't be necessary, Truck! Jim said. What we have here will be sufficient. Although, the luxury of having more warriors is tempting, the time consumed marching them all north is the biggest problem."

"In dat case, Jimbo, I think I'll take my squad to dat stream and get rid a dis crud clinging ta me. It's starting ta make me itch!"

"Not to mention the smell! Greg mocked, taking a step back from his large brother.

"It's just a little dirt, from some honest labor. Truck shot back, winking at Jim. Ya oughtta try it sometime. As a matter a fact, I think ya should try some, right now!"

Before Greg could react, he was engulfed in a truck-sized bear hug, his head mashed against his brothers massive, dirt-encrusted chest.

As Greg struggled to free himself, from Truck's grimy embrace, Jim roared with laughter.

"Let go of me, you smelly gorilla! Greg protested.

"Ya gonna apologize for hurting my feelings?" Truck asked, increasing the pressure on his squirming sibling.

"Yes! Anything! Greg, quickly, agreed. Just let me catch my breath."

Releasing his young brother, Truck joined in on Jim's laughter. They stared at Greg, who was, now, encrusted in dirt and sweat from his forehead to his waist.

Looking down at the filth clinging to him, he shook his head and was, soon, joining them in their laughter.

"I believe I'll just tag along with you to that steam." He said, slapping Truck on the back.

# CHAPTER 11

The first "Sister" sun nudged the slumbering village awake, with her warm embrace. Activity was already afoot. Evinced by the start of breakfast fires, children beginning their daily play routines, water being dipped from the deep wells and other early chores tended to, as the natives prepared for the new day. Activity outside the village was limited to tending the large herd of Lurdas, penned up just outside the village gate. Since the departure of the rescue cavalry, six days earlier, the normal activities outside the village, foraging, hunting, exploring were restricted. Leota felt it was best to keep everyone close to the village, until this conflict with the furry invaders was resolved.

Sentries manned the elevated catwalks, surrounding the settlement, in continuous shifts. The community storage huts held an ample supply of dried meat, edible roots, fruits and vegetables. Their dietary needs were, also, supplemented by the many small gardens, throughout the village. No one would go hungry! The restriction of their outside activities was a sacrifice they had to accept, to insure their overall safety. For many of the most avid hunters and gatherers, confinement wouldn't be easy.

Graci stared across the small fire at her mate. She was well aware of the agony he suffered, in his heart and mind. There was very little she could do to alleviate his pain, other than to give him her unquestioning support. The strength of a leader dictated the well being of his people. His emotional tortures would never affect their happiness.

"Leota! When all of our warriors have returned from their journey, I believe a big celebratory feast is in order!" She had put the emphasis on the word "all".

It brought a slight smile to Leota's saddened countenance. He had been, truly, blessed while serving as the leader of this village. To be surrounded, by so many positive proponents, made even the worst day tolerable. Other than the time he and Graci were captured and separated, by the Nevoans, she was always there for him. Her, pleasingly, mundane outlook on life in general, was often the deciding factor in many of his decisions.

"My love! If we are fortunate enough, to embrace that day, I promise you the biggest celebration in the history of our people."

Graci stared across at him, with a scolding look. She remained silent.

"What is it I said to cause such a look on that pretty face? He asked. Before she could answer, it dawned upon him. Forgive me! "When" that day arrives, we shall have a celebration surpassing all others."

The glowing smile, on Graci's face, informed him he had answered correctly.

"It is fortunate, for you, our Earth brethren are not hear to listen to your negative talk. She replied. They would have added more than, just, stern looks!"

"What you say is true, mate of my heart! However, there are times when I feel the weight of my responsibilities to be overwhelming. Maybe I have grown too old to bear up under them. Maybe, the right thing to do is to pass the reins of leadership onto my son when he returns."

Graci refused to give in to his melancholy. The beautiful smile had not left her face. "The man who shared my furs, this past night, did not seem old to me!" She said, with a sensual lilt in her voice.

Leota rocked back with laughter, his gloomy mood forgotten. "Woman! Every day you provide me with another reason for loving you. Thank you for keeping this man on the right path."

"Thank you" is not necessary! She replied. Besides, we have twenty years to make up for that were stolen from our lives. We must not allow anything to disrupt this."

"When you put it in that light, neither one of us can afford to get old." He said, smiling back at her.

There was a pause between them, as they enjoyed the moment. It was Leota who broke the silence.

"Your suggestion, of a celebration, has given me an idea!"

Before Graci could ask what was on his mind, he continued.

"Finish your tea and help me gather our people, at the "Meeting" hut. He said, excitedly.

* * * * * * * * *

A short time later, most of the village was congregated in the meeting place. The morning sun cast her warmth on the large crowd, anticipating the reason for this sudden gathering.

Leota stood before them and raised his arms, above his head. The murmurings ceased, almost, immediately.

"I welcome you to a new day, my people! He began. First, I would like to extend to you my appreciation for the sacrifices being made. It has not been easy, over these last few days."

He paused and looked around at all the faces, filled with questioning looks.

"The quality of our everyday lives, over this dire period, has proved to be rather monotonous. Yet, I have heard few complaints. My mate, Graci, mentioned to me, just this morning, her desire for a momentous celebration on the return of our brethren. It started me thinking about our present situation. The restrictions, we are forced to adhere to, to ensure our safety, have removed some of the joys from our everyday lives. I have a proposal that could alleviate some of the tedium from our present situation."

The attentive crowd started buzzing with excitement at the mention of an occasion that could put a little spark back into their daily routines.

"I have been told by many elders, in the past, each new day creates a new beginning. Embrace and celebrate it, as if it were your last. If we are in agreement that is, exactly, what I am about to propose. Our natural passions for hunting, foraging and exploring, put on hold, during this trying period, could be slightly mollified by inventing new distractions, such as, contests with bow and arrow, races, feats of strength, anything that will help us all weather this crucial period as one. Your input on my proposal, if you accept it, will be most appreciated." Leota finished, taking his seat next to Graci.

The positive cheers, emanating from the large crowd, told him the entire village was in agreement. Every man, woman and child was more than eager to liven up their daily routines.

For the next four hours, Leota was bombarded with ideas ranging from "beautiful baby" contests, arts and crafts events, spitting contests, eating contests and many more. Every one of his people, it seemed, had an idea.

There were enough suggestions to fill out an entire year's worth of activities.

The second sun of the day had almost exhausted her warmth, before the large crowd melted away to take care of personal chores. The overall demeanor, of the people, was elevated to a high pitch of anticipation.

"Graci, my love, I think we are going to be busy, for quite some time!" Leota said, with a big smile of satisfaction on his face.

# CHAPTER 12

Early the next sunrise, the excited villagers were gathered at the target field. The children would exhibit their skills, with bow and arrow. No less than seventy-five, nervous youngsters, between six and ten years of age, lined up in anticipation. The older children, between the ages of eleven and fifteen, would get their chance to compete in later tournaments. The idea, for this event, was that of "Treban". He was the most skilled bow and arrow maker among them. To possess one of his creations, assured the hunter deadly accuracy and a lifetime of use. It had been decided upon, the person who promoted the idea, for a certain activity, would be in charge of that given event. Treban had the honor, for the moment.

Raising his arms and gaining the crowd's attention, he began.

"In fairness, to all our young warriors, I have separated them into age groups. The winners of each group will compete against one another, until there remains only one."

Bending over, he lifted a long hide bundle from the ground. Untying a cord, he raised a brand new bow and a quiver of arrows above his head, products of his expert skills.

"When our champion is fully capable of mastering the power of a bow, such as this, he or she will pay me a visit and claim their prize. Your sires will inform me, when you are ready."

A large group of women sat behind the competitors, ready to cheer on their offspring. Bomar and Tomal, sons of Jim and Sanda and Greg and Lona, respectively, were counted among the first group. Their dark hair distinguished them, in the sea of blond tresses.

"Bomar's excitement kept him awake most of the night, Sanda said. I hope it will not affect his accuracy."

"If he was just competing against Tomal, they would be evenly matched. Lona replied. He was awake most of the night, also."

"Rest assured, all of these young warriors have spent restless nights, in anticipation of this contest. Mara chimed in. Salba will be competing in the next age group, if he can stay awake long enough."

The laughter, shared by the anxious mothers, was long overdue. In the last few days, of this trying period, tension had blanketed any attempts at humor.

Treban now stood in front of the young competitors and held his arms above his head.

"The targets have been placed twenty-five paces away. Each one, of our young archers, have been given five arrows. The ones who place the most arrows, in the accuracy circle, will move on to the next level of competition. He continued. If the possibility of a tie occurs, the targets will be moved five paces further. This will be repeated, until only one remains. Let us begin!"

Along with Bomar and Salba, there were fourteen others, in this age group. After each contestant had exhausted their five arrows, Treban walked over and checked the targets. Six of the competitors had each placed three arrows in the center of their respective targets. These six would now shoot at targets five paces further out. All others, in this age group were eliminated, returning to their parents with eyes full of tears.

Bomar and Tomal were among the five existing competitors. Playmates, almost from birth, they were used to competing against one another.

"I wish all the fathers were here to enjoy this with us. Sanda said. They would be so proud."

"I guess we'll just have to do this again, when they return." Lona responded, with hope reflecting from her eyes. We wouldn't want them to miss all this excitement. Would we?"

Tears of understanding, leaked from the eyes of the women, as they hugged each other.

"Everything will turn out just fine!" Sanda replied, joining them and adding her tears to the emotional moment.

Leota, Graci and Cinda had been circulating through the spectators and observed the three women clinging to each other.

"What have we here? Leota asked, knowing full-well, the heartache each woman harbored. Don't let your sons see this! It might affect their accuracy." He added, trying to alleviate some of their sorrow.

The three women smiled at the leader and, silently, sent him their thanks for his concern.

The second round of the competition was just getting underway. So, their attention, once again, was riveted on the young archers.

As the last of the arrows were sent skyward, a collective hush shrouded the large audience.

Treban, once again, studied the six remaining targets. Three of the archers had placed two arrows in the circle of accuracy. The targets were, again, moved another five paces further out.

Bomar, Tomal and a youngster named Feldo were the final entrants, representing the six and seven year old competitors.

"Already, these three young men have established evidence of a secure future for our village. Leota commented to the small group he was with. Our new generations of defenders will, equally, be as strong as our present warriors."

As the final three toed the line, Treban gave the signal to begin.

The three youngsters expended a little more patience, as they launched their arrows toward the targets. Their nervousness overflowed into the crowd of anxious spectators.

Each. of the three competitors, had sunk one arrow in the middle of their target. A three-way tie, again!

Treban strolled to the center of the target area and held up his arms. "Our three remaining archers will each shoot one arrow, at the target, from the same distance. He announced. Tomal! You will shoot first!"

The youngster, nervously, approached the shooting line and notched an arrow. Drawing his bow, to full capacity, he let loose. The arrow formed a perfect arc, as it whisked through the air toward its target. "thwack!" It buried itself, slightly, outside the small accuracy circle. A well-placed shot, that would have brought down whatever it was he was aiming at, if he were hunting. But, not perfect!

"Feldo! It is your turn!" Treban commanded.

Moments later, Feldo's arrow was buried inside the white circle, an inch or so closer than Tomal's arrow. Tomal was eliminated!

Hanging his head, in dejection, he made his way out of the target area. Bomar intercepted him and laid a hand on his shoulder.

"You did very well, my friend!" Trying to ease some of Tomal's disappointment.

"Not well enough! Tomal replied. It is yours to win, now."

"Bomar! Treban shouted, interrupting them. You're up.!"

Smiling at his friend, Bomar made his way to the shooting line. Widening his stance, he set his arrow on the taught cord. "Father! He said to himself. If you can hear me, help me to remember all you have taught me!"

He drew back on his bow and sent his arrow through the warm air, as he held his breath. It hit the target and, suddenly, everything around him stood still.

Treban hurried over to the target, to check the results. A moment later, he was walking toward the middle of the field, to address the crowd.

"We can all be proud of our contestants, here today. The future hunters and defenders of this village are well represented. He said, stretching out the suspense. Unfortunately, there can only be one winner in a competition, such as it is. In the hearts of everyone, they are all winners."

The crowd was stirring, impatiently, awaiting the announcement of today's winner, sometime today.

"The youngster, who will bask in the glory, for today, is Bomar! His final arrow was, nearly, dead center. Congratulations, Bomar."

The, elated, youngster was, quickly, surrounded by his peers. The smile on his face reflected his happiness. Pats on the back, hugs and words of praise fell on him from all directions. This would, surely, be one day he would never forget. The only thing that could, possibly, make it better was if his father were here to share it with him.

# CHAPTER 13

Shortly after the first sun of the day had cast her warmth over the settlement, various activities were already in progress. The responsibilities of the small cavalry had become second nature, by now, mending or replacing damaged equipment, tending to the welfare of their mounts and keeping themselves prepared for battle. Sentries, on the high wall surrounding the Nevoan city, were relieved every four hours to maintain a constant state of alertness. Small groups were scattered about, breakfasting on the Nevoan produce, dried meat and tea. A hunting party, of fifty men, had been sent out earlier. By now, everyone was more than ready for a change in the menu.

In four cycles of the "Sister" suns, they had accomplished much, cleansing the city of its putrid carnage, locating Mokar and the other surviving residents, forming an alliance with them to fight the marauding beasts from the north and recovering the weapons cache. The one last obstacle, they had to surmount, was the successful application of the Cerebral implanter. If all went well, in a cycle or two, they would commence with the search for their brethren.

The Earth brothers, Roca and a handful of men, sat around the dying remains of a small fire. Anxiety was evident on all faces.

"We should be hearing from Mokar, very soon. Jim said, using a stick to stir the dying embers back to life. Whether this experiment works or not, we'll be on our way in a couple of days. I just hope we haven't traded any of our brethren's lives for this delay."

"None of us had any way of knowing, whether they still lived or not, when we left our village. Greg replied, noticing the concern on his brother's face. Try not to hold yourself accountable for something you have no control over!"

"Da pup is right, Jimbo! Truck joined in. It don't make no difference if dere alive or not. We gotta make dose heartless bastards pay for what dey did!"

"I agree! Roca added. These vicious assaults on our peoples most be avenged."

Before any more input could be shed, on the subject, a Nevoan messenger came among them.

"Mokar has requested audience with him, at this time!" He announced.

The Earthmen and Roca made their way, immediately, across the large, open, square. Moments later, they were standing before Mokar in his library. Delcor and Froban were already in attendance.

"Greetings to the new day, Mokar!" Jim offered.

"Likewise to you, also, Earth friend. The Nevoan replied, nodding to his other three guests. Delcor, here, has informed me all is in readiness. We may proceed with this experiment, after certain details have been discussed."

"Where would you suggest the two captives be taken, for the initial transition?" Greg asked.

"I have a small chamber set aside, for the beginning process. Mokar answered. The second area selected, will depend, entirely, on the number of recipients you wish to be educated."

"Mokar! Would it be possible for the entirety, of our joint forces, to benefit from this knowledge, at the same time? Jim asked. With everyone on the same page, it would increase our chances of succeeding."

"Delcor! What say you? Mokar deferred. Is this possible?"

"Yes! It is possible! He responded. All that would be required is an enclosed area large enough to accommodate all recipients. I would, also, have to make adjustments to the volume control, to insure everyone receives the information."

"Dat old banquet room of Zarnog's, would fit da bill. Truck suggested. If dat's okay with you, Mokar!"

"Anything, within this entire settlement, that would increase your advantages over these heartless beasts, is at your disposal, Earth friend." He replied.

"The banquet room will serve our purposes, adequately!" Delcor agreed.

"If there is nothing further, to discuss, I will have my men deliver the captives to you, immediately, Mokar." Jim said.

"You have my permission, Earthman. And know this, I will be counted among the participants!"

"Ya coming with us ta kick some butt, Mokar?" Truck inquired.

"No, my friend. Mokar replied. I am many years removed from battle. I wish only to understand the rationale of creatures, compelling them to commit such heinous acts."

Observing the befuddled look on his brother's face, Greg interjected.

"Those are, precisely, the same reasons my brother, here, is submitting himself to this experiment."

Jim looked at his two siblings, shook his head and smiled.

"We'll see you very soon, Mokar. He said.

As they filed out of the room and made their way to the outside, Truck still had a baffled look on his face.

"Ya wanna explain ta me what ya said ta Mokar?" He asked his younger brother.

"I, simply, told him of your reasons for participating in this experiment." Greg replied, winking at Jim.

"And what reasons did ya give him?" Truck asked.

"I related the fact you were having difficulties adopting one of the little fur balls, because of the language barrier."

Jim roared out in laughter. Truck stopped dead in his tracks and Greg sped up a few paces.

"Ya better be careful, dwarf, or your gonna adopt a little pain. Truck replied, shaking his big fist. And believe me, ya won't have time ta understand da language."

# CHAPTER 14

Over twelve hundred men, Human, Native and Nevoan, were gathered in the banquet hall. Mixed apprehension, from the three races, was highly evident. However, it was most prominent in the Native ranks.

As seats were being sought, by the aspiring participants, Delcor and an assistant were busy working on a machine mounted on a tripod. This sat upon the raised platform formerly occupied by Zarnog's throne. A few steps above the vast audience, it was in the most advantageous position for transmitting the recovered knowledge to its subjects.

Seated at a large table, directly below the platform, was Mokar, Froban, the three Earth men, Roca and Tonio.

Mokar was relating the results of the first phase of their experiment.

"Entire lifetimes of accumulated knowledge, once possessed by the captives, now reside in that apparatus. He began. Delcor has informed me, the extraction process went without mishap. Transmitting this recovered data, to all of the given subjects, will be more complicated. In order to achieve total comprehension, an intellectual median must be established."

Memories came flashing back in Greg's mind. While held in captivity, nine years earlier, by the maniacal ruler, Zarnog, he and his brothers were forced to endure this same ordeal. The excruciating pain they were subjected to while the machine sought out their intellectual levels, caused involuntary shudders to ripple up and down his spine. The thought of repeating this agonizing procedure was unsettling.

"Mokar! He interrupted. Is this the part where you inform us Nevoan intelligence is far more superior to that of humans?"

The Nevoan leader stared back at him, for an instance, before he responded.

"The level of intelligence, to which one has aspired, would, ordinarily, be a matter of a few degrees of difference if it were to be measured among persons consisting of the same race. However, that luxury does not avail itself to us on this occasion. He hesitated a moment and stared at the three Earthmen.

"The depraved minds, responsible for creating this deplorable device, have set the standards. Not I! Success can only be realized, if all involved are in total compliance."

"Of course! Forgive me, Mokar! Greg apologized. The sting of past grievances is still felt. You cannot be held accountable for Zarnog's cruel behavior toward us."

"No apology is necessary, Earthman. Realistically, all Nevoans could be held accountable for allowing this to happen for such a long period of time."

"Mokar! Would it be feasible to begin the initial intensity probe at the lower end of the spectrum and, gradually, increase it to a comfort level compatible by all? Jim asked. To begin at the "Nevoan" level could be rather painful, for many of us."

The Nevoan intellectual level had been used as a barometer, in the past, while employing the device. Aside from the Earthmen, countless numbers of unwitting beings, throughout the universe, had experienced this same pain before the machines' intensity was reduced to their level of intelligence. Zarnog's thirst for universal knowledge, was the catalyst of his cruelty.

"An excellent suggestion! Mokar replied. I shall discuss it with Delcor, immediately!" With that, he rose from his seat and hurried up the steps leading to the raised platform.

"Am I to understand, there will be a lot of pain involved during this experiment?" Tonio asked, nervously.

"That is, precisely, what we are trying to prevent! Greg answered. When my brothers and I were forced to endure this procedure, Zarnog, the former leader, thrived on the suffering of others. His whole empire was founded on cruelty. Mokar will not allow this to happen."

"What if he can't change nothing? Truck interjected. Do we still put ourselves through dis crap all over again?"

"Speaking for myself, Truck, the answer is "yes" Jim answered. If it will increase our chances to help our lost brethren, I'm willing to make the sacrifice."

"Don't worry about it, Truck! Greg chided, with a grin on his face. I'll hold your hand during the entire procedure. You'll be just fine!"

"Keep it up, shorty, and I'll hold your throat at da same time." Truck shot back, also, grinning.

Their verbal joust was interrupted by Mokar's return,

"I have spoken to Delcor! He started, as he sat at the table. He has reversed the settings on the "Implanter". The final aspects of our experiment will be conducted with a comfort zone taken into consideration."

A modicum of relief reflected from three Earthly faces. A few pounds of apprehension melted from the countenances of Roca and Tonio, as well.

"How soon before we begin?" Greg asked.

"Delcor is attending to the final adjustments, as we speak." Mokar replied.

"How long do you think it will take to complete the experiment?" Jim asked.

"Delcor has assured me, once the appropriate level has been established the duration of the transmitting period will be, approximately, one third of a sun's cycle, (about two and one-half hours Earth time).

"I guess, all that's left to do is wait." Jim said, looking around at the large room

"Do you recollect the last party we attended in this room, Truck?" Greg asked.

Not long after their introduction to this strange world, Zarnog had ordered them to join in on a celebration commemorating the Nevoan's one hundred years of settlement. Truck, shortly after festivities began, became involved in a duel to the death, courtesy of Zarnog's undying thirst for blood. Truck had, quickly, dispatched his opponent. It seemed almost certain, at the time, their stay on this cruel world would be a short one. A short while later, the three of them were attempting to avenge the murder of Bantor's new-born daughter, (again the casualty of Zarnog's cruelty). Jim and Greg were purposely indisposed by a draco wielded by Mokar. Truck and Bantor were chained together and, later, sent away to toil in a Nevoan labor camp.

Upon regaining consciousness, the next morning, Jim and Greg were informed their brother had been slain and his body was fed to voracious beasts.

Because Zarnog had rued the fact he hadn't imposed the death sentence, on Truck and Bantor, in actuality, he salvaged a little sadistic satisfaction by ordering Mokar to tell the brothers Truck was dead. Their painful grief was Zarnog's solace.

"Now dat was some shindig! Truck replied, sarcastically. At least it was a lot more exciting den dis one."

"Well, why don't you go and pick a fight with someone. Jim kidded. I mean, if you're that bored."

"Dat's all right, Jimbo! I'll save it for dos furry bastards."

About this time, Délcor was motioning for Mokar's attention, beckoning him to approach the platform. After conferring, briefly, Mokar held up his arms for silence and addressed the huge audience.

"We are about to begin our experiment. He shouted. To insure its success, silence will be maintained through out. Lower your heads to the tabletop and breathe deeply. Nothing more will be required of you."

Returning to his seat, at the table, he nodded to Delcor. You may begin!" He said, lowering his head to the table.

Instantly, the vast banquet hall was infused with a relentless droning, emitting from the machine. The probing vibrations saturated everyone's minds, sedating all with its offered knowledge. Soon, they would become quite familiar with their enemy.

# CHAPTER 15

"Lumar" is a small planet, located thousands of light years away from nowhere. Its sole inhabitants are known as "Lumas". Nature had imbued these creatures with the ability to self-reproduce every six months, upon reaching maturity. This involved the creature, literally, splitting into two separate beings, cloning itself.

The group they were born into was called a pod. These pods roamed, endlessly, over their world, constantly at war with one another. One massively large village existed on the entire planet. Within the fifty foot high barricade, completely encircling a one thousand square mile area, thrived over ten million "civilized" Lumas. The feral, roaming pods refereed to them as the "controllers".

Over-population was the constant concern of the "controllers". Their main purpose in life was to regulate the reproductive rate, forestalling a short future. Their ancestors, referred to as "The Ones Before", had foreseen an abrupt end to their kind. They were, literally, eating themselves into extinction. The great wall was built, over a period of many years, and the growing metropolis evolved into a self-sustaining community. Agricultural specialists performed miracles, nurturing the voracious appetites. Feed animals were cloned and dwellings were built to sustain the increasing populace. Their endeavors were dynamic, but, soon, they would realize them to be far from adequate. It wasn't until their experiments with aero space-technology came into fruition and provided them with a solution. They had to expand their boundaries.

Cannibalism was rampant in all the out-lying areas, surrounding their settlement. The hunger-driven, wild, Luma pods attacked time and time again, nearly succeeding in breeching the walls on numerous occasions.

Using their newly developed aircraft, the "controllers" initiated a plan to rectify this problem, as humanely as possible. Those who resided, within the settlement, were averse to killing. However, their very existence lay in the balance.

Armed with metallic nets, the aircraft swept down upon the ravenous hordes attacking their settlement, ensnaring as many as a hundred wild Lumas in one pass. When a thousand of the half-starved creatures had been culled from the menacing throng, they were deposited, a short time later, onto much larger air ships. These space vehicles would be sent into orbit around the planet for two eternities. Shuttles would dock with the "garbage barges", (as they were referred to by the passive citizens miles below) periodically, providing vast amounts of food to the incarcerated unfortunates.

A great deal of time and energy was expended on this project. However, not one pacifistic mind, in the Luma settlement thousands of miles below, suffered from guilt. Over an extended period of time, No less than twenty of these "garbage barges", with their living cargo, orbited Lumar.

A meteor shower, occurring five years earlier, struck one of the barges. It was ripped from its present orbit and propelled into the unfathomable depths of space. The furry occupants, inside, were unaware of this catastrophic occurrence. Weeks passed by, followed by months. Eventually, a bright green planet happened to intersect its course. The crash, that ensued, allowed over five hundred surviving inmates out on "parole"

They soon discovered, this new world was more than capable of feeding them. When their numbers had reached ten thousand, food in this area was becoming scarce. If their large pod was to exist, they had to keep hunting.

* * * * * * * * *

An hour after the strange experiment had been completed, men sat around in groups digesting the alien knowledge they had just inherited. Some found it difficult to accept that another race of beings existed, solely, for the purpose of eating and reproducing. This two-dimensional lifestyle threatened their survival. The knowledge they now possessed was beneficial and troubling at the same time.

"If it weren't for their vicious assaults, one might be inclined to empathize with these discarded creatures. Greg said. At one time, they were innocent products of their society, just keeping the status quo."

"I understand what you're saying, Greg! Jim replied. However, if we don't stop them, they'll scour the face of our world like a swarm of locust."

"Dat means we gotta kill everyone a dos bastards! Truck added. If only one a dem survives, dis crap starts all over again."

"That's the way it looks, Truck. Jim replied. We don't have much of a choice."

They were sitting on the wide steps, fronting Mokar's "House of Learning". The first of the three "Sister" suns was halfway through her cycle. The ordeal, they had just under taken, had taxed their mental capacities. But, the knowledge they had gained, made it worthwhile.

"In the mean time, gentlemen, might I suggest we pay a little visit to our two guests?" Greg suggested.

"Good idea! Jim responded. Let's do it!"

Rising from their perches, they made their way across the open square. In a matter of moments, they were standing outside the small dwelling, housing the captives.

"Bring the prisoners out for questioning!" Jim ordered.

Two of the four sentries, guarding the aliens, entered the dwelling. Moments later, they returned with the two "Lumas" in tow. They were forced into sitting positions, directly in front of the Earthmen. Taking seats on the mossy sod, as well, they stared across at the two creatures. Tension permeated the morning air, as they weighed each other out. Unflinching human eyes fixed on alien arrogance.

"What is it you want from us?" Jim asked, breaking the eerie silence.

Greg and Truck looked at their brother, surprise written on their faces. The strange language, flowing from Jim's mouth, was, at once, comprehensible.

The two captives stared at one another, registering their surprise as well. One of them turned his gaze on the Earth trio and responded.

"We desire, only, what the "Ones Before" have promised." He said, in a voice filled with grunts and groans, similar to an injured canine.

"What is it the "Ones Before" have promised?" Greg inquired, testing the alien language.

"To join them in the "Forever" and partake in the eternal feast." The Luma replied.

"How does one aspire to this exalted status?" Greg continued.

The haunting eyes stared, piercingly, at the Earthmen. Intimidation was a big part of its personality. But, it had little affect on the three humans.

The other creature, silent until now, spoke. "To join the "Ones Before" the domination and consummation of all others is necessary. Only the remaining survivor, of a pod, is accorded this esteemed reward."

"Why did you mangy bastards attack the settlement?" Truck barged in.

Staring, questioningly, at the big man, they remained silent. Although, they did not understand most of the question, they understood the anger carried with it.

"What he means is, why was it necessary to slaughter all of these innocent beings?" Jim intervened.

Both of the Lumas stared, menacingly, at Truck. The yellow, in their eyes, glowed with hatred. A slight grin, on Truck's face reflected, unflinchingly, back at them.

Finally, one of them broke his gaze and turned to Jim.

"The area we crashed in, many years earlier, is no longer capable of sustaining our numbers. Our hunger dictated our actions. It was necessary!"

"Do you not feel any remorse for the blatant decimation of innocent life?" Greg asked, heatedly.

"What is "remorse"? The Luma answered.

The three Earthmen looked, sadly, at one another. They already knew how cold and calculating these creatures were. But, witnessing it with their own ears how uncaring they were, of life in general, made their human blood cry out for vengeance.

After a few thoughtful moments, Jim spoke.

"What has become of the other small group you attacked, the people of my pod?"

"What alternatives can there be, when war ensues? One of the creatures answered. Some were killed and consumed. Others were taken captive."

"Where are dey, ya sonnuvabitch?" Truck shouted, quickly, regaining his feet.

Jim and Greg were on their feet, instantly, doing their best to restrain their infuriated brother.

"Take it easy, Truck! Jim urged. We have to keep them alive until we can get more information."

"Gimmee about ten minutes with da bastards. I'll make dem talk!" Truck protested.

The four sentries had been watching and listening in silence. When Truck had jumped to his feet, they, quickly, surrounded the two captives, pulling them roughly to their feet.

"I don't believe we are going to accomplish anything more here today, gentlemen. Greg said. Tomorrow's another day!"

"Take the two prisoners back to their dwelling!" Jim ordered.

Moments later, the three men made their way back to the main square.

"Truck! You really should work on your interviewing skills." Jim said, with a big smile on his face.

"A big amen ta dat!" Greg added.

"Hell! I was just getting warmed up." Truck replied.

# CHAPTER 16

Shortly before the first sun made her appearance, a small group was gathered around the three Earthmen. As they related the results of their recent interview with the Luma captives, the stunned silence of the audience reflected back at them with shocked and nervous stares.

"Unfortunately, we were unable to detect any signs of weakness. Greg informed them. Their main premise, in life, is to become part of an elite group known as the "Ones Before".

"The only requirements, for reaching this plateau, are their never-ending need to reproduce and the destruction and consummation of all others in their path. Jim interjected. The last surviving member, of its given pod, earns this status."

"So you see, gentlemen, we are confronted with a foe whose existence depends on very few basics, to make its life complete. Greg added. Their demented obsession, to aspire to this level, leaves little room for anything else."

"I can get da information we need, about our friends, da old fashion way. Truck joined in. Dere ain't a creature in da world dat can take too much pain."

"You forget, my brother, they are not of our world. Jim replied. Their entire lives revolve around pain and suffering. I don't think your method would accomplish much."

"There might be another way!" A voice shot from the small crowd.

"What is this way you speak of, Sovan?" Greg asked.

"During my security watch, over the beasts, I overheard them talking. I don't believe they were aware of the fact I was capable of understanding their language."

"What did you hear them speak of?" Jim asked, anxiously.

"One of them asked the other if he thought we, as their captors, dismembered our victims. The other replied that if it were our practice, neither of them would ever join the "Ones Before". To do so, one had to be whole in body, as well as in mind."

"That would explain why they hacked all those Nevoan citizens to pieces. Jim replied. They couldn't allow them to join their ancestors. Or so they thought."

"Excellent work, Sovan! Greg exclaimed. Your diligence may, just, have provided the leverage needed to obtain information about our brethren."

Jim understood, immediately, what his brother meant.

"Truck! Grab an axe! He ordered. It is time we paid our furry friends another visit."

Moments later, the three Earthmen and twenty others were congregated around the captive's dwelling. The four sentries were informed, as to what they proposed doing.

"Bring those two hideous creatures out here. At once!" Jim shouted loud enough so the captives, inside, could hear and in their own language. Within moments, they were kneeling in front of the gathered mob. All was silent, until Truck stepped forward, from the crowd.

Their eyes went wide with uncertainty, when they noticed one of their very own axes dangling from the Earthman's right hand. Their arrogance abandoned them completely. Breathing became a full-blown pant.

"What do you intend doing with us?" One of the cowering fur bags asked, nervously.

"We're gonna have a little celebration ta honor all dos poor people ya slaughtered. Truck said, in his most threatening voice. Guess who da guests of honor are gonna be?" He finished, smiling at the quivering creatures.

"Our customs dictate the removal of one limb, from the authors of our anguish. Greg joined in. It is cut into many pieces, so every survivor is able to sample a part of their murderers and regain a slight compensation for their losses. The amputee is, then, set free to wander our world."

"By continuing this tradition, we have found our future enemies much easier to defeat. Jim continued with the charade. Because we are a humane race, the choice of which limb, offered up as a sacrifice, is left to the contributor."

Nods of agreement and murmurs of affirmation echoed from the mob.

"You cannot do this to us!" Shouted one of the beasts, in panic. He was shaking, so violently, he was shedding some of his fur.

"If this sacrilegious act falls upon us, we will never be invited to feast with the "Ones Before". The other wailed.

"Ya shoulda thought about dat crap before ya murdered all dos people! Truck bellowed. Now, who wants ta be da first one ta dis feast?" He finished, shaking the big axe in their frightened faces.

The two creatures, convulsed with fear, were unable to sit upright. They squirmed on the ground in physical and mental agony. Yet, not one, Earthly, native or Nevoan hand had been laid upon them. The shuddering thought of being excommunicated from their furry nirvana was a pain far worse than any torture ever conceived.

The onlookers stared upon them with satisfaction. All of the atrocities, committed by these heartless aliens, entitled them to the most severe punishment. No one would feel any remorse, while they were made to pay for their sins.

After a few moments, one of the beasts composed itself, enough, to sit up.

"Is there nothing that can be done, to prevent this ritual from occurring?" He asked, pleadingly, in his whiney voice.

No one answered. The distaining stares, from the crowd, felt almost physical to the two quivering aliens.

"Over the ages, there has been but one annulment of this practiced ritual. Greg broke the silence. An ancient document stated the contributor, at the time, had something to offer more vital to the people than one of his limbs. Whatever it was, he had to offer, has been lost in the dust of time."

"You two ain't got nothing but da fur and fleas on your on your asses dat ya came with. And, dat ain't enough! Truck goaded. Let's just take em both and cut off what we want." He said, raising the large axe and striding toward them.

"We have information about those of your kind who were captured. The trembling creature said, hurriedly, pulling his comrade up into a sitting position, as if to bolster his own confidence. Would this be considered vital, enough, to keep us whole?"

This was, exactly, what they wanted to hear, from the two murderers. But, if they reacted too hastily, to an agreement, their little ruse might be exposed.

Turning to face the small mob, Jim addressed them in the strange language. He did not want the creatures to miss any of this melodramatic farce.

"If all are in agreement the ritual will be delayed, long enough to learn the nature of their offer and decide, whether or not, it carries the weight of truth. Let us take a short break and confer in private."

In a few moments, they moved to a safe distance from the captives, out of earshot.

"I think this movie is up for an academy award, gentlemen. Greg joked. Keep up the good work!"

The quizzical looks, on the men's faces, made him smile.

"Let's get this over with! Shall we, Jim?"

"Ya know, we gotta kill dem, after we get da information. Don't ya, Jimbo?"

"I'm aware of that, Truck! Jim replied. We don't have much of a choice. Do we?"

"Whatever we do, we'll be able to live with our decisions. Greg interjected. Future generations are in the balance."

"You're right, my brother. Jim replied. Let's get this done!"

"Relax, you guys! I'll take care a da dirty work, when da time comes. Now, let's get dat information and get da hell outta dodge!"

A few moments later, the crowd of onlookers assumed its former position. The two creatures stared up at them, fear and uncertainty reflecting from their cold eyes.

"We have decided to listen to your words. Jim began. If they convince us, you are telling the truth, the ritual will be suspended. You may begin!"

"Before I do so, I would ask if we should trust your kind. After hearing our words, you could then mutilate our bodies."

"That is true! Jim replied. We know little about one another. But, under the circumstances, this is the only option availing itself to you. So, make up your minds!"

The two captives stared at one another, indecision and desperation battled within their minds. Their only glimmer of hope would be entrusted to the integrity of these unfamiliar creatures. Reluctantly, a silent agreement passed between the two. "I will relate to you all I know. One finally spoke. Shortly, before our great victory over the strange beings of this settlement, we encountered and did battle with men of your kind."

Greg noticed Truck's reaction to the Luma's mention of a "great victory". He nudged the big guy with an elbow, to get his attention and shook his head.

"Some were killed. He continued. A great many Luma warriors were, also, killed."

"Where were the survivors taken?" Jim interrupted.

"Where our pod has settled. Twelve long marches, to the north. It lies toward the top of tall, rocky structures that rise up toward the sky. Moving water runs beneath these structures. At the very top of this high structure, many of those green living units are clustered together." The creature held both arms above his head and swayed slowly left and right.

"I believe he is describing trees on the top of a mountain, with a stream running below it." Greg said, in a whisper to his brothers.

"The captives were herded into a large hole, in these rock structures and men were ordered to watch over them. The rest of my pod departed to do battle in this place." He finished.

"How many captives were there?" Jim asked.

The creature looked at the Earthman and hesitated. Then, he looked at the group standing behind the brothers. Pointing at them, he said; "As many as they and almost as many as they again."

Looking at Greg, quizzically, Jim asked. "Did you understand that?"

"I believe what he meant, Jim, is almost twice as many as our group here."

"That would mean there are between thirty-five and forty survivors. Jim replied. Bantor started out with a group totaling forty-five men and five women."

"Dat means dos bastards killed about ten of our comrades." Truck did the math.

"What do they intend doing with the captives?" Greg asked, hoping the answer would not be food related.

"They have been set to work, digging big holes in the rocklike structures. My pod will settle there. Much food lies in this area."

"It sounds to me like he is describing the excavation of caves, Greg. We have to look for a mountainous area, twelve marches to the north, with a stream running at its base. An uneducated guess would put it about two-hundred miles away."

"I agree, Jim! We haven't seen too many mountains, since arriving on this world. If we get in the general vicinity, we should be capable of picking up the trail. Knowledge of the number of men in their pod would be helpful. We could get a rough estimate as to the size of the area needed to support them all."

"Go ahead and ask him, little brother. Said Jim. He had a hell of a time conveying the number forty to me."

Before Greg could decide, Truck spoke.

"I wanna know what your gonna do with da captives after dere done digging all your caves."

"When one has exhausted his usefulness in life, all that is left of him is to feed the living. Is it not the same ideology practiced by your kind?"

His fingers, wrapped around the axe handle, turned white from the powerful pressure applied by them. The anger and disgust, emanating from his eyes, made the two creatures cringe.

"Truck! Not now! Jim yelled, trying to intervene in a potential slaughter. They may have more useful information!"

Breathing a little easier and allowing blood to regain its place in his cramped fingers,

Truck stared down on the two beasts.

"I just wanna let you two bastards know dat you just made da job, I gotta do, a lot easier." He, then, dropped the axe at his side and walked away.

As the third sun of the day was closing in on darkness, the entire native army was gathered around a large fire. All had been updated on the information gleaned from the captives. Mokar and Froban were preparing their army for the departure. The rising of the first sun would escort them on their way. A new confidence had taken root in each of the men. Mentally, their enemy was already familiar. Soon, they would introduce themselves to them physically. Not only were the lives of the native captives at stake. The continued existence of every living creature, on this world, hung in the balance. There were no alternatives. One race of beings had to be exterminated, in order for three others to survive

# CHAPTER 17

The archery competition continued for the next three days. A fourteen year old lad, by the name of Harlo, was the over-all winner. He was the envy of every youngster in the village, when he took possession of Treban's tailor-made bow and arrows.

Leota was happy this event provided a much needed distraction. As he walked through the settlement, arm and arm with Graci, he could feel the positive energy emanating from his people.

"To ease the minds of the people, from their emotional burdens, is a goal all leaders strive to accomplish. Leota mused, aloud. However, not often enough, is credit given to their mates, who stand beside them during these trying times. Look around you, my love! All of these happy faces are the results of your idea."

"My idea? Graci replied. I only suggested a celebration, upon the return of our people. You were responsible for orchestrating the events."

"Ah! But, you planted the seed in this hard head of mine. Leota answered. I, too, was in emotional depths. Concern for our son and our brethren had stagnated my thinking. I am fortunate to have you by my side." He finished, looking down into her caring eyes.

People greeted them, as they made their way through the village. Offers of hot cups of tea or food were plied upon them. Truly, the warmth, radiating from his people, far surpassed the warmth emanating from the rays of the first "Sister" sun.

Huddled around a small breakfast fire, in front of Cinda's hut, was a group of women. Sanda, Mara, Lona and Cinda were enjoying each other's company. Their smiles and laughter invited anyone, within earshot, to join in.

"Good morning my daughters! Leota greeted. What form of humor has visited you, on this beautiful morning?"

"Good morning, Leota, Graci! Please, sit with us!" Sanda invited.

"Cinda has some good news, I know you will enjoy hearing." Lona said.

Staring across at their son's mate, Leota and Graci waited.

"I am with child, once again!" The beautiful woman, finally, said, happiness flowing from her eyes.

"Oh, Cinda! I am so happy for you!" Graci replied, as she crossed over the few paces and embraced her.

"That is wonderful news! Leota replied, adding his hugs. At times, such as this, it is most welcomed!"

"Did you tell Bantor, before he left?" Graci asked.

"No! Cinda replied. I wanted it to be a surprise for him, on his return. A small flicker of uncertainty reflected from her eyes. He has many things he must concentrate on, during his quest. I did not want to add to his burden."

"This will, surely, multiply his celebration when he returns home. Leota replied. I think you did the right thing by keeping it a secret."

Tears, induced by all the encouragement, started to flow from her dark eyes, as she nodded her head in acknowledgement.

"Maybe, I shouldn't have told my children. Cinda said. Already, Julo is making a bow and arrows for his new brother. Loshana and Jenjo are making dolls for their new sister." A slight smile started to leak through her sadness.

"By the time Bantor does return, every man, woman and child, in the village, will be aware of your "surprise". Mara chimed in. I hope you are the first one to greet him!"

Laughter returned, once again, pushing foreboding thoughts a little further back in their minds.

A short time later, Leota and Graci continued with their walk through the village. As they approached the park-like area, in its center, they marveled at all the contrivances conceived from American ingenuity. Swings, slides, seesaws and many other Earthly inventions amused the youngsters of the village for hours on end.

A tall wooden pole rose from the center of the play area. At its very top, waved a woven replica of the Americans red, white and blue flag. It had been adopted as the village's banner of identification.

"Our Earth adoptions have, truly, left their mark on this world, Graci. Leota said, smiling at his mate. Their assimilation, into our lifestyle and, freely, sharing ideas from their world, has gained the gratitude from everyone in this village."

"I agree, Leota! Graci replied. However, a share of that gratitude belongs to you, also."

"All of these inventions were their ideas. Leota said, with a questioning look on his face. What makes you say I am entitled to any praise for their accomplishments?"

"Many leaders have a reluctance to "change", of any kind. She answered. You did not hesitate to open your mind to the, possible, betterment of your people's lifestyles. Had you rejected their ideas, none of this would even exist."

Leota laughed and hugged his mate, tightly, against him.

"If every leader had a mate, such as you in their lives, decisions of any kind would be easier to make. I know you make me eager to accept the challenges each new day brings."

Shouts of anger disrupted their intimate mood. A group of children formed a circle around two young combatants. As the two novice gladiators rolled around in the dirt, striking out at one another with tiny fists, the juvenile audience yelled out support for their chosen friend.

Leaving Graci's side, Leota strode, quickly, through the circle and separated the two.

"What is the meaning of this?" He bellowed, as he held them an arms length apart.

Both youngsters, breathing heavily, froze, staring at the ground beneath their feet.

After a brief pause, it was Julo, Bantor's eight-year-old son, who spoke first.

"It is my fault, grandfather! He began, tears leaking from his eyes. Salba and I were practicing for the wrestling competition. He was getting the better of me and I struck him in anger."

Salba, Truck and Mara's seven-year-old son stood, silently, tears also misting his Earthly, blue eyes. Although, younger than Julo, he was bigger than all the eight year olds in the village and, even, some of the nine year olds.

Looking, sternly, at the two youngsters, Leota shook his head.

"You two have been inseparable, almost since birth, and you are both old enough to understand harm, of any physical nature, to another person within this village, will not be tolerated."

Winking, slyly, to Graci, he continued.

"I think the best thing to do, for the future safety of all, is to send the both of you off to two of our "sister" villages. This separation will prevent harm from coming to either of you."

Julo and Salba stared at the leader, in disbelief. The young audience was stunned into silence.

Before the situation could erupt into an emotional volcano, Leota continued.

"However! Because this is the first time this has happened, to the best of my knowledge, if both of you swear to me this will never occur again, we can put this behind us."

"It will never happen again, Grandfather! Julo replied, with tears of relief flowing down his cheeks. I swear to you on my ancestors!"

"I am sorry, also, my leader! Salba echoed. I swear it will not happen again!"

Satisfied his approach had gained all of their attention, he needed to instill upon them the important roles, each would play, in the future.

"Take a seat on the ground, my children. He commanded. I have a story to tell you."

Graci watched with pride, as her mate continued. Many villagers joined her, wondering what all this was about.

"Years ago, before many of you were old enough to walk on this world, two men from very distant tribes, were captured by our enemies, at the time, the Nevoans. A long chain was placed around their necks, joining one to the other. For a very long time these two men, were forced to eat, sleep, and work together, linked as they were. They were as different from one another as two beings could possibly be. Language, goals, cultures all ran contrary to each man's beliefs."

Leota paused, as he looked around at his rapt audience. Smiling at Graci, he continued.

"Only two options were at their disposal, kill the other person to free oneself from the constant weight tugging at them, from the other end of the chain. Or, accept the other person. They chose the second option. Setting aside their differences, they, eventually, learned each other's language and became fast friends. Bantor and Ta-rok remain loyal comrades to this day."

Surprised gasps, from the young crowd, echoed back at him. Stories of the past were always their favorite and Leota knew how to tell a tale.

"If these two strangers, under duress, could find ways to settle their differences, anyone in this village is capable of doing the same, without the use of violence."

These last words were directed toward Julo and Salba.

"There may come a time, in your life, when you have to rely on another. Treat those around you with respect, always, so you are not left standing alone. Go, now, my children! Enjoy this beautiful day. But, remember what I have said."

As the youngsters raced away, to enjoy their playful endeavors, Leota rejoined Graci.

"I believe your words reached into every one of those young minds. Graci said. Your skills as leader, have not diminished."

"They are our future, my love! We can only guide them along that path, to prepare them. Of course, your words, of encouragement to this old man, are always appreciated. Leota replied, with a big smile on his face. Now, let us continue to the meeting area. The wrestling competition will soon be starting."

# CHAPTER 18

As the first of the "Sibling" suns cast her glowing warmth over the horizon, an improbable scene was enfolding below. For eons the "Sisters" had been nurturing this world with her life-giving rays. Never before had the activity, taking place below, been revealed to them. Former enemies marched across the moss-covered plains, united in a common goal.

Two hundred native cavalrymen, mounted on, the once, wild and vicious Lurda, rode four abreast. One thousand Nevoan warriors were strung out behind them, each carrying the lethal "Dracos" on their shoulders.

James, Gary and Gregory Stonedeer, abducted from the planet Earth, were directly responsible for many of the changes, in the mundane realities indigenous to this wild world. Now, the "Sister" suns shone down on a planet wrought with anomalies. Their major achievement, thus far, was uniting "Native" and "Nevoan" races to fight for a common cause. Enemies for more than one hundred years, they were, now, confronted with a warring horde of beings who threatened their very existence.

The native riders goaded their mounts to maintain a steady, yet, comfortable pace. The sturdy beasts could endure many hours of travel time, before rest was needed. The long strides of the "Nevoan" infantrymen, allowed them to follow, closely, behind. They, too, could endure the rigors of a long trek. Therefore, rest periods were only needed every five or six hours. Many miles flowed in their wake, because of this. Men and mounts proceeded with no problems. A fatigued army, thrust into battle, could suffer dire consequences.

Four scouting parties, each consisting of five men, had been deployed one mile away from the advancing forces. They were situated to the north, east, west and south. The crusaders had to do everything in their power, to insure invisibility. Their small force was greatly outnumbered, by the invaders. To be engaged in battle, at this point, would severely lessen their chances of rescuing their brethren.

Information, gleaned from the "cerebral implanter" machine, revealed little about "Luma" battle tactics, other than their swarming attacks. Did their egos permit the use of scouts, for security purposes? Or, was their overwhelming wickedness enough to instill fear in their adversaries? They had to be certain!

Confidence was high, among the men, as they advanced, steadily, over the mossy terrain. The knowledge, each contained about their enemy, was a big advantage. Especially, after learning these creatures had, but, one intent; to consume their world! No prisoners would be taken.

The Luma faction needed to be completely annihilated, in order to assure a future for all.

The Nevoan soldiers, eight years removed from their own war crimes against the native tribes, marched, explicitly, for revenge. Their wrath made them a welcomed ally.

"We'll make our first stop in that valley, up ahead! Jim informed his brothers. I hope the pace, we have set, hasn't been too much of a burden on our Nevoan friends."

"They appear to be doing just fine! Greg replied. We can ill-afford to slow it down, if we wish to accomplish anything."

"I did inform Froban, before we started out, to notify me, immediately, if any of his men indicated any signs of fatigue." Jim added.

"I ain't heard no complaints, so far. Truck enjoined. I, on da other hand, have lost about six pounds of rump roast."

"That poor animal, you are riding, isn't complaining about that, my brother. Greg teased. It, probably, owns the most polished backbone in the entire herd."

"When's da last time your jawbone got polished, shorty?" Truck fired back.

Jim just shook his head and smiled. His two siblings had managed to put fifteen miles behind them, before this verbal joust. It was long overdue

"I can't help it! Truck continued. Dese long trousers are so hot dere turning my butt into soup."

Before they had left their village, each man had been outfitted with leather riding britches, to eliminate the chaffing from the Lurda's stiff hairs. As uncomfortably hot as they were to wear, the chaffing would have unseated the men from their mounts long ago.

Jim couldn't resist.

"You can change your diaper when we reach our first rest stop, Truck."

Greg rocked with laughter when he saw the strange look on Truck's face.

"Okay you guys! I get da message!" He replied, adding his own laughter.

That was Jim's way of telling either one of his brothers, they were acting like babies.

The mid-day sun pelted them, mercilessly, with her heated attitude. Sweat gleamed on the faces of the mounted warriors. But, yet, their determination shone through. Whatever hardships they must endure, or sacrifices they must make, it no longer mattered to them. They had to rid their world of these murdering creatures or suffer dire consequences.

About a mile away, a riderless Lurda raced steadily toward them.

Being the first to notice, Greg pointed. "That looks like trouble, gentlemen!"

All eyes were focused on the beast, as it neared them.

"Tonio! Roca! Hold everyone here! Jim ordered. Come on, you two! Let's go check this out!"

As the three men galloped across the flat landscape, to intercept the animal, Truck noticed movement about fifty yards behind it.

"Dere's a man out dere chasing his ride, by da looks of it." He announced.

"Go pick him up, Truck! Greg and I will recover the animal."

Moments later, all had returned to the main caravan. It had proven to be nothing more than one of the scouts, stopping for a moment to stretch his legs. His mount had yanked the reins from his hand and raced off to join the mounted herd in the distance.

"I was on my way back here to report that all was clear ahead. I decided to walk for a few moments. My mount must have caught scent of your animals and bolted away from me."

"You gave us quite a scare, Nomac! Jim exclaimed. For a moment there, we thought the battle had already started. Go claim your mount!"

A few, uninterrupted, miles later the entire army entered the small valley. After watering their animals in the stream, flowing through it, natives and Nevoans clustered in small groups. Others replenished water skins or bathed in the invigorating stream.

The Earthmen, Tonio, Roca and the Nevoan commander, Froban, sat separately from the rest.

"Are any of your men finding the pace we have set, too, difficult?" Jim asked Froban.

"No complaints have been voiced in my direction, thus far. He replied. Our objective takes priority over the hardships."

"That is commendable! Greg joined in. However, the physical well being of your men is just as important. We cannot allow this long journey to diminish the strength of our warriors."

"Your concern is noted, as well as appreciated, Earthman. Do not trouble your mind any further, with this matter. We have endured much worse than this, in the past. When it is time for battle, we will be prepared physically as well as mentally.

"If any of your men get tired, dey can always ride with us on one of da animals." Truck offered.

"That will not be necessary! Froban couldn't refuse fast enough. Our legs are adequate enough to carry us into battle."

"Actually, our animals would be capable of carrying three at a time, with no trouble. Greg added, watching Froban squirm. Four hundred of your warriors could rest at one time."

"It is a very thoughtful suggestion, Earthman. I will take it into consideration." Froban answered and hurriedly made his departure.

"I think the two of you just scared the hell out of that guy. Jim said, smiling. I don't think we have to worry too much about riding double.

# CHAPTER 19

Four days later, the midday sun cast her relentless heat upon the weary army. As they zigzagged through a range of low hills, a rider was spotted lumbering toward them. His Lurda was glistening with sweat and lathered around its muzzle.

Jim held up an arm and brought the marching crusaders to a halt. The scout pulled up, stopping his panting mount directly in front of them.

"What brings you here with such haste, my friend?" Jim asked, concern reflecting from his eyes,

"I was ordered to bring word to you as fast as I could. He said, panting in sync with his tired beast. About three miles north of here, we came across the remains of both native and Luma bodies."

"Roca! Trade mounts with this man and follow our trail. Jim ordered. Greg! Truck! Let's go have a look."

After the two natives had switched mounts, the Earthmen followed the scout, as he led the way toward the discovery. They did not tax the abilities of their beasts, but maintained a steady pace. A short time later, they came across the other four natives, making up this particular scouting party. They were standing together, talking. When the Earthmen and scout had dismounted and approached, they noticed the sullen looks on the faces of the four men. They, also, took in the native and Luma carnage strewn around them.

"Ya think dis was da place where Bantor and his men was attacked?" Truck asked.

"It's hard to say, Truck. Jim answered. There doesn't appear to be much left that we can identify for certain."

One of the scouts, with his back to them, turned and said, with tears in his eyes, "Bantor's party was involved in this battle."

"How can you be so certain?" Greg inquired, as they approached him.

"My younger brother, Lato, traveled with Bantor. Moments ago, I discovered his head resting among the scattered remains of our brethren." A new flood of tears poured from his eyes. His whole body shuddered in the throes of grief.

Truck reached out and enfolded the young native in a consoling bear hug. "Don't worry, my friend! We'll make dos bastards pay, big time!" He replied, tears leaking from his own eyes, as well.

The same native, who had traded mounts with Roca, was sent back to guide the rest of the caravan back to this spot. They would make camp here for the night, to honor their fallen comrades.

The rest of the men, began searching the entire area to collect the gruesome remains. Wood was gathered and stacked around the mound of dismembered flesh.

It was difficult to ascertain just how many of their brethren had contributed to the carnage. The Luma dead were left to rot where they lay.

An hour before the third sun had expired, the entire entourage was comfortably ensconced in the tree-lined valley. All had been apprised of the fatal encounter that had taken place here. Many had relatives or friends participating in Bantor's expedition. They knew not whether the gory mound embraced them. None-the-less, all would be properly mourned.

Extra security had been positioned around the large camp. If the funeral fire was discovered by the Luma, so be it! Let the battle begin this night! Their brethren would be accorded a proper ceremony, to guide them to their ancestors.

"I counted the remains of more than thirty Lumas. Jim announced. Bantor's men put up one hell of a fight."

The three siblings were sitting alongside a small stream. They had just completed washing the gore from their bodies. The heartless, disregard for life, exhibited by the Luma horde, placed them in this gruesome position for the second time.

"I'm really getting tired a dis shit! Truck said. One bloody mess ta clean up after another!"

"Hopefully, it won't be too much longer, my brother, before we cleanse our world of these ruthless murderers. Jim replied. We'll have our revenge!"

"If our endeavor is successful, Jim, we will have attained something much more important than revenge. Greg interjected. The survival of our people and future generations lay in the outcome."

"Da bottom line is, kill or be killed." Truck added.

"That is, precisely, what it amounts to, my brother. Greg continued. This will be an unconventional struggle, devoid of prisoners, contingencies of any kind or divisions of land. Winner takes all!"

As the three men sat, ruminating over the outcome of their impending encounter, with the defilers of their world, Roca approached them.

"Pardon the interruption, my Earth brothers. He said. Many are anxious to know how soon before we light the funeral fire."

"We will proceed, immediately!" Jim answered. Rising from their mossy seats, they accompanied Roca back to the awaiting army.

The ghastly remains, of their slaughtered brethren, had already been placed atop the huge mound of dried wood. One of the natives stood to the side, a lit torch in his hand.

The brothers recognized him as the bereaved sibling of the man whose head had been found. Tears, from a wounded heart, flowed freely from his eyes.

Jim raised his arms above his head, to get the crowd's attention. When the murmuring trickled down to a low hum, he began. "My friends and fellow warriors we gather this night to bestow honor and recognition to our fallen comrades. Sarna, you may light the fire and send these brave souls home."

As the torch set the dry wood ablaze, Jim continued. "Let the heat and smoke from this fire carry them safely into the embracing arms of their ancestors and inform them they had not died in vain. Soon, all will have ample opportunity to avenge their deaths. If we are not victorious, the memories we harbor of all our past loved ones, will die with us. We cannot allow this to happen!"

The collective voices, of all the gathered men, shattered the nocturnal ambience with their shouts of agreement.

"Go, now, and rest! Jim ordered. Tonio! Roca! Deploy ten more men for security. I want this entire area safely blanketed against surprise attacks!"

As the small army was disbursing, Greg and Truck approached their brother.

"Well said, James! Greg complimented. You're getting better with practice."

"Thanks, Greg! You can have the honors the next time!" Jim replied.

"We can only hope our next ceremony revolves around happier circumstances. Said Greg. Giving eulogies is not my forte."

"We could always train the big guy, here, to handle it." Jim chided, with a big smile on his face.

"That is an excellent suggestion, Jim! His command of the languages would make him suited for the job."

"Fat chance a dat happening! Truck replied. You two should know by now, I leave da easy stuff for you."

Moments later, the three Earthmen were the sole occupants, around the dwindling funeral fire. The night sparkled with a myriad of stars. They had taken a big risk, building a fire and announcing their presence. Never the less, its warmth was appreciated, as it warded off the night's chill.

"I've been doing a little thinking. Jim broke in on the quiet setting. Back on our world, we were considered pretty efficient, at tracking game. Tomorrow I'm going to put Tonio and Roca in charge of our troops. The three of us will join the scouting parties. How do you feel about that?"

"I think it's an excellent idea, Jim! Greg replied. Our Earthly skills may uncover a sign the scouts have missed."

"I was getting kinda bored leading dis parade around da countryside. Truck added. Count me in!"

"That will be welcomed news to the hundreds of men who have been down wind of you during this entire march. Greg teased. Now, at least, they will keep closer ranks with their leaders."

The offended expression, on Truck's face, elicited laughter from his two brothers.

"How would ya like me ta realign your snot locker, squirt?" Truck fired back, shaking his fist.

"Good night, you two! Jim said, smiling. I'm going to bed."

# CHAPTER 20

As the first sun roused the world below with her bright warmth, activity among the united forces had already commenced. Riders recaptured their mounts and packed their gear. Scouting parties were deployed. They were spread out approximately two miles from the main caravan, covering its front, rear and flanks to prevent surprise attacks from any direction. The three Earth men, along with seven others, were responsible for the area directly ahead of the advancing army.

One hundred riders, in total, comprised the security net around the rest of the crusaders. If evidence was discovered, by any of the patrols indicating a possible trail used by the enemy, riders would be sent out to alert the other scouting parties and the main force.

The terrain, they were traveling over, was becoming much more hilly. Higher peaks could be seen in the distance. The absence of trees in this area eliminated any possible enemy concealment. However, it made their advancement much more visible.

As each of these high rises were surmounted they would call a halt, long enough, to scan the rolling landscape ahead.

They hoped, eventually, it would reveal evidence of their enemies passage.

"This terrain is prime area for ambush". Jim said. I suggest we spread out a little and make ourselves a little less visible."

"I agree, Jim!" Greg replied. According to those two captives, we should be nearing their settlement in a few days. Every mile we advance, from here on out, increases our risk of being observed."

"We can only hope those two were telling the truth. Jim said. By the way, Truck, you never did tell us what you did with them, before we left."

"Nothing! The big man answered. Mokar had dem locked up in one of dos cages in da zoo. He said he wanted to watch dem reproduce."

"Our old friend thrives on knowledge. Greg enjoined. If ever we meet again, I would be interested in learning his results."

"One thing will be certain" Jim chimed in. Those two will be accorded more decency than we ever received from Zarnog."

"It's a waste a time, if you ask me. Truck disagreed. He should a let me destroy da bastards."

"It won't be too much longer, my brother. Everyone will have their fill of killing. Jim replied. I just don't want to be taken by surprise."

As they scanned the rolling vista, they couldn't rid themselves of the feeling of being watched. Five miles in the distance they spotted, what appeared to be, a small forest.

"Greg take two men and head west for about half a mile. Truck, You go east with two others. Then, both of your squads will proceed forward, once again," Jim ordered. I will proceed forward from this point with the rest of our men. If anyone uncovers a sign of our enemy, send a rider to notify the others. We'll rendezvous in that small forest up ahead."

As they split away from one another Jim called after them, "Good hunting, my brothers."

Greg and Truck each lifted an arm in acknowledgement and soon were gone.

The pace slowed considerably, to allow for a more accurate search, in Jim's group at least. One set of eyes searched the rolling landscape, ahead of them, to guard against any surprises. The others concentrated on the ground, in pursuit of clues.

The first sun was nearly spent when they crested a large hill. The forest, they had detected earlier, was less than a mile off in the distance.

"A rider approaches from the west!" one of the scouts announced.

As the shaggy beast lumbered up the hill to join them, anticipation grew. Had a trail been discovered? Had the battle begun?

When the messenger pulled even with them he announced. "Your sibling wishes you to join him. We have come across another mound of bones."

Turning to his three scouts, Jim ordered, "You men remain here and hold this position. I'll go check this out."

A moment later, he and the messenger were racing across the hills to join his brother.

They, soon, came upon a scene similar to the last gory encounter. However, the remains were not of native or Luma nature. This heap of carnage had once belonged to a Lurda Bull.

Dismounting, Jim joined his brother, who was kneeling alongside the grisly remains.

"What is it about this dead lurda that has caught your interest, my brother?" Jim asked, kneeling beside him.

"My first thought was that a Kazor had cornered and killed an old bull because of the way the bones are scattered around. Greg answered. But, on closer inspection, I noticed the bite marks, on some of the bones. They are much smaller then that of the old lizard. Then one of my scouts found this." He said, as he produced a broken spear.

"Look familiar Jim?"

It was, indeed, one of the Luma's weapons. Many had been scattered about in the Nevoan settlement after their invasion.

"Good work Greg!" Jim responded. Finally! Our first indication we are going in the right direction. Any ideas on which way they went from here?"

"Not yet, Jim! But, I think our blood-hound brother might be capable of helping us with that."

Within moments, riders were sent out to retrieve the other scouting parties. Another was sent back to the trailing caravan.

Once, all the warriors converged on this site, camp would be established and their next strategy would be discussed.

The third sun was well into her cycle before all parties were accounted for. Men bustled about, tending to their animals, their own needs or resting. No fires would be enjoyed from this point on. Dried meat, water and their sleeping furs would be the only luxuries realized for quite some time.

Security teams had been dispersed, two miles from their encampment, in all directions. The majority of the men had already turned to the comforting warmth of their furs. Armed with exhaustion, sleep quickly won the battle.

As darkness won its battle with the last sun of the day, a small group of men clustered together. Earlier, the entire encampment had been informed of the latest discovery. This helped to raise the spirits of the weary travelers. However, a shadow of apprehension settled over them. Encamped on grounds, once again, desecrated, by their enemy, caused more than a little consternation. Anticipation of a conflict can cause as much damage to one's psyche as the actual physical aspect. During the many tedious miles of this trek, spirits had started to diminish. Unfortunately, the only solution to rectify the situation was a full-blown battle. There was, absolutely, no way of knowing how far in the future this would occur. The mind of the men had to be kept sharp until then.

"Truck! When the first sun rises, I want you to take ten men and pick up that God-damned trail. Jim ordered. I have a gut feeling those beasts are close. Move as fast as the terrain allows, but, maintain discretion. We can't afford to be careless, at this point."

"I already got dat figured out, Jimbo! Truck replied. I'll post two a my men a mile ahead for security. When we catch up with dem, I'll move em ahead another mile. Dis way I can go as fast as I want and still have my ass covered.

"Leave markers, while you're at it, Truck. Jim added. We'll bring the main force forward at a slightly slower pace."

"If you uncover evidence, revealing a definite trail, send word at once. Greg enjoined. We'll catch up with you on-the-double."

"I'll go right now and pick da men I wanna take. Truck said, getting to his feet.

Dey'll be ready ta ride first thing in da morning."

When Truck had left, Jim stared out at the rolling terrain. A rocky peak rose majestically over the hilly landscape, about three days ride in the distance.

"Greg! You see that high ridge?" He asked, pointing.

Looking in the direction his brother had indicated, he grasped the meaning of this observation.

"I would make it out to be about a three and a half day march, he replied. That would definitely coincide with the information gleaned from the two captives. Plus, the geological profile would be, ideally, conducive to the formation of caves."

The long, hot marches endured by the army, over the many long days, left many with the feeling they were wandering aimlessly through unfamiliar wilderness. The only motivating factor they had to guide them was a vague direction given them by the two luma captives. North! Doubts, as to the validity of these words, were harbored by every one of the crusaders.

Now! The possibility of a tangible objective heightened their excitement. Did that forbidding ridge hold their brethren in its stony clutches? If so, would it play witness to the decimation of an entire culture?

# CHAPTER 21

Half-way through the afternoon sun, Truck rode into their midst. Stopping ten paces from the advancing caravan, he sat on his shaggy mount with a big smile plastered on his face.

As they pulled up even with him a halt was called.

"I hope that look on your face is an indication of good news," Greg ventured.

"You can bet yer ass on dat, little brother." Truck replied.

When he didn't expound further, Jim asked, impatiently, "Well! What did you find?"

"About three miles north of us, we came across a wide stream. He finally answered.

Dere was footprints in da mud, on both sides of it. Native and luma!"

"You're certain of this?" Greg asked, excitedly.

"Dos tracks, I saw were old. But, dey are definitely, what we been looking for."

"Good work! Jim exclaimed. I knew we could count on you!"

Modestly, shrugging off the compliment Truck replied, winking at his older brother.

"You just sent da right man ta do da job, dat's all —
nothing to it!"

He was game-playing with Greg's ego and knew a
response was eminent.

"All the experience you've had tracking your rowdy
friends, from one bar to another, this must have been a walk
in the park for you, eh, Truck?" Greg shot back.

"It was a little harder den dat, dwarf. Dis place didn't
have any bars in it."

Shaking his head and smiling at the big guy, Jim
interrupted his brothers' war with words.

"Would you be so kind and lead us to this spot?" he
asked.

"Follow me!" truck answered, as he turned his shaggy
beast and headed north.

Less than one half hour later, they converged on the area
in question. Two of Truck's trackers were standing near a
wide stream. The others had been deployed further ahead
for security purposes.

As the majority of the troops started setting up camp,
the three Earthmen joined the two men alongside the
stream. Kneeling on the muddy bank, they saw the spoor
evidence by the passage of many feet. Sandal-shod prints
were interspersed with the wide talon-toed tracks of the
luma.

"Any idea of how many bodies passed this way, Truck?" Jim asked.

"It was hard ta tell!" he answered. So many a da tracks overlap. We followed da trail up ahead for a few miles. "Da closest guess I got is about forty natives and a hundred or so of dos bastards."

"What's the terrain up ahead like, Truck?" Greg asked.

"In less den a mile it starts ta climb. I think da trail is headed toward dat small mountain, about three miles off."

"Well! At least this area is free of dead natives." Greg interjected.

"Dey probably wasn't hungry yet." Truck stated, morbidly.

"I hope they stay that way, for a while longer." Jim added.

"Amen, ta dat, big brother."

The remainder of the evening sun was utilized in preparations for the imminent battle. The discovery of their brethren's trail elicited excitement throughout the camp. Minds, dulled by the long, monotonous march, became active with anticipation. The tangible evidence, that lay in the mud, enhanced their fervor for battle ten-fold. Awareness was taken to the next level.

"It appears this trail is headed right up the side of that mountain," Jim announced.

"We'll have to hobble our animals a safe distance away and ascend on foot when we get nearer."

The entire army was clustered, closely, around their leaders. The last sun had surrendered to the conquering night, only moments before. The eerie glow cast a surrealistic ambience on the gathered men. Soon, this too would capitulate to a star-filled sky.

"Fifty of our men, armed with bow and arrow, will be spread across the trail in advance of the main body. Jim continued. Stealth is of the utmost importance, from this point on. Once the enemy settlement has been located, the remainder of our men, armed with dracos, will veer to the east and west in a flanking maneuver. Froban will spread his Nevoan warriors across the trail, approximately, one quarter mile to our rear, advancing at a slower pace."

"Hopefully, we will be able to position ourselves close enough to establish the whereabouts of our brethren, before the fireworks begin," Greg interjected.

"Dat means, any unfriendlies we run into along da way, have to be killed quickly and quietly. Truck added. We don't need no alarms going off, before we get into position."

"Exactly! Greg responded. Bows and arrows or knives must be used to dispatch any enemy between us and their settlement."

"There's no way of knowing what harm would fall upon the captives were we to be discovered prematurely. Jim piped in. We must not let this happen!"

Nods of acquiescence bobbed through the crowd. Anxiety, as well as the anticipation of a battle elicited equally from the weary men.

A short while later, most of the encampment was tucked, exhaustedly, into their furs. For many, it could be the last respite they would ever enjoy, other than death.

No less than one hundred sets of watchful eyes had been deployed, encircling the sleeping warriors with an umbrella-like formation.

Every few hours they would be replaced to insure alertness. Thus far, the clandestine methods used by the avenging army, had managed to deposit them near their enemies doorstep. Vigilance would become even more vital, to their success, as they closed on their objective.

While the rest of the camp was well on its way in the pursuit of dreams, the three Earthmen sat together talking. Furs were draped over their shoulders, to ward off some of the night's chill. A myriad of twinkling stars sent their nocturnal glow down on them. The irony of such peaceful ambience, at this crucial time, left little to enjoy.

"I would imagine, you have decided which positions the three of us will be assuming during the assault," Greg ventured.

As a matter of fact, I have," Jim replied.

"You and Tonio will take command of the second wave from the west. Truck! You and Roca will control the second wave coming from the east. I will lead the frontal attack."

His two brothers looked at each other, disagreement written on their faces.

"Why can't da three of us lead the frontal attack? Truck argued. Ya know we fight a lot better when wer covering each other's ass."

Before Jim could respond, Greg interrupted.

"There is no use in debating the issue, Truck! Our brother here, always does his best to see to it the three of us are separated during any battle."

It was true! Jim had explained to them, many times in the past, they were the only Earth beings on this entire planet. He would not allow for one battle, to totally eliminate their legacy.

"Isn't that what big brothers should do? Jim replied, with a big smile on his face. Protect his younger siblings!"

"Dats a crock, Jimbo, and you know it! Da three of us know how to handle ourselves."

"I am fully aware of that, Truck! Jim shot back. I just think this will cut down the odds of all of our children becoming orphans at the same time."

"Dat ain't gonna happen! Truck said, vehemently. "Because wer gonna squash dos furry bastards!"

Seeing how worked up his large brother was getting, Greg couldn't resist.

"There might be another strategy we may consider employing, Jim! Every one of us can remain here, while we send Truck into battle."

Calming down a little, Truck looked sheepishly into the smiling faces of his brothers.

"Now dat ya mention it, a little protection could come in handy," he responded, smiling back.

A short while later, the three brothers sought out the warmth of their sleeping furs. Where would their dreams take them, on this night?

# CHAPTER 22

Fourteen cycles of the "sister "suns had become history, since the mounted army had departed their village. The drudgery of waiting for friends and loved ones to return was alleviated, slightly, by the games and contests taking place. Morale had improved considerably.

A small group of men and women sat around Leota's hut reminiscing about days gone by. They debated about which figure, past or present, they believed had made the biggest impact on their village.

"I remember your brother, Julo and I hunting together quite often in our youth. "A man named Talas was saying. Age wise he was undoubtedly the senior citizen of the village.

"One day, as we emerged from a large forest, I remember we were trying to decide which area we would hunt next. Our day had begun with the rising of the first "sister" sun and we had nothing to show for it. So distracted by our discussion, we did not notice the approach of that old kazor. We almost walked directly into him before we reacted. Julo ran one way and I another. The beast chose to pursue Julo. Maybe he looked tastier than I did. Talas continued, with a big smile on his wrinkled face. When I finally noticed the kazor wasn't chasing me, I turned back to help my friend. The scene I came upon moments later sends shivers up my spine, even as I sit before you, on this day, relating that long ago experience. The beast was sprawled, unmoving, over a pile of rotting logs the point of a spear protruded from its back. As I came closer, I noticed an arm and a leg sticking out from underneath that blanket of death. Then, a shallow moan drew me even closer. Julo lived! I exalted and started tearing at the pile of vegetation between him and the beast. The weight of the kazor was crushing the life out of my friend! After a long while, I managed to drag him free. From head to toe, his body was covered with gashes none of them were serious, but the amount of blood they had caused made it appear so. When Julo regained consciousness he told me what had happened. That old death stalker was almost upon me when I dove into that woody pile. He said. I, somehow, ended up on my back with my spear poking through that tangled mess. The heavy beast fell on me, knocking the air out of my lungs and I passed out. When he was stable enough to walk, I helped him to a small stream and washed his wounds. It took us quite some time, but we eventually made it back to the village. While Julo stayed behind to recuperate, I gathered a group of men and returned to the kill site. It took twelve of us to roll that beast over, It was then we discovered, Julo's spear had inadvertently, entered a very soft spot in the creatures tough leathery hide. Knowledge of this vulnerable area in the man eater has saved many lives since that day." Talas finished.

Leota smiled across at his brother's dearest friend. It made him realize, once again, how close Julo had always been to him.

"Thank you Talas, for sharing that with us. It is the first time I have heard that story told since Kaba was among us. Kaba was Graci's brother. During the time Leota and Graci were held in captivity, by the Nevoans. He had been a surrogate father to Bantor. His old brother in law had taken the journey to meet his ancestors five summers earlier.

"Speaking of Kaba, a thought has just occurred to me. Leota continued. The majority of our village has, already, agreed, the three Earthmen have made the biggest impact upon them. We cannot dismiss their strange inventions which have truly improved our daily lives and paved the way for more enjoyable futures. But, had old Kaba not intervened in their lives shortly after they came to our world, they would never have been counted among us. He recognized the possibility they might be the siblings of Ta-Rok. Even though they were ignorant of each other's language, at the time, he managed to convey his suspicions to Jim and Greg. Then, as old and weak as he was, he led them to our village."

Leota paused and scanned the faces of his attentive audience, before continuing. "Yes! We are all amazed by the fruits of our Earth brethren's labors, but we should never forget it was Kaba who brought the trees among us."

Murmurings of agreement resounded from the small group. When put in that perspective, Kaba did indeed, make a significant contribution to their welfare, even though it was vicariously.

"We are, indeed, fortunate to belong to a village teeming with contributors. The leader went on. All are to be commended. Our beloved ancestors nurtured our desires for change and improvement. Through their sacrifices we have evolved into an industrious community. It is the responsibility of all here today to honor their endeavors with the continued pursuit of improving our existence."

Before the collective cheers of agreement had finished echoing into the new day, they were interrupted by a young man who rushed among them.

"Forgive my intrusion, Leota! He began, slightly out of breath. One of the sentries has sighted a kazor headed for the lurda herd."

Addressing the messenger, Leota ordered him to procure five of the Nevoan power weapons from the village arsenal.

"As soon as you have them, meet me at the front gate."

As the messenger rushed off, to do his bidding, Leota made his way to the village entrance. He designated five men the task of destroying the beast. Moments later, each arrived with a lethal Nevoan weapon. They made their way out through the gates, quickly mounting five lurdas, they raced toward the murderous intruder.

A short while later, the whining sounds of bolts of energy emitting from the weapons, could be heard. A handful of moments later, the five hunters were safely ensconced in the village, once again.

"We arrived, just in time to destroy the monster before any damage was done to the herd. One of the men in the detail reported to Leota. It's scattered remains have been added to the fates of its brethren.

"Excellent job!" Leota exclaimed, nodding to the five men involved. Once again, the alertness of our sentries and the quick response of our hunters has averted another potential disaster, he thought to himself, as he walked away.

When he returned to his hut, Graci and Cinda were sitting around the dwindling breakfast fire. He noticed tears running down Cinda's cheeks as she looked up at him.

"Leota!" Graci acknowledged him. "Cinda has experienced a disturbing dream."

Taking a seat next to the women, concern reflected from his eyes.

"If it would ease some of your distress by talking about it, I would listen." He said,

Staring across at her father-in-law the sadness in her heart continued leaking from her dark eyes. Finally, she began.

"Bantor was in a dark, cold place, surrounded by his comrades. Hairy creatures were Hacking away at them with stone axes. It seemed so real, I could actually smell the blood and feel the fear emitting from each one of the poor men. She sobbed, heavily, as she continued. I could feel Bantor's devastating anguish as if it were happening to me. Then everything turned dark and I awoke, screaming. The next thing I realized, my children had their arms around me asking me what was wrong."

Pausing for a moment, while his mind digested Cinda's traumatic dream Leota responded. "When we love and miss someone at the same time our minds have a tendency to distort the true picture, especially in our dreams. When the physical nearness of that significant other is removed, rampant scenes are projected because of our concern for them." Smiling at the saddened women, he continued "I also have dreamt of Bantor and the other brethren. Some were frightening! Some were pleasant. My methods for dealing with these moments of fear and doubt have changed considerably especially since our "Earth" citizens have made our village their home. Ta-rok once said to me, at the time I thought Graci was lost to me forever, we have to will ourselves to carry on and focus on today. Tomorrow will take care of itself. So, my daughter, keep hope foremost in your heart. Do not become a victim of thoughts and dreams. And, most importantly, keep yourself strong. Not just for those around you, but for that day in our futures, when we all must cope with its uncertainties, whether they be good or bad."

Looking across at Leota, tears drying on his face Cinda spoke. "I will not allow myself to become trapped by my dreams or thoughts, my father. I will make a conscious effort to dwell only on the happier episodes." She finished, crossing over to leota and embracing him. Graci joined them.

I pray there is enough hope left to see us all through this ordeal. She thought to herself.

# CHAPTER 23

Gia limped through the village. A wooden bucket swung, unsteadily, from her right hand as she made her way toward one of the village wells. The wooden leg, Ta-rok had made for her, was causing a lot of discomfort. Her adoptive father would make weekly adjustments to the artificial limb, insuring her comfort. But, he was not here!

"I will endure this pain! She said to herself. Ta-rok and the others are probably suffering much more than I am."

Gia was just three years old when she was out hunting with her mother and father. A group of Nevoan invaders discovered her hiding in a tree. Her father had placed her there before he set off to decoy the Nevoans away from her and her mother.

Later, he had returned. He thought he had been successful in leading the enemy away from them. He was mistaken! As he climbed the tree to retrieve his daughter, they returned. He was blasted to pieces, by the Nevoan sharp-shooters before he could reach her. When they noticed the young girl, clinging to a limb high above them, they fired upon her, knocking her from her lofty perch. Her right leg, below the knee, was blown away. As the young innocent fell toward the forest floor, a branch embedded itself into her cheek.

As her young body hung suspended, the Nevoans assumed she was dead and departed the area.

A short while later her mother, Mara, climbed the tree and recovered her daughter. She had witnessed the devastating scene from concealment, a short distance away.

The physical wounds healed after a while but, it took much longer for her to recover from the psychological damage. For many years, after being dealt this devastating blow, she did not utter a single word.

From the very first moment the big Earth man had noticed her, hobbling along with the aid of a wooden branch, he had adopted her into his heart. In a short period of time, her life regained normalcy. She started to talk again and interacted with the other youngsters in the village. She adapted so comfortably to her make-shift prosthesis she had no trouble keeping up with her peers.

"I am a woman now! The fifteen year old said to herself. Only children complain about the little aches they suffer."

As she, finally, reached one of the two wells, in her village, she filled the bucket with water and proceeded back to her hut. She hadn't taken three paces when she, suddenly, tripped. The bucket of water splashed over her, as she slammed into the ground. Before she even thought about righting herself, a hand was thrust before her face.

"Are you injured?" the young man asked, concern reflecting from his eyes.

He was tall for his age, perhaps sixteen or seventeen years of age. His long, blonde hair hung down to his shoulders. It appeared to be wet.

She accepted the proffered hand and he helped her to her feel.

It was then she noticed his damp hair. "I apologize for getting you wet. I am so clumsy, at times." she said, hurriedly.

He paused a moment and stared at her, questioningly. Then, he erupted into a fit of laughter. After a short while it subsided into a warm smile.

The embarrassment on Gia's face turned a deeper shade of red.

"Why do you laugh at me?" she asked.

"I was not laughing at you," he replied, still smiling. You thought my damp hair was caused by your mishap. I have just come from bathing in the stream."

Gia's face broke into a smile, erasing her embarrassment.

"I am Rojari, son of Corbon." He introduced himself. "I am a woodcarver apprentice."

"I know of Corbon. Gia replied. His work is famous throughout the village."

"And, what name are you called?" Rojari asked.

"I am Gia! Daughter of Ta-rok and Mara," she replied.

"Ta-rok!" he exclaimed. He is the most powerful warrior in our entire village. I did not know he had such a beautiful daughter."

Staring at the handsome youth, something inside Gia wasn't right. In a panic, she reached down and gathered up the empty bucket.

"I must go!" she said, limping away as fast as she could.

Rojari stood there with a baffled look on his face, as he watched her -move away.

"What did I say to offend her?" he wondered. "I vow I will find out though. And, hopefully, much more."

He walked across the open area toward his hut. A big smile of anticipation lit up his face.

When Gia returned to her hut, she sat down, dejectedly, on one of the logs circling the cold fire pit. The empty water bucket lay at her feet. When Mara emerged from their dwelling, she took one look at her saddened daughter and the empty bucket and knew, immediately, something was wrong.

Taking a seat, beside the young woman, she put her arm across her shoulder." I would be willing to listen to whatever is bothering you, Gia." She said in a consoling voice.

"I am sorry, mother! But, I cannot explain this strange feeling I have inside me." She replied.

"Perhaps, if you tell me how this feeling got started,I may be able to help. Mara responded. "What is it that happened to you when you went for water?"

Gia told her the whole story. The confused expression had not left her face.

A smile, of understanding, reflected from Mara's face. Gia had just experienced her first platonic encounter with a member of the opposite sex. To a young woman, making the transition from childhood to womanhood was, sometimes, a very difficult task. As she grew older and more knowledgeable, she would realize these incidents were only nature's way of initiating relationships.

"I felt the same emotion, when I was your age. Mara said, after explaining this to her daughter. The first time your father spoke to me, sent me into a panic. It took me a while before I was able to carry on a conversation with him and feel comfortable being near him."

Looking at her mother's eyes filled with gratitude, Gia let out a noticeable sigh of relief.

"This Rojari? Mara continued. Did he seem like a pleasant young man?"

"Oh, yes, mother! Gia replied. He is tall and strong and very courteous."

A shadow of despair flickered over her daughter's features.

"It was I who was the discourteous one. I did not even think to thank him for coming to my aid."

"Don't worry yourself over that, my daughter. If a young man is interested, that minor affront will not deter his intentions."

Little did she realize, at the time, how prophetic her words would prove to be.

# CHAPTER 24

The first "sister" sun was still in her infancy, as the crusaders pushed onward toward the dubious mountain. The pace was considerably slower, as caution guided their footsteps. A silent course was maintained toward a small glade, approximately, one mile from the base of the mountain. Many scouts had been deployed to help ensure their stealthy approach. The wooded objective had been agreed upon, earlier, for two reasons. It formed a natural shield from enemy eyes before they began their assault on the mountain. Their shaggy mounts would be hobbled near a shallow stream, which ran through its middle. This area, also abounded in the mossy vegetation vital to the lurda's diet.

From this point on, the rescuing army would make their way on foot. Even if their shaggy beasts were capable of navigating the steep paths, they had decided their best chances for success lay in the maneuverability. Ten men had been assigned the task of tending the herd, when the time arrived.

The three Earthmen, leading the caravan, scanned the rolling landscape, hoping it would shield them long enough to reach the sanctuary of the impending forest. Danger increased with every step they took toward their objective. Along with the two hundred natives and the Nevoan infantry of one thousand warriors, anxiety hitched a ride.

"One of our scouts approaches." Tonio announced. Within moments, the rider was among them. He, excitedly, divulged his information to the leaders.

"Before our scouting party entered the forest we hobbled our mounts and proceeded on foot. We penetrated it's depths for, approximately, fifty yards before we heard noises. Soon, the source of the disturbance revealed itself. He paused for a moment, catching his breath. We counted twenty of the enemy beasts overseeing a work detail. Five of our fellow men were busy cutting down trees. We cautiously retreated to the fringe of the forest."

"That was a wise choice, my friend. Jim replied. At this point, we can ill afford the risk of alerting them to our presence."

"Da hell with alerting dem!" Truck jumped in. We gotta get our men away from dose cannibal bastards, Right now!"

"I agree with Truck! Greg added. We might as well begin this war, today!"

"And I couldn't agree more with the two of you! Jim responded, taking in the surprised expressions in his brothers faces. If you had allowed me to finish, I was about to suggest a fifty man rescue team. But, now, I think I'll just send you two instead."

Greg and Truck stared sheepishly at each other, taking on the guise of scolded children. Smiling at them and shaking his head, Jim continued "Truck! You take twenty five of your men and enter the forest from the west. I'll take twenty five more and enter from the east. Greg! You take the rest of the caravan and converge on the area where the scouts have hobbled their lurdas. Close in behind us, at a slower pace, after hobbling your mounts. Truck! Once you enter the forest swing your men wide and come at them from the rear. Your main objective is to cut off any possible retreat. I know I don't have to tell you, If, just one of those beasts escapes to spread the alarm we're in for a rough time."

"Dat ain't gonna happen, Jimbo!" Truck said, assuredly.

Nodding at his brother, Jim continued. "I'll hesitate twenty minutes to allow you time to get behind them. Then I'll make a push from the front. A silent kill is in order only bows, arrows and knives will be used. Any questions?"

When none came, men were assigned and the two advance units moved out. A short time later, mounts tethered, they entered the forest on foot.

The cool grasp of the gloomy wood became even colder as they pushed ahead. The dubious aspects of any given conflict always produce feelings of dread.

Moments later, Jim halted his party at the edge of a man-made glade. The stumps of many trees dotted the area. This particular copse of trees had been harvested repeatedly for quite some time. Rotting remains stood alongside freshly amputated cuts.

An eerie sound arrested their attention seconds before they caught site of movement up ahead. They froze and looked on in disbelief.

Twenty five yards, from where they hid, a Luma was bent over at the waist making wretching sounds. As they watched, the jaws of the creature opened so wide that they actually dislocated. The creatures throat swelled many times out of proportion. Slimy liquid flowed from the open mouth. The choking grunts of pain, emitting from the creature, announced its distress. Then, it vomited a long viscous mass onto the forest floor. The pale gray object quivered into movement and started to grow right before their awestruck eyes. The vomitor's jaws and throat returned, immediately, back to their normal proportions. By this time the quivering mass had become a wet reproduction, identical in every detail, to its host. The two creatures ambled off to join their comrades, gathered together less than fifty yards from the hidden men. The horrified looks on his men's faces registered the effect of having witnessed such a disgusting display. Before it had a chance of unsettling them further, Jim gave orders. Whispered from one man to another, they nocked arrows and prepared themselves for the mad dash to engage their enemy. Jim hoped Truck was in position.

If he wasn't it would be a devastating blow to their cause, sealing the fates of their comrades.

The tree stumps, standing only a couple of feet above the mossy, forest floor offered very little coverage. The only ally, enlisted in their cause, was the brash act itself. Hoping to catch their enemy unaware might reduce casualties. Roca stood on his right side, eyes wide with anxiety.

"Be quick, my friend and let your aim be true. Jim offered in encouragement. We'll come out of this okay."

"I am ready earth brother." The young native replied.

Word was, again passed down the line to leave all gear behind except their weapons. Jim rose, slowly to his feet and gave the word. "Now!" He said in a loud whisper.

The small assault team launched itself into the open. Dodging the low stumps, they flew silently across the forest floor. The mossy carpet cushioned their charging feet and absorbed any sound they made. They were half–way across the open glade before the enemy stirred into action. Grabbing up spears and axes, they rushed to meet the intruders.

Twenty yards from the nearest creature Jim let loose an arrow. It buried itself, to the hilt, in a furry chest. Even before it tumbled to the ground, he had another arrow ready. It, too, found a home in an enemy body. A spear flew by Jim's left ear. The creature that had hurled it, stood less than five yards away. Jim quickly, dropped his bow and drew his knife, as he covered the distance. Before the creature could pull his axe from the leather thong encircling its waist, Jim was on him. The earth man's knife lashed out and the creature's blood spurted from its slashed throat. Looking toward the uncut trees to the north he spotted Truck's party making its way toward them. It was over! Every furry creature was dead or dying. Not one of his men suffered as much as a scratch.

Jim assigned three of his men to make sure all of the creatures were dead. If not, a quick death would be administered to prevent them from crawling back to their settlement and sounding the alarm. When the two units finally joined in the middle of the glade, Jim noticed the five filthy natives Truck had in tow.

"Good work, my brother! He said as they shook hands. Did you suffer any casualties?"

"Not a nick, Jimbo. He answered. You guys did all da work for us. When dey rushed out ta meet your party all we had ta do was put a few arrows in dere furry asses."

Glancing behind his brother Jim pointed. "Looks like our five brethren are accounted for"

One of the rescued men came forward and stopped in front of him.

"Is this the way Earth men greet their brothers?" He asked

Looking through the filth, caking the native from head to foot, recognition sped home.

"Bantor! My brother!" He yelled pulling his native friend into a welcoming embrace.

"Ta-rok didn't recognize me either, when first we met" He said as they stood apart.

"How, many, of your party still walk this world?" Jim asked

"How far away are dos bastards?" Truck added.

"If you can find me a cool stream, in which to remove this filth, and treat me and my men to a little food I will be more than happy to answer all your questions." Bantor replied.

The dead Luma warriors, along with their weapons, were collected and thrown into a hastily dug pit. After they had covered them with leafy debris, they retraced their footsteps back through the glade. The entire army was there to greet them. Bantor was amazed to see one thousand armed Nevoans counted among them.

"I, too, will have many questions when we talk."

Then, followed by his four filthy comrades, he raced a few yards away and plunged into the cool stream.

# CHAPTER 25

"One day, during our long journey, we came across the path of a lone native traveling back to his village. We had established contact with this particular village, one year earlier. He informed us of a settlement to the northwest. He had lived with them for a short time. I decided to extend our travels a little further and investigate, unfortunately, it was the wrong decision."

Bantor was regailing them with the exploits of his exploratory expedition. The entire camp with the exception of the many security patrols, gathered around him. The night sky was close to adopting its ebon cloak. Furs were draped over shoulders to fend off the cool breeze. Fires were out of the question.

"When we finally located this village, a few days later, we were surprised by its size, or lack of size I should say. Little more than four hundred men, women and children, living in branch huts, eked out an existence in this barren area." (For the sake of his allies, Bantor didn't mention the reason why these people choose to live in such an isolated area.) Half starved and filthy in appearance, they subsisted almost entirely on roots, vegetables and whatever small game wandered into their vicinity. (Needless to say, their quality of life started to diminish fifty years earlier when they were driven to live in this desolate region.)

"Our visit managed to produce a little hope in their lives. When we informed them war had ended and they were free to live and travel wherever they wanted, they were ready to adopt us. Not wishing to add to their economic burden, our stay with them was a short one. Maps were given to the elders showing the way to other villages. I have confidence they will relocate near one of them, in the near future."

"One of my scouting parties detected evidence of habitation in an area six days march to the south," Jim interrupted.

"It could be the very same village you are describing."

"That is very possible." Bantor acknowledged.

"How did you guys end up getting captured by dese furry bastards?" Truck asked.

"During our brief visit, rumors were circulating through the village about a tribe of strange people living seven days march to the north," Bantor continued. "After discussing this with my men, it was decided we would leave the following day and investigate. Once, again, it would prove to be the wrong decision," the native added, his brow wrinkled in regret.

"Bantor!" Greg interjected, "The decision was a collective one. You cannot hold yourself responsible for exploring the unknown, especially when that was your objective to begin with."

"True! It was unanimously agreed upon. But as the leader, the weight of responsibility is much heavier."

"I suffer that same dilemma with every order I give. Jim joined in. The risks we take, when dealing with other's lives, are necessary if anything is to be accomplished."

"Amen ta dat," Truck said. Da little guy and I don't always agree with big brother, but we know he'd give his life for us. I know your men feel da same way about you. So, knock off dat negative crap or we'll send you home." He finished with a big smile on his face.

A slight smile erased some of the sadness from the native's face. He knew the Earth men were right. But, a part of him would always retain a measure of guilt.

"Please, Bantor! Continue with your story," Jim said. The more we learn about these creatures the better prepared we'll be."

"Five days after leaving the village we were entering a small forest. Suddenly, we were surrounded by the beasts. Those uncanny howls still ring in my ears. They came at us relentlessly, brandishing axes and long spears."

"We managed a good fight and killed many, but, their overwhelming numbers finally subdued us. Eight of my men were killed and devoured, before our very eyes. Two others died from their wounds as we were being marched back to their settlement. They, too, were torn apart and consumed. By the time we reached their caves, most of the men were in a state of shock."

Bantor paused and looked around at all the saddened expressions reflecting back at him.

"For the next few weeks we were forced to dig into the mountain, cut trees and do any filthy task they ordered us to do." He continued.

"At night we were herded together, into a large cave, and given roots and fruit to eat. The hard labor and lack of enough food, made us weaker as each day went by."

"How many of our people are still up there?" Jim asked, interrupting.

"As of yesterday, thirty-two men and two women still lived," Bantor answered.

"Eight days earlier, two of my men died a most horrible death. At the time, they were in a weakened state, unable to work. Four of the beasts dragged them from the cave and commenced cutting off their arms and legs. The mutilated men, screaming in agony, as well as the rest of us, looked on in shock as their body parts were passed around and eaten by the beasts."

Tears flowed from Bantor's eyes, as he continued.

"From that day forward we combined what little strength we had left to ensure every man was able to rise and do the job, regardless of their condition. In spite of our futile efforts, they killed and consumed four more men since."

"Bantor! Could you give us a rough estimation of their numbers?" Greg asked.

Pausing a moment, to consider, he answered.

"My nearest guess would be about five thousand strong. Work parties, as well as hunting parties were leaving and returning to the settlement, at different times throughout the day."

"Did you notice more than one approach to their settlement?" Jim inquired.

"We traveled the same narrow defile each day, always downhill from their village. To the best of my knowledge, there didn't appear to be any other trails. A tall cliff with many small caves sits at the other end. About one-hundred feet above, trees grow to the very edge."

"It would appear, we are confronted with a natural cul-de-sac, gentlemen. Said Greg. One way in, one way out."

"Not necessarily, Greg!" Jim chimed in.

"If we are able to locate a route taking us to the tops of the cliffs, we could make our way down from there."

"About a half mile, down the trail from their caves, it is crossed by a narrow ravine. Bantor added. It runs east and west. I know, for certain, the eastern route bends back toward the mountain. We were marched over this path to collect wood. I am not certain where the trail to the west leads. One of these trails could be the route you are seeking."

"What kinda security do dey have around dere caves? Truck asked. Any look-outs or patrols close to da trail?"

"I do not recall having seen any. Bantor answered. Our weakened state, at the time, didn't allow for much more than the ability to place one foot in front of the other. If any were present, they were unnoticed."

"Given the remote location of their settlement, there is a strong possibility they feel the need for sentries is unnecessary," Jim replied.

And so it continued, long into the night. The entire army listened avidly, absorbing vital knowledge of their enemy.

Bantor's questions about their Nevoan allies, were answered directly by its leader, Froban. A friendship started to develop between them, putting aside all past differences.

"Roca! Tonio! At sunrise you will take four men to this ravine," Jim ordered.

Roca's company was comprised of the youngest men in their army. They would proceed along the eastern route and, hopefully gain the top of the cliffs overlooking the luma caves. Tonio's company would take the western trail to search for a path headed back toward the mountain. These two groups would be given a half-day head start.

The three Earthmen would then lead their troops up the narrow trail in three waves. Jim would lead the first patrol, followed twenty minutes later by Truck's men. Greg's men would follow another twenty minutes later. Froban would follow shortly after with his Nevoan army. They were counting on this procedure to circumvent the possibility of one massive ambush devastating their entire forces.

Men were assigned to the care of their shaggy mounts, that would be tethered just outside the small glade. They protested, almost to the man, the fact they would not be involved in the battle. Not until they were made to realize the importance of this assignment did they relent.

If a retreat was imminent, these beasts represented their last means of escape. They had to be kept in a state of readiness.

The first wave of assaults, proceeding up the mountain, would be limited to the use of bows, arrows and knives. It was their hope, this silent approach would remove all threats from their path without alarming the main bulk of the enemy. They would then await the rest of their comrades on the outskirts of the settlement.

If, either, Roca or Tonio succeeded in finding a way to the summit, overlooking the luma caves, a flaming arrow would be loosed into the sky, notifying the main force. Then the right to survive on this world would, finally, be decided, by one faction or the other.

The cool night was half spent when the three Earthmen retreated to their sleeping furs. Many questions and doubts still lingered. Each one knew, full well, the new day could prove to be their last.

# CHAPTER 26

As the first sun cast her glow on the ominous mountain, the avenging army converged on the narrow ravine crossing the trail. Because of the proximity to the enemy settlement, no camp was established. They concealed themselves as well as they could, among the rocks, crags and any natural structure afforded by the small defile. Sentries were posted at highest points, along either side. Here they would remain until word was brought to them from Tonio's or Roca's scouting parties, signifying their success in locating a route to the summit of the escarpment hovering above the Luma settlement. This would secure a dominant position, coinciding with their frontal assault. This vantage point could prove to be paramount to a victorious endeavor. One way or another this day would witness a clash of two cultures fighting for the right to survive. Three Earth men, a little more than two-hundred natives and one thousand Nevoan soldiers would be pitted against an army consisting of over five thousand Luma warriors. Victory would not be achieved by bravery alone. It would be determined by the faction which cherishes life the most and has the unflagging will to continue it.

"How long we gonna squat in dis pile of rocks? Truck asked. We're so close I can almost smell dos bastards."

"We have to give the scouting parties, at least until the end of this day to report in. Jim replied. If we receive no word, by then, we must assume they were not successful."

"We can only pray they were." Greg chimed in. "To secure that advantageous position would drastically, reduce the overwhelming odds confronting us."

"One way or another, my brothers, tomorrow's first sun will signal the beginning of our assault." Jim added, with a sullen lilt in his voice.

Observing the worried expressions on his brothers' faces, Truck shook his head. "You guys sound like we, already, got our asses kicked. Knock off da bullshit thinking. We're gonna come out a dis just fine."

"Let's face it Truck! Jim responded, staring at his large brother. We have no actual way of knowing how the tide will turn. Do we?"

"Dat's true, Jimbo! But, it ain't gonna do no good worrying about it, either."

"Jim! Greg joined in. Our large sibling here will never understand. Worrying is a part of human nature. Something he doesn't qualify for."

Jim burst out laughing, when he observed the quizzical look on Truck's face.

"You two think dat's funny, don't ya?" Truck retorted. Well, think about dis den. Dos animals aren't gonna worry about us being in dere backyard. Dere gonna try ta do something about it. Dey ain't gonna sit on dere furry asses and try ta worry us away. Dey ain't gonna waste dere time and I know deep down in my bones, dey ain't got much a dat left."

Now, two questioning stares reflected back at him.

"You guy think about dat for a while. Truck said with a big grin on his face. "I'm gonna take a little nap before all da fun starts."

Jim and Greg sat silently, as they watched the big man walk away. The rest of the day was spent, silently making preparations for the imminent battle. Weapons were checked and rechecked for readiness. Men sat in clusters, drawing confidence from one another. All were aware, by this time tomorrow many of these familiar comrades might not be counted among them. To dissipate a few pounds from the gloomy atmosphere, some of them were relating stories about their families and past experiences. For many, these tales represented a last desperate attempt at being, simply, remembered. Naturally, with no way of knowing who would survive the battle, these stories of their personal antics would be all that remained of their legacies.

The Earth trio sat huddled together with about twenty of their native warriors. Jim was regaling them with one of his adventures that had occurred on his home planet. "That old she-bear was only about thirty paces behind me and gaining rapidly. He related. My old grandfather, Joseph, was in camp and watched as I approached. Stop! He yelled out to me, as he turned and confronted the bear. With arms raised to the sky, he started chanting in the Sioux language. I froze, trying to catch my breath, only five feet behind him. What I witnessed next will live in my mind until I meet my ancestors. The bear stopped dead in her tracks a few paces in front of my grandfather. I watched in amazement as the bear lay down on the ground and stared up at the old Indian. The chanting seemed to have a calming effect on the furry beast. Its large head started swaying from side to side. After a short eternity, the chanting stopped. The bear rose from the ground and made its way, slowly, towards my grandfather. Her eyes locked onto his with a glazed stare. Our weapons were out of reach. I was eight years old and I was petrified with fear. Jim paused for a moment, taking in the intent looks reflecting back at him. This true story always drew undivided attention. He continued. "The old bear rose to her full height, almost seven feet, and placed her massive forepaws on my grandfather's shoulders and stared into his eyes. The next thing I know grandfather Joseph raises his right arm and places his hand on the top of the bear's head. They stood that way for many moments before the bear dropped down on all fours and dashed off toward the forest in search of her cubs."

Jim had explained the unpredictable nature of a bear to his native audience when he had described the beast to them. They were, also, made aware its ferocity was unequaled in the area where the earth men were raised. The elements of danger and bravery, in the story, made for rapt listeners. "After the bear was long out of sight, he continued, I asked my grandfather to explain to me what had just occurred. "I talked to the bear in the language of the people, he said. I let her know we had no quarrel with her. It was her concern for the safety of her two cubs that had prompted the chase." I remember the next thing grandfather did was to place his two hands on my shoulders and stare into my eyes. The next time you discover any wild animals that comes across your path, do not touch them! The scent of yourself, was on the cubs. But, grandfather! I remember saying. How did you know there were two of them and that I did indeed touch them?"

"When we talked, she told me!" He replied.

The small audience was shaking their heads in amazement at the conclusion of Jim's tale. Some questioned its validity while others believed Earth people just might be capable of doing such things.

As the day wore on, anxiety multiplied. Tempers were close to flaring, while confidence was starting to ebb. The emotional and physical strain they were subjected to was starting to show.

"If we wait too much longer, I fear this war will begin among us. Greg broke the silence, as they made their way through the pensive troops. "And sooner than we think.""

"There isn't a hell of a lot we can do about it, at this moment." Jim replied. In less than four hours, our strategy will be decided for us, a full frontal assault, or a more methodical attack, from two positions."

"I kinda like plan 'B' myself. Truck interjected. It evens up da odds a little."

They continued with their sojourn through the ranks, offering encouragement to bolster spirits. They were interrupted a short while later by one of the sentries. He brought their attention to a group of men, approaching, hurriedly, from the west. As they neared, Jim recognized the group as Tonio's party. Soon, they were among them.

Sweaty, filthy and out of breath Tonio began "After following this narrow ravine for two cycles of the "Sister" suns, we found ourselves getting further away from the designated mountain. It was useless to continue on. So we marched all night to return."

"Did you run into any unfriendlies along the way?" Jim asked.

"No sign of them was discovered, during our entire mission." Tonio answered.

"The efforts from you and your men are appreciated, Tonio." Jim said. "Go, now and get some rest. Tomorrow, the battle begins.

After Tonio and his men had left, the three Earthmen and a few others sat around talking.

"We can only trust, Roca had better luck." Greg said. His was the more logical route to begin with."

"I hope we learn the answer to that soon. Jim replied. We're running out of time!"

"Dat reminds me! Truck said as he rose to his feet. I got one more thing ta do before da battle starts."

With that said he rushed off.

"What was that all about? Jim asked no one in particular. He's been prepared since we started this march."

"I have no idea! Greg replied. There aren't any bars, nearby. Are there?"

That brought a smile to Jim's face. "It's hard to tell, when our brother is concerned."

A short while later, Truck returned. He carried an eight foot long sapling that had been stripped of its smaller branches. As he sat down, next to his travel pack, he noticed all the quizzical looks. Smiling at them, he reached into the hide pack and pulled out a three foot long banner. It had been dyed red, white and blue. "I asked Mara to make dis before we left. He answered the questioning gazes. We can't go inta no battle without our colors. Can we?"

Smiles of approval emerged from the sullen faces, as they watched the big man tie the banner to the sapling. When he finished, he rose to his feet. "Dis is what it is all about! Right?" He said, as he raised "old glory" above his head.

"Amen ta dat, Truck! Jim agreed. That is exactly, what it's all about."

"And here I thought you were out looking for a bar." Greg enjoined

"Nah!" Truck responded. "Da only good one is in a peaceful village miles away from here. After we get done kicking dese furry asses off of our world, da drinks are on me."

Almost in sink the small group echoed "Amen to dat!"

Shortly before the final sun of the day surrendered to the night, they were again, interrupted by one of the sentries. "A man approaches from the east." He announced.

The three Earthmen rose immediately and followed the sentry to a high point above the ravine. Moments later, they spotted a figure running, rapidly, thru the semi-darkness. Soon, he was among them. Covered with dirt, he bled from several superficial wounds. Collapsing into the arms of a couple of native warriors he made his announcements.

"Roca has located a path to the top of their mountain. He said, trying to regain his breath. He waits there, now, as we speak."

A collective sigh of relief was audible from the gathered warriors. This encouraging news couldn't have arrived at a better time. "The very instant he observes the approach of our army, he will let loose a merciless barrage from above." The exhausted courier finished as he crumpled to the ground.

"See to this man's comfort! Jim ordered a couple of men nearby. The rest of you get some rest! Our battle will begin when the first "sister" sun smiles upon us."

# CHAPTER 27

Shortly before the first of the "sister" suns spilled her waking warmth, over the horizon the allied army was in motion.

One isolated incident occurred as the invading army moved up the narrow defile to within a half-mile of the enemy stronghold. One of the luma beasts was in the middle of its repulsive, reproductive process. It was spotted, earlier, one mile below its settlement. It was, quickly, dispatched by a well-placed arrow from one of the forward scouts. The body was dragged off the trail and concealed beneath a piece of rocky debris." If we could catch everyone a dos son of a bitches throwing up dere babies on da ground, we could kill two with one blow." Truck had commented.

The three Earth brothers were at the head of the vanguard, Tonio and Bantor at their side.

Because of the timely success, Roca and his party had attained, they would attack in an all-out, frontal surge. Roca and his young troops, already concealed above the settlement, would begin a merciless barrage, into the backs of their enemies, immediately after they were engaged by the charging army.

The narrow ravine began to widen as they approached the settlement. Natives and Nevoans spread out from one side to the other, using what scarce coverage availed itself. Every one of them was aware of what must be done. No captives would be taken. No one would stop killing until the last of this murderous infestation was erased from their world. If they allowed for the slightest act of mercy to dictate their actions, on this day, their own survival would be placed in jeopardy.

As they made their way, stealthily forward, one of their scouts moved in their direction. The three Earth men raced ahead to intercept him, while the rest of the advancing army came to a stop. When the scout came within earshot, he made this announcement. "About a quarter of a mile ahead, this trail spills into their village. No sentries are posted. Few are stirring at this hour, although, we did notice four armed creatures guarding the entrance to a large cave. It sits at the back of the village, in the base of the mountain."

Unnoticed Bantor had joined them. "It is there they keep our brethren. He replied. Those four must be killed first."

"Would dey have any guards inside?" Truck asked

"Because of the weakened condition of the occupants, they found it unnecessary to do so." Bantor answered.

As they rejoined their comrades, Jim looked around at the sea of nervous stares emanating from the native faces.

Even the battle tested veterans, from the "Nevoan" war, had flickering shades of doubt in their eyes.

"Men! Today you will be tested. Jim began, in a voice loud enough to be heard by many of the massed warriors. We must prove our worthiness to survive this world. To do so, we must eliminate an entire culture. Peace has reigned on our world for many years. To insure our continuance and the future of our children we must remain strong." Nods of enthusiastic agreement bobbed throughout the crowd. "You have opened your homes and your hearts to my brothers and I. We will not allow this to come to an end. Let us go, now, and earn our right to survive.

Turning, abruptly, he led them toward the Luma settlement at fast march. Moments later they were a shouting distance away. The stronghold came, suddenly, to life. The furry beasts were, now aware of the approaching threat. They poured from their caves, like ants out of an anthill. Brandishing spears and axes, they charged.

The first volley of arrows was directed at the four Lumas guarding the entrance to the "hostage" cave. Half of them ended up buried in four furry bodies. Wave after wave of arrows and blast after blast of "Draco" fire power poured, relentlessly, into the charging beasts. The steady barrage from Roca's party, one hundred feet above the battlefield, added to the murderous storm. But on and on they came. Death was not a novelty among their kind. Their over whelming numbers would soon turn this battle into a hand to hand affair. They had to reduce their numbers considerably, before that happened, or the outcome would be obvious. Heedless to the rain of death falling upon them, the Luma's lust for survival was as ardent as that of the attackers.

Jim dodged, just in time, to avoid being impaled by a spear. Charging forward, his knife found a home in a furry throat. Because of the close proximity of the two warring factions, Roca and his party ceased their barrage of arrows and began repelling down the escarpment on vines clinging to the cliff's face. Soon they were attacking from the rear.

Truck waded onto the furry hostiles, using his Draco as a staff. Heads were crushed, right and left. Blood, trickled from his body, most of it was of the "Luma" flavor. Picking up a fallen Luma axe, he hewed his way through a carpet of fur. The rocky ground was slippery with gore. Footing was becoming treacherous.

Greg had fought his way to the cave harboring his captive comrades. Five furry hostiles, armed with spears and axes, were pressing him back. One of those spears stabbed, deeply into his right leg just above the knee. He lost his balance and fell heavily, to the ground. Warding off blows, he tried to regain his feet before anyone of the three remaining beasts could deliver him a fatal blow. A swarm of filthy, emaciated men rushed past him and pounded them to jelly. The large stones they held, in their grimy hands dripped with blood and brain matter. Helping Greg to his feet, they ushered him into the cave. The battle waged on for the better part of the next two hours. Casualties were mounting most of them were furry. But it seemed like their vast numbers would, soon, dictate the outcome. Jim took a risk. He ordered everyone to fall back immediately. The surprised Lumas, not expecting this sudden change in the action, came to a standstill. They were even slower to react when Jim ordered his Nevoan artillery forward and to commence firing. Wave after wave of lethal energy spat out of their weapons. The sky rained Luma flesh and gore. Soon, all that remained were small groups of Lumas, isolated from one another. Truck led a small body of men into their mist. All swung the heavy Luma axes. Their fear of dismemberment drained enough of their courage to cause a slight retreat. Jim, fighting side by side with his brother now, shouted to his men. "Use the axes on them. We wouldn't want them visiting the "ones before", in one piece would we?"

Soon, axes wielded, by native and Nevoan alike, left a gory path of body parts as they pushed the beasts farther back. The relentless surge of the avenging army, soon had the enemy pressed against the base of the cliff. Not one of the remaining beasts opted to surrender. Neither faction could afford this option. On and on they fought.

The avenging crusaders pressed forward, sensing victory, through the quagmire of carnage, slipping and sliding, unwavering from the task at hand. Covered with the gore of their enemies, weapons were becoming hard to grasp. The putrid smell of the dead and dying grew almost unbearable as the battle wore on. The hot rays of the second "sister" sun added to the morbid ambiance.

And then it was over.

The last of the creatures dropped their weapons and made pleading overtures for surrender. Not on this day! Only with the total decimation of this murderous culture would other cultures be allowed the chance to exist.

Jim, Truck and Bantor stared long and hard at the gore slickened battlefield polluted with body parts. Men were, already sorting through the carnage for their dead and wounded comrades. Others went about searching for any surviving Lumas. If only one was left alive, it would eventually, bring about a reenactment of this brutal onslaught in the near future. They could not allow this to happen!

"Make certain every cave and possible hiding place is thoroughly searched. Jim ordered a group of men near him. We must insure future generations against ever having to go through this. Tonio! Take your men and do what you can for our wounded."

"Where's da little guy?" Truck broke in, looking around him expectantly, panic building.

Before he could rush off on a frenzied search for his sibling, an emaciated replica of a man approached him. "Your sibling is safe. Ta-rok! He announced. He suffered a wound in one of his legs and is resting comfortably in the cave."

"Thanks, pal" Truck replied, as he tore off across the bloodied battlefield toward the cave.

Bantor smiled and shook his head. "Even if you had not told me, long ago, how much your siblings care about each other or the barbs they hurl at each other is a game they play. I would have learned the truth this day. The genuine concern on Ta-rok's face would have lifted all my doubts." Jim stared back at his native friend. "And, I pity the man who is not aware of this and tries to do harm to one or the other."

The rest of the day was spent scouring every inch of Luma real estate for any enemy survivors. Parties searched the out-lying areas, as well, on the chance one of the residents may have gone there on "maternity leave". Piles of body parts were investigated to be sure none of their comrades lay buried beneath, living or dead.

Thirty seven of their native brethren now walked with their ancestors. Two hundred and eighty seven Nevoan allies would not be making the journey home. Over five thousand Luma perpetrators would not be attending their "last supper". The price, paid for with native and Nevoan blood was devastatingly steep. However, if this alien infestation was completely erased from their world, future generations would feel it was worth every one of the sacrificing souls.

"Tonio! Jim called out. Take a detail of men and retrieve our lurdas. We will set up camp where the ravine crosses the trail and await you there."

"Good call, Jimbo! Truck said. Dis place is starting ta smell like buzzard puke."

"Now how in the Hell would you know what that smelled like, my brother?" Jim asked with a smile on his face.

"Obviously, you haven't gotten close to some of his dates, have you Jim?" Greg interjected. Watching his brother laugh so hard the blood and grime, that had dried on their faces, actually, cracked and fell away. Truck responded. "You need a little more pain midget?" He said, shaking his fist. But the smile in his eyes and relief in his heart told a different story to those seated around him. A short while, later, they finished setting up camp. A, small stream was located nearby. The reviving cool water cleansed the gore and grime from their bodies. But minds would be tainted forever by the horrors they had just waded through. All the wounded had been tended to and were, now resting comfortably. Their fallen comrades lay on a bed of branches, awaiting the fire and smoke that would carry them to their ancestors. Native and Nevoan warriors lay side by side on the leafy pyre. Unforseen allies in life, they would be united in their final pilgrimage.

The twenty seven survivors of Bantor's exploratory party sat with their leader. He was to learn, seven more of his party had died horrible deaths since his rescue. A small detail was sent to collect their remains, if any could be located. They returned a short while later. Vine baskets, slung on poles between them, carried the grizzily remains of their comrades.

"Aside from the men we lost during our first engagement with the beasts, all in my party are accounted for. Bantor said with a heavy heart and sadness leaking from his eyes. Let them join their brothers on the final journey." Many hands volunteered to, reverently, place the remains alongside their other fallen comrades.

"Rest assured Bantor! "Those slain in that first battle are already with their ancestors. Jim said. We accorded them a proper send-off."

Bantor nodded his head in appreciation. The Nevoan commander, Froban, had, agreed to a similar funeral, earlier.

"When Tonio returns with our animals, we will start the ceremony. Jim announced. Rest up, men! Mourn your fallen brethren! But, take solace in knowing you have won the struggle for existence, not only for yourselves, but, for your children, and the generations to come. I am honored to have fought alongside every one of you."

"Amen ta dat!" Truck chimed in.

# CHAPTER 28

Tonio and his men galloped up the narrow trail. They were followed, closely, by the entire herd of lurdas. Social creatures, by nature, they also depended on their numbers for protection. As they thundered toward the encampment, Tonio and his men slackened the pace a little until they literally walked into the camp.

Men were already capturing their mounts, putting reins on them and leading them to an open area a safe distance away.

"I take it there were no problems with the animals, Tonio?" Jim inquired.

"A few of them managed to free themselves from their hobbles. But, they remained close by and caught up with the herd, as we made our way back. I believe they are all accounted for. They, almost, seemed as happy to see us as the men we left behind to tend them."

"Good work, my friend!" Jim replied. "In a day, or two, all should be rested enough to begin the journey home."

As the last "sister" sun plunged over the horizon, the entire army gathered around the bed of branches embracing their fallen comrades.

Jim, Truck, Bantor, Roca, Tonio and the Nevoan commander, Froban, stood before them. No campfires had yet been lit, as an act of deference to their slain brethren. The funeral fires, carrying the spirits of friends and relatives, into the embracing arms of their ancestors, would be the first.

Men stood near each mound of branches, holding lit torches in their hands, awaiting orders.

The honor of bestowing the eulogy was accorded to Bantor.

"Let us all remember our brethren who have relinquished their spirits to insure a future for our people, he began. A big reason why we stand here, on this night, is due to the fact we believe in one another. Our Nevoan comrades, once enemies, have proven beyond all doubts, a powerful coexistence is possible, between the cultures. The Luma invaders sought to prove otherwise. They are no longer! When we return to our homes, there will be joyous celebrations. Our victory, today, means we are worthy and deserving of this.

Bantor paused and looked into the intent eyes of the gathered mourners.

"Upon our return home, there will also be anguish in the hearts of those, closely, related to these fallen souls. Each of us must make a concentrated effort to ease some of this pain by making them aware their loved ones did not perish in vain."

"Let us, now, send these brave warriors on their final journey. They are gone, in body, from our lives. But, their spirits will forever be our companions."

"Light the fires!" he ordered.

Soon, the night was turned into day, as the branches ignited, casting its warm glow over them.

A short while later individual fires dotted the encampment and small clusters of men sat around them talking. There wasn't a single soul among them who was not anxious to begin the long journey to their homes. When their wounded were deemed fit enough, to withstand the arduous trek, upon the backs of their mounts, they would depart. In spite of this necessary delay, spirits soared. They had survived this perilous ordeal, by overcoming their physical and emotional inadequacies. The only battle, left unwaged, was against their own impatience.

Greg made his way, slowly, through the camp aided by a stout branch, he limped around the many small clusters of chatting warriors. When he spotted a group of men consisting of his brothers, Bantor, Tonio and Rosa, he joined them.

"Nice of you ta show up! Truck said, in greeting.

"Ya slept through da whole show!"

"I can't imagine what it was you gave me, Tonio, but it sure knocked me out," Greg replied, taking a seat by the fire and ignoring Truck's comment.

"Shara always prepares that special tea for me, when I have trouble sleeping. Tonio answered. Of course, she never makes it that potent."

"How's that leg feeling, brother?" Jim asked.

"It's a bit stiff and a little sore," Greg answered. But, I'll be ready to saddle up when the word is given."

Looking over at Bantor, he apologized for having missed the funeral.

"Apologies are unnecessary, my Earth brother. I know you would have wished them all a safe journey, had you been here. Besides, you and the other wounded must regain your strength before we can make the journey home."

"Any idea how soon that will be?" Greg asked.

"That would depend on the status of our worst casualties, brother. Jim replied. We were just discussing this before you arrived."

"Ta-rok has suggested we build litters to be dragged behind our beasts. Bantor said. Similar to those used by the people of your tribe, back on earth."

"A travois?" Greg chimed. "That is an excellent idea! Good thinking, Truck!"

"Naturally!" Truck replied with a big grin on his face.

"If we can complete the construction of the litters and accustom our animals to pulling them, it may be possible to depart the day after tomorrow," Jim said.

"How many a dem poles we gonna need?" Truck asked.

"Roca! You were helping with the wounded, earlier. How many of them do you feel, will be unable to ride?" Jim inquired.

"There were fifteen men, for certain, who would not be able to ride. He answered. I will check to be certain."

"You want me to do the math for you, Truck, or are you capable of adding it up?" Greg jibed.

"Keep it up, runt, and we're gonna need at least two more." He responded, shaking his fist.

The feigned expression of menace, on Truck's face, made them all laugh.

"Before you sleepy heads drag your tired asses outta da furs, tomorrow, my men and I will have "thirty" of dos poles ready." Truck replied, making it a point to emphasize the word "thirty" and staring at his young brother.

"Well done, Truck! I'm proud of you!" Greg shot back.

"I didn't sleep through all of dos classes in school." The big man responded, with a big grin on his face.

# CHAPTER 29

As the first "sister" sun lifted her bright head over the horizon, most of the men in the allied camp were already, up and about.

Anticipation was so vivid, in their minds, a euphoric cloud of happiness settled over them as they finished their preparations. Even though sleep had eluded most of them, due to their eagerness to return home, the adrenalin coursing through their souls would be more than enough to carry them safely through their journey.

Truck had returned, with ten of is men. A stack of thirty stout poles, each eight feet-long, had been trimmed of branches and were ready for use.

Others were in the process of braiding hide cord. These would be used in securing the travois to their beasts. Large furs, used for sleeping purposes, would be stretched between the poles.

The journey home would be at a much slower pace, to insure the comfort of their wounded comrades. In spite of their overwhelming eagerness, every man was more than willing to make this sacrifice for their brethren.

Jim was over-seeing a small party of men, a short distance from their camp. Ten of their Lurdas were being butchered. Because of their loss of so many men, a good number of riderless mounts existed.

"It has been a long time since I have eaten fresh roasted meat." Bantor said, as he piled fleshy chunks on a hide spread on the mossy turf.

"It won't be too much longer before we are all in our own homes, sating our appetites, my brother," Jim said.

"I know all will be appreciative of the feast tonight, Earth man. It is well-timed idea.

"It seems a little morbid at the same time, Bantor, when you stop to realize we will be dining on the beasts to honor the ones who rode them."

"Do not worry yourself, my Earth brother. I do not believe anyone will taste the difference."

Jim started laughing so hard, he almost toppled into the pile of flesh.

Men had, already, started many large fires. Soon, the smell of roasting meat permeated through the entire encampment. After many weeks, subsisting on dried tasteless meat, roots and berries, anticipation of this succulent event was just what they needed to take their minds off the hell they had waded through. Aside from the much needed nourishment, it would, also, nurture their spirits.

"Dis was a great idea, Jimbo! Truck said, as they sat around chatting and watching the meat cook. "What made ya think a dis?"

"I was getting hungry, earlier, and started thinking about how nice it would be to have a fresh piece of roasted meat. Then, I thought about all of the rider-less mounts that would be following us home. Sadly, there will be more beasts than natives making the return trip."

"One can only hope you put that poor beast Truck was riding, out of its misery. Greg interjected. I don't think it's capable of lasting much longer."

"Dat was da first one slaughtered, you crippled dwarf, and were saving dos nice greasy back straps just for you." Truck shot back.

"After that long trip, Truck, it should be the most tenderized meat in the herd," Jim joined in, with a big smile on his face.

Bantor, Tonio and Roca, also added theirs.

Looking across the fire, at his three native friends, Truck shook his head.

"Ya see what I had ta put up with, all my life?"

A short while later, the meat was done roasting, burned in some places, rare in others, none seemed to mind. Their appetites, completely sated, they sat around with a sense of ease they had not known for weeks. Their return journey would begin at first sunrise. They would retrace the same route which had brought them here. They could not leave this mountain of anguish behind them soon enough.

Discussions varied, throughout the camp, as men sat around the many small fires that fought against the night's ebony embrace. A mild breeze filtered through their midst, as they huddled together. A chandelier of stars looked down on them, adding to the peaceful ambiance.

"Do you think you're going to be capable of riding?" Jim asked, as he watched Greg changing the moss dressing on his injured leg.

"I'll be just fine, Jim. He answered. The bleeding has ceased and I will be able to tolerate the little pain involved."

"We could, easily, build another travois or you could ride double with Truck." Jim said, smiling mischievously.

"Not if you wish to continue calling me your brother, you won't! Greg, quickly shot back. I would rather walk all the way home, before subjecting myself to that abuse."

The hurt look on Truck's face elicited smiles from the gathered men. Bantor, Tonio and Roca led a chorus of laughter that was quickly picked up by others sitting nearby.

"Dat's okay by me! Truck retaliated. I didn't want dat midget taking up my space, anyway."

"What space?" Greg rejoined. That poor beast barely has room enough to breath, with you sprawled across its back."

Truck stared, sheepishly, at the small group, as they rocked with laughter. It was so infectious, he was soon joining them.

"Rest assured, one way or another, we will all get safely home. I hope!" Jim said smiling.

A short while later, the allied encampment slumbered. Pleasant dreams of family and friends, back home, accompanied them.

The storm had run its course. Most had survived it. From this moment on, every day of their lives would stand as a living testament to the bravery of their deceased comrades that would, forever, be remembered.

# CHAPTER 30

"I dreamt throughout the night, Graci. Leota said, as they sat at their morning fire drinking tea."

It was, both, unsettling and reassuring at the same time, very disturbing!"

Graci remained silent. She knew her mate well enough to recognize the expression on his face. She knew, whatever it was troubling him, he would soon share. His restlessness had kept her awake half the night, also.

"I felt the agony of many men. He continued. Their fears, hopelessness and pain were so vivid, it was as though I were actually among them, experiencing the same."

He paused and took a sip of his tea. The pensive look in his eyes told Graci that his mind was focused on a faraway place. She remained quiet.

"After a long period of time, I cannot say exactly how long, the feeling of fear and hopelessness vanished. I could still feel the pain, however. Sleep must have over-taken me then. In my dream I was awakened a second time. I was in the company of many men. I could sense them rejoicing and an overpowering wave of relief flowed from them. I awoke before I could determine what it was they were celebrating."

He stopped and stared at Graci. The confused look in his eyes almost pleaded with her to provide the right answers to his dilemma.

Smiling across at her mate, she simply asked, "Wasn't it you I overheard telling Cinda not to get caught up in one's dreams, and to not allow them control of your mind?"

"Yes! I did say those words, my loved one," he answered with a half smile in return.

"But, this dream felt so real! None I have ever before experienced, have troubled my mind to this extent."

"I am not as knowledgeable in these matters as you, my mate. But, I would offer you my perception of what you have described to me." Graci replied.

"Please! Do so!" Leota responded.

"Fear, hopelessness and pain are all symptoms experienced by warriors before or during a battle, are they not?"

"Among others! Leota answered. Please, continue!"

"Maybe, such a battle did occur in your dream and you became a part of it. Did you not also mention in the end, you were among rejoicing men?" she concluded, with a big smile on her lovely face.

The sullen expression, slowly, melted from Leota's face, as comprehension took hold of his mind.

"If they were rejoicing, they had to have won the battle!" He deduced, as a big smile enveloped his face.

"That is, also, what I pictured from the telling of your dream." Graci replied.

He rose and crossed the few paces to her, engulfing her with an affectionate embrace.

"Woman! You never cease to amaze me!" he said, staring down into her eyes.

"Does this mean we will, both, get a restful sleep this evening?" she asked, smiling back.

"I promise! "Some" of the night will be restful!" he said in a sensuous voice.

Life in the village had reverted, once again, to limited activity. Since the completion of the contests, three days earlier, daily routines were almost uneventful. For a short period of time minds had been alleviated, somewhat, distracting them from the constant worry over the plight of relatives and friends. They were, now, left to their own devices for dealing with the emotional anguish they harbored, on an individual basis. For some, this was more difficult. As a leader of people, the emotional burden was multiplied. Every conscious moment, in Leota's mind, was shadowed heavily with concern for his son and brethren. Even, his unconscious mind prevented him from enjoying a restful sleep. And, it would continue until final closure became definite, figuratively and realistically!

# CHAPTER 31

As the victorious army made its way across the mossy terrain, the palpable energy exuding from it, belied the fact they had fought and survived a battle against overwhelming odds. Many of their brethren, along with "Nevoan" comrades in arms, had been lost during the bloody conflict. Every appreciative step they took toward their homes, was a tribute to the ones left behind.

The shaggy lurdas adapted quickly to the travois, pulling them easily behind them. The pace was much slower than their outward march. But, no one seemed too concerned. They were on their way home!

It had taken them six days to reach this area from the Nevoan settlement. Jim estimated, at the rate they were traveling, it would take them eight days to return.

Truck rode to the head of the caravan and joined his brothers.

"I checked all da litters! He announced. Dey all seem ta be holding up okay."

"I'd love nothing better than to pick up the pace. Jim replied. But, for the safety of our injured comrades, I am not going to risk it."

"We ain't in no hurry, now, Jimbo!" Truck said.

"Da war is over! We can take our time."

"And, I hope it is our last, brother," Jim added.

"What, on two worlds, is our large sibling going to do with his time, now?" Greg inquired, smiling.

"Ta-rok is always welcomed to accompany me on my expeditions." Bantor joined in. He was riding double with Tonio, trailing the three earth men.

"I don't think dat's what my tiny brother meant, Bantor." Truck interjected, staring at Greg.

"He thinks dat if I ain't fighting or raising some kind of hell I ain't gonna be happy."

"Well, now that it's over with, just what exactly are you going to do with your time?" Jim asked, playing along.

"One a da first things I'd like ta do is put da runt, here, on a weight training plan, add a little meat to his bones, you know? Make him into man size."

When they all laughed, Greg couldn't help but to join them.

"That may take some time!" Greg replied. But, at least for the present, we have that luxury."

"Amen ta dat, shorty!"

As the day wore on, spirits remained high within the ranks. Naturally, there were those who wanted to rebel against the snail-like pace they were subjected to. But, they did not allow their anxieties to surface. They consoled themselves, with the fact, they were fortunate to have earned the opportunity of making this return trip.

Shortly before the second "sister" sun had retired below the horizon, a halt was called in the shade of a small forest. Animals were tended to after their injured were made comfortable. Men cooled themselves by taking a dip into a small stream nearby. It was decided, earlier, a prolonged stop wouldn't make any difference in their travel plans, given the slow rate of advancement. Fires dotted through the encampment as night settled in.

It stirred the coals into waves of even greater brightness as it reflected off the faces of the many men gathered around them.

Devoid of their stress-related symptoms, evident in every one of them just a short while ago, they were now transformed into living canvasses exuding relief and happiness. The only thoughts in their minds were the overwhelming desires to be home with their families.

Friendly banter emanated from each group as they clustered around the fires, corralling the warmth. Mention of families and personal objectives to be accomplished on their return, dominated most discussions. They thrived in this peaceful ambiance of which they had been deprived for so long.

"I'd like ta invent a machine dat can grind up meat. Truck was saying. I'd give my left nugget for a big, juicy hamburger right now!"

"What is hamburger?" Bantor asked.

"Ya take a handful of dat ground meat, shape it into a patty and cook it. Truck answered. Den ya put it in between a couple a slices of bread and eat it."

"I cannot understand why you would choose to do this to a good piece of meat." Bantor replied, shaking his head.

"It is just another method of preparing meat, used by the people of Earth. Greg said. If prepared properly, I must admit, it is delicious."

"Truck! That is a great idea!" Jim joined in. "There are many elderly people, in our village, who have difficulty chewing meat. If you manage to succeed with your invention, they will no longer be deprived."

"It would, also, cut down on the chances of a toddler choking on a piece of well-cooked meat," Greg added.

"Dat's, exactly, what I had in mind when I thought of da hamburger," Truck piped in.

"I bet it was! Jim said, skeptically. I know it had nothing to do with that bottomless pit you call a stomach. Did it, Truck?"

"Maybe a little!" Truck replied, smiling, sheepishly, back at his brother.

As the night wore on and the fires burned low, some men had already retired to their furs. Sentries had been posted around their encampment. Creatures of habit, they would practice security measures all the way back to the safety of their village. They needed no more surprises! Everyone wanted to believe the furry invaders had been totally eliminated from their world. However, if by a small chance, some still existed, they would not be caught off guard. To do otherwise, at this point, would undo everything they had accomplished.

# CHAPTER 32

Six more, uneventful, days later, found the weary warriors within a few miles of the Nevoan settlement. Roca, who had been riding lead scout had just informed them.

"I happened upon two Nevoan sentries. He said. They are now in the process of spreading word of our success."

"How long of a lay-over can we expect, once we have gained the settlement?" Greg asked.

I think a day or two would be appreciated. Jim replied. It would be an affront to them were we to deposit their warriors and rush off. Without their assistance, the outcome of the battle may have been, tragically, different."

"I agree, Jim! We cannot discount their loyalty with a hasty departure. Greg said. Besides, if those two furry captives still live, our brother here, has two more left to kill. We wouldn't want to deprive him of that, would we?"

"Dat aint gonna happen, squirt! Truck rebutted. I had my fill a killing."

His brothers stared at him with mock disbelieve reflecting from their faces. Looking pointedly, at Greg with a mischievous grin on his face, Truck couldn't resist. "However, you keep up with dos insults, midget, and I might change my mind before we get home." He finished, shaking his big fist in Greg's face.

Bantor, Tonio and Roca, riding directly behind the Earthmen, started to laugh.

"I thought we agreed, the war was over." Bantor joked.

"For most of us, it definitely is!" Roca joined in.

"But not all of us." Tonio added, staring at Truck.

"You'll have to forgive our brother, here. Jim replied. When he goes long periods of time without sex and his favorite foods, he has a tendency to take it out on others."

"We can all be thankful he hasn't taken it out on the lurdas, yet!" Greg ventured, as he spurred his mount away from the one truck sat.

Laughter peeled from his comrades when they noticed the look on the big man's face. "Dat was a low blow, you little shit!" He yelled at his brother. Then the infectious laughter over-took him and he soon joined them. A short time later, the walls of the Nevoan settlement stood out over the flat mossy plain.

Sentries, posted at the top of the walls spotted them and soon, the massive gates swung open. There to greet them was "Mokar" the Nevoan leader.

Dismounting, the three Earthmen, Bantor, Roca and Tonio approached him. They were joined moments later, by Froban, The leader of the Nevoan forces.

"My greetings, warriors! Mokar began. I assume I am looking upon a victorious army?"

"You are, indeed! Jim responded. The sad part is, we left many brave souls behind."

"It is the nature of all wars, my earth friend. Mokar replied. In the pursuit of peace we are all expendable."

"We feel certain all invaders have been eliminated! Greg joined in. Peace resides, once again, within our world.

"All except dos two furry bastards in your cages, dat is! Truck added.

"The two you speak of, had grown to four since your departure." Mokar replied. Having documented their strange reproductive process, for my own knowledge, they were quickly terminated."

"I hope you are not too disappointed, Truck!" Greg joked.

"Aw, shut da front flap, will ya shorty?"

Truck responded, semi serious, or you're gonna go home with more den a bum leg." He finished with a big grin on his face.

"Did I not do the right thing, concerning the captives?" Mokar asked, alarm showing on his face.

"Pay them no heed, Mokar! Jim answered. They are just being brothers."

"I find it difficult, at times, to understand the relationship between earth siblings." Mokar said, shaking his bulbous head.

"Believe me, when I tell you this Mokar. Jim replied. I do too!"

A little later, camp was set up in the same open area they had used before. Their animals roamed the same mossy tract as on their previous visit. A small group of men accompanied Mokar to the "House of High Learning". There they regaled him with all that had transpired during their mission. Praise and appreciation was doled out to Froban and the Nevoan army. Mokar was also apprised of the fact, all his slain warriors were, ceremoniously, sent to their forbearers in the native tradition.

"Stay among us as long as you wish, my earth friends. Mokar said. Your leadership has avenged my fallen citizens. This will not be forgotten in the annuls of Nevoan history,"

"Your offer is appreciated, Mokar. Jim replied. But, many are anxious to return home. Meaning no disrespect to your hospitable offer, I must decline. We will depart when the first sun wakes our world."

"No offense is taken, my Earth friend! Mokar said. It is understandable."

Taking their leave, the small group made their way back to their temporary camp. When word had spread among the men they would be leaving at first sun, a joyous shout of approval echoed off the Nevoan walls. Sleep would have a hard time embracing anyone this night.

# CHAPTER 33

Amply fortified with fresh meat and fruits, given generously by the Nevoan people, camp was struck in quick fashion. Travois were attached to their beasts and the injured were settled comfortably in.

The three Earthmen, Bantor, Tonio and Roca stood among a group of Nevoans watching the native convoy flow out through the massive gates.

"Many years ago I witnessed this very scene. Mokar said. It was an overpowering sense of relief I had, as I watched you depart our settlement."

"The mental devastation, at the time, ran much deeper than the physical turmoil of our ruined existence."

"Hatred, for your kind, was prevalent in most minds. On this day however, every citizen here is compelled to offer their gratitude. Our gates will forever remain open to you."

"What we have accomplished would never have been possible without the assistance of your warriors, Mokar. Jim responded. Our gratitude is offered, also. May, our next meeting, be under less stressful circumstances."

Froban, who had been standing alongside of Mokar, held his arm out to Jim." I would offer my hand in eternal friendship, Earth friend. He said. Should you ever ask, your battles, will become my battles."

As Jim grasped the tong-like aperture in his Earthly hand, sealing the bond between two cultures, he nodded in compliance. "Like wise my friend."

Mounting their shaggy beasts, they followed the last of their comrades through the gates. Spurring them into a steady gallop they, soon, assumed their position at the head of the procession.

"When we get home, I'm going to make a suggestion to Leota. "Jim said. "I believe it is time we establish commerce between our cultures."

"After experiencing the efficient manner in which the Nevoan soldiers deported themselves, I don't believe there is a man among us who would object to that idea, Jim. Greg replied. We may not have been successful without their assistance. As for myself, I would love nothing more than to have access to their shops. Just imagine the inventions we could contrive!"

"Da only inventions I can think of dat could help us, at dis time, are da wagons we built. Truck joined in. If old Stinky and da gang was here ta pull em we'd get home a lot quicker."

He was referring to the four alien beasts they had rescued from Nevoan captivity shortly after winning the war with them, nine years earlier. With a lot of work they had managed to make them tractable enough to cart their injured comrades home by pulling two large wagons. The last of these alien beasts had died three years earlier.

"They sure would have made this part of our trip a lot easier." Jim agreed.

"You still miss that creature, don't you Truck?" Greg asked, with a mischievous smile on his face.

Jim noticed the expression. Here they go again! he said to himself.

"Course I do!" Truck answered. She was my friend!"

"I won't ask how you discovered it was a female." Greg instigated.

Looking at his younger brother, for a moment, Truck shook his head. "Dos animals helped us out a lot, so don't say nothing bad about dem." He warned.


Jim interrupted them. "We should have walked through the zoo while we were there, Truck. Maybe we overlooked an animal or two that could have helped us."

"I did! Yesterday! He replied. Da only animal dos bastards didn't kill was da "xarta". Dat sunnuva bitch is only good for one thing. Eating!"

"The two of you would have had, at least, one thing in common." Greg jabbed.

"Back off, a little, Greg!" Jim, intervened,trying to suppress the laughter ready to erupt.

Tonio, Roca and Bantor didn't hold back. All it took was one look at the expression on Truck's face and they let go.

"You think dat's funny, you primitive piss ants?" Truck bellowed, as he stared back at the native trio.

"Truck! Take it easy! Jim cut in. They were only joking."

Staring back at his brothers, he replied. "I must a been joking, too, Jim. I ain't killed no one yet. Have I?"

With that said, he reined in his mount, sharply to the left and retreated toward the rear of the column.

"What was all that about?" Jim asked no one in particular.

"He's been edgy all day long, Jim. I was simply, trying to cheer him up."

"You did one hell of a job, Greg! Jim replied sarcastically. Next time make sure you don't talk about the animals. He's a little touchy about that. Especially since the Lumas slaughtered all of them."

"It won't happen again, Jim!" Greg answered.

"The hell it won't!" Jim said with a half-smile on his face. Not until you get your next chance, that is."

"What is piss ant?" Bantor asked, from behind them.

The two earth men looked at each other and broke out laughing.

As the third "sister" sun was getting closer to losing her battle with the encroaching darkness, the final halt of the day was called near a wide stream. The hilly landscape, surrounding them, was treeless. The injured were settled in, mounts were hobbled nearby, grazing peacefully on the mossy terrain, and fires were lit. The little tiff, between Greg and Truck faded away like the countless others they had been involved with their entire lives. It was a given, whenever the two of them occupied the same space, their verbal wrestling was inevitable.

"Comrades! In five cycles of our "sister" suns we will, finally be home. Jim announced to the large group gathered around a blazing fire. By now everyone was more than aware of this. Never the less, their shouts of approval were sincere. The brave souls we left behind will, also, accompany us in spirit. He continued, as more men gathered around. Each and every one of you can take pride in the fact, our future generations will be born to a world free of strife. Their right to thrive in peace is attributed to the sacrifices we have made. My siblings and I consider it an honor to be counted among you."

Cheers of approval attacked the nocturnal stillness, reverberating through the darkness. After the joyous outburst had subsided into a cheerful drone, Bantor spoke.

"All are aware, also, the leadership provided by our Earth brothers, contributed greatly to our victory." Another roar of approval echoed from the crowd. There is not a man among us who would hesitate to follow the three of you into any battle.

But," he concluded with a big smile on his face, "Let us hope this was our last."

"Amen to dat, my brother!" Truck shouted. The night hadn't grown too much older, before every tired soldier retired. The pursuit of restful sleep was a war of another kind. Their hearts and minds, filled with the overwhelming desire to be with their families and to resume their normal lives battled the whole night through with the Gods of slumber.

# CHAPTER 34

Four, long, marches later found the native cavalry one day removed from their village. The vibrant atmosphere, inundating the hearts and minds of the weary travelers, almost reached the outer limits of constraint. Were it not for their injured comrades, trailing comfortably behind in the travois' and the cohesiveness developed among them during their life and death struggle, many would have bolted in a frenzied stampede to be with their families. Any delays, at this time, were viewed as personal deterrents, preventing them from assuming their normal lives. Patience had started depleting many miles back. The last sun of the day was close to surrendering her hold on the world. Camp would be established shortly. During the last few days, marches had become increasingly longer. Not one complaint evinced from the eager travelers. Even the injured warriors adapted themselves to the extended marches, in anticipation of their homecoming. Left, to their own devices, the entire army would have gladly, continued their trek throughout the night.

Holding up an arm and reining his shaggy mount to a stop, Jim took in the familiar surroundings. Low hills dotted the landscape, directly in front of them. A small brook reflecting the last of the sun's ebbing light, wove its way through them in a snake like fashion.

"We, camp here for the night." He announced as he dismounted.

Disgruntled murmurings rippled through the anxious ranks. To stop, now, this close to their homes was unsettling. After a short while their minor protests dwindled into compliance. Camp was quickly established as men busied themselves with tending to their beasts, starting fires and making their wounded comrades comfortable. Many, splashed into the shallow stream nearby. Even though hearts and minds rebelled against another delay, to their homeward surge, the distraction alleviated some of the anxiety, if only temporally. The obvious factor was, by this time tomorrow they would be with their loved ones. Clustered around the many fires, more for comradery than warmth, stories were being told to while away the time.

"When we were forced into digging out their caves in the side of that mountain, we came across a strange substance. Bantor was recalling some of the ordeals he and his men were subjected to, while held captives by the Lumas.

"The oppressive darkness was lighted, slightly, by torches. Quite often they would reflect off of patches of bright yellow rock as we hacked our way deeper into that depressing opening, with our stone tools. The floor of the cave became littered with large pieces of this yellow stone"

The three Earth men looked at each other knowingly.

"Bantor! Greg interrupted. Can you give us a further description of this yellow substance?"

He stared at the Earthman, for an instant, wondering why a rock was so important to him. "When first we started uncovering this strange rock, I did indeed examine it. Bantor continued. It was unlike any rock I have ever seen. When struck with a stone pick, it did not break. The stone tool managed, only, to make indentations. It, was soft enough, I could leave marks in it with my fingernails. What is it, about this yellow rock, that interests you?"

"Sounds to me like you struck gold." Truck joined in, excitedly. You're a rich man, Bantor!"

"It is one of the most precious and sought after metals on Earth. Greg intercepted. It is the foundation of our monetary system. The people or governments controlling it are exceedingly rich while the people controlled by it remain poor."

Observing the confused look on bantors face Jim tried to explain. "On this world a man places high value on family, friends and homes. That person is considered very fortunate. On my mother planet, Earth, there are people who feel this yellow rock is much more important,"

"But it is only a rock! Bantor replied, astounded. Nothing has more worth than family!"

Many of the men, clustered around voiced their agreement.

"Suffice it to say! Greg chimed in. It would have no meaningful use on this world."

"Whatta ya talkin about, shorty? Truck disagreed. We could make a lotta things with it.

"Truck, other than ornamental un-necessaries, it would serve no practical purpose."

Jim joined in. It's too soft to be made into weapons or tools."

"I guess your right, Jimbo!" Truck recanted. Dis ain't Earth! He said, with a big smile on his face. Dere ain't no banks here!"

"On the other hand, Jim, now that the war is over with, this may provide the hobby our big brother, here, is looking for." Greg said, with a mischievous grin on his face. Observing the look he had seen so many times in his life, Jim knew what was coming. Truck can spend his time gathering the gold making jewelry. He continued. Then he can open up a gift shop for all of the visitors to our village. He'll, eventually become the richest man on this planet."

Looking around at all the smiling men, who were an instant away from bursting into laughter, Truck sat, there, silently.

"How could we afford to purchase this jewelry if he has all the riches?" Bantor Joined in.

"We could, always, make trades!"Tonio took his shot.

The bemused look on Truck's face, grew in proportion, as he listened to this friendly gang of tormentors. Then he spoke. "You Bozos keep dis shit up and I ain't gonna tell ya about da surprise I was gonna make outta dat gold." He paused and looked around at all the smiling faces.

After a moment or so it was Roca who asked "what was it, you would have made for us Ta-rok?"

"I was thinking about getting enough a dat gold ta build a monument in da middle of our village. I think everyone woulda liked it too. A long sharp pole so you laughing jerks can take turns sitting on it." He concluded, breaking into laughter.

His infectious humor was soon joined by the entire group.

When the last ripples had subsided, Jim spoke. "On a more serious note, when we reach our homes, tomorrow, it will mark an end to this arduous adventure. But, it will also mark the beginning of an even greater one. Our futures! The lives of our comrades, willingly given to insure the peace and prosperity of our people, will always remain the foundation of all generations to come. Go now, my comrades! Get what sleep you can. The morning sun will signal the beginning of an emotional day."

As the cool night closed in on them, warm thoughts accompanied them to their furs.

# CHAPTER 35

Shortly before the first "sister" sun had announced the beginning of a new day, men were finishing their meager breakfast of dried meat, fruit and tea. Most were too excited to eat. Every mile of this last march would be a battle against their pent up anxieties.

All that remained was to harness the travois' to their animals and settle in their injured comrades. Personal gear had, already, been secured to their mounts.

"Let's hook up the cabooses and go home, my friends!" Jim ordered, in a voice loud enough for all to hear.

These long anticipated words fell upon their ears like a blazing fire over a forest of kindling. In short order, travois' were connected and the injured were fastened securely, upon them.

"I am amazed none of them deserted during the night." Greg commented, as the three brothers led the parade of anxious natives out of camp.

"Had we delayed any longer, I am sure we would have witnessed it." Jim replied.

"You're right about dat, Jimbo!" Truck added "I woulda been leading the stampede, too."

Jim turned and looked sadly, behind him. The long column of mounted warriors trailing them, was, unfortunately, shortened by the absence of their slain comrades.

Bantor, riding double, with Tonio directly behind the earth trio, noticed the sullen look on Jim's face.

"The losses we suffered were few, my Earth brother." He said. However, to the ones who loved them, the losses will be great. It is the misfortunate consequence of any war."

"You're right about that, my friend! Jim agreed. No matter where a war is being waged the winners and losers, alike, suffer from it."

"This was much different than most wars. Greg joined in. The very existence of an entire culture verged on the outcome."

"At least our people will survive ta mourn da losses of dere loved ones. Truck added. Dos furry bastards don't have dat option."

The injury-fri endly pace, they had begun with, was gradually increased. As more and more miles were left behind, the recognition of familiar terrain marking the proximity of their village, pushed the anxiety level to the utmost. If it were not for the men leading this parade a mad dash would have ensued miles ago.

"You don't suppose we should stop for a short rest, do you Truck?" Greg joked.

"Dat ain't even funny, Squirt! Truck responded. Dese guys are kinda in a hurry ta get home."

"And I suppose you're not?" Greg asked.

"I got patience, shorty! When we get dere we get dere."

"In that case, Truck ! Jim joined in. Maybe we should stop for a while, you know? Freshen up a little and make ourselves more presentable."

The shocked look on Truck's face, thinking his brother was serious about delay, almost caused him to rein his mount to a stop.

"We all want to look our best, when we enter our village. Don't we? Greg goaded.

Bantor, Tonio and Roca started laughing. The Earthmen are playing their word game again. Bantor thought.

"Dere ain't nothing wrong with da way I'm dressed, Jimbo. Truck shot back. If I get dere bare-assed, I don't care!"

"Oh, please! Greg interjected. People may be eating at that time!"

The second of the "sister" suns had just crested the horizon, as the caravan pushed forward through the low-lying hills dotting the mossy plain.

The audible excitement, exuding from the travel-weary warriors permeated their surroundings. With every mile they won toward their homes, it gradually increased like dams holding back a flood of emotions. They were at the cresting point. Yet, they remained disciplined, step after agonizing step. The climatic culmination, of this arduous quest, would soon be realized. Nature dictates, the closer one gets to his heart's desires the further away it seems. And, to these home sick heroes, their village remained A world of anticipation away.

The third "sister" sun, of the long day had recently taken her position in the clear sky, casting her thermal brilliance down upon the home-coming parade. The orderly formation they had maintained, during the entire venture was now abandoned. Eager riders jockeyed for position toward the front of the caravan, as close to the leaders as they could get without passing them by.

The three Earthmen now rode abreast of Roca, Tonio and his passenger Bantor. They had whiled away the monotony of what was, purportedly, the longest ride in their lives, by talking about family and friends. It distracted them enough, from their own desires, to keep them from spurring their mounts into a stampede for the village.

"The two large hills, you see in the distance, over-look our village. Bantor said, pointing over Tonio's shoulder. Our journey will, soon be at an end."

All, within earshot of Bantor, looked in the direction he had pointed. Anticipation mounted once again, but no one deserted.

"These last few miles will, undoubtedly, prove to be the most trying. Greg said. How are we going to keep our brother, here, from inciting a jail break?"

"Don't start, squirt! Truck warned, shaking his big fist. I got something here dat could incite a couple a black eyes."

The laughter, surrounding them, induced the two verbal warriors to join in. A little better than an hour later, found the caravan skirting the two large hills one half mile from their village.

# CHAPTER 36

Leota and Graci sat outside their hut, sipping tea. They had just built their night fire to ward off the coming darkness. Their evening meal completed, they took comfort from each other's company. For many, agonizing, weeks they had done their best, presenting a positive outlook to instill confidence in their native charges. The anguish, seeping from their troubled minds, grew more and more noticeable as the long days wore on. Their personal war with worry was becoming a losing battle.

"Graci! My mind is being pulled in so many directions, it is becoming difficult to concentrate. Leota said, looking sullenly at his mate. I fear, it may not be too much longer before all this turmoil causes me to make a bad decision."

"Leota! There is not one person in this entire village, who feels any differently. You cannot perform miracles to erase their anguish."

"But I must do something, Graci! I am their leader! Leota responded, with a dejected look on his face.

"Remain true to yourself, mate of my heart. Said Graci, with a big smile, on her face. Time will, soon, Sort out all of our problems."

"Time has just about consumed all of my patience, Graci. He replied. What is left?"

"There is always hope! We cannot stop believing. These sad times, we now experience, will become better."

"My heart is receptive, Graci. It is my mind that fights against it." He replied, with a vague stare in his eyes.

Rising to her feet, she walked over and gave Leota a kiss on his cheek.

"Come! she said. Let us take a walk through the village. We may find a distraction that will ease the burden from your mind."

Getting to his feet, he hugged her to him.

"That, we can do, my love!" he replied, as they started away.

As they approached the play area, in the center of the village, a youngster, maybe nine or ten years of age, came rushing up to them.

"The gate sentry has sent me to fine you, he said, slightly out of breath. People are approaching our village!"

Without a word of acknowledgement, Leota turned and started running toward the front gate, Graci trailing close behind him. His mind was bombarding him with questions. Was it the return of his people, Visitors from another village, friend or foe?

When he reached the front gate, he practically flew up the ladder leading to the catwalk above. People, standing nearby, were astonished by the agility exhibited by their old leader. When he approached the sentry, he took in the scene he had, long, anticipated. Men, mounted upon lurdas, made their way toward them from half a mile away.

"They have returned!" he said to himself.

"Open the gates, quickly!" he ordered. "Our warriors have returned!"

He turned and scrambled down the ladder. Graci awaited him at the bottom.

"They are home, my love!" he said, as he engulfed her in a warm embrace. Tears of relief poured from their eyes, as they clung to each other. The many weeks of pent-up emotion, keeping them all in a quandary concerning the welfare of their loved ones, erupted ecstatically from flowing eyes and gladdened hearts.

People were already, pouring through the gates, with hope in their hearts that they would find their loved ones counted among the returning army, as they rushed to meet them.

"Shall we join them, Graci?" Leota asked, looking blurrily through moist eyes into the even moister eyes of his mate.

"Oh, yes, Leota!" she replied, excitedly taking his hand in hers. An instant later, they were joining the happy exodus from their village.

"Dat is da prettiest sight I ever saw in my life." Truck said, as he watched the people erupting from the village and rushing toward them.

"Amen to that, my brother!" Greg agreed.

"Shall we join the, men?" Jim shouted.

He didn't have to say it twice. Almost on cue, every man spurred his tired beast into a fast gallop and raced across the mossy stretch to intercept the surging horde of family and friends.

# CHAPTER 37

After turning their mounts loose, in the paddock outside the front gate and assisting their injured comrades, the victorious warriors entered the village. Equal amounts of joyous celebrations and mournful lamentations, for the slain relatives, formed an imperfect opera as it assaulted the early evening. Two hours later they were sitting around the large space outside the tribal hut. Fires reflected off the faces of almost the entire village. A small group, consisting of Leota, Graci, Bantor, Cinda and the Earthmen and their mates, sat in the middle of the merry mob. They told of their exploits and fielded questions.

"Is it safe to assume, all of these murdering creatures no longer pose a threat?" Leota asked.

"I sent out many search parties, after the battle was over." Jim answered. "They discovered no sign of any living Luma."

The avid listeners hung on every word, as the tales unfolded. Jugs of "tova", the fermented fruit wine, were passed liberally through the crowd. Preparations for the big victory celebration were discussed. It would commence two nights from now.

"If it were not for our sturdy beasts, our journey into battle would have been much more difficult. Jim said. They performed, admirably, and brought us safely home."

"That is true Jim! Greg interjected. However! The poor beast, our large brother was riding, had a miserable time of it."

"Was it not one of the animals we slaughtered to provide for our victory celebration?" Bantor asked.

Truck stared at Bantor and his younger brother with a sheepish grin on his face. He remained silent as their laughter spread into the audience.

"We had no choice, but to put the poor beast out of its misery!" Jim answered

"Ya see what I had ta put up with on da entire trip? Truck replied. All da work I put into making dat meat nice and tender, for dos ingrates, and dis is da thanks I get." A big smile enveloped his face and he joined in on the laughter.

They talked long into the night. No one gave a thought as to how late it was becoming. Relief and thankfulness was etched, deeply, in the minds and hearts of all. The next day, Lifestyles would revert, once again, to the normal. All restrictions had been lifted, allowing them to pursue their pleasures, hunting, exploring, wondering through the beauty of their world, living.

# CHAPTER 38

The first "sister" sun was only an hour old. Making her way through the heavens, she warmed her world below. After many long weeks of anguish, serenity had returned to the village. Unburdened from the weight of worry, which had enslaved them for so long, the seeds of their complete lifestyles had been re-cultivated. They awakened now, to a day filled with the promise of adventure, excitement and accomplishment. No longer would their desires be put on hold.

The three Earthmen and their mates sat on log seats watching, as their children capered about in the play area. Greg stretched his injured leg out in front of him. The scar would always be a reminder of the hell he had gone through, for the rest of his life. But, it was healing nicely.

"How's it feeling today?" Jim inquired.

"It's a bit stiff, Jim, but the good news is the infection is long gone."

"Dat's da way I was feeling, all last night." Truck said with a big smile on his face, starring at his mate.

Mara blushed, suddenly, and averted her eyes from the others.

"It must run in the family!" Sanda replied smiling at Jim.

Their collective laughter was the first shared among them, since the onset of the "Luma" war. The six participants pursued it with total abandon. Since the stagnating cloud, that shrouded minds with doubts and fear, had been eliminated, people were free, once again, to rejoice in life. No matter which way you turned, in the large village, the enjoyment of existence was reflected.

"May we join you?" Bantor, accompanied by his mate, Cinda, broke in on their gaiety.

"By all means!" Greg replied. "Have a seat!"

"Your laughter caught our attention, as we were on our way to see Leota and Graci." Cinda said. "What was so funny?"

"Our earth mates were just discussing what a "hard" time they had sleeping last night."Lona answered, with a twinkle in her eye.

This re-kindled their previous laughing attack. Bantor and Cinda looked confusedly at each other

"I had no difficulty in that area, once Cinda was finished welcoming me home."

Bantor replied grinning sheepishly at his mate.

"Dat is exactly, what we been talking about." Truck put in.

Lights of acknowledgment flickered in Bantors and Cinda's minds as they burst out laughing. This time they were joined by the others

"It's great to be home! Isn't it gentlemen?" Greg asked, after a while. "What we share, at this very moment, makes all the hell we waded through worthwhile."

"We can only pray nothing like this will ever happen to us again." Jim replied.

"Two wars in less den nine years. Truck joined in. Dat's it for me! From dis moment on, nothing is ever going to bother me again!"

They sat there in silence, cherishing each other's company. The time, stolen from them because of this world-shaking ordeal, was forever lost to them. They would live their futures to the fullest, cherishing each day. After a short while Mara spoke. "In all the excitement of your home-coming Ta-rok I forgot to mention Gia has a boyfriend.

"What? Truck roared. She's too young for dat!"

Jim and Greg looked at each other, with knowing smiles on their faces. Maybe their large sibling did have more things to worry about.

# CHAPTER 39

The third "sister" sun had just taken up residence in the sky, spraying her warmth on the world below. Activity abounded in the large native village. Preparations for the "victory" feast had been completed. Anticipation ran rampant in the hearts and minds of every citizen. Stories will be told. Ceremonies, honoring their slain brethren, would be held. Mountains of succulent food and drink would be consumed.

But, most importantly, the cohesiveness of the village would be reestablished. Their right to existence had come at a high price. Many lives had been forfeited in the ordeal. The survivors would pay honor to their slain comrades by making each new day a celebration and more certain these martyred soles would never be forgotten.

Every citizen in the village took their place in the joyous crowd. The most seriously wounded veterans were carried to the celebration on stretchers. They were made comfortable toward the front of the boisterous gathering.

Seated at the place of honor, next to Leota and Graci, were the leaders of the victorious cavalry, the three earth men, Bantor, Tonio and Roca. Their mates sat by their sides.

Leota rose from his log seat and held his arms above his head, turning, slowly, from left to right, he scanned the entire mass of elated faces. In moments, the noise level softened to a happy murmuring.

"I welcome all of you, my people!" he began in a loud firm voice.

"The celebration we share, this night, is more than just an acknowledgement of our victory."

He paused, letting his words settle among them.

"It is a tribute to the men and women who were determined to do whatever was necessary to insure the continuance of our very culture. Their deprivations and sacrifices have won, for each and every one of you, your futures."

The roar of appreciation, erupting from the grateful horde, was so dynamic it nearly knocked the night into day.

When the exuberant elation dwindled down, a few decibels, he continued.

"Our dear comrades, who are no longer counted among us, relinquished their lives, willingly, for everyone here. They have afforded us the gift of pursuing long and fruitful lives. Remember, them, forever, in your hearts and minds."

Another, tumultuous, roar of acceptance reverberated from the on-lookers. Turning his back on the mob of merry-makers, Leota addressed the small group sitting behind him.

"Would anyone care to speak?" he asked.

"Father! I would speak!" Bantor replied. Leota nodded and they traded places.

"Forgive me, my people! I do not have my father's gift, when it comes to manipulating words. But, I will do my best!" he started. This elicited laughter from the large audience. Bantor turned and smiled at his father. It was returned in kind.

"I would let everyone here know there were three significant factors which contributed to our victory. While all fought valiantly, the decisive outcome was due to our Earth brethren."

Once again, the nocturnal ambiance was shattered by loud voices of acknowledgement.

The three brothers looked, sheepishly, at each other. The unexpected praise made them feel, slightly uncomfortable.

"Aside from sharing with us the weapons, of the world they came from, and their ability of employing animals to do their bidding, their leadership skills are unequaled," he continued. "During the most trying times, they were able to deflect some of the seriousness from the situation and put minds at ease. They saved my life and the lives of most of the men in my company."

He paused, again, for a moment, his eyes misting over. "I love them as the brothers I never had." He walked over to the three earth men and they rose to meet him. Then, they clustered together in one huge embrace of friendship.

"May I say a few words, Bantor?" Jim asked.

"Please, do!" the native replied. Turning to the massive gathering, Jim smiled.

"My siblings and I appreciate the praise. But I wish you to know a commander is only as efficient as the men he leads. Without their loyalty and ability to carry out orders, he is, but, one man. We are honored to have fought, side by side, with so many brave men. I hope we never have to do this again!" he said with a big smile on his face. "The only one who had trouble following orders was my brother, Truck. But, we're all used to that by now."

One look at Truck's face incited the audience into raucous laughter.

A short time later, after everyone had eaten their fill, people sat around in small groups. "Tova" flowed freely through the vast crowd. Already, many had become overwhelmed by its potency and returned to their huts to sleep it off.

Much later, the three Earth brothers, their mates, Bantor and Cinda were the last of the celebrators. They sat around the dwindling flames of the tribal fire, talking. The night had cooled off and the heavens twinkled back at them with a myriad of stars.

"Do you realize, nearly, ten years ago, we were enjoying a solitude, quite like this, in the wilds of our own world?" Greg said. "None of this was even remotely conceivable!"

Staring at her mate, Lona asked, "Do you suffer any regrets for the world you left behind, Gug?"

"I wouldn't, exactly, call them regrets, Lona," he replied. "There were people there who were very dear to me and important to my development. But they are long gone. The memories I have of them, however, will always remain a part of who I am!"

"I agree, Greg!" Jim joined in. People come from all walks in life. Some of them are good and some of them bad. But, the fondest memories always revolve around the ones who made the biggest impact in our lives."

"Since da old Indian died, dere ain't a thing on Earth, dat I miss," Truck added.

Jim noticed the mischievous grin on Greg's face. "Here we go, again!" he said to himself.

"Truck! Be honest!" Greg began. "Are you going to tell us you don't miss that herd of women you hung around with?"

Looking, questioningly, at Truck, Mara asked, "Earth women travel in herds?"

"The ones our brother knew did." Jim couldn't resist, bursting out in laughter.

"Dey was just friends, Mara!" Truck said, looking nervously at his mate. "Dey didn't mean nothing to me! Honest!"

"They must have been more than that, Truck!" Jim continued. "You even had names for them."

"Let me see, now. There was Betty Bovine, Annie Angus, Hilda Holstein and that bow-leggd buck-toothed one. I can't remember her name."

"Lola Longhorn!" Greg added as he and his brother erupted into a side-splitting burst of laughter.

"Don't listen ta dos two trouble makers!" Truck pleaded with Mara. "Dey was always making fun a my friends."

Winking at Jim, Mara decided to get in on this game with words.

"Where will Ta-rok be sleeping tonight?" she replied, repressing the laughter rolling inside her.

After a short while, the familiar stillness of the evening returned.

"My brothers! Do you realize how fortunate we are? Blessed, with wonderful families, good health and many friends. We have, indeed, acquired the best that two worlds could, possibly, offer!"

As they shared this appreciative moment, each one gave silent thanks. The battle they had won, would insure its continuance, not only for themselves, but for future generations.

"Should we call it a night and head for home?" Greg asked. "We have a lot of catching up to do tomorrow."

"And 'you' have a lot of catching up to do, tonight," Sanda said, looking, passionately into Jim's eyes.

"Amen ta dat, Sanda!" Truck seconded.

And, they all laughed, happily ever after.

# CHAPTER 40

On a faraway mountainside, two furry creatures looked upon their devastated settlement. All of the former residents were long dead. Stillness pervaded the macabre scene.

One of the two remaining creatures had been gone for some time, while giving life to the clone, standing at his slide. The death and destruction, amongst which they stood, didn't sadden either of them, in the least. Devoid of all emotion, they deemed this scene as an advantageous means of attaining their life's quest. To be the last survivor of their pod and sit with their predecessors at the final feast was the ultimate culmination of their furry lives. All else mattered little.

Lifting his axe, from the throng circling his waist, the furry creature swung it in a vicious arc at the neck of his clone.

The severed head rolled to a stop a few feet away. Dark, dead eyes stared back at him, as the body crumpled to the ground.

"I am the last!" he exalted in a loud voice, dropping his axe.

Racing to the base of the mountain, he began to climb. An hour later, he was standing on the summit. One hundred feet below him lay the remains of his entire culture. Stepping off the lofty escarpment, he plummeted to his death, into the waiting arms of the "one's before."

# BOOK THREE

## Resolve

# CHAPTER 1

The menacing tremors rippled over the wild landscape, flattening trees, leveling hills and redirecting the flow of many streams. Large tracts of mossy sod were swallowed by the gaping cracks left in its devastating wake. Animals panicked, rushing headlong into the yawning chasms. The very air vibrated in protest of this catastrophic intruder. The first sun of the alien planet had barely crested the horizon. Many of its occupants would not survive to welcome another tomorrow. All in its path would be sacrificed to its fury.

A large village, many miles away, had just begun to untangle itself from the night's embrace. Breakfast fires were being lit, water was scooped from the two wells and other morning chores were tended to, in the preparation of the new day.

Sitting in front of a hut, consisting of wood and thatch, a man and woman surrounded a small fire pit. As they sipped hot tea and made plans for the new day, their three children slept.

Sanda braided her long, blonde hair as she stared across the short space at her mate. Her dark, kind eyes sparkled in the early morning glow. Her honey bronze complexion radiated health. She was an exceptional example of the Kletta people, who were all dark of eyes and blonde as well.

Her mate, however, posed quite a contrast. Dark brown hair and light brown eyes, he was taller than most men in the village. He was not from her village. He was not even from her world. James Stonedeer (Jim) and his two siblings, Gary (Truck) and Greg were abducted from their home planet, Earth, many years before. Their physical and mental prowess made it possible to carve a happy existence, for themselves, on this alien planet. Much of their Earthly knowledge was prevalent throughout the village, making native life considerably more comfortable and fun. Their heroic involvement, in two separate wars, earned them love and respect from the entire village.

The "Nevoan" empire was responsible for employing the "Space" traders who brought the three Americans to this wild world. A bloody war had ensued eight years later. After their eventual defeat, the Nevoans became their allies in another war against a murderous faction known as the "Lumas". After the thorough erasure of these creatures from their world, Nevoan and native relations became more compatible through commerce and the exchange of knowledge, benefiting both cultures. Once again, peace reigned on this world for the last six years.

"Sanda! Could you please find me a length of sinew? Jim asked. I looked in the storage hut and couldn't find any."

"What, on this world, would you do without me?" She replied, smiling across at him.

"I can only think of one thing. Jim returned, with a mischievous glint in his eyes. But, it wouldn't be as exciting without you."

She stood and walked over to him. Giving him a kiss on his cheek, she made her way toward their storage hut.

Staring after her Jim thought to himself, once again, how fortunate he was. A beautiful, loving mate and three healthy children, living among people who cared and sharing a peaceful existence. On this world, such a man is considered rich. His two siblings agreed with him, wholeheartedly. It took two worlds to get it right. They would not change a thing, even if it were possible to do so. Memories of their Earth experiences were pushed further and further toward the back of their minds. Life on this new world occupied every waking moment, offering very little time for reminiscing. They were more than comfortable with this tradeoff in lifestyles.

The large village, in which they lived, consisted of approximately four thousand inhabitants. A wooden picket fence, ten feet high, completely encircled the large area, adding to its security. Laid out in a relatively oval formation, wooden huts were strung out along the entire perimeter, inside the wooden stockade. Two fresh water streams flowed through its middle, one on either side. Wells had been dug years early, providing pure water for their safe consumption. These were just two examples of the Earthmen's ingenuity. Gates were located to the north and south ends of the village. Catwalks had been constructed around the entire perimeter on top of the fence, for security purposes. Although they were no longer at war, sentries were posted upon it around the clock, to ensure their security.

In the central part of the village Earthly contraptions abounded for the enjoyment of all. Swings, slides and other American apparatus entertained young and old alike. A flagpole sat in the center. Fluttering from above was almost a perfect likeness of the Earthmen's red white and blue flag. It had been adopted as their village symbol. Wooden bicycles, carts and wagons littered this area.

Leota, the head man of the village, had given the three Americans a free reign to implement their Earth-born ideas. There existed not a soul in the village who hadn't made use of their devices.

Without a doubt, the most substantial contribution made by the Earth trio was their introduction of the bow and arrow. Up until that time, hunting was done with spears, knives or hurled stones. This new weapon made it easier and much safer for everyone to provide sustenance for their families. In their two wars with the Nevoans and Lumas it proved to be the deciding factor in their victories.

At first, the villagers were skeptical and reluctant to try some of their new concepts. But, when their three adoptees attempted to domesticate the ferocious Lurda and succeeded, all future inventions were unanimously accepted. The Lurda had been hunted for generations, providing them with meat and hides. Standing six feet high at its shoulder and weighing more than fifteen hundred pounds this animal was second, only, to the murderous "Kazor" in its ferocious, and unpredictable nature. Hunting parties, throughout history, would usually return minus a few hunters. The shaggy, muscular beast sped across the mossy terrain on four thick legs. Its flat, elongated head sporting one large eye ended with a horn that could reach eighteen inches in length. The animal used it to tear up the mossy turf, before mulching it up with its wide mouth. The large molars, quickly, ground up its meal. When hunted, the long horn became a lethal weapon. Many hunters met their fate, impaled upon it. Its tenacious penchant, for survival, made it extremely hard to kill.

The three Earthmen had started their experiment by capturing the young bovines, shortly after they were weaned. Along with a small group of selected men, they slowly accustomed the beasts to being around people. Their horns were removed to ensure safety. After a long while, as the herd grew in numbers, they became almost as tractable as the herds of cattle on their home planet Earth.

It wasn't long after that, their next experiment came to light: Training the shaggy bovines to accept a rider. The entire village was in agreement, The three Earthmen were foolhardy for risking their lives in such a dangerous and, to them, unnecessary endeavor.

After many painful and ungraceful landings in the thick sod turf, they decided to lead the animals into the middle of a small stream and mounting them there. The water counteracted some of the beast's power and tired them. It wasn't long before they had a stable of complaint Lurdas. Now, they had over two thousand available "rides". Hunting was far less dangerous and travel was more comfortable. Exploratory parties ranged far and wide on the backs of these animals, seeking out other villages which had been isolated to them, during the period of Nevoan domination.

The beasts were also trained to pull large wagons; hauling wood and other supplies needed in the village. It also provided a comfortable means of travel for the elderly, children and the infirmed. Needless to say, anything conceived by the three Americans from that day on was welcomed by the entire village.

Truck's invention of a meat grinder made life more enjoyable, especially for the toddlers and the elderly. Mothers could feed their youngsters meat without fear of them choking. The senior citizens of the village, minus some or all of their teeth, gave silent thanks to the big man with every mouthful of meat they gummed.

As the three Americans adapted themselves to this alien lifestyle, so too, the natives adapted and accepted their Earth-born concepts. Everyone benefited and there was never a shortage of eager volunteers to implement these new ideas.

His musings were interrupted, as Sanda approached him and laid a bundle of cord at his feet.

"Will this be sufficient?" She asked.

"It will, indeed, my love. Thank you."

"How many weapons does one man need?" She asked, as she seated herself by the fire pit, once again.

"I really can't answer that question, Sanda. He replied. I guess when a man stops making them he has convinced himself he is too old to use them."

"In that case, keep making them forever." She replied, with a big smile on her face.

Staring back at his beautiful mate, he returned her smiled.

"This particular bow is for Bomar. Jim continued. He is old enough and responsible enough to merit a powerful weapon. I want to surprise him!"

"I am certain, he will be. Sanda returned. He has been awaiting this day for a long time, now."

As the new day continued, more and more people were out and about. An atmosphere of friendly chatter surrounded them.

"Good morning, Jimbo, sanda! Truck said, as he joined them. What's da plan for today?"

At six inches above six feet tall and weighing two hundred and forty pounds, he carried himself with the ease of someone much smaller. His unique way of talking was not by choice. A near fatal head wound sustained in the Vietnam war, on their home planet Earth, was the author.

As big and strong as he was, his real strength lay in his compassion for people and animals, especially the underdog. He acquired the nick name "Truck" as a high school football player. His powerful runs over opposing linemen and anyone else in his way made it the appropriate handle. Not very many people who knew him called him by his christened name, "Gary".

"And a good morning to you, also, Truck. Jim returned. What brings you out so early on this gorgeous day?"

Before he could answer, Sanda held a hot cup of tea out to him. Good morning, Ta-rok. She greeted. (All of the natives had difficulty pronouncing the "T" and "R" in their language. Especially, when they ran together. Thus, "Truck" became "Ta- rok".) Is Mara up and about, also?"

"She went up to da community hut about an hour ago with "Lona". Dey was both carrying bundles of fur and didn't even say goodbye."

"I think I will join them. She said. See you two men later!" With that said, she left.

Truck shook his head, as he sat down on a log across from Jim. "I think dos women are up to something, Jimbo."

"What makes you say that, my brother?" Jim replied.

"Da three of dem were at my hut last night, talking. Whenever I came near dem dey would hush up."

"I gave up on trying to figure out how a woman thinks, while we were still on Earth, Truck. The women of this world are a whole new breed."

"Ya. I know dat. Truck countered. But, da last time dey acted weird like dis we became fathers. Alarm, suddenly, flared in his eyes. Ya don't suppose we done it again, do ya?"

"Why are you asking me, Truck? I didn't have anything to do with Mara's pregnancy the first time. Jim said with a big smile on his face. Why don't you just ask her?"

"I hope ta God ya didn't!" Truck replied, with a big smile on his face, which caused them both to break out laughing.

After a while, Truck said, "dat's a nice bow yer makin, Jimbo. You must have about fifty of dem, already. Any special reason for dis one?"

"It's for Bomar. I think he's ready for it!"

"I made one for Salba last year. Truck added. Dey sure grow up fast, don't dey?

"You're right about that, Truck! It must be something about growing up in the wild. People mature much faster here than back on Earth. Of course, the three of us were exceptions to that rule. Fortunately for us, Grandfather Joseph gave us the guidance we needed to make our transition into adulthood much easier."

"I know what ya mean, Jimbo! After mom and dad died and we was put in dat orphan's home, we had no choice!"

John and Martha Stonedeer were killed in an automobile accident, when the three boys were quite young. They were, adopted by their grandfather, Joseph, a full-blooded Sioux Indian. He taught them how to survive any circumstances Earth could throw at them. Under his stern, but, loving tutelage they became quite skilled in hunting, tracking, fishing, surviving. Those were the happiest days of their young lives.

"I really miss dat old Indian! Truck said. I know he was a big part of what I am, today. I think he can still see and hear us from dat "High Hunting Ground" he's at."

"I couldn't agree more, Truck! We owe a lot to that man. I know he is proud of whom we've become."

"Good morning, Jim! Greg called out, as he joined the two men around the fire. I see you are still not too particular as to whom you entertain at your hearth."

He was the youngest of the Earth trio. Standing a tad under six feet tall, his slender build carried one hundred seventy pounds of hardened muscle. His light brown hair and blue eyes made quite a contrast to his brothers.

"Morning, Greg!" Jim greeted.

"Well, look what da cat dragged in. Truck added. Mornin shrimp!"

Greg and Truck had an, age old, game they played, stemming from childhood. Their frequent, verbal jousting actually made those around them convinced they were the worst of enemies. In reality, they would die for one another.

"What got ya up dis early, squirt? Your old lady kick ya outa bed?"

"No, you big ape! But yours did." Greg shot back.

Jim burst out laughing, when he saw the look on Truck's face.

"Dat ain't funny, Jim! Truck replied. Then he, too, started laughing.

Ah, maybe it was a little bit." He allowed.

In a more serious tone, Greg said; I would appreciate your opinion of my latest invention. He reached into a pouch at his side and withdrew a piece of tubular-shaped wood. When he pulled on the ends it expanded three times its original length, in telescopic fashion.

"What have we here?" Jim inquired.

"I've been experimenting with the development of a telescope." Greg answered, handing it to Jim. The hardest part was the construction of the lenses."

Jim put the wooden tube up to his eye and moved it in and out.

"This is fantastic! He said after a moment. By moving it in or out you can adjust it to suit your own vision. Check this out, Truck!" He said, handing it to the big guy.

Truck looked through the tube and adjusted it to his vision. "Chalk another one up for da squirt! He's done it, again!"

In the past, Greg had been instrumental in the development of many inventions. He had a knack for figuring things out.

"Like I said, the biggest challenge I had was the lenses. After heating many combinations of sands, from various locales, I almost, gave up on it. Then, one day, I discovered a substance resembling the mica we find on Earth. I crushed it and added it to the sand and it worked. I nicked out concave depressions in a slab of stone and used it for a mold. "It took a little doing. But, I made it work."

"You sure did, little brother! This will be a big help in hunting and exploring. Jim replied.

As they sat there, passing the new invention back and forth, sighting in on different objects around the village, a strange vibration emanated from the ground they sat on.

"What da hell is dat?" Truck asked, as they rose to their feet.

"I believe we are experiencing another earthquake, gentlemen." Greg said.

Over the past two years the village had been shaken five times by seismic tremors. None, to this date had been too severe, causing only minor damage. But, each one seemed to last longer than the previous one. Because it was becoming such a frequent occurrence, no one had been too concerned.

But, this one was different. The tremors grew in the next few minutes. In the past, it would have abated by now.

"Go! See to your families!" Jim shouted. The panic in his voice sent his brothers away from his hearth in a flash. Racing into his hut, he roused his three children from a deep sleep and herded them toward the south gate of the village. "Go into the hills! He directed. I'll find your mother!"

The village air was filled with a chorus of paniced voices. People were rushing in all directions. Children were crying. Others were screaming.

The vibrations, underfoot, were increasing to the point where walking was becoming difficult. People were struggling to stay on their feet. Some were crawling about on all fours. Loud cracking noises, in the near distance, overwhelmed the loud mayhem of the paniced natives.

Jim stumbled through the village toward the community meeting place and found it abandoned. The entire population was making its way toward the gate.

"Sanda! He yelled over and over again until his voice was reduced to almost a whisper. Hoping, with all his heart, she had joined the wild stampede toward the gate. He made his way in that direction.

The ominous cracking sound rose in a shuddering crescendo. Homes were collapsing all around him. A wide chasm was snaking its way through the village, swallowing everything in its path. The air was so thick with dust, it was becoming difficult to breath.

More screams filled his ears, as he approached the gates leading toward the hills above his village. Just as he was about to pass through a part of the stockade collapsed and fell on him.

The dust stopped filling his lungs. The loud pandemonium, suddenly, went silent. Everything went still and black.

# CHAPTER 2

The first of the "Sister" suns sprayed her solar splendor down upon a scene of abject horror. Where once a village had stood, only half remained. As the dust slowly settled on the ruins, hundreds of natives made their way down from near by hills. Only to discover their worldly possessions and some of their loved ones no longer existed.

The wide chasm, caused by the quake, engulfed over half of their village. Closing over it, again, it sealed the unfortunate in a gargantuan tomb. The string of huts, lining the left side of the village, no longer existed. Fortunately, not all of them had been occupied at the time. The huts on the right side of the village sustained minor damage. A large portion of their Lurda herd was annihilated.

Greg and truck, accompanied by their families, were among the first to reenter the scene of devastation. Sanda had found her children and trailed a little behind them.

As more and more villagers returned, The sounds of mournful cries increased in volume. The owners, whose huts had been thoroughly demolished, had nothing left to recover but their composure. The descendants, of those who knew for certain their loved ones still occupied the entombed huts, added a loud lamenting chorus to the somber symphony.

At this end of the village, the meeting center was left unscathed by the disaster. The storage huts, containing their surplus store of meat and vegetables, were also undamaged.

Truck and Greg bade their families to stay in this area, while they organized search parties. As they moved on their way, Sanda rushed up to them in a panic.

"Gem" is not among us!" She cried.

Greg gathered her in a comforting embrace.

"Don't worry Sanda! We will find him! Stay here and help watch over the children."

Walking alongside the area of the village which had almost completely vanished, they came upon Bantor and his family. They were huddled together, crying on each others shoulders. Bantor, the son of Leota the village leader, wept the hardest.

The two Americans joined them. Not a word was spoken for a few, long, moments.

"My father and mother were in their hut, when this curse came upon us. Bantor broke the silence, tears flowing freely from his eyes. I had no chance to warn them. I had to see my own family to safety."

As another wave of sorrow gushed from his aching heart, Greg put an arm around his shoulders.

"Be strong for them, Bantor! He said. They would want that!"

Pushing himself, brusquely, away from Greg, he responded. "For what? There is nothing left!"

"You are alive! And so is your family." Isn't that enough?" Greg countered.

"You do not know our ways, Earth man! Tend to your own affairs and leave me to mine!"

"Ya better cast your self pity in a different direction, mister! Truck jumped in. Your da leader of dese people, now, and dey need your help. So ya better get your damned ducks in da huddle. We feel your pain, but, life has ta go on. Come on, Greg! Let's go help someone!"

With that, they left Bantor. All he could do was stare at their backs, as they made their way through the mourning mob.

A short while later, Greg, Truck and about twenty other men were busy digging through collapsed structures, searching for survivors. So far they had discovered six with minor injuries. Unfortunately, at the same time, they had uncovered the bodies of eight elderly people and three children. Along with some of the surviving relatives, the eleven unfortunates were carried outside the perimeters of the village stockade and placed on piles of branches. When the gruesome ordeal was over, hunting for the missing, a massive funeral would be held. Their huts, as well as that of their brother Jims, were situated on the side of the village suffering the least amount of damage. All of these huts were, also, checked. No other casualties were found among them.

"After discovering Sanda was not at the meeting place, our brother must have made his way toward the gate. Greg said. Let's search in that direction, Truck."

"I agree! Truck replied, anxiously. He's gotta be somewhere between here and dere."

"If anything has happened to him, Truck, we had better start being a little nicer to each other. Greg said, in a tone lighter than he really felt.

"Don't start talking like dat, shorty! We'll find him!"

As they finished covering the distance to the gate, they were joined by Bantor.

"I would have a moment of your time, if I could. Earth brothers."

They stopped and turned as Bantor closed the gap.

"I have allowed your words to travel above my heart and into my mind. He started. His eyes were still red from his somber ordeal. I do realize Earth people mourn as well. You two and your sibling were deprived of your parents for a much longer time than myself. I did not mean to offend you, with my words, when last we met. They came from my mouth, not my heart, because my heart had been wounded. I will lead these people, as my father would have wished.

I would, also, ask you to forgive me for discounting your feelings when you extended them to me and my family."

Truck grabbed him up in a crushing bear hug. "My brother, you are forgiven! We will continue to help you like we did your father."

"Amen ta dat, Truck!" Greg added.

When they had apprised Bantor about the disappearance of their brother, he insisted on joining them in their search.

A short time later, they reached the fallen gates.

"If he had traveled beyond this point, we would be aware of it by now." Greg surmised.

"I guess we'll just have ta retrace our steps." Truck said. Where in da hell did he go?"

"I think he went right over there!" Bantor said, pointing at the fallen gate.

It took them only seconds to detect the sandaled foot jutting out from beneath the fallen structure.

They rushed over to it in a flash. Truck squatted down and put both hands under one of the thick logs that made up the gate, as Bantor joined him.

"Truck! Let me get more men!" Greg pleaded.

"No time! Truck returned. When I take da weight off a him, you two, pull him out!"

Tensing every fiber in his body, he started. Veins bulging, grunting out his frustration, he cried out. "Come on, ya sonuva bitch!"

The heavy gate moved up an inch, then two. Greg and Bantor grabbed Jim's leg and pulled him free.

"We got him, Truck! Greg yelled in relief. You can drop it now!"

Instantly, the big man let the gate fall back onto the turf. He fell, exhausted, beside it.

"How's he doing?" He shouted, gasping for breath.

Jim's body was tattooed with scratches and black and blue blotches.

Greg, immediately, checked for a pulse.

"He's alive! But, his pulse is weak. His breath is a tad shallow, also. He answered.

Bending over his brother, Greg pinched Jim's nostrils closed and tilted his head back.

He opened his brother's mouth and put his over it. Breathing three quick breaths into his brother, he rechecked the pulse and was about to repeat the process when Jim's eyes fluttered open. He coughed and sputtered for an instant then took a deep breath.

"What's going on?" He asked, dazedly, trying to sit up.

"Take it easy, big brother! Truck said. Da little guy, here, was just given ya a little lip service. Enjoy it while ya can!" He finished, laughing in relief.

Noticing Bantor for the first time, he said; See how these two take advantage of their old brother when he's on his back?"

"Don't worry, Jim! Greg added. The engagement is over!"

They all laughed, then, and helped him into a sitting position.

"Oh, dear God! He said, when he noticed the devastation around him.

"My family!" He shouted, trying to regain his feet.

"Relax, Jim! Greg said. They're all fine. They're over in the meeting area. We'll take you over there, in a minute or two. Just rest!"

When we are positive there are no more casualties or departed to honor, we will all join you there. Bantor said. With the death of my mother and father, I must decide what is to be done with our futures."

"Leota? Graci? Oh, no! Jim cried out. Bantor, my brother. I am so sorry."

"Your concern is appreciated, Earth friend. If I receive half the support the three of you rendered my father, the future will heal all wounds and lessen the ache of my loss."

Nods of agreement and smiles all around confirmed it.

"Help me up you guys! I want to see my family." Once on his feet, he was steadied by his two brothers. Fortunately, the most serious injuries he had sustained were deep tissue bruises and a myriad of minor scratches. The spongy turf had absorbed most of the impact.

As they approached the village meeting area, Sanda spotted them and rushed into his arms. Wincing, as she threw her arms around him, caused her to withdraw. But, he held her tight.

"Don't worry, mate of my heart, nothing ever hurt so good." He said, with a big smile on his face.

The confused expression on her face only made the battered Earth man smile even more broadly. A short time later, every living villager was gathered at the meeting place.

The three Earth men and their mates sat in a tight circle next to Bantor and his mate, Cinda.

It was almost uncanny how subdued this huge gathering was. But, on the other hand, death does not leave an individual much to celebrate.

Standing and walking toward the front of the gathering, Bantor raised both arms above his head.

When the noise level dropped and he had their undivided attention, he began.

"As all of you are aware of, by now, Graci and Leota have been counted among the departed unfortunates, on this day. My first words to you, as your new leader, are to offer my heart-felt condolences for your losses. And, I assure you everyone will receive the assistance of the entire village in repairing your futures."

Pausing, he took a moment to look out upon the sea of sadness, wishing for some way to take their pain away.

"I loved my father and mother for making me the person that I am. He continued.

"But, I am not my father! I am only Bantor. That man, who lies buried with my mother beneath our village, led his people through the dictates of his heart and mind. I believe he was the equal or better of any leader who walked this world. If I am to be compared with him, I would loose that distinction for many years to come. Only when I have proven myself, as worthy of leading my people, would I share that honor. All I can say to you now, my people, is to give you my solemn promise to lead with an open mind and a just heart. I know I will make mistakes, along the way, but, have faith in me. We all have to begin somewhere. I will start this sad evening."

The head of a Lurda is useless unless it has the support and desire of its legs and heart. You, my people, are those necessary parts!"

A cheer of agreement rose from the crowd. It was the first positive act evinced from them for quite some time.

He continued, once again, after the crowd had quieted.

"Vegetables and meat will be doled out to any needy individual. I am sure we have a few of them among us tonight." He said with a big smile on his handsome face.

This prompted a trickle of laughter from the audience. It, also, told them their leader believed nothing would be taken so seriously it would prevent them from rising from the ashes of despair.

"The next issue I wish to discuss, with you, is the idea of moving our village to a safer location."

This prompted a little consternation among the gathered people. They started talking all at once, one person trying to out shout another.

Holding his arms up, Bantor regained their attention. Waiting a few moments for the noise level to drop a few decibels, he continued.

"Only an hour ago, one of our Earth brethren brought a serious matter to my attention. I will let him explain it to you." Bantor traded places with Greg, who made his way to the front of the assembly.

"Everyone is aware, in the near past, we have experienced many of these quakes. Obviously, none with the intensity displayed this day. We had these quakes on my former world, Earth, quite frequently. Most seismologists contend that a quake will follow the same fault lines, repeatedly, each time getting stronger."

"What is a seismo- whatever? A voice from the crowd, queried.

"Similar to a shaman who specializes in tracking and predicting these quakes." Greg answered.

"So, in reality, if we rebuild our village on its present site, or even a short distance from here, there is a good possibility we may suffer the same consequences as we did this day, on a frequent basis. Or we may not experience another for years. I, for one, do not wish to gamble the safety of my family. I am sure, many would agree."

Turning toward Bantor, he motioned he was finished and took his seat next to Lona once again.

"Very well said, Gug! The parts I could understand, that is." Lona replied. (The natives had difficulty pronouncing "G" and "R" when they were together. Thus, "Greg became "Gug".)

"I will explain it all to you another time, my dear! If that is what you wish! He answered.

Bantor stepped back in front of the crowd.

"On one of our exploratory treks, a few years ago, we completed the longest journey any of us had ever taken. He began. Thirty complete cycles of our "Sister" suns found us in a land far to the south. It was so rich in fruit, vegetables and game, a man did not have to travel far to collect it. Lurdas and other large non-predatory creatures practically walked right up to us. I've spoken of this to Sanda and a few others, in the past. Because the journey, itself, is so long and somewhat dangerous, I stored it in the back of my mind. In light of this devastating occurrence, which has taken so many, it is at the forefront of my mind, once again.

For the safety of my people, I would ask this proposal be considered."

A voice from the crowd piped up. "Today I lost my wife and three of my children. If what the Earthman said is true, I may lose the rest of my family the next time it occurs. I would move my family to this far land you have mentioned."

Another voice escaped the noisy crowd.

"How are we to be sure this strange land is far enough away from the shaking monster?"

"Earth brother! Would you care to answer that?" Bantor gestured to Greg.

The Earthman rose and made his way forward.

"Thirty days of traveling, averaging approximately twenty-five miles a day, would put us safely seven-hundred and fifty miles away from this danger." He finished and returned to his seat.

"My people! We all suffer this day. Some, more than others. Bantor said. You now have at least one option to think about, which could prevent further danger and suffering to all of us. Tomorrow we will use the voting stones. White stone for "yes", black stone for "no".

"We will now proceed to the funeral byres outside the south gate. There we will pay our last respects to our departed loved ones, as they make their final journeys to be with our ancestors."

These last words were spoken, haltingly, by the young leader, as they passed from his heart to the solemn tear drops flowing down his cheeks.

Cinda was at his side, hugging him to her. "Mourn them well, my mate! She said to him. I will help you bear the burden of this loss."

He hugged her back in acknowledgement.

When they arrived, outside the village, a huge mound of branches rose in front of them. Laid, reverently, over the top were the bodies of the eight elderly villagers and the three children. Another one-hundred and seventy-three residents were unaccounted for. They all had dwelt in huts swallowed by the devastating cataclysm, entombing them forever.

The morbid thought of rebuilding their village upon the eternal resting places of their departed loved ones revolted the minds of even the most stoic residents.

Taking a lit torch from a youngster, nearby, Bantor raised it above his head. The murmuring, emanating from the long procession, dwindled to a respectful silence.

"Let the souls of these eleven individuals guide our other missing brethren to the abodes of their beloved ancestors. Bantor began. "We honor every one of them for the contributions they had made while among us. Our lives became much more fulfilled because of their endeavors. Remember them in your hearts, always, and give individual thanks for their leadership, love and forgiving ways. We are the reflections of their guidance. We can honor them by using the tools they have given us."

Placing the lit torch on the wood pile, Bantor took a few steps backward.

"Travel a safe and happy path, my brethren!" He said, as fresh tears ran from his eyes.

Shortly before the last "Sister" sun was defeated by the night's army of darkness, people were settling in. The doors of existing huts were opened to accommodate the homeless unfortunates.

Travel tents were obtained from storage and, soon, everyone shared a warm place in which to spend the cool night. The natives were already more united. This devastating tragedy would only make them stronger.

# CHAPTER 3

As the first "Sister" sun peeked her brilliant head over the horizon, a group of twenty five men, mounted on Lurdas, ranged over the mossy terrain. Led by the Earth trio, they searched over the rolling hills for their "Lurda" herd. Scattered by the invasive quake, which shattered their village, the paniced beasts had bolted in all directions. Three other herding parties, led by Bantor, Tonio and Roca, also, joined in the search.

Their animals' fear-driven stampede exhausted them and brought them to a halt within five miles of the village. This made the round-up much easier for the "cowboys". In a short while they had the wayward bovines herded together and were coaxing them back to their familiar grazing grounds just outside the wounded village.

"I estimate we lost, approximately, five hundred head. Greg said, as they urged the last of the surviving beasts together. Along with his two brothers he now rode alongside Bantor, Tonio and Roca.

"Dere's a few wild ones mixed in with our animals. Truck said. Whatta we gonna do about dat?"

"After the decision has been made, whether we leave this area for a new site or not, we'll kill them off for their meat. Jim answered. Many of the meat caches have been depleted. We'll need to replenish".

Ten minutes later, they were taking the reins off their mounts and setting them free inside the large corral with the rest of the delinquent bovines. They, then, joined the stream of villagers headed for the community meeting area.

Their mates, Sanda, Mara and Lona awaited them at the head of the main fire pit. They were awarded this prestigious position by Leota. Their earthly input and counseling in warfare and other matters, concerning the welfare of the village gained them the trust of everyone. Their other-world concepts proved, more than once, to be the deciding factors in dire situations.

As they sat next to their women, cups of hot tea were pressed into their hands.

"Were you able to gather all of our lost animals?" Sanda asked.

"Not all of them, my dear! Jim answered. Greg thinks we may have lost around a hundred or so."

"Oh my! Lona joined in. That many?"

"It could have been a whole lot worse! Greg added. If the quake had traveled through the other side of the village, we may have lost the entire herd."

"At least we didn't lose very many of da riders. Truck joined in. We can always get more of da meat animals."

"Good morning!" Bantor greeted, as he joined them. Cinda was at his side. In his arms he carried the large, clay, "voting" jug. Placing it on a small stand, off to their left, they took a seat around the cold fire pit.

The "voting" jug was used to catch their votes. Each villager, in favor of a proposal, would deposit a white stone in it. If their vote was against the proposal, they would deposit a black stone. Whichever way they voted was not revealed to anyone else. The stone of choice, black or white, was concealed in the voter's hand. He would, then, put his hand through the slot, in the leather lid, and deposit his vote.

"Good morning to da two of ya!" Truck returned for them all.

As the last of the villagers straggled in, joining the vast crowd, the excited murmuring grew louder. This would be the hardest decision any of them would ever have to make. To abandon the familiar confines they had accustomed themselves to, their entire lives, and uproot their lifestyles in pursuit of a land far away, offering them little more than chance. Their lives were in jeopardy if they remained. Would they be in jeopardy if they sought this mysterious land?

"Perhaps, I should have postponed this issue until a later date. Bantor said. The emotional devastation, suffered by my people, might cloud their judgment."

"That probability always rears its head, whenever any major changes are being discussed. Greg replied. However, their anguish is fresh, at present. If no changes are made, they will become complacent. They will start rebuilding the village and continue with their lives. The biggest quandary we face today is do we stay here and heal our wounds, hoping and praying it will not be repeated. Or, do we venture a relocation into an unknown area?"

"Even then, Greg, we are not guaranteed complete safety, in this new land." Jim interjected.

"Life is full a risks! Truck joined in. If ya think da grass is gonna be greener on da other side of da mountain, den, ya gotta get off yer ass and try ta get dere. I ain't gonna let dis happen ta me again! At dis very minute, all we got left ta lose is our lives. And dere too damned valuable ta risk."

Silence reigned, for a few brief minutes, as they digested the logic in the big man's words.

"I have to agree with my mate! Mara said. I do not wish to dwell in an area that would put my children's lives in jeopardy."

Bantor stared at the others, in their small group. The weight of this recent, leadership role pressed heavily upon him. Fear and indecisiveness bombarded his mind. Anguish filled his heart.

"I can not disagree with what you have said, Ta-rok. Which ever way the balloting favors, to stay or relocate, as their leader I must cast the final vote. My position does not allow me the luxury of personal choice. I must base my decisions on the welfare of the entire village.

"Bantor! Jim responded. You and your exploration party are the only ones to have seen this new land. If you feel, in your heart, it is worthy of an attempt, trust in your decision!"

"Amen ta dat! Truck chimed in. Home is where da heart is!"

"Which ever way you decide, my brother, you can rely on us for our total support." Greg added.

"It is easy to see why my father valued your counsel! Bantor replied. It is even more appreciated at times such as this."

Nodding at the small group, he rose from his seat and made his way toward the front of the anxious villagers. Raising his arms above his head, he awaited their silence.

"Today, my people, we begin a new page in the chronicles of our village history. He began. Future generations may hear the story of how their ancestors healed their wounds and rebuilt their shattered village upon the scarred site where a natural disaster had reaped its havoc, only to return in all of its fury years later."

Bantor paused, looking into the sullen eyes of his people.

"Then, again, they may hear the story of how those brave survivors collected the remnants of their possessions and made a journey to a land far away, a land abundant in food, water and hope."

"I, Bantor, along with many among you, have seen this land. It would take us many marches to reach this area. But, together, we can rebuild our lives and become strong once again. For the sake of our children and, indeed, the sake of our futures, this endeavor would be worth considering. We can not live with a veil of death hovering around us. Its next visit could mean our complete destruction."

"What of our memories and all we have shared, in this village? An older citizen piped up. Would it not be a disrespect to our deceased loved ones were we to abandon them?"

"Our departed loved ones will travel with us, in our hearts!" Another voice chimed in.

As agreement and disagreement clashed, through out the boisterous crowd, Jim approached Bantor and said something to him.

Raising his arms above his head, he got their Attention.

"One of our Earth brethren wishes to speak."

As the volume of voices lessened, Jim began.

"If any one of us was told, for certain, we had only one month to live what use would we make of that time? Perhaps, some would mope about their last days, listlessly, awaiting their fate. Yet, others might spend that time preparing for their closure and giving their legacy a memorable boost."

"What has this to do with our decision to leave or not?" A voice from the crowd sang out.

"Simply this, my friend. Jim replied. All of us have received many warnings in the near past. We choose to ignore them, picking up the pieces time and time again. Soon, there will be no one left to pick up those pieces. We, now, have an option to consider. I choose not to resign myself to this Imposing fate. I would strive, with every fiber of my being, to help insure happy lives for my family and friends. Because it is not too late, I embrace this opportunity. We owe it to ourselves and to the future generations of this village to take this journey.

Turning away from the crowd, he returned to his seat.

As the large gathering absorbed the Earthman's words, Bantor took his place in front of them. "At this time, we will begin casting our votes. He announced. Do so with an open mind and hope in your heart."

A short while later, as the last of the people deposited their votes and made their way back to their abodes or temporary shelters, an eerie pall blanketed the wounded settlement.

The three Earthmen, Bantor and their mates occupied seats around the fire pit. Moments before, a fire had been started to ward off the encroaching darknes.

"The first sun of the day will not arrive soon enough to suit me. Bantor said. I will sleep little this night."

"I may have a remedy for you, my mate." Cinda said, with a big smile on her face and a glint in her eyes.

This caused the small group to break out laughing, slightly melting the somber mood.

"Here, alone, are four good reasons for wanting to live forever." Bantor replied, pointing at the women and hugging Cinda to him.

"I have a feeling logic will prevail, Bantor. Said Greg. The desire to live far surpasses complacency."

"Well, we will find out in a few short hours." Jim added.

"You guys worry too much! Truck joined in. Take dat time and start thinking about da stuff we gotta get ready for da move."

"That's my brother! Jim said. Full of optimism."

"He's full of something!" Greg added.

The bemused look, on Truck's face, prompted more laughter.

A short while later, the entire village slept. The new day would reveal the answers to their dilemma.

# CHAPTER 4

Before the first sun of the day had risen to her full stature, Truck walked, briskly, through the wounded village. His restlessness had battled against sleep most of the night. His mind was on overload. He was almost certain the villagers would opt for relocation. His thoughts were swamped with the necessary mechanics for making the big move. Transporting this huge mass would require extensive planning. Through out his entire life, whenever his siblings discussed the "whens" and "wheres" of any given objective, he focused on the "how". Even though it wasn't a certainty, the villagers would vote in favor of a relocation, his mind was already in motion. Transportation, food, weapons and all the other elements, relating to an exodus of this proportion, dominated his thoughts.

As he continued on his way, through the most devastated section of the village, he came upon an elderly gentleman sitting on the ground near a large depression littered with broken possessions.

"Good morning ta you, grandfather!" He greeted. All senior men of the village were used to this Earthly title of respect, he accorded them.

Turning, slowly, he focused in on his intruder.

"Ta-rok! He said. This old man has seen the last of his good mornings. Along with joy, comfort and love. They lie here, buried forever." He pointed to the debris filled hollow. Jana was my life! I should have been with her!"

Truck remained silent. As he gazed into the old man's eyes, reddened with anguish, he could almost feel the pain himself.

"It matters not, to me, how others have voted. I will remain here to watch over my mate."

The man was called "Murto". He was counted among the oldest citizens in the village. His expertise was in gardening. People always joked, old "Murto" could grow something good to eat out of a boulder. The morning the quake had targeted his village, he and a small work crew were in the Lurda corral collecting fresh manure. It would be dried and mixed into their large vegetable plots. Another Earth-born idea shared by the Americans.

Truck reached deep into himself for a proper response. Arguing with someone whose mind was emotionally devastated, would prove futile.

"I'm really gonna miss ya, old timer. Dose vegetables ya grew were da sweetest and juiciest I ever ate. If we lived only on meat we'd all starve ta death. Especially da children! I just hope we can find somebody ta grow da proper garden, when we get ta da new home. But, ya won't have ta worry about dat, anymore, now. Will ya?"

Murto stared at the Earthman. His eyes seemed a bit more lucid.

"Well, little buddy, if dey do decide ta leave, I'll stop by and wish you well."

As he turned, to continue on his jaunt through the village, Murto called after him.

"Ta-rok" do you believe there may be a problem starting a garden in this new village?" He asked.

"Dere's always a chance of dat happening. Truck replied. I just hope ya taught dose youngsters well enough."

Murto spoke again, quickly, when he saw that Truck was ready to leave again.

"Maybe I should go along, after all. I could stay in that distant land long enough to see a new garden growing. I can always come back to visit Jana."

"Dat's a great idea, my friend! Truck kept at it. Maybe ya can call da garden "Jana's Field," in her honor." He said, as he walked away with a big smile on his face.

They had lost enough people, in the catastrophe. Every survivor would be needed, to rebuild their futures. Today, at least one more would be added to the list.

....................................

As the last of the stragglers gathered at the meeting place, a cloud of anxiety settled over their minds. No matter which decision was decided upon, their futures held a modicum of fear. To stay, they would be living with the constant fear of another murderous onslaught, waiting to happen. To leave, they would have to battle their way through the unknown.

The three Earthmen, Bantor and their mates were in their usual place in front of the anxious crowd. The ballots had been tallied by the village elders. More than once, actually, to insure accuracy.

"It is time!" Bantor announced to the small group beside him. He rose to his feet and walked to the front of the nervous horde. Other than he and the four village elders, in charge of the counting, knew in which direction their futures dwelt.

He raised his arms above his head, signaling their attention. An eerie silence had already prevailed over the large gathering, as they awaited the decision.

"I welcome you to this new day, my people! He began. Before I give you the results of our voting, I would hear your arguments on this issue, one more time. As a leader, the true feelings of his people should be heard and respected. We may agree or disagree. But, all opinions will be considered, from the youngest to the eldest."

"I would say a few words, Bantor! A voice rose from the crowd. With no objections, he continued. Until this morning, I had convinced myself no matter which decision was decided upon I would remain here and mourn my mate, forever. A wise man from another world made me realize none of us can afford to be selfish with our feelings. The loss of loved ones shouldn't mean the loss of the survivors. By all means, the living should mourn. But, to give up on themselves they are depriving friends, families and their village of the valuable support they are capable of giving to help them rise from the ashes. I will honor my deceased mate by helping to make our village strong, once again."

Greg and Jim looked at one another and, then, at truck. The large satisfied grin on his face answered their unspoken question.

"Wise man?" Greg mumbled, in a low voice, shaking his head.

"Thank you, Murto! Bantor said after a few moments. Anyone else wish to speak?"

"I would speak, Bantor! Another voice piped up. How could you expect a man of my years and others, such as myself, to make such a long journey even if we agreed to do so?

Jim rose from his seat and approached Bantor. "I can answer that, my friend!" He said to the leader.

"Answer away!" Bantor returned.

Jim turned and faced the curious crowd. "At present, we have twenty-four large wagons at our disposal. I have been informed another five are nearing completion. Our stable of Lurda rides was mostly spared by the disaster. We have proven in the past, they are capable of carrying two riders for long distances with little effort. If it is decided we make this journey, no one will have to walk unless they choose to do so."

As the pensive gathering mulled over this information, Jim returned to his seat alongside Sanda.

"You truly believe we will have cause to use them, don't you "Gem?" She asked in a low voice.

"Yes I do, my darling! He replied. The desire to survive will always conquer the fear of the unknown."

As the crowd became more impatient, it became louder.

"Bantor! A voice carried above the loud murmurings of the gathering. If you please. Tell us in which direction our futures lie!"

Shouts of agreement filled the air as all attention focused on the young leader.

"My brethren ! He began. The votes have been counted. In a short period of time we will embark on a journey. All who make this journey will do so under duress, however. Our fears and doubts will march right along with us. Together, we can conquer the unknown. At the least, we will be facing it head on. Our present situation, we cannot defend against. Not knowing when it will come upon us next."

He paused, starring at the agitated audience.

"Our ancestors, he continued, bonded together making our village strong and safe. To honor them, we must do the same!"

All were aware it was, literally, a damned if you do, damned if you don't situation. Emotions ran rampant through out the crowd. They sparred with one another. Each one trying to convince the other, theirs was the logical choice.

It wasn't until the night was nearly spent, before the last of the disgruntled congregation retired. The new day would witness no miracles.

# CHAPTER 5

"Dat's da last one! Truck announced, as he rolled the wagon wheel across the dirt floor and stacked it with fifty-seven others. The four foot high, eight inches thick disks would be used as "spare tires" for the twenty-nine "Land wagons". Each would carry two, for emergency purposes.

The large pole shed, they worked in, contained the wooden vehicles in various stages of construction. Each of the wagons was twelve feet long and six feet wide. The large bed was completely enclosed by four foot high side rails.

Axles, sleeves, pivot posts and all other metal hardware were products of Nevoan workshops. Commerce had flourished, between the two cultures, since they united to repel the near annihilation of the Nevoan settlement, at the hands of the invading "Lumas".

Hides, furs, wooden implements and various food stuffs were traded for the higher "Nevoan" technology.

Greg and Truck headed a group of one hundred eager volunteers in the "transportation" department. The twenty-four existing wagons, along with the five recently built, were made travel-ready. For the last twelve sunrises, they had worked diligently at their arduous task. A mass exodus, such as this, demanded no details, large or small, be overlooked.

Twenty-nine sets of double wooden yokes were stacked in another pile. Once enclosed around the Lurda's neck, they would be attached to the heavy wooden tongues, already attached to the wagons. Each was lined with fur to prevent abrasion to the animals. Many lengths of braided leather harness hung from a wall.

"I believe we are as prepared as we're going to be. Greg said, looking around at all of their inventions. He had been primarily responsible for their development.

"Come on, Truck! Let's find Bantor and notify him all is in readiness."

As they made their way through the village, people were scurrying about in various stages of preparation. Some worked around smoking fires, curing mounds of Lurda meat for their consumption on the long trek. Travel equipment, such as tents and sleeping furs were being repaired by others. The last of the produce was gathered from the large garden and stowed away in stiff leather containers.

Individuals sifted through their personal belongings, building small piles in front of their huts. They would be limited, only, to those things necessary to their survival during the long journey. Years of accumulated heirlooms would be left behind. Their focus, now, was strictly on their futures.

A small group of people sat with Bantor, as they approached his hut. It appeared they were in the middle of a heated discussion. The two Earthmen took seats around the fire and listened in.

"We cannot abandon the homes of our ancestors. One elderly man said. Too many memories have been shared in this place to disregard. Taking an uncertain journey, in pursuit of a new village, would show disrespect!"

"If we remain and die, another argued. Who will be left to honor their memory?"

"My brethren! Bantor interjected. We must always remember our ancestors paid a heavy price in their endeavors to secure a safe abode for the people. For many years their sacrifices earned for us a happy lifestyle. I cannot believe they would want us to remain, putting our lives in danger, just to pacify their memories."

As feelings rose, the verbal battles waged among the small group, were elevating toward hostility.

"Bantor! Greg intoned in a loud voice. May I speak?"

"Please do, Earth brother!" He returned.

"On the world I come from, we had a saying. He began. "United we stand. Divided we fall."

Absorbing he questioning looks of the small group, he continued. "It simply means a country, in this case, a village will become weak or disappear completely if its inhabitants abandon the principles which made them strong in the beginning. On any world, the one in which I came or this one, It matters not. We made a conscious effort to avoid as much peril in our lives, so the lives of our children could be extended. Thank you for hearing my words!" He finished.

"Your words are appreciated, Earth brother! He replied.

Turning to the group, he said; "We will talk more on this at a later time. Now, I have other things to attend to."

As he and the two brothers watched the disgruntled group filter away, stress hung heavily in the air.

"We didn't mean ta interrupt yer party, Bantor! Truck said. But, we thought we'd bring ya some good news."

"Your arrival was well-timed, Ta-rok. He answered. I had exhausted all of my arguments to convince them to join us on our journey."

"We thought you should know, immediately, all reparations to the wagons have been completed." Greg joined in. We're ready to roll!"

"That is good news, Earth brothers." Bantor replied. But, the tone of his voice and the sad look in his eyes belied his true fee;ings.

"Don't beat yerself up over dis, little buddy! Truck interjected. I got a feeling, deep inside, dat dey will change dere minds."

"I can only hope, Ta-rok. Bantor replied. To remain strong, this village must stay together. Every man, woman and child plays a vital role in developing our futures."

A short while later, the two Earthmen were on their way to find their brother. They were told he was in the Lurda corral, breaking in the last of the animals. Every ride would, soon, be needed.

As they continued through the village, each man thought about the arguments they had listened to at Bantor's fire. Who had the right answers? Soon, they would all learn Truck's consoling words to Bantor would prove to be prophetic.

# CHAPTER 6

An eerie stillness hung over the village, as people completed final preparations for their impending journey. Anxiety settled over them. The, once, vibrant atmosphere was reduced to a funeral state. For the first time in their long history the people were, clearly, divided. Individual groups sat around in heavy discussion, justifying their reasons for staying or their reasons for leaving.

The majority of them would be making the long journey. Approximately five hundred chose to stay with the bones of their ancestors. Soon, people would be saying their final farewells to brothers, sisters, aunts, uncles and all other loved ones and friends. That day was soon approaching!

The Earthmen, Bantor and their mates were the sole occupants of the "meeting" place.

As the first "Sister" sun bathed their world, with all her splendor, it was not enough to dispel the somber atmosphere shrouding the village. Since the onset of the devastating quake, which nearly annihilated it in its entirety, people moved about in a mechanical manner, some still in a state of shock. The fear if another unforeseen disaster invaded their thoughts.

"I am unable to make them understand how important it is for all of us to remain together. Bantor said. If this breech in our unity remains unchecked, the future of our village will be in jeopardy. I cannot impose my will upon them!" He finished in frustration.

"Absolutely not! Greg agreed. That very same method was imposed many times, on people back on Earth. It only resulted in driving nations further apart."

"I talked ta some a dos people, Truck joined in. Nothin I said got through ta dem."

"Well! That would explain their reluctance to join us!" Greg chided, starring across at his large brother, with a grin on his face.

The puzzled look on Truck's face elicited a trickle of laughter from the small group.

"Keep it up, midget! He replied, shaking his big fist at his younger brother. You might miss da train too!"

"That is, precisely, the type of behavior that will not win friends or influence people!" Greg shot back.

Before Truck had the chance to fire a second verbal round, Jim interjected.

"Bantor! I think your decision, allowing people to follow their own fate, was a wise one. A show of force, at this crucial time, may have resulted in even fewer people making this journey."

"My Earth brother! I know you say these words in an attempt to lessen my burden. They are appreciated! Now, if only you could offer me a solution to this dilemma I would be one happy native!" He said, with a big smile on his face.

"I keep telling you guys, things like dis always have a way of working demselves out. Truck said. Stop worryin about da things ya can't control. Take care a da stuff you can do right now."

"Ta-rok! If your wisdom was as easily accepted as your words, none of us would every worry." Bantor replied.

"That is the second time, today, I've heard someone refer to our brother as "wise". Greg interjected, looking across at Jim.

"Why is dat so hard ta believe? Truck asked. I been da brains of dis outfit all our lives.

"I will admit, you have delivered us from many precarious situations." Greg replied.

"And, we also have to agree, he's gotten us into a few of those precarious situations you've suggested." Jim added, with a smile.

The sheepish grin on the big man's face, caused the group to laugh, lifting some of the constraining tension.

Suddenly, the ground started vibrating. Shouting erupted throughout the village.

"Here we go, again!" Truck said, as they all rose to their feet, looking around.

Turning to the women, Jim shouted. "Get out of the village! Now!"

Soon, they were joined by a multitude of others, as they made a mad dash toward the gate. The tremors increased with every step they took, sometimes throwing them to the ground. As Bantor escorted the women, the three Americans headed for the Lurda corrals.

"Where are you going?" Sanda shouted after them.

"We have to lead the animals to safety! Jim answered. They are vital to the success of our journey!"

"Just keep going! Greg added. We'll meet up with you later."

As they raced away, Bantor hurried the women through the gates. The tremors raced after everyone.

When the three Earthmen reached the corral, Greg and Truck opened the gate. The animals paced, nervously. Before they could bolt through the open gate, each man leaped upon the back of a frightened beast. As they coaxed them through the opening, they turned their mounts toward the low hills on the north end of the village. Looking over their shoulders, they noticed the entire herd following them. Had they not taken control, the crazed animals would have scattered in every direction, miles from the village. The herding instincts of the beasts took over and they followed the leaders. By the time they reached the hills they had calmed down, considerably, and slowed their pace.

The three men, quickly, dismounted and raced back toward the village. Soon, they were among the throng of frightened people. Slowing their pace, they wended their way through and reentered the village. The quake had run its coarse. A few huts were in shambles. A small amount of debris was scattered in front of them.

Compared to the last quake, which tore through their village with its ground pulverizing violence, this one had departed quickly, with little damage and no casualties.

As the long line of fear stricken inhabitants made their way back inside the village, an eerie silence followed them. Although, a major catastrophe had been averted, this time, their fragile emotional status had reached its limit.

"After we assess the damage and ascertain our wagons and supplies are still in tacked, we will gather at the meeting place." Bantor announced looking around his twice wounded village. With him were the three Earthmen and their mates.

"I'll bring the herd back in after they've settled down a little." Jim volunteered.

"Truck and I will check on the wagons!" Greg added.

"Us women will check on the food supplies and the whereabouts of our children!" Sanda volunteered.

"You'll find them safe and sound over by the large corral!" Jim chipped in.

As they made their way through the excited crowd, Bantor thought to himself. For many days his mind had been in a constant state of turmoil, trying to discover a way to keep his people together. It was ironic, but, this recent quake may have provided him with a solution.

# CHAPTER 7

Every man, woman and child walked through the village toward the meeting place. Some made their way in a state of urgency. Others, in a trance-like procession. Soon, all were gathered in front of the large fire pit.

The Earthmen, their mates and Cinda sat in a small circle, off to the side. Bantor stood in front of the weary mob. As the last "Sister" sun fought to keep her fading light kindled, he began.

"On this day, my people, I believe we have all witnessed a sign from our ancestors. They are telling us it is time to leave this land, to seek out a new haven in which to heal our wounds and make this village strong once again. As most of you, I was frightened at first when this new "land shaker" descended on our village. Then, I started to realize what it meant. After the loss of so many in the previous disaster, not everyone got the message. Some had, already, chosen to remain."

Bantor paused and scanned the saddened faces staring back at him.

"As your leader, he continued, I will force no one to join us in our journey against their will! However, as your leader, I will not allow these signs, given to us not only once, but twice, from our ancestors to go unheeded!"

"Bantor! A voice rose from the crowd. I would speak, If I may!"

Borton was the designated spokesperson for the faction choosing to remain behind.

"Please do, my brother!" Bantor invited.

"I, also, have searched my heart and mind, exhaustedly, seeking the reasons behind the recent occurrences. We gathered earlier and reached the same conclusion you so, aptly, addressed. All, except for a handful of minds, have changed the direction of their thinking."

"And, what was decided at this gathering?" Bantor asked, hope rising in his heart.

"If it is not too late, my leader, we wish to join with the rest of our people on this journey." He answered.

A rousing chorus of ecstatic acceptance erupted from the crowd. Tears of relief were shed among loved ones who thought they were to be separated forever. Embraces of happiness were shared, now, instead of the sad embraces of farewell later.

"I believe you have your answer! Bantor shouted over the elated celebration of the crowd. We welcome you!"

The Earth brothers hugged their mates. Cinda joined Bantor and they shared a long embrace.

A short time later, as the crowd of people became a few decibels less boisterous, Bantor held his arms up.

When the demonstrative, celebrants had tamed their emotions, somewhat, he spoke.

"My people, I have purposely avoided discussing plans of departure for many days because I could not convince myself it would be the right decision. An emotional war waged in my mind. To seek a place of safety for the majority of my people fought on one side. On the other was the unprotected abandonment of the few who wished to stay. This night I stand before you not only as your leader, but as the most ecstatic man who ever walked this world." Tears of unlocked emotions poured from his eyes.

An appreciative roar erupted from the gathering. Cinda, still standing by his side, enfolded him in a loving embrace and wiped some of the tears from his cheeks.

As the noise level dwindled enough to be heard, he continued.

"The time to begin our journey is long overdue. Our Earth brethren have informed me, the "land" wagons and animals to pull them are in readiness. Food and other supplies, sufficient for a long journey, have been prepared. In three risings of our morning sun, our journey will begin!"

The loudest vocal demonstration of the young evening shattered the air, announcing to the world the relief they felt. Distancing themselves from the oppressive cloud of uncertainty, which hovered over their minds, was a breath of new life. They were more than eager to confront all new challenges and uncertainties. On with their futures!

# CHAPTER 8

Tonio, Roca and twenty of their men turned their animals loose in the large corral. They had just completed a twelve-day jaunt to the Nevoan settlement. Their mission was successful. They had notified the Nevoan leader, Mokar, of the impending exodus and acquired the metal parts to the wagons, vital to their long journey. Extra pivot pins, wheel rims, sleeves and other hardware was unloaded from their pack animals. A leather pouch, containing maps of the region they intended traveling, was also acquired.

They were apprised of the second quake that had occurred during their absence and the happy changes resulting from it. Some of them had relatives, among the group which had opted to stay. Cheers of joyous relief erupted from them as they left to find their relatives and friends.

Bantor, the Earth brothers, Tonio and Roca sat around the small breakfast fire, in front of the meeting hut. As they sipped their tea, they studied the Nevoan maps.

"That is pretty much, the way I remember it! Bantor said. Their maps end far short of our destination. But, we can follow them for the better part of our journey"

"It is amazing how far the Nevoans ranged to secure this information. Greg put in. It is no wonder the native tribes were scattered so far from one another."

"Their nomadic existence kept them from becoming extinct. Bantor chimed in. After many years and the loss of many men the Nevoans finally realized they could not rid this world of my people."

"Do ya think dere are more villages out dere dat ain't been discovered yet, Bantor?" Truck inquired.

"One can only hope, my brother. He answered. When the Nevoans came upon a village it was so sudden it left little time among the people to communicate their whereabouts. Many families were separated, living their entire lives apart from one another."

"Maybe we'll get lucky and find more a dose people along da way. Truck said. We can take dem all with us!"

Before anymore could be said, a group of youngsters rushed into their midst.

"Father! Come and see what we have captured!"

It was Julo (Bantor's sixteen year old son). He was followed closely by Marus and Bomar (Jim's sixteen and fourteen year old sons). Salba (Truck's fifteen year old son) and Tomal (Greg's fourteen year son).

Friends since birth, they were inseparable. Spending almost every waking moment together. Days upon days were filled with hunting, exploring, teasing the young girls and getting into mischief.

The three Earth fathers referred to them as the "Posse".

"Excuse my son's rude manners, my brothers! Then, turning toward the youngster.

"Julo! I hope you have good cause to interrupt men at their meeting!"

His voice was stern, but, everyone was aware Julo was his pride and joy.

Knowing smiles passed among the other men.

"I apologize, father! Julo replied. It can wait until a later time!"

Before he could walk away, Truck spoke.

"We're just about finished here. Ain't we fellas? Let's go see what dey have!" He finished with a wink at Julo.

"I guess we can continue with our discussion a little later." Bantor said, smiling.

The six men rose as one and followed the youngsters. A short time later they stood outside one of the small corrals. There were four of these enclosures. They were used to Hold the youngest of the Lurda calves. This one, in particular, held only one occupant. A cream colored infant, maybe two or three weeks old, stared back at them with its one dark eye. It didn't look to be more than fifty pounds in weight. Aside from its unusual coloring, it stood on only three legs.

Its right front foreleg was malformed. An obvious birth defect, the small limb was barely seven inches long.

"Where in da hell did ya find dis little fella?" Truck asked.

"About three miles north of here, near that small forest." Salba answered his father.

"He was laying next to his dead mother. Bomar joined in. I think she was killed by a Kazor. The body was pretty mangled!"

"She must have put up a pretty good fight, protecting her young one." Jim said.

"Obviously, he isn't weaned yet." Greg added.

"Without its mother's care it will, soon, die. Tonio joined in. It would have been best to have left this little one where it was."

"But, father, we had to do something! We just couldn't leave it!" Julo pleaded.

Bantor stared at his son, with pride.

"My son! We cannot interfere with the ways of nature. Left to its own devices, it balances everything out." Roca! Take it away from our village and end its suffering!"

Truck strode over to the blonde leader and put an arm around his shoulder. "Come over here! I wanna talk ta ya!"

When they were out of earshot of the others, he began.

"Your da one dat believes in signs. Take a good look at dis situation! Dat little animal was born da wrong color ta ever be accepted by da herd. It's crippled and it's an orphan because his mother died protecting him. If dose aren't signs telling ya it should live den maybe we shouldn't believe in dem."

"What are you suggesting, Ta-rok?" Bantor asked.

"I think dat we should give da kids a chance ta save da little thing." Truck answered.

"I agree, it is time they learned about responsibilities, Ta-rok. However, we have much to prepare for our departure. And, we do not need any unnecessary distractions!"

Truck paused for a moment, starring at the blonde leader. He would not give up!

"Back on Earth I took care of a lot a animals. Some a dem died. But, da ones I brought back from da dead, made me feel dat I gave dem another chance at life. I can teach dem how ta do it!"

Bantor looked at the big man, but, before he could say a word Truck continued.

"Dat little creature ain't gonna take up much room. One a da boys can be with it at all times. And dere's one more thing. On any long journey in life, distraction is a good thing! Dis will keep da boys from getting inta any mischief. Dey'll be too busy."

After a moment of thought, Bantor spoke.

"Very well, Ta-rok! They will have their chance! However, I will hold you responsible for any mishaps."

"Dat's fine by me, friend! Truck replied, with a big smile on his face, slapping the native on his back.

When they rejoined the small group, all were informed the animal would be allowed a chance to survive.

The youngsters swarmed Truck and Bantor with hugs of appreciation.

When the other men returned to the village, Truck related to the boys how they would go about saving the young orphan. The five students were getting an education. But, more importantly they were being led to understand more effort should be devoted to the preservation of life, rather than its devastation.

# CHAPTER 9

Two sunrises later, Bantor sat near a small fire. Seated around him were fourteen others. This small group of senior citizens comprised the entire contingency of those who would not be making the long journey.

"Barta! Is there nothing I can say to dissuade you from this decision? Bantor asked. Our new village will not feel complete without the sage wisdom and experience of this group!"

A saddened smile transformed the face of the elder spokesman, as he looked into the young leader's eyes. "Bantor! Your father and I romped through these hills and forests, in our youth. We competed with one another to be the best. We talked much about everything. One particular conversation, I recall, concerned an aging warrior in our village. His name was Pallo. He was Leota's father, your grandfather."

"Leota told me all about the man's heroic exploits. His battles with the Nevoan invaders and his fearless endeavors while killing the dreaded Kazar to protect his village."

The small group listened in respectful silence. Stories, such as this, were also apart of their history.

"As Pallo grew older and his strength started to wane, Barta continued. Each new day increased his frustrations.

No longer capable of his, once virile potential, he began to retreat within himself."

"I remember a conversation I had with him, shortly before he took the journey to be with his ancestors. Leota and I sat with him, at the time, in front of his hut.

"If a person is loved, respected and remembered he has led a fruitful life. He said to us. Once that has been accomplished they most make way for the next person, allowing them to do likewise."

"Take a look around you, Bantor! Remember us not with sadness, but, celebrate our accomplishments and contributions in life."

The native leader stared across at the old man, tears threatening to force their way from his eyes. He knew no further arguments would sway them.

Rising to his feet, he embraced the elderly spokesperson and the others in turn.

"We will meet again at the hearths of our ancestors, the old man replied. Have a safe journey!"

"Live happy, my friends!" Bantor returned and started to make his way toward the village gates, tears trailing in his wake.

The sullen atmosphere, he had left, was replaced with an excited vibrancy. People bustled in all directions, making last minute preparations for the journey.

Their twenty-nine "land wagons" were strung out in a long line, pointing to the south. Mounted riders with other Lurdas in tow, coaxed the beasts toward the wagons, where they would be harnassed in their traces. Others were busy loading food, furs and all other equipment, necessary for their journey, into the first ten wagons. The rest of the wagons would be used in transporting the young, old and infirmed.

Most of the two thousand mounts would be carrying double riders. Because of the vast distance to be traveled, their pace would be slow and steady. None of the animals would suffer from over-exertion.

As Bantor entered this beehive of activity, Jim rode up to him on his mount. He was holding the reins of another animal trailing behind him.

"I spotted you leaving the village! He said, handing him the reins of the second animal. "Thought you might want to check on the progress!"

"Thank you, my brother!" Bantor replied. A trace of sadness was in his voice.

"I can tell by that look, your meeting was not a successful one!" Jim said, as the blonde leader leapt upon the back of his Lurda.

"Sad, but true, my brother! He answered, as they goaded their rides into a slow walk, alongside the long line of wagons. Those fourteen old souls will not be accompanying us on our journey. I did not wish to add to the weight of their decision by arguing with them any longer."

"You've done all you could, my friend! Jim responded. There are things in life which are, simply, out of our control."

They rode in silence, for a while, absorbing the joyous sounds emanating from the anxious people.

Truck and Greg joined them as they were completing their inspection.

"All of the food and equipment is stowed, Bantor! Greg said. We've almost completed hooking the Lurda teams to the wagons!"

"All we gotta do, now, is load everyone onta da train and get da hell outta Dodge." Truck added.

"What is this "dodge" and "train" you speak of, Earth brother?" Bantor asked.

"Allow me to interpret for my "wise" brother. Greg interjected. What he meant was, we are nearly ready for departure!"

"Interpret dis, shorty!" Truck replied, shaking a big fist at his sibling.

Looking over at the two brothers, Bantor replied, with a big smile on his face. "And da sooner da better. Right?"

That caused the three Americans to bust out laughing.

"Amen ta dat!" Truck finished.

# CHAPTER 10

The first sun was only half way through its cycle, as the long caravan snaked its way through the low hills outside the village. The large wagons were strung out in single file formation. Fifty-foot gaps were maintained between them for safety purposes. Columns of one thousand mounted Lurdas paralleled the wagons, one on either side. They remained a constant one hundred feet away from the slower moving wagons.

Bantor, Tonio and Roca led the column of riders on the right side. The three Earthmen led the column on the left.

The pace, they had established, would gain them approximately twenty-five miles per day. Thus, assuring them, no undue exertion would be put on their animals.

Following this ribbon-like procession was the remainder of their "feeder" animals. Three quarters of the large herd was slaughtered for the preparation of their travel jerky. The two hundred or so, that still existed of their "feeder" cattle followed their herding instinct. No riders were necessary to goad them along.

The most time-consuming exercise they had encountered, at the beginning of their journey, was the placement of the people. Women with young children, the elderly and those with physical afflictions were made comfortable in the wagons. The twenty designated coaches were not overly crowded. This was dew to the hard work and patience of the Earth brothers. Over the years, there were not many people in the village who did not desire the opportunity to learn how to ride the shaggy beasts. Many became adept at handling them. No one could foresee a day, such as this, ever coming. But, they were prepared!

Husbands and wives, brothers and sisters, friends and relatives, alike, rode in double tandem. The animals would be alternated after every rest stop, to alleviate some of the extra burden put on them. The only arguments evolving from the passengers were "who" would be in control of the beast. None-the-less, their exodus was moving along smoothly.

Bantor gazed straight ahead, unseeing. His mind dwelt on the small group manning the forsaken village. As the leader of these people, he knew for the rest of his life, nothing would dispel the feeling of guilt he harbored. He could have, forcefully, abducted the senior citizens away from their beliefs. All that that would have accomplished would have been a quick fix to alleviate his conscience. Now, he must live with it!

"Father! He said in a low whisper, looking skyward. What would you have done? Maybe this son of yours is not capable of leadership!"

His thoughts were interrupted by the approach of Roca. He had been sent ahead, earlier, to find an adequate resting area for the large caravan.

As he guided his animal alongside Bantor, he noticed the saddened expression on the leaders face. He did not need to ask what was causing it. He remained, respectfully silent, waiting for Bantor to speak.

"What have you discovered, Roca?" He finally asked.

"About one mile ahead, my leader, is a large forest. A well-worn trail runs through its middle. A large stream is near by. I believe it will accommodate our needs." Roca finished.

"Good job, my friend! Bantor replied. Drop back and notify our column we will soon be stopping for a rest."

"Tonio! Bantor addressed the man following closely behind him. Make sure our Earth brethren are made aware of this, also!"

As the two men rode away to do his bidding, he looked into the near distance and spotted the forest.

The second "sister" sun of the day had nearly run her course. If this resting area was compatible enough, he just might call a halt to this day's travels. There would be many prolonged marches in the near future. He was almost positive. He wanted to accustom them slowly, to any hardships ahead of them. The only deadlines they really had to adhere to would be decided by the dictations of each individual day. Some would be long. Some would be short.

About an hour later, the entire caravan was comfortably ensconced in the depths of a cool forest. People were busy helping the passengers out of the wagons, leading their animals to water, unhitching wagons and getting settled once they had been informed this would be their camp for the night. Fires were started, animals were hobbled, while others were busy setting up traveling tents and preparing meals. As exhausted as they were, from the hectic activity of this first day, everyone cooperated.

Shortly before the last sun of the day surrendered to the oncoming night, a myriad of small fires dotted the peaceful landscape. People sat around them discussing the day's events. Many moved about just to stretch out cramped muscles they hadn't used before. The morale of the "refugees" was high, as laughter trickled from every direction.

Truck sat with the "posse", watching as the boys fed the "Lurda" orphan. He had constructed a feeding bag made out of stiff hide. It was funnel shaped, with a small opening in the narrow end. After showing the youngsters how to go about milking one of the nursing animals, they had become quite proficient. It took the halve-starved calf no time at all to accept the artificial teat.

The young men had alternated during the first leg of the passage, sitting with the young animal in one of the wagons. The animal adopted his surrogate mothers, also. It had become so calm and accepting, it often napped with its head in one of their laps. They even named the three-legged misfortunate "Lucky".

"Just remember, every time we make a rest stop ya gotta feed him. Truck said. Dese little guys gotta eat a lot. And don't forget ta clean up any messes he makes in da wagon. No one wants ta lay dere head down on a pile a shit. Dey might complain a little. And, we don't need dat. Do we?"

"No, Ta-rok, we don't!" Julo replied, smiling.

"How long before he is able to eat the moss and other plants?" Bomar asked.

"Not for a while, yet. Truck answered. When dere dis little dey need all da milk dey can hold."

Noticing the looks of frustration, he quickly added. "Dese little fellas grow up pretty fast, doh. In da wild dey have no choice. If dey don't get strong in a hurry some sonuva bitch'll eat it. You guys ain't gonna give up on dis little fella, are ya?"

"No, Ta-rok! Marus chimed in. We will make him strong!"

"Dat's what I wanna hear! Truck replied. When dat day comes, yer all gonna feel good about dis. Bringing dis little creature back from da dead will make all you guys better men."

"Why is that, Ta-rok?" Salba asked.

"It'll make ya appreciate life more. Jus knowing dere are people in dis world who won't turn dere backs on ya when yer sick or dying. I know if you guys make dis little fella strong it'll tell me I can always count on ya ta help me if I ever need it."

"We won't let you down, Ta-rok!" Tomal replied.

"Dis ain't about me! Said Truck. Da main thing is ya never want ta let yourselves down. Ya start something, ya make damn sure ya finish it"

The five young men nodded their assent in unison.

"I'll see you men later. Truck said, rising to his feet. When ya put dat little guy ta bed for da night cover him with one a dos Lurda furs. He'll think he's snuggling against his mama."

As he walked away, the young men smiled. There was nothing on this world that would keep their little charge from living to adulthood.

# CHAPTER 11

The first "Sister" sun of the day had barely begun her cycle, as the large caravan resumed its march south. As soon as it had been safe enough to navigate by the dawn's dim light, the eager travelers had broken camp. After breakfasting on hot tea and bowls of hearty stew, left over from last night's repast. Short work was made of harnessing the teams of Lurdas, reining in their mounts and loading the wagons.

A nomadic existence ran contrary to the life style of these people. Years of complacent contentment, derived from village life, made them more than anxious to resettle. The efficient manner in which they went about completing their assigned tasks helped them to survive another day on the trail. Many of these, linked together, added up to them making a home in the new land.

As Bantor led his column of mounted men he was in deep thought, once again. Although his heart still ached for the ones left behind, he was no longer sad. Convinced he had done everything within his power to rectify the situation, he focused on the things he had done to make their lives more comfortable. Fifty of their feeder cattle had been left in one of the large corrals. Smoked meat and dried vegetables were packed to the rafters in one of their storage lockers. Although they were elderly, some of them were still capable of hunting, if the need arose. Ten of the powerful Nevoan firearms were, also, left with them. Many of the seniors were well versed in there use.

The gates to the village had been repaired, as well as their living quarters. Some had chosen to live together. Others had opted for a more private existence. All had their personal reasons for remaining behind. Obviously, they were important to them.

Bantor was happy he had not put pressure on them. It would have sent a message to them, telling the seniors their reasons for staying were irrational. He had left them their respect.

Barta was the only one among them who had any living kin. His granddaughter, Alijo, had lost her mate in the disastrous, first quake and she was reluctant to leave. The broken hearted, twenty year old relented only after her grandfather had reminded her that she was the last of his bloodline. Roca had, already, taken quite a liking to her.

Bantor sent Tonio and Roca ahead to secure an area for their first rest stop. The morning sun would soon be exhausted and the animals needed to replenish their strength.

On the other side of the wagon train, the three Earth siblings rode side by side. They had talked through the morning about the development of their new home. Each was excited about implementing new inventions they had in mind. The slate of old ideas had been swept almost entirely away by the first quake. It was time, now, to draw on new concepts.

"One of the veterans, who had been on the long expedition with Bantor, had mentioned a large body of water existing in the area of that far away land. Jim was saying. I'd like to build a big boat and see if we can't catch some fish."

"Dat's what started dis whole damn thing in da first place. Truck joined in. I told ya before. I'm never going fishing with you two, ever again."

"Well, no one invited you this time, you big ape!" Greg interjected.

"Our bait will last us longer, this way." Jim went along with his brother's chiding, with a big smile on his face.

"Our brother is convince we're using sushi for bait." Greg continued, breaking out in laughter.

"Keep it up you two clowns and I ain't gonna tell ya about da new things I got in mind." Truck shot back.

"You know, eventually, you're going to tell us, Truck! Jim said. You never could keep a secret!"

"I ain't saying another word about it! Truck replied. And dat's final!"

Jim and Greg gave each other knowing looks and smiled.

They rode in silence for the next minute and a half.

"Okay! I'll tell ya about one a my ideas. Just one!" Truck said, excitedly. Causing his brothers to laugh.

"I didn't think our brother was capable of keeping us in suspense for that long!

Did you, Jim?" Greg said after a while.

"Not since we were younger and he backed into that campfire. Jim returned. His pants were on fire for nearly five minutes before he informed us."

All three broke out laughing at the memory.

Before they could continue their conversation, Roca rode up to them. "Up ahead, about two miles off, is a small valley. He reported. There is water there. We will be stopping for a short rest."

"Thank you, Roca! Jim returned. We will notify the others."

"It's about time, too! Truck said. I need ta take a plunge in dat water and wash off some a dis stink."

"Boy, do you ever! Jim said. But, please, try to restrain yourself until the rest of us have had a drink, first."

"Especially, the animals." Greg added.

Laughing as they went, Truck and Greg peeled off and goaded their mounts toward the rear of their ranks to apprise he others.

A short time later, the entire caravan was safely tucked into the small valley. The hills grew high on either side.

Enough shade trees were scattered down the middle to provide comfort for the weary travelers. Two large springs bubbled at the base of one of the large hills. They were far enough apart to separate bathers from drinkers.

No fires were lit. People sat in the shade eating some of their travel food. The beasts of burden were unhooked from the wagons and led, in tandem, to the watering hole. When their thirsts were slaked they were reconnected to the wagons. As they rested in their traces, they tore up mouthfuls of moss and munched away, contentedly.

All of the animals were checked over to assure they sustained no injuries.

The second "Sister" sun radiated down on them, with all her thermal glory. Bantor, the Earthmen and a handful of others sat in the shade of a large tree. The Nevoan maps lay, unfolded, in front of them.

"In a day or two, these maps will end. Bantor said. Then, we will all be at the mercy of my memories."

"Is any of this starting to look familiar?" Jim asked.

"Yes, my Earth friend! Bantor answered. Up until this point, it is all still fresh in my mind. I believe, in four or five days, we will come upon twin mountains that touch the sky. I remember traveling between them. Beyond that, however, things become a little hazy.

"As they say on Earth, Greg joined in. We will cross that bridge when we come to it." Until then, we at least know we are going in the right direction."

"When we get to dos mountains, we can send scouting parties ahead. Truck added. Maybe dey will find a landmark dat'll jump start your memory again."

"Until we get to that point, my friends, nothing else can be done. Let's get this "Train" moving again. Shall we?"

Many hours later, they were camped for the evening. Low rolling hills surrounded them. A small stream snaked its way along one side. The travel-weary "Nomads" attacked their sleeping furs and were soon lulled by their dreams.

# CHAPTER 12

Five days later, the caravan was cresting a rise to a low hill. In the distance they saw two large mountains, approximately, twenty miles off. The rolling terrain was working against them. It sapped the strength from their animals at an alarming rate, forcing them to make rest stops more frequently. It had been decided, earlier, to continue on a straight course, up and down the low hills, rather than expend the extra time going around them.

They had been fortunate, up until this point. Since the beginning of their journey, only one mishap had befallen them. For some, inexplicable, reason one of the mounted Lurdas had bolted from the orderly caravan and thrown its rider. The youngster was bruised by the fall, but, otherwise okay. The same could not be said for the unfortunate animal, however. In its wild dash, it had plunged into a small ravine and broken its neck.

With many helping hands, it was butchered in short order. The meat was cooked when they made their nightly layover.

As the third "Sister" sun marched halfway through her cycle, a halt was called. Large hills pressed in on them from one side. A wide, but shallow, stream bordered on the other.

Trees were scarce in this area. But, it didn't matter. The day was cooling down, as it slipped into nightfall.

As people settled around small fires eating leftovers and sipping tea, it was becoming obvious the long journey was starting to catch up with them. At least half of their enthusiasm had waned. And there was a long way to go, yet. Many of them had never been on any trek, of any length, their entire life. Chores were now being carried out in a perfunctory manner. Morale was sipping!

Bantor, the three Earthmen and their mates surrounded a small fire.

"My people are weary from traveling. Bantor said. Village life has a tendency to make a man bury himself in complacency. Ahead of us lies, at the least, twenty-five long marches." He finished, shaking his head in frustration.

"I have, yet, to hear anyone voicing their desire to turn back. Greg joined in. But, I can clearly see your concerns. If despondency is left unchecked, we may have a rebellion on our hands."

"Dat won't happen!" said Truck. Dese people have nothing to turn back to. Dey're a little tired and impatient, but, dey'll be just fine."

"I agree with you, Truck!" said Jim. But, as Bantor has pointed out most of these people are not accustomed to the hardships of a long journey."

"All of us are anxious to start building our new home. Sanda replied. They were aware, from the beginning, it would take much time."

"Saddle sores and fatigue have a way of making a person forget what lies at the end of any journey." Jim added.

"Is there nothing we can do to encourage them? Mara asked. When we were in our village we could always hold a celebration to dispel some of the boredom."

"Why couldn't we do that now, Bantor? Lona asked. At least minds would be distracted from the hardships ahead, if only for a short while."

"This is why we give thanks to our ancestors for all the women they have put into our lives!" Bantor said, with a broad smile on his face."

All eyes around the fire pit stared back at him, questioningly.

"You have given me a wonderful idea!"

All remained silent, waiting for him to explain himself.

"Not too far ahead there lies a small glade. Through its middle runs a wide stream with fast water. It empties into a deep pool. If I dig deep enough into my recollections And I can locate this area we can rest there for a few days. It will become our temporary village. We can hunt and relax our travel-weary bodies. It will be known as our "Half-way" celebration."

"Amen ta dat!" Truck replied.

"I think it is just what the doctor ordered!" Jim added

"Bantor! Greg asked. Have we, actually, reached the halfway point in our journey?"

"Not quite, Earth brother. But no one need know. He replied. Do they?"

"Absolutely not!" Greg answered, with a big smile on his face.

"How long before we reach this ideal spot?" Jim asked.

"After we pass between those two mountains, tomorrow, Maybe one or two days should put us in the vicinity, If my memory hasn't failed me." Bantor replied.

"Are there any identifying structures, in this area, we should be aware of?" Greg asked.

Staring across at his Earth friend, Bantor searched his mind.

"I do remember one thing." He said after a while. Shortly before we discovered it, we were traveling downhill. It was extremely warm. So, the second "Sister" sun must have been watching over us at the time."

"Was da sun overhead, in front of you or at your back, at da time? Truck asked.

"She was more than halfway through her cycle so she would have been at our backs, I think." Bantor replied. Why do you ask?"

"That meant you would have been traveling in a southwesterly direction. Jim concluded. So, after we pass through the mountains and find that downhill stretch we should travel in that direction."

"I can only hope it will be as easy as you say, my Earth brother. Many years have passed since then." Bantor returned.

"Don't worry, Bantor! We'll find dat spot!" Truck added.

"Even if we don't find this place, there will be others in which to hold our celebration." Sanda chimed in.

"Everyone is ready for a break, so it won't make much difference to them where we stop." Mara added.

"Amen ta dat, again. Truck said. If it was left up ta me, we'd be partying right now!"

"If it were left up to you, old "wise" one, We'd be no more than a block and a half from our old village, at this time." Greg chided, smiling.

"Why do you say that, "Gug?" Lona asked.

"We've seen our brother celebrate many times before, my dear." Greg answered.

The "I'm guilty" look on Truck's face caused a round of laughter.

A short while later, the entire caravan was in pursuit of dreams.

# CHAPTER 13

Two sunrises later, the last of the caravan had just snaked its way through the twin mountain peaks. Their progress was further impeded by a gradual rise in the rolling landscape.

Their beasts of burden were more than capable of meeting the challenge. However, to alleviate some of the stress on the animals, they went at a much slower pace.

A few miles ahead of the lumbering wagons, Bantor and five men scouted the wilderness. The men, he had selected, were members of the original exploratory expedition who had accompanied him on this same journey years before.

They had stopped their mounts on top of a high hill. Below them sprawled a wide, lush valley. They could make out a large stream, far ahead, that meandered its way into a thick forest.

"I remember this place! Bantor announced, excitement echoing from his voice.

Before this day is ended, all of my people will gaze upon a land so beautiful it will be a struggle to make them leave it. Let us hasten back and inform them." He said, turning his mount and goading it into a fast trot. Relieved, now, his memory had not failed him, he smiled to himself.

A short time later, as they skirted the base of a large hill, he spotted the advancing caravan one mile away.

"Here comes da boss!" Truck said, when he noticed the mounted party headed in their direction.

"They've been gone all morning. Jim replied. I hope they have some good news."

Bantor's five scouts broke off and headed back to their column to notify Tonio and Roca. Bantor headed toward the three Earth men, turned his mount and fell in alongside them. The big smile on his face told them, almost, everything they wanted to know.

"I have been successful, my Earth brothers! He said. Before the second "Sister" has exhausted herself, we will make camp in this wondrous setting I have told you about!"

"I told ya it would all come back to ya!" Truck said.

"That you did, Ta-rok! However, there are times in a person's life when the faith others have in you is greater than the faith one has in himself."

"We will notify the others of this good news, immediately!" Greg said, as he started to turn his mount.

"Do not trouble yourself, my Earth brother. Bantor told him. I wish this to be a surprise!"

"Good idea, Bantor! Jim agreed. Their excitement might put a little undue stress on the animals."

"We will Talk later, my friends!" With that, he swung his animal to the right and trotted off to rejoin his column.

"Let da party begin!" Truck bellowed, with a big grin on his face.

"There goes the neighborhood!" Greg shot back.

Less than one hour later, the two long columns of weary nomads were swallowed up by the cool embrace of the lush forest. The wide lane, in which they traveled, easily accommodated the entourage. The mossy floor absorbed any sounds of their approach.

The uncanny stillness, together with the leafy shroud, hung over them, putting nerves on edge. Their minds had convinced them that every shadow in this gruesome setting was hiding one form of monstrosity or another.

Soon, they found themselves in an area where the trees had thinned out and the encouraging rays of the sun trickled down upon them. A wide stream merged with their path from the right, her water racing swiftly down the channel. The merciless heat of the second "sister" sun, which had pelted them throughout her cycle was dispelled, somewhat, by the wild water as it splashed over rocks and anything else in its path, cooling the area. When the waterway turned sharply to the left, her rumblings grew louder.

Going around the next bend, they discovered the reason.

The wide stream had now become a small river and had plummeted ten feet down into a large pool. It continued its southerly course through a small opening at the far end of the pool.

Raising his voice slightly above the liquid symphony, Bantor spoke. "We will rest here, my people, long enough to heal our travel-weary bones. If that takes a few days or more, so be it!"

An enthusiastic roar of approval erupted from the tired mob. Some would never get used to this nomadic existence. A little time off, for good behavior, was just what they needed.

In no time at all, wagons were unhitched, animals were tended to and hobbled in a large mossy area, at the edge of the pool. Maintenance checks were made on all their equipment. It didn't stop there! Traveling tents were pitched, fires were started and meals were being prepared. When all chores had been completed, they gathered at the edge of the small lagoon.

As the rampant water plummeted, with all her wrath into the large pool, it cooled the air and lulled them with her liquid music.

Never before had anyone observed more than a shallow stream, moving no faster than a man could walk. A degree of fear was added to their excitement, as they watched, mesmerized by this strange occurrence.

"We have traveled far from our former village. Bantor began. Up until this moment it has been a tedious trek. A new horizon looked much the same as the last. I wanted to share this scene, from my past memories, to make you aware there are places on this world of ours filled with wonders such as this."

He paused, looking over his rapt audience. Thanking his ancestors, once again, for being able to trust in his memories.

"My brethren, I promise you! In the days that lie ahead there will be many more strange and exciting adventures!"

Cheers of approval roared from the large crowd.

"Everyone of us must take this opportunity to rekindle our strength so we can better prepare ourselves to face any challenges we may incur in the near future. Rest well, my people!"

A thunderous roar of acceptance erupted at his back, as he rejoined the small group seated directly behind him.

"Knute Rockne, eat your heart out!" Jim said, as Bantor took a seat.

Looking questioningly at the Earthman, He asked. What is knute Rockne?"

"He was a great leader and motivator of men on Earth. Jim answered. For many years the physical feats he extoled them into performing were astounding."

"I am honored by the comparison, Earth brother. I hope I will still be worthy of the compliment by journey's end.

"Dere ya go again, little buddy. Truck joined in. Worrying about tomorrow when ya still got so much of today ta think about."

"It is a necessary burden one must carry as a leader of people. Bantor replied. Making certain all the tomorrows in their futures are safe and fulfilling takes priority over the events of most days."

"Dat's well and fine, my friend. Truck responded. But, ya still gotta learn how ta relax and enjoy every day as it comes. When ya learn how ta do dat, ya might discover dere are ways of havin fun and finding new things dat can help everyone at da same time."

"Please tell us, my philosophic brother. How would you go about doing that?" Greg interjected.

"Well, my underfed brother. Truck began. In a little while I'm gonna take dese hot riding pants off and cool myself in dat water. As long as I'm in dere I'm gonna find out how deep it is, If it's safe for da kids ta swim in it and if dere are any fish in it. Any more questions, shorty?"

When none were forthcoming, he rose to his feet, removed his long leather riding pants and plunged into the cool, inviting water.

# CHAPTER 14

In the next few days many new discoveries were made in this strange section of their world. Fish did, indeed, occupy the depths of the large pool. Some, almost, seven feet long and sturgeon like in appearance, wended their way over the bottom feeding on the fern-like growth covering it. Truck had discovered them on his initial dive. At first glance he thought them to be logs, carried over the falls and sunk to the bottom. It wasn't until he prodded one with a foot and watched it slowly ungulate through the water, that he knew for sure. He, also, discovered smaller sardine-like fish in the shallows, along the perimeter of the pool.

A strong current also existed, caused by the tons of water pouring over the ten foot drop and exciting through the narrow channel on the far side of the pool.

It wasn't long before everyone was feasting on the aquatic creatures. After braiding lengths of sinew into long lines, they attached hooks made from "Lurda" bone, Truck had shown them how to make. Baiting them with the smaller, sardine-like fish and attaching a stone it sank to the bottom. It wasn't long before the people on shore were involved in a grueling tug of war.

When the first of these monsters was pulled up on dry land and started flopping around the novice fishermen dropped the end of the line and ran for cover. The three Earth brothers were the only ones laughing.

The only water these people had ever seen, in their entire lives, were the slow moving, shallow streams they had waded across. Needless to say, none of them knew how to swim. They were reluctant to venture into water that went past their waists.

Under the direction of the three Earthmen, it wasn't long before the pool was filled with people of all ages, splashing about in its cool depths. There, also, remained a large number of natives who adamantly refused to join in. But, never the less, everyone enjoyed the clean, fresh taste of the monster's flesh. The Earthmen, also, showed them how to smoke the fish, preserving its flesh to last a long time. It would become a welcomed addition to their travel stores.

Hunting parties discovered, immediately, the Lurdas indigenous to this area, were much smaller and of a different color. Instead of the shaggy dark hair, their bodies were covered with a light tan hair. When they had approached the beasts, instead of stampeding into a frenzied dash for safety, the animals, literally, walked up to them out of curiosity. The hunters killed no more than they needed.

The herd of Lurdas, which had followed them all the way from the old village and were used as feeder cattle, were long gone. Many had been butchered during the trek. others had, simply, wandered away. Now, they had an unlimited supply to replenish their traveling fare.

The women and children, who foraged the area, discovered a plethora of exotic fruits and vegetables. Bantor was happy this new land would, amply, provide for his people.

Only one incident, of note, occurred during their entire stay in this area.

One morning, a woman's scream brought them running to the edge of the pool. Jim was first to arrive on the scene. The woman pointed to the far end of the pool, where it excited through the narrow channel.

"My baby!" She cried, tears flowing from her eyes.

Looking in the direction she had indicated, he spotted the child being tossed by the rapid current running through the middle of the pool.

He dove into the water and swam toward the misfortunate urchin. Soon he was in the same current, being swept toward the fast exit. He was only a few yards behind the toddler when its head went under. Taking a deep breath, he plunged beneath the surface. The clarity of the water allowed him to see the child, a few yards ahead. Kicking his legs with all his might, he reached out and grabbed the child's leg.

Struggling to the surface he noticed he was about to be swept into the churning channel of the pool's exit. Holding the child above the water he knew he was about to be sucked through the narrow outlet. Just before the current forced him through the narrows, something grabbed his leg. The next thing he knew, he was being lifted backward and out of the water. The small child, still in his grasp, he lay on the shore looking up at the smiling countenance of Truck's face. The toddler, lying on his chest, cried out her fear, but otherwise was unhurt.

Assessing the situation, the big man had raced down the shoreline. Knowing the current was pushing his brother and the child toward the outlet, He charged toward the area to intercept them. He arrived not a moment too soon.

They found out later, the mother had taken her child down to the shallow end of the pool to bathe. The little girl became excited by the tiny fish swimming around her feet. She tried to catch one and fell face first into the water. In an instant, the current carried her away from shore. The mother happen to be one of the reluctant ones who did not wish to learn how to swim.

When people talk about this incident, they marvel at the athletic ability displayed by the Earthmen, on that day. How Jim could move through the water so fast and catch up to the child. And, how Truck, given his size, could run in sand as fast as he did and catch his brother and the child before they would have been sucked out of existence through the narrow chute.

For five more days, the displaced villagers basked in the rejuvenating atmosphere. Even the most skeptical among them were starting to believe this sudden change in their lifestyle could be for the better.

Bantor had already declared, in two risings of the morning "Sister" they would continue their journey. Minds and bodies had strengthened. But, more importantly, their desire to learn more about this new area, they would soon be calling home, had increased.

"Will ya take a look at dat!" Truck said, pointing across the way. He and Jim were over-seeing the small fires, smoking the last of their fish and "Lurda" meat for the journey.

Walking down the shoreline, from the direction of the falls, was Gia, Trucks adopted daughter. Following, closely, at her side was "Lucky", the three legged orphaned "Lurda". The young animal, untethered, matched her step for step. The other workers, around the fires, smiled at the sight.

Gia stopped well short of the smoking fires, as did her companion.

"Ta-rok! We have not talked much since this journey began. Did I come at a bad time?"

"We're just about finished here, little darling. He answered. What's on yer mind?

Before she could answer, Jim joined them. "Gia! Good to see you." How are you doing?"

"I am fine, uncle! She replied. Rojari and I have been busy planning our new home."

They had just married the previous year and were inseparable. Rojari was the son of the best carver in the village. He had followed his father's trade and become quite adept in his own right.

"Let's go over dere and sit down. Truck invited." It's not as smoky over dere."

As they made their way to a group of log seats, the little animal followed them.

"Looks like ya got a new friend, Gia." Truck said, watching the little creature Nuzzle Gias hand as she sat down.

"It started about five days ago, father. Bomar and his cousins asked me to watch over Lucky so they could go hunting. Now, he comes into my camp every day, looking for me. He follows me everywhere I go!"

The big smile on her pretty face told the brothers she didn't mind at all.

"Sometimes when I take my leg off to adjust it, he lays down in front of me and stares, she continued. He looks so sad when he does that."

"Maybe he wants ya ta make him a leg, too."

"Ta-rok! Would that be possible?" She asked, excitedly.

"I don't think it would work on an animal, sweetheart."

When he saw the disappointed look on her face, he quickly added. "But, den again, we could give it a try when we get ta our new home."

When the smile returned to her face he asked. "What was it ya were gonna tell me, darling?"

"I am going to have a baby, Ta-rok!" She replied, her eyes sparkling with happiness.

Truck just sat there, speechless, his mouth hanging open.

"That is wonderful news, Gia!" Jim said, running interference until Truck could collect himself. How soon?"

"It won't be for quite some time yet. She answered. I can hardly wait!"

Truck got up and gave her a big hug. "I'm so happy for ya, sweetheart." He said, tears running down his cheeks. I'm gonna be da best Grandpa dat kid will ever know."

Sitting down, again, Truck wiped his eyes. "Did ya tell your mother yet?"

"We had breakfast together, just, this morning. Before I had a chance to tell her, she looked at me and said, "You're pregnant, Gia! Aren't you?"

"How did she know?"

"Mothers know dese things. Truck answered. She could always tell, when ya were little. Da slightest little ache or pain ya had she could fix it before ya knew ya had it."

"Well, Ta-rok, uncle, I have to find Rojari. She said, as she rose from her seat. We'll come and visit you and mother, later, and talk more."

The two brothers hugged her and watched as she made her way toward her camp.

Her three legged companion loped at her side.

"Congratulations, brother!" Jim said, shaking the big man's hand.

"Thanks Jimbo!" Truck returned, with a worried look on his face.

"What's that look all about, my brother? You should be the happiest man in this village!"

'I am!' Truck replied.

"But?" Jim shot back at him, with a questioning look on his face.

"I'm kinda concerned about her keeping her balance when she starts ta get bigger. When women get pregnant dey ain't very graceful. What if she falls?"

"She'll be just fine, brother. Jim said. I couldn't detect more than a slight limp."

"I guess yer right, Jimbo! She can take care a herself. She always did."

"Amen ta dat, my brother! Jim replied. Let's finish up here and go tell Greg the good news!"

# CHAPTER 15

Two days later, as the morning "Sister" had just begun her trek across the heavens, the long caravan was on the move. Continuing on their southern course, their progress was impeded by the many stops they made to investigate a new plant, new river or any other anomaly the new terrain introduced to them. The tediousness, plaguing most of the journey, thus far, was replaced with these new and exciting discoveries. The world, as they once knew it, metamorphosed into a transition of exotic tastes, smells and sights, all were eager to sample.

Palm-like trees, many fifty feet or taller, shaded them with their sprawling frond branches. Clusters of seed pods covered the ground beneath them. When cracked open, a citrusy odor permeated the air. After a few brave individuals had sampled them, the sweet, almond- flavored nuts were added to the traveler's menu.

By trial and error, the foreigners to this strange new land, were trying to adapt to the unfamiliar environment, experimenting with all she had to offer.

Shortly before the morning sun was finishing her visit, the long line of travelers rested in a large palm tree laded glade. An enormous spring bubbled its bounty of cold water into a large pool.

Once all of the chores had been completed, people set off in small groups, exploring their surroundings. Others rested in the shade, sampling many of the new foods collected along the way.

Even their sturdy mounts and beasts of burden adapted to the change in their menu. The thick moss, they were accustomed to, was now replaced by grasses and other plants. They munched, contentedly, on the leafy green vegetation.

Bantor, Jim, Greg and their mates sat in a small circle, talking. Truck and Mara were out exploring. In front of them lay a small collection of exotic fruits and vegetables, all sizes, shapes and colors.

"Back on Earth, Greg and I used to give Truck anything we felt unsure of. Jim was saying, pointing to the mound of strange produce at their feet. If he ate it, we knew it was safe!"

"Or so we thought! Greg added. One time, we were in this farmer's field. I remember, he grew all kinds of vegetables. We came across these low plants. They were covered with small red peppers. Truck, always hungry, reaches down and picks one. He pops it into his mouth and starts munching away at it like it's the sweetest and juiciest thing he'd ever eaten. We asked him how it was."

"Delicious! He says." So, Jim and I each grab one of the small peppers and popped them into our mouths. After just three chomps, fire exploded. I remember Truck laughing his ass off, as we raced across that field looking for water or anything to put out the inferno inside our mouths."

"Later! Jim picked up the story. He informed us, they were the hottest peppers he'd ever eaten. When we asked him why he hadn't reacted to them like we did, he said he was teaching us a lesson. And, what lesson would that be? We asked."

"He replied. Every individual in life must take their own risks!"

"That is sound advice!" Bantor agreed. Never allow another to do something you are capable of doing yourself."

Right on cue, Truck and Mara approached their little circle. In one hand, Truck was carrying a round object. It was about twelve inches in diameter, yellow, with black spots.

"Now, what did you find?" Jim asked, as the late-comers took a seat.

"It kinda found me! Truck replied. Mara and I was walking through some bushes. I tripped and fell flat on my face inta one a dese things. My whole head was a sticky mess. Before I could wipe it off, some of it kinda got into my mouth. Pointing to the object, lying at his feet, he said. You are looking at da sweetest melon on two planets.

Mara and I, already, ate one."

"Are you, absolutely, certain it is safe to eat, Earth brother?" Bantor asked, casting a questioning glance at Jim and greg.

Taking an ivory knife from his belt, Truck split the melon in half. As the other's watched, he cut it into smaller pieces.

"Help yourselves, my friends!" He said, as he took a piece for himself and started eating.

No one took him up on his offer, until Mara took a piece and started to eat it.

A short while later, all that was left of the melon was a small pile of rinds and eight broad smiles covered with sticky juices.

The second "Sister" took up residence in the heavens, as the caravan departed the spring-fed glade. Curiosity stops were held to a minimum, as the weary refugees became more adapted to their surroundings and all the treasures it held.

Scouting parties combed their environs in all directions, diligently seeking out any hostiles or hazards that could, possibly, threaten their progress. The flat, grassy plain, in which they traveled, was studded here and there with low-growing shrubs. Small, reddish-brown berries grew on these plants. They were extremely bitter to the taste, as a few adventurous samplers found out. However, the indelible stains on their hands, informed them it would make an excellent dye. They would file this knowledge away for future use.

This new land was proving itself to be an enormous warehouse, abundant with a plethora of helpful products. The exciting thing about it was they had their entire lives in which to explore and implement these gifts.

As the three Earth brothers led their column steadily on, under the hot, mid-day sun, Jim scanned the distant landscape using Greg's ingenious telescope.

"We have riders approaching!" He announced to his brothers riding on either side of him. About a mile ahead of us."

"I see dem! Truck acknowledged. It looks like da" Posse"

Moments later, the five young men rode into their midst.

Julo, Marus and Salba led the way. Trailing, closely, behind them were Bomar and Tomal. Stretched between these last two youngsters, on lengths of braided, leather ropes, a furry creature struggled to free itself.

"What in da holy hell did you boys find now?" Truck asked, as they came to a stop in front of him.

"We were kind of hoping you could tell us, Uncle!" Marus replied.

"How did you happen upon this strange creature?" Greg inquired.

"About three miles ahead, lies a large patch of strange looking bushes. Julo answered.

When we approached, we noticed about twenty of these animals eating the strange fruit hanging from them. We took a few of them, also." He finished, tossing a round, purple object to Greg.

Catching it, smoothly in one hand, he studied it for a few moments.

"Here, Truck! Lunch is served!" He said, handing it to the big man..

As Truck sampled the strange object, Jim dismounted and walked toward the cowering creature. It ceased struggling, warily eying the approach of this two-legged stranger.

The furry animal stood, barely, two feet tall and balanced itself on four stubby legs.

It appeared to weigh in at, approximately, one hundred and fifty pounds. The tan colored hair, covering its entire body, was about two inches long. The hair around its neck stiffened, more noticeably the nearer Jim came to it. Its red eyes locked on to the Earthman's. Its short round head swayed in warning. Small ears stood erect from both sides of its head. The short, flat muzzle had small openings on either side. Panting heavily from its struggles, its mouth hung open. Large molars filled it, front to back, top to bottom. Strictly a plant eater, Jim guessed.

Its over-all shape was that of the wild pig, found on his former world. Its large belly hung, just, inches from the ground.

"Be careful, uncle! Tomal warned. He has, already, tried to take bites out of our mounts.

"It sure looks like da wild pigs we had on Earth. I wonder if dat one tastes as good." Truck added.

"Since you are so anxious to place this creature on our menu, get down here and give me a hand." Jim invited.

Jumping down from his mount, he joined his brother. "What's da plan, Jimbo?" He asked.

"A little rodeo action is in order. I think. Jim replied, taking two lengths of thongs from the pouch on his belt and handing one of them to his brother.

"Bomar! Tomal! When I give you the word, I want you to take all the slack out of your ropes and keep it taut." He ordered.

"You and I, my brother, will attempt to hog-tie it."

"You ready?" He asked the two mounted lads.

By this time, curious spectators from the halted caravan had made their way forward to find out what was causing the hold-up. They stopped short of the spectacle, starring at the strange animal.

Affirmative nods from the young men signaled their answers.

"Now!" Jim shouted.

Goading their mounts, slowly, in opposite directions, the leather rope pulled taut between them. The animal struggled, violently, but was unable to move off the spot.

The two Earthmen dove in from opposite sides, pinning the thrashing beast to the ground. Careful not to come into contact with the snapping jaws, they flipped the beast over and wound the leather cord around its legs. Truck, also, secured its jaws with another cord.

"Good job, Truck!" Jim said, staring down at their handy work.

"Let's get this critter secured to the back of your mount!"

"Wait a minute! Truck protested. Why do I have ta carry dis thing?"

"It's the obvious choice! Greg chimed in, as he sat his mount. The natural odors, emanating from your ride, will keep the little animal calm" He finished with a smile on his face, winking at Jim.

"A couple a black eyes would calm you down, too, dwarf!" Truck replied, shaking his fist.

"Come on! Let's tie this thing off and get this show back on the road!" Jim said, before his two siblings could exchange any more verbal blows.

Truck vented some of his displeasure. He grabbed the animal by its trussed up legs and in one smooth motion flung it onto the rear quarters of his mount. With another leather cord, he secured the dangling legs beneath his Lurda's belly and remounted.

As they continued on their march, once again, side by side, Jim made it a point to place his animal between those ridden by his brothers.

"By the way, Truck! How was that fruit the boys found?" Jim asked, breaking the silence.

"Delicious! He replied, staring straight ahead.

Jim looked across at Greg and smiled.

# CHAPTER 16

The next few days proved to be the most exciting and, at the same time, the most frustrating period of the entire journey. As the new discoveries mounted, people were becoming more and more reluctant to leave these beautiful areas. They were weary of traveling. Their only desire, now, was to settle into one of these abundant locations long enough to, thoroughly, enjoy all of her gifts.

"When will this journey end? Why isn't this place suitable for our village? What is it you are looking for? And, many more questions were pressed upon Bantor, daily.

The beleaguered Chieftain was deep into his thoughts, as he led his people further south. Exactly what he was seeking, he did not know. The ideal setting was out there, somewhere. He must keep searching. He was confident this location would reveal itself to him, when he came upon it.

Many scouting parties were dispersed. Their orders were to report any significant changes in the territory ahead of the slow moving caravan, anything different than what they had already experience.

The third "Sister" had, just, started her visit. A halt had to be called, soon, to set up their evening camp. A range of high hills rose in front of them. The exhausted travelers would reach them, within the hour.

"Bantor! Tonio called out. A rider approaches!" He pointed in the direction of the high mounds.

Soon, a rider galloped into their midst and fell in alongside Bantor's mount.

"What brings you here with such haste, Toma?" Bantor asked.

"My leader, on the other side of those tall hills lies a body of water, so vast, one cannot see the far shore. Roca sent me to tell you it would make a good night camp."

"How long do you think it will take, to reach this location? Bantor asked, excitement rising, as he dug deeply into his collection of old memories.

"We should be able to reach it long before the third "Sister" retires for the evening. Toma replied. There is a safe path through the hills. I will show you!"

"Excellent, Toma! Tonio! Notify the Earthmen! Tell them to increase the pace, slightly."

It wasn't too long before the caravan emerged from the shadows of the large hills.

In front of them, no more than a mile off, The third "Sister" cast her brilliance on the vast, shimmering, magnificence of an immense body of water. The palm-like trees, studding the shoreline, swayed in time to a slight breeze. The grassy turf, on which they had traveled forever, thinned out, until it was replaced, in its entirety by coarse, white sand.

To the people, accustomed to narrow streams of water, the sight was overwhelming.

A halt was called to the caravan, beneath the shade of the swaying trees.

Bantor dismounted and walked toward the edge of the water. He was, soon, joined by the three Earthmen.

Truck knelt down close to where the waves lapped at the shoreline. He cupped a hand and dipped it into the water. He brought it up to his mouth and tasted.

"Dat's clean, fresh water he announced. What we got here is a damn big lake, not a salty ocean."

"What is "lake" and "ocean"? Bantor asked.

"On our old world those were names given to bodies of water. Greg replied. Usually, when a body of water contained salt, it was classified as an ocean. Most of the lakes were salt- free."

"My people will never be thirsty!" Bantor said, smiling.

"Dat's for sure!" Truck agreed.

As the people busied themselves, setting up camp, taking care of the animals and cooking meals, Bantor leaped upon the back of his "Lurda.

"Take a ride with me Earth brothers!"

A short while later, the four of them were at the summit of one of the lofty hills, overlooking the bay. Scanning the wild vista, in all directions, they spotted herds of "Lurda", grazing on the plains to the south of them. In another direction, they spotted groups of the pig-like creatures the "Posse" had captured, a few days before. They dined on the succulent fruit, that grew, profusely, in this area. When they had butchered and sampled the animal, for the first time, the brothers all agreed it did, indeed, taste like pork.

All of the strange fruit and vegetable plants, they had sampled along the way, they would soon discover, growing abundantly near- by. Grazing for their animals was unlimited, on the vast plains surrounding them.

"My friends, I believe our search has ended! Bantor spoke. When we left our previous village behind, I wasn't quite sure of what it was I sought. But, at this very moment, I feel I have found it! Do you feel this wondrous area is worthy of the attempt to build our new village?" He asked.

"It is, indeed!" Greg replied. It abounds with the necessary criteria one must consider, while searching for a new abode; An ample food supply, fresh water, and the security of high hills at ones back and the water protecting our front door."

"I'm more than ready to settle down, again. Jim added. I agree with you, Bantor. This is, definitely, the right decision!"

"Amen ta dat! Truck chimed in. I know da people are more den ready!"

"Well, my brothers. Let us go and find out what they think. Shall we?"

Spurring their animals into a slow trot, they retraced their steps back to the camp.

Moments after dismounting, all were summoned to meet at the edge of the water.

A short while later, Bantor stood staring at the small waves, as they chased one another across the broad, liquid expanse.

At his back, sat every member of the expedition, waiting expectantly for him to begin..

Looking up to the sky, his silent thoughts filled his mind. "Father, let the decisions I make be the right ones! Our people are weary and need a place to call their home.

Today we plant the seeds of our futures. Help me to guide them the way you would have and help our people to flourish."

He turned around and looked into the fatigued countenances of anticipation, fatigue,

And, yes, even hopelessness.

"My people, our journey has been long. He began. You have weathered it well! I am proud of every one of you. Your efforts have kept us all united."

He paused, taking in the travel-weary faces.

"On this day, I have but one question I must ask. Are you ready to end this arduous journey and begin building your futures?"

A tumultuous roar exploded from the crowd, sounding out their relieved assents.

When the emotional crescendo dwindled, somewhat, He continued.

"It is confirmed, then. He proclaimed. From this day forward we will refer to this place as our home."

Another boisterous cheer echoed out over the big water. The elated immigrants held nothing back, as they celebrated. All their pent up fears and anxieties dissolved. Their lives had been put back on track, once, again and they embraced their new futures, zealously.

Later, as the exuberant implants to this new land retired for the evening, their minds were not bombarded by fear, frustration or uncertainty. They would dream, peacefully, of rebuilding futures, once more, restored to them.

# CHAPTER 17

In the many days that followed, a large settlement was carved into the façade of the uncharted wilderness. Gradually, its permanence became as indigenous to the area as the forests, hills and all other natural landmarks.

A thick, wooded glade, two miles from the village site, provided an ample supply of material for the construction of private dwellings, storage sheds and the ten-foot stockade, surrounding the entire village. Starting at the shoreline, on one side, it bent around, enclosing all the homes, in various stages of completion, curving its way, once again until it met the far end of the shoreline. It was, virtually, in the shape of a horseshoe. The lakeshore ran across its entire front. In essence, it was protected on three sides by the wooden barrier and the fourth side protected by the lake.

Four Lurdas were hitched up, to each of the wagons, in order to move the enormous amount of lumber.

Crews, consisting of many men, women and older children were divided up between the laborious tasks. While some cut the trees down, others hauled them. As others split the trees into usable lumber, others focused on the construction of dwellings, storage huts and all other necessary buildings. Three springs bubbled within the village site. Wells, with buckets hanging over them were built, providing them with a constant source of uncontaminated water. Two large corrals were built outside the village, one on either end.

The village meeting place was built on the shoreline, just a few yards from the lapping reach of the pristine lake.

Hunting and foraging parties didn't have to venture far, in the pursuit of sustenance. Soon, their storage sheds were filled to capacity. The contentment of the people was reflected by the overall acceptance of their new life style. No longer did the impending fear of death and destruction loom over them. Every day was a new adventure.

However, shortly after their arrival on the village site, a strange occurrence shocked them all to a standstill; "Rain".

Living their entire lives in the arid north, shallow streams and springs were their only watering sources. What little evaporation, transpiring in the area, balanced out natures growing process, without the need of any rain.

So, one day, soon after they had arrived in this area, dark clouds formed, blotting out most of the "Sister's" sparkling rays. This new phenomena caused panic among the villagers. They rushed for the protection of their shelters and peered out, nervously, as the rain started to fall.

After the three Earthmen had assured them it was a natural occurrence, they gave it no more thought. The children and, even, some of the adults could be seen frolicking in it after that.

Exploratory Parties ventured in all directions. Accurate maps were made of the region, encircling the large settlement for many miles. Some of these expeditions lasted many days. Roca and his twenty men were one of these Far-seeking groups. No one had heard a word from them in the last twenty days.

Narrow catwalks, which ran on top of the three-sided enclosure, were manned day and night by a half dozen men. This was, still, virgin territory, so, no security risks were taken. Young boys and girls alternated as runners. At least one was stationed at all times, along the interior of the wooden barrier. Given a discovery by one of the sentries, the news was then imparted to one of the runners, who raced through the village, broadcasting the information.

The three Earthmen headed a small crew outside the north gate. They were driving in more posts around the large corral. The day before, they had completed the large corral around the south gate.

Lurdas were prolific creatures, giving birth twice yearly. Usually, they gave birth to two calves each time. Triplets were a rarity. In the short time since their homecoming, forty new calves had been born. These would be added to their future riding stock and beasts of burden. Milk was gathered from these animals for the making of butter and cheese.

Herds of the smaller "Lurdas", indigenous to this area, were hunted for their meat and fur.

"I gotta idea. Truck said, as he worked alongside his two brothers. How bout we build six or eight foot sections of da rails already connected ta da posts. Dis way, when wer ready ta expand, dere ready ta go. Kinda like dos prefab houses dey got back on Earth.

"That is an excellent idea, Truck! Jim agreed. We'll be able to stay ahead of their population explosions much more efficiently. Tomorrow, we can begin their construction and start stock-piling them for future use."

"Good thinking, you big ape! Greg added, as he finished driving a post into the ground with a rock hammer. And, here I thought that round thing sitting on your shoulders was just for decoration."

Tapping the side of his head with a finger and smiling broadly, Truck replied.

"Dere's a lot more in here den you think, Shorty!"

"And, I'm certain, most of it can be used as fertilizer." Greg shot back, smiling.

Before Truck had a chance to retaliate, Jim intervened.

"We're just about finished with this section. Let's take a little break."

"Ya read my mind, Jimbo! I was jus thinkin about breakin something myself." He finished, giving his younger brother the evil eye.

A chorus of laughter accompanied them, as they made their way to the village gate.

Soon, they were seated around a fire, in front of Jim's hut, eating a hearty stew and flat bread. Their mates had joined them and they were re hashing the day's events.

"I talked with Alijo this morning. Lona was saying. She is deeply concerned about Roca's absence. Worrying about here mate isn't helping her pregnancy any."

"Groups such as this have been known to spend long periods of time away from home." Greg replied. If any problems had occurred, they would have dispatched a rider to notify us."

"But, what if they were unable to do so?' Sanda asked.

Before the situation became emotionally out of control, Jim Replied.

"If they are not back in the next two days, we'll send out a search party."

"Dey shouldn't be too hard ta find." Truck said. Roca and his men were following the lake shore to da north. He told me he wanted ta find out how long it would take dem ta travel around da whole thing."

The second "Sister" was halfway through her splendor, when one of the runners carried word from the sentries. In a loud voice, he announced the approach of a large party of men, nearing the village.

The three Earth men raced to the nearest ladder leading up to the catwalk.

Greg took the telescope from his belt and focused on the direction indicated by the sentry.

"It's Roca's group, he announced. And, they have a guest with them."

"Let me have a look!" Jim said, Taking the glass from his brother.

On the back of one of the Lurdas sat a creature, clinging to the rider in front of him.

"What in the hell did they find, now? Jim asked no one in particular, handing the glass back to his brother and racing down the ladder. Followed by his two siblings, they Made their way to the south gate.

The patrol was fifty yards away, when they arrived. They through open the large gate and waited.

Roca and his men dismounted and turned their and turned their animals loose in the large corral. Walking at his side was a creature, approximately, six feet tall, with a muscular build. Its skin was a deep, reddish brown, almost black. The black hair, on his head was in the shape of a long topknot, hanging down to his shoulders. It resembled a tail. The eyes were slate gray in color. Anatomically, it matched the human form. It wore a green, kilt-like garment made from some form of rough leather. The sandals on his feet were made from the same material.

Bantor and many curious onlookers had joined the Earthmen at the gate.

"Welcome home, Roca!" Bantor greeted. Staring at the stranger, he smiled.

"It is good to be back, my leader!" Roca returned.

Without any prompting, the dark visitor stepped in front of Bantor and placed his right hand on his left shoulder. "I, Ponsel, am honored to meet with you, also." He replied.

The look of surprise, on Bantor's face, brought a smile to the stranger's face, also.

Turning in place, Bantor ordered his people to gather at the meeting place, at once.

To Roca and his guest he said; "It would seem you have much to tell us, Roca!"

Looking into the dark man's eyes, he offered a "formal" invitation.

"Ponsel! We are the ones who would be honored, if you joined us!"

A short while later, every man, woman and child was gathered on the shoreline, in front of their village.

Bantor, Roca and the three Earth men, along with their mates sat, facing the villagers,

who murmured among themselves in anticipation, anxious to learn about this mysterious, dark stranger.

Ponsel sat between Bantor and Roca, staring back at the villagers, trying not to show how nervous he really felt.

"Honored guest! Bantor began. I must ask, first off, how is it you speak and understand the "people's" language?"

"When your men found me and saved me from my "last journey", I was compelled to express my gratitude. Ponsel replied. Once they got over the surprise, I was fully capable of conversing with them in a common language, they asked me the same question. Since the very moment I sprang from my mother's womb, thirty-five years ago, it was the only language I have I have known.

"Could it be possible our ancestors, from the distant past, coexisted?" Roca asked.

When no one volunteered their opinion, Greg joined in. "On the world my brothers and I came from, people were known to migrate and settle in areas far from their birth place. Physical characteristics evolved, through many generations, making them more compatible to their chosen location. Dark skin in the hotter climates made it easier to cope with the heat, to go for longer periods without drinking when settling drier areas and whatever nature deemed necessary to make one comfortable with his environment."

Ponsel stared at the Earthman, before he spoke. "What other world is there, but, this one?"

"That story will have to wait for another time to be told, my friend. Bantor injected. Now, my people are curious as to how you came among us."

"Leader of the people, Ponsel replied. I would defer to your man, Roca. He is responsible for extending my life. He owns the right to tell his story."

Nodding in appreciation, of the dark man's humble gester, Bantor turned to Roca.

"Well, my friend, Your audience awaits you. Tell them a good story!"

# CHAPTER 18

"For many days we followed the shores of the big water. Many detours were taken when mighty cliffs grew flush with the big water's edge or forests were so dense we were forced to seek other paths."

Roca paused and looked out over the big crowd. The gathered people were intrigued, as they listened to the story of his latest expedition.

"About eight days ago, we were traveling a stretch of shore covered with pure white sand. Roca continued. A small tree had broken away from a forest and the waves of the big water had embedded it into the sandy shore. Upon investigation, we discovered Ponsel tangled in its branches. He was alive! But, his breathing was very shallow. As we carried him into the shade of nearby trees, he began mumbling in his delirium. To our surprise, he was speaking in the "people's" language. We gave him water and made him as comfortable as we could. After a while, he revived long enough to tell us his name and ask who we were. We camped on that spot, for a few days, while he regained his strength. The story he told us was one of the strangest I've ever heard. We had no way of knowing how much further it would be, around the big water, so we retraced our steps and made our way home."

Looking toward the small group, clustered on his right, he addressed the dark stranger.

"Ponsel! I believe it is time we heard your story!"

The dark man rose to his feet and stood alongside the native. Before Roca joined the small group, they both placed their right hands on one another's shoulder. All would soon learn, this gesture was as common to Ponsel's people as the American's handshake.

The large gathering was, unusually, quiet as it awaited answers to all of their questions..

"I greet you, people of the land! He began. I am Ponsel of the "Tepu" clan. Many days ago, I was cast into the big water to begin my final journey." Noticing the questioning looks, reflecting back at him, He continued.

"My people live on floating craft called "Turboks". We travel endlessly on the big water, competing with other clans for new hunting territories. The clan which controls the majority of these areas is the stronger clan."

"Before the last sun of each day, dips below the horizon, we make landfall on whichever land mass we are closest to at the time. Not to do so would put us at the mercy of the mighty "Krada". It prowls the big waters only during the dark hours, destroying and consuming all in its sight. Some worship this vicious creature, but, all fear it!"

"It was shortly before nightfall when I was cast into its watery lair. Why had this happened to me, you are wondering. I will tell you my new friends!"

"When a Tepu man or women reaches the age of thirty-five years, they must give up their space on the Turbok to prevent over population. Each of these craft have, but, one leader. He will remain so as long as he is able to thwart any challenges from his subordinates. Nemor, the leader of my clan, is the oldest person among us. Through the years, he has successfully met and defeated all of his challengers. He is big and powerful, leading his clan by intimidation and cruelty. Before my allotted time was up and my opportunity of a challenge, he had some of his deceitful cohorts beat me and throw me from the craft. Nemor knew I was capable of wresting the leadership of the clan from him.

"I struggled, for what seemed like an eternity, to keep my head above water. I spotted a large plant floating nearby. With the last of my strength, I made my way to it and managed to climb on top of it. For two cycles of the suns, I drifted. Eventually, I lost consciousness. The next thing I can remember, was looking at Roca's face. When he talked to me in my people's language, I was convinced I had, actually, arrived at my final journey's end. My story has been told! Know, then, Good people, that, I, Ponsel will devote the rest of my life repaying the debt I owe every one of you. With those last words spoken, he rejoined the small group.

Bantor rose to meet him. Laying his right hand on Ponsel's shoulder, he spoke. "Stay as long as you wish my friend."

Returning the gesture, he nodded and took a seat next to Roca.

Turning and facing the crowd, Bantot spoke. "My people, I know there are many questions you would have asked. But, for now, return to your daily duties. Or guest will be among us for a time. Enough, so we will all have a chance to learn about one another. Tomorrow is another day!"

As he rejoined his group, the large crowd started to disperse, talking among themselves, as they went.

"Ponsel! Tell us more about these turboks." Jim asked.

"What is it you wish to learn, villager?" Ponsel returned.

"The dimensions, method of propulsion and how they are constructed. Jim shot back.

"The turbok I called home was the largest one of all the clans. More than three hundred people shared its space. Each family had its own shelter, above deck. Flat stones, gathered from dry land, keep fires from eating the deck. Ten feet below them are two large storage units, filled with the bounty of our hunting and gathering. One is located near the front of the turbok, the other toward the rear. No one ever went hungry. Between these two storage units, below deck, were double rows of seats, running almost the entire length of the vessel, on either side. Men alternate shifts at the long oars, dipping into the water."

The three Earthmen, listening intently to the dark man, stared at each other knowingly. Slave galleys, Viking ships and all other vessels in ancient times, back on Earth, were propelled across oceans by the sweat of man, either slaves or free.

"Have your people ever used sails?" Greg asked.

Looking, questioningly, Ponsel replied. "What is a sail?"

"Sails are large sheets of wind-resistant material, stretched high above the deck of watercraft. Attached to masts or spars they can be directed to catch a breeze and propel the vessel in any direction." Greg answered.

"In my many years spent on "Kressa", our name for the big water, I have seen no such invention." Ponsel returned.

Bantor, Roca and the women had left moments before to attend other matters. The three Earthmen had the dark stranger to themselves.

"Ponsel! Jim asked. If you had it in your means to challenge Nemor for leadership, would you do so?"

"When one is cast to the fates of his final journey, he loses everything. Said Ponsel. I have never mated, so, I have no women or young ones to weep my absence. My weapons and clothing were all I possessed. However, my status as 'first" hunter was a high one. I have no doubt in my mind

Nemor promised this position to Zorboth, one of the two henchmen who cast me into the waiting arms of Kressa. To answer your question, villager, if it were possible I would wreak my vengeance on them and reclaim my status."

"Would you consider helping us to build a water craft suitable enough to navigate Kressa? Greg asked. Assuming, of course, you have knowledge of their construction."

"Every member of the Tepu clan learns, at a very young age, how to build a Turbok. Ponsel answered. Its maintenance is paramount to our survival. If it will defer the debt I owe you and your people, for extending my life, I will gladly assist you."

Truck had remained quiet during this exchange, listening and analyzing the conversation. He was not entirely convinced of the validity of Ponsel's words. His nature dictated to him, until complete trust was earned, a part of him needed to know more about an individual. The reserved approach had made it easier to deflect consequential incidents in the past. For the moment, he would go along with whatever plan was realized. But! He would keep a close eye on the stranger.

"Truck! Jim said, bringing Truck's mind back into the present. Is there anything you wish to add?"

"Ya! I'd like ta know more about dos monsters ya was talkin about." He replied, hiding his suspicions.

Looking at the big man with a bewildered look on his face, Ponsel hesitated before answering. "Your speech is different, villager! Are you from another clan?"

Jim and Greg couldn't help but laugh.

"I can assure you, ponsel, our brother comes from the same clan. Greg answered. Do you wish me to translate for you?"

"Keep it up, half pint, and da broken jaw, yer gonna get, will make it hard ta translate anything." Truck shot back.

"Pay those two no mind, Ponsel! Jim intervened. Since childhood they've played this word game with each other. Believe me, it's harmless!"

Looking at Greg and Truck, ponsel noticed the smiles on their faces, adding to his bewilderment. Finally, he spoke.

The Krada is half as long as the longest of our turboks. Its flat head makes up for one third of its size. The gaping jaws can open wide enough to swallow three men standing side by side. Its sleek gray form has a dorsal fin running the length of its body. Two, powerful legs in front, it propels itself through the water with its webbed paws. Long talons, extending from each paw, are ideal for catching and holding its prey. The massive jaws, filled with double rows of razor-sharp teeth, make short work of anything coming into contact with it. The long, flat tail pushes it through the water at speeds faster than our most powerful oarsmen. I have seen, with my own eyes, the carnage it causes."

"It is, certainly, no wonder your people seek the shores at night." Greg commented.

"Sounds like you just described a cross between a crocodile and a shark." Jim added.

"One, nasty son of a bitch!" Truck chimed in.

Starring at the big man, once again, Ponsel asked. "What is sunnava bitch?"

All three Earthmen broke out laughing, leaving him even more bewildered.

"It's just an expression, my friend. Jim said. Do not concern yourself!"

"I don't know about you guys, but, I'm getting kinda hungry!" Truck said. Let's go and git something ta eat!"

# CHAPTER 19

The morning sun was barely half-way into her cycle. Her warm rays trickled through the leafy canopy, down upon the men as they cut their way through the forest. Many trees, fifty feet or longer, already lay dormant on the forest's floor. Nearby sat five wagons, each hitched to four Lurdas, waiting to haul the woody produce to their village. Rough-hewn planks would be coaxed from each of the green giants.

Ponsel acted as over-seer to the project. He selected the trees most apt to contain the necessary lumber needed in the construction of a ship. Many were the volunteers, anxious to be part of, yet, another mysterious invention contrived by the Earthmen.

When it was decided a sufficient number of trees had been harvested for their project, they started loading the wagons. Many trips were necessary to transport it all to the village. It was deposited on the shoreline, fifty feet down from their meeting Area.

Using stone awls, wedges and hammers, in time, they amassed a large stack of planks.

Large, flat stones ground gritty sand over each board, until they became somewhat smooth. Long boards, bent around the wide staves of the ship, were secured with wooden pegs. The projected dimensions of the finished craft would be, approximately, seventy feet long from bow to stern and twenty-five feet wide amidships. It would be small, in comparison to the Turboks of Ponsel's clan.

Many days, of intense labor, produced the skeletal outlines of the vessel. Long boards were being bent to its shape and pegged into place. When completed, there would be, approximately, seven feet of draft from keel to water line. Five foot high railings, called gunwhales, encircled the entire upper deck of the ship. The area, below decks was divided into three compartments. The forward hold would contain extra rope, ballast and other equipment necessary in maintaining the vessel. The aft compartment would be used to store food, weapons and bedding.

The large compartment amidship would act as their berthing compartment. Woven grass hammocks would be strung for the sailor's comfort.

A fifteen foot mast was fixed amidships. Its bare yardarms would soon hold a sail twenty feet wide and ten feet in height. A plant had been discovered, near the village. The fibrous growth, that covered it, was woven into waterproof, and hopefully, wind- proof sheets. The same material was, also, woven for the construction of their hawsers and other lengths of rope, in different diameters, to secure the sail, lifelines, hammocks and a thousand other uses.

A large rudder was carved and installed that could be operated by one person from the after deck. The fortuitous discovery of another tree, growing in their vicinity, solved the problem of leakage. This gnarly looking gray plant exuded a sap-like substance. It hardened the instant it came into contact with the air. When huge chunks of this hardened sap were heated over a fire it became liquid once again. When applied to all of the seams under and around the entire ship it hardened, creating a water-proof seal. Many chunks of the hardened material were put into storage for future use, if needed.

Large boulders lined the center-line inside the hull. This ballast was necessary to insure the vessel did not become top-heavy and keel over. By adding or subtracting these stones, they could control how high or how low the vessel rode in the water.

Many days went by before it was completed. It sat on huge wooden blocks, at the edge of the shoreline, just out of the reach of the lapping waves.

To launch it, a wide and deep, trough had to be dug, connecting it to the water. When the trough was thought to be deep enough, beneath the ship, the blocks would be pulled out from under her. Hopefully, it would float. Tomorrow would reveal the culmination of all their efforts.

Shortly before night cloaked the world with her darkness, the three Earthmen and their mates sat around a fire in front of Jim's hut.

"I have exhausted the limited store of knowledge I have, concerning ship building. Jim admitted. From the deck down, Ponsel has shared his expertise. But, the mast and sail I'm not so sure about."

"Don't worry yourself so much, my brother. Greg replied. At least we have a prototype, now. We can iron out the glitches through experience."

"Dat's right, Jimbo. Truck joined in. If it don't work we, just, start all over!"

"I cannot believe something as big and heavy as that will even float, in the first place." Sanda said.

"Have you not noticed, while washing out our wooden bowls how they float upon the water? But, when they are filled, they sink. Jim explained. If anything is made water-tight, it will float, regardless of the weight. My main concern is not having enough ballast in her bottom to keep it from keeling over."

"We'll make sure there is a pile of stones at hand." Greg added.

"I don't know if I want to go out on the big water in that thing! Mara joined in. After what Ponsel told us about the monsters lurking there, I think I'd be too afraid!"

"Don't worry yer pretty little head about dat! Truck said. Were gonna have plenty a fire power on board! If we see one a dos bastards, we'll blow it back ta hell!"

"Will we be close enough to the shore in case something does happen?" Lona asked, nervously.

"Don't you worry, my love! Greg answered. We will have thoroughly tested it out before we risk any ones lives."

"Has any one thought of a good name for her? Jim asked. She has to have a name before her maiden voyage."

"Why is it a "she" and not a "he"? Sanda asked.

In our Navy, back on Earth there were many explanations given describing its gender. Jim volunteered. The one I always preferred was its association with "Mother" nature. The ship was assumed to be one of her daughters, she had trained to sail the seven seas."

"I guess dat would make sense! Truck agreed. I was kinda thinkin about dat a few days ago and I think I got da perfect name for it."

"This ought to be good! Greg said with a big smile on his face. And, pray tell, my large brother what did you come up with?"

"You guys remember when we went up to Alaska on dat fishing trip? Dat one guy dat almost rammed us with his big boat?"

When his brothers both nodded their acknowledgement, he continued.

"I'll never forget da name a dat boat! The "Raw Dawg". He finished.

Looking at Jim, Greg replied. "And our large brother, probably, thinks "Dog" is spelt correctly."

"That is a good name, Truck! Jim said, quickly, to defuse another, possible, verbal spat. However, other than the three of us, no one on this world has ever heard of a "dog".

"Besides the fact, it needs a feminine title." Greg added.

"How about a feminine title and a message, at the same time?" Jim replied.

"What did ya have on yer mind, Jimbo? Truck asked.

"Hope"! Jim answered.

"Perfect fit! Greg said. We hope to find Ponsel's people, restoring his status among them. We "hope" our creation floats. Brilliant!"

The others agreed. Tomorrows were always full of hope. They would, soon, find out how much.

# CHAPTER 20

The first "Sister" sun had barely trickled her warm rays over the horizon, as the village stirred. Morning meals were rapidly consumed. People were, already, congregating around the land-locked object of their curiosity. Pessimism and optimism ran together, equally, in their thoughts.. The hard work, invested in this project over the last two months, would soon be realized. Some believed the heavy, wooden structure would sink out of sight immediately after launching. Others, who had worked on projects contrived by the Earthmen in the past, felt they would, soon, be witnessing another amazing creation.

One of the first things they noticed was the bold lettering spelling out the word, "Hope", stained into its transom. Greg had gathered the dye-producing berries from a bush, one mile from the village, earlier, this morning. After crushing them, he used a piece of discarded leather and daubed the letters into life. The reddish-brown color stood out in vivid contrast to the light colored wood.

Many men, using wooden shovels, dug out a huge pit around the vessel. Only a narrow sand ridge, at the shoreline, prevented the water from reaching in and carrying it out into the waiting arms of "Kressa". Once it was deemed, the pit was deep enough, this barricade would be removed. On the other side of the sand ridge, the shoreline dropped to a depth of ten feet. It was this sudden drop-off that had decided the location of the launching. Soon, the excavation crew climbed out of the seven-foot deep pit.

"Remove the barricade!" Jim shouted.

In less time than it takes to tell, The obstruction was removed. Water gushed into the pit, over-flowing the shore. For an instant, the small vessel did not move. Then, suddenly, it started rocking back and forth as the incoming waves reached into the small lagoon, they had excavated beneath the vessel.

"I believe she's floating free, Jim!" Greg announced excitedly.

A triumphant cheer rose from the crowd, watching in disbelief, as the incoming waves surrounded the craft and gently nudged her into the open water.

A heavy rope, made from the resilient fibers of another plant growing near the village, had been attached to a wooden cleat located in the bow of the vessel. The other end was secured around a large tree near the shoreline, preventing it from escaping too far off shore.

"Come on, you two! Jim said, indicating his two siblings. Let's go for a swim!" Walking to the water's edge, they dove into the drop-off and swam out to their floating creation. One by one, they navigated the rope ladder hanging from the bow. Gaining the deck, seven feet above the waterline, they turned and waved to the jubilant crowd hugging the shoreline.

This sent another loud cheer, echoing back to them.

"The first thing we have to check for is leakage. Jim replied. Greg, check the after hold. Truck, you check the one forward. I'll check amidships."

As they hastened to inspect the given areas, the small ship rocked gently beneath their feet. A short time later they met above deck, beneath the thick mast. No leakage was discerned. They did agree, however, that she sat too high in the water. More ballast would be added to counter-act this problem.

"Before we take her out for the maiden voyage, I suggest we build a dock. Greg suggested. Some of the people still have an aversion to swimming."

"Especially, after hearing about the monster Ponsel described." Jim agreed.

"We gotta build some small fishin boats. Truck chimed in. Ta get dem used ta bein on da water.'

"That will be our next project, Truck, after we get our dock built. Jim said. But, for now, we have to make sure our ship is seaworthy. We don't want all of our hard work sinking from under us."

Staring at the many faces, gathered on shore, Greg spotted the dark man. "It's hard to believe people, living most of their lives upon a body of water, are incapable of swimming." He said.

"I think the stories about the terrible "Krada" they've actually, experienced, has a lot to do with it. Jim replied. Plus the fact, they associate the water with their "final journey".

"Dey was always tellin people about sharks, octopussy and other monsters dat could eat ya liven in da oceans back home. Truck added. But dat didn' keep da people from swimming in it."

"You'll never have to worry about that! Will you, my brother?" Greg interjected, with a big smile on his face, winking at Jim.

"Why da you say dat?" Truck asked.

"Because they'd probably spit you out, anyway." Greg answered.

Jim broke out laughing.

"Come here, midget!" Truck bellowed.

Before Greg could take one step, he was caught in Truck's iron grip, raised into the air and flung over the railing in a perfect arc.

"Let's see if dat big bastard likes da taste of chicken legs."

Jim was still laughing. Before he was aware of it, he, too, was flying through the air.

As the two heads broke the surface, Truck looked down at them.

"Now, dat's funny!" He said, with a big grin on his face. Vaulting the railing, he cannon-balled his two brohers and swam for shore.

A short while later, they discovered the lake bottom was almost solid bedrock, only two feet below sand. It would have been near impossible to fix pillars permanently at the end of their dock. Not to be deterred, a portable, floating dock was constructed. Twelve feet long and four feet wide, it could be, easily, moved in or out of the water. A designated swimmer, carrying the ends of two ropes, would attach them to the anchored ship, twelve feet off shore.

All that day and most of next, saw a constant line of curious spectators crossing the floating dock to inspect the strange vessel. To prevent over-crowding, only twenty people at a time were allowed on board. They were impressed with the buoyant stability of the large invention and the efficient use of space below decks.

The three Earthmen and Ponsel acted as hosts, answering questions, directing traffic and assisting people on and off the small ship.

The third "Sister" sun had almost spent her allotted time, before the last of the curiosity seekers stepped ashore. Only a handful of natives, from the entire village, adamantly, refused to set foot on the floating creation.

Two large boulders acted as anchors. Attached to thick, braided ropes one hung from the stern, the other from the bow.

Roca worked at the far end of the dock, detaching it from the ship. The twelve-foot utility walkway was, quickly, hauled up on the shore.

As the people melted away to take care of personal chores, a small group assembled in the meeting area. Bantor, Tonio, Roca and Ponsel sat around a fire pit, watching the flames attack a large log. Although the nights were far less cooler than in the region of their former home, fire always provided comfort and security.

They had been discussing the proposed attempt to search for Ponsel's people.

"How many men will be necessary for this mission?" Bantor asked.

Jim had, already, given this much thought. "Besides myself and my two brothers, Ponsel, Tonio and roca, I would say twenty more men would be sufficient. He answered. We cannot risk overcrowding."

Bantor paused for a moment, before responding. "Twenty-six men against a force of thousands?, how can you even hope to accomplish anything, given those overwhelming odds?"

"We have, at least, three vital elements in our favor. Greg interjected. Surprise, maneuverability, and Nevoan fire power!"

"If we can, successfully, locate Ponsel's Turbok and he initiates his right to challenge Nemor for leadership, we will have accomplished our mission." Jim added.

"And, what will become of you and your men if ponsel should lose the challenge?" Bantor asked.

"I will not lose the challenge! The dark man spoke for himself. For Many years I had no other choice, but, to bide my time, while watching Nemor bully and instill fear among the people. I would have made a difference in how my people lived their lives, if I had not been denied my right! He is big and strong, but chooses to employ others to do his dirty deeds. In my eyes, that makes him a coward. My only concern is of the henchmen who serve him."

"Don't worry about dat, my friend. Truck said. We'll keep dos other bastards off your back!"

Ponsel nodded his appreciation. How soon before we begin this improbable adventure?" Bantor inquired.

"I believe, in about two weeks, we should have all the kinks ironed out. Jim replied. We'll take the "Hope" on a short cruise to see how she handles. The men I've selected will be well-versed in her behavior, by then."

As the night's dark forces marched in, capturing the day's light, the village slept. The few, still awake, rebelled. Heavy thoughts, bombarding their minds, fought against dreams. A voyage into the unknown was unsettling. Could any survive it?

# CHAPTER 21

As the first "Sister" sprayed her warmth onto the world below, a small ship sliced through the rippling façade of "Kressa", the big water. The third day into her training cruise, "Hope" was performing admirably. The pivoting mast, they had installed, could be turned by two men in any direction, to catch the prevailing winds. The extra ballast, they had added, lowered her in the water by two feet. No longer top-heavy, she answered her rudder more quickly. As the crew became more familiar with her nuances, they became more at ease, especially after what had occurred the previous evening.

The star-lit night had revealed one of the monsters, trailing in their wake.

The thirty foot long "Krada" had made its way to within twenty-five yards off their stern. Most of the crew was still awake, performing their shipboard duties, when one of the look-outs sounded the alarm.

Moments later, Truck and a few others, armed with 'Dracos", the powerful Nevoan weapons, blasted the creature to fish bait. In no time at all, the surrounding water was filled with no less than a dozen more of its relatives, in a violent, feeding frenzy. Any evidence of their fallen comrade was quickly devoured. Needless to say, all look-outs were more alert, after this incident.

Ponsel had told them, the carnivorous creatures traveled in packs. Each one of these consisted of ten or more of the veracious fish. Patrolling their own territories, from sun down to sun up, they sated their enormous appetites by consuming all in their way. If it wasn't for their curious habit of surfacing, when quarry was detected, no prey stood a chance. The eyes, of this creature, shone an evil red glow, before attacking. These two lanterns of death are, probably, what brought it to the attention of the look-out.

It was decided, immediately after this incident, to end their training cruise and return home. There they would rest for a few days, before re-outfitting the ship for their main voyage.

As the morning "Sister" continued on her journey through the sky, the steady breeze nudging "Hope" across the water, suddenly, slackened. Ponsel was showing a few people how they fished. Large nets had been constructed of supple vines. Two of them hung at the ends of braided leather ropes, trailing out from each side of the stern. Wooden floats were attached to each net. When the floats sunk out of sight, it signified the net was heavy with fish or, possibly, debris floating in the water. In any case, it was pulled aboard.

Soon, The after-deck of "Hope" contained a writhing mass of colorful fish of many shapes and sizes. After ponsel had educated them as to the tastiest of the flopping creatures, the rest were thrown back into the water.

A short while later, every crew member not on duty, was gathered amidships. They sat around the stone fire hearth, as the dark man showed them how his people cooked the fish.

Letting out a loud belch, Truck throw another handful of bones into the fire. "Dos were delicious, little buddy! Tasted kinda like da walleyes we caught back on Earth."

"This "Earth" you speak of, Ta-rok, this was the world you and your siblings came from?"

"Dat's right! Truck replied. As a matter a fact, we was onna fishin trip ta one of our favorite lakes when dos bastards captured us and took us here in one a dere space ships."

"From what world did these "bastards" come from?" Ponsel asked.

Jim and Greg sat there, listening to their brother describing how they came to be on this world. Smiling at one another, they knew Ponsel was about to be thoroughly confused, after hearing Truck's description.

"Dey was either martians or some other alien assholes dat traveled in space." Truck answered.

Shaking his head, in disbelief, Ponsel stared at Truck.

"Before your people brought me back from my final journey, I had no idea so many worlds existed. Worlds populated by "bastards", "martians", "Earthmen" and "Alien assholes". I have much to learn!"

Jim and Greg broke out laughing. The dark man stared at them, questioningly.

After a while, Jim addressed his brother. "Truck"! I think you've confused, I mean explained, enough for our friend here!"

"What? Truck replied. I was jus tellin him da way it was."

"And, you did a superb job, my brother! Greg joined in. At least, two of us understood where you were coming from."

Ponsel looked at each of the Earthmen, in turn, and shook his head. "This race of people was difficult to understand." He thought to himself.

Two days later found the voyagers in close proximity to their village. In the last two nights, they were fortunate not to have any more encounters with the "Krada". After observing how easily the Nevoan power weapons dispatched the monsters, the crew set aside some of their fears. In a few more hours they would be home. Some were eagerly anticipating the venture still to come.

Jim was taking his turn, manning the rudder. Ponsel kept him company.

"Well, my friend! Jim asked. How did you feel our maiden voyage went?"

"I am still amazed at how you managed to harvest the wind. He replied. It propels this vessel at a much greater speed than any Turbok I've ever seen."

"After you defeat Nemor, maybe you will think about converting one of your ships into a sailing vessel. Jim said. It would save your people from having to labor over the water using oars."

"If that day ever comes, my Earth friend, I would ask your help in its construction."

"When" that day comes, you mean! Jim corrected. We will be happy to assist you!"

Shouts, coming from the forward part of the ship, interrupted their conversation.

The village was in sight!

# CHAPTER 22

The "Posse" surrounded Bantor at the village meeting place. The five young men, Julo, Marus, Salba, Bomar and Tomal were seeking permission from the leader to be counted among the men making the voyage to locate Ponsel's clan.

"The five of us can outshoot most men in the village with either bow or the Nevoan weapon." Julo said to his father.

"And, there are few who can keep up with us, when moving through the water." Marus added.

"Bomar, Salba and I can run faster than, almost, anyone in the village." Tomal piped in.

Bantor smiled at the five youngsters. "I am, more than, aware of your capabilities, he said. However, a mission as dangerous as this requires tested warriors."

"Father! How will we ever be able to show our true worth, unless we are involved? Julo asked We have not, yet, been given the opportunity."

"My son! When you are older you will realize a man will have many occasions in which to prove himself."

"Many, younger than us, have fought in the last two wars. Marus said.

Julo and Marus had always been the leaders of the "posse" Salba, Bomar and Tomal would follow them anywhere. Their childhood ties had evolved into adulthood loyalties. Bantor found this admirable. However, he was not willing to relent.

"I have, already, given you my decision, my young warriors.!" He said, with finality. Your time will, soon, come!"

Almost as one, the five discouraged young men rose from their seats and stalked off.

Bantor watched them go and smiled again. "This village can rest assured their futures will be secure." He thought to himself.

He remained seated for a long while, digesting the conversation that had just transpired. A part of him wanted to relent. However, the fatherly part of him rebelled against it. He was younger than them when the Nevoans had invaded his land. His father and mother were captured away from his younger life. His mother's brother, "Kaba", had raised him and nurtured his warrior instincts, at a very young age. At that time, young and old, alike, had no choice. Fight or die!

The imminent mission to locate Ponsel's clan was not imperative to the safety of his village. The men involved did so on a voluntary basis. No other lives had to be put in jeopardy, especially young lives.

"Their anger and frustration, caused by my decision, will soon be forgotten. "He said to himself, as he rose and made his way back to his hut.

A short while later he sat at his own hearth, talking to Cinda.

"Those young men are anxious to prove their worth. She said, after Bantor had told her about his earlier confrontation. They remind me of someone I know quite well!" Her accusing smile let him know who that someone was.

"Cinda!" He said. In those days there were no other choices. Our lives were being threatened. Everyone was involved!"

She looked across at her mate and shook her head. "I do not understand your concern, then." She replied.

Before Bantor had a chance to respond, she continued.

"Wouldn't it be more productive for one to develop his skills in a nonthreatening situation to better prepare himself for the dire emergencies?" She asked.

"In most cases, that is true Cinda." But….

"But, in this case we are talking about Bantor's son." Cinda finished for him.

The sheepish grin on Bantor's face, told her she was correct.

"I just think they are much too young to get involved in matters such as this! He said, defensively. Besides, our Earth brothers have already selected men for this mission."

"I have talked with some of the mates of these chosen men. Cinda said. It sounded to me as if a few of them are close to rescinding their voluntary status. Life on the big water wasn't what they expected."

"Are you suggesting we replace them with these youngsters?" Bantor asked.

Looking out on the shimmering, liquid expanse, Cinda replied. "Why don't you discuss this with them? They have returned!" She pointed out toward the big water directly in front of them.

Following her gaze, he spotted the "Hope" in the distance, slicing through the gentle waves, as she made her way toward them.

Not too much later, he was overseeing a group of men as they man-handled the floating dock into the water. Two men stood on the far end with ropes, ready to secure the small ship when she arrived. A large gathering had made its way to the shoreline to welcome it home.

Soon, the small craft was tied off and both anchors were dropped. The sail was secured, tightly, to the yard arm.

As the last of the sailors disembarked, the entire crowd made its way to the meeting place.

"Did your maiden voyage go as expected" Bantor asked.

The three Earthmen, Ponsel, Tonio, Roca, along with their relieved mates sat in the circle of honor. Almost the entire village sat around them, anticipating the story of their voyage.

"Everything went smoothly! Jim answered. The "Hope" performed admirably. A few leaks were detected, but, they were sealed up, quickly, with the extra resin we had on board"

"I am relieved to hear that, Earth friend." Bantor replied.

"Other than our encounter with the sea monster, "Krada", a few nights back, it was an uneventful cruise." Greg joined in.

"Tell me about this creature!" Bantor insisted.

"May I be permitted to describe this encounter to your leader?" Ponsel asked, addressing Jim.

"By all means, Ponsel! Jim replied. Tell away!"

"On this particular night, all was as quiet as most evenings on Kressa. He began. Until, one of our look-outs shouted an alarm. Krada was out hunting this night. Its eyes glowed blood red, when it surfaced and began chasing the ship. I have seen this many times, while living with my people. We would man the back rails of our Turbok, armed with long spears. Most of the time we were fortunate enough to ward off the creature with little or no damage. Those Turboks less fortunate, will lie forever beneath Kressa's cold shroud".

"This was not to be in our recent encounter with the creature. He continued. Immediately, after the alarm was sounded, men with short weapons, rushed toward the back of the ship. Moments later, balls of energy erupted from these weapons, destroying Krada instantly. As the rest of the pack fed on their pulverized companion, we made our escape. I am amazed how easily this dreaded killer was dispatched! No men should ever fear traveling on Kressa's back with a weapon, such as this, in their possession."

The crowd had barely uttered a whisper, as they listened to Ponsel's narrative.

"Dat bastard is now fish crap lying on da bottom of da lake!" Truck contributed.

"Speaking of fish, Ponsel introduced us to a method his people use to catch them." Jim added.

"He, also, educated us on the ones safe to eat. Greg said. We shared many delicious meals together."

"The gratitude of all my people is yours, Ponsel." Bantor replied.

"It is I who is the grateful one. Ponsel answered. Had my life not been restored to me, the little I have to share with you would not be possible."

Giving the dark man an appreciative nod, Bantor changed the subject.

"So, Earthman! How long before you begin your voyage to search for Ponsel's people?"

"I think three or four days should be sufficient enough to re-outfit the "Hope" and rest up." Jim replied.

Staring at his Earth friend, deep in thought, Bantor replied. "I would speak to you and your entire crew in private, in the morning! Now, everyone return to your homes and rest!"

A short while later, the village surrendered to the night.

# CHAPTER 23

"The first "Sister" had just crested the horizon, as the village woke. People sat around small fires finishing their breakfasts. The morning breeze nudged rolling waves against the shoreline. A small group of men sat in the meeting area, sipping hot tea as they talked. Bantor's insistence on an early meeting had them all wondering what was on his mind.

The three Earthmen, Ponsel and the rest of the men, who had made up the crew of the "Hope", waited for Bantor to arrive.

"You don't suppose Bantor has changed his mind about this mission, do you?" Greg asked no one in particular.

"I can't think of any reason why he should. Jim fielded the question. He wants to help Ponsel return to his people as much as we do."

"I kinda had da feelin dat he was thinkin about something else, during da meeting last night." Truck joined in.

"And you're an expert on that feeling, aren't you Truck?" Greg goaded.

Truck stared at his younger brother, registering the implied insult before he replied.

"It's kinda early for black eyes, ain't it shrimp? Don't start!"

The crew, seated around the fire, chuckled. During the short cruise, the verbal sparring between the two Americans was a constant.

"Here comes Bantor, now!" Jim announced.

As the leader took a seat among them, he was handed a cup of tea. Nodding his thanks, he smiled at sight of all the serious looks given him by the gathered men.

"Rest assured, my brethren, this meeting reflects no serious undertones. I, simply, want to verify a situation brought to my attention, recently. Also, I would welcome your input on a proposal I have."

He paused for a moment, watching as the expressions reflecting back at him became more relaxed.

"It is well-known the tongues of our mates never cease wagging." He continued, with a smile on his face.

"When they reach my ears, however, I must decide if it is something important enough to act on. The success of any endeavor, in life, relies on the cohesiveness of the people involved. This impending voyage, you plan to undertake, is of vital importance to our friend, here. He nodded, indicating Ponsel. All must be willing to do his share, with no reluctance."

"You need not worry yourself, in that regard! Jim interrupted. I could not have asked for a better crew."

"Perhaps you will change your mind, slightly, after you have heard me out." Bantor replied.

Staring, questioningly, at the native, Jim just nodded.

"Sitting among us, at this moment, are a handful of men who, were it not for their pride, would have rescinded their decisions to become members of this mission long ago."

Looking at the curious faces, he continued.

"There is no shame or reduction of pride if a person attempts something and later finds it was not to his liking. Shame exists only if that person refuses to attempt anything in their lifetime."

"You have all volunteered for this dubious mission. Now, I would ask for your complete honesty, as to your commitment. This will insure that the men who do sail the "Hope" do so with no lingering doubts to impair their judgements."

In the next twenty minutes four men made their apologies and resigned their mariner status.

"Go, now, my brethren! Bantor replied. Rejoin your families!"

Before the four men left, Ponsel rose and placed a hand on each one of their shoulders, in turn. "Your efforts toward my cause will not be forgotten." He said.

After they were gone, Ponsel regained his seat.

"I had no idea those men were unhappy with their situations. Jim said. They were good shipmates and hard workers."

"Sometimes pride can keep a man employed much longer than he expected." Bantor replied.

"In any case, I'm sure I can recruit a few more men for our venture." Jim said.

"That would bring me to the second reason I've called this conference. Bantor interjected. Just recently, it so happens, I was approached by five young men seeking employment in your venture."

"Who are these men you speak of, Bantor?" Greg asked.

Staring, pensively at his Earth brother, he paused for a moment, before he spoke.

"Everyone refers to them as the "posse", our sons!" He answered.

"No way! Truck bellowed, vehemently. Dere too damn young for dis kinda stuff!"

"What answer did you give to their request?" Jim asked.

"I told them, exactly, what Ta-rok has said. The native answered. That they were too young to become involved with something as dangerous as this."

"I believe you made the proper decision." Greg interjected, with relief. His two siblings nodded their heads in agreement.

"However, after giving this much thought. Bantor continued. Allowing my mind and heart to battle out their differences, I have changed my decision. Sons and daughters are a person's most valued contributions to the growth of any world. My heart belongs to the father in me, while my mind leans toward the future security of my people. Without the experience to guide them, our young men and women face uncertain roles in life"

Tonio rose from his seat. "Maybe the rest of us should leave and let Bantor and the Earthmen discuss this in private." He said, addressing the rest of his crew mates.

"That won't be necessary! Jim intervened. They may be our sons, but, if it is finally decided they go with us, it concerns us all."

Tonio nodded and returned to his seat.

"Bantor! Greg joined in. The men you see, here, take these risks voluntarily so the youngsters and elderly, of this village don't have to. Our children will have ample opportunity to test their metal, throughout their lives."

"I gotta agree with my brother. Truck said. Dere time will come soon enough."

"May I ask why you've changed your mind?" Greg inquired.

Bantor looked at the Earthman and smiled. "After I had spoken to the five young men, memories from the past flashed into my mind. I was trapped in the years, between boyhood and manhood, wanting desperately to prove myself. However, people such as ourselves, kept passing me by. Until that time came, my world was quite small."

"You had no choice at the time! Jim argued. Your people were involved in a life or death situation with the Nevoans. This is a much different situation!"

"Danger arrives in many forms, from many directions. Bantor returned. How old should one be before he is responsible enough to do something about it?"

While the group pondered his words, he continued. "My friends, what better time is there to train and guide young minds? He asked. With no pressure from a war, weighing on them, their minds will be more receptive."

"Bantor! Greg chimed in. You realize the magnitude of responsibility you are placing on us, don't you? This voyage is not a pleasure cruise!"

"I am aware of the possible dangers that might occur. He answered. However, if we shield our sons or anyone else in this village, for too long a time, the consequences could be disastrous. How will they react when these same dangers confront their untrained minds?"

"I agree! Jim replied. It is our duty to prepare the younger people to face these conflicts, but, I don't feel this is the appropriate time to begin!"

"If da shit hits da fan, were gonna have a hard enough time dealing with it. Truck jumped in. If we gotta worry about da kids, at da same time, it'll make it harder!"

"Not if you transform those youngsters into men, before any conflict arises." Bantor shot back. Besides, I would not consider entrusting the safety of my son to anyone other than this group gathered here, today. I implore you to give these youngsters an opportunity to absorb your wisdom."

Silence settled over the debate, for a moment, while they pondered Bantors words.

It was Truck who broke the silence.

"It might be kinda fun after all, you guys. I ain't spent much time with Salba, lately, and I think dis might give me da chance ta do a little catchin up!"

"I know for certain, Tomal could use a bit more discipline." Greg added.

"My two run with the same pack. Jim said. So I guess there's nothing left to do but take them all aboard."

"Dere goes da neighborhood!" Truck finished, causing laughter.

# CHAPTER 24

A few days later, the "Hope", restocked and re-manned, pushed her prow through the dancing waves of Kressa. They had set sail shortly after sunrise. Ponsel acted as their compass, guiding them into a northeasterly direction. Born into the arms of the rolling vastness, the homing instincts, inherent of his kind were the only tools necessary for finding ones way home. In ten to twelve cycles of the suns, he had informed them, they would reach the territorial waters controlled by his clan. The perimeters of these unmarked domains had been set generations before. Locating one's own territory was as easy for them as it was for a "landlubber" finding his own village.

The five new ship mates were kept busy maintaining the ships cleanliness, tightening or loosening guy lines, standing look-out watches, manning the rudder, or anywhere else they were needed to fill in. So far, any duties given them, they completed without complaint.

Truck sat with his back against one of the gunwhales, on the after deck. His son, Salba, was manning the rudder. The night wind had increased, slightly, sending the small ship skipping over the rolling waves. A chandelier of brilliant stars reflected down upon them.

Jim's eldest son, Marus, stood look-out duty on the bow, nervously anticipating an encounter with the dreaded "Krada". Thus far, the night had remained silent.

It had been decided, by the three Earthmen, while any of the youngsters stood a night watch, at least one of them would be with them to supervise. Until more experience was gained, the young sailors would not be left alone.

The excitement, they brought aboard with them, spilled over to the rest of the crew. Morale was at its highest. From the very moment they had been informed they would be included in this endeavor, they eagerly embraced any directive given them. Of course, the pre-boarding consultation they had had with their fathers laid out the rules and what was expected of them. Life in the fast lane, so to speak, called for quick decisions, no questions asked.

The night was halfway through her ebon clutches, when a high-pitched shout echoed from the bow.

In a matter of minutes, the bow deck was crowded with men, rudely awakened from a peaceful slumber.

Some of them were armed with the Nevoan power rifles. Jim was first to reach Marus. He pointed to a spot, approximately, one hundred yards, directly in front of them.

Two glowing orbs floated above the surging waves, as they made their way closer to the tiny ship.

"Well done, my son! Jim exclaimed, with fatherly pride. Your vigilance has prevented the monster from closing up on us, unaware."

As Jim brought the lethal weapon up to his shoulder and sighted in on the monster, he changed his mind and handed the weapon to Marus.

"You have earned the right to be in on the kill!"

Smiling at his father, Marus turned, locked In on the creature and began firing, adding his firepower to that of three others.

Soon, the hope sailed through the scattered debris of the obliterated Krada.

"Nice work, little buddy! Truck said, slapping the youngster on the back. Dats da way ya stand a watch!"

"Thank you, uncle! Marus replied. But, I was just doing my duty."

"He's yer boy, all right! Truck said, turning to Jim. A chip off da old block."

The serene peacefulness returned to the evening, moments later, as men returned to their hammocks, to recapture blissful dreams. The look-out watches and helmsman had been replaced with fresh bodies. Greg assumed duty, as he supervised the replacements. Julo, Bantor's son, assumed the bow watch, while Greg's son, Tomal manned the rudder. The rest of the night wore on, peacefully, with no more interruptions.

Shortly before the first "Sister's" rays sparkled off the liquid surface, Greg had stoked the sleeping coals awake in the large stone hearth, located amidships. Tea was already brewing, before the first of the rising crew set foot on deck.

"Good morning, Greg! Jim greeted, as he helped himself to a cup of tea. Anything to report?" He asked.

"Negative, Jim, he answered. After our encounter with the Krada, it was a very calm night."

"That's always good to hear. Jim returned. Why don't you go hit the sack for a few hours? I'll take it from hear."

"Gladly, Jim! There's something about nights spent on the water. They lull you into a dreamlike state, you wish would last forever."

"Good morning you guys! Truck bellowed out his greeting, as he took a seat among them.

"Then, again, one could be awakened by a nightmare." Greg piped in, staring at the big guy.

Jim chuckled, when he noticed the questioning look on Truck's face.

"Huh? Truck asked. What did he say?"

"I was just telling Jim what a drastic difference there is between night and day. He said, winking at Jim. I'm going to bed!" With that said, he got up and made his way below decks.

"Da little guy was never much of a night owl, was he?"

"I guess not, Truck! Jim replied, smiling.

After a brief silence, Truck changed the subject. "Ya gotta be mighty proud of dat kid a yours, Jimbo! He proved ta everyone last night dat he can be trusted."

"You know as well as I, Truck, the unconditional pride we have in our sons. My elation comes from the fact, Marus has taken his first step into manhood, "responsibility.""

"Who do ya think he got dat from? Truck asked. We have a lot ta do with setting dos standards."

"That's true, in a sense, Truck. Jim responded. But, kids don't always listen to adults. As they get older they start making their own decisions. Marus is at that point in his life where he owns the results of those decisions and no one else can be held accountable."

"Den how come I always get blamed when Salba belches or farts when he's in a crowd a people?" Truck asked.

"In that case I think Salba would be considered an exception to the rule. Jim said, trying to hold back his laughter. "Like father like son.""

Truck stared at his brother for an instant, registering what he had just said.

"Ya know, sometimes you can be just as much a pain in da buttocks as dat squirt. Why do I even try ta talk ta you guys?"

"Because, you love us, Truck!" Jim replied.

'Dat's probably da only reason I do it, too." Truck said, as he too, broke out in laughter.

# CHAPTER 25

The new day proved to be uneventful, until the third "Sister" assumed her position in the azure heaven. Sails had been tightened to capture the diminishing winds. Men sat around in groups, talking. Some had retired below decks, napping in their hammocks. Others were preparing their evening meal.

A shout of alarm erupted from the bow watch, shattering the peaceful ambience. Men scurried from all directions and assembled on the bow deck.

"What have you detected, Roca?" Greg asked.

Pointing ahead, a few degrees off the starboard bow, he replied. "It appears to be a ship of some kind, or I should say what's left of one, about two- hundred yards ahead." Handing the telescope to the Earthman, he moved to the side.

Greg peered through his invention and sighted in on the object in question.

"It is, indeed the remains of a ship! He confirmed. Ponsel! Have a look!" He passed the telescope to the dark man.

After scanning the horizon for a moment, he handed it back to Greg. It was one of my of my people's Turboks." He confirmed, shaking his head.

"Looks like one a dos monsters smashed da shit out of it". Truck exclaimed, after looking through the glass.

"The Krada was not responsible for this!" Ponsel replied.

By this time, they had closed to within fifty yards of the derelict vessel.

""If not the Krada, what else could have caused this?" Jim asked.

"A rogue ship is on the prowl, once again." Ponsel answered.

"Rogue ship?" Greg echoed.

"Many times, in the history of our people, groups have broken away from the norm, built their own Turboks and waged war on other clans. Attacking, only, under the cloak of night, they board other vessels and then throw the men to the mercy of the dark waters. After pillaging food supplies and equipment, they sink her. Women and children, from the unfortunate vessel, are forced into slavery."

As they neared the wreck, movement was spotted near the stern.

"There appears to be, at least, one survivor!" Greg announced, handing the scope to Jim.

As he looked through the glass, he spotted a young woman struggling to free herself from a tangle of rope. Fighting to keep her head above water, she flailed about in panic.

Tossing the glass to Greg, he quickly vaulted the railing and splashed into the water. By this time, the small ship was within twenty yards of the wreck. In a quick moment, he was at her side. The eyes of the frightened woman went even wider when this white stranger held her head above the water as he untangled the lines, snarled around her legs with the other. In the next instant, they were both being hauled aboard the "Hope".

As they lay sprawled upon the deck, catching their breath, Ponsel made his way to the woman.

"I am Ponsel of the "Sirka" clan. He said. Are you injured?"

Relaxing, somewhat, when she discovered the presence of one of her kind, she shook her head. "I am not injured, Ponsel of the "Sirka" clan." She answered. Then, in a low voice she asked, who are these strange people?"

"They are members of the "Kletta" tribe. He answered, smiling. A clan of people who live almost their entire lives on the hard land. They are assisting me to locate my clan."

She was surrounded by the curious crew, as they stared at her. She, nervously, returned their stares.

Jim noticed this and took control. "All right, men. Give the lady room to recover. Assume your duties!"

As they moved off, Ponsel helped her to her feet. "What is your name?" He asked.

"Forgive my bad manners! She apologized. I am "Raina" of the "Terin" clan. Her eyes saddened. At least, a short while ago I was. My clan is no more."

Ponsel placed a comforting hand on her shoulder. "Our fates are similar! He replied. Your clan has been lost to you. I have been lost to my clan!"

"What do you mean?" She asked.

"Come with me!" He said.

They sat around the hearth, a while later. He watched as she ate some food and drank some hot tea.

He related his story to her and a warm friendship was starting to evolve. Ponsel had never mated. His energy and time was always directed into his hunting skills.

Raina had never invested her time or emotions in a serious relationship. Their worlds were about to expand.

Shortly before the third "Sister" had exhausted her visit, everyone except the bow watch and rudder man was gathered at the hearth. Raina was relating to them the devastating malady that had befallen her.

"The fog was thick, as we made our way toward hard land to prepare for our nightly layover. She began. All of a sudden, people began shouting and running in all directions. Strangers were among us, brandishing spears and sharpened lengths of wood. Women and children were screaming, as our men did their best to repel the invaders. We were a small clan, overwhelmed by their numbers. Our brave men voiced not one sound as they were tossed into the eternal arms of Kressa To begin their final journeys.

The women and children were gathered up and taken aboard their Turbok. I hid beneath a pile of fish hides in a storage room. An hour later they began boring holes in our Turbok, then they left! When water started rushing into my hiding place, I made an attempt to escape. I became entangled in ropes and hides. All that dark night, I fought to keep my head above water. I must have passed out. When I came to, I found myself floating in a tangle of debris. When I tried to free myself, I managed, only, to make matters worse. That's when you found me. I am compelled to express my gratitude to all of you."

"Thank you, Raina, for sharing that with us. Jim said. An ordeal, such as this, is not easy to talk about. Go, now, and get some rest." Ponsel escorted her to one of the storage rooms below decks. A hammock was hung, there, for her comfort and privacy.

"Sleep well, Raina! The dark man said, as he left.

# CHAPTER 26

The first "Sister" climbed over the horizon, spilling her warmth and brilliance down upon the small ship.

A slight wind prevailed, pushing gentle waves against her bow. Tonio stood the forward watch, while Roca manned the rudder.

The "instinctive" compass, inherent in Ponsel's mind, kept them on a steady northeasterly course.

The only other occupants, awake at this hour, were the three Earthmen and Ponsel. They clustered around the ship's hearth, sharing its warmth. Early mornings, on the water, were often cool and damp.

They were discussing the course of action they would take, if they came in contact with the rogue ship.

"Because of the presence of women and children, we can't very well blast it out of the water, can we? Greg surmised."

"And, because of the overwhelming odds a night raid is out of the question!" Jim added.

"I agree! Ponsel replied. Also, the use of your powerful weapons, in such a confined space, would amount to a lot of innocent people being injured or killed."

"We gotta approach dis like it's a hostage situation." Truck joined in.

"And, pray tell, how would you go about doing that, Sherlock?" Greg replied, sarcastically.

Ignoring his brother's slight, Truck answered. "With da use a dat spy glass ya built. We're gonna spot dem long before dey spot us! We follow dem, from a distance and watch where dey make dere overnight stay. Den, we nail da bastards!

"Good idea, Truck! Jim replied. They'll be more spread out and the chance of innocents getting hurt will be minimalized."

"Do you have any suggestions, Ponsel?" Greg asked.

"Only, one! He replied. Post more look-outs. Have them scan the water for any strange debris."

"How would that help us?" Jim asked.

A Turbok can handle only so much weight, given the number of people she carries. When new supplies of any kind are added, useless items are cast overboard to equalize the weight. Other Turboks follow these watery trails, at times, salvaging useful items."

When the entire crew was up and about, a short time later, all were apprised of future procedures. Extra look-outs were assigned, providing eyes in all directions.

The wind had increased, bulging the sail with its propulsion. The bow of the "Hope" sliced through the attack of the marching waves, sending her smoothly through her ranks. Truck fought against the rudder, keeping it from having its own way. Because of the strenuous effort it took, to keep the ship on a true bearing, the rudder watch was relieved every two hours.

"Are you ready for a break, Ta-rok?" Tonio asked.

"You bet. Truck replied. She's buckin like a sonnuva bitch, today. Ya, really, gotta lay on her hard." He said, as they, quickly, changed places.

A moment later, he approached the ship's hearth. His two brothers, ponsel and Raina were seated around it, talking.

"Mornin everyone! You too, squirt. He said, as he took a seat and helped himself to a cup of tea.

Jim smiled, prepared for the usual morning exchanges between his two siblings.

"I haven't spotted any icebergs yet. Greg said. At least you haven't sailed us to the north pole."

"I could send you ona bruise cruise if ya want, midget." The big man said, shaking his fist.

Raina's eyes went wide with alarm, as she observed this verbal jousting between the Earthmen for the first time.

"Pay them no mind, Raina! Jim said, smiling, when he noticed her look. My two siblings have always found it impossible to be civil with one another for any length of time."

Smiling across at the distraught girl, Ponsel pointed at the three Earthmen, before he spoke. "You will learn in time, Raina, these three men come to our world with some strange mannerisms. Their dual with words most be inherent among their people. It is harmless!"

The questioning look, on raina's pretty face, ran even deeper.

"I will tell you the story at another time, Raina. Jim said. As soon as I figure out what happened to those two." He finished, pointing at his two brothers, with a big smile on his face.

When the three Americans began to laugh, Raina and Ponsel joined in.

As the day wore on, the sky started to fill with ominous, gray clouds. The wind, howling through the mast, agitated the rolling waves, turning them into four-foot white caps. Men scurried about the ship, securing any loose equipment before it was blown over-board. Sheets of rain blanketed them and turned the deck into a dangerously, slick surface. Except for a few men, all were ordered below deck. The sail was lowered and secured. Two men struggled with the rudder, doing their best to keep the small vessel from straying too far off course.

Two hours later, the clouds parted, ushering in the warm rays of the third "Sister" sun. The diminishing winds sent, only, two-foot rollers against the "Hopes" bow. The battering waves of the storms fury had not opened any seams in her skin. All hands returned above deck.

Sail was raised, once again, Soon it became pregnant, bulging out as it captured the wind. Men, pushing wide, reed brooms, soon, had pockets of storm water racing over the side.

Ponsel pointed out the corrected course and all returned to normal.

The fire was relit in the hearth. Soon, the aroma billowing from a hearty stew, permeated the tiny ship. Men sat around, eating, more confident, now, knowing that their tiny vessel had not failed them.

She had survived her first encounter with the elements, with minimal damage. "Landlubbers" from birth, a collective sigh of relief was experienced by every man aboard.

# CHAPTER 27

Two days later the second "Sister" sun of the day, took her place in the blue sky. Men sat around talking, as they repaired fish nets. A few were below deck, resting in their hammocks. They had fished, on and off, the past few days. The over-flowing drying racks, spread out on the after deck, gave evidence of their success.

Three more Krada had paid them a visit, the last two evenings. None of them had come within fifty yards of the tiny vessel, before their pulverized flesh sank to the lake bottom. With the addition of four extra look-outs, the murderous fish stood little chance of surprising them.

Other than a few scattered clouds, the weather remained clear. The prevalent winds favored the tiny ship, urging her along, right on course. Ponsel had informed them, in approximately three days, they would be in the territory of his clan.

Shortly before the third "Sister" had assumed her position, an alarm was sounded by the starboard look-out. In a matter of moments, he was joined by others.

"What do you see, Roca?" Jim asked.

"I can't say for sure. He replied. But, I definitely saw something bobbing in the water, about three hundred yards ahead of us." He finished, pointing in the general direction."

"Bomar! Jim ordered. Run to the bow and get the looking glass!"

A moment later, he handed the telescope to his father. Scanning in the direction indicated by Roca, he soon located the object.

"There it is! He shouted. Ponsel, what do you make of that?" He asked as he handed the glass to the dark man.

"It appears to be a tangle of fishing nets and floats. He answered. They resemble the type made by my people. But, if you look further ahead and off to the right, you will see something even more interesting."

Taking the glass from Ponsel, Jim scanned the horizon.

"It's a ship without sails!" He exclaimed, excitedly.

"We call them "Turboks." Ponsel said, smiling.

"Is it of your clan?" Jim asked.

"I do not recognize the markings on her side. It is a little far off to tell for sure". He answered.

"Maybe it's dat boat dat slaughtered Raina's people!" Truck joined in.

"We won't know for certain, until they have made landfall." Greg added.

"For the time being, we'll maintain a safe, parallel course. Jim said. We can't let them out of our sight!"

"They will be making their landfall very soon. Ponsel said, still peering through the looking glass. There is an island in their path, directly in front of them."

Handing the glass back to Jim, he pointed to a spot about one hundred yards in front of the Turbok.

"That must be their destination! Jim assumed, as he observed the faint outline distorting the horizon. Tonio! Take your crew and tighten up the sail! He ordered. Rudder man, put us hard to starboard!"

"Whatta ya got in mind, Jimbo?" Truck asked.

"We'll observe where they put ashore and anchor the "Hope" in the shallows on the other side of the island." He answered.

An hour before the third "Sister" retired for the night, they watched from a safe distance, as the Turbok emptied her occupants. Raina looked through the glass and became excited when she recognized her people.

The "Hope" was maneuvered around a craggy point, out of sight of prying eyes. After she was anchored, in a shallow cove, the sailors, then, began wading to shore. Five men were left behind, including Raina, to protect the ship. The shore party, armed with the Nevoan power rifles and bow and arrows, assembled beneath a stand of trees.

The island was small and thick with vegetation. They estimated their distance from the raiders was less than a half mile.

"I don't have to tell you, stealth is our only ally this night! Jim said. Because of the overwhelming odds against us, we must fight as a unit. Once it begins, each one of us must do his part. Not to do so, will bring defeat upon us." These last words were directed toward their five young ship mates, who stood, nervously, among the men.

"Rest at this time, my friends! When Roca and Ponsel return, be prepared."

A short while later, the bushes rustled and the two scouts appeared.

"They are guarding the captives in a small clearing at the back of the beach, the women on one side, the men about twenty-five yards away." Roca reported.

"The majority of the raiders, approximately two hundred, are congregated about ten yards from the water's edge." Ponsel added.

"How many guards do they have around the captives?" Jim asked.

"We counted five around the men and three around the women. Roca replied. Their backs are toward the forest, facing the water."

'Dere's our advantage!" Truck said. We come from behind dem, take out da guards with da bows and arrows and drive da rest a dos bastards inta da water."

"How are they armed?" Greg asked.

"All clans use similar weapons. Ponsel answered. Long lances called "Seneks" have sharp points on one end and curved hooks on the other. They, also, carry long knives called "Torbs.""

"We'll go with Truck's idea! Jim said. Roca and Tonio! Take one third of the men, armed with bow and arrow. You'll be responsible for taking out the guards. The rest of us will attack from the two sides flanking you. Truck and Ponsel will take one group, Greg and I the other. Are there any questions?"

"What's da signal gonna be?" Truck asked.

"When the guards are taken out and the prisoners are secured, the rest will open fire. If any show signs of surrender, cease fire immediately."

When no more questions were forthcoming, Jim gave the order to move out.

A short while later, the three squadrons of men were in position. The raider's camp sat twenty yards, directly, in front of them. A huge fire burned brightly, lighting the entire kill zone.

Bows started twanging, sending a fusillade of arrows into the backs of the unsuspecting guards. Before they fell dead to the sandy beach, a barrage of lethal fire power was released upon the rest.

The raiding villains started racing in all directions seeking out their weapons, while searching for the author of this devastating attack. Further and further they were being pushed back to the water's edge. By this time, the mangled bodies of many of their comrades littered the beach. Soon, many of the survivors were dropping their weapons and falling to their knees in surrender.

In a handful of moments, it was over.

"Cease fire! Jim called out. Advance, slowly, and keep your eyes open."

The small army made its way to within fifteen yards of the raiders, groveling in the sand. No words were spoken, as the defeated clansmen stared in shock.

"Who were these white strangers who, so easily, defeated them?"

"Which man among you claims to be leader?" Jim asked.

Many dark heads turned and indicated a man cowering in their midst.

Jim pointed at the individual. "Stand and come forward!" He said.

The man hesitated for a moment, then, struggled to his feet. Visibly shaken he staggered to the front of his cohorts and stopped ten feet before the American.

"What is your name?" Jim demanded.

"I am Fosa of the Pelon clan." He exclaimed in a trembling voice.

Staring in disgust, at the cringing coward the Earthman spoke.

"The heads of your deceased comrades lay heavily upon your shoulders, Fosa. You, alone, are responsible for the cowardly attack upon people of another clan. I am not in the position to pass judgement. However, there is one among us who has that right. Had these atrocities been perpetrated against my people, none of you would be breathing, at this time!"

The dark creature, before him, was trembling almost to the point of convulsing.

"Ponsel! Jim summoned. Please join us!"

Their dark comrade had been mingling with the captives, checking on their welfare.

Of the fifty men, forty women and a handful of children, only one man was close to death.

In a moment, he was at the Earthman's side.

Jim pointed at the defeated perpetrators. "Their fate will be determined by your decision, my friend."

Ponsel nodded in understanding.

"An act, as vile as this, would have already been avenged were it against my clan, also. He began, staring threateningly, at Fossa. However, The cowardly Pelon clan choose, instead, to war against a small clan unable to protect itself. To send preying Kradas, such as you, on a quick journey to meet their makers is not enough. That would be too kind."

The rescued captives, at this time, moved closer, hanging on Ponsel's every word. Given the opportunity, every one of them would be more than willing to tear their tormentors apart with their bare hands. Observing the blood-lust in their eyes, Ponsel addressed them.

"My friends, let us not become them! There are more than enough of you to commandeer their Turbok and continue with your lives."

"What will become of these cruel men?" A voice rang from the group of captives. They will go unpunished?"

"They will spend the rest of their useless lives on this small island. Ponsel replied, with a big smile on his face. I am sure they have much to think about."

For the condemned men it was a death sentence, worse than swimming into the jaws of a Krada. Most of them buried their heads in the sand and wept. This would be a long death.

In a little more than an hour the entire rescued party was safely ensconced on their newly acquired Turbok. They had a more than ample supply of food and equipment to keep them comfortable for quite some time. Raina joined them, rekindling friendly ties.

They, gladly, accepted an invitation to follow the "Hope" home and become acquainted with the white clan.

They had left the marooned raiders their weapons and whatever food they had taken ashore, before the battle had begun.

Not one tear was shed as the hope, followed closely by the turbok, sailed into the early night.

# CHAPTER 28

The following day, toward the middle of the second "Sister" sun, A turbok was spotted a mile away off the port bow. The friendly, Turbok following them, kept pace one hundred yards astern. To prevent the Turbok from keeping a back-breaking pace, the "Hope" dropped her sail by half, allowing the slower vessel to stay close to her.

As they gained, on the distant Turbok, Ponsel announced to them that it was, indeed, his clan's vessel. "Drop sail!" Jim ordered.

"Why do you choose to stop your ship, now, when we are so close?" Ponsel asked, anxiously.

"We have to notify our friends behind us and let them know what we intend to do. Jim replied. I want to keep them out of harm's way."

Nodding his head, in acknowledgement, Ponsel joined the others as they waited for the Turbok to come up on their starboard side.

When the clan vessel came within earshot, they were apprised as to what was happening. They would hold this position, while the "Hope" sailed ahead.

"We gonna use da same tactics we used on dat other ship?" Truck asked.

"No! Jim answered. We'll sail close enough to them to allow Ponsel to make his intentions known." Jim answered.

As they closed to within one hundred yards of the Turbok, their spy glass revealed increased activity on the clan ship. Men could be seen scurrying in all directions, arming themselves and pointing at the "Hope".

They decreased their speed, by lowering their sail, slightly, and glided into a matching Pace, approximately twenty yards off the port bow of the bigger vessel.

The three Earthmen and Ponsel stood on the bow. The rest of the "Hope's" crew lined the starboard side. Each was armed with a Nevoan power rifle, they kept hidden below the gunwales. They did not want to reveal any threat to the clan ship. However, if they showed any sign of aggression toward them, they were prepared.

As the clansmen of the Turbok stared across the short space, Their stares were returned by the crew of the tiny "Hope". An eerie silence shrouded the scene. It was shattered, suddenly, as Ponsel raised his voice and addressed his former clan.

"I am Ponsel of the Tepu clan! He began. I would have words with your leader, Nemor!" He announced.

In moments, a giant of a man strode forward. "This cannot be possible! He replied, brusquely. Ponsel has taken the final journey, a short time ago."

"And I would have! Ponsel shot back. However Zorboth and your other henchmen failed to complete the deed you ordered them to carry out."

The tall man standing alongside Nemor blanched when, he heard his name mentioned.

"You cannot deny who I am, Nemor, as once you denied me my right to challenge. I have returned to claim that right. It is time the Tepu people stopped living in fear!"

Murmurings filtered from the Tepu people crowding the deck. "Honor his right to challenge!" Someone shouted.

Ignoring their derisive chants, Nemor chose to side-step the situation.

"Who are these strange, white creatures in your company? He bellowed. They must be ghosts that followed you from the after world!"

Turning to face his crowd of clansmen, he raised his voice. "We cannot allow them to defile the decks of our home!" he attempted to discourage them.

Ponsel responded in a confident voice. "These people are my friends, Nemor. They discovered my, nearly lifeless, body after you had your henchmen toss me into the dark arms of Kressa. They are not from the after world."

Nemor looked across at the tiny ship, now only ten yards away, and a cruel smile formed on his face. "Your handful of white rabble is no match for our might! He shouted. You will not set one foot on my Turbok!"

Ponsel returned his smile, as he walked casually up to Roca, whispered in his ear and pointed to a spot on the bow of the Turbok.

Roca lifted a Nevoan rifle from concealment, sighted in on a net-covered staff protruding from the bow of the Turbok. He fired once, disintegrating the target.

The entire gathering of clan people dropped to their knees in abject fear.

Pausing for a moment, to allow the devastating demonstration time to sink in, Ponsel walked, slowly, back to the bow of the "Hope".

"I will say this for the last time, Nemor! My right to challenge will not be denied me again! Make your layover on that island, dead ahead. The leadership of my people will be decided on this night! Am I understood?"

Rising slowly to his feet, visibly shaken, Nemor nodded. I will do as you ask, Ponsel."

An hour later, the crew of the "Hope" watched as the Turbok's entire company waded ashore. Shortly after, Ponsel, accompanied by the three Earthmen, Roca and Tonio did likewise. All were armed with Nevoan rifles except Ponsel. As Truck always says, dis will even up da odds a little.

As his comrades spread out at the edge of the shoreline, with no one behind them, Ponsell continue across the sandy beach until he stood five paces from Nemor. Zorboth and three other men were close by, staring menacingly at the challenging clansman. The three Earthmen paid particular attention to them, moving a few paces closer in their direction.

The rite of challenge involved as much formality as that of a wedding or funeral ceremony. The Earthmen and their two native partners, watching their backs, were about to get an education.

"I, Ponsel of the Tepu clan, claim my birth right to challenge the present leader, Nemor, for the leadership of this clan."

An elderly man approached from the crowd and stood between the two combatants.

"Ponsel, of the Tepu clan, is entitled to this challenge!" He said, placing his right hand on Ponsel's shoulder.

Turning, quickly, the old man now faced Nemor. "Does the present leader acknowledge this right to challenge?" He asked, placing his right hand on Nemor's shoulder.

"I will allow it!" Nemor replied.

Turning back to face Ponsel, again, The old man asked. "Is this challenge made, free of any underlying grievances?"

"No, it is not! Ponsel replied.

"The people would here of these grievances, at this time!" Said the old man.

"Let it be known, Twenty years ago Nemor murdered my father. He was known to you as Selbon, your previous leader. The night before Nemor was to execute his right to challenge with my father, He had one of his henchmen poison him. I was very young at the time. However, I remember my mother telling me what she had seen. Nemor laced my father's tea with the bile from a Krada's liver. Zorboth had, also, aided him in this vile deed. My mother, mysteriously, disappeared shortly after!"

"Is there anything more you wish to discuss?" The old man asked.

"Yes! Ponsel replied. Since Nemors dubious assent as leader, a cloak of fear and doubt has settled over this clan. Tonight, his reign ends!"

Turning to face Nemor, once again, the old man asked. "Nemor! Do you wish to make comment on Ponsel's grievance?"

"Yes! Nemor responded. I will not relinquish my leadership to the son of that, pathologically, weak Selbon!"

Hatred flashed in Ponsel's eyes. He was about to break protocol and Nemor's neck at the same time.

The old man sensed this and intervened, quickly, by announcing in a loud voice: "This challenge will be determined by the final journey of either Nemor or Ponsel! Let the challenge begin!"

As the old man filtered back into the crowd, the two combatants backed away from one another until they were ten paces apart. Two men raced in from the crowd of onlookers and handed each man a "Senek".

The two warriors balanced the lethal staff in their hands, as they eyed each other.

The three Earthmen moved in closer. Nemor's henchmen, they had noticed, made their way closer until they were only ten paces behind Ponsel. The Americans were in a good position to thwart any subterfuge on their part.

Nemor moved in, swinging his weapon in a vicious arc, aimed at ponsel's head. The younger man dodged, quickly, out of reach. As they continued to circle one another, Jim noticed the three henchmen keeping Pace with Ponsel, sticking closely to his unguarded back. Another vicious slash was launched at Ponsel's midsection. As he leaped back to avoid it, he tripped over another weapon that had been tossed at his feet by one of the goons. Down he went! Before he could regain his feet, Nemor slashed down at Ponsel's head.

He caught the descending weapon on the end of his Senek and deftly rolled to his feet.

The three Americans started in action, the instant they spotted the intentional trip, by one of Nemor's men. They were on them, quickly. Three punches, thrown in unison, crushed the cartilage in three Tepu noses. Down and out, they went!

The two warriors froze for an instant, taking in the scene. Ponsel nodded his head in appreciation toward the brothers. Nemor's eyes went wide with panic when he realized he no longer had the advantage. In an act of sheer desperation, he charged in on Ponsel with his weapon raised above his head. He would end it now!

He didn't even come close. Ponsel ducked low and brought the spear point up in a savage arc. It buried itself in Nemor's midsection and exited on the other side, two feet beyond his spine.

The tyrant dropped his weapon and stared through wide, frightened eyes at his younger foe.

Poncel yanked the lance, viciously, out of Nemor's inards.

As the soon-to-be, ex-leader watched his own entrails curl their way to the sand, Ponsel shifted the senek in his hands. With one, swift movement, he sliced Nemor's head off, with the sharpened hook blade at the other end.

"Mother and father!" He said to himself. This beast will never harm another soul."

Before Nemor's body was finished twitching in the bloody sand, Ponsel walked over to the Earthmen. Emotionally spent, he placed his hands on their shoulders, in turn. "Forever friends!" He said, trying his best to smile.

# CHAPTER 29

Early the next morning, as the first "Sister "spilled her warmth over the world. Three vessels plowed through the rolling waves of Kressa. The Hope, with her sail at half-mast, Led the way, many of the occupants of the three crafts, were still in slumber.

A meeting had transpired, shortly after Ponsel's victorious challenge had ended. Every man woman and child from the three vessels had attended. It had lasted for the better part of the night. The majority of spectators came away from the meeting satisfied Ponsel's ascension to the leadership role would make their lives more comfortable. Many changes would be made. Changes in traditions dating back to the beginning of their history. The right of challenge was abolished. The people would be given instead, The right to select a leader on the basis of his contributing factors. Gone, also, was the tradition of the ruling family receiving more food and exemptions than the rest of the people. All would share equally!

It was, also agreed upon the survivors of Raina's clan would merge with the Tepu clan. When Ponsel brought to their attention how much stronger and safer they would be as a two-turbok clan It was unanimous.

Their enthusiasm grew when Jim invited all to visit his home and establish commerce between the two peoples. Of course it helped, considerably, when he promised to help them erect sails on their turboks, thus eliminating the back breaking ordeal of propelling it with man-powered oars.

If there remained any doubts among them about any proposals up until this time, they were removed completely after Truck gave a demonstration with the power rifle. It frightened them at first. However, once they recovered from the initial shock and realized how effective such a weapon could be in maintaining security, they embraced it. Especially so, after Jim promised to train men is its use and would include them in a trade.

Raina had moved to Ponsel's turbok. It was obvious, in everyones eyes, they were intended for one another.

Nemor's Henchmen, which amounted to twenty after being ferreted out by the people, were given their weapons and lifetime exiles on the small island. Only Zorboth made threats vowing one day to have his vengeance on Ponsel's people. It wasn't until later they found out Truck had offered him swimming lessons. Zorboth had flunked the final test.

The three Earthmen sat around the small hearth. They were accompanied by the "posse". The five youngsters listened as the three men related an adventure from their youth, back on earth. A steady breeze stirred the embers in the fireplace. The third sun bathed them in her warmth. Gentle waves broke against the small vessel, rocking her into a soothing rythm. The three days since leaving the small island, had been relatively uneventful. Four more Kradas were sent to the lake bottom, as the "Hope" acted as gunship for the small fleet. The clans people, lining the railings of their turboks, were amazed how easily their major nemesis was defeated.

'We were a few years younger than the five of you boys, When our grandfather, Joseph, took us to his hunting camp, deep in the northern woods of Minnesota." Jim said "Grandfather was a full blooded Sioux Indian. His tribe had a long history, much the same as our Kletta people. A test of manhood was to be left in wild parts of the country. Our only possessions were a small hide tent, Knives, bows and arrows, and wool blankets. He must have felt sorry for us kids, because, he left a big pot filled with his homemade beans. In the tradition of the manhood test, we were supposed to hunt and forage for our own food." And as everyone on this world is aware of our large sibling here has a bottomless pit for a stomach. Greg joined in indicating Truck, with a smile on his face. The guilty look on the big man's face caused them to laugh. "Well anyway ", Jim continued, "It wasn't long before that pot of beans was empty. It was getting late, at that time, so we banked our fire, wrapped our blankets around ourselves and crawled into the small tent. It wasn't long before we were asleep. A short while later Greg and I were wide awake. Truck was farting like there was no tomorrow. The tent was filled with odors only mating skunks would appreciate. When our watering eyes cleared enough for us to navigate, Greg and I grabbed our blankets and raced out of the tent."

The five youngsters were roaring with laughter soon, others gathered around the story tellers adding their laughter.

"I remember laying there on the ground Jim and I were trying to clear our heads."

Greg took over. "The roaring spurts from our brother continued. We started laughing. It was a cool quiet night otherwise. So we decided to move a little further away from our brother's eruptions, if we intended to get any sleep at all. Jim continued. We moved under some trees about fifty feet from the tent, we could still hear Truck's poop locker talking. Before we could get to sleep we heard rustling in the woods nearby. Suddenly there was a huge black bear among us. You've all heard us describe this big, powerful animal in the past. The one that visited us on that night must have weighed over five hundred pounds. We froze, hoping it would go on its way. But, It didn't! It headed straight for the tent. Greg and I raced to recover our weapons lying by the fire pit. As we fitted our arrows to our bows, we turned, just as the bear stuck its head into the tent. Before we had a chance to fire, it let out a whimpering roar, Jumped straight into the air and raced off into the woods. We quickly ran over to the tent and lifted the flap. Our large brother was still asleep. Snoring, farting away, not a care in the world. We quickly retreated from the happy gas and after our coughing stopped, we curled up in our blankets once again, and fell asleep. The next day we told our brother what had happened. To this day, he doesn't believe us."

"Dats right!" Truck replied. "and don't you youngsters believe a word of it either!"

"I don't know Truck!" Jim said "I think when that old bear took one whiff of the occupant of that tent it decided to go on a diet."

"Our brother could have made us all rich back then." Greg chided "If he could have found a way to bottle that poo poo vapor obviously it would have made an excellent bear repellent." Everyone roared with laughter, as Truck lifted a cheek and polluted the air right on cue.

# CHAPTER 30

On the third day of their voyage, the three earth men transferred over to Ponsel's turbok. Each carried one of the "Nevoan" power rifles. For the next three hours, they instructed the Tepu people in its use. Debris was thrown overboard into the vessel's wake. Most of the clan, eagerly, took their turn firing at it. Few were reluctant to try. Ponsel had become quite adept in its use, during his deployment aboard the Hope.

Before the Earth men hailed the "Hope" to come alongside for their transfer, they left one of the weapons in Ponsel's safe keeping. If, for some reason, a krada slipped past the watchful eyes of the "Hope's" crew, the turbok would be able to protect itself. The next day they repeated the exercise aboard the turbok of Raina's people. One of the weapons was, also, left with them for their protection.

Greg was, slightly, skeptical of Jim's magnanimous gesture.

"I don't feel they're ready for that weapon." He argued. "Do we really, know them well enough to trust them with such a potent weapon?"

"I took that into consideration before I made the offer, Greg. Raina's people would have remained in slavery for

1026

God knows, how long?" Jim replied. "They have never been so happy or secure their entire lives. I know, damn well they will pose no threat. And, as far as Ponsel's people, when we delivered their lost son back into their fold, they became excited about the new changes in their lifestyles. So what's the problem?"

"You know as well as I Jim, throughout history either this world *or on Earth,* Saints have turned into sinners when given enough power."

"Da trouble with you squirt, you don't know how to trust people." Truck joined in.

"Not when it places my ass in the line of fire I don't." Greg replied

"You might be reading more into this then there really is, Greg." Jim said

"I just hope you're right, for all of our sake." Said Greg. "I've had enough of war to last me the rest of my life.."

"Amen ta dat, Shorty." Truck replied.

As the day wore on, the weather started to change. The winds increased, making it necessary for them to furl their sail. The lake became agitated, slamming four foot waves against the Hope's bow. The sky darkened to an ominous gray. Footing became treacherous as the wind lashed water inundated her deck.

Jim fought against the rudder, doing his best to hold the Hope on course.

"Want me to take over for a while, Jimbo?" Truck yelled through the roar of the wind.

"If you don't mind!" He answered quickly changing places with his brother, "This storm is worse than the last one."

Both men were soaked to the skin, but their Lurda hide ponchos kept some of their body heat from escaping. Jim looked in the direction of the two turboks, trailing in their wake. Because they were much bigger than the Hope, they were less suseptical to the elements. Their bows cut through the attacking choppers with ease. "I'm going to go below and check for any leaks. He said. I'll have someone relieve you in an hour."

Truck nodded his head in acknowledgement and watched his brother walk away.

"I hope we don't lose sight of Ponsel's turbok!" He thought to himself. "Dat'll make it a little harder for us ta find our way home."

About two hours later, the wind diminished almost as fast as it had arisen. The torpid water was reduced to two foot rollers. Activity increased on the small ship as men resurfaced from below decks. Water was already being swept from her deck and sail was raised, once again

The man powered turboks had managed to keep pace with them through the onslaught, keeping to a steady course one hundred yards astern.

"Take us alongside Ponsel's turbok !" Jim ordered Tonio, who now handled the rudder. "He can put us back on course."

Tonio swung the rudder to starboard, sending the "Hope" into a gentile turn toward the trailing turboks.

As they pulled twenty yards off the port bow of the turbok, Jim stood on the bow.

"Did you suffer any damage from the storm?" He shouted across the short gap between the ships.

"Nothing major!" Ponsel shouted his answered.

"I hope it didn't push us too far off our course." Jim replied

"Actually the storm was a benefit to our journey." Ponsel answered. It pushed us further in the right direction."

Jim breathed a sigh of relief. He was anxious to return to his village. The thought of having to make up for lost time was unsettling." That is good news, my friend." He replied. "I'll check with the other Turbok and talk to you later."

Ponsel waved as the "Hope" swung astern and made its way back toward the other turbok. After checking on the welfare of the other ship, the Hope resumed her position at the head of the small fleet. Pointed in the right direction, they continued on the journey. Home was not too far off. The wet miles, which lay ahead of them, would be long ones.

# CHAPTER 31

The three Earthmen stood at the bow scanning the horizon for any signs of land. Ponsel had informed them, the day before, they were getting very close to their homeland. Naturally, any anomaly on the far horizon elevated their level of anticipation. Their anxieties had authored long days and sleepless nights, during the voyage. Soon they would be delivered into the arms of their loved ones. However! Until that moment arrived, the ache in their hearts and longing in their minds continued to grow.

"When we get home, you guys ain't gonna see me for about a week." Truck said. "Me and Mara gotta lot a catching up ta do."

"That should take care of the first five minutes." Greg replied. "what are you going to do with the rest of the week?" he finished with a big smile.

"Maybe I'll come over ta your house and see if you need any help." Truck shot back. Jim laughed as he listened to his siblings taking shots at one another.

"I don't believe that will be necessary." Greg returned, quickly.

Their verbal banter was interupted, when Julo approached them.

"Uncles!" he said "May I have words with you?"

"Sure, Julo! What's on your mind?" Jim replied.

Staring down at his feet, Julo paused for a moment. When he finally raised his head, enough to gaze into their eyes, it was obvious something was bothering him.

"What is it that troubles you Julo?" Greg asked.

The youngster's eyes started to moisten, as he answered.

"Back on the island, when we killed those clan men something happened to me." He replied in a trembling voice.

"Were you injured in the battle?" Jim asked in alarm

"Yes uncle!" He answered "Not physically! But things have not been right in my mind since that day. I keep reliving the destruction I caused to another person, when I fired my weapon. I have been asking myself, since that day, If what I did was really necessary."

Nodding his head in acknowledgement, Jim asked. "Have you talked with the other boys about this?"

"Yes uncle." He replied "they all told me the same thing."

"And what was that?" Greg asked.

"They told me those me those men were bad and had hurt a lot of people. We had to stop them from hurting anyone else."

"You know, what they told you is true. Don't you Julo?" Jim said.

"Yes uncle," He answered," but, Part of me feels bad for killing those men, just the same."

"It is normal to feel remorse for ending another man's life." Greg added. "The three of us always feel that way after a battle. However, were we to do nothing to stop atrocities against us or others, while we have it in our power to do so, would be a bigger offense to mankind."

"Dats right!" Truck agreed. "A man has ta do da right thing when he has da chance."

Julo paused for a moment, digesting his uncle's words.

"My father would be ashamed of me, if he knew the way I was feeling about this." He said, tears leaking from the corners of his eyes.

"On the contrary!" Jim replied." He would be proud to know his son had a very healthy conscience."

Looking, questioningly at Jim he replied "I do not understand uncle."

"If you were a remorseless killer, ending men's lives for pleasure, your father and many around you would be ashamed to be in your company. But, you, Julo, are a compassionate person who shows concern, even for his enemies. No my nephew! Because of that, your father would be extremely proud of you."

A smile broke through the boy's sad mask, "Thank you uncles! I think I understand, now, why I harbored these feelings. I will not dwell on them any longer." With that said he left to find his friends.

"You can tell dat boy is a chip off Bantor's block, can't cha?" Truck said after the boy had left.

"Your right, about that Truck! "Jim replied "I think he's going to be fine. All of us deal with death in different ways over time. We all learn to accept it as one of life's strange necessities, as ironic as it sounds."

"And, there are those who seem to enjoy it." Greg said, staring over at his large brother. After doing their deadly deeds, they show no remorse."

Truck smiled back at his brother, before responding. "I'll tell you what, Dwarf. After I strangle you, I'll shed a few tears. Will dat change your mind about me?"

Jim burst out laughing and was quickly joined by his brothers.

The third "sister" was making her way into position. The winds had subsided to gentle gusts and sail was stretched as taunt as could be, to catch the dwindling air current. Men sat around talking

"Land Ho! Dead ahead!" Tonio shouted from the bow watch. In moments, he was surrounded by the entire crew.

# CHAPTER 32

When the "Hope" was less than a mile away from her home port, orders were given to reduce sail by half. Slowing her progress the tiny ship made a sweeping turn to starboard.

The village lookouts had spotted the small fleet, about an hour ago. The portable dock was already in place, waiting to receive the "hope" as the entire village swarmed to the beach. Their excitement increased when they noticed the two strange vessels in her wake.

"It appears, we are about to play hosts to quite a few visitors, Cinda!" Bantor said as he and his mate stood on the far end of the dock, awaiting the arrival of their brethren. Both were deeply concerned about the safety of their son. They did their best not to reflect these concerns to the other, to alleviate a few pounds of parental worry.

As the Hope nudged her starboard side to the dock, mooring lines were quickly thrown up to them. The two anchors were dropped and the sail was frapped tightly to the mast. Each of the turboks glided to a stop closer to the shoreline on each side of the dock.

Jim was the first one down the ships ladder.

"We brought a little company with us!" he said, as he shook Bantor's hand in greeting.

"They are all welcomed to our village!" Bantor returned, with a smile on his face. His smile widened noticeably when he spotted Julo and the other members of the "pose" awaiting their turn to scramble down the ladder.

Jim noticed the relief in Bantor's look. "All of the Hope's crew is present and accounted for, my friend."

"Thank you, Earth brother!" Bantor acknowledged, gratefully.

A little more than an hour later, as the third "sister" was nearly spent, the entire collection of natives and clanmen gathered in the meeting place. Fires were lit to ward off the night chill and to provide an aura of security. Bantor, the three Earthmen and their mates sat with Ponsel, Raina and a few other head men of the clan in the place of honor. Friendly murmurs emanated from the large crowd. The anticipation of many new stories elevated their excitement. Nearby, huge roasting pits were being dug to accommodate the vast amount of meat, to be cooked for their celebration the next day. Bantor had, somehow, anticipated their arrival and sent out hunting parties. Fifty large Lurdas were butchered, along with fifty of the wild pigs. Dishes of vegetables and fruit were, also, being prepared. Small loaves were formed from a variety of crushed seeds and berries. They would be fried on hot flat stones in Lurda fat and then covered with honey. The celebration was destined to become the largest in the history of the people.

Staring out, at the huge gathering, Bantor smiled in appreciation of his brethren returning safely from their voyage, Ponsel wresting leadership from the tyrant, "Nemor" and commerce was developing between the two cultures. Days, such as this, far outweighed the multitude of turmoil and frustration he had experienced as their leader, thus far.

Rising to his feet, he stood before the merry mob. Raising his arms above his head, he waited for them to rein in their excitement enough for him to be heard. "On this day, all people in attendance have much cause to rejoice." He began "The dubious voyage, led by our three Earth brethren, has managed to set one clan free from slavery, another free from a leader who instilled fear among them, resulting in the merging of the two clans. I was informed, this was the first time this has ever occurred in their long history."

"I welcome all of you to our village!"

An enthusiastic cheer erupted from a balanced chorus of native and clan voices.

As he waited for their enthusiasm to subside a few decibels, tears seeped slowly from the corners of his eyes. "I must admit, my joy on this evening derives itself from a more personal direction, a father's selfless love for his son. They took our five boys on this voyage, tutored their naïve minds and safely returned them as men. To me, that deserves as much gratitude as their other accomplishments."

Another cheer rose from the crowd. When it dwindled to a quiet moment, he continued. "The feast, we celebrate tomorrow will be a momentous occasion for all of us. The concept behind it was derived from our Earth brethren. I will defer its explanation to them." He said nodding at Jim.

As the two men changed places, the crowd became a tad quieter in its anticipation.

"Some of you are familiar with the story about how my two siblings and I came to be on your world." He began. "Suffice it to say we were abducted by space traders, employed by the Nevoans, from our home planet, "Earth." All that was held dear to us, was suddenly ripped away. We fought our way across this world seeking a new beginning. It wasn't until we came upon an old friend and relative of the Kletta people that our lives changed. His name was Kaba, Bantor's uncle. Through his patience and understanding a new life opened before us."

Jim stopped and looked around at the large gathering, some of the heads nodded in understanding, recollecting those days long ago. "There isn't a day goes by, that my brothers and I don't give thanks to that old man and others who have since joined their ancestors. A few days ago, as we were making our way home, my brothers and I were discussing our celebration. It was, actually Truck who mentioned a celebration Earth people enjoy once each year. It is called "Thanksgiving!" This tradition had started when my ancestors first settled our homeland called America. The people, who existed in this area at the time, were called Indians. They were tribes such as the Kletta and clan people who lived off the land and water. These natives helped my people survive this wild land. So they held a big celebration to give thanks to the tribes.

The term "Thanksgiving" was given to this momentous day. It was appropriate! Because of the cooperation between Earth people, Klettas, and clan people, we have all joined on this day and we are all grateful to one another for our survival. Everyone here has earned the right to participate."

Nodding to Bantor, he returned to his seat. The night was halfway through her journey before the gathering broke up. All the travel tents were set up in the meeting area to accommodate Ponsel's people. A light rain started falling as the last person pursued his dreams.

# CHAPTER 33

The new day dawned bright and clear, as the village stirred. Men, women and older children began preparations for the up-coming feast. Fires were lit in the huge cooking pits. Once the bed of hot coals was established, the quartered sections of lurda meat would be spitted out over them, slow roasting to perfection. Many side dishes were already in their first stages. To accommodate their more than three-hundred guests, more wooden serving platters were being made. As they worked diligently at their given chores, the air around them vibrated with excitement.

The tova fruit, once used to make their intoxicating beverage, did not grow in this region. This, however, did not stop a few men from experimenting with local fruits and berries. They managed to create a tasty drink called "ferma." It proved to be even more potent than their familiar "tova."

An ample supply of hide bags, filled with the nectar of their labors, hung ready to alleviate the thirsts of the celebrants. Lona created a succulent pudding made from crushed nuts and berries, mixed with cream and honey. Stirred vigorously until it thickened, it was stored in a hide casing.

The bountiful region, in which they lived, amply provided the luxury of an extensive meal. All took pride in their creations. The aromas emanating from all areas of the village, advertised the promise of a most succulent feast.

A group of people sat around one of the morning fires, drinking tea and discussing the coming events of the day. Competitions, such as racing, wrestling and marksmanship would be held. People of all ages were invited to join in.

"We encourage wrestling among our youngsters! Ponsel said. The throwing of the "torb," for accuracy, has always been a favorite pastime. Some take it more seriously than others, wagering huge amounts on the outcome."

"Can I have a look at dat knife a yours?" Truck asked. Ponsel removed the fourteen inch weapon from his belt and handed it to the earth man. Truck balanced it in his hand for a moment, admiring its workmanship.

The hilt was made from some type of dark wood, about five inches long. The blade, itself, was made of bone or ivory. It was narrower at the hilt and widened toward the tip, ending in a sharp point.

Truck noticed two stones, one on either side, imbedded in the thicker part. When thrown, this added weight would drive the point home into whatever was targeted.

"Dis is beautiful!" he said. What is it made out of? Bone or ivory?"

"Neither, my friend!" Ponsel replied. It was made from the single tooth of a "Krada."

"Dat must a taken a long time ta make! Truck said. "It did, indeed!" Ponsel answered. However, we have many expert carvers who devote most of their time to making tools and weapons."

"How do your people go about killing those monsters?" Jim asked.

"We use seneks twelve feet long. The eyes and throat of the beasts are the kill spots. If we are fortunate enough to hit these areas and kill the creature, it is then towed into the shallows and butchered. This keeps us safe from its comrades. They will not venture into shallow waters. We only have use for the bones, teeth and hides. Its meat is unpalatable."

"Now, ya got a weapon dat'l kill dat bastard from a safe distance and even butchers da sonnuva bitch for ya." Truck added, smiling.

Ponsel stared, questioningly, at the Earth man. "These are tribal names in which, you refer to the "krada?" Ponsel asked.

"No, Ponsel! Greg chimed in. My large sibling here, just has a different way of describing things. It would be much too simple for him to call it a "krada" he said with a smile on his face.

"How would ya like ta describe a split lip, midget?" Truck said, shaking a fist.

When the Earth men started laughing, Ponsel and the others joined in.

As the day wore on different contests took place outside the village. Both clan and native youngsters competed. No prizes were awarded. None were needed. Each of the youngsters took their satisfaction in the pride of representing their people. Winners and losers alike, were congratulated on their worthy attempts.

The three Earth men entertained the crowd with their amazing skills with the bow and arrow. Ponsel and some of his clanmen demonstrated their accuracy while throwing the torbs.

The wrestling contests got a little heated. Especially, the scrap between Salba, Truck's son, and a clan youth by the name of Lekor. Physically, they matched up evenly. Lekor was the taller of the two. But Salba outweighed him by a few pounds. For twenty minutes they grappled, trying their best to put the other in submission. Neither youngster would bend. An accidental elbow caught Salba squarely on his nose. It stunned him for a moment. As he backed away from Lekor, wiping the blood from his nose, he dodged a kick to his mid section. A smile formed on his face as he waded in on his adversary. Then Lekor launched another kick, Salba was ready. He veered to the side, stepped behind the clan youth and wrapped his arms around him. Turning quickly, he flipped Lekor in the air. As the youth hit the ground, Salba leaped upon him and had him pinned.

Try as he would, Lekor could not throw him off. Moments later, he slapped the ground at his side in frustration. It was the sign of submission.

Salba offered him a hand and helped him to his feet. A smile, now, formed on Lekor's face also, and he placed his right hand on Salba's shoulder. The crowd cheered the two combatants, not only for their efforts, but for their sportsmanship.

Shortly before the second sister was nearly spent, it was announced the food was ready. So, too, were all the eager appetites.

Ponsel assumed the place of honor and led all of his people to the front of the line. None of them had seen as much food in one place their entire lives.

Soon, everyone was seated with platters, filled with the delicious food, balanced on their laps. Praise could be heard emanating from the crowd, how wonderful all of the native dishes were.

Voracious appetites were, soon, reduced to nibbling. To Ponsel's people, this was an eating experience they would never forget.

They were, also, amazed how four trays, heaping with the succulent food, disappeared into Truck's stomach and, then, watch him return for more.

"Your sibling has quite an appetite! The clan leader exclaimed. He sat with Raina, Bantor, the three brothers and their mates.

"Greg and I always said he was born with two stomachs," Jim said.

Ponsel looked quizzically at the Earth man. "I do not understand!" he said.

"Ever since we were youngsters, our brother has always eaten enough for two people," Greg joined in.

"I believe I would burst if I consumed that much!" Ponsel replied.

"My brother does that on the lay-away plan!" Jim joked.

"We call that farting!" Greg added.

Everyone was laughing, just as Truck returned with another heaping platter in one hand and a hide bag in the other.

"What did I miss?" he asked, taking a seat. "By the looks of that platter, I don't think you missed anything, my brother." Greg said.

When they all started laughing again, a sheepish grin took over Truck's face.

"I was a little hungry!" he replied.

As the day stretched into a glorious, star-lit night, most of the gathered people were still seated in scattered groups, picking at leftovers and talking. The skins filled with the potent "ferma" were passed around liberally, causing some to slur their words and stagger through the early evening. Voices were raised and laugher became contagious over the antics of any inebriated individual. Ponsel and Raina, along with the rest of their clan partook, sparingly, of the potent beverage. To be congenial, they sampled it because they thought it was part of the village people's celebration ritual. They, politely, refused when more was offered.

A short while later, festivities were winding down and people were making their way home.

This, indeed, had been a day of "thanksgiving"!

# CHAPTER 34

The three Earthmen, Ponsel and a handful of his clan men gathered on the deck of Ponsel's Turbok. They were assessing the materials needed to install sails on Ponsel's two vessels.

The larger of the two Turboks was over one-hundred feet long and forty feet wide amidships. Its deck leveled off twelve feet above the water line. The other ship measured seventy feet long and twenty-five feet amidships. Their flat-bottomed hulls could navigate in water less than five feet deep.

"I think a twenty foot mast would be appropriate for this ship. Greg was saying. A fifteen foot mast should be adequate for the other Turbok."

Ponsel had been anxious to get underway, shortly after the celebration. But, the allure of fitting his ships out with sails was too much for him to pass up. Life on the water was the way of his people. The openness and freedom was in his blood. The confining restraints of land life could only be tolerated for short periods at a time. Bantor's magnanimous invitation to stay with his people until the Turboks were fitted out with sails, was hard to refuse. He did not want to burden the villagers. However, many of his people had been invited to learn how to ride the Lurda and join the hunting parties. The Tepu women were eager to go foraging with the village women. After last night's feast, everyone was eager to improve on their diets. The deciding factor was the sails. To harness the wind and use its power to guide them swiftly over the water, would provide security for his people and eliminate the hours spent laboring over the oars. He would share this knowledge with the other clans.

As the first sun rose to her midway point, crews were already cutting down the trees to be used as masts and yardarms. They were trimmed of the smaller branches and debarked. Women had already gathered the necessary materials for the sails and were busy weaving them into windproof sheets. Others braided the fibrous membrane, of another plant, into lengths of strong, pliable rope.

Large ballast stones were collected to offset the weight of the masts, yardarms and sails, keeping it from becoming top heavy.

Holes were cut into the decks of both Turboks and seating sleeves were pegged to the inside of the hulls.

Eight days later, the two Turboks were ready to receive their masts. They were floated out to them and hoisted aboard. With the aid of many willing hands, they were man-handled into their seating sleeves and secured. The rotating yardarms were attached to the masts and sails were stretched into place. Ballast was set, securely, on the inside of the hulls. They could always pick up more ballast along the way, if needed.

The third "Sister" of the day was just making her appearance, when the two Turboks pulled up anchor and embarked on a trial cruise.

Jim, Ponsel and Roca commandeered the larger Turbok, while Greg, Truck and Tonio handled the smaller one. Ponsel's men were divided among the two ships, acting as crews. It was surprising how quickly they caught on. Soon, they were zigzagging their way over the water, learning all the intricate nuances of their ships.

Ponsel had appointed a man named Janto as his "First Hunter". This status carried with it almost as much authority as the leader. He would commandeer the smaller of the two Turboks. Janto was a quick study. A few hours later, Greg, Truck and Tonio sat and watched as the young clan man navigated his ship.

Shortly before night fell upon them, the two Turboks were anchored, once more, in front of the native village.

A large group surrounded a fire in the village meeting area. They talked, excitedly, about the maiden voyages under sail. "I am still amazed how easily the wind pushes us across the water!" Ponsel commented.

"It is, indeed, a relief after the hours I've spent pulling on oars." Janto added.

"I wouldn't get rid of your oars, for a while. Jim said. Not until you've become more comfortable with the sails."

"Dey'll come in handy if da wind dies down and ya gotta get ta shore in a hurry." Truck joined in.

"I believe we have adapted the proper amount of ballast. Greg said. Both ships were cutting through the water smoothly enough. You know what to do, now, if they start to feel a little top-heavy."

"Yes we do! Ponsel replied. Thank you!"

Looking over at Bantor, he continued. "Village leader, because of your generosity and aid, my people will be indebted to you forever. You have opened a new way of life to us. The time you took to help a perfect stranger in his endeavors and the hospitality you so graciously extended to us will never be forgotten. We can only repay all of you by remaining your ally until we make that last journey to be with our ancestors."

"Then, I consider the debt paid in full!" Bantor replied.

The first "Sister" sun of the new day shone down on the two vessels, as they weighed anchored and set sail across the sparkling waters of Kressa.

# CHAPTER 35

On an early morning, a few days later, the three Earthmen, Bantor and their mates sat around the community fire place, eating flat breads covered with honey and drinking tea. They reminisced about days gone by.

"The years we have spent on this wondrous world have been more than fruitful. Greg said. I feel we have accomplished more, here, Than we ever did on our home planet".

"I agree, Greg! Jim replied. The first couple of years was a little rough. But, it just kept getting better after that."

"I never thought dat after being locked in dose cages by da Nevoans we would have it so good. Truck joined in. I didn't think we was gonna make it dere for a while."

"The people of this village are happy you did! Bantor chimed in. Your Earth inventions have benefitted everyone. Your fearless leadership in the two wars made the difference in our victories."

"Dat was a team effort! Said Truck. We couldn't ta done it without their help!"

As the morning wore on, more people joined them at the fire, listening in.

"I know one thing I learned long ago, little buddy. Truck continued. When we was chained together, dat time, I learned how ta trust another person besides dos two rascals, dere. He said, indicating his two brothers.

"We didn't have too many choices, Tarok. Bantor replied. It was either kill the person at the other end of our chain or learn to live with him. As it turned out, we made the right choice!"

"Amen ta dat, my brother! Truck returned. Da hardest thing for me was learnin your language."

"I find that hard to believe! Greg interjected, with a big smile on his face. With your excellent comand of the languages, I would have thought it would have been easy for you."

Everyone within earshot, laughed when they saw the blank expression on Truck's face.

"And, he did it without the use of an interpreter." Jim instigated.

"It was difficult, at first! Bantor joined in the game. However, over the years I'm, just, starting to understand him."

"How bout I take all you jokers for a swim, tonight. Truck offered. When one a dos Karaks is biting yer skinny little asses and ya start yelling for help, we'll see who understands who."

Everyone laughed, including Truck.

Jim spoke, in a more serious tone. "Personally, the most significant accomplishment for me, since my arrival on this world, was to find this little lady, sitting at my side, and falling in love. Something I could never achieve on Earth. If I had never crossed the stars, I would still be searching."

Sanda reached up and kissed him on the cheek, hugging him to her.

"No argument dere, Jimbo! Truck said, as he gave Mara a big hug. I never had much luck with da women back home either."

"At least, not the sober ones. Greg added, with a mischievous grin on his face. Although, there were a few who stuck around a few hours after they came to."

The crowd erupted in laughter at the sight of the big man squirming nervously, as he stared at Mara.

"Where will Ta-rok be sleeping, tonight?" She asked, trying to subdue the laughter bubbling inside her.

"Dose women didn't mean nothing to me, darling! Truck defended. Honest!"

When Mara finally unleashed her laughter and hugged the big guy, he relaxed.

"I love you, you big oaf!" She said, and kissed him.

They talked for a few more hours, before everyone left to attend to chores.

The three brothers were, now, the only occupants left around the big fire pit.

"I have a great idea, you guys. Let's go fishing tomorrow!" Jim said.

# EPILOGUE

Forty-five years later, an old man makes his way, slowly, through the sleeping village. He leans, heavily, on a staff, to ease some of the pain in his aching joints. People he passes, along the way, nod in respect. His destination lies on the other side of the large village. More than seven thousand natives make their homes, here, now, more than double in its size, since he had helped settle it, many years ago.

He stops on the shoreline, in front of the meeting area. A dozen ships, with tall masts, bobbed against the long docks. Gentle waves rock them in their caressing liquid arms. One ship, in particular, catches his eye. She was the smallest vessel in the native fleet. The name on her transom was faded, but still legible. "Hope"

Memories flowed back into his ancient mind. It had been the first ship built, shortly after settling into the new village. The exciting escapades he shared, while sailing over the liquid expanse, brought a smile to his wrinkled face. It was so long ago he couldn't remember the exact date. He did know for certain, only five others besides himself, were alive today to recount these memories from experience.

As the sun beat down on the old man, he stopped, again, to rest on a large rock. Ordinarily, he wouldn't have stopped, in his morning routine. But, his tired body begged him for a reprieve. Long gone were the days he was active from sunup till the last "Sister" ushered in the night. Leaning on his staff, he hauled himself back onto his feet and continued on his way. When he reached the center of the village, he took in all the apparatus scattered there. Swings, slides, seesaws and other instruments of amusement were a few of the things he had had a hand in inventing. Twenty feet above the play area, on a stout pole, a flag rippled in the breeze. Red white and blue, it was a copy of a banner from his birth country, Earth. It symbolized freedom. The natives had adopted it when they had adopted him. It made the old man proud when he thought about the significance behind it. He had fought for freedom on two worlds and survived.

As he continued on his way, he stopped at one of the two wells in the village. Again, he was instrumental in its creation. Dropping a bucket attached to a long rope into the well, he waited a few moments as it filled part way with the pure cold water. Turning the handle on the winch, he retrieved it. When it reached the top he Hauled it over the side. Taking a hollow gourd, hanging at the side of the well, he dipped it into the bucket and quenched his thirst. Dumping the rest of the water on the ground, he wiped his mouth and continued on his way. His objective was in sight, now. A few moments later, he was there. Slowly easing himself to the ground, he sat in front of six rectangular slabs of stone. Resting a moment to catch his breath, he began reading the scripture chiseled into the stone. Tears of remembrance flooded his eyes when he had finished. The first headstone read; Gary M. Stonedeer (Ta-rok).

The second stone read ; Mara, his loving mate.

The third stone read; Gregory J. Stonedeer (Gug)

The fourth headstone read "Lona" his loving mate.

The fifth headstone was blank, awaiting its occupant

The final headstone read; Sanda, his loving mate.

After a few solemn moments, The old man wiped his eyes and rose, slowly, to his feet.

I will be with you very soon, my loved ones. He said to himself. But, not this day.

Before shuffling on his way, he remembered something Truck used to say.

"Amen ta dat! He said aloud. "Amen."

Printed in the United States
By Bookmasters